# A PLAGUE
# OF ANGELS

# A
# PLAGUE
## of
# ANGELS

*Sheri S. Tepper*

SPECTRA™

BANTAM BOOKS

NEW YORK     TORONTO

LONDON     SYDNEY     AUCKLAND

A PLAGUE OF ANGELS

A Bantam Spectra Book / October 1993

Spectra and the portrayal of a boxed "s"
are trademarks of Bantam Books, a division of
Bantam Doubleday Dell Publishing Group, Inc.

**Library of Congress Cataloging-in-Publication Data**

Tepper, Sheri S.
    A plague of angels / Sheri S. Tepper.
        p.  cm. — (A Bantam spectra book)
    ISBN 0-553-09513-7
    I. Title.
    PS3570.E673P58   1993                    93-158
    813'.54—dc20                            CIP

*Published simultaneously in the United States and Canada*

PRINTED IN THE UNITED STATES OF AMERICA

RRH  0  9  8  7  6  5  4  3  2

Michael:   *And though man plays at being good,*
           *yet he does rue*
           *the dreadful deadly Godly goods*
           *God's angels do.*

*The Michaelmas Play*
*ca. 1465*

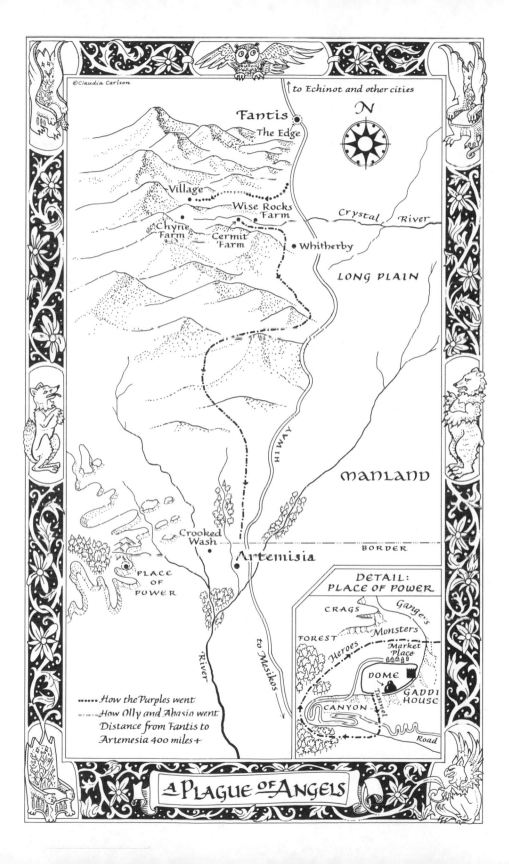

©Claudia Carlson

↑ to Echinot and other cities

N

**Fantis**
The Edge

Village

Wise Rocks
Farm

Crystal River

Chyne
Farm

Cermit
Farm

• Whitherby

**LONG PLAIN**

**MANLAND**

HIWAY

Crooked
Wash

**Artemisia**

BORDER

PLACE
OF
POWER

River

to Mesikos

..... How the Purples went
— · — How Olly and Ahasia went
Distance from Fantis to
Artemesia 400 miles +

**DETAIL:
PLACE OF POWER**

CRAGS

Ganges

FOREST

Monsters

Heroes

Market
Place

DOME

Tunnel

GADDI
HOUSE

CANYON

Road

**A PLAGUE OF ANGELS**

# CHAPTER 1

*M*oonset, just before dawn; swollen moon collapsing into a notch between black mountains; river talking quietly to itself among the stones; pine and horsemint scenting the air as Abasio brushed by them on his way down the farm lane. Big Blue whickered softly from the corral, more a question than a good-bye, but for that brief moment Abasio longed to be back on his bed on the back porch, curled under his light blanket in the morning cool. It was the same home-longing that had stopped him a year ago at the valley road and last winter when he got as far as Wise Rocks Farm. This time the doubts and longings didn't sneak up on him, didn't send him scurrying back to the farm before anyone found out he was gone. This time wasn't practice, it was real.

Besides, he could always come back.

Ma had come back. She'd run off to Fantis when she wasn't much older than he, been picked up and sold as a conk to somebody or other, she never would say who, but she'd come back. Grandpa said yes, she had, but she wasn't the same. Abasio couldn't imagine her any different. She was just Ma, quiet and busy, sometimes clucking after him like a mother hen and sometimes going off into the woods and losing herself. She always came home eventually, sometimes grabbing him, holding him close, and crying, "Abasio, oh, Abasio, don't ever leave me! Stay here where it's safe!"

It was safe, no question about that. Every day was like every other day. There were critters to feed, there were fields to sow or harvest, there were crops to store, there were repairs to be made to this thing or that thing. Once every twenty days or so, they'd load the wagon with wool or grain or root crops and drive into Whitherby to trade for sugar or salt or lantern oil. Once or twice a year there'd be trouble with a troll, or they'd sight a dragon hovering over the western mountains. In the cloudy mirror beside the wash-basin on the back porch Abasio saw his face slowly changing, getting solider and bonier, with soft hairs sprouting on his chin and lip. His body was changing too. He could feel life roiling and surging inside him, beating at his skin from inside, like some wild thing wanting to get out. He felt like the gullies in spring when the snow-melt came bashing down the mountains, eating furious holes in the banks and running off in all directions. If he went on feeding the chickens, harnessing the horses, putting out porridge for the goblins, letting life boil away like the water in the gullies, then like them he'd dry up, and his whole life would be gone.

The decision had been some time amaking. When he'd been a kid, maybe nine or ten, he'd figured adventure could come to him on the farm. In stories it did. A Hero from some archetypal village could come by and recruit him as a squire. A dragon could come, or a giant, for him to slay, which he'd do cleverly, surprising everybody. He really expected something like that to happen. Every day he sort of looked for it, but years went by, and no dragon appeared closer than the distant peaks, no giant came anywhere near, and the only Hero he saw was the one in the archetypal village over the high ridge, and then only when Abasio climbed up there to peer down at the villagers and wonder about them. He finally had to admit that adventure wasn't going to come to him. He had to find it.

So he was going, early in the morning while Ma and Grandpa were asleep. It was cowardly, he admitted that, even sneaky. But giving them a chance to argue with him would only make everyone unhappy. No matter what they said, he had to see all the stuff the truckers talked about: festivals, games in the arena, women who danced and sang and flapped their bodies like fish. Young ones, not all gray-haired and anxious, the way they mostly were in farm country. He had a right to see that, and he didn't need to feel guilty about it. He wasn't taking anything that didn't belong to him: his own life, his own body, his own clothes, his own books. Even though Ma'd told him over and over nobody read books in the city, he had to take a few. He'd take Big Blue, too, if there were some way to do it, but everyone said there wasn't any place for horses in the city. No place for any animals there, except maybe dogs and rats.

The moon was already half-sunk behind the hills when he came to the end of the farm lane. He turned right between the two ruts of the valley road, seeing an occasional glimmer where the bounding waters of the Crystal River dodged back and forth among big rocks, making deeps and shallows and music all at once. He passed between the two abandoned farms north and south of the road, then trudged past Wise Rocks Farm, where the two arms of the mountain flattened out into Long Plain, county-wide and three counties long, so said Grandpa. It was more flat-land than Abasio had ever seen before, that was certain, dotted with farms and fields and little streams and with several roads running north and south along it, including one highway. The Long Plain highway went north to Fantis, and it even had a lot of pavement left.

The sky was gray when he got that far. He'd counted on getting away unseen by anybody, but as he came through the last copse before the plain, he saw three men approaching from the south, Whitherby direction, one of them leading a donkey. Grandpa had often said that prudent men avoided confrontations, particularly when outnumbered, so Abasio slithered back among the trees and sat on a stump out of sight. He wasn't out of earshot. He could hear every plop of the donkey's hooves and every note of the eerie melody one of the men was whistling. Then both the footsteps and the whistling stopped.

"This is your valley, is it not?" asked a powerful baritone voice.

"It is, Whistler, it is."

The answering voice was higher, older, with an edge of accustomed sadness to it. Abasio surprised himself by thinking the man, whoever he was, had seen some unhappy times.

The baritone again. "Sudden Stop and I, we wish you well. Take care."

A bass rumble of agreement, more thunder than words.

The high voice. "That's kind of you and Sudden Stop, and it was kind of you to accompany me this far. I don't imagine much care will be needed hereabouts. Farmers are peaceful folk."

Bass and baritone laughter in doubtful duet, words Abasio only partly heard, something to do with there being other things around besides farmers.

Footsteps again, two people moving on toward the north, more swiftly now, one man and donkey turning slowly up the hill toward Abasio. Hastily, he got to his feet. He didn't want anyone to think he was lurking, like some villain.

At the fringe of the copse they met.

"Well now," said the donkey-man. "Aren't you out early."

"Yes, sir," mumbled Abasio, digging one toe into the ground while the old man gave him a looking-over that missed nothing, not his dirty fingernails or the sack he carried or the expression on his face, which any chicken-eating dog would have recognized as one of guilty defiance.

"Running away to the city, are we," the old man said with a sigh. Sadness in that sigh, but a thread of amusement too.

Abasio pulled himself up straight and said firmly, "Going to the city, yes, sir. I'm old enough."

"Oh, indeed you are. The average citizen of Fantis is just about your age. About fourteen, I'd say."

Abasio was trying to think of a dignified reply when the left-hand pannier on the donkey wobbled, catching his eye. Two tiny hands were holding on to the rim of the basket, and a tousled little head emerged from its depths, the eyes regarding Abasio thoughtfully. He knew at once it was a little girl, though there was no outward evidence to indicate her sex. No hair ribbon. No ruffles.

"Man," said the child.

"Thinks he is, at any rate," the old man agreed, grinning at Abasio.

"Go," said the child, jiggling herself in the basket as though annoyed at this unscheduled stop. "Go!"

Without even thinking about it, Abasio stepped forward and lifted the child from the basket. He seldom got to handle children, and he liked them a good deal. They shared many of the interesting qualities of animals, besides being able to talk.

"What's your name?" he asked, jiggling her, while the old man regarded him thoughtfully.

"Orpn," she said, leaning forward to give him a hug and several wet kisses. "Orpn."

"Orphan," clarified the old man. "She's going up there"—and he pointed up the valley—"to the archetypal village."

"I hope you're sure-footed, old man," said Abasio, concern making him sound suddenly older than his years. "That's a break-bone trail. The better road comes in from the north." He looked at the baby girl worriedly. The donkey could no doubt make it without trouble, but still . . .

"Too many people north of here," said the old man. "Too many other things as well."

The old man reached for the child, settled her in the pannier, then took Abasio's hand in his own and held it for a moment as though taking his pulse.

"You're the Cermit boy, aren't you?"

"How'd you know?" challenged Abasio, suddenly worried this man might seize him up and carry him back up the valley.

"I knew your grandma," the old man answered. "She was a lovely woman, your grandma." He nodded a polite farewell, then turned to lead his donkey up toward the dawn-lit mountains.

Abasio stood a moment looking after the unlikely group before going on his way. The two men called Whistler and Sudden Stop had already moved northward out of sight. He didn't know how long he would have to wait beside the highway for a ride, but one would come along, sooner or later.

The sun was well up before one did. Abasio was leaning on the signpost chewing on a grass stem when a trucker finally slowed to a crawl and leaned from the vehicle window. The boiler on the back of the truck sputtered and steamed, and the turbine warbled a few times with loud screeches, like harpies.

"Where y'goin'?" the driver called.

Abasio gave him a grin full of good-natured insolence and pointed up at the sign he was leaning against. Fantis, it said, on an arrow pointing north.

"Goin' to try the city, huh!" The driver beckoned, leaning across the seat to open the door on the other side. Abasio tossed his sack onto the seat before getting in himself, and the books inside hit with a thump that made the driver blink.

Abasio stuck out his hand. "I'm Abasio Cermit. Folks call me Basio."

"Barefoot Golly," grunted the trucker in return.

Abasio looked down at the driver's feet, finding them as advertised. "You got somethin' against shoes?"

"Nothin' except they hurt my feet. Always did. Never found a pair yet that felt as good as skin." He put the truck in gear, and they picked up speed as the boiler built up pressure.

"What do you do when it snows?"

"When it snows here, I'm somewhere else. Maybe down in Low Mesiko."

"It doesn't snow there?" The kid dropped his jaw as if he'd never heard any such thing.

"Where you from, boy? Don't they teach you any jogaphy?"

"I know where Low Mesiko is. It's way south of manland. I just didn't know it didn't snow there."

"Well, it doesn't. Not often, anyhow. Where you from?"

"Up there." The kid gestured toward the hills at their left. "Up the valley."

"Farm kid, ainchu." It wasn't a question.

"So!"

"Hey, no 'fence. Just sayin', you look like a farm kid."

"How come?"

The driver looked him over, all of him. The kid was no lightweight. Six one, maybe. Dark skin. Dark curly hair. Eyes full of the old devil. "Oh, hair. Clothes. You'll see when we get to Fantis."

"You goin' all the way there?"

"All the way. Got a load of batteries from the Place of Power for the battery stores in the market. Got some weapons for Sudden Stop at the Battle Shop—"

"Who?" asked Abasio, alertly.

"Sudden Stop. He runs the Battle Shops, includin' the one in Fantis. Then, when I'm unloaded, I'll run back empty as far as Whitherby, pick up a load of wool there, and head south around Artemisia to High Mesiko, to the blanket weavers."

"Whitherby's where my grandpa sells his wool."

Abasio settled back, wondering at the coincidence of almost meeting Sudden Stop and then hearing about him, wondering but not liking to ask about the other man he'd almost met, Whistler. Just knowing who Sudden Stop was made him more than ever curious about who the old man with the donkey might have been. One of the things Grandpa had hammered home, however, was that it was often wisest not to ask questions of people one has just met.

So Abasio let his curiosity feed on itself except about things he saw as they went along. After a mile or so, the road came up alongside the highway, where southbound traffic was on one road and northbound traffic on another. It wasn't much smoother than the narrower road had been. Whenever they hit a rough spot, which was every few yards, Abasio grabbed at the handles set into the roof of the truck.

"Nobody fixes the roads in manland anymore," said Golly. "Another five years, there won't be any roads, and the trucking brotherhood'll have to do something else for a living."

"No trucks?"

"Maybe the Edge'll come up with something else. They're part of manland too."

"How far does manland go, exactly?"

Golly twiddled his toes. "Well, it sort of starts where the forests give out, two, three days' drive east of here. And it includes all the farm country on the prairies, and the farm villages. And it ends up three or four days' drive north, where the badlands are, and three, four days' drive south, at the border of Artemisia."

"How far west does it go?"

"Don't know as anybody's ever said. These little old foothills along here, they're in manland right enough, but once you get back in the real mountains, they don't call that manland. They call that wilderness!"

This more or less accorded with Grandpa's version of matters. Everything east of the mountains, Grandpa said. All the cities and Edges and towns and farms as far as a person could go in any direction before running into forests or some other country. Abasio nodded to himself, pleased to have the matter confirmed. Manland was a sizable piece of ground, even though it was mostly open space.

They trundled along. After a considerable time they came up a long ridge, and Abasio sat up straight, looking far ahead. "All that sparkle there, what's that?"

"Those're the walls around an Edge, boy. Didn't you never hear about Edges?"

"I know about Edges! They're where the people went who left the cities, but I didn't know they'd look like that."

"It's the morning sun on 'em."

Abasio stared at the glistening walls until they dropped over the ridge and he lost sight of them. For a while there was nothing but farms and fields with trees furring the waterways. Then, after a good many miles, they crested a rise and saw the walls again, coming up close on the right, farther away on the left, across the divided highway. Tall they were, and slickly shining, with complicated barricades at the top. No bushes or trees along them, either.

Golly pointed upward, saying, "Weapons they call laser cannons up there, and all kinds of alarms. You try and climb that, the guards'll pick you off like an apple out of a tree." Then he looked back at the road and abruptly stood on his brakes, cursing.

"Oh, shee-it!"

"What?"

"Damn goblins!" the trucker growled as they screeched to a halt. "Look at that, will you! They've cut a trench right across the road!"

They climbed out, Golly muttering and hitting the side of the truck angrily. The excavation was two feet wide, four feet deep, straight-edged as a grave across both lanes of the road they were on, with another one to match across the two lanes on the other side of the grassy strip.

"Shee-it," the driver growled to himself.

"What do we do?" Abasio asked, more excited than annoyed. "Do we fill it in?"

"We do not!" Golly exploded. "I got other things to do with my time besides fillin' in goblin trenches or defusin' kobold bombs or any of that. My aunt Hettie, but there's more of 'em every time I turn around! You help me get the flaps out."

They had to unload several crates of batteries before they could get at the flaps, solidly constructed minibridges that they lugged to the front of the truck and dropped neatly across the trench. When they'd driven across the flaps, they got out and went back to reload.

Abasio was bent over the flap, trying to get a good grip on it, when he suddenly got a sick feeling, as if he were going to throw up. He took a deep, shuddering breath, frightened, wondering what was happening to him, and at that moment Golly put a hand on his shoulder and made a surprised noise, a little whuff of air. There in front of Abasio's eyes were two sets of booted feet, and legs covered with shiny black stuff that looked stiff, like the carapace of a beetle. Golly's hand was pressing Abasio down, so he stayed where he was.

A voice said, "You." The voice was windy and hot, as though it came across a desert.

"Yessir," said Golly, standing very still.

"You travel this road often?" The words seemed to come from far away. Abasio shut his eyes and concentrated on breathing. The words came out here, but they started somewhere else.

"Yessir," said Golly. "All the time."

"On your journey today, have you seen anyone along the road?"

Golly swallowed audibly. "Him," he said, tapping his finger on Abasio's shoulder. "Just him."

Abasio felt his head being lifted. Not by hands, not *by* anything he could see or feel. It was like somebody had a fishhook set into his scalp and was pulling. He could feel the pain of it, as his eyes traveled up the legs and the stiffly armored black torsos to two identical expressionless faces, and two pairs of hot red eyes. It was the eyes doing it to him. He could feel them like levers, pressed into his flesh, as though their gaze had physical reality. His feeling of nausea increased. He wanted to shake or vomit or yell, but that seemed like a bad idea. The easiest thing was to hold real still, like when you meet a bad dog or come near to stepping on a rattlesnake.

"Did you see anyone?" the windy voice asked.

"Yessir," he said, aping Golly's manner. "Two men walking along, goin' toward Fantis—"

"With a child? Children?" the voice demanded.

Abasio had no particular reason not to mention the old man and the donkey, but this avid question brought back the feel of the toddler in his arms, her lips on his cheek. Though it was no doubt a very risky thing indeed, he decided the questioners didn't need to know about every damn donkey.

It took more resolution than he'd ever used before to tell them just what he did. "The two men didn't have any family with them. When I saw them last, they were just two big men walking north along the highway." The effort not to say anything more left him limp and wet all over.

Without farewell, the two shiny figures moved away, also northward. Even sweaty and distracted as he was, Abasio noticed they moved faster than men should be able to move.

"Shee-it," murmured Golly, panting as though he'd been holding his breath. "That's all I needed. Damn it to all hell, I went an' peed my pants." He pulled the fabric away from his groin and flapped it, cursing vividly, though in a subdued voice.

"Who were they?" asked Abasio.

"People call 'em walkers. Last couple of years, they've been all over the place, asking about babies. Little girls. Anybody seen any little girls that didn't have folks. Any little girls bein' fostered. Hellfire, the way people're dyin' all over, there's always kids bein' fostered. I don't know what they think they're lookin' for."

Abasio, who thought he did, kept his mouth shut.

"Show you something," whispered Golly. He went over to the place the walkers had stood and peered at the earth, beckoning with one hand toward Abasio. Abasio went over next to him, looking down to see whatever it was.

"There," said Golly, stirring the grasses with his foot.

At first, Abasio didn't see what it was, but then he noticed the dry black fragments all over Golly's bare toes, the grasses where the two things had been standing, dead and burned right down to their roots. Abasio looked the way they had gone, figuring he'd see footprints.

"Nope," whispered Golly. "They move too fast for that. It's just when they stand still a bit. You see places like that, stay away from 'em. You camp on toppa that burned dirt, pretty soon, you don't feel so good."

He heaved a heavy sigh, as though deeply troubled, and then the two of them reloaded the flaps. They got back into the truck and went forward at a slow trundle for some little while. Golly seemed of a mind to let the walkers get a long way ahead. Even now they had become small black dots, far down the plain.

"What are they? Really?" Abasio murmured.

"Boy, I don't know. I try not to think." And Golly began singing to himself, rather tunelessly. For a long time, neither of them said anything more.

Finally Golly seemed to get his spirits back, and the truck picked up speed as they rolled past the high walls, past the steel-spiked gates with their guard posts. Through the gates, Abasio could see greenery, trees and lawns and flower gardens, with elegant houses set wide apart, and beyond them the squat, glistening towers where the Edgers worked.

"What makes those buildings all lit up like that?"

"Science, boy. These folks still got science. Used to be lights like that ever-where, you believe that?"

They passed three sets of gates without even a wave from the guards, but as they were approaching the fourth, Golly muttered to himself and reduced speed once more.

"Now if this ain't the end! First goblins, then walkers, and now this!"

The next pair of high gates was standing open, serving as a backdrop for a crowd of pale-skinned and brightly dressed people, all so clean-looking, they made Abasio's eyes smart. In the midst of them stood a girl clad in green, her hair a knee-length flow of pure gold, a flower wreath around her head, her feet in crystal slippers. Drawn up outside the gate was a melon-shaped carriage, red lacquer and gilt, polished so bright, it reflected the sun like a gemstone, six white horses harnessed to the shaft and a coachman up top with a high plumed hat.

"What?" murmured Abasio, awestruck.

The driver shook his head. "She's a Princess, boy. Look at her. A Princess if I ever saw one. They're taking her away from her home in the Edge, off to a archetypal village, I'd say. Poor thing. She's cryin', and they're all pattin' and pettin' of her. Shee-it. This is goin' to take a while."

He shut down the engine and twiddled his toes while Basio shook his head at the wonder of it. "There's an archetypal village near our farm. Up over the mountain. I used to climb up the top of the gap and look down into it. There's a Hero there, and an Oracle and a Poet, and a bunch of other archetypes. Do you suppose she's going there?"

"Does your village have a palace?"

"It has an old castle, mostly fallen-in."

"I'd say no, then. No, that Princess isn't for any old fallen-in place. She'll go someplace shiny-new, probably with a Prince already there. Either that, or to an enchanted tower."

"Who's the old fallen-in castle for, then?"

Golly pursed his lips, thinking. "Oh, I'd say prob'ly a Ghost. Or a Wicked Witch."

Abasio shook his head slowly, reflectively, as he settled himself for a considerable wait. "No," he said at last. "There wasn't any Wicked Witch."


Somewhere, of course, there had to be a Wicked Witch.


South and west of the Long Plain and the area known as manland, west of the land called Artemisia, past mountains and valleys, arroyos and mesas, at the top of a sinuous, canyon-climbing road, the Place of Power spread fingerlike at the eastern edge of a massive tableland where carved chasms fell away between the fingers, changeable under each shifting cloud or turn of season, now light, now dark, turning from rose to amber to gray in an instant, and in an instant rose again. Thunderheads often massed behind the towering rimrock, great cliffs of cloud spitting lightning and ruminous with

thunder. Whether from this ominous backdrop or for some more conse-
quential reason, the Place was considered to be strange and threatening,
perhaps even dangerous. Some said that parts of it might be evil.

They meant the Dome, a building squatting on the eastmost canyon rim,
bulging ominously upon that prominence like a lopped and swollen head.
Everyone knew the misshapen Dome had at one time been an observatory,
used by astronomers, creatures of night, who had peered through its slitted
eye nearsightedly into the heavens. Many thought the building was still used
by creatures of darkness, though for purposes less benign, for now it was
the Witch who went there, the Witch and her minions, shedding shadow
behind them as a dog sheds hair, dropping a dander of malevolence to itch
those who dwelt in the Place.

The Witch's given name was Quince Ellel, *The* Ellel, head of the Ellel
clan. Quince Ellel had a longtime though unwilling servant named Qualary
Finch. Although Qualary was not the only person to think of Quince Ellel
as the Witch, no one called her that out loud. When Qualary spoke to her
or of her, she said "Madam Domer" in tones of absolute subservience and
groveling respect.

Each morning, while others in the Place were having breakfast or talking
with friends or engaged in other ordinary pursuits, Qualary Finch was standing immobile on the high, spidery platform beneath the rusty Dome, holding
open a heavy leather-bound book, while the Witch, robed in black and masked
in gold, read the words of her quotidian litany.

"'Hunagor is gone,'" she chanted in a harsh metallic voice, lingering
over the words. "'And Werra is gone....'"

Hunagor had died fifty years or more before, and Werra had been gone
for at least two decades, but this made no difference to the Witch. Hunagor
and Werra had been residents of Gaddi House, and the Witch hated all present
and former residents of Gaddi House.

"And always will," laughing Berkli had remarked, not caring who heard
him. "Ellel will not be happy until Gaddi House is rubble, then she'll dance
on the shards." Berkli was *The* Berkli, head of his clan as Ellel was head
of hers.

Ellel had not been amused by his comment. When Ellel spoke of Hunagor
and Werra dying, her voice pealed like dissonant bells, an enjoyment Qualary
perceived but did not question. Qualary had learned painfully not to react
to anything Ellel did or felt, not by so much as a tremor. At home she'd
held a stone weight at arm's length for hours, practicing, so she wouldn't
let the heavy book quiver. " *'Heavy as cobble, heavy as lead, let the book
wobble, I'll end up dead.'* " So she told herself mentally, quoting one of
her many "Rhymes for trying times." Her only chance of remaining unscathed was to remain unseen, unnoticed, taken for granted like a chest or

a chair. While the Witch's words fell in descending echoes among the blotched arches below, Qualary stood like furniture, utterly still.

" '. . . their heritage has been ended,' " the Witch cried triumphantly, speaking still of Hunagor and Werra.

"Amen," chanted the minions from the floor far below, the words coming as a hot wind, as a burning and stinking exhalation.

Qualary bit the insides of her cheeks, steeling herself against that heat, that smell. The first few times she had been dragged up here, the Witch's voice hissing obscenities, the Witch's fingers twisted deep into Qualary's hair, that hot stink had surprised her. She'd been only thirteen then, but now, twenty years later, she still bore the scars of Ellel's initial chastisement. Now, even when the robed figure turned from the book to lean over the railing, peering downward, Qualary remained rigid, for she knew what lay below and had no desire to see it.

Down there was a mosaic floor, set with the signs of the Zodiac and the orbits of the planets. The designs were shattered now, the tesserae scattered. Even if they'd been whole, Qualary couldn't have seen them through the serried ranks of Ellel's myrmidons, thousands of them, arranged in lines like necklaces, their complicated helmets mere beads of black or gold or red, so thickly gathered they completely hid the floor.

They were not things of this time at all. They were utterly foreign to this age, creatures of an almost forgotten era, found in a vast and ancient cavern far underground, laid up like cordwood as they had been stored long ago against some unimaginable future need. The Witch's father had found them. They had been his. Now they were hers.

Her father had never used the things effectively, so said the Witch. Not that she said this to Qualary. She didn't talk to Qualary. She talked very little to anyone, but she sometimes murmured to herself when Qualary could hear.

The Witch drew back from the narrow rail and ran her finger down the page until she found her place once more. An illuminator had been brought all the way from Low Mesiko to letter this book, to make these words gleam with gold and bright ink. Qualary sometimes wondered about that, about the Witch's going to all that trouble when she had written the words herself and knew them by heart. The Witch needed no page, no writing, no servant to hold the book. Except that the gold and the bright ink and the motionless servant were part of the Witch's aura, her design, her imagined self, her vaunting and voracious ambition.

" 'Impotence holds the gate of Gaddi House. The time trembles,' " the Witch cried.

The lips of the golden mask could not move, but the eyes that glared from the eyeholes shifted and glared, bloodshot and yellowed. Years ago, the

Witch had shown her face. In recent years, she had shown only the mask. All in all, Qualary preferred the mask. It was inhuman and therefore easier to deal with. When Qualary had seen the person, face to face, she had expected human responses, humane attitudes, and had suffered for it.

The echoes still ricocheted from pillar to pillar below. "Time, ime, ime, ime. Trembles, emmles, emmles."

Time always trembled, thought Qualary. Something was always breaking apart or unraveling. As for Gaddi House, everyone said there was only one old man living over there: old, old Seoca, doddering his way toward death. And best he get to it, for if he didn't die soon, Ellel would kill him! The Witch wanted desperately to get into Gaddi House. That closed, enigmatic space infuriated her. She assumed there were wonders hidden away in there, and she wanted to get her hands on them.

The Witch moved to the rail and leaned over once more.

" 'The days of Seoca are numbered!' "

The words were almost a scream, far too loud for this enclosed space. The golden fortress of Gaddi House was only a few hundred yards away, on the rim of the mesa. Perhaps Ellel wanted the old man to hear her.

"Amen," her creatures chanted once more, the sound of their voices surging toward the high balcony like the rush of a boiling, inexorable wave. Qualary held her breath. Sometimes she woke in the night, dreaming of drowning in those voices, in that smell.

The Witch's voice rose in an impassioned howl. " 'What was false shall be true, what was true shall be false. Destiny calls the people of the Dome to stand upon the power of the place, to renew the might of man, to bring progress upon the earth!' "

"Amen," her creatures said for the third time, as they had been programmed to do. Qualary believed that Ellel valued the creatures most because they would always do precisely what they were programmed to do. Unlike creatures of flesh. Unlike human beings. Unlike Qualary herself, as the Witch frequently pointed out, who had to be repeatedly disciplined to assure she did what was required.

The third *Amen* had been the final response. Silence gathered.

"Go," Ellel murmured, the whisper as clear as the ritual cries had been.

The creatures rose silently and departed as silently. Their feet made no sound as they crossed the cracked pave, ebon and gold and bloodred strings of them flowing like beaded serpents, slithering out among the arches. They spiraled and eddied as they departed. Even Qualary could not keep her eyes from them. They were like oil on swirling water. The patterns were different every time.

Besides, they were going away. The only tolerable thing about them was when they went away.

The Witch stood watching until only a few were left, those retained for the day's duties. Ignoring Qualary, she sat upon the automatic lift chair and swirled her way along the spiraling track, past the little mezzanine with its information console, around the cylindrical walls to the floor. Left behind upon the balcony, Qualary wrapped the book and put it away, then plodded slowly downward, careful step by careful step, holding tight to the railing. The track wasn't made for feet, but Ellel didn't care about that. Ellel was quite capable of telling Qualary to fly, then beating her when she didn't immediately sprout wings.

Halfway down the long spiral, Qualary heard the creatures below as they greeted their mistress.

"Ellel, Empress," they chanted together in their metallic, uninflected voices.

"My faithful followers," the Witch returned the greeting in a voice not unlike their own. "Have you found me the child?"


Far northeast of the Place, Abasio and Golly trundled quite slowly past the last of the Edge, where the walls bent away east and west to make a circle around the city, then across a strip of wasteland along the shallow river and up onto the bridge that crossed it. Though Abasio had kept an eye out for the walkers, he hadn't seen them. Either they'd moved faster than the truck, or they'd turned off somewhere.

When they got right up on the top of the bridge, Golly stopped his truck again and just sat there, twiddling his toes against the pedals, thinking.

"Whatso?" asked Abasio, impatiently. It had been a day for delays!

"Well, boy, before we go on in, I was just considerin'. Did your folks tell you about IDDIs?"

Abasio flushed and muttered, "My ma did."

"Well then," said Barefoot Golly. "Well then, you think on what she told you, boy. Just you think on it." He went on twiddling his toes, moving not an inch.

"You mean now?" Abasio asked, incredulously.

"I do mean now. Just you sit there and think what she told you."

Though considerably annoyed, Abasio cast his mind back to the time Ma'd told him about IDDIs. It had been about a year ago, summertime, like now. They'd eaten their supper outside under the willow tree, and there in the dusk with the stars pricking out overhead, Abasio, who was even then thinking about running off, had asked his ma why she'd come back from the city.

"I was pregnant with you," she'd said. "And it's not good for babies there. Sure not good for women."

Then she'd looked him straight in the face, using the dusk as a kind of veil to hide her blushes, and she'd told him about IDDIs, slowly, painfully, as though she had to force each word out against her will.

Abasio hadn't known where to look, or what to say. He hadn't known even whether to believe her! Maybe it was just horrible talk, to scare him, to make him stay home.

But Grandpa nodded the whole time she talked, and when she'd finished, he'd said, "Believe her, boy. Every word she says is true." Then he'd pointed eastward, where Orion was heaving himself up over the horizon, the huntsman of the heavens. "I've always believed our kinfolk went to the stars partly to escape the IDDIs. No IDDIs among our brothers on Betelgeuse. They were smart to get away, smart to go."

Abasio had been hearing about mankind going to the stars since he was a tiny baby, but he'd rather talk about that than what Ma was talking about!

"When did they go, Grandpa?"

"Oh, in my great-great-grandpa's time, boy. A hundred years, maybe a hundred fifty."

"Why didn't they take us with them, Grandpa?"

"We weren't born yet. Some people chose not to go, and we're descended from those folks."

Abasio wished he had been born then. If he'd been born then, he'd have chosen to go! There'd have been no problem with seeking adventure. Going to the stars was adventure, all right!

Still, Grandpa said the important thing was that men had gone. He puffed out his chest when he said that. Whenever Abasio thought about it, it made him puff up like a cockerel, too, just to think that men had gone. Men like him. Even though he hadn't gone with them, he still owned the stars sort of by proxy. If men had gone to the stars, there was nothing they couldn't do!

So now, sitting on the bridge beside Barefoot Golly, he felt a familiar confusion: danger and sex all mixed up in his adventure. So it was too late to go to the stars, but it wasn't too late to see the world. But Ma had warned him, and Grandpa had warned him, and now here was this trucker warning him. He, Abasio, was no fool. They didn't need to keep telling him the same thing over and over. He knew about IDDIs!

"All right, I thought on it," Abasio growled. "I thought on everything Ma said about it."

Golly gave him such a speculative look that Abasio thought he might have to come right out and tell what he knew about IDDIs, but after a minute the trucker grunted and let the truck roll down the incline of the bridge toward the city.

Despite Abasio's attempt at nonchalance, his first view of Fantis came as a shock. At the foot of the bridge were half-fallen buildings, walls that went nowhere, exposed floors teetering over cracked and littered streets, surfaces painted in gaudy colors and contorted patterns, steel grills over doors and windows, a wildly disintegrated scene that Abasio's eyes took in but his brain refused to interpret. Nothing seemed to connect to anything else. He felt his bowels clench and grab, not quite letting go but almost.

The truck stopped at the side of a virtually intact building, and Barefoot Golly got out, waving at somebody inside.

"Is this it?" Abasio asked in a voice that didn't sound like his own. It was nothing, nothing like he'd thought it would be!

"This is it, boy," Barefoot told him, giving him a look up and down and then heaving a sort of sigh. He moved in on Abasio, coming very close, talking quietly so nobody could hear what he was saying but Abasio himself. "Look past my shoulder, boy. You see those men down there at the corner. There's some in green, and some in other colors, you see?"

Abasio saw.

"Those are what you call recruitment teams. Any young ones come to Fantis, male or female, they got to go that way to get on into town. This's all neutral territory along here, but if you don't have a pass, you've got to hook up with somebody. Try and stay away from the Greens, Abasio Cermit. That's all I'll say to you, but it's meant in friendship. Try to stay away from them."

Then he was gone, and there were men swarming over the truck, unloading the cases of batteries and the heavy weapons boxes with BATTLE SHOP all over them in big black letters.

Abasio took a deep breath and started for the corner. When the green-clad men with the long green-dyed braids came toward him, he moved quickly and got himself among some other men, nearest to two with high purple hair crests and purple tattoos all over their hands.

"New to the city, boy?"

"Come meet the family, boy."

A quick glance over his shoulder showed him the Greens snarling and showing their teeth like farm dogs, so he said yes quick. The two purple men put him into a flashily painted vehicle that spouted black smoke as they drove past streets painted in blue and green and red before getting to a street where all the paint was purple.

"Purple House!" one of his guides said unnecessarily. It was four stories of decaying brick with snaky designs in lavender and wine and deep violet covering it from broken sidewalk to curly shingled roof.

"Whatso?" called a guard from the front stoop.

"This here's Basio," announced one of his guides. "Come to have supper with us."

"Welcome to Purple House." The guard smiled around his gap teeth. "You enjoy yourself now."

It wasn't what Abasio expected at all. Not that he was exactly sure what he expected. Sometimes when Ma described the city she said one thing, another time she'd say something else. What it really was, this first night, was him, Basio, sitting on the floor on a mattress while people brought him food and gave him stuff to drink he'd never had before. On the mattress beside him was a girl wearing, so far as he could tell, only two scarfs, one around her top and the other one sort of between her legs.

"What's your name?" he asked her.

She shook her head, opened her mouth as if she were trying to say something, only no words came out. The man on the other side of her said something to her, low and hard, and the girl grabbed on to Abasio as if she were drowning and he were a log that'd keep her afloat. She still didn't say anything.

"You like her?" the man on the other side of him asked.

"Sure," Basio said, his tongue so thick and his lips so unmanageable, he was scarcely able to get the word out. "Sure. She's fine." He'd thought a city girl would be more fun, somehow, and she didn't seem to be able to talk, but otherwise . . . she was fine.

"She's yours, for tonight," the man whispered. "Enjoy."

Later he and the girl were in a little room together, only she scuttled away from him and crouched in a corner like a whipped pup.

"I'm not . . . not gonna hurt you," he said.

"I ain't never," she wept. "I ain't never. They had no right!"

"What you talking about?"

"My daddy had to sell me," she wept. "And they bought me. To raise up tots for the Purples. But I ain't never, and I'm scared."

Abasio whispered to her he hadn't never, either, but he'd watched dogs and cats and sheep, and there didn't seem to be much to it. He was right, there wasn't. It didn't take him anywhere near as much time as it did dogs, not any of the times he did it. By the third or fourth time, she even quit crying about it and just let him. It was pretty much how he'd thought it would be. Some of the books he'd read said it was like a miracle or marvel or wonder, but it wasn't like that. It wasn't all that different from doing it himself, because she just shut her eyes and held her breath and waited for it to be over.

Next day they were still half-asleep when the two Purples showed up again to drag him out to see the arena and the market and all the homegrounds of the Purple Stars and Blue Shadows and Green Knives and Renegades. At first, all Abasio could see was the dirt. Dead animals. Sometimes dead people. Puddles of stuff in the streets and alleys, stuff he didn't want to step in even though he had his boots on. Turds everywhere, where dogs or people had just squatted and let go, and on the turds masses of flies that rose up in clouds and stuck to his lips and around his eyes until he thought he'd have a fit getting rid of them.

The Purples he was with didn't seem to notice. They just brushed the flies away, not even stopping whatever it was they were saying. They were full of stories about the Purples, the battles they'd fought, the victories they'd won over the Renegades and the Blue Shadows and the Green Knives. "You gotta watch out for the Greens," they told him. "They torture prisoners. Their Chief, Wally Skins, he likes doin' it."

"Why do they call him that?" Abasio wanted to know.

"'Cause he wears prisoner skins. Fresh ones, usually."

"Who's . . . in charge of the Purples?"

"Soniff, he's warlord. Old Chief Purple, he got him so much money he bought him a place out in the Edge. Said he was retirin' from the binness and Soniff should take over."

"Jus' 'til Old Chief's boy Kerf grows up," said the other, with a snigger. "Little Kerf."

"Watch your mouth," warned the first, turning Abasio's attention away from this remark by pointing out the sights. "That there's the Battle Shop, Basio. Man named Sudden Stop, he runs it, and he runs the shows at the arena too. He's got the best weapons, new ones all the time."

Abasio blinked. Twice on the road, and now here, he'd heard that name. *Three times is meant*, the old adage ran, so he took a good look. The Battle Shop was big and fairly clean. It had glass windows without any bars over them and enough weapons piled up inside to wage a pretty good war.


After a few days, Abasio had to admit Grandpa and Ma had been right about a lot of things. At the farm there'd been a windmill to pump water right to the house, but here in the city the only water came from the water-men's water-truck that arrived every few days and pumped the tank on the roof full, just enough for cooking and pot washing and the like. Dirty clothes went to the neighborhood laundry, and people went to the neighborhood baths. Both of them had water piped in from the river, and filters to clean it, with slave teams stoking the boilers and walking the treadmills to keep the water moving. When Purple women went to the baths, Purples went along to guard them. Purples escorted the tots to and from school, too, keeping the kids from getting too close to dead bodies and from being stolen by other gangs.

The first day Abasio was on escort duty he got jumped by Blue Shadows. It made him so mad, he didn't even have time to be scared. When he came to himself, there were two Blue Shadows on the sidewalk and two more running and his fellow escorts clapping him on the back, crowing like cocks. That night they asked Abasio if he'd like to join the Purple Stars. Basio had his doubts, but he wasn't silly enough to be disrespectful and refuse the honor. People who were disrespectful didn't last any time at all. His fight against the Blues got counted as First Fight. They showed him the Book of the Purples and gave him a copy to memorize; they added his name to the roll of honor on the wall; they pricked the first of his tattoos onto his hands, then everybody got buzzed.

Two days after that, he was on his way out back to the privy, when he heard a sound from one of the back rooms. He'd been past that room a hundred times before, but the door had always been shut. This time it was open, so he looked in: three beds with men on them, a hag washing bloody rags in a basin.

The hag looked up at him. "You don't want to come in here," she whispered.

Abasio's memory was trying to tell him something while he stood there stupidly with his mouth open. Wounds were treated upstairs. He'd seen knife cuts being sewn up and bones being set up there. They had a special hag to do all that, one who'd had lessons from a real doctor.

"What's wrong with them?" he asked the hag.

"You don't want to know," said one of the men. He had great black lumps sticking way out from his neck. His mouth bled. He had no teeth. When he spoke, the blood in his mouth made a shiny red bubble on his lips. He looked old, but Abasio knew he wasn't.

The hag shooed Abasio out, muttering at him, "Fool boy. Why you think they gave you that new little girl? Why you think, stupid?" He was on his way back from the privy before he realized what he'd seen. It was what Ma had warned him about, what the trucker had tried to tell him.

"Those men in the back room, they got IDDIs?" he asked one of the men he'd been on escort with. "They goin' to die?" He thought he knew, but he wanted verification. The reality of what he had seen was nothing he'd ever imagined, and he had to be sure.

"Yeah, well," the man said, looking over Abasio's shoulder at nothing. "Maybe they been here in the house too long."

The next day the door was open and the room was empty and stinking with some strong chemical smell.

Ma had seen men die like that. She'd told him so, or tried to. Dying like that was what she'd run away from. Men dying like that, and kids, and women too. If the mother or father had it, babies even, born with an IDDI— an immune deficiency disease, Grandpa said. It hadn't meant much to Abasio until now. Now, having seen, it was all different. Having seen and having heard what the hag muttered at him: *Why you think, fool boy? Why you think they gave you a new girl?* A girl who hadn't, ever. A girl they thought probably wasn't infected. *Why, fool boy?*

So she'd get pregnant with a healthy baby, he answered himself. So the baby wouldn't die before it was born, the way IDDI babies often did. So the Purples could raise up some healthy tots, to make them strong.

The girl they'd given him got pregnant right away, so they took her upstairs to women's quarters and she wasn't available anymore. Though she'd been his first, Basio decided she was going to be his only. No point seeking adventure if all it did was get you dead! The other Purples laughed at him. They called him Basio the Cat, because when the gang went to the song-houses, Basio would go along, but he wouldn't get his feet wet, though they weren't talking about his feet. They were talking about cock-hole. "Cuckle," they said. "What good's a man without cuckle and chuckle." Or fuck and luck. Or screwin' and doin'.

"Short life and wild!" they cried. "Cuckle and chuckle until you buckle!" and "Nobody lives forever!"

No matter how they said it, Abasio wouldn't. Sometimes he woke up sweating, hearing that voice through its bubble of blood: *"You don't want to know."* No, he didn't want to know. He wanted more than cuckle and chuckle. Something more. A lot more, though he didn't know exactly what that might be.


Young Kerf, the Old Chief's son, was younger than Abasio by a couple of years, but he already had a woman of his own, one Elrick-Ann, a virgin girl from the Cranked-Up gang, bought for Kerf by his daddy when the boy was only ten. As far as anybody knew, she was a virgin still and was likely, so some of the Purples whispered to each other, to remain that way forever.

Whatever her sexual status, Elrick-Ann was that impossibility among conks, a popular woman. She never flirted with any man, but she was sisterly toward them all. She listened to their troubles and offered good advice if they wanted it. She supervised the hags in the kitchen and made them produce food that was tasty and looked nice. Most gangers' women stayed all their lives in the women's quarters on the roof, but Elrick-Ann buzzed around Purple House like a bee, always busy with something. Even the other women liked her, and that was an unheard-of thing, for about all the amusement the women had besides going to the baths was fighting with each other.

To Abasio, Elrick-Ann took the place of a ma, or maybe an older sister. He told her how he felt about IDDIs, and she told him being scared was real sensible if a man cared about living. Elrick-Ann suggested Abasio make it his business to find amusements for Kerf, because that would get him in good with Soniff and keep him away from the whoring and drugging, which was mostly where the IDDIs came from. When the young Chingero brothers, TeClar and CummyNup, were recruited for the gang, Elrick-Ann told Basio to look out for them and them to look out for him, because a man lived longer with somebody watching his back. When he told Elrick-Ann how much he liked books, how he'd brought books with him but couldn't read them because the Purples didn't respect people who read or who used unusual words, Elrick-Ann suggested he move out of Purple House and find a place of his own.

"Purples don' have to live in the house, Basio," she whispered, looking around to be sure they weren't overheard. "Not if they've got some other place. No reason you shouldn' do stuff you like. I even got me this idea 'bout a place for you."

The place was a solid old shack on top of a tenement a few blocks away, where he could keep the books he bought secretly in the market and read the night away if he liked, or as much of it as he was able to find lantern fuel for. Kerosene was scarce, and torches were too smoky to read by.

All the caring wasn't one way. When Elrick-Ann confessed one lonely night that Kerf would probably never be a normal man, but that she wasn't a normal woman, either, having been born without the right organs to make babies, so the doctors said, Abasio hugged her and told her he was sorry.

"Is okay," she whispered. "With Kerf, I'm safe. My daddy figured so. Nobody'll bother me so long as I belong to Kerf."

Abasio respected Elrick-Ann. When she told him, four years after he came to Fantis, that it was time he went home to tell his ma he was all right, that he owed his ma that much, he paid attention to what she said, borrowed a horse from the Patrol Post outside the city, and went.

Ma wasn't there. Somehow he'd never thought of her not being there.

The old man, much thinner and grayer, wouldn't say where she'd gone. When Abasio asked, he only shook his head, and he didn't invite him to stay, not even for a visit. In the end, Abasio came back to Fantis because it was the easiest thing to do.

"I thought you might stay there," whispered Elrick-Ann.

He hadn't intended to tell anyone about it, but he told Elrick-Ann, and he cried tears, and Elrick-Ann patted his shoulder and told him he'd just left it too long, she should have mentioned it to him sooner.

"Don't tell anybody about me going," he begged. "She was always scared somebody from the city would come looking for her. If they knew about the farm, they might hunt for her."

Elrick-Ann said she wouldn't tell. When she said it, she really meant to keep her word.

.    •    •

In the archetypal village over the ridge from the Cermit Farm, she who had been old Cermit's daughter and Abasio's mother—though she no longer remembered that fact—dwelt in a cave beside the waterfall. Her new name was Drowned Woman, and she was visited, time and again, as today, by a girl-child about six years old who was known as Orphan.

"Tell me a story," the girl begged.

"Come sit on my lap," said Drowned Woman.

"You're all wet," Orphan objected.

"So I am," Drowned Woman agreed. "I'll put on something dry, how's that."

Orphan put her thumb in her mouth to pass the time it would take Drowned Woman to find dry clothes. Oracle said Orphan was too old to suck her thumb, that six-year-olds were virtually grown up. Orphan didn't suck it in front of Oracle, only with Drowned Woman, who didn't care, or when she was in her own hovel, about to fall asleep. It was comforting. Sometimes she needed comforting.

Drowned Woman found something reasonably dry, and when she sat down beside the fire, she patted her lap invitingly.

Orphan took her thumb out of her mouth and crawled into the waiting lap. Drowned Woman's lap was bony. Oracle's lap was more cushiony, but Oracle was grumpier than Drowned Woman.

"What story do you want? 'Sleeping Beauty'? 'Three Bears'?"

"Not one of those. I want an Artemisia story."

Drowned Woman looked doubtful. "I don't know many Artemisian stories. Only the ones I've heard from Oracle."

"The Bear Coyote one."

Drowned Woman settled herself. "I think I remember that one. Let's see. Long and long ago . . . "

"How long ago?"

"Before you were born, or I was born, or our parents or our grandparents. Way back then. Coyote and Bear were married once, you know, when Bear was a woman, but this story comes after that, after Bear changed into a furry thing, with big teeth. Well, Coyote and Bear were walking along in the woods, and they saw a whole bunch of men hiding in the trees, with bows and arrows and throwing sticks and ropes, waiting to kill Bear and Coyote when they came along."

"And Coyote said to Bear, 'Way-oh.' "

"Right. Coyote said to Bear, 'Way-oh, there's men in the trees and men in the rocks and men in the bushes and men in the reeds along the stream, and they want our hides to keep them warm, but we want our hides for ourselves!' And Bear said, 'Way-oh, let's go up this rock and through that cave and go the long way round.' "

"So they did!"

"So they did. But the next day it was the same thing, and the day after that, and Bear and Coyote got tired of always having to go the long way round, just to keep their hides for themselves.

"So, one day, Coyote said, 'Let's ask our big brother the Water Sprinkler to send a huge flood, to wash all the men away.' "

Orphan said eagerly, "And Bear said, 'If the flood washes all the men away, what's to keep it from washing us?' "

Drowned Woman agreed. "Exactly. So Coyote said, 'Let's go to the Sun and ask him to send a great fire to burn all the men up.' "

"But Bear thought he might get burned too."

"Yes, he did. And after that, Coyote said, 'Let's go to our sister, Cold Woman, and ask her to send ice and cold to freeze all the men to death.' But Bear said, 'I have to sleep through the winters now, and that's cold enough. What's to keep me from freezing when the men freeze?' "

"So, finally . . . " said Orphan, expectantly.

"So, finally, Coyote said, 'Let's go to the Woman Who Changes Everything, and let's ask her to make monsters to eat the men so they won't bother us anymore.' And Bear said, 'But if the monsters eat all the men, they'll still be hungry, and then they'll probably start eating us.'

" 'Not if the Changing Woman won't let them,' said Coyote."

Drowned Woman's voice trailed away. "I've forgotten the rest," she said fretfully. "It's something about the monsters, but I've forgotten what it is."

Drowned Woman did forget things sometimes. Orphan snuggled more deeply into Drowned Woman's lap, trying to think of a story Drowned Woman couldn't forget.

"Tell the story about when I got here," she said. "You remember that one."

"Well, yes. It happened four years ago, one summer day when the villagers saw a little man coming down the mountain leading a donkey. And when he got to the market square, he opened one of the baskets on the donkey, and a guardian-angel came out and perched on the edge—"

"But people didn't know it was a guardian-angel," Orphan interrupted.

"No, none of the villagers had ever seen a guardian-angel, so they didn't know, but there it was, on the basket. And when the little man got down into the village, into the market square, he turned round and round and cried out in a loud, loud voice, 'My name is Herkimer-Lurkimer, and I've brought you your Orphan.' "

"So what did people do?" Orphan asked. She liked this part.

"So Hero went down to the square, and Oracle went down to the square, and Poet went, and Bastard went—"

"No, no!" cried Orphan, outraged. "Bastard didn't go. Bastard didn't get here until later!"

"Sorry. You're quite right. Bastard didn't go. And of course, I didn't, either, because I didn't come until a few days later. But Fool went, and Faithful Sidekick—"

"Faithful Sidekick got eaten last year."

"Quite right. He got eaten last year by a monster—"

"An ogre," said Orphan with a shiver. She remembered a huge shagginess, with teeth, a thing that roared and smelled dreadful. She buried her face in Drowned Woman's side. "Ogres are dreadful because they eat us up." She shivered.

Drowned Woman pulled her face away and kissed it. "But that ogre is gone now."

"And it won't come back!"

"No. It won't come back because Hero hunted it down and killed it. Now, where was I? Oh, yes. Everyone who was in the village went down to the square, and the little man opened the other basket and took out—"

"Me!" cried Orphan.

"Exactly right. You were two years old, more or less. Then Herkimer-Lurkimer handed you to Oracle, and Oracle almost dropped you because she had never had a baby and had no idea which end was up."

"But you did."

"When I got here, seemingly I did, though I don't remember how I knew. Even Oracle knew you were hungry and wet and needed tending to. Even Herkimer-Lurkimer knew that, for the other pannier was full of food and diapers."

"And I stayed with you for a long time!"

"Until you could go to the privies by yourself, exactly. Then I took you up to the Orphan's Hovel, which is where the Orphan is supposed to live. And you've lived there ever since, among all of us villagers."

"But specially you and Oracle."

"Especially me and Oracle. And we look after you, seeing you get the things you need, and between the two of us, we feed you, and everything is—"

"Just fine," said Orphan, bringing the story to its customary close. "Except I'd rather live here than in the hovel."

Drowned Woman hugged the child, smiling. "Well, Bastards can live anywhere at all, but Oracles have to live in caverns and Heroes have to live out under the stars and Misers have to live in dirty old houses crammed full of stuff and Orphans have to live in hovels. That's how things are.''

"And Princesses in palaces and Virgins in bowers and Milkmaids among the cows,'' chanted Orphan. ''Because we're archetypes. That's what Oracle says.''

"Oracle is quite right. We're archetypes, and we have to act typically. Otherwise, we'd be sent back into the world that has no room for us.'' Drowned Woman lifted Orphan out of her lap, set her on her feet, brushed the cloud of dark hair out of her eyes, and tugged her tattered smock down straight. ''Now, pretty girl, you're having supper with Oracle tonight, aren't you?''

"Yes.''

"Well, then. You get along up to the cavern before Oracle eats it all up.''

"All right.'' Orphan yawned. She'd spent most of the day swimming with the Water Babies, and the rest of it climbing the rocky gorge along the stream above the pool, looking for wildflowers to make Drowned Woman a crown, so she was tired. She smoothed down her smock, gave Drowned Woman a parting hug, and left the cave. As she came out, her guardian-angel flew down to her shoulder and nibbled on her ear with its long, sharp beak.

Walking up the path from the pool, she admired the fall, like glass slivers falling, and the pool making little jiggles that were part water and part light. Sometimes things were so pretty, she got all shivery inside. As soon as she got to the cavern, she'd ask Oracle for a story, right away! If she did that, maybe Oracle would forget to put ashes on her face, and she could stay pretty too.

No such luck. First thing in the cavern, there was Oracle coming with ashes on her fingers, swiping at Orphan's cheeks and forehead, at her arms.

"You're clean, again,'' she said in an annoyed voice. ''Drowned Woman has a fire. She has ashes. Why doesn't she dirty you?''

"Because she likes me better when I'm clean!'' cried Orphan rebelliously.

"Orphans aren't clean,'' asserted Oracle. ''And I don't know how many times I have to point that out. Every time I get you properly dirtied and your hair draggled, Drowned Woman washes you and combs you, and you don't even remotely resemble an Orphan!''

"My smock has a hole in it,'' said Orphan, tears in her eyes. ''I don't have any shoes!''

"There, there, child. I didn't mean to yell. It's just . . . you're not typical.'' Oracle turned her large self around and began stirring something in the pot over the fire, looking grumpy and dissatisfied, the way she usually did.

Orphan sat down and watched the firelight through her tears. When she squinched her eyelids, it made a blurry brightness that danced across the piles of books at the back of the cavern and made slender licky shadows around the pillars and half pillars as it glanced way back into corners and reflected from lots of little twin moons glowing there. Squirrels' eyes, maybe. Or bats. Or maybe something else, wandered in from outside. It had been gnomes once, because Orphan had seen the gnome-man and his wife and their baby, tiny as a peach pit, all warming themselves by the fire. But not monsters, because Oracle wouldn't let them.

When she got tired of making visions with her tears, Orphan wiped her eyes, sneaking a glance from under her lashes. Usually, if she cried right away, then Oracle was nice to her for the rest of the visit.

"I asked Hero to teach me to fight," she said.

Oracle gave her a surprised look. "You're not old enough."

"He says I am, but at first he said he wouldn't teach a girl. He said it wasn't—wasn't becoming for women to fight."

"According to Hero's lights, I'm sure that's true. According to Hero, most of what he does is in defense of womanhood." Oracle snorted a tiny snort and shook her head.

"He said violence is unfeminine and women's kinfolk should protect them, and I told him since I'm an Orphan, I don't have any kinfolk, and he said he'd protect me, and I said he might not be around when I need protecting. He sort of grumped, but he said he'd teach me."

Oracle stared blindly at the wall. Orphan was too young to have reasoned this out so well. Orphan was too young to come up with a lot of the things she came up with. "That was kind of him. Will you need weapons?"

"He says no. For the first years, it's just exercises. Jumping and spinning and kicking, like that. He says I'm very well coordinated and have a good spatial sense. He says my feet are already nice and hard from going barefoot all the time. And I'm not a scaredy-cat."

Oracle humphed to herself and went on stirring. A rustling noise overhead ended in a plop on the sand, and there was Orphan's squirrel, climbing onto Orphan's knee. Oracle's Pusscat saw him and came over to sit on the other side and lick his black whiskers. Pusscat had designs on the squirrel, so Oracle said, but Orphan protected him.

"Bastard invited me to his house. He wants to read to me," said Orphan.

Oracle stopped stirring and gave her a serious look. "You stay away from Bastard. He can read to himself."

Orphan found a nut in her pocket and fished it out for Squirrel. "I told him you would say that because he's dangerous, to females especially, and he said a lot of dirty words."

Now there it was again. Oracle could not remember ever having said that particular thing about Bastard, and yet Orphan knew it was true.

"That's typical." Oracle spooned the contents of the pot into two bowls, added a chunk of bread, and handed one such assemblage to Orphan.

"Will you tell me a story tonight?" Orphan begged, seeing it as a propitious time.

"What kind of story?" asked Oracle, her face softening. "What story would you like, child?"

"The end of the Artemisian story about Bear and Coyote. Drowned Woman started to tell me, but she forgot the ending."

"Which story about Bear and Coyote? The one where they get married?"

"No. The one where they ask Changing Woman to make monsters, to kill the people, so they can keep their hides. Drowned Woman only got as far as Changing Woman crying because men were her children too."

"Oh. Well, Changing Woman told Coyote and Bear she didn't need to make monsters to kill men, because when her sons, the Hero Twins, had killed most of the monsters, they'd left certain ones alive, and their names were Sa, that is Old Age, and Hakaz, that is Cold. But Coyote said men had become too clever for Sa and Hakaz, that worse monsters were needed.

" 'But it was through me the worst monsters were slain,' Changing Woman cried. 'My sons slew the bad monsters so that man could live.'

" 'Now men are killing everything! Don't other things need to live too?' cried Coyote."

"And Changing Woman was sad," said Orphan.

"Oh, indeed she was. For though Coyote and Bear were her children, men were her children too. And at last she said she would do another thing so Coyote and Bear could keep their hides. At the beginning of time on this world, men and animals had talked the same language, so Changing Woman said she would make them speak the same language again."

"And she did!" cried Orphan.

"She did indeed. And Bear and Coyote told the hunters to leave them alone, and the hunters were so surprised, they did! You can still hear Coyote out on the prairie at night, telling all his family how clever he was to talk to man."

"Hero says man started killing them again, though."

"Well, yes. But that was another age. Another time." Oracle gave the pot a final stir.

"If Changing Woman's sons got rid of all the monsters when the world began, why do we have monsters now?" Orphan asked.

Oracle stared into the darkness, her eyes half shut, her mouth pursed. After a long time, she said, "Same reason, Orphan. This is a different age, another time."

•  •  •

In the Place of Power, two shiny black creatures came unseen by a secret way, quick as snakes through tunneled stone, deep beneath the Dome, then upward to the place where the Witch lived. To them she had no human name but only a coded impulse, a unique mastery, a key that fit their particular lock. She was the reason they had brought the six-year-old child they carried with them, the child who cried for her aunty as she had ever since they had taken her.

"Where did you find her?" the Witch asked.

"South. Almost to Artemisia," said one of the creatures.

"Come here, girl," the Witch said, setting aside her mask.

And she, the child, seeing a human face, even one like this, was foolishly glad, for she thought people were kinder than the creatures that had brought her here.

"Go look again," said the Witch. "This is likely not the right one."

Obediently, the beetle-black creatures returned to their seeking, and the woman drew the child through doors and down hallways, deep into her apartments.

"What's that?" the child screamed hysterically. "What's that!"

"It's only a chair," she said, putting the child into it and strapping her there.

"What's that?" the child screamed again. "Don't do that! Don't!"

The woman did not answer, but merely lowered the helmet, down and down until it hid the child's eyes.

"Now," said the Witch. "Now, let's see!"

For a brief time the child went on crying.

# CHAPTER 2

*I*n the village there had always been a Miser's House, back of Wicked Stepmother's House, just below the ruined castle, but there'd been no Miser in it for a long time. Then one day, groaning over the notch in the ridge, came one truck and another one and one more yet, all of them making a rackety-clack and smoke from the boilers on the back, with the men in them red-faced and yelling, boistering, roistering, asking where was Miser's House. Three truckloads of stuff they put in Miser's House, piles and stacks of paper, and teetering towers of boxes, and lumpy sacks of this and that, and old falling-apart furniture, going back and forth, up and down, cursing and spitting and laughing and yelling. When the trucks were empty, they went away and a little vehicle came, rattling and smoking, to bring Miser himself.

He was thin and papery with a voice like cards being shuffled. He scuttled like Orphan's squirrel, quick, quick, out of the truck, into the house, then one side of his white, wrinkly face showed at a window behind a tattered curtain like a mouse peering from a hole. Miser's lips always trembled as though about to say something, but they very seldom did.

"What's he scared of?" Orphan had asked Oracle.

"Everything," said Oracle. "But mostly that someone will steal something from him."

Orphan hadn't seen anything going into the house that was worth taking out of it, but as Oracle said, that was typical. As it turned out, Orphan was about the only one Miser wasn't afraid of. Every now and then she'd go sit on his porch and sing to him, because she thought he might be lonely. She sang "Big Bad Ogre Had a Farm," and "Eensy Weensy Wivern," and "This Old Troll." Miser would peek at her from the corner of the window, and after a while from the corner of the door, and later yet, from the open door.

" 'This Old Troll, he played eight, he played nick-nack with his fate. With a nick-nack, paddy-whack, throw the imp a bone, this Old Troll came trolling home. . . . ' " she finished up with a long note.

"Very nice," whispered Miser, easing the door a crack.

"Poet says men went to the stars," she told him. "I want to know about it."

"True," said Miser. "Yes. They did. Rats. Deserting a sinking ship."

Through the open door Orphan could see Miser's hallway and stairs, both piled with boxes on the sides leaving only a narrow trail between, all the edges softened by velvety dust, the banisters draped in cobwebs that trailed lumpy pennants of dead flies. She wondered once again how Miser could stay so rusty black and papery white living in all that dust, but it didn't seem to stick to him any more than spiderweb did to spiders. Oracle said it was his natural milieu. He swam in it, like a fish in water.

"Can you tell me about it?" she asked. She wouldn't have asked if she wasn't so curious because Miser wasn't a good storyteller. He pinched his words as Oracle said he did his pennies.

"Men went," he said reluctantly. "That's all."

"How?" she demanded. "When?"

He sighed, a rusty sigh. He went away from the door, and after a time he scraped back, dragging a rickety chair along behind him that he set inside the door, close enough that he could close it quickly if a thief came along.

"Long time ago," he whispered, "men were profligate."

"What's *profligate*?" Orphan asked.

"Wasteful. 'Waste not, want not,' that's the motto, but men forgot it!" His voice actually rose beyond a whisper for a moment, then sank back and started over again. "They used up their inheritance. They didn't save things. They didn't take care—take care of things." He gestured at the hallway behind him. "You have to take care of things, Orphan." He panted and bit his lip.

"How did they go? On ships?"

"They built a station up in space, a great wheel that rolled and rolled, between earth and the moon. They mined the moon for minerals. They took hold of the sun for power. They built sky ships, and they went away. To the stars . . ." His voice trailed off.

Then he said, "That's all," got up from the chair, and shut the door.

Just as Orphan was about to leave, the door cracked open a little, and Miser's nose came through the crack. "And they should have taken their awful walkers with them!"

Orphan had no time to ask what awful walkers were, for the door was shut tight.

Later that day, she found Oracle and Bastard and Ingenue and two or three others sitting in the park, so she asked about awful walkers.

"Walkers?" Oracle mused, pausing in her crocheting. She was making a coverlet for Orphan, who had only two raggedy blankets to her name. "I've never heard of walkers, awful or otherwise."

"Maybe those damned impudent things," spat Bastard, who had been leaning back with his hands behind his head, taking the sun. "Arrogant creatures. Stopped me when I was coming here for the first time! Asking questions!"

Oracle raised her head and asked, "What were they like?"

"Like each other!" Bastard growled, rubbing his fingers across the red scars on his forehead where the letters B and R were branded. "Like as twins! Wearing black helmets. I told the driver to go through them or over them, but he wouldn't. Coward!"

"How many of them?" asked Oracle.

"Two. Driver told me they always go by twos."

Oracle asked no more questions then. Later, however, when Hero returned from his most recent stint of rescuing maidens or killing monsters, she asked him about walkers.

"Oh, yes," Hero replied, applying oil to the muscles in his arms and flexing them slowly back and forth, one-two, one-two. "I've met them. Always the same, striding by twos throughout the world, helmeted in black, with voices like fire. They say they are looking for a girl-child. At first it was for a toddler; later, year by year, for older children. They ask if I am aware of any children being fostered, or of any adopted, and I tell them no, I am not aware of any such. My quests seldom include children."

Oracle believed Hero's awareness pretty much stopped at Hero's skin, which in this case was probably fortunate. "What do they do if they find such a child?" she asked in a studiedly offhanded tone.

"I have heard they take them away," said Hero, with equal but genuine uninterest.

He had heard the truth. Whenever the walkers found dark-haired, dark-eyed little girls who were adopted or being fostered, they took them, deaf to protestations, unmoved by tears, leaving the protesters alive or dead, depending on whether they had contented themselves with screams and tears or whether they had tried to keep their children by force. None of these girl-children ever returned, and yet it seemed none of them had been the right one, for in years following, the walkers were searching still.

So much Oracle learned by questioning this one and that one, as time went on.

Following his abortive visit home, Abasio fell into habit as into a pit. Though he had not forsaken the idea of adventure, days spun into seasons and seasons into years while he did nothing at all about it. The fact was, he was too comfortable as he was. He had his rooftop shack, his books, his meals at Purple House or at a songhouse, his forays on behalf of Young Kerf. He did almost exactly what he wanted to at any hour on any day. He had a wide assortment of acquaintances among truckers and travelers, many of whom spun flavorful tales that both amused and intrigued him. Over the years, he had made himself useful to Soniff as well, and Soniff used Abasio for all manner of errands to do with *attending to business*.

"Got to attend to business," Soniff told him. "Got to make sure the little shop guy pays his dues regular and doesn't get hassled by some other gang once he does. Got to be sure your drug shipments are coming in regular. Got to pick up the brothel receipts every day and make sure new whores—new faces, anyhow—are coming in from next-city-north and old faces are sent on to next-city-south."

He sent Abasio to Echinot, next-city-north, to straighten out a problem, which he did in timely fashion, seeing nothing new or different in Echinot to make him stick around. So far, experience had taught him one city was almost exactly like another.

Late in the afternoon he caught a ride back with a water-trucker, not realizing until they were on the highway that the man was buzzed out of his skull and likely to kill them both. Abasio was trying, with no success, to get the driver to stop when two black-clad figures stepped from the borrow pit along the road, flashed across the pave like dark lightning, and laid hands on the vehicle. The truck stopped running, as though commanded to do so, and slid to a stop, half into the pit.

"Get out," commanded one of them, or both in unison, the command coming from some unimaginable distance.

Abasio got out, but the trucker, who was simply too far gone to understand what was happening, stared blearily through the glass as though wondering why the truck had stopped.

"Get out," the voices said once more.

No action on the part of the trucker. With growing apprehension, Abasio jittered from foot to foot, wanting to pull the man out, uncertain whether he should try.

He was given no opportunity. One of the walkers reached into the truck and pulled the man out. Abasio saw the trucker rising at the end of the walker's arm, straight up, that heavy man held at arm's length as though he weighed nothing, nothing at all, then the walker's hand let go and the trucker went on rising in an arc, impossibly rising, like an arrow shot from a bow.

"Have you seen a dark-haired girl about thirteen?" the other walker asked Abasio, coming close to him and glaring with its red eyes, drawing Abasio's eyes down, away from that arc in the air he'd been trying to follow to its end.

Abasio gulped. Yes, he had. He'd seen girls like that in Fantis, various places. And in Echinot too. He said where, painfully. As he spoke, spit ran out of his mouth and down his chin. He didn't even try to wipe it away.

"Girls without families," said the walker.

Abasio said he didn't know if they had families or not. He hadn't spoken to them. He'd just seen them, one place and another.

The walkers turned and went away.

Abasio stood heaving for a few moments before slowly, unwillingly walking across the road and out into the prairie land beyond, trudging along in the same line the trucker had been thrown, keeping on even when he was certain he'd gone too far, way too far. He finally told himself he'd take another dozen paces, and on the tenth one he found what was left of the trucker smashed onto a rock outcropping. Abasio turned aside to empty his stomach, noisily and messily.

He drove the truck on into Fantis himself. All the way there, he kept going over and over the incident in his mind, how he'd felt, what he'd heard and smelled while it was going on. He told himself he should have either been more scared or less! He should have been more scared because of what the creatures could do. He should have been less scared because they didn't look menacing. It was almost as though the walkers themselves had controlled exactly how terrified he was; as though they'd decided just how much to frighten him, enough to make him answer fully and at once, but not so much as to make him fall down in a fit.

Could it be some kind of ray they broadcast? Some smell they had, maybe. Pheromones. Grandpa used to talk about pheromones. Could there be a smell you didn't even know you were smelling that would make you weak and trembly and sick to your stomach? Or a sound you didn't know you were hearing? And if they could do that—was there anything they couldn't do?

He left the truck at a truckers' hostel, telling the people there what had happened and where they could find what was left of the trucker. He wanted to talk to someone about it, and he briefly considered discussing it with Elrick-Ann. He decided not to. Better to keep such matters to himself.


Orphan was walking in the woods one day when she found a baby griffin. She was shuffling along, kicking up clouds of last year's oak leaves, when the guardian-angel began whistling in her ear, shifting its weight from one side to the other, fluttering its wings and generally making a nuisance of itself. When Orphan looked to see what had upset the angel, she saw the baby griffin, half-buried in leaves at the foot of a tree. It was all crouched down, trying to hide its pinky-bronze body under its little wings that were hardly sprouted yet, and when she picked it up it tried to bite her with its tiny soft beak that couldn't even pinch.

The angel froze against Orphan's neck, making no noise at all. Orphan sat down and put the griffin in her lap.

"Where's your mama?" she asked the baby. "What are you doing down here all by yourself?"

The baby quit struggling and crouched again, making a tired little noise.

Orphan took off her knit hat that Drowned Woman had made for her and stretched it around the baby to keep it warm while she looked around. She stood back from the nearest tree and looked it all up and down, seeing if there was a nest. Then she did the next tree to that, and the next half-dozen, but there wasn't a nest anywhere.

She thought of taking the baby home, then sighed, knowing what Oracle or Hero, either one, would say about *that*. Orphan fetched all kinds of animals home, all the time, but none of the people in the village were what she'd call *supportive*. Orphan knew perfectly well what the animals wanted and what to do for them if they were hungry or hurt. They were like kinfolk, so she told herself, feeling it to be so, but none of the other villagers understood that.

The guardian-angel fluttered off through the trees and landed on a rock outcropping, where it sat and whistled at her, over and over, *quirrup, quirrup, quirrup,* meaning "Come over here and look," the way it did when it heard grubs under bark or found wild raspberries. When she got there, the angel flew up the wall a little way, and when Orphan stepped back to see where it was, she saw the griffin nest, or at least she saw the neatly arranged sticks sticking out of a small cave about halfway up the rock wall. Griffins built neat nests, according to Hero. Like little log cabins turned upside down.

"You crawled all the way over there, didn't you?" she asked the baby. "All the way over under those trees." She could certainly see why it had gone in that direction. All the other directions were more or less straight up, which is the way she would have to go if she was going to take the griffin back to its mother. She briefly considered asking Hero to do it, setting the idea aside almost at once. Hero wasn't sentimental about baby things. Certainly not about baby monsters. If he climbed up there, he would probably kill the other hatchlings, if there were more, and the parents, too, if he could find them.

No. If this baby was going to be returned to its home, Orphan would have to do it herself.

The hat would serve as a carrier if she tied it around her waist with her belt, which she did. She had no shoes to take off, but she did hike her smock up between her legs and stick it through the belt in front. These preparations quickly accomplished, she started up the wall, reciting to herself Hero's instructions for removing oneself from pits, chasms, and crevasses.

"Three points in contact before you let go of the fourth. Keep your eyes on where you're going. Don't look down. Don't worry about how far up you have to go. Just worry about the next grip up, the next step up."

There were plenty of handholds, though some of them were slimed with one thing or another. She only slipped twice, neither time very badly. The baby began to whimper when she was almost there, which is no doubt why the big one reached the nest almost at the same moment Orphan did.

The first Orphan knew of it was when she looked up to find her view of the rock wall blocked by a pair of fully expanded, scaly wings, the sun glinting off an open beak that was unmistakably stabbing at her.

"I'm bringing it back!" shouted Orphan, more angry than frightened. "By the wind's knees, monster, I'm bringing home your child!"

The beak slammed shut like the door to a vault. Orphan climbed over the ledge into the cave, where she untied her belt and unfolded the hat, disclosing the baby, which she hurriedly placed in the nest before standing back to await whatever would happen next.

The baby cried. The mother nuzzled. Or maybe it was the father. Orphan had no idea which. Obviously, the two could talk to one another, because what was going on was not mere baby-parent babble. It was a conversation. If Orphan had to attach words to it, it would go something like, "How did you get down there in the first place?" "Mama, I was just climbing on the nest walls." "How many times do I have to tell you, don't climb on the nest walls! You could have been killed!"

And would have been if Hero had found it, thought Orphan as she sat down to catch her breath and to consider how she was going to get down.

Even Hero admitted that going up was often easier, since one's eyes were at one's top end.

The Griffin had to ask twice before Orphan realized the question was aimed at her.

"I ask again, what is your name?"

"Orphan," said Orphan, turning to see the large Griffin's eyes fixed on her with a fierce bronze glare. She dropped into one of the defensive positions Hero had taught her.

"Not eating you," said the Griffin. "No need for apprehension."

Orphan slowly straightened up.

"Is Orphan your name? Or is that merely what you are called?"

Orphan shook herself. "I don't know," she mumbled.

"Were you merely born? Or were you created for a purpose?"

Orphan could only stare, wide-eyed. The Griffin nodded to itself, talked to the little one a moment more, then grasped Orphan quickly and firmly by both shoulders and stepped out into the air.

A moment later, breathless, Orphan was released at the bottom of the wall.

"Griffins live long," said the Griffin, thrusting down with its great wings. "I will remember you."

When the Griffin had flown up to the cave once more, the guardian-angel came out of hiding and sat on Orphan's shoulder, chortling in a puzzled-pleased fashion.

"Fine lot of good you were," grumped Orphan, turning about to go back to the village. "Fine lot."

When she got back to the village, she wanted to tell someone what had happened, so, spying Poet ensconced on the doorstep of the Creative Artist's House, she decided to tell him. Before she could get there, however, a high reedy voice called from inside the house. "Your lunch is ready, John. Wipe your feet when you come in." The Poet's Spinster Sister. All the time she'd been in the village, Orphan had never heard her say anything but "Your meal's ready, John. Wipe your feet when you come in."

So Poet was at lunch, and there was no one else around to tell, and when night came, Oracle said she was in no mood to be pestered.

"Well, tell me this, at least," begged Orphan. "Was I merely born, Oracle? Or was I created for a purpose?"

"Eat your soup," said Oracle, with a frown. "And don't ask questions it would take an Oracle to answer."

"But you are an—"

"Eat your soup!"

Seasons came and went, and though at first Orphan remembered the Griffin clearly, as time went by, the incident became fuzzy. Stories and dreams and actual happenings got mixed up in her mind, and sometimes she wasn't sure whether she actually remembered events or had been told about them or had dreamed them. Griffin got all mixed up with Changing Woman and Coyote and Bear and the dream Orphan kept having of the house in the woods with the three tall chairs. In the dream, she was tired and wanted to sit down, but she couldn't climb onto any of the chairs. They were too high, too far. There were no handholds, no place to put her feet. In the dream she tried each of the chairs in turn, but all of them were huge and gray and carved all over with fearsome creatures.

Whenever she had the dream, she would wake up with her heart pounding, sitting straight up in her narrow bed, clutching her raggedy blankets around her, only to hear her guardian-angel whistling and chortling from the head of the bed.


Oracle had taught Orphan to read and write when she was tiny. By the time she was seven, she had read quite difficult things with long words, and by the time she was fourteen, she had read all the books in Oracle's cavern—at least, those that were at all interesting and had started over.

Orphan was delighted, therefore, when a new inhabitant moved into the village, one who had among his belongings shelf after shelf of books. His name, so said Oracle, was Burned Man. His people came and went for days, stowing wagonloads of his belongings into the house next to Orphan's Hovel, which was known as Martyr's House, and when they went away at last, leaving him behind, they cried.

It took a little while to get used to Burned Man's appearance, which was dreadful, but Orphan, who managed it at first for the sake of the books, found she could ignore how he looked a good deal of the time. Burned Man taught her arithmetic and algebra and geography, she seated on the bottom porch step of his house, he seated a step behind her where she wouldn't have to look at him, marking maps and equations in the dust with a long pointy stick.

During geography lessons, he spoke of the great forests to the east, seas of trees that stretched all the way to the eastern ocean, speckled with warrior tribes. West over the mountains lay the desert, and beyond that the western sea, the Faulty Sea, with towns along its shores. South lay Artemisia, then High and Low Mesiko and the land bridge to a whole other continent full of huge snakes and alligators and birds as tall as men. He talked of the traders who moved among these peoples and places. Mostly, however, he talked of manland, so called because the men who lived in the cities and Edges and farms shared a language and, more or less, an economic system. Mostly, he dwelt upon the cities and the gangs who ran them.

"You make city people sound just awful," Orphan complained. "They don't sound very civilized."

"Some of them aren't," he had mused. "The wall between civilized and natural man is a flimsy one. Natural is born in our bones. Civilization is received from our parents and passed on to our children, as a gift. If we don't have it to give, our children don't get it."

"Why doesn't somebody give it to the cities, then?"

He didn't speak for a long time. She sneaked a look at him, a quick one. It was very uncomfortable to look at Burned Man for long. About the time she decided he wasn't going to say anything more, he did.

"Perhaps one reason for children being born little," he said painfully, "is so their parents can teach them to control themselves while they're small enough to be controlled. If a person grows up without controls, it's very hard to civilize him. Like trying to stop a truck without a brake."

"Like Bastard," said Orphan.

"Exactly like Bastard. The cities are full of people like Bastard. No way to stop them at all."

There was another long silence.

"But *why* are they that way?" Orphan persisted.

"Think of it this way," he whispered to her. "Imagine that people are tiny. Imagine that they can live on the surface of a cube."

She shut her eyes and imagined it. "All right. I'm pretending."

"Imagine the cube is a foot each way. There are six square feet, one to each side of the cube. And there's one cubic foot inside, right?"

She pictured this without difficulty. "Right."

"Imagine one more thing. Imagine one of these little persons can live on each square foot of outside, one person can live in each cubic foot of inside. How many outside to how many inside?"

"Six," she said. "Six outside to one inside."

"Now, if you make the cube bigger, the number of units inside increases faster than the number of units outside. Can you see that?"

It took her a little time, but she did see it. "Since this has something to do with people being civilized, I suppose you mean a little cube is like a family. And a bigger one is like a city. Is that it?"

Burned Man laughed his uncomfortable laugh. "You're right. Both cube and family have an outside and an inside. Outsiders know of the world, they're experienced, they've learned what works. Insiders haven't. They have only wants and urges. In a family, if Grandma, Grandpa, Mama, Papa, Older Brother, Uncle are all working to civilize one child, the child can hardly escape, can he?" Burned Man laughed, the way he sometimes did, all breath and no ha ha. "Even if there are two or three working to civilize one, it works out. But if there is only one to civilize each one, or one to civilize two, or three, or if the insiders grow up never learning what works and have children of their own . . . "

Orphan shook her head at him. "You're getting upset."

He breathed heavily. "You're right."

"You shouldn't get upset. It's not good for you." Oracle had told her as much. "Stop thinking about cities."

He made a funny noise, not quite like a chuckle. More painful, somehow. "I'll try."

Orphan tried to help. "When men went to the stars, they should have taken everybody."

He started to say something more, then stopped. Orphan waited. Suddenly he stood up and went into his house, shutting the door firmly behind him.

Orphan stayed on the porch steps until she was sure he wasn't coming back. When she got back to her hovel, she found Oracle waiting for her.

"What was Burned Man going on about?" Oracle asked her softly.

Orphan quoted Burned Man as best she could, concluding:

"He said the cities were too big to be civilized by anybody."

Oracle sighed. "Poor man! I wish he'd understood that before."

"Before what?"

Oracle hummed and jittered. "Well, Orphan . . . before he burned himself. He thought immolating himself would make someone do something."

Orphan felt unaccountably angry at this, for it made no sense. "He burned himself! Why did he do that?"

Oracle patted her, calming her down. "Burned Man was an Edger."

"What's an Edger?"

"Someone who lives in an Edge. That is, not in the city itself, but in the protected Edge, which has retained much of what the cities lost long ago. Technology. Law. Arts and sciences. The Edges, so I am told, are blessed places where a remnant of true humanity has saved itself. The Edges, so I am told, are damned because the people there turned their backs on those in need when they fled the cities. Whichever, or perhaps both, Burned Man was an Edger, and he was also what is called a reformer, you understand? He saw suffering in the cities and wished to alleviate it."

"He told me about that," Orphan said.

"He tried to help and couldn't. He tried to get other people interested, but they weren't. Finally, he went to the Council Building of the Edge where he lived, he sat down on the steps, poured fuel on himself, and set himself alight. He left a letter of protest saying he hoped his horrible death would draw attention to the problem and something would be done."

Tears seeped down Orphan's cheeks. "Poor Burned Man," she whispered. "He went on living, and nobody did anything."

Oracle shrugged. "What was there to do? As you said, it was too large a problem to have an acceptable solution. Some fires cannot be put out, they must consume themselves. Some knots cannot be untied; they must be cut. But people can't accept that. Burned Man couldn't. Poor man. He's an archetypal Martyr, a walking accusation, an uncomfortable neighbor. So they sent him here.''

"Are all of us here uncomfortable people?'' asked Orphan.

"Most of us.''

"Including me?''

Oracle looked into her eyes, stroked her cheek, said tenderly, "I imagine so, child. I imagine so.''

"I tell you one thing,'' said Orphan angrily. "Before I'd go burn myself, I'd be sure it would do some good.''


People came and went in the archetypal village. Glutton came one spring, but died of overeating by fall. Poet died, and in his place came a Painter with an irascible little wife of faded beauty who sounded almost exactly like Poet's Spinster Sister. Conspirator came for a time, then disappeared under mysterious circumstances. Sycophant arrived and pitched his tent next to that of Hero, just in time to be eaten by a huge stinky troll that came down from the hills. The troll had finished Sycophant and was about to start on Gossip when Hero returned from somewhere all out of breath and killed it dead. Orphan didn't sleep well for a long time after that.

Everyone got older, even Ingenue, who went on saying she was nineteen just as she always had.

Every now and then Oracle asked Hero about the walkers, being as casual about it as she could manage, and he said they still stalked the roads of the world, asking the same question they had asked for years. "Have you seen a dark-haired girl, a fosterling perhaps. A girl of seventeen? A girl of eighteen?''


Lately, Bastard had made a habit of hiding where Orphan couldn't see him, then whispering to her in a voice out of nightmare. Sometimes he was in the trees along the path or outside her window.

"There are other villages,'' he whispered in the dark night, his voice like a ring of smoke, circling, infiltrating.

"There are villages where the Hero is the Fool, where the Oracle is the Idiot, where the Bastard is the Hero.''

Orphan sat on the stool beside her fireplace and tried to pay no attention.

"There are villages where time turns back on itself and the old wonders rise again,'' he whispered. ''Where man is the lord of creation and woman his willing servant. Where pain is pleasure, Orphan.''

She turned, seeing him peeking at her at the window corner. His eyes had red sparks in them, like the eyes of an animal at the edge of firelight. His teeth showed between his lips, very white.

''There are villages where my kind and your kind are allies,'' he said to her. ''Maybe, even . . . lovers.''

Orphan got up and ran out the door, toward Oracle's cavern, where she'd feel safe. Behind her she could hear Bastard's soft laughter, a clinging sound, a sucking sound, making her think of the bats in Oracle's cavern, who made that same sound as they digested the blood they had drunk in their nightly forays.

One time she saw Bastard talking with Fool. Bastard never talked with Fool, no one did, really, and Fool never listened to anyone. Usually, he just stood beside his gate, looking up the road, crying ''Mama, Mama.'' Now there was something evil in the line of Bastard's back, something horrid in Fool's fascination.

Neither of them had seen her. She stopped around the corner of Fool's shack, where she could hear without being seen.

Bastard chortled. ''Oh, she was young, just the age I like 'em. She had long hair, down to her sweet little ass. She kind of twitched, the way they do, walking along. And I said to myself, 'I'm going to have a piece of that or know the reason why!' ''

Fool repeated the words after him: '' . . . piece of that.''

Orphan poked her head around the corner of the house to see Fool rocking to and fro, petting himself between the legs. He did that sometimes. In fact, he did that a lot of the time.

Bastard said, ''I asked around until I found out where I could find her. I take what I want!''

''Take what I want! Take! What I want!'' Fool giggled and bounced. Then he became very still and took his hands away from himself. ''Mama said no,'' he said to Bastard in a strangled-sounding voice. ''Mama said no.''

Bastard poked him and laughed. ''Ah, well, but your Mama didn't know this girl. So that night, I went in through her window with a knife . . . ''

''Through her window,'' Fool cried with a sidewise glance, licking his sloppy lips. ''With a knife.''

''Just to keep her quiet and respectful.'' Bastard laughed his sucking laughter. ''I like women who are respectful!''

Orphan felt her shoulder seized firmly in a large, hard hand.

''What filth are you listening to?'' Oracle demanded in a whisper.

"Bastard's talking about raping someone," Orphan replied, rubbing her shoulder.

"No doubt," said Oracle, pulling her around the back of Fool's shack and away toward the cavern. "What did you think the R branded on his forehead was for—reformer?"

"No," grunted Orphan. "I know what it's for. Oracle, it wasn't what he was saying. It's that he's talking to Fool."

Oracle frowned and nodded.

Orphan went on. "Fool doesn't usually talk with anyone. He just stands at the gate of his house, staring up the road."

Oracle sighed. "That's the way his mother went, after she left him here years ago. At first he stood there at the gate and howled, day and night. Finally, I told him if he howled, his mother would die and never come to him, but if he would be a good quiet boy, his mother would come fetch him, eventually."

"Will she come back?" asked Orphan.

Oracle shook her head. "Only metaphorically. She had an IDDI. It's why she brought him here."

Orphan didn't need to ask what IDDIs were. Oracle had been disgustingly specific and boringly historic about sexual diseases, going over and over them until Orphan could have listed them and all their causes and symptoms in her sleep. Since IDDIs were what killed most people, it wasn't surprising that Fool's mother had died from one.

Orphan shook her head and said, "That's too bad. I wish Fool could be happy. I wish something nice could happen to him."

Oracle sighed. "Sometimes there are no nice things, only bearable things. There are no acceptable solutions to some problems."

Orphan knew that. Oracle had told her often enough.

Seasons came and went; snowfall and summer sun. Oracle asked the farmer, when he came to deliver milk, whether he had ever encountered walkers. Oh, yes, he said. They were wandering the world asking the same question they always asked.

"Have you seen an orphan girl of nineteen? Of twenty?"

# CHAPTER 3

*A*basio was lounging around Purple House
one afternoon, feeling bored and restless, when the door banged open and
one of the kid-Purples came in with blood running down
his face and arm, one eye rapidly swelling shut and a
bad cut on his shoulder.

"They took Elrick-Ann," the kid cried in a voice
that squeaked. "They took the Young Chief's
woman!"

Everybody sitting around was up, shouting, everybody asking questions so loudly, no one could hear the
answers. Abasio yelled at them, his voice bellowing
over theirs: "You all shut up and let me ask the
questions!"

"Tha's right," piped up TeClar Chingero. "You lissen
to Basio."

"Now," he said. "One of you go get the medic-hag.
One of you go get some hot water from the kitchen. The
rest a you sit down and hush."

There was some toing and froing, then the medic-hag

had the worst of the bleeding stopped and was busy setting stitches into the boy's shoulder while he bit his lips and tried not to yell.

"What happened?" Abasio asked, keeping his voice steady and calm.

"We was doin' escort duty," the boy muttered between clenched teeth. "Five of us, takin' some of the women to the baths. We got to the corner, you know, where the odds-shop is. And these Greens came bustin' out, ten of 'em, maybe more—"

"You're positive Greens?" Abasio asked, puzzled. The word was, Old Chief Purple paid off Wally Skins to keep the Greens at a distance until Kerf was old enough to be a good Chief, which meant—so said the smart mouths— never.

"Sure it was Greens!" the boy shouted. "I'm not color bline. They was wearin' colors, they had green braids, they was yellin' war cries. There was two of them to ever one of us, and some of 'em grab Elrick-Ann an' make off down that alley while the rest keep us busy. We was down all over the place, you know, cut up some. I think Little Truck's dead. When we kine of got it together, I tole the others t'go on, and I came back to report."

Abasio didn't like the smell of it. "Was Carmina with you?"

Carmina was Soniff's woman, and she was eight months pregnant. Why take Elrick-Ann when they could have Carmina, who'd bring a big ransom? Pregnant women always did.

Asking the question might not be smart. Abasio looked for Soniff, but he wasn't around.

"I'll tell the Young Chief," he said. "You all wait here."

Young Chief Purple was asleep. He sat up in his bed, staring bleary-eyed from his smooth round face, not meeting Abasio's eyes.

"Oh, those rotten Greens," he said.

His voice was usually petulant and never strong, but to Abasio's ear it seemed more than usually nervous. Young Chief stroked the few scanty hairs on his upper lip, hiding his mouth.

"I can arrange a rescue," Abasio offered, somewhat disconcerted by the Young Chief's manner. Young Chief usually greeted bad news with screams of rage or hysteria. This calm was uncharacteristic.

"We can be there in half an hour," he continued softly.

"No, no. We wait for the ransom deman'," Young Chief mumbled, still looking everywhere but at Abasio. "They be makin' a ransom deman'. No doubt."

"No doubt," agreed Abasio, narrow-eyed. "Poor Elrick-Ann."

"Wha'?" Young Chief asked, with a darting glance at Abasio. "Oh, yeah, yeah. Poor Elrick-Ann." His voice lacked conviction.

Abasio waited, forcing himself to be calm. The ransom demand arrived twelve hours later. Abasio read it before taking it to the Young Chief. It was for a ridiculous amount—a golden crow. A stupid amount, one that seemed calculated to arouse fury rather than permit payment.

"They crazy, askin' this," said Young Chief after he'd glanced at the demand.

"Too much?" asked Abasio, even though he knew it was.

"Too much even for a pregnant woman, and she not pregnant."

Which was restating the smelly part of the case from Abasio's point of view. Why had the Greens taken Elrick-Ann at all?

"You want me to negotiate?"

"Nah. Wait till they come down with they ransom. Jus' wait."

Abasio had no intention of waiting, though he gave every appearance of doing so. He knew the Greens' reputation. He could imagine all too clearly what was happening to Elrick-Ann. He rounded up TeClar and CummyNup and swore them to secrecy. "You my men?" he demanded.

TeClar said, "We your men, Basio. Our mama, she say you save us more'n once, so we got to do what you say. An' Elrick-Ann, she our friend too."

CummyNup asked, "What we gone do, Basio?"

"We're going to be audacious," Abasio told them.

"What that mean?"

"That means we're going to do something nobody would expect."

They waited until it got dark, along about suppertime, when all the Greens would probably be downstairs. Abasio strapped every knife he owned to various parts of his anatomy and hung two guns at his waist. TeClar and CummyNup had bags full of smoke bombs and noisemakers. They sneaked into the alley half a block down and across from Green House, and while the Chingeros stirred up a racket that brought the Greens swarming out like hornets from a nest, Abasio shinnied up a drainpipe and got through a back window at Green House. The room he got into was empty, so were the next two, and in the third one he found what was left of Elrick-Ann.

She was still breathing, though he couldn't imagine why. Looking at her made him so sick, he didn't try to think about what he was doing. He just wrapped her in a sheet from the bed, slung her over his shoulder, shinnied back down the pipe, and sneaked back to Purple House, picking up the Chingeros en route, as planned. After some confused talk, they decided to leave her on the Purple doorstep for TeClar to find with a convincing display of surprise. TeClar was good at that. Nobody had any idea how she got there, least of all Elrick-Ann herself, who had stayed conveniently unconscious throughout. She was taken upstairs to the women's quarters while the younger men stood around in chattering clusters, wondering who'd brought her back, and why, and Abasio added spurious conjectures of his own. Strangely, Young Chief was absent from the house and so were most of the older Purples, including Soniff.

The fact that the Greens had been so easily suckered firmed up Abasio's opinion that they hadn't expected a rescue attempt. They hadn't even set a guard on her. And the fact that they'd cut her up meant they hadn't planned to ransom her, either. Which meant—which meant that somebody, the Young Chief or somebody, had paid the Greens to make off with Elrick-Ann.

Why?

Abasio didn't have to wonder long. Less than an hour later, the Young Chief came in, smiling all over his fat little face, surrounded by his usual entourage of elders and bringing a new conk he'd just bought from the Bloodrun gang. Sybbis, her name was. Sybbis, bought not leased. She was younger than Elrick-Ann was by a good bit and certainly more . . . Abasio groped for a word to describe Sybbis. He didn't find one. Mostly, he had a feeling, men didn't try to describe Sybbis. They just looked at her with their mouths open. The minute she got inside the house, she took off the full robes women wore in the streets, and after that, everyone could see just what she was like.

Having seen, everyone was most congratulatory to the Young Chief, including Abasio. Nobody was so tactless as to mention that Elrick-Ann was back, though Soniff eventually found out from Carmina. Once he knew, he should have declared war on the Greens. At the very least, he should have sent a few retaliation teams. Tally teams were sent out on the least excuse, because that's how kid-gangers earned their reputations. Soniff didn't even do that, and the rumor was, the Old Chief told him not to.

"Why Soniff not sendin' tallies?" TeClar whispered to Abasio. "Why the Old Chief not lettin' him?"

"You know what's good for you, you don't ask," Abasio whispered back. Everyone knew why, but nobody was saying. Elrick-Ann had been leased from the Cranked-Ups, so much a year for life. If she were dead, the Young Chief wouldn't have owed another black-penny on her. If the Greens had killed her, it would have been the Greens' debt to pay, and the Cranked-Ups probably wouldn't have attacked the Greens because of their reputation. No cost to the Purples, and Young Chief rid of Elrick-Ann. A smart plan. So smart, the Old Chief had probably thought it up.

Maybe she'd still die. It would be best, all around, if she did. Abasio knew that now. He should have killed her there in that room, killed her to put her out of pain, but he shouldn't have brought her back. Not the way she was.

It was too late to think about it now. He'd just have to hope that she died, preferably without ever coming to and seeing what it was the Greens had done to her.

"Were you always an Oracle?" Orphan asked.

Oracle stared into the flames and slowly stirred the pot that was sending up aromatic little puffs of steam.

"You mean, was I always called Oracle?"

"Were you somebody else, before?"

Oracle nodded, putting the lid back on the pot and seating herself in her rocking chair.

"Will you tell me about it?"

"It's a long, dull story, child."

"The meat isn't tender yet. And it's raining. So why not tell me?"

There was no good reason why not. Oracle settled herself in the rocking chair, leaned back her head, and told the story:

"Oracle was a child once," she said. "Her name was Seraphina.

"She lived far west of here on the hills beside the Faulty Sea, where the ocean had flowed in to fill a great fault in the land. From the hills where Seraphina's people lived, they could look across to the Caliph Islands, the treasure islands where the Caliph's gold was buried. Long ago, a great city stood there, but it was all fallen down.

"Inland from Seraphina's home the mounded hills breasted the horizons, blotched with brush, grown up with grass, sun-scorched and dry for most of every year. Some days the sun glinted from the growth as from burnished metal, like the hot hard light of her father's forge where he labored at the anvil, hammering red iron into horseshoes or candlesticks or tall, fancy gates. Some nights she dreamed of the forge light, the huff of the bellows, the clangor of the iron, waking with her heart pounding like the blows of the hammer, full of terrible apprehension at that burning, terrible light. She spoke of it to her mother, her father, but they told her hush, hush, it was only a dream.

"Sometimes she dreamed other things. One night she saw where gold was buried in the old city. By morning, she was all in a fever of excitement to go there and find it. She begged and begged, father, uncles, nothing would do but they take her at once. She told them she'd seen gold in the ruins.

"So they went in a boat to the Caliph Islands, and when they set foot upon the shore, she went straight to the place in the tumbled city where the gold was, as she had dreamed it. But there were other things there, things she hadn't dreamed, skulls that grinned at her when she uncovered them, the eyeholes gleaming with buttery metal, chains and rings and bracelets, uncorroded by the burying earth. And when she saw the skulls, they spoke to her, telling her things she couldn't bear to hear.

"So she did not speak of gold again, and when the dreams came, she was silent. But her father, who had hushed her often enough, would have none of her silence now. Fool-child, he called her, always screaming and whining. The bones wouldn't hurt her, the bones wouldn't kill her—why couldn't she be good for something? Come now, he commanded, come tell Uncle Netse where gold will be found, for Uncle wants to go digging.

"She was an obedient child. She shut her eyes and summoned the image of gold: *A white building, all tumbled down. If you stand on the tallest hill, facing the Faulty Sea, with the bridge across the sea to the left and the broken tower to the right . . .*

" 'Not clear enough. Make her go with me!' Netse demanded.

"And at this she screamed and fell and foamed at the mouth, for she couldn't bear to go again among the bones. Father and uncles didn't know what it was like, remembering what all those bones had felt and thought when the world fell, the howls of pain, the maimed bodies, the crushed skulls. Seraphina thrashed and foamed at the mouth and went on howling until they sent Uncle away and let her lie by herself in her room, lulled by the sounds of the waves."

"Was it beautiful there?" asked Orphan.

"Oh, yes. It was beautiful there," said Oracle. "It was home."

"And she . . . you didn't see bones all the time!"

"Not all the time, no, but she did see them and she did see other things. Seraphina thought it strange that her father and her uncle believed her dreams of gold but denied her dreams of shaking and fire and death. They wanted to believe in gold. They didn't want to believe she saw the other things."

"What did she see?"

"She saw a little fire in the canyon bottom, a thin wraith of smoke in the dusk, a wind that would come with morning, dispersing the smoke so that no one would know it was there, then a larger fire in the dark hours, an earthquake in the night, a holocaust that would come with dawn of the second day, a firestorm driven on a fierce wind that shifted in every direction, up every canyon, down every hill.

"She tried to tell them, but no one would listen but Aunt Lolly, and even she laughed.

" 'When will all this happen?' Aunt Lolly asked.

"Seraphina didn't know when. Maybe soon. Maybe later. But Father would still be alive, for Seraphina saw him die in the fire. Others in the town would be alive as well, for she saw them burning as well. Then, after that, she saw villages of stilt houses being built over the sea, where the recurrent fires couldn't get at them. Little houses with bottoms like boats, so they'd float when the earth shook. She had begged her father to build such a house, live in such a fashion. . . .

" 'Nonsense,' her father had said. 'There are far too many of us to live like that.'

"And Seraphina knew he was right. There were too many men to live in such a sensible fashion. Men had to live dangerously because they were so many. Lives are cheap when men are many."

"What happened?" begged Orphan, after a long silence.

"It was not long," Oracle said, "before people heard about Seraphina's talent for seeing gold. People outside the family; people outside the town! They came demanding to know where treasure was. They bothered Father at the forge, they woke the family at night, knocking at the windows. Some begged and some threatened. Father said he could do without the gold easier than he could put up with such a fool-child, so he named her Oracle and sent her away, across the sunny hills and the baked desert, over the high mountains to an archetypal village, where distance veiled the images and she seldom dreamed of fire."

"Did Seraphina's town really burn down?" asked Orphan.

"Oh, yes," said Oracle in a distant voice. "Just as she had seen it happening."

"What happened to the people?"

"Most of those not crushed by the shaking burned in the fire."

"Her family? Her father and uncles?"

"Gone. All but her aunt Lolly. When she smelled the little smoke, she remembered what Seraphina had said and got out in time. It was she who sent word here, to me, to Oracle, telling me what had happened. She needn't have done. I already knew. Just as I knew when they built the first of the little boat-bottomed houses, out over the sea."

"I'm sorry about your family," said Orphan.

Oracle smiled a weary smile with sadness in it. "Sorry-ness has no part in it, child. I did what I could do. My people believed what they wanted to believe. Just as every seeker who comes to me for a prophecy believes what he wants to believe and never one jot else."


In Purple House, days and days went by, but Elrick-Ann didn't die. She regained consciousness, and the hags gave her drugs for the pain. When she saw what they'd done to her, she begged for them to kill her, but nobody had the right to lay hands on her but Kerf; he wouldn't do it; she couldn't do it by herself. Gradually her wounds healed, leaving hideous scars behind them.

She had no duties any longer. She was not Kerf's woman any longer. She was not welcome in the house where anyone could see her. She was just there, hidden away in the women's quarters, with nobody going near her for fear of Kerf, imprisoned, virtually alone, and with no other place to go. Abasio fretted over it, waited for a propitious moment when Soniff was relaxed, and suggested the Young Chief award Elrick-Ann a pension, just as he would any disabled gang member.

"Why would he do that?" Soniff asked lazily.

"To save talk," Abasio answered in a careless voice. "Wouldn't do to have the young ones thinkin' people disrespect the Purples."

"Why would people disrespect the Purples?" Soniff sat up, frowning.

"Well," drawled Abasio, "we didn't go to war over her. We didn't send tallies. Greens musta disrespected us quite a bit, takin' her, doin' that to her. She's a Crank girl, and they might disrespect us, too, considerin' all the talk that's goin' round."

Soniff frowned, but he saw the point. A pension was cheaper than any of the alternatives. Soniff sent Abasio to the Cranks to settle them down so far as the Purples were concerned. Though Abasio started out cool enough, his anger ruined his diplomacy. He couldn't forget what had happened to Elrick-Ann. He found himself saying too much, describing too much, and then he had to blame somebody. He couldn't come right out and blame Soniff and Little Purp, so he had to lay it on the Greens. When he left the Cranked-Ups' homeground, it was with the strong feeling the Cranks were going to fight the Greens over Elrick-Ann.

Things took off faster than he expected. That same night when he left Purple House to go to his own place, all the talk on the street was that the Cranks had challenged the Greens for that same night, a war that would be shown on the public amusement screen. Instead of going home, Abasio went to the entertainment district to see what the odds-shops were predicting. They were giving five to one on the Greens, which was more or less the way Abasio would have called it himself. He decided to stick around and see how it came out.

"Where's this war gonna be?" he asked the odds-shop man.

The man shrugged. "Out east, toward the bridge."

It was probably as good a place as any. Plenty of open ground; plenty of wreckage around for cover. Of course, there were some occupied buildings out there, too, but while the war was going on, the inhabitants would bottle themselves up inside. Abasio paid a silver mouse for a seat in the screen room and sat himself down among the crowd of bettors who were jabbering and yelling at one another while a Whisper-High commercial filled the screen. Whisper-High was known as a woman's drug. Men's drugs were advertised mostly at the arena and in the songhouses.

"There they are!" somebody shouted.

And there they were on a stretch of open ground littered with old car bodies and tumbled walls, lit by bonfires. In the foreground, Greens capering, black and orange in the firelight, legs raised, backs bent, stomping out their war dance, howling out their war cries: hoo-wah, hoo-wah. Wally Skins bending and shuffling, scalps bobbing on his belt and headdress. In the background the Cranks were setting off red and yellow flares, Crank colors, leaping high in a dance of their own. It went on awhile. It always went on awhile, working the men up to it. Then finally, the two gangs drew into formation for the attack, after which things got confusing: smoke and men running, this way, that way, men down, men up again. No question, the Cranks were getting the worst of it. They were outnumbered, and Wally Skins had better weapons. The word on the street was, he'd spent the whole Green war chest on Sudden Stop's fanciest weapons.

"Where those Cranks goin'?" somebody said. "They runnin' into that buildin'! There's people livin' in that buildin'!"

"Scared, I guess," snorted somebody else. "Want to hide where Wally Skins won't come after 'em."

"What's he doin'?" asked the first voice.

"He's—he's fixin' to burn that tenement," said the second in awe. "He's really fixin' to burn the Cranks out. . . . "

And there it was on the screen, Wally Skins manning a big, complicated flame gun and the building going up like a bonfire while the screen peeked into every window where the grandmas were, and the mamas, and the little kids, watching them as they came jumping out of windows and off the roof, listening to them as they burned and screamed.

Words marched across the bottom of the screen: "Odds-shop pool for minutes to insurance cancellation."

Abasio went to the counter and bought himself a ticket on fifteen minutes.

Fourteen and a half minutes later, the words said, "Insurers announce cancellation. Winners fourteen and fifteen."

Abasio went to pick up his winnings. A silver rat, which was nothing to be sneezed at.

"He's dead," said a bearded bettor, shaking his head.

"Who's dead?" asked Abasio.

"Wally Skins is as good as dead. Ten to one, he's in the debt-arena by next week. Ten to one they'll make the Greens fight the Survivors! Wally Skins went way too far this time."

Abasio shook his head. It could happen. The Greens would have to pay the damages, insurance or no insurance. Their slaves, tots, conks, and hags could be sold at auction, but that wouldn't bring nearly enough, so the Greens would be summoned into the debt-arena, where half the ticket sales went toward payback. Even matched against average fighters, most gangs only lasted four or five bouts in the arena. Matched against Survivors, the Greens would be lucky to last one time. Somebody was set on making an example of the Greens.

When Abasio got outside, the whole city smelled of smoke, and the first person he saw was TeClar.

"I gotta message for you, Basio. Kerf, he tole me you should go to Purple House, quick."

"Now what does he want?"

"It not him. It's that Sybbis. She's goin' to a ark-type village to consult a Or-a-cle, an' Kerf, he knows you go to the country sometimes, he wants you along. You be guide and fight off the trolls." TeClar almost broke himself up laughing at this idea. But then, TeClar had been born in the city and had never seen a troll.


Though it was early morning in the village, the Water Babies were already playing under the waterfall, their infant voices heard everywhere in the village, raised either in joy or in complaint, as shrill as treble bells.

Orphan, still abed, pulled the blankets over her head, made a nose-hole to breathe through, and tried to go on sleeping. She'd been cleaning Burned Man's House until long after dark and felt much aggrieved at this early-morning racket. Every morning it was something! If it wasn't the Water Babies, it was Hero, clanging his sword on his shield and declaiming in the village square. If it wasn't him, it was Fool, standing by his fence calling "Mama, Mama" in his cracked voice, or Oracle chanting versicles into the predawn silence. Each of them seemed determined to break the night-still with some particular vehemence of his or her own, let lesser folk lie wakeful if they would.

Another peal of infant laughter!

Orphan sat up, ready to rage at the world!

Silence. Silence more unnerving than the noise.

She cocked her head and listened. Nothing. Babies suddenly quiet. No clangor of swords. No chanting voices. No Bastard shouting imprecations at this one or that one. Only the waterfall muttering to itself as it always did. Only the subliminal crackle of psychic flames from the Burned Man's House.

"What's happening?" Orphan asked sleepily.

"Somebody coming," said the guardian-angel from its perch by the door-post. "Horses over the hill, the hill, galope, galope, galope."

Orphan sighed. It was a conspiracy. On days she got up early, nothing much happened. On days she wanted to sleep, something always interrupted.

As though the universe had her in its sights and aimed to keep her always on the verge of exhaustion.

She rolled off her cot to land half-squatting beside the hearth where she stirred up the coals, threw on a sparse handful of dry twigs, and swung the kettle over the resultant blaze. Out back she pumped a gush of icy water for her morning ablutions, scrubbed her teeth with her fingers dipped in wood ash, and pulled a comb through her hair. Inside once more, she dragged the cleanest of her three smocks over her head, thereby reminded it was washtime again. Everything she owned was dirty, not ritually dirty but really dirty. Sweaty. Stinky. Everything but her underwear. Oracle had given her the silky chemise and panties last spring as her twentieth birthday present. Or eighteenth arrival-day present, actually, since no one knew when her birthday was. The garments were still in their original box in the back of the cupboard, too precious to be worn. Orphan was saving the underwear for—for special.

Back in the hovel she set out her tea chest along with her new cup, a chipped one Bastard had thrown away. Breakfast would be tea and a wrinkled last-year's applcot yet again. The applcot tree outside her door was laden with fruit, but it was yet inedible, hard little orbs of so dark a green as to be almost black. Lunch she would—well, skip, and supper . . . maybe Oracle would invite her to supper. Or Drowned Woman.

"Somebody, galope, galope," remarked the guardian-angel.

"Well, who?" she asked impatiently, dipping her fingers in the cold ashes at the edge of the fire to mark her face and rubbing a little into her hair for good measure.

The guardian-angel didn't say. It merely turned its head so that one eye could stare at her while the other looked down the dusty street toward the notch in the hills where the road came through from the lands beyond. Orphan went to her crooked door to see for herself. A glittering there, moving nearer. Dawn light reflected on something shiny, quite a lot of it. Too many people to be from faraway, and farmers didn't travel like that, which meant it was probably some businessman from an Edge or some gang-lord from a city, probably come to consult the Oracle.

As though to verify this, Oracle came striding from her cave, tattered robes swirling around her dirty ankles, to stand in the middle of Main Street staring northward toward the sparkles. "Oh, woe," Oracle cried, lifting her arms prophetically. "Oh, woe."

The effect of her dramatic posture was somewhat diminished by the gather of giggling Water Babies who came dripping from the pool all by themselves. Drowned Woman was probably still asleep.

Bastard slammed open several windows in rapid succession. Burned Man came out of his house and screamed something unintelligible but agonized.

From the far end of the street, Fool tumbled from his ramshackle shanty to cry, ''Somebody coming,'' and strike out wildly with his slap-stick, crackety-crack, batty-bat. ''Maybe Mama!''

Whoever it might be, it wasn't his mama, Orphan was sure of that. By now, everyone could see it was a procession: one high-somebody gang-lord carried in a chair by sullen slaves (rent-a-slaves, Bastard sneered to Burned Man, pointing out the tattoos), he with his cockscomb hair dyed purple and bracelets halfway to his pudgy shoulders, followed by several other purple-crested high-somebodies, older men, riding horseback and making hard work of it, then a closed litter, with a few young gangers bringing up the rear. The youngsters were the source of all the glitter, for their leather jackets were covered with shiny studs and they carried brightly plated weapons. Orphan thought they were fire-squirt guns, though they might be bullet-shooters. Except for blade and bow, Hero's choice, she knew very little about weapons.

The gang-lord clippy-clopped down the village street, shouted his slaves into a stumbling halt, then just sat there, staring at Burned Man and the Water Babies, his mouth making a moist round hole in his plump, hairless face. Oracle gestured impatiently and pushed through the throng until she stood at the visitor's side.

''Why do you come, ome, ome, ome,'' she said in her echo voice, the one that sounded as though it came from a limitless cavern, far far under-ground. Orphan almost snorted. She could do that voice too. Almost anyone could if they practiced.

The smooth-faced gang-lord seemed impressed, but one of the older men answered: ''We have come to consult the archetypal Oracle.''

''Yeah, the Oracle,'' affirmed the gang-lord in a childish tenor with a squeak in the tail of it. Three oldish men from among the high-somebodies stood nearest him, watching him as a magpie watches a cat.

This is the son of somebody important, Orphan thought with sudden in-sight. Either that, or he's a puppet, set up by those old men. Men like *him* didn't command men like *that,* so somebody else was pulling the strings somewhere. That was what Hero would say, at any rate.

Oracle was making her usual pronouncement:

''I am the archetypal Oracle, whose words are a window into the future, whose visions are the truth of tomorrow! If you will come into my cavern . . . '' She bowed the gang-lord the way he was to go, but it wasn't he who went. Instead, the door of the litter opened and a purple-gowned woman stepped out. She wore shackles on her ankles, but the chains were only a few links long, not even joined, two tinkles of gold that didn't impede her progress as she minced after the Oracle toward the gaping darkness of the cavern.

Interesting, Orphan thought as she sidled around the corner of her hovel to the stone outcropping that crowned the Oracle's cavern. According to

Burned Man, gangers' women were close-kept and much-controlled in the cities. Certainly it was rare for a city female to visit the village, and rarer yet for one to consult the Oracle. Now what would this one be wanting?

The best way to find out was the listening hole she'd discovered some years back, a snaky crevice that went all the way through to the cavern from the ledge behind Orphan's Hovel. Kneeling at its outer orifice, she could hear everything Oracle said as clearly as if she were standing next to the tripod. Orphan scrabbled over a bench of rough stone and knelt, her ear close to the hole, eyes half-closed.

The first sounds were ritual ones: gongs and bells. Orphan caught a whiff of incense, then heard Oracle grunting as she heaved herself up on the tripod. If Oracle kept putting on weight, pretty soon she'd need a stouter tripod.

"What ask ye of the Oracle, acle, acle, acle," her voice demanded, the echo going all the way back into the mountain.

The woman spoke in a petulant treble that sounded much rehearsed, the words unfamiliar, or pronounced in an unfamiliar way: "I ask if I, Sybbis of the Bloodrun gang, gold-bought conk—concubine of the gang-lord Young Chief Purple, will bear the lord a son."

Orphan could almost see the pouted ruby lips forming around the words, the sidelong glance beneath lids so heavily lashed, they looked like underbrush, the heavy ringlets falling at either side of her face, the breasts that jounced and bobbed like fruit on a bough. Sybbis was what Bastard would call doable. Burned Man would say she was an archetypal Helen, from some old myth. Both of them would mean the same thing: Sybbis was sexy.

Orphan plucked at the smock over her own modest chest and sighed. Biology, as Burned Man sometimes remarked, was both bewildering and immoderate.

More gongs and bells, another whiff of fragrant resin. A long silence while a filmy wisp of smoke seeped from the listening hole. Finally Oracle's voice:

> "*Shall the applecot tree be blamed that she bears no fruit*
> *When the Maker-of-trees has adorned her with flowers*
> *That bloom all undisturbed.*"

Silence again.

Orphan almost giggled, stopping herself only just in time with a hand clamped over her mouth.

"I don' unnerstan'," the concubine replied in her pouty voice.

Oracle snorted. "I think you do. If you do not, the advisers to the gang-lord no doubt will."

"Howdja know 'bout them?" the concubine asked.

Oracle snorted again.

"You gonna tell all them wha' you tole me?" the little voice persisted in a calculating tone.

"Of course not. You're the one prophesied for."

More gongs and bells, more smoke out the listening hole. Orphan got to the edge of the outcropping just in time to see the concubine mincing back toward her litter. The gang-lord squeaked a command, and his slaves started, a nervous movement that made the chair sway and dip before steadying. When Oracle came from the cave, the gang-lord commanded his chair directly at her, as though to trample her, but Oracle stayed rooted like a tree. Unflappable, Oracle.

"D'ju say wha' I wan', woman?" the gang-lord demanded in his squeaky tenor.

"The words are not mine, Young Chief Purple. They come as they will." Oracle waved a dismissive hand. "Of course, they must be paid for by someone."

The gang-lord gestured toward one of his advisers and turned his slaves away, lashing at them with his whip and screaming in aggrieved fashion. One of the old men bowed and muttered something to Oracle, probably an apology, as he presented a purse.

It was then, just then, that one of the younger men, the youngest one riding a horse, turned in his saddle and caught sight of Orphan. His face changed in a way Orphan could not quite describe, except to tell herself that his eyes opened like windows; at first opaque, they became suddenly clear, fixed on her own with a force like gravity. She felt herself falling toward his eyes, flying into his gaze like a diving bird.

He was extremely handsome, her senses told her, though some reluctant mind-part denied this. What was he, after all, but a purple-crested savage? One of those whom Burned Man would have given his life to civilize? His hands disfigured with tattoos, his open vest showing a massive brown chest between its laces, his knees gripping the horse he rode as though they had grown there. A savage, of course, but his eyes stayed fixed to hers, even when someone shouted in his ear, jerking him around to begin the ride out of the valley once more.

She knew him. She was certain she knew him. Well, how could she know him? He was ten years older than she, at least. He had never been here before, so much she was sure of.

All well and good, but she knew him nonetheless. She felt their mutual gaze fall away as though it had been a physical thing, now unfastened, felt it drop like a rope, like a heavy chain, something she had had hold of but had now lost among the leafy clutter at her feet. Her eyes searched for it, wanting to pick it up and reattach it. Then she raised her eyes to search for him, but he was lost somewhere among the others.

"Well now," she said to herself, almost panicky at her feelings of loss when there had been nothing to lose. "Well now, forget this business of looks and burning eyes and think what's happened here.'' So she did, telling it off laboriously: A gang-lord came, and he paid for a pronouncement, and no doubt he will regret the payment when the concubine tells him her blossom lacks a workable bee! The gang-lord, though young, was either infertile or impotent, most likely impotent from the looks of him. Surely he knew that. What had he been hoping for, a miracle?

So she told herself, keeping her mind away from that other thing, that wondrous recognition she had no words for at all.

Whatever the gang-lord had hoped for, away he went with what he'd received, the slaves plodding along under the weight of the litter; the purple-crested men glumly slumped in their saddles, no doubt bored to tears . . .

Except for one man, that one man, he, he alone turning to peer back at Orphan once more, their eyes meeting again, as though drawn by some force outside themselves, as though they would never have enough of looking, enough of seeing. Then the trees came between them, and he was gone.

She felt his eyes still. It was a cable of gold, reaching from somewhere inside her into the distance where the road went. She felt her face. It was flushed and hot, as though she had been bending over the fire where that cable was forged.

The villagers stared after the visitors, murmuring to one another. Orphan thought they must have seen what had happened to her, but they seemed not to have done so. The world could be on fire, still they would mutter and clack like chickens, seeing nothing but the corn between their toes.

And so, thought Orphan, another morning. And so, she thought trembling, a morning like no other.

"I take it no son for the gang-lord," said Burned Man, who had come out onto his porch to observe the proceedings.

"Not from his loins, no," Oracle replied. "How did you know what she asked?"

"I know the cities," said Burned Man with a painful shrug, "at least as well as any Edger knows them. In the cities a high price is paid for virgin girls who have no sign of disease, for it is believed they will produce healthy tots, no matter what sickness the ganger himself may carry. Tots are desired for the strengthening of the gangs. The young gang-lord will be very angry when he learns what you said."

Orphan took all her will to pull herself together, turned her back on the Bastard, who was approaching from his house, and said firmly, "The conk won't tell him. She'll make up something interesting. Then she'll find some way to get pregnant by someone else and convince the lord it's his. That's what she'll do."

Bastard arrived in time to hear the end of this remark.

"Such an imaginative young woman," he sneered, with a tentative clutch at Orphan's backside. "So opinionated, for one who knows so little of life."

Orphan moved away from his groping hand with a feeling of revulsion. Despite Oracle's prophecy and Hero's threat, Bastard continued to be free, both with his hands and his nighttime whispers.

"Getting pregnant by someone other than the gang-lord would be diffi-cult," mused Burned Man, moving toward his porch railing. "She probably shares women's quarters, and they're usually well guarded."

"Nonetheless, that's what she'll do," said Orphan stubbornly, knowing it was so. Sometimes she knew these things. It wasn't the way Oracle knew them, seeing them in a vision. It was just knowing, the way she knew two and two made four. They just did.

"Listen to her," said Bastard with an unpleasant sneer in Orphan's di-rection. "Sounding all grown up, which, of course, she is. You know, Orphan, you're getting a little old for your archetype. A little big for your . . . panties."

"There've been Orphans older than she is," objected Oracle in a troubled voice.

"Older and uglier," agreed Burned Man, with a gallant bow in Orphan's direction and a smile that would have been charming had he had any lips.

"Very little older," Bastard insisted. "What are you, girl? Twenty-one? Twenty-two?"

Orphan shrugged, aware of a sudden apprehension. "No," she almost shouted. "Nineteen. At most."

Bastard sneered. "You sound like Ingenue. But let's count it up. You were a toddler when I came, and I've been here what? Seventeen, eighteen years?" He grinned at her, a flesh-eating grin. "Watch it, woman. Any day now, they'll be sending us a new Orphan, and then what'll you do?"

"Stop cleaning house for you," Orphan said vehemently. "That's the first thing."

It was some satisfaction, seeing his face as he turned and stalked away. Let him think about doing his own work! Last time it had taken her four days to get his house clean. Piles of stuff all over everything, wherever he'd dropped them! Compared to him, Miser was neat!

Lately, she'd been doing entirely too much housekeeping. There wasn't a wide choice of employment in the village, and archetypes who had no wherewithal coming in—like Orphan—had to earn from those who did— like Bastard, who had remittances from his family, or Oracle, who had money from her fees, or even Burned Man and Drowned Woman, who had Martyr's and Suicide's pensions from their families. Orphan had nothing at all.

"Poor as a churchmouse," she reminded herself, eyes fixed on Bastard's departing back. "As a gnawed bone. As a handful of ashes. As a knacker's horse."

Enough of that. Orphan gestured toward the chairs by her door as she said to Oracle, "Have a cup of tea with me."

Though the fire had burned to ashes, the kettle still steamed. Orphan rinsed out the pot with hot water, measured in the tea, then filled the pot to let it brew while she fetched her other cup. It was cracked, but it would hold tea if you squeezed it while you were drinking.

Outside the door, Oracle leaned back in one of the two rickety chairs watching Bastard as he walked away. "Hateful though he is, Bastard's right about one thing."

Orphan, who was desperately trying to keep her mind off the young man on the horse by making a mental shopping list for the next time Peddler came, did not ask what Bastard was right about. She emerged from the door to see Oracle unfolding a napkin on the rickety table between the chairs, a napkin holding half a dozen buttery scones.

"I tucked them in my pocket before all that fuss this morning," mumbled Oracle. "I thought you might be hungry."

"I'm always hungry," Orphan admitted as she grabbed a scone. "I can't remember a time I wasn't hungry. Except that feast, that time, when the warlord from that coastal gang paid you in gold because you foresaw a great naval victory, and you paid Huntsman to bring us a whole pig. I actually got stuffed that time."

"Ah, yes." Oracle licked her lips at the lubricious memory. Roast pig. Fat crackling over the flames. Everybody loved it but Burned Man, who couldn't stand the smell of meat roasting, and who could blame him for that? "Too bad the victory I foresaw was for the other side."

"You said you foresaw a great victory. It was his own fault that he assumed you meant it for him." Ruminatively, Orphan bit into another scone. Despite being crumbly they were wonderfully filling.

"Where was Hero this morning, while all that was going on?" Oracle wondered, looking down toward Hero's tent, still closed tight, with its banners hanging limp in the morning still.

"I heard his horse go clopping by in the early hours of the morning. He's still asleep, I suppose, though he often wakes me with his morning declamations."

As though in response, Hero's high peaked tent bulged feraciously and produced Hero himself, who yawned, stretched, then strode to the center of the marketplace, where he rattled his sword on his shield and declaimed in a deep voice:

*"Look upon the world's Hero, rescuer of maidens, restorer of kingdoms,*

*remedy of dragons. Queens and priestesses regard me with favor. The sun admits my glory, and the moon my integrity.''*

"No false modesty there," murmured Oracle.

"Bassos don't need modesty," remarked Orphan. "Any more than peacocks do."

"True," Oracle acknowledged as Hero went on:

*"My power comes from purity of purpose. Only the wicked die at my intention; I am unstained by their deaths. I am goodness's executioner, honesty's hangman. I am the blameless warrior who descends into the pit of evil and emerges unscathed. I take no account of law, but I put my finger upon the scales of justice and bring the balance. I am the restoration of righteousness.*

*"I am maleness incorruptible who takes celibacy as a wife. I am he who honors all women but knows none. I am the preserver of innocence, the champion of virtue, the paradigm of purity. In me is all chastity, my heart is the house of decorum.*

*"Yea, though I seek corruption, I am incorruptible; though my weapons are bloodied, my soul is unstained.''*

He clanged his sword three times on his shield, strode around behind the tent, got on his horse, and rode slowly up the village street, gravely saluting Oracle and Orphan as he passed.

When he had gone, Oracle shook her head in amusement. "Like a big archetypal Boy Scout."

"He's sort of in love with himself," said Orphan.

"That's what I just said," said Oracle. "He has to love himself; he's not allowed to love anyone else."

"Hero says he loves honor."

"Yes, well, some love honor, some love the ideal, and some love God. But it's always one's own honor, one's own ideal, and one's own God, isn't it. There's a certain narcissism there."

Orphan was stubborn about it. "He's been very nice to me. He taught me a lot of things."

Oracle frowned at herself. "He has been nice to you, and I shouldn't criticize him. He's typical, God knows, which is what he's supposed to be. Besides, I didn't come to discuss Hero. I baked the scones to lure you into a time of quiet talk, and we must talk. It can't be put off any longer. Bastard uttered a truth this morning: You are old for an Orphan."

Orphan banged her fist on the step, not wanting to hear any more about it. "Damn it, Oracle!"

"It's true!"

"Well, hell, then I'll be the Spinster Sister!"

"We already have an Artist's Wife, which is practically the same thing. And you're too pretty and loquacious, besides."

"Pretty!" Orphan's jaw dropped. What did the woman mean, pretty?

"Try though I may to make you look waiflike, it doesn't take! Whenever you wash yourself, your hair shines like polished ebony, your skin is smooth and sweet! Orphans are supposed to be pale and washed-out-looking, but you're a lovely brown when you've had a little sun. Orphans are supposed to slouch, and you've never mastered the slouch. Your features are interesting." Oracle stared at her, taking inventory. "Nice straight nose, wide mouth, fringy lashes. Your eyes are a lovely nut-brown and big enough for any two young women. All in all, you're an attractive, shapely person who has become more un-Orphanish with every passing season!"

She glared angrily, as though Orphan had failed in some simple but important task.

"Was that why one of those purple men was staring at me all the time he was here?" Orphan asked, her face growing hot.

Oracle turned toward her, staring in her own right. "Who? When?"

Orphan swallowed deeply. "When the concubine came. One of the men— he kept staring at me."

"Perhaps it was only curiosity," said Oracle, half doubtfully. "No doubt that was it. Because you don't really look like an Orphan."

"I'll be something else."

"My point is, there's nothing else you can be."

Which was probably true enough. The village afforded little opportunity. There weren't many vacancies she might fill. The ruined castle waited for any member of a Royal Family, but there hadn't been anyone in it for a generation or more. Privately, Orphan thought it fit only for an archetypal Ghost. Both the Temple and the Parsonage were empty, but Orphan didn't aspire to either priesthood or preacherdom. Ingenue was old for her job, but Orphan didn't know how to flirt or giggle.

Oracle went on doggedly, "The matter worries me enough that I'd like to offer you a prediction."

Orphan looked up from under her lashes. "What prediction?"

"Yours. In the cavern. You should be entitled to a prediction."

"I can't pay you. Never in a million years."

"I know I'm not supposed to predict without a fee, but I can set whatever fee I like. I'll set this fee at—this cup of tea!"

"A prediction for me! What will it say?"

"Child, how the hell do I know? I never know until the time comes. I'm no phony soothsayer, no carnival trickster! I'm Oracle! I've told you my history! How they sent me here from my home by the Faulty Sea because

I'm Oracle. I light the fire and burn the incense, I sound the gong, I mount the tripod—all that because it's customary—but whether I do it or not, the words come. They come out of nothing, or out of the smoke, out of the echoes, out of goodness knows where. I don't make them up, and I don't know what they'll be until I hear them pouring from my own lips!''

''I thought—''

''No matter what you thought. Never mind. I'd never have ended up here if I weren't the genuine article. Look around you, girl! The Bastard is really a Bastard, isn't he? And Burned Man? Can you look at him and think he's a phony?''

He wasn't, of course.

''And remember when the ogre came down out of the hills, eating this one and that one—wasn't he monstrous? And when Hero killed him, wasn't he the quintessential Hero? Wasn't the Faithful Sidekick exactly what he should be?''

''It was too bad about him,'' sighed Orphan. Though it had been a long time ago, she could still remember.

''So it follows that our Orphan must be the genuine article,'' Oracle went on, not to be sidetracked into sentiment.

Orphan shrugged. ''How would I know, Oracle? All anybody knows is some little man dumped me off a donkey and said, 'Here's your Orphan.' ''

Oracle got to her feet and shook herself. ''Well, child, you can do as you like about the prediction, but if I were you, considering that I'm giving it away practically for free, I'd take advantage of the offer.''

Orphan stared at her feet and didn't answer.

''Another day, another duller,'' said the guardian-angel.

''Hush,'' she murmured, not really hearing. ''Be still, angel.''

''Well?'' demanded Oracle.

''Oh, all right!'' Orphan grumped, getting herself out of the chair and following Oracle as she strode back toward the cavern. The air smelled of dust and resin and crushed herbs, all with an overlay of Hero's horse.

The path to the cavern went through several small caves littered with stuff people had dropped or thrown away in anger or despair. Clockworks and bedsprings and petitions written on scrolls. Mostly prayers that the petitioner wouldn't die of IDDIs.

''You ought to clean this place up,'' grumped Orphan, staring at the sandy floor, which was covered with bare footprints and sandal prints and even donkey prints where Woodcutter had led his beast down into the Cavern of Prophecy. The way got darker the farther they went, and she stopped at last, unable to see where she was going.

''One moment,'' murmured Oracle. ''The fire's gone out.''

Darkness drew away from a tiny flame, which became a torch, which became a fire in the pit. Familiar light flickered across the rising pillars and half pillars of rock, the hanging forest of stony branches and twigs. Orphan found it comforting and warm, even the pairs of eyes peering from the corners.

"Stand there," said Oracle, pointing to a low circular podium near the fire, "where the petitioner stands."

Orphan moved into the circle while Oracle threw incense on the fire, whanged the gong a couple of times, then heaved herself onto the thick leather pad atop the tripod. Smoke blew into her face. Her eyes rolled back.

"What question do you bring to the Oracle?" she cried in a strangled voice.

Orphan shook her head, puzzled. What question? Where she had come from? Where she was going next? What she should be doing? What would happen to her?

"What question should I ask?" she blurted.

Oracle's eyes snapped open, white, no see-parts showing, just blind ivory orbs, like somebody dead. She trembled and stretched her arms into the darkness. Her voice came from some far-off, echoey place:

*"Ask one only child.*
*Ask two who made her.*
*Ask three thrones that tower,*
*Gnawed by four to make them fall.*
*Find five champions,*
*And six set upon salvation,*
*And answer seven questions in the place of power."*

Orphan heard the words as though through a heavy fog. Only one of them was clear, the word *thrones*, which rang in her head like a mighty bell. The other words she heard, remembered, but that one permeated her, shook her, she shuddered with the sound of it, the pictures it evoked in her mind: inchoate, terrible, yet as seductive as the smell of food when she was hungry. A need. An appetite.

Oracle panted. The smoke rose around her like a blown veil, and she began to cough, the pupils of her eyes sliding down out of her head and coming to rest at the center of her eyeballs with an almost audible clang.

"Damn!" she gasped, struggling down from the tripod. "All this fragrance is getting too much for me." She coughed again. "How did you like it?"

"I—it did something in my head," said Orphan fearfully, her eyes wide.

"I should hope so," snapped Oracle. "Prophecies should do that."

"I mean something strange," she cried. "Like somebody calling me, Oracle."

"Well now?" Oracle sat down with a thump.

"I didn't understand it. Don't. Understand it."

"I didn't expect you to. If you understood it right off, it wouldn't be worth much, would it?"

"I didn't understand it at all. And I don't know why I feel this way. As though I should be . . . going off somewhere. Right now. At once!"

"I thought parts of it were unusually clear," grunted Oracle. " 'Ask one only child' and 'ask two who made her' are easy enough. You're supposed to ask who you are and who your parents were. Those questions are universal. Everyone wants to know who he or she is; everyone wants to know who his parents were. That's our anchor in time. Also, it tells you you have no siblings, which is interesting."

"All right," said Orphan fretfully. "Who am I, and who were they?"

"I haven't any idea."

"You said I was supposed to ask!"

"You are! But don't ask me. I've already given you your bargain-rate prophecy, the answer to your question. Your question was, what question should you ask, and I've told you."

Orphan felt a familiar black wave of despair rise up inside her, one she knew well, one she kept afloat on only by resolutely ignoring it. She cried, "I hadn't thought about who I am! No matter what you prophesy, that doesn't change what I am, does it?"

Oracle sighed deeply. "Hush, child, hush. Some roles are permanent, like Oracle or Bastard. But Orphan is a temporary role, like Baby or Student, or Young Lover, or Bride. One outgrows those archetypes. One should, at any rate."

"I didn't mean to sound ungrateful," Orphan managed to say. "But . . . if there's no room for me here, no answers here, it means . . . " It meant terror, was what it meant. It meant letting the waiting blackness beyond the notch in the hills well up and drown her. It meant answering the call, the voice she heard in her head, going to some unknown place, to do some unknown and totally strange thing.

Oracle turned her face away, hiding her expression. "Yes, it means going out there somewhere." She gestured at the road, leading away over the mountain. "That's where the answers to most things are. Out in the world."

Orphan's jaw was rigid, her hands were clenched tightly. This whole subject was one she had learned to avoid ever since she'd been old enough to think. She'd learned not to think about it. She'd taught herself not to think about it, but now . . . with this summons ricocheting about in her head. Like people calling her. Not "Orphan," but some other name. Her real true name. Whatever that was.

She could not deal with this matter of her own identity and existence. She had no picture of herself as a person. She was only Orphan, only what she had been raised to be. Any other way led to panic and horror and dreams in the night that made her wake up in terror.

Oracle put an arm around her. "Don't be disconsolate, child. We must all leave the nest sooner or later to make our home elsewhere."

"But you've warned me about going out into the world!" she cried in panic. "There are monsters! The mountains are full of them! Look at all those people who came with the concubine, just for protection against trolls and ogres and dragons. People traveling alone don't have a chance. Then there're the cities! Burned Man warned me about cities."

"It will be difficult, but you can avoid monsters, and you can stay out of the cities."

Orphan felt herself snarling. "I'd need money."

"I'll give you what you need," said Oracle. "Everyone who comes for a prediction pays me in silver rats or golden sparrows. I've a case of coin back in the cavern, with nothing whatsoever to spend it on."

"It all sounds thrilling, Oracle. I can't wait." Orphan wept, tears streaming down her face.

Oracle got a certain look on her face, as though she wanted to say one thing but had to say another.

Orphan knew that expression. "You *know* something," she said, wiping angrily at her face. "That's what's brought this whole business up this morning. You know something."

Oracle looked at her feet. "A little vision," she said uneasily.

"Vision of what?"

"Of your being here when a new Orphan comes. Of your being—disposed of, to make room." She threw up her hands. "Child, do think about it. If the time comes, it'll be easier if you've thought about it. And while you're at it, think of a name for yourself. You can't go out into the world calling yourself Orphan."

Orphan tried to think up a name for herself and failed. She tried to think about going, but her mind veered away from the idea, refusing to consider it. Why not wait until the time? Wait until the new Orphan arrived. Then she'd worry about it.

Except then it might be too late. Then they might just take her out of the village, not give her time to—time to decide anything. Time to pack, even.

Ludicrous! What did she have to pack? Three smocks, two blankets, a coverlet, and two towels, one of them with holes. Two cups, one cracked, one chipped. She couldn't take the tea chest or the cot or the kettle. They'd been here in the Orphan's Hovel from the beginning.

She wouldn't go. She wouldn't consider it. She'd make this tocsin inside her head go away. She'd ignore it. She wouldn't listen to it. Nothing would change. She would go on just as she always had.

So she told herself. So she tried to make happen. It did no good. At night she dreamed and wakened, dreamed and wakened, each time with the horrid feeling that someone she knew and loved was calling her name and she was refusing to answer!

# CHAPTER 4

*U*nder the Dome at the Place of Power, upon
the small mezzanine halfway up the cylindrical interior, a corroded console was
set crookedly into the wall and connected by a tangle of
cables to complicated receptors far below. Into these
receptors, information flowed automatically, much of it
from great distances, causing numbers to flicker upon the
console if anyone cared to observe them. *So many thou-*
*sands of walkers present beneath the Dome. So many*
*assigned for duty elsewhere. So many people born, died,*
*killed here, there, everywhere. So many acres under cul-*
*tivation. So many farm animals bred and born. So many*
*animals, formerly thought to be extinct. So many crea-*
*tures sighted, formerly thought to be mythical. . . .*

It was Jobo Berkli's habit to consult this console at
least once every three or four days, out of curiosity if
nothing else. He was careful to do it when Ellel wasn't
about, not that there was anything wrong about his being
there. He was The Berkli, head of his clan just as she
was The Ellel, head of hers. Even though the Dome itself

had become known as Ellel territory, she had never said a word about his
not reading the console if he liked. It was just that he found her presence
intensely and increasingly disturbing. With every passing day, she became
more strange and discomforting. Despite that, he felt it was important to
know what was happening out in the world, away from the Place of Power.
Also, as a purely personal idiosyncrasy, he needed to know precisely how
many walkers there were actually in or near the Place. They gave him the
horrors. He pretended otherwise to Ellel. It was never wise to let Ellel know
if one was frightened or embarrassed or upset, but nonetheless, the walkers
sometimes terrified Berkli into complete immobility. Knowing how many
there were helped. Then he knew how frightened to get, whether he could
risk wandering about behind his well-practiced mask of mocking unconcern,
or whether it was wiser to lock himself in his rooms for a few days.

So now he examined the number flickering upon the console with a good
deal of interest. Ellel wanted a certain number for "security," and Fashimir
Ander, The Ander, wanted some set aside for "settlement." Ellel said "security" meant protection against the monsters who roamed the canyons and
forests outside the wall, which had some sense to it. "Settlement," however,
at least in Berkli's opinion, was ridiculous! Fifty years ago Fashimir Ander's
granddaddy had wanted to reopen the moon mines. After he died, the notion
had been forgotten for decades (an appropriate neglect, to Berkli's mind),
only to reemerge recently when Fashimir had remarked:

"Since the shuttle will be finished soon, and so long as we're going to
the space station anyway, we'll flit on over to the moon and reestablish the
settlements, as my grandfather suggested long ago."

Berkli had not been paying attention—he couldn't bear to usually, because
when one listened to Ander, one simply couldn't keep a straight face—and
it was only the insouciant arrogance of that "flit on over" that caught his
awareness. Then, when Ellel had responded with enthusiasm, Berkli had
realized what was going on and reacted with an explosion of choked breath
that covered hysterical laughter.

He still giggled every time he thought about flitting on over to the moon,
yet another one of the Ander-Ellel series that had begun when they were
children: *I'm going to be Queen of the earth someday. You be Queen, and
I'll be King. We'll finish the shuttle and go to the space station. We'll flit
on over to the moon.* It was all part of the Ellel-Ander style. Dramatic.
Ritualized. Egocentric, with either of themselves at the center of the stage.
Witness the way Ander dressed! Witness this new conceit of Ellel's, going
always robed and masked, unseen except for her glittering eyes!

Though it was not Berkli's style to be confrontational, when he had heard
those words, *flit on over to the moon,* he had put aside his usual pose of
teasing uninterest to ask:

"How are you going to flit on over anywhere when you don't have a guidance system?"

"We'll get it," Ellel had asserted with the absolute conviction that she had displayed since her father disappeared, the tone of pure purpose that always made the hair on Berkli's neck stand up. "We'll find the person we need, and we'll get it."

She had turned her eyeholes on him then, those two shadowed caverns she hid behind, watching him like a dragon from a lair. He had only kept himself from trembling with some effort. She did that to him. She had an answer for everything. She had even managed to come up with a reason for moon settlements: "As security against a sneak attack from space."

Neither she nor Ander had said who was going to mount such an attack. Mutated members of the human race? Their own earth people, back from Orion or Alpha Centauri or wherever it was they'd gone? Some wild tribe from Low Mesiko who had reinvented space travel? Some previously unperceived alien presence? Moon monsters? Little green men?

Ellel seldom felt it necessary to identify a threat specifically. Her paranoia had room for enemies unlimited. "Some inimical force!" she had cried, not bothering to name it.

Of course, Ellel and Ander were right about one thing: Ellel's walkers could succeed on the moon where humans evidently hadn't. Walkers could assuredly *survive* there, forever if need be. And one had to admit the effort to put them there was no more useless than nine-tenths of the things men did now or had done once.

"In my opinion," he murmured to himself now, with a moue of self mockery. "Only in my humble opinion."

He heaved a self-conscious sigh and returned to his examination of the console. Whatever the ostensible reason for having walkers in the Place, there were too damned many of them. Berkli stumbled over them every time he turned around. He pressed a button and other numbers flickered by, receiving only a glance. Estimated population here and there, number of square miles under cultivation, number of square miles in desert, in wasteland, and so on and so on. Reforestation. Fisheries. Animal herds. Precipitation.

For generations the Four Families, the Ellels and Anders and Berklis and Mittys, had been collecting information about the world at large, including places and peoples over whom they had little influence and no control. Not that Ellel didn't try to control them. She was always threatening war or withdrawal of trade. So far, Jobo Berkli and Osvald Mitty—The Mitty— had been able to dissuade her. The Families needed imported food and fiber and ores and lumber far more than manlanders or Artemisians or tribesmen needed manufactured goods. Convincing Ander of that was getting more and more difficult, and convincing Ellel of anything was impossible. She had always preferred to prevail by force rather than by diplomacy, and Ander trailed after her like a puppy.

Even though the figures were worthless in a utilitarian sense, Berkli enjoyed following the trends. Eventually, when the Four Families got around to rebuilding civilization, as Ellel was determined they would, the data might be used for something.

Unfortunately, it would probably be Ellel who'd end up attempting the rebuilding, and her idea of civilization did not accord with Berkli's definition. She'd been a tyrant even as a child. He remembered himself at age twenty coming upon her at age eight, playing she was Empress of Earth and readying herself to behead several of her playmates. She'd been furious with Berkli for taking her sword away, sharp as a razor it had been, and God knew where she'd found that! At the time Berkli had thought it was the game of a lonely child who hadn't been properly socialized. Later, he'd realized it wasn't a game at all.

At least, Berkli giggled to himself, she'd learned not to use a real knife on other Family members where anyone could see her. Not that it was funny, it wasn't. Just that one had to laugh, or one would be sick!

The memory spoiled the morning for him. He wouldn't bother with the rest of the figures. Instead, he shut down the console and went through a narrow door that led to the spiderweb balcony running around the outside of the Dome. The view was splendid. He could see the entire Place of Power, together with the surrounding countryside. Or chasmside, as it were.

North of the Dome was the golden bulk of Gaddi House, looming at the very rim of the canyon, impenetrable and enigmatic, just as it had been when the Ellels had first arrived. After their arduous journey, they'd expected welcome, at the very least. Wasn't the Place derelict, and weren't the people there in need of succor? Not according to Gaddi House, which had met the arrival with total equanimity, not to say uninterest. Gaddi House had not even opened its gates. Despite that huge bulk standing there, virtually empty so far as anyone could tell, the Ellels had been forced to camp under the dilapidated Dome until they'd built homes for themselves. As had the Berklis and the Anders and the Mittys, each in their turn. It was during those times that the newcomers began referring to themselves as Domers, while calling those who lived in and around the great cube of Gaddi House "those damned snooty *Gaddirs*."

Snooty, because taciturn. Or often, just plain silent. The Gaddir habit of saying nothing, and that in the fewest possible words, was infuriating, and though the other three families had become more or less accepting of Gaddir silence, the Ellels continued to be enraged by it. While the Domers chattered and rumored and whispered, loquacious as magpies, the Gaddirs merely smiled and nodded and refused to confirm or deny anything.

Of the three original families in Gaddi House, there were now only a few feeble oldsters left, said the Domers. Maybe only one, said the Domers. Gaddi House had no purpose, said the Domers. The reason Gaddirs wouldn't say what went on inside was because nothing went on inside, said the Domers. Meantime, the Gaddirs took no notice of all this conjecture but merely went on about their inscrutable business. Gaddi House might be virtually unoccupied, Gaddi House might be only a monstrous vacancy, but it remained mysteriously and impenetrably closed to non-Gaddirs, for all that.

When Berkli tired of looking at Gaddi House, he turned his attention to the silo, which had held a quarter-finished shuttle when the Four Families arrived, and now, after lifetimes of effort, held one that was virtually complete. The original plans had been followed, the original specifications adhered to, except in one case, and except for that case, the bird was almost ready to fly. Berkli supposed it was exciting, if one cared about that kind of thing.

Extending from the base of the silo south and west was a Domer clutter of storage depots, foundries, factories, shops, greenhouses, stables, barns, and residences, all of which, down to the least tool shed, were contained within a massive and well-guarded wall. The Four Families had seen to the building of the wall, designed as much to keep the residents in (so Berkli often accused) as to keep the monsters out. Outside the main gates was the marketplace, a level, graveled area where local farmers brought their produce and truckers brought their imports and Artemisians brought whatever they thought appropriate to trade for whatever they had decided they needed.

Berkli rather admired the Artemisians, not least because Ellel disliked them. Artemisians were relentless in their application of common sense, eschewing sentimentalism, refusing to be moved by eloquence or ceremony, disregarding lineage and pride therein, making no claim of nationhood. They might be wrong, so they admitted even to themselves, but they were damned well going to live as good sense demanded, in accordance with the needs of earth itself, of which the people of Artemisia—or any humans—were only a part.

Ellel had no respect for this point of view. In Ellel's worldview, humans were the apex of creation, Ellels were the apex of humanity, and she herself was at the very peak of Elleldom. It was her intention to "civilize" the Artemisians. She'd probably end up killing every last one of them in the attempt.

When Berkli tired of looking at the Place, he considered the scenery for a while, finding it as always marvelous but unrevealing. Anything could be hiding out there, anything at all! From time to time, so the guards said, trolls came howling out of the canyons to prowl along the base of the wall. From time to time minotaurs bellowed there, or giants and ogres came from the canyons to scratch at the stones. No assault by monsters had ever succeeded in breaching the wall, and as though the monsters knew it to be impossible, no one had ever seen them really try.

Berkli turned and turned again, finding the view as usual. The world had not changed in the past few days. The world changed little, if at all.

Sighing, Berkli returned to the mezzanine, sat in the chair, and let it carry him around the curve of the wall in a slow spiral downward. The ramp turned lazily, a long curving drop, like a swerving seed blown from a tall tree. Once at floor level he strolled toward the residential annex where he had his own apartments. Considering the number of walkers about, he would stay sequestered for a few days!

"Berkli!" he was hailed.

He turned to greet the colleague who had crept silently up behind him: Fashimir Ander, his velvet slippers soundless on the floor, his dark hair waxed into complicated coils, his silken draperies wafting gently on the air.

"Ander," Berkli greeted him in a carefully neutral voice. He hadn't seen The Ander for some days. All the Anders spent a good deal of time among themselves, disappearing periodically into familial retreat.

"Was there any significant information on the console this morning?" Ander asked.

Berkli frowned impatiently. Had there been significant information? Some of the population figures had seemed a little low. That might be significant, but he decided against mentioning it. Why let himself in for an argument! If he said something was important, Ander would simply run to Ellel with it.

Berkli decided upon diversion. "There was nothing about this Gaddir girl The Ellel is looking for, if that's what you mean. Have you considered that whole business may be based on false hope?"

"What is false will be true," Ander said, almost indifferently. "That much is doctrine."

Berkli snorted, truly amused. "Oh, for our forefathers' sake, Ander! Ellel *made* it doctrine. Let's not fall into the trap of believing our own propaganda! She's the one who made up the ceremony. I admit, we've picked a few things we want to change and said so, but *we* said them. *We* said agriculture could use a boost, and *we* said certain areas should be resettled, and *we* said population should be increased to support a higher level of technology. They weren't the words of God."

Though Ellel would make them words of God, herself as deity, given half a chance.

"Ellel is frequently right," Ander said stiffly. "And she's convinced she'll find the Gaddir child. When she does, what will you say then?"

Berkli grinned to hide what he actually felt, a cold hollow behind his breastbone. "What could I say? I'd bow down before you both; I'd admit defeat. Until that unlikely day, however, allow me to believe this Gaddir offspring is pure mythology."

"When the old Gaddir, Werra, was alive, I myself heard him say   "

Berkli forced himself to interrupt. "As you yourself recorded the incident, what Werra said was Delphic at best! *'Gaddir girls, particularly those without family, often display a patterning talent useful in steering the heavens.'* Now that could mean a number of things, Fashimir. Some of them metaphysical!"

"You forget. Werra was asked specifically if such a Gaddir child had been born recently."

"And he didn't answer."

Ander made a face, the superior Ander face, lips pursed, eyes narrowed. "If the answer had been no, he would have answered. Think, Berkli! The very fact he didn't answer tells us there is such a child. Gaddirs don't tell lies, we know that. Besides, later he was asked, by no less a person than Jark Ellel the Third, Quince's father, if such a hypothetical girl could provide a guidance system for the shuttle. Jark knew it would save us a generation, at least, if we didn't have to build a system. And what did Werra say? He said hypothetically yes, she could."

"He said it unwillingly! Only when pressed!"

"It's the very unwillingness that makes us believe it! It's all of a piece. Call it myth if you like." Ander nodded, slipped a fan from his sleeve, and fluttered it purposefully. "Such stories are often based in truth."

"They are as often based in wishful thinking," Berkli muttered. He raised a hand in farewell and turned once more toward the annex, only to hear the sluff-sluff-sluff of Ander's slippered feet restlessly following him.

"How long now?" Ander called.

Berkli turned, trying to control himself but failing. He threw up his hands in exasperation. "Ander, damn it, what is it with you and Ellel? Why ask me how long it will be? Ask the engineer in charge! Or ask Mitty. He's the only one with any technical knowledge."

Ander smiled serenely. What Berkli said was untrue. Ellel had considerable technical knowledge, so she assured him, knowledge hard won by solitary struggle with old books, ancient records. No one except Ander knew of her capability, so she whispered, and he must keep her secret.

"You were seen talking to the engineer yesterday. How long did he say it will be?"

Berkli snarled, "According to Dever, the damned thing is almost finished. A few days or weeks, and it'll be done! But as there's still a great gaping hole where the guidance system is supposed to sit, and as building a guidance system is going to take years more, it doesn't matter whether the rest of the shuttle is finished now or later!''

Ander withdrew the fan from his sleeve once more, flipped it open, and ruffled the air before his long nose, pinching the nostrils slightly to show his annoyance. ''Very little matters to you, Berkli.''

Unable to maintain the calm he knew was wiser, Berkli let his anger show. ''Well, the shuttle doesn't matter unless you can make it go somewhere. And Ellel's damned orphan doesn't matter because she'll never be found!'' He turned his back upon Ander, stomping off toward the shining hallway that led to his own quarters, unable to resist one last taunt.

''Because she doesn't exist!''


Orphan was unable to regain the peace of mind she remembered in her childhood. Though Oracle continued to be generous with her buttered scones, Orphan lost weight and began to show dark circles around her eyes. She was not sleeping well. The dreams awoke her more and more frequently. She noticed Oracle looking at her with concern and heard Burned Man fretting over her, though others in the village seemed to notice nothing amiss.

Until one afternoon Orphan heard Fool howling like a dog, ''Mama, Mama, Mama's dead!'' She looked out her window in time to see Bastard walking back from the Fool's shack, a white ape's grin showing below the red glitter of his eyes.

Orphan went to get Oracle and found her outside her cavern holding her head in her hands.

''Bastard told Fool his mother's dead,'' Oracle muttered deep in her throat, like a growl.

''Why did Bastard do that?'' asked Orphan.

''Bastard did it because he's a bastard,'' said Oracle. ''He's angry at me for preventing his getting at you, angry at you for being out of reach, and angry at Hero for telling him what would happen if he tried it anyhow.''

''What'll we do!'' Orphan cried, putting her hands over her ears to shut out Fool's howling.

''We'll tell him his mother waits for him in heaven, I suppose.''

''Is that a lie?''

''It's what we tell fools and children.'' She sighed. ''Postulating a heaven gives man an out for having been unable to retain the paradise he was given here on earth. What else can I do?''

Oracle had become so accustomed to Fool, she had not realized how big and strong a man he was. Only his awkwardness saved her, for at first he would not let her speak. When she tried to speak of his mother, he struck at her, shrieking "Mama, Mama, Mama!"

She murmured, and murmured, over and over and over. At last he listened to her. At last he quieted. When she went back to him later in the day, he said, "Mama gone." He said it, however, almost gloatingly, almost with satisfaction. "Mama gone. Mama said no, but Mama gone."

He hunkered down beside the fence, looking at Oracle out of the corner of his eye as she walked wearily away. He stayed there, once in a while looking over at Bastard's House and whispering to himself.

"Mama said no, no, no, but Mama gone," Fool said.

"I take what I want?" Fool said.

"Through her window, with a knife," Fool said, looking first at Bastard's House, then at Orphan's, his tongue feeling its way between his laxly parted lips.

Orphan overheard him. His words went into her mind like a key into a lock, little doors opened, little cuckoos came out, fragments of this and that suddenly added up to more than their sum. She went to Oracle, though sadly, and told Oracle what she thought. Oracle put her hand to her forehead, shut her eyes for a moment, then agreed, also sadly, before going to Hero with the story. Hero was waiting when Fool tried to climb through Orphan's window with his knife. Bastard must have given him the knife, for Fool had never had one that sharp.

None of them felt it was really Fool's fault. After Hero and the village Smith had buried Fool, Hero went to Bastard's House to settle the matter, only to find Bastard gone. Bastard had fled the village, as he had no doubt planned to do all along, hoping to leave wreck and tragedy as a monument behind him. Oracle was proven right once again: There were no acceptable solutions to some problems.

It was only one day later that Orphan was wakened in the predawn hour by Oracle, who shook her and mumbled urgently into her ear.

"Get up, girl. Get up. Your time's run out. Oh, lag-about woman, your time's run out! I've seen it in the smoke: Bastard talking and talking. It's what he went to do; he's done it. He's told someone. They know you're here, and now they're coming!"

"Wha . . . when?"

"Now. With the sun. Here. While you've dallied, I've been busy. I've sewn you a coat and bought you a pair of boots. Silver rats and silver mice in the linings of the pockets. Golden sparrows in the soles of the boots. It will make for heavy walking, but you've no choice at all!"

The things thrust at her were a pair of high-cuffed boots that came above her ankle and a new coat, a flow of gray wool, warm and whole.

"My underwear!" cried Orphan.

"Well, put it on; it'll keep the wool from scratching. Here's the chemise, and here the pantaloons. Here are trousers and a shirt, with another set for spare, gray like the coat, to fade into the shadows. You can only take what you can wear or carry! Put these things on! Where's your other blanket?"

"I don't know!" Orphan cried. "I aired them out on the fence some days ago, and one of them went missing."

"Well, take the one, and the coverlet I made for you. Here's a canteen to hang on your belt."

So there she was, wearing her chemise and panties under unfamiliar trousers and shirt, the new coat over that, her bedding and spare clothes in a bundle on one shoulder and the guardian-angel on the other, new boots on her feet and a sack thrust into her hand, containing, so Oracle averred, food for both angel and woman, including breakfast, for Orphan had no time to eat before she must go.

"My animals!" cried Orphan. "Who'll care for my squirrel, and my jay, and—"

"I will," grated Oracle. "I promise. Danger comes from that way," she cried, pointing to the northern notch. "So you must go the opposite direction!"

"Nothing there but mountains!" cried Orphan, half-hysterically. "And monsters. That's what Hero says."

"So much the better. The men aren't likely to go looking for you there. Take the path down by the pool. Say good-bye to Drowned Woman. She'd never forgive me if you left without doing that."

Orphan's feet stumbled along the path as though by themselves. Drowned Woman was waiting at the poolside, her face very pale in the first light.

"Oracle thought it would be soon," she whispered. "You're going."

"Oracle says—"

"I know. She's seen it coming. Creatures striding silent through her dreams, blades in their hands. She hoped it would change. Sometimes things do. But not this time. No. They're bringing another Orphan, and they will make room for it."

"Make room?"

Drowned Woman shook her head. "I don't know. But someone's coming, Oracle says. Someone with the authority to clear away one Orphan to make room for another. If you stay, you won't survive it."

Orphan shivered. She wanted to cry.

"Go, my dear. Go south, over the mountain. Move steadily along. There's enough food in that sack to last you for some days. We can't take time to cry over you. There's only time for you to get gone and for us to clear every sign of you out of the hovel." She made a grim line with her lips. "And for Oracle and Hero to be sure Bastard left nothing behind that will betray you, for it was he told them you were here! Go now, before it's too late.''

Orphan turned away and went weeping over the pool on the stepping-stones, up along the fall to the top where the canyon led upward into the mountain beside the warbling water, stumbling higher and higher, farther than she'd ever climbed before. The light was barely enough to see the path. Late summer blossoms crushed beneath her feet. The scent made her cry all the harder, but she didn't stop.

She had topped a ridge when the sun rose at last, and she turned from this pinnacle to see the village spread out beneath her like a quilt. Far off in the notch was the glimmer of sun on metal, as she'd seen it before.

She could not go without seeing what happened! She knelt behind the stones and watched through a crack. Oh, a long procession this, and not a typical manland one. This had cultic folk in it, dancing and prancing. Drummers. Trumpeters. A litter, like last time, only this one held a woman naked to the waist with the traditional white cloth around her head and a baby at her breast. Not only an archetypal Orphan, but an archetypal Wet Nurse as well! Someone had a sense of drama, and the power to indulge it!

The procession stopped at the door of Orphan's hovel. Two helmeted creatures threw open the hovel door. Even from the height, Orphan could see the glitter of sun on their complicated helms and on the naked blades that they carried into the hovel and out again. Servants carried baskets inside, the Wet Nurse carried the infant inside, and the strangely helmeted creatures went striding through the village, stopping this one and that one, no doubt asking questions, but searching only one house.

Bastard's House. They went through it like a storm, into it and out of it again, shaking their heads at one another. No, no, they had found nothing. So Oracle and Hero had been right. Bastard had been—what? An informer? But for whom?

Even from this height, Orphan knew the two questioners were not merely guardsmen or soldiers or any other thing she might understand by a simple label. Oddmen, she said to herself, making her own name for them. Odd, for they moved with a terrible alacrity, a sinuous grace. They got where they were going too swiftly and returned too quickly. They moved like a snake striking from an unseen crevice, like a jab of sudden lightning from a clear sky. Unexpected. Even though she was watching them, looking right at them, each motion happened unexpectedly, in a direction or with a force that she could not anticipate.

If she had been in the hovel when these men came, she would have been dead or captive by now. Oracle had been right. These oddmen were not guarantors of the safety of the child they escorted; they were killers or abductors sent to clear the way. The child was a mere excuse, a sham. A feint. A mockery, perhaps, of Herkimer-Lurkimer, to say "See, here's how you install an Orphan, old man!" Someone had told these creatures she was there. They had come for her, particularly. If she had been there when they came . . .

But she hadn't been. She was here. She was here, high above the fall. Because of Oracle, they hadn't found her.

Below her, the oddmen returned to the procession, which re-formed itself, turned about snakelike, and went back the way it had come. The sound of drums came like a rattle of gravel on a slope. Trumpets brayed, their triumph tattered by the wind.

And she was Orphan no longer. She had been driven out. She wasn't an archetype anymore. She was merely homeless, a wanderer woman, out in the wide world, no place to lay her head.

And no idea in the world why those . . . creatures, those oddmen had wanted her, or wanted her dead.


Quince Ellel's father had been Jark Ellel III. Third Jark hadn't been able to beget himself a son to carry on the tradition. Instead, he got him the one girl-child, Quince, whom he had babied and spoiled and called his Princess for as long as it amused him to do so. When it became apparent she was going to be the sum total of his posterity, however, he avowed his disappointment with life, left his daughter with the womenfolk, and moved into the apartment that his own father, Jark II, had ordered built in an annex of the Dome of Reflection.

It was a wing where astronomers had worked once, comparing photographs of stars, recording data that came in from elsewhere, wearing out their eyes and their minds looking farther and deeper than anyone had looked before. Jark II had simply cleared the place out, had the space elaborated and complicated, and had then crowded the resultant rooms with handmade furniture and rugs and a hundred rarities from distant lands. To this initial complexity, Jark III had added exotic plants, a tank of brightly colored fish, a cage of flamboyant birds, hand-blown bottles full of fragrances, and a hundred different knickknacks he found on expeditions to buried cities as far away as the lands beyond High Mesiko. A great traveler was Jark III, a great digger-up of ancient things, and a great man to his daughter, Quince.

When he had moved to the Dome, she had followed after him like a puppy, like a puppy putting her head where it might encounter his hand, just to feel petted, even though the hand might pinch or buffet or draw away as often as it stroked. She had longed for the touch of his voice, though that voice might curse or tease roughly as often as it called her Princess. She had told tales of him to her playmates, tales of wonder, for Jark III was a shining idol so far as she was concerned. Though she was disciplined for telling other lies, she was never even admonished for burnishing Jark's reputation, no matter how much the glitter owed to fabrication.

So matters had gone on until Quince Ellel was twentyish, at which time Jark III had announced his intention of departing on yet another journey of exploration. Quince had offered to go with him, so much was common knowledge, but he had refused her. That, too, was common knowledge, as was the fact that he had sneaked away in the dark hours with only one or two of his recently discovered walkers as companions. He had gone surreptitiously to spare her the pain of good-byes, so Quince Ellel had said.

Whatever he sought to spare, he spared permanently, for he had never returned from the trip. When his absence stretched from one year to two, the Ellel clan had met to declare him officially dead and redistribute the Family offices. Confounding everyone's expectations, daughter Quince had not grieved herself into a decline but had set about taking the reins of Family power into her own bony hands, managing this with such firmness—not to say vehemence—that she was elected to head the Family over the candidacy of several male cousins. The day following the election she moved into the quarters that had been built by Jark II and occupied by Jark III. It was her wish, she said over a discreet glimmer of sentimental tears, that everything in the place be kept precisely as her father and grandfather had arranged it.

Thereafter, it was her place. She did not entertain there or welcome visitors there, but she existed there, as a kind of custodian of past glory—or at least, so said Ander, the only member of the Four Families who had ever entered those rooms.

Quince's solitude did not exclude servants. One of the first projects conducted by the Four Families after their arrival at the Place of Power had been the "recruitment" among neighboring tribes of persons to do the work the families preferred not to do. Over time these recruits and their offspring were trained to be useful and taught to be civil. Descendants of the original "recruits" were now the gardeners, mechanics, tool makers, engineers, maintenance people, computer programmers, and data analyzers who made up the preponderance of the population.

Their numbers included Qualary Finch, who, in addition to her morning duties under the Dome, was also housekeeper for the Witch. On her first day, Qualary had found one of the bright birds dead and had been beaten for it. When she found some of the fish belly up, she was beaten for that as well, and then beaten for moving something an inch from where it had been before, and beaten again for complaining about being beaten.

Domer servants were not slaves, so the Domers self-righteously claimed.

They were servants, paid for their labors, and moreover paid quite well. But still, servants could not be allowed to complain. Or quit. Or refuse to do the duty they were assigned. Servants had to know their place.

So now, years after those initiatory bludgeonings, Qualary Finch always arrived at the apartments while the Witch was occupied elsewhere, which gave Qualary time to steel herself for the day's duties. Getting into the mood of the place, was how she thought of it. Accustoming herself to junkiness and unattractive clutter. Then, too, some things had to be accomplished in Ellel's absence, such as the removal of dead fish and sick or dead birds, both to be replaced, when possible, with healthy ones. Qualary maintained cages of birds and tanks of fish at her home for just this purpose.

Presumably Ellel didn't know of the substitutions. She had never seemed to notice. So long as the cage was alive with movement and song, so long as the tank moved with glittering bodies, that was all Ellel cared about. Qualary had not been beaten over birds or fish for quite some time. Over other things occasionally, but not over birds and fish.

One of the doors in the apartment was locked and had been locked as far back as Qualary could remember. It was not wise to be seen cleaning next to this door, or she might be accused of snooping. Nor could she move anything, for that would be impudence, a claim to refinement that she, a simple maid, could never possess. So Qualary, who had never desired to be refined, who wanted only peace and to be let alone as much as possible, fluffed cushions, dusted windowsills, washed bric-a-brac, and tried not to think about it. The dust was a constant. Other parts of the Dome had filtered air supplies, but this apartment had been blocked off for fear someone might sneak in through the ducts. They were very small ducts, but perhaps the Witch knew of very small creatures who could get through such tiny openings. Sometimes Qualary amused herself by imagining such creatures. She equipped them with huge appetites and incredible teeth and imagined them coming upon the Witch in her sleep and eating her entirely, starting with her feet. Such imagining had gotten her through many an otherwise impossible morning.

On a particular day she was on her knees, wiping up the floor, when the Witch came in.

"Still at it," came the hard, metallic voice from behind the mask. "You should have finished hours ago."

"Sorry, ma'am," murmured Qualary. She had learned this was acceptable verbiage.

"I'd get rid of you, except I've just got you broken in," the voice went on, as though to itself. "Maybe I could trade you to Ander. He's got some good servants."

Whom Ander treated very well, thought Qualary to herself, busily brushing. Ander hired very highly trained and qualified people, after which Ander mostly ignored them, which was fine with them.

"Let the rest of it go," the voice snapped. "Get up off the floor."

Qualary stood obediently, eyes down. Looking into those eyeholes was also impudence. Or arrogance. One or both.

"This just came in."

Something was thrust into Qualary's hands. Cloth. Not too clean. "Yes, ma'am," she murmured.

"Take it down to the labs. Give it to one of Mitty's men, Pelly or Josh, one of them. Tell them I want a genome match to the samples they've got."

Qualary bobbed respectfully, picked up her cleaning supplies, backed away, and went out the door, hearing the voice snarling behind her. "Quickly, tell them!"

Qualary went swiftly away in the direction of the labs. The Witch hadn't really needed to specify Mitty's men. The people in the labs were mostly Mitty's men. And in the shops. And in any other place involved with technical or scientific matters. Only the Mittys knew about such things. Maybe the Ellels had known once, or the Berklis or the Anders, but no more.

Once out of sight of the doorway, Qualary spread the fabric between her hands and looked at it. A raggedy blanket. What did the Witch want with a raggedy blanket? Qualary shook her head and sighed. How could any normal person tell what the Witch wanted with anything?


In the apartment Qualary had just left, Ellel moved slowly to the front door, shut it firmly, and locked it. Then the mask bent toward the door, forehead almost touching it, as though listening. After a time, a bony hand reached out, unlocked the door silently, and jerked it open. No one there. No one eavesdropping. The door was shut and locked once more. Then there was a slow search of the cluttered rooms, a careful check behind each door, behind each drapery, in every closet and cupboard. Only when all of these possible hiding places had been eliminated did she go to the inner door, the perpetually locked door, open it, and go down the long corridor beyond and into the very private room.

In the opposite wall a tall window filtered green and watery light through a green veil of creeper. As she walked to this window, the hem of her robe raised ankle-high puffs of dust that fell at once into the luxuriant layer blanketing every surface. No pattern could be seen in the thick carpet; the carvings on the paneled wall were softened, and the bewildering wall of draperies around the lofty bed was so encrusted, it might have been carved from sedimentary stone. Only the windowsill was relatively free of dust, its surface abraded as though something had been repeatedly and recently dragged across it. Between the creeper tendrils, the window stared blankly across the canyons through panes rendered barely translucent by the accumulated filth.

Ellel's robed figure leaned on the abraded sill, the eyeholes of the mask stared through a peekhole rubbed through the grime on the glass. "We have her," she whispered in a voice that even Qualary had seldom heard, one that would have horrified her to hear.

"We have her!"

Silence. Outside the tendrils moved gently in the light wind. Cloud shadows skimmed the convoluted canyons like enormous bats. No sound came into this room except when the narrow window was opened. No one could see into this room.

"A pair of our walkers brought us a blanket," the voice said conversationally. "The blanket the Gaddir child slept in. It was worthy of a carnival, a circus, so I sent one! A parade. Drummers and dancers and a Wet Nurse. Surely they've got her by now."

The answer came as a breathy crepitation, like dried leaves scratching.

"Good! That's good, daughter."

A long pause, during which not even a breath disturbed the air.

"That's my Princess."

The Witch turned from the window to stare at the chair beside the bed, a strangely contorted chair that had been clumsily gilded and padded with a velvet cushion. On the arm of the chair was a diadem, one made for a younger and smaller person. On the cushion lay a jeweled scepter. Her toys. Things she had had since she was a child. Soon . . . soon to be replaced with real ones.

She turned back to the window, bony fingers drumming on the sill. So much work yet to do! First the shuttle, then collect what was needed from the space station, then back here. Then the fall of Gaddi House. And of the Berklis. And of the Mittys. Yes, and most of the Anders, too. She had her walkers. She needed no other allies.

"Yes, daughter," sighed the whispery voice.

No one could have done better, she told herself. Not even a son, if he had had a son.


After seeing her hovel occupied by others, Orphan moved resolutely upward and southward among ramified ridges, keeping one distant peak before her, stumbling onward along a rocky defile even after sight of this peak was lost. It was evening when resolution gave way to weariness, and she sagged onto a rounded stone to rest. Abruptly, the sun dropped behind the western peaks and she realized she could not go on. All the sky glowed alike, dusk gathered, and there were no directions. Food sack in her hand, she merely sat, staring at stones, thinking nothing.

The guardian-angel nibbled on her ear, chuckled at her, and said, "Come on, come on."

She was unable to respond. She wanted Oracle. She wanted Drowned Woman. She wanted her squirrel, and her jay, and to be sitting by Oracle's fire, warm and comforted.

"Come on!" demanded the guardian-angel yet again.

She got up, wandered a few steps farther, then sat down again, blinded by tears. She couldn't move. It wasn't possible.

Darkness came, and reality with it: hunger and chill and herself without proper shelter because she'd spent the last of the daylight feeling sorry for herself instead of attending to business. Hero would be ashamed of her, she told herself as she crawled beneath the drooping branches of a nearby spruce, where she wrapped herself in her cloak and blankets, cuddled the angel under her chin, and fell into exhausted slumber.

Only to be awakened, breath caught in her throat, by something she heard. The angel stirred alertly at her throat but, unlike itself, made no sound.

It came then, a keening hum, as though something moved through the air high above her. The hum was succeeded by silence; the normal sounds of bird and beast and insect stilled.

" . . . Orphan . . . ," called a voice.

She opened her mouth to answer. Her guardian-angel shuddered, putting its beak to her lips, and she changed her mind. Perhaps it was not a good idea to answer. Not until or unless she knew what it was that called her name in the night.

Not *her* name. As Oracle had made clear, she was not Orphan any longer. There was a new Orphan. She was someone else. She didn't know who she was.

" . . . Orphan . . . "

Sweet, that voice. Like a mother calling. *Come, dear one. Come, daughter. Sweetheart, come on. Don't hide. Come on, lovely. . . .*

" . . . Orphan . . . "

It was like the call inside her. A summons. A beckoning voice that she should recognize. Or was it the place it was summoning her to that she should recognize? The angel shuddered again, and Orphan held her breath, tears in her eyes.

*You must answer me, sweetheart. Don't make Mother angry. Don't upset your loving mommy. Dear one. Answer Mother.*

The tears rolled down her cheeks. She thrust a knuckle into her mouth and bit down on it, hard. Only silence abroad in the night, only silence and that voice, and somewhere the place the voice wanted her to go. To Mother. To Father. Home.

Something moved through the trees nearby. Something large and heavy, at least as large and heavy as a person, though it moved more quickly than a person could have moved in the dark among the trees, among the clutter of branches and twigs, across the stumbling stones.

Oddmen, she told herself, knowing it was true. Here were the deadly creatures, abroad in the night, hunting for her. So Oracle had been right. There was danger. More than mere danger.

"*. . . sweetheart. Daughter. Dear one . . .*" The voice came from the place the other sound had come from, accompanying the sound of movement. Orphan bit her finger until she tasted the salty, metallic tang of blood.

A long silence. From somewhere nearby a bird made a sleepy whistle. A cricket began its continuous count of night moments, creaking them off one by one. Something trumpeted far off, a kind of bellow-roar she hadn't heard before, but still a natural sound, an animal, bull-like noise. It could be an animal. It could also be a minotaur, or a manticore, in which case, might it come this way?

She felt herself growing dizzy and realized she'd been holding her breath. She gasped.

Slowly the normal night noises resumed. Eventually, though she tried to stay awake and listen, she slept once more.

Morning brought breakfast and determination, after which the day went better. Wherever she might end up, staying where she was was not an option! So she followed a stream up onto the heights, making her way slowly, inspecting each new type of growth or soil as Hero had taught her to do. Here there were oddly burned places scattered across the hillside, almost like footprints, with a smell that made her guardian-angel squawk and flutter away all draggle-winged. She followed it to find an easy path into the next valley. She went downward most of the day, stopping well before dark to find shelter and firewood—both from a huge old tree with many dead branches fallen around it and a large, nicely smoothed hollow among its roots. According to Hero, places occupied by wolves, bears, or lions usually smelled strongly of animal; places occupied by monsters stank of decay. This one smelled of nothing but mice, moss, and punky wood.

Sound came again in the night, this time moving lingeringly, east and west, north and south, as though searching. She heard the voice again, but it was some distance away, a mere murmur. She knew what it was saying because she could feel it. The message came to her via some other organ of sense than her ears; apprehending the actual words wasn't important. The voice wanted her to come home. She wanted to come home. But not with the voice.

She knew it had gone when she felt mousefeet running across her blanketed body and heard the angel making querulous comments above her. Though she lay awake a long time, she neither heard, saw, nor smelled anything else that seemed dangerous. There were not even any ogre howls or griffin shrieks, sounds she had heard many nights from the village.

Early the third morning, she came to a farm where a youngish looking but gray-haired woman offered her food in exchange for a few hours' labor. Orphan was willing enough, accepting the burden of a canvas sack and the scrambling climb in the Farmwife's wake up the hillside to a barren, much-eroded tract of land edged by feathery growths of new trees. The canvas sacks contained more trees, tiny ones only a handspan tall, and the Farmwife showed her how to make a slit in the earth and insert the roots, how to put stones around it to make a catch basin for moisture and prevent its washing out. It took a long time, finding stones and fetching them and making sure they would stay where she put them. After some hours mostly on her knees, her smock tied up between her legs, bedeviled by black, triangular flies that bit like snakes, she followed the Farmwife down the hill and watched as she made a mysterious tally on the side of a tool shed.

"Eight thousand thirty-five," said the woman, with weary pride.

"Eight thousand trees?"

"When I have done ten thousand, I will be a Sister to Trees," she said.

"Will they give you a medal?"

The Farmwife laughed briefly, almost silently. "Unlikely, child. I must content myself with the title."

"Who will give you the title?"

"I, myself. It is a title I must earn for myself, in expiation for the evil done by others. Once I have earned it, I may, if I wish, petition to join a community of Sisters, to live and work with them."

"Where do they live?" Orphan asked.

"Here and there. Mostly in the mountains, in this part of the world, though there are Sister Houses among the forests to the east, so I've heard. Tush. Listen to me go on and on. Come into the house. I've some ointment to put on those deerfly bites you're scratching."

At the pump behind the house Orphan washed the dirt off, applied ointment to the fly bites, and was given a substantial meal of apples, cheese, meat, and biscuits.

"How have you kept out of the clutches of the monsters?" the Farmwife wanted to know. "And where are you headed?"

Orphan shook her head. "I didn't hear any monsters except maybe once," she said, deciding to keep quiet about the other things. "I came over the mountains from the village, but I don't know where to go from here. Where is the nearest city?"

"If you go to the bottom of the valley and turn north, you'll reach Fantis. But I wouldn't go there if I were you."

Fantis. Where the purple people had come from. Where *he* had come from. Where *he* was now.

"I don't know where to go," Orphan said, fighting down the urge to talk further about Fantis. "It's kind of . . . "

"Fearful, I should think," said the Farmwife with a pat of sympathy. "I'd offer you housing for your help, which I could well use, but my man wouldn't have it. He's suspicious of strangers. Not without reason."

"Maybe it'll be easier when you have children," said Orphan, with a glance at the Farmwife's bulging belly. "They'll be a help."

"It's some years before they become helpful," she replied wearily. "My recollection is that about the time they're able to be helpful, they decide to leave home. Also, I'm old to start another family. Never mind. Until some help comes, I'll have to get by."

"Maybe angel and I'll come back this way and drop in again," Orphan offered.

The Farmwife tickled the angel's neck with her finger as she said, "Best you not, unless you see I'm here alone. Best you avoid the next few places down the valley too. There's some feeling against villagers there."

"But why? We do no harm. And if it were not for the villages, none of the archetypes would be preserved. Where else would one find Oracles, or Wizards, or Fairy Godmothers? Where else would there be Preachers and Princesses and Private Eyes?"

"Well, no doubt *someone* wants them preserved," ruminated the Farmwife. "For *someone* sends messengers to cities and towns, to Edges, to farms, telling this Queen or that King, this Milkmaid or that Virgin they must go to such and such a village which has need of their archetype. Also, for those who petition for residency rights, villages are no doubt a convenient place to put persons who can't get along elsewhere, such as Demagogues and Bastards and Fools. But there are those who say the villages are the centers around which the monsters gather, that if there were no villages, there'd be no dragons, no ogres, no trolls."

"Just because two things exist at the same time, doesn't mean one causes the other!" cried Orphan. Burned Man had taught her that.

"I know, child. I'm only telling you what people say." She shook her head sympathetically. "I'd stay close to the road, for the monsters avoid roads, but I wouldn't stop along the way until you get to Wise Rocks Farm, almost at the bottom of the valley. You'll see five pillar stones, sandy red and leaning together. Farmwife Suttle is mistress there; she'll feed you. Maybe even give you work. And no one there will bother you, as some might."

Orphan nodded. "Hero taught me to protect myself, so I'm not as unprepared as some might be."

"Lord, child, I hope not. Most of us leave death out of our reckoning, don't we? We think death won't come for us, then we find him lurking behind every door. I did. I thought life would be berries and cream and a handsome prince to bear me away to his kingdom—" She laughed abruptly. "Listen what a fool I sound!"

Orphan said soothingly, "I've had those same dreams. According to Oracle, most young women do. And young men dream too, vasty dreams of slaying dragons and rescuing maidens."

"More likely slaughtering someone in the arena to the roar of cheering crowds," murmured the Farmwife. "Don't forget the cheering crowds. Do you watch the public amusement screens?"

Orphan shook her head. "I've never seen one."

"My husband bought a screen. For me, he said. So I wouldn't be lonely when he's away. Him that's as close with his coin as a bee with its honey, he bought me a screen, and the batteries to run it, and a generator thing that runs from the windmill to keep the batteries full of whatever they're full of, if you can believe that! Now I can sit in my kitchen and watch people killing each other all day so I won't be lonely." She laughed again, bitterly, tears at the corners of her eyes. "And perhaps that's how he meant it all along! If I see enough of it, I'll reconcile myself to solitude! Time you were going on. Don't forget. Farmwife Suttle, at Wise Rocks Farm."

"Farmwife Suttle," repeated Orphan, obediently.

"Tell her Farmwife Chyne sends word that she is expecting a child in thirty days' time and would be glad of help. For which, my thanks. And I'd take it as a kindness if you didn't mention having been here to anyone else."

Orphan nodded that she'd do her best, then bowed politely before starting on her way once more. She could cover a good bit of territory by nightfall if she kept moving. Also, she had discovered that moving kept her from thinking much about a certain person, and she did not want to think about him.

She walked for an hour on one of the parallel ruts that extended from the farm-gate down the valley, stepping aside once to allow a heavily laden wagon to come up past her.

"You there, girl!" the driver shouted.

She stood quiet, waiting.

"Where you from?"

"Just walking," she said.

"You stop anywheres along here? You been talkin' to anybody?" The voice was both frightened and threatening.

Orphan took a deep breath. "Nobody, mister. Didn't see anybody around."

"Well, keep it that way. Don't stop anywhere."

"Bastard," said the guardian-angel in her ear. "Don't stop anywhere."

Orphan answered neither man nor angel. She merely lowered her head and trudged away, feeling eyes on the back of her head, listening to the sound of creaking wheels slowly diminish behind her. By the wind's knees, but these were a strange bunch.

When she approached the next farm, identifiable by the sound of animals lowing, dogs barking, the lessening of weeds in the ruts she was following, and a slender pillar of smoke rising over the next hill, she moved to her left, into the trees, and stayed hidden among them until she passed the gate leading to a cluster of gray buildings. She saw no one. No one saw her.

Once well past, she took to the ruts again, seeing no one at all at the next three farms, two of which were invisible from the road. From the top of the last hill, a wearyingly long one, she saw the five pillars of red stone standing above the tops of the trees like gnarly people gossiping with their heads together. These were undoubtedly the Wise Rocks, as well described by her informant of the morning. Here she would find Farmwife Suttle.

She first found a child who was making its androgynous and curious way down a brook, turning over the stones as it went.

"Is this the Wise Rocks Farm?"

"Mostly," said the child. "What isn't somebody else's farm. What sort of creature is that?"

Orphan took the angel onto her finger. "It's a guardian-angel."

"What's it for?"

"It's to keep me out of trouble."

"I've never seen one like that before."

"Nobody has," said Orphan. "This is the only one. I've had it since I was a small child." She furrowed her brow, thinking. "Is Farmwife Suttle near about?"

"My ma. Near enough, I should think. Near enough to find me right away if I do something she thinks I oughtn't." The child turned a thoughtful face on Orphan, as though trying to decide what naughtiness to commit in order to summon her mother.

"Don't do any such thing on my account," said Orphan. "I'd just as soon look for her."

"You wouldn't say that if you knew what you were talking about," said the child darkly. "You might come upon the Widow Upton first, and she's a pain. Or Silly Sim, him the gangers knocked all the sense out of. Or my dad, and you wouldn't wish that on your worst old cow, her that the Knackers are coming for."

"Why is that?" asked Orphan, curious despite herself.

"He's mad at the world, Ma says. It won't lie down and accommodate itself to his uses, so he's mad at it. Since it does no good to beat at the world, he beats at other folk, me for instance, or anybody wandering by. Like you."

"But not your ma?"

The child snorted. "She'd never stand for *that*. And he's not here often, so we've little to worry over."

"Well, I really should find your ma. I've got a message for her."

"And you shouldn't go saying things like that, either. People claiming to be carrying messages might be Up To No Good." The child climbed out of the stream bed and dried her feet on the grass. "If you and your angel sit over there under that tree, I'll find her for you. Take cover if anybody else comes by." The child glowered at her threateningly. "And don't come galloping out until you see me!"

The child trudged off down the lane without a backward glance, leaving Orphan to look after her with her mouth open. Such a very verbal young person! And so very opinionated. Orphan could not recall having such definite opinions at that age, or at any age.

The indicated tree spread a patch of dense shade at its base, and Orphan sat there, prudently hidden behind the trunk from casual passersby. The guardian-angel whistled and nibbled her ear. The angel's feathers smelled sweet, like a mild spice. The smell always came as a surprise, and while Orphan was inhaling, the angel flew off into the trees, all in a flutter of green and blue wing feathers with raggedy red tail plumes fluttering behind. It had been doing that more and more lately, Orphan thought, falling into a doze.

"Whsst" was the next thing she heard, a piercing whistle not unlike a bird's whistle.

"Here's my ma!"

Orphan stuck her head around the tree trunk to watch the woman approach, a stout figure with braids of dark red hair wound into a tight helmet around her head.

"Seelie says you have a message," she said when she had looked Orphan over from head to foot.

Orphan repeated her message from Farmwife Chyne.

"Ah. Well."

"I'd say she's very lonely," said Orphan, forgetting to be laconic. "And she was very big." She gestured how big, which was big enough.

"The message alone would earn you supper," said the Farmwife, looking both glad and sorry at the same time. "She'll need help, but Farmer Chyne's so foolishly afraid of outsiders . . . Have you other news from up the valley?"

"A little way back I saw two people high up on the mountain."

"Hunters," the woman grunted. "After goats. Or maybe deer. There's more deer up there all the time."

"I got passed by a man in a wagon, but he told me to keep moving."

"Farmer Chyne. He could have stopped here and told me she was having a baby, but he wouldn't. Oh, no. He'll do it on his own or leave it undone, no matter who dies of it." She sighed. "Ah, well, I shouldn't say that. He lost his first wife and children to outsiders, strangers, citymen. They thought he had money hid, so they tortured the children to make the wife tell, then killed her for not telling what she couldn't. He's been leery of strangers since."

"How'd you get to know her at all?" Orphan asked. "Seems like you people aren't very neighborly."

"She's another who had family slaughtered before her eyes," snapped the Farmwife. "After that, she lived here with me for ten years. Dear to me as my own sister, she became, and I wish she'd stayed. But she was longing for children of her own. When Farmer Chyne made her the offer, she took it, the more fool she. She'd be better off among the Sisters to Trees." The woman shook her head sadly before going on:

"I'll offer you supper, girl. I'll maybe offer you more than that, if you can keep your own counsel. You came from an archetypal village, didn't you? What were you? Virgin? Half of a Young Lovers? Princess?"

"Orphan," she admitted.

The woman snorted. "Orphan! You look no more like an Orphan than I do like a banty hen. You're too old and too pretty!"

"Which may be one reason I was supplanted," said Orphan, depressed by the subject.

The guardian-angel cried from among the trees and came fluttering to take its place on Orphan's shoulder.

The Farmwife snorted. "So there's the other one of you. Two draggletailed refugees! Well, I can't go calling you Orphan. So far as the people here are concerned, you're my oldest sister's husband's youngest sister's middle girl. Kind of a round-about cousin."

"What's my name?" whispered Orphan, aware that something meaningful was taking place. A name—exactly what Oracle had said she needed.

"Olly Longaster," answered Seelie promptly. "All Ma's kin are Longasters, even by marriage."

"Not a very pretty name," said Orphan, doubtfully, wishing she'd spent more time choosing a label for herself.

"All the better for that," said the Farmwife. "My family didn't go in much for pretty names. A pretty name would have a suspicious sound. You're Olly, now. Olly—say it over to yourself and answer to nothing else! You were sent here to help me by your pa, Leesnegger Longaster, one of the

Longasters of Longville. You were dropped off a freight wagon near Whitherby village, and you walked from there.''

She took the new Olly by the arm, murmuring as she did so, "See, Olly, there's Widow Upton with her son, Sim, come to meet us.''

The stout iron-haired woman who came bustling toward them was followed by a shambling figure carrying a rake over one shoulder.

"Silly Sim,'' Seelie hissed. "Be careful what you say.''

"Hush, Seelie,'' her mother muttered. "Olly has quite enough to think about.''

"Who's this, who's this?'' the widow cried.

"Stranger,'' her son replied. "A stranger, a danger. Whack, whack. Beat my back.''

"Hush, Sim,'' Farmwife Suttle said. "This is no stranger, this is my kinswoman, Olly Longaster, come to spend a time in the country with her cousins.''

"Cousins by the dozens,'' the guardian-angel piped, flying to the silly's shoulder and pecking with its long, sharp beak.

"Ouch-grouch, stranger-danger,'' Sim sang. "Word-bird.''

"Hush, son,'' his mother directed. "Well, my dear. I'm the Widow Upton, and this is my son, Simile. Dear Origenee didn't say a word about your coming—''

The Farmwife interrupted, "Because her coming is a surprise. But your aunt Ori is glad to see you anyhow, dear girl. Come along, now. I know you and your pet must be weary. Seelie, run ahead and put fresh water in the spare room.''

"Far-star,'' Sim sang as he leaned toward the former Orphan, peering at her through faded eyes in which a strange, liquid glow pulsed. "Sorrow-borrow.''

"Hush, Sim,'' his mother said again. "Forgive him, Olly. Sometimes he doesn't make much sense.''

She, who had seen that same glow in the eyes of Oracle, merely nodded. Here was another one telling strange truths about somebody or other, but evidently no one realized it. So long as everyone told him to hush, she ought to be safe enough.

CHAPTER 5

*W*hen the Purples returned from visiting the Oracle, they were edgy, partly because Young Chief had been unusually petulant and unpredictable, but mostly because they had not known how to behave among the unknown dangers of the countryside. They had seen a manticore and two trolls, though at a distance, and had been much troubled at the sightings. Danger in the city was ubiquitous; death was likely on any given day; but IDDIs and stray gunshots were familiar while monsters were not. Abasio could not reassure them without betraying more familiarity with the area than he chose to. Besides, he himself was dismayed at the sightings. In all his years at the farm he had not seen so many in such a short time.

Add to this general unease the specific irritations felt by Abasio and the Young Chief: The Young Chief had been promised a son (so Sybbis said), but since he didn't know what to do about the prophecy, he remained touchy and wrathful about everything. Abasio had been promised nothing. He was merely under a spell.

He tried various mental contortions to deal with the girl in the village, telling himself she wasn't all that much, that he'd soon forget her, that she was, after all, merely a woman. None of it worked. He couldn't stop thinking about her. He couldn't minimize her, forget her, or categorize her. She was unlike any woman he'd ever known. She was certainly unlike the girl he'd been given when he first came to Fantis, who'd later miscarried and been traded off. And though he'd learned a good deal about sexual enjoyments from the farmers' daughters he'd dallied with occasionally while visiting the countryside and from the songhouse singer with whom he'd had a brief, careful, and thank God, inconsequential liaison, the girl in the archetypal village was totally unlike any of them.

Of course, he had never thought of himself as being in love with any of them. It was not a word he often thought of, or a phrase he ever used. Gangers did not speak of love, though the word appeared frequently in the books he read. Ma and Grandpa had said they loved one thing and another. Grandpa had loved his wife, so he had often said, loved her and grieved over her leaving him. Ma had loved him, Abasio, so she had told him time and again as she begged him to stay in the country and be safe. Abasio had loved them both, he now thought, though he did not recall if he had told them so.

Why did he think he loved this girl? She was a dozen years younger than Abasio! He'd held her when she was a toddler. She'd kissed him then and put her arms around his neck, a mere baby. Orphan. Which meant she had no one. No one at all. Except, perhaps, himself. . . .

So, well, maybe he did love her. Maybe that was what love was, this tumbled, troubled, pit-of-the-stomach feeling, this ache in the groin, this habit of sighs, this suddenness of dreams that he woke from trembling, unable to remember what they'd been about. Except one, which was of someone and himself on Big Blue, walking slowly into darkness with her arms tight around him. He wondered about all this as he shaved in the morning, as he ran one errand or another; thought it as he went about the daily routine of living, seeing the world around him through love's eyes. What would she think of this, he wondered, as he traveled through the filthy streets. Though she'd had ashes on her face, she'd seemed immaculate to him, living with only cleanly woods around her, with pure water to bathe in and to drink. What would she think of this place, of the way he lived?

What did he think of it?

And that question stopped him in his tracks, stunned and gaping as he realized he didn't think of it much. It was, that was all. Not really chosen. Not really believed in. Just a way of going along, day after day, not making any decisions at all. A way of life he'd fallen into and never cared enough about to change. He wore the crest. He bore the tattoos. He had memorized the Book of the Purples, gibberish though it was. He could recite the names of the Chiefs and the reason the Purples gave for not having gone to the stars when other men went. Not necessary, they said, for every Purple was a star, a sun, with woman-planets revolving about him, his worlds to make fertile, to raise a crop of tots from. Over the centuries Purples would become more numerous. Eventually, they would fill the world. So said the Book, and so parroted Abasio when necessary.

What was his current life to him? It was merely easier than going home and admitting he'd been wrong to leave in the first place. It was merely easier than seeking the adventure he had left home to find. So he thought soberly, not liking the thought at all.

He was not allowed to continue these uncomfortable meditations uninterrupted. Soniff sought him out, told him the Young Chief continued to be in a miserable mood and that Abasio had better find something to amuse him. Abasio complied, snorting to himself. Young Chief, indeed. Kerf was thirty, at least, and if it weren't for his daddy, he wouldn't have lived this long. Old Chief Purple might've bought himself a place in the Edge, but it was still his men who kept Kerf strutting and crowing. It was still Old Chief's men who sent Abasio running through the District, looking for something to amuse his sulky son.

Sybbis ought to be sufficient amusement for any man. Sybbis, with her undulating form drifting out the door on the way to the baths. Sybbis, with her already-legendary tantrums in the women's quarters, screaming the House down almost daily. Sybbis, spending hours and hours at perfumers and the clothiers, as though it mattered what she smelled like, what she wore. Sybbis, spending her afternoons in the conk section at the arena, eating popcorn and drinking beer. Wasn't she sufficient amusement?

Abasio gave her credit for being sly. So long as Kerf thought she might bear a son, he wouldn't do to Sybbis what he'd done to Elrick-Ann. Poor Elrick-Ann, slowly healing in the women's quarters. One thing Abasio was sure of: When Elrick-Ann was well enough, he intended to get her out of Purple House. If he could do nothing else for her, he would see to that. Thinking about love had decided the matter; it was needful to say something or do something about people one cared for, and he cared for Elrick-Ann. She was the nearest thing he had to family, and toward her he would not be merely a ganger, not merely a Purple, careless and heedless of the disposable people around him, all destined for an early and messy death.

He set these thoughts aside as he set out on his assigned errand. One could not afford to be absentminded in Fantis. One had to be especially alert in the District, where the streets were lined with woman brothels, boy brothels, eunuch brothels, smugglers' stores, drug boutiques, weapons stores, battery-shops and odds-shops, some of them owned by gangers, some by Edgers.

The Battle Shop was the biggest store in the area, always with a display of new weapons in the window. It was said in Fantis that four out of five kills were done with Sudden's weapons or in the arena that Sudden managed. Sometimes, however, Sudden Stop had other things than weapons. Sometimes he had toys, playthings, gadgets. Among the array, Abasio had occasionally found amusements for Kerf. Today, however, the only thing that caught Abasio's attention was the way Sudden was looking at him, a kind of measuring stare, strangely disquieting. As soon as he could, Abasio eased himself out of the shop and away. When Sudden got interested in people, they often didn't last long.

Abasio had no better luck elsewhere. At night, with the gaslights lit and crowds milling about, the District sometimes felt exciting, but now the shops were faded and tawdry, the area reeking of smoke. As a last resort, Abasio stopped at a smuggler's shop for a bottle of good stuff, paying the extortionate price without complaint as he dropped the bottle into the capacious pocket of his baggy trousers. From there he dodged swiftly and watchfully through the warehouse district to the South Bridge. Though this was neutral territory, one never knew when some kid might try to make a reputation. At the far end of the bridge was a Patrol Post where Abasio sometimes picked up information. This morning he slouched his way into the commander's office, grinning amiably and making clinking noises with a coin against the bottle in his pocket.

"Whatso, Basio?" said the lieutenant, wondering thirstily what might come of the visit.

"Not much." Abasio smiled, putting his elbow on the lieutenant's desk and letting one hand languidly support his chin. "Whatso with you?"

The lieutenant shrugged. "Truck came in from Hanurg this mornin'. Loaded with honey-beer."

Basio shrugged. He had drunk the beverage mentioned and found it merely average, though TeClar and CummyNup sloshed it down by the gallon when they could get it.

The officer furrowed his brow in thought. He wouldn't get whatever Abasio had in his pocket unless he came up with something. "Whistler's down from the hills. His people came up with this new drug. He calls it Starlight. Dreamy stuff, he says. It's a sex thing."

Basio pulled out his pocket notebook and ostentatiously made a note. He'd bought drugs from Whistler before. Sex stuff was always in demand.

"He'll be sellin' the stuff in the market pretty soon."

Abasio made another note, smiling noncommittally.

The lieutenant slogged on. "When the patrol come in this mornin', they said there was a refugee reported out in the farmlands."

Bells clanged in Abasio's head, like a tocsin ardently rung. "What sort of a refugee?"

"Just a refugee. Prob'ly from an ark-type village. They said a female. Looked to be young, dark-haired."

Abasio went cold, then hot. He had no reason to think the refugee was anyone who would interest him. It could be an aged Ingenue or a well-preserved Wicked Stepmother whose stepchildren had grown up and gone. He told himself this, knowing it wasn't true. The refugee was from the archetypal village he'd recently visited and could be only one person. He knew it as simply and absolutely as he knew his own name. The girl was Orphan, his Orphan (for so he had labeled her), out wandering around by herself.

Still, he couldn't go all that way on mere intuition. "Who saw the refugee?" he asked from a dry mouth. "Who told the patrol?"

"Hunters. They was out there above the Wise Rocks tryin' to get a few deer or wild goats for that roast-kitchen near the arena—Hub's Kitchen, you know—and they saw this refugee down below makin' for Long Plain."

Abasio kept his face expressionless. The Purples had gone into the archetypal village from the north, where the road was. The girl must have come out from the south, over the gap in the hills, the way the old man and the donkey had gone, the way Abasio himself had used to go to spy on the village. Why? Why that break-back trail? What trouble was she in?

He reminded himself, with some effort, that he was supposed to be looking for amusements for the Young Chief. He would no more bring such a girl to the city to amuse the Young Chief than he would attempt insurrection among the Purples!

His attempt at being dutiful did no good. He had to go see. He presented the bottle with an expansive gesture.

"Little present," he muttered. "If you'll let me borrow a horse and wander out there to take a look."

The officer, with a gap-toothed grin, waved at the paddock visible through the window where half a dozen horses lazed under the shade of a large tree, tails flicking. He had no objection at all. A man who brought such acceptable gifts could borrow a horse anytime he had a mind to.

Abasio rode with a natural grace, though he'd done it seldom since coming to the city. Gangers preferred their smoke-wagons; nongangers rode bicycles or walked. Edgers, so it was said, had clean vehicles that ran on electricity. Only farmers and patrolmen used horses, and those in the paddock were an unexciting lot, uniformly lazy, underexercised, and fat.

Why then, this thrill of anticipation that went through him as he went into the tack room for a saddle, a canteen, and blankets? Why this feeling of energy and liveliness as he mounted? He sat stiffly for a moment, waiting for the feeling to abate or clarify itself. It didn't happen. Instead, there was a sort of clenching in the pit of his stomach, a feeling of alertness to his skin. Was it the girl? Was it something else? He had a sudden recollection of his dream about himself and someone else on Big Blue, walking off into the darkness.

The officer, holding the open bottle by the neck, was watching Abasio curiously from inside the door. Abasio waved one hand, trying not to let his confusion show.

"Ride careful," called the patrol officer.

"Ayeh," he called over his shoulder. The horse was already moving off in the right direction, as though it knew where he wanted to go.

Morning beneath the Dome. Standing immobile, Qualary held the book. The Witch leaned upon the railing, watching the walkers depart.

"Mine," the Witch muttered, turning her head slightly. The mask glittered in the motion, almost as though it smiled.

Qualary did not move. It was unwise to hear the Witch when she spoke, as now, privately to herself. It would be only a few moments longer. The last of the serpent lines was leaking away.

Almost the last. Caught by an unusual sound, Qualary risked a glance from the corner of her eye. One of the creatures had fallen over. It was making crawling motions, arrhythmically thwacking itself against the marble floor.

The Witch muttered an obscenity under her breath, whipping her robes around her as she descended in the chair to the console, where her fingers flew across the buttons. Qualary knew what she was doing: summoning certain of her creatures by number, particular ones she had taught to obey her. In the marketplace, in the community tavern, Qualary had heard Mitty's men say that the creatures should be on a regular maintenance schedule, that they would begin malfunctioning otherwise. Was this what they meant? Was the thing broken? If so, it seemed determined to break the rest of the world as well. Already it had shattered great chunks out of the floor and fractured one of the pillars. The balcony trembled with the creature's flailing, and Qualary reached out a hand to steady herself. Luckily, the Witch was concentrated on the event below and did not see the movement.

Half a dozen beetle-blacks came silently from the shadows to carry the crippled one away. It went on mindlessly thrusting with arms and legs. Qualary had never seen a broken walker before. From the way the Witch was half crouched over the console railing, like a vulture about to drop, neither had she.

"Malfunction," muttered the voice from behind the mask. "Was it?"

Qualary didn't reply. The question hadn't been directed at her.

"Or was it sabotage?" the voice hissed, then paused, as though awaiting an answer.

"Berkli, perhaps?" the voice asked. "Or perhaps Gaddi House?"

Qualary gave no evidence of having heard. In her mind she quoted one of her rhymes for trying times: " 'When you're bitten by a louse, blame the bites on Gaddi House.' " Everything was the fault of Gaddi House, to hear Ellel tell it.

"Ellel?" called a voice from below.

Qualary knew the voice well. *The* Ander.

"May I come up?"

The Witch did not reply, but one arm beckoned. Fashimir Ander came whirling up the spiral trackway, his gown fluttering, his sleeves like kites. Qualary took no notice of him, nor he of her.

"I saw one of the walkers being carried out," he cried, his flutelike voice giving the words a tremolo of concern.

"Malfunction," said the mask.

"Ah. Well, I suppose one has to expect some of that," he said dismissively. "Is there anything interesting on the console?"

Even from where she stood, Qualary could hear the careless complacency of Ander's voice, see the irritated quiver of the Witch's shoulder. They would be amazed to know she had heard them, seen them, knew what they felt. So far as Ander and Ellel were concerned, servants were deaf and blind and mute.

The Witch did not answer her visitor. She merely stood aside from the console, letting Ander approach it, which he did diffidently, with a sycophant's shuffle.

"Some of the population figures look odd," he said after a few moments' perusal. "I don't remember their being this low before. Berkli was here a few days ago. He should have seen it."

"Was he?" The Witch turned from the railing and peered through her eyeholes at her follower.

"Here, you see," Ander chirruped. "Population is down in segment AN 856, and has been for weeks."

"Where is segment AN 856?"

The words were hollow, distant. Qualary had only recently realized what the Witch sounded like: She sounded like her own creatures. Like the walkers. She moved like them. Even her masked face copied their inhuman quality.

"Let me find it for you," said Ander, manipulating the console, which honked at him several times before displaying the desired information. "It's a piece of manland, farmland mostly, though it includes a couple of cities and Edges. Well, you don't need to worry about that, Ellel. The Edges keep their population stable, but in the cities, every time they have a little gang war or a flare-up of plague, the population goes down. Afterward, the birthrate soars, and the population rises again.''

He cast a sidewise glance at his colleague, and received no encouragement, so went back to fiddling with the console, bringing some display onto the screen. From where Qualary was, it looked to be a star chart, little lights all clumped together in one area.

''What's this?'' Ander asked curiously. ''You've got many of your walkers gathering in one place?''

The Witch laughed.

Qualary bit her cheeks, tasting blood. To those who knew the Witch best, that laugh carried terrible associations.

''I think we've found the Gaddir child,'' she said.

''You're joking?'' Ander was incredulous.

The Witch laughed again. ''Berkli jokes; I don't. I remember what my father told me years ago to expect from Berkli, from you all. Expect nonsense from Gaddi House, he said. Expect machines from the Mittys; aesthetics from the Anders; balks from the Berklis.''

Silently, Qualary completed the list, well-known among the servant class: *''And tyranny from the Ellels.''*

''Why are you here?'' the Witch asked.

''You asked me to meet you,'' Ander reminded her. ''You wanted to see the shuttle this morning?''

''Ah.'' A long silence. ''I want to check what we've been told, yes. There's always the possibility we've been lied to.''

Ander sighed, one of his much-put-upon sighs. ''I don't know why you think Berkli or Mitty would lie about the shuttle. They don't care about it enough to lie about it.''

''I will see what has been accomplished.''

He frowned at her obdurate tone, but he got into his chair in response to an imperious gesture, swirling down the track and clearing the way for her to follow him.

Only when the two had gone off down the long corridor leading toward the silo did Qualary ease her rigid muscles, relaxing them slowly. Sometimes by the end of the morning's ceremony they had grown so stiff and unyielding, she thought her bones would snap when they let go. She took a deep breath, let it out, moved her head, her arms. If she hurried, she could have the Witch's apartments cleaned before the Witch got back from looking at the shuttle.

•   •   •

Ellel and Ander made slow progress down the long corridor between Dome and silo. The distance was not great, but there were a multitude of niches and closets and storage rooms for Ellel to examine as they went by. Then came a door giving onto the raised side aisles above the noisy, bustling Domer shops where tools and equipment were manufactured for trade with those beyond the wall; then a tortuous ramp that led them a considerable distance underground; and finally the huge double doors with their multiple locks, which gave upon echoing space where curving walls forced their eyes toward the cylindrical structure before them and thence upward.

Ander shut his eyes as he always did when he came to the silo. Though he was looking up, not down, the perspective made him feel vertiginous. Everything dwindled away to an infinite distance: the circular wall, the vast cylindrical construction held in its protective arc, the zigzagging ladders that went up to the limits of vision. He could never convince himself he was not falling.

High above, in the gloom, the lights that sparkled like stars could have been an infinite distance below. Voices echoed from aloft; tools whined like trapped insects.

"They're working," said Ellel.

"What did you think they'd be doing?" asked Ander in the slightly sardonic tone he sometimes, though rarely, dared use with her. "Having a nap? Shall we go up and ask the workmen if Berkli is sabotaging the ship? Or maybe make a tour of inspection? In that case, do tell me what to look for!" He knew she would not. She didn't intend to display her knowledge, at least not yet. Ander knew of it only by inference. But then, Anders were notoriously good at inference.

She did not dignify his sarcasm with an answer but merely strode to a nearby control panel and keyed a summons. After what seemed a very long time, a mechanism high on the side of the ship began to hum shrilly as it moved downward, finally stopping against the floor with a metallic cry of protest. A stocky man with a much-lined face emerged, pausing to remove his protective helmet before approaching them.

He bowed. "Madam Founder. Sir." He knew them well enough, but Domers never remembered anyone's name who wasn't a family member, so he introduced himself. "Dever, project engineer in charge."

The Witch's question was flat, unemphatic: "How near is the shuttle to completion?"

He took off his helmet and rubbed his forehead thoughtfully. "We've made excellent progress recently, mostly because we've had everything on hand we've needed. Search and salvage teams have been scavenging materials and fuel for a long time, but you know that. It was members of your Families who sent them out in the first place."

"We do know that," said Ander, with a sidelong glance at his companion. "It's taken a long time," said Ellel. The words were an indictment.

The engineer stared from face to face, a little fearfully, wondering what had sparked this inquiry. "I know it's been frustrating," he commented, assuming what they did not say. "Finding the materials was the big problem. Sometimes a team couldn't find what it expected to; sometimes teams didn't come back. More than once we had to pay ransom to the Tribes to get our people back, and them empty-handed." He sighed and rubbed the sides of his face where the protective helmet had made reddened welts. "Most of the delays were early in the project, however. We have everything we need now. Except the guidance system, of course, but you know about that."

"How long?" breathed the implacable voice from behind the mask.

Dever shrugged. "Since we're doing everything for the first time, it's been hard to judge the time any specific job will take. Barring any unforeseen difficulties, however, I'd say a few more days for the shuttle itself."

"Which is exactly what we've heard before from Berkli," remarked Ander, jittering uncomfortably from foot to foot. "Do we need to know anything else?"

"One more thing." The woman turned back toward the engineer. "Dever, what's the status of the space station?"

The engineer was momentarily confused. "Status?"

The robed woman merely waited.

What did the woman want? "No one's looked at it. I mean, we can't get there, can we? Not until this shuttle is finished." He rubbed at the furrows between his eyes. "When I came on the project, I was told there'd been a complete computer review before the project even started. Of the moon bases too."

Ander made a finicky gesture. "We've *seen* the records, Ellel. Our grandfathers used the orbital telescope to look at everything visible, and they got the station and settlement computers back on line as well. Everything up there is just as it was left when men departed for the stars."

The engineer nodded assent, wondering why the hell they were asking these questions now. A little late, wasn't it? He was given no answers. Without farewell, the woman turned and left, Ander tottering after her, miming exhaustion. Heaving a deep, relieved breath, Dever put on his helmet and went up to the shuttle tip once more. Around him, surfaces gleamed with polish and paint, each component individually made and finished. The control section was complete. He ran his fingers along the enclosed bunks for the flight crew, the doors of the toilets and the galley. Behind them was what had been cargo space on the plans, now divided into personnel cubicles, each with its own bunk and storage space. And behind that, the moon lander folded neatly into its own compartment—a salvage crew had found that in a museum, so they hadn't had to build one, though getting it to the Place of Power had been a three-year nightmare. Behind the lander were the engines. They'd had to build a plant just to create the fuel they needed. Twenty-some-odd years of his life.

Sighing once more, he went back to what he'd been doing before the interruption: making the connections between the engines and the booth, the control panel and the booth. He called it *the booth* to himself, though it was actually a reclining chair. With a helmet. With automatic mechanisms to insert filaments through the helmet and through the skull of the person sitting there. The so-called guidance system.

Dever still found the concept unsettling: a human brain of a particular genetic type that was uniquely specialized to guide the ship anywhere at all. If not for the detailed plans that had been found rolled up inside something else, Dever would have considered the whole thing impossible. The funny thing was, he'd been through that set of specifications—for the fuel injection system, it was—a dozen times, and he'd never noticed anything called the Organic Guidance System before. The whole thing was just a little too pat, and he'd tried to tell Jark III so, but Jark was so excited, he'd heard none of it.

Not that Jark had accepted it right away himself. The plans said it had to be a Gaddir brain, so Jark had asked Werra about it. Twenty years ago, that had been. Right before Jark went away, and just before Werra died. The conversation had taken place down on the floor of the silo, and Dever had heard the whole thing. Old Werra, tottering around on his cane, exclaiming at this, that, the other thing, and Jark III asking, oh, so casually, if it were true that there were Gaddirs who could guide ships in space?

Werra had hemmed and hawed, finally saying something about the talent applying "historically" to Gaddir females who were reared away from other Gaddirs, and yes, a girl-child had been born with the talent, and *well, yes, but*.

Well, yes, but, was right, so far as Dever was concerned. So an electronic system would have required at least another decade to build and to test. What was the hurry? You put a human brain into this thing, the brain wouldn't be removable. Not alive. Not thinking. And suppose something went wrong? How would you fix it? With an electronic system, at least one could carry spare parts!

He swallowed, fumbled in his pocket for a lozenge, and put the ultimate purpose of what he was doing out of his mind. As a purely technical exercise, it was going well. As it should. This was the one task connected with the shuttle with which he'd had an opportunity to gain experience in advance.

He sucked noisily on the lozenge, thinking about being sick when they raised this shuttle. He'd already decided on that. If they asked him to go, he was going to be too sick to go along. He was going to be too sick even to watch.


Across the Place of Power from the Dome, high behind the forbidding facade of Gaddi House, the one surviving Gaddir, he sometimes called Old Man Seoca in his absence though usually Your Wisdom in his presence, lay in his bath thinking soothing thoughts. The Witch beneath the Dome was planning to murder him. According to the telltales and the spies, however, she did not plan to do so until she returned from her extraterrestrial voyage. At the present time, no action was needed, and it was pleasant to procras tinate, to temporize without feeling guilty about it.

"Your Wisdom," murmured Nimwes, his favorite helper.

"Umm," he acknowledged.

"Would Your Wisdom like a little more hot water?"

"A touch, perhaps," he said. "And a few more drops of the cedar oil."

Water flowed; resinous scent rose around his face. The world had so many simple enjoyments. Warmth and fragrances and tastes. Why did people constantly find it necessary to complicate things? Like those . . . he fumbled unsuccessfully for a word to describe the Domers that was sufficiently pejorative.

He muttered, "Those damned *chatterers*!"

"Your Wisdom?"

"Nothing. Nothing important, at any rate."

"Does Your Wisdom have work to do tonight?"

"Yes." Yes, he did. All kinds of work: A book-burning team had returned, and he wanted to go over the reports. There were several long-planned jobs to be implemented if his assistant, Fuelry, had everything arranged. The old man shifted uncomfortably. He was depending upon Fuelry entirely too much. Fuelry was a layman, as was Nimwes, and it wasn't appropriate to involve them in this way, but since Werra was gone, Seoca had no choice. . . .

Seoca had warned Werra to stay in Gaddi House, to stop mixing with the Domers, but longtime Gaddirs had their own failings. A kind of lofty complacency was one of them. Werra had thought himself inviolable. Unfortunately, Gaddirs were not immune to poison. Which meant Seoca was now all alone, facing a task that he could not do alone. He had to rely on Fuelry. And Nimwes.

"How long has it been, Nimwes?"

She interpreted his expression, one of sadness. Or perhaps loneliness.

"Since Werra—passed on, Your Wisdom? Twenty years, I think, or a bit more. It was a year or two before you went out that last time. I remember, because Mama worried until you got back."

"I haven't seen your mama in years. How is she?"

"Well, generally. She fusses over these walkers!"

"As do we all," he said grimly. "That trip you mention was the last one I made outside the wall."

"It's getting harder for any of us to go outside the wall. Sometimes the walkers stop us as we enter or leave Gaddi House. Sometimes they ask us questions."

He sat up, water sploshing, anger surging. He had not thought himself capable of such anger any longer. "Walkers asking questions! At the doors of *my* Gaddi House? Of *my* people?"

"Yes, Your Wisdom. All the gardens along the front wall have died because the walkers parade there. And the lawn is all black." Her voice rose, distressed. "Including my rosebushes!"

He patted her hand. "Who sent them there?"

"Who other than the Witch," she murmured.

"That unmitigated bitch," he mumbled. "Bitch-witch. Amazing how tyrants sprout, like mushrooms, out of nothing."

Though it wasn't really out of nothing. The Ellels had been power-mad for at least four generations, digging through old cities and prying through ancient books, endlessly seeking anything that would give them an advantage. With every generation they had grown more inbred, more psychotic, and more clever. Ellel had twice the mind her father had had, and that was saying a good deal. Until she'd put on her black robes and her golden mask, she'd never looked particularly clever or malign, which had been one of the most dangerous things about her. Like a clay-colored snake, crawling quiet in the sun, venom oozing from every pore. It was she who had poisoned Werra, almost killed him, shortened his life!

He thrashed, getting himself in position to be lifted from the tub. Nimwes pressed the proper button and stood, head down, holding the soft drying robe. The lift raised him, turned him, put him upon his feet. He wrapped the robe about himself and sat in the chair, which promptly buzzed him onto the terrace. Whenever the weather was appropriately warm, the old man went to the terrace after his bath. Even at night, as now, he could feel the soft winds, watch the stars, smell the trees.

He sniffed. The forest immediately below the terrace was mostly spruce and pine. Farther down the canyon, the trees were piñon, stout little nut trees, mixed with cedar and sage. Through his telescope, he could watch the people who came to gather nuts. Watch them spreading their blankets beneath the trees and beating the branches to dislodge the seeds from the cones.

Some were Sisters to Trees in their green ceremonial robes, gathering the nuts for planting rather than eating. Animal Masters sometimes came as well, and a few Guardians from time to time. And of course, there were the Artemisians. Seoca was always interested in seeing the Artemisians, assessing their numbers and their habits. They were, as he had often pointed out to Nimwes, a very hopeful sign.

"Does your family still gather nuts in the fall?" he asked her now, trying to regain his calm. He did not want to be angry. It was not wise to act when angry. Hot blood made bad decisions.

"Umm," she agreed. "My oldest brother is usually away this time of year, but my younger brothers sneak out very early in the mornings sometimes."

"Sneak?"

"Well, this year was a good year for nuts, but it's getting more and more difficult to get past the marketplace. The walkers are patrolling the road, now, and they don't let us by."

"Gives the damned Domers something to do, I suppose," he snorted. "Except for conspiracy and murder, God knows they have nothing else to occupy them."

"Except," she whispered, "you know. The little journey they're planning."

He nodded with a wry grimace. "Which, please Creation, they may soon begin!" He fumed silently, wishing many things, gradually calming himself. "Is Fuelry here?"

"He is, Your Wisdom."

"Tell him to come out here. It's warm enough, and I like the smell of the night."

Nimwes left silently, and Fuelry came as silently, standing just outside the door as he waited for his eyes to adjust to the dark. The terrace was set invisibly into the eastward side of Gaddi House, the side that formed a seamless part of the barrier around the Place of Power. From this vantage point, one might look into the outside world without being seen by anyone but jays, the occasional buzzard, or any flying monster with a taste for staring at the forbidden.

It had been a long time since old Seoca had been seen by anyone but Nimwes and Fuelry and a half-dozen other Gaddirs. In the dim glow from the windows, Tom Fuelry thought the old man appeared just as usual, just as he had for as long as Tom could remember, or Tom's father before him, except that he now stayed in his chair most of the time. The chair kept him massaged and exercised. The geriatric drugs kept him capable and intelligent. Eventually, none of it might do any good, but though the old man must be, well, extremely aged, there was no sign of dissolution yet.

"Your Wisdom," Tom Fuelry said formally, keeping any trace of affection out of his voice. Affection embarrassed His Wisdom. He seemed never to feel he had quite earned it.

"Sit down, Tom," said the old man. "Pull a chair over close so we needn't shout. I shouldn't be surprised if those yattering Domers have someone out there trying to listen, even at this time of night."

"It would be an unsuccessful try," said Fuelry, as he brought a chair from the side of the terrace. "I've put a sound screen across this whole side of the building."

"Clever." The old man nodded. "But then, you always were. An instinctive technological genius is what your teachers called you. Or was it a preeminent gadgeteer?"

"Thank you, Your Wisdom." He blushed, embarrassed by this praise.

"What brings you tonight?"

Fuelry arranged his thoughts. "A couple of things," he said, raising a finger to mark the first of these. "Our information shows a drop in population in several local districts."

"Which districts?"

"City districts in manland, mostly. Both around Echinot and up toward the lakeshore."

The old man nodded slowly, heavily. "Yes, that would be probable. What else?"

"There's been some shuttle visiting and a lot of message traffic back and forth from the Dome. Signs of unusual excitement."

"The shuttle must be very nearly complete. A bit sooner than I'd anticipated, but ambition breeds efficiency, does it not? Have they—or should I say, has *she*—made definite plans yet? Has she specified what they're going to do?"

"You mean, if she finds the guidance system?"

The old man grimaced painfully. "Assuming they find what they're looking for, yes."

"Quince Ellel has always said they're going to salvage materials from the space station. Recently there's been some talk among the Anders about reopening the moon mines, or even going to the stars, but basically they say what she does: They're going for salvage."

"Have they said why?"

Fuelry shrugged. "Because it's what they've been planning to do for several generations."

"Just going to be going? No particular material that they expect to find up there?" He hummed to himself, tapping his teeth with a fingernail. "I don't believe that for a moment."

Fuelry shrugged again. "You know the Domers, Your Wisdom. They're devious."

"Not all of them. The Berklis are true to their heritage. They're thinkers, not doers; they don't take themselves too seriously, so their influence is limited. The Mittys are so completely dedicated to their own field, they're not even aware of what else is going on. The Anders come from a sycophantish strain. They're essentially unctuous and truckling, admirers of power without wanting to hold it in their own hands." He nodded to himself slowly. "Unlike the Ellels, who do."

"Odd that the entire Families are . . ."

"Not really," said the old man. "They're inbred. Like certain kinds of dogs. Self-selected for certain characteristics. Mittys quit breeding with other Families because they considered them technical nitwits. Ellels quit breeding with other Families because they didn't trust them. The Berkli sense of humor rubs everyone raw save other Berklis, and no one's sensitive enough for an Ander save another Ander.

"So what do you think they're up to?"

Tom Fuelry shook his head and said blandly, "I try not to think, Your Wisdom. I think too much, I get all rattled."

The old man hid a smile. "Very well, Tom. I'll do the thinking. I think it is time for Plan B. Let our friends know they may be needed soon."

Fuelry nodded. "Oh, yes, sir. They're not only ready but eager. I'll send word tonight."

The old man nodded. "How are the other stocks building up? Contingency items?"

"About completed, sir. I think we've prepared for all the contingencies you've brought to my attention."

"Provided we've foreseen them all. Which is unlikely. We didn't foresee those damned walkers. If we had, all this would be over. Well. Justice demands that we be sure of Quince Ellel's intentions. She has a person working for her. One Qualary Finch. Get next to her."

"Get next to her?" Fuelry shook his head, confused. "I'm sorry, sir. . . ."

"Cultivate her. Get acquainted with her. Make friends with her."

"Oh, sir, I—"

"You don't like women?"

"Of course, but—"

"Everything I've found out about her tells me you are precisely the kind of man Qualary Finch might hope for." The old man was careful not to smile. What he said was true, but he didn't want to explain it. "Tom? All right?"

"Yes, sir," he said, still shaking his head. He doubted it was ethical.
And he wasn't all that sure it was possible.


Sybbis, concubine of Young Chief Purple, chewed the end of her pen
reflectively, crossed out several words she had just printed with great effort,
printed several others, then nodded to herself as she regarded the much-
corrected page with baleful satisfaction. It would do. Settling herself, she
took a clean sheet and copied the text laboriously but clearly, then folded
the single page and put it in an envelope that she taped and addressed to her
younger sister Posnia, at Bloodrun homeground.

The letter invited Posnia to visit her. Such visits weren't exactly encouraged, but they were common enough among sisters, or even between mothers
and daughters, if the gangs involved weren't enemies or if the Chiefs hadn't
forbidden it. Young Purple hadn't forbidden it, and the Bloodrun Chief was
Sybbis's own father. He'd always babied her. He'd let Posy come. It was
absolutely essential he let Posy come.

She rose and stretched like a cat as she peered through the grating of her
private room at the roof garden she shared with the other homewomen and
their tots. The Warlord's woman, Carmina, was nursing her new baby. Half
a dozen of the younger women and mostly grown girls were playing patty
ball. Two hags were mending bed sheets under the arbor. Sybbis felt no
desire to join them. They didn't like her because of Elrick-Ann, even though
Sybbis had had nothing to do with Elrick-Ann. It wasn't her fault the Greens
had chopped on Elrick-Ann. She knew whose fault it was, but she wasn't
going to say anything about that, or the same thing might happen to her—
unless she could make something else happen instead. The Oracle had been
the first step toward that! This letter was the second. The Young Chief would
read it before he'd let it go, but let him. The day she wasn't smarter than
the Young Chief would be the day she'd deserve being cut on!

Later, in his room below, the Young Chief ripped open Sybbis's letter
and read it carefully several times.

"Why's she want her sister?" he grunted to Soniff, who was dozing in
the window.

The Warlord shrugged. "I suppose she's lonely, Young Chief."

The Young Chief grunted, rubbing his smooth cheek with one pudgy hand,
a habitual gesture with him, feeling for whiskers that had never come. If
he'd grown whiskers, Old Chief would have let him run the gang himself
instead of having Soniff do it. If he'd grown whiskers, Old Chief would still
be at Purple House instead of living in the Edge and never coming here
anymore. Kerf never got to see him. Soniff saw him, but not here. Old Chief
met Soniff somewhere else to give him orders: What Kerf could do, what

Kerf couldn't do. Kerf couldn't go to the baths where the men might make fun. Kerf couldn't go to the songhouses.

Not that Kerf wanted to! What was all the fuss about? Not that it was painful or anything, but it was boring. Elrick-Ann hadn't expected him to do it hardly at all, but then, Elrick-Ann couldn't make a baby. She'd told him that, just this past spring. He'd said he didn't like it, and she'd said well fine, he didn't have to do it with her because she couldn't make babies anyhow. She was sterile.

If she hadn't told him that, he wouldn't have . . . he wouldn't have needed Sybbis.

"I guess it's okay." He handed the letter to the man who'd brought it. "You can take it on over to the Bloodruns."

Posnia, who was a year younger than Sybbis but looked much like her, came with her escort the following morning. The men delivered her at the front door, then camped out in the street, waiting to take her back. Two of the Purples escorted her upstairs, being careful not to touch her on the way. Touch some Chief's daughter he was holdin' for a good price, and you might find yourself eunuched before you knew it.

Posnia found her sister smoking a drug called Dreamland and listening to recordings by a newly heralded street singer.

"I hear you went to an Oracle," whispered Posnia, when she had divested herself of her red-and-green-striped street gown. "It all over Fantis how you go gettin' a pro-phe-cy."

Sybbis pursed her mouth, as though to spit, rolled over, and turned the music up so they could not be overheard.

"How the hell you hear that?"

"What she tell you?" Posnia whispered.

"What you think! I not goin' get pregnant 'less I cn get fucked!"

"He still can't do it?"

Sybbis made a face. "I don' think he has any li'l bitty idea what 'it' is. He goes through the motion, like maybe he seen somebody do it, or somebody maybe tole him about it, but he just pushin' nothin' 'round. It this dinky thing the size my thumb, Posy. You wouldn' believe! After a while he sigh and sorta yawn and say somethin' like, 'Is that enough, you think?' "

"He doesn' come?"

"He doesn' get close."

"He's never seen one stiff?"

"Posy, don' ask me. He's smart enough 'bout some things, but he just doesn' know nothin' 'bout that. I think he never did grow up. I think he like a baby still. I think his pa made sure he never fin' out he not like other men."

"How could he keep from findin' out?" Posnia cried, surprising herself at the sound. She put a quick hand over her mouth. Someone could be listening.

Sybbis whispered, "He got these Old G's. His daddy's men. His daddy's Warlord, even. They always close aroun' him. They tell him he can talk to this one or that one, he can do this or that. Tha's what Carmina say. She the Warlord's homewoman, an' I figure she should know."

"You think his father know? Old Chief Purple?"

"'Course he know! But I think maybe he hope."

Posnia shook her head in confusion.

"Little Chief not thirty yet. Maybe Old Chief, he hope like, Little Chief's just slow. Maybe he hope if his son is a good Chief, the res' will come. Like you train a dog to fetch, later you train'm to roll over." Sybbis laughed, chokingly. "Train'm to kill enough Blue Shadows, maybe he can do t'other thing."

"What are you going to do?"

Sybbis sobered, her eyes narrowed. "I not goin' like that other one, that Elrick-Ann, tha's for sure. She at the baths, an' I see what happen to her." She shuddered, remembering the livid scars that crossed Elrick-Ann's face and body.

"I hear she get away from the Greens. Nobody knows how. People say even Wally Skins don' know."

Sybbis pouted. "That don' matter. What matter is, what that Oracle say. It got to be up to me. He don' know it his fault I not pregnant, and don' look for me to tell him, tha's for sure. I got to get me pregnant some other way. Otherwise it be me the Greens are cuttin' on."

Posnia looked apprehensively at the curtained door leading to the Chief's quarters. "Sybby, you can't."

Sybbis settled herself, placed a hand across her sister's mouth, and leaned toward her ear.

"We go to the baths. Two, three times a week. The men stay outside when we go in. There a back door. You 'member that hag we use to have? She our nursemaid at Bloodrun House. Nelda?"

"She got sold to—"

"I know where she got sold to. She got sold two or three times, but now she got a songhouse on Happy Street. I wrote her a letter askin' her to meet me at the baths nex Fifth-day." Sybbis patted her breast, pulling up a corner of the note so Posy could see it. "You take it when you go."

"You want *me* goin' to a house on Happy Street! Sybby! Why don' *you* send the letter?"

Sybbis spoke between gritted teeth. "Because I don' wan anythin' direc from me to Nelda. Jus in case Little Purple start askin' questions. I don' wan' anything lead from me to her."

"She won' come."

"She will. She use to steal things at Bloodrun, and we both know 'bout it. She goin' to remember that. She goin' to be afraid we tell on her if she don' do what we want. Either you or me."

"Why do *I* have to be there?" Posnia whined.

"You have to be there, 'cause when the time come, you goin' to preten' to be me!" her sister snapped.

Posnia was much tempted to lose the letter. Her prior experience with Sybbis, however, had been that when Sybbis was frustrated, it was Posnia who felt the pain. Therefore, out of apprehension rather than any sense of sisterly helpfulness, Posnia paid one of the bath girls to deliver the note. The bath-girl, almost as a matter of course, unsealed the missive and read it, hoping for something juicy she could sell to a gang Chief. Finding nothing at all, she delivered the letter out of fear of what might happen to her if she did not.

Nelda, in her turn, remembered the Bloodrun girls as fully capable of retaliation, so she took herself to the baths on the following morning, where Posnia drew her into a private room already occupied by Sybbis.

"Sit down," Sybbis snapped when the two of them had been left alone.

Nelda stiffened, gripping the knife in her pocket. What was this one up to?

Sybbis, however, seemed more confiding than threatening. "I got me this problem, Nelly."

Nelda sat down and leaned slowly forward, feeling her shoulder gripped by Sybbis's strong hand, hearing Sybbis's whisper, too low to be overheard by anyone.

At the end of Sybbis's recital, the brothel mistress shook her head in mingled amusement and apprehension. "What do you want from me?"

"I cn come here, then I cn go the back way an' get me to your place, Nelly. Or some other place, nearby. I put on a blackie robe, like you outside women wear, and I go someplace. Someplace, Nelly. You pick it. And you have to find me a cock. A quick one, one guarantee to make baby roosters."

"What am I to tell this cock?"

"Tell him nothin' 'cep he gets paid. Don' tell him who I am 'less you want your throat slit. I wear a mask when the time come."

"Tattoos," Nelda reminded her.

"Daddy wan' to make it up to me for sellin' me, so he tell Young Chief he musn' tattoo me. It not in the contrac'."

Nelda laughed. "Determined, aren't you? Well, you always were. How come you let your daddy sell you to that one at all? The whole city knows Little Purple has no balls at all, no more than a bitty child."

"Daddy need the money real bad. His insurance was goin' up and up, and he los' a big sponsor. One those battery-shops, they decide on the Renegades 'stead of the Bloodruns. Daddy sits me on his lap an' call me his sweet baby an' say he sellin' me to the Purples, but I should be patient for a little, 'cause Young Chief prob'ly sen' me home again pretty soon.''

"You think he won't?"

"He sen' me in a basket! Or dead! Only reason I tell you is so you understan' why I got to do this, Nelly. I got to get pregnant. Young Chief got to think it his, too. It lucky he so ignorant. He believe anythin' anybody tell him. And his daddy, he wan' to believe it too!''

"When's your baby time?" Nelda asked. With infertility rampant, the mechanics of conception were well understood by the women of Fantis.

"Nex Third-day," said Sybbis, who'd kept close track of her timing for months.

"That's real soon," said Nelda. "Maybe I can't get everything put together so soon.''

"Well, it then or it a month from then," said Sybbis. "One or the other."

They talked awhile longer, Sybbis explaining how she would manage this, how she would manage that. Nelda asked for a hefty price, and Sybbis granted it almost without bargaining.

"When I get pregnant, he be so puffed up, he give me the whole Purple war chest 'f I ask for it!''

Sybbis had her bath and went home with her escort, believing things were well begun. Nelda, for her part, slipped down the mucky alley to her song-house considering which of the cocks in Fantis she should make aware of this opportunity. Next Third-day was only six days away, and no matter what Sybbis said, this business was not simple!

She made a mental list: Whoever she picked must be reasonably like Young Chief Purple in coloring. Since this was a gang-lord's child, his heritage could include ferocity, or at least good physical coordination. Perhaps the assignment would appeal to the Survivors—a supergang made up of men who'd survived battle in the debt-arena. Survivors were the quickest, the strongest—or at least the luckiest—Fantis had to offer. That would be a good heritage for Sybbis's child.

Problem was, all the Survivors drank and boasted. The word would get out in no time. No. No, a Survivor was not a good idea.

And there were three additional problems, from Nelda's point of view. The first was merely logistical: bringing the cock and hen together secretly and frequently enough to assure success. Sybbis's ideas on that matter were innovative, but they needed methodical refinement. Luckily, Sybbis had a healthy heritage on both sides, giving no reason to doubt her fertility.

Which brought up the second problem, one Sybbis hadn't even mentioned. If Nelda wanted no problems later on from Sybbis or the Bloodruns, this baby would have to be healthy, which was true of few babies these days. Many had drug-induced deformities. Many had genetic or transmissible disease. Men who frequented the brothels were likely to be tainted with one of the nasties. Ball-rot. Twinky-droop. Blood boils. All of which were sexually transmitted. In addition to these, many men had one of the IDDIs, which were invariably fatal. Sometimes they knew they had it; often they didn't. Sometimes they didn't care. Women who mated with such men usually didn't survive pregnancy.

There could be none of that. Not if Nelda wanted to keep her neck intact. No, this one had to be clean, which meant a casual. Someone who only rarely came to a brothel. No, better someone who didn't come there at all.

Which brought the third problem to mind: keeping him quiet afterward.

And though Sybbis was in one hell of a hurry, Nelda knew she must not be. This matter must be accomplished carefully, she told herself. Very carefully indeed. If it were done, it should be well done so that she could retire to the country on the proceeds.

Among the crowd gathered with their market baskets, waiting to go out the gate of the Place of Power to the marketplace beyond, Qualary Finch was an undistinguished member, being a brownish woman, a monotone of skin, hair, and clothing that resembled a carving as much as a living person. As though to increase this likeness, she had transferred into her daily life her workaday pose as furniture: a slightly wooden manner, a stillness of face, and a gracelessness of movement that suggested the unpracticed manipulations of an unpainted marionette.

This carryover was understandable inasmuch as she had worked for the Witch for two decades, and it explained the lack of reaction she displayed when greeted by a fortyish, graying, round-faced fellow carrying a market basket of his own.

"You're Qualary Finch, aren't you?"

She nodded the least possible nod, turning slightly away so as not to encourage him. She did not recognize him as a Domer, which meant he was probably a Gaddir. It wasn't forbidden to speak to Gaddirs, but neither was it discreet.

"You don't know me," he went on, undiscouraged. "But I know your brother Bossik. He's told me all about you."

Qualary shuffled her feet, more than a little embarrassed. Unlike the rest of the family who had always given at least lip service to the Domer notion that Gaddi House was at best obsolete and at worst up to no good, her older brother Bossik was a renegade, a heretic, a man who actually said that Gaddirs might be decent folk, for all anyone knew to the contrary.

How had Bossik gotten to know this one? And how did one respond to such an introduction?

She was spared the necessity of deciding when the man went on:

"Whenever I see Bossik, he tells me something new and wonderful about you. He says you make the best venison stew in the world."

Bossik Finch had indeed told him this, though it had taken a good deal of time and maneuver to get him to do so.

Unaware of all this effort, Qualary flushed. "Oh, well," she murmured. "You can't believe everything Bossy says."

"On the contrary." The stranger beamed. "He said you were the prettiest woman in the Place, and I'm inclined to agree with him." This was a lie, but not unwelcome.

Her mouth dropped open as she considered what one might say to this. Pretty? She? He must be joking!

He gave her no time for rebuttal. "My name's Tom Fuelry. No laughter, please. Ma was a jokester, and it really is my name. Are you on your way out to market? Me too. I'll walk with you."

And she found herself walking, talking about nothing much, all at a loss what to say or do about this assault upon her daily routine. They went through the gates, which allowed free egress on market days—though no one could come back inside without a the proper permanent identification—and once outside strolled through the chatter and tumult of the market itself, full of hawkers and merchants and peddlers and traders, in addition to the local farmers with their produce and grains and meats.

Under Fuelry's watchful eye, Qualary bought a rat's worth of sausage, a few mice worth of fresh vegetables, several packets of seeds, two potted flowering plants, a small bird in a cage, a jar of honey, a sack of crushed grain that she planned to cook with meat and raisins—so she said—and a freshly killed chicken. To Fuelry's astonishment, she asked if anyone had live little fish for sale and was distressed that no one had. Meanwhile, Tom Fuelry bought venison chops, potatoes, late sweet corn, and two bottles of wine transported all the way from the shores of the Faulty Sea.

Both of them summoned Domer tote-boys to carry their baskets and strolled back to the walls together, where they waited in line with their tote-boys to be approved by the sensors.

When they were safely inside, Fuelry said:

"You don't know me at all, but your brother does. If you consult him and he recommends me, and if you'd like to do so, would you join me for dinner in my quarters tonight? I can't drink all that wine alone. It would be a sin to try."

Without quite knowing how it happened, she found herself agreeing. On her return to her own placid and lonely house, she didn't even call

Bossik to ask him about his friend. She told herself it wasn't necessary. In fact, she would have been embarrassed to do so, for Bossy would tease her as he always had when they were children, and she didn't think she could bear it. It wasn't anything she'd ordinarily do—have dinner with a Gaddir (she no more than any Domer making the distinction between Old Seoca and those who served him)—but since he was a friend of her brother's . . .

All this consideration was to no point. Had she tried to reach her brother she would have found him gone. Fuelry had made quite sure that Bossik Finch would be elsewhere when he approached Qualary.

She went to the Gaddi House gate at sundown, where Fuelry waited to escort her through the checkpoints to a labyrinth of halls and rooms and stairs and lifts inside.

"I've never been in here before," she whispered. "None of us Domers have. I thought it would be . . . strange."

"Nothing strange about it," he said offhandedly. "Just a big apartment house for people to live in."

Elsewhere and below in Gaddi House, there were indeed strange places, some of which Tom shuddered to go into and most of which he had never even seen. He knew of them only because the old man had spoken of them as he spoke of many marvels in the place. Sometimes Tom thought the old man merely imagined what was behind certain huge doors or down certain winding corridors. Imaginary or not, Tom didn't mention them to Qualary. Tom was one of half a dozen people the old man talked to, but none of the half-dozen ever talked about what he said, not even to one another.

Tom's own quarters were roomy and pleasant, facing on a sizable balcony that extended over an interior courtyard.

"You have windows," she cried. "I didn't know Gaddi House had windows."

"Oh, yes," he remarked. "All the living quarters are built around these atriums. It's really quite comfortable. Different from the separate houses most of you Domers live in, and I must say I envy you your gardens."

She agreed that the gardens were enjoyable and went into some detail about her own small house, her own small garden.

"I often think it would be nice if we could visit back and forth more," asserted Fuelry. "Domers and Gaddirs seem to be getting more and more isolated all the time. We share the Place, we ought to be friendlier."

She hadn't thought about it. She did so now, trying to do so honestly. "There are fundamental differences in philosophy," she said seriously. "Ander says there are variations in the essentialities of our experience. Dissonant intellectual matrices."

Fuelry gave her a long, level look, and she blushed again, wondering if he had understood her. Wondering if she had understood herself. She knew she had used the right words, and she thought she knew what she meant. Of course, the differences were philosophical, and Domers said Gaddirs couldn't understand philosophy. Gaddirs were unregenerate pragmatists. They cared only for what worked. They served no higher purpose. The Domers, on the other hand, cared for eternal verities. World order. A united mankind. A civilization of philosophers.

Fuelry, who thought it interesting that she quoted Ander rather than Ellel, made no attempt to dig into what other things Ander might have said. Instead, he turned the conversation to gardening, a comfortably pragmatic subject that the Founders were not greatly interested in and had therefore never bothered to invent a jargon for. He chatted, and filled her glass, and asked a few questions as though the answers didn't matter, and when the wine had been drunk and the food eaten, he helped her into her jacket and escorted her to the gate, where he planted a chaste kiss upon her cheek and let her go back to her quarters, totally unscathed and thereby reassured.

Reassuring her had been his intent. Qualary Finch was shy, diffident, defensive. She had every right to be. He thought he had a notion why she had wanted the fish, why she had bought the little bird. She had not told him specifically, but she had described Ellel's apartment, speaking of the caged birds, the bright fishes, and her hands had gone to her shoulders, like a child protecting a hurt place. Fuelry could put two and two together as well as the next man. Particularly inasmuch as he'd received substantiating information about Quince Ellel from a number of other sources.

Qualary was a Domer only because she'd been born one. She had no reason to be loyal, but she had good reason to be discreet. She would have to know Tom Fuelry a good bit better before she would come right out and tell him what Quince Ellel was up to. If she knew.


In the time of the current Ander's youth, a number of the older clan members, including Ander's parents, had built themselves a family retreat in a forested area near the back wall of the Place of Power. It was a fanciful pavilion, much gilded and ornamented with carved dragons. Craftsmen had been brought all the way from the Faulty Sea to do the work, and craftsmen were still summoned at intervals to repair the lacquer or regild the finials of the roof peaks, architectural conceits that did not stand up well to those violent changes in temperature and humidity that the locals called climate.

The pavilion was exclusively an Ander hideaway. Family members were so excessively refined that prolonged contact with persons from other clans inevitably sent them retreating to the sound of tinkling waters, the feel of silk robes loosely belted, the sight of blossoms artfully arrayed, and the smell and taste of fine foods, elaborately prepared. All Ander servants were well schooled in artfulness and elaboration. The pavilion servants were especially so. The simple handing of a dish could take up to five minutes and require full orchestral accompaniment. Such lengthy conceits embodying mime, music, and ballet were encouraged. There was no hurry in the pavilion. There were never any voices raised there. No business was ever discussed. In the entire history of the structure, this latter rule had not been broken until now. The fact that it was being broken now, and by general consent, conveyed more than a little of the importance the Anders attached to Quince Ellel's imminent flight to the moon.

Ander's uncle, one Forsmooth Ander, stood at the center of the gathering, pivoting gracefully and extending his arms to display his sleeves. The sleeves were pure silk, spun in the boat-towns of the Faulty Sea. Their elegant pattern of pine cones and siskins had been printed by a dyer near Whitherby in manland, one Wilfer Ponde.

"We all know what she's like," Forsmooth said for perhaps the fifth time. "Every person in the Place knows what she's like. If she thought the air in Berkli's lungs carried a scent she needed, she'd put a clothespeg on his nose and suck his breath. She's not going to let him sidetrack her, not him nor Mitty. Quince Ellel is going to take power. She may think we haven't noticed, but she's already taken over for all intents and purposes."

"We do know that, uncle," said Ander, with a graceful gesture. "You're quite correct when you say we all know her."

"Then you know what she wants?"

Ander knew what Ellel said publicly. But he also knew what she hinted to him privately, pretending she jested, just to see his reaction.

He said, "She wants weapons. And the starship."

"The starship?" gasped Forsmooth, amid a chorus of other gasps. "We assumed she wanted weapons, but what starship?"

"The one that's up there."

"Our records don't say anything about a starship," he said in amazement. "Not a word!"

"Hers do. Or perhaps it's something she heard from her father. One of the Gaddirs told Jark the Third there's a starship there, and Ellel wants it. If not this first trip, then sometime later."

They glanced at one another, nodding.

Forsmooth said, "We needn't concern ourselves with that now. She certainly doesn't intend to break it down for salvage!"

"That's true, uncle."

"So what she wants is weapons. What does she *say* she wants them for?"

"Salvage. She says they have self-contained power sources we can use in the shops."

"Power is one thing the Place doesn't need any more of, Ander. We're sitting on top of the world's last fusion plant. Why would we go flying to the moon to get self-contained power sources?"

"Uncle, I wouldn't go flying to the moon to get a lifetime supply of tea and cakes. Don't ask me why Quince Ellel is going to do this or that. She does what she does, that's all. You've all studied her far more diligently than I!"

Forsmooth Ander brought his brows together. "Fashimir, my boy, if Quince Ellel is going into space to get weapons, then you may be sure she has plans for them. Thus far, we four Domer Families have managed to keep things reasonably well balanced among ourselves. None of us has been preeminent; none of us has been at the bottom of the ladder. Life has been equitable. None of us has had an advantage over the others. But things are changing. We can feel it. Surely you can feel it. Look at the symbolism of the mask Ellel wears! She has hidden her face. What does that say to you? She doesn't realize what the act betrays! She's planning secretly. And more and more, Ellel is at the root of events. More and more, when things happen, we find that Ellel has caused them to happen. And weapons are an advantage, my boy."

"Indeed," said Aunt Bivina. "And if she's going after weapons, then in the interest of family equity, it should be with our help, with us as allies, share and share alike."

Ander sighed. "What makes you think I can convince her of that?"

It was Aunt Bivina who answered. "She'll listen to you just now, Ander. You're right that we've been studying her. Analyzing her. Ellel believes Berkli is her enemy, and because Mitty gets on well with Berkli, she mistrusts him as well. That's two to one. She needs us to balance the equation, to keep it two against two. Without us, she feels isolated. She counts on us to be her ally, and she'll welcome our statement of support. She doesn't have all power gathered into her own hands yet. That's what she wants the space weapons for."

"I don't understand."

"The Edges, Fashimir, the Edges. With the walkers, she could conquer any place on earth except the Edges. The Edges have technology of their own. So she needs weapons powerful enough to subdue the Edges. Trust us. Until she has them, she'll welcome our support. Before she has them, we have to assure that we don't become her next victims."

Forsmooth nodded agreement. "Talk to her, Ander. Convince her it should be a two-family expedition. Some Ellels, some Anders. Share and share alike. Helping one another to keep Berkli and Mitty at bay.''

Ander spread his arms in a graceful gesture of acceptance, one that showed off his robe to advantage. There was just time for a murmur of appreciation from those assembled before the master of ceremonies announced dinner.

# CHAPTER 6

W hen the sun edged the mountain crests to the west of Long Plain, Abasio stopped at the first farm he came to and dickered for some meat, salad stuff, and salt. He also asked for potatoes, though he couldn't remember whether it was late enough in the season for the farmers to have dug their root crops. Living in the city so long had put him out of touch with the soil. The Farmwife said of course she had potatoes, who wouldn't have potatoes by this time of year, smooth and brown and smelling of earth. He bought six of them and a sizable lump of butter in a gourd pot, and he filled his canteen at the farm well. A mile or two farther south, he made camp on a breeze-swept height far enough from any stream to be free of mosquitoes, close enough to the north-south highway to be relatively safe from monsters, so he told himself, and beside a copse littered with fallen tree limbs and grown up with clumps of burdock.

He gathered a handful of burdock leaves and a bundle of deadfall branches, shaving some of the latter into paper-thin kindling. Once his fire was burning well, he tipped his canteen onto the clayey soil, stirred the resultant mud into a paste, wrapped his potatoes first in burdock leaves and then in an even layer of clay, and buried the sticky bundles in the coals of his fire. He ate the meat and lettuces while he waited for the sun to set, the stars to come out, the fire to burn down. When nothing was left of it but grayed embers, he dug out the blackened balls, cracked off the clay, and put all but two of the cooked potatoes in his saddlebags. Those two he buttered copiously and ate with salt and enjoyment before drowning the fire, rolling up in the blankets, and falling asleep.

Deep in the night, he came awake to the sound of growling, like animals fighting. Huge animals. He sat up, stood up, went to the edge of the copse, and peered out at the night, suddenly aware that the wind was blowing from behind him toward the sound. His awareness was matched by something else's. The snarling stopped. A long silence, followed by a questing howl, then another, joined together and coming toward him.

Cursing under his breath, more than a little panicky, Abasio untied the horse and slapped it into motion, rolled his possessions inside a blanket, strapped the untidy bundle on his back, then climbed the tallest of the nearby pines, up the dead and broken lower branches, stopping to kick off the stub of each dead branch behind him, then on up among the living branches, prickled by the needles and stained with resin. These were lessons learned in youth, drilled into him by Grandpa. "If what's chasing you doesn't have wings, go high, cut off your route behind you, get hid if you can." So he went high, so far up that the trunk diminished alarmingly, bending and swaying under his weight.

The yammering howls came closer. He put his folded blanket on the best branch he could find, cushioning his seat so discomfort would not make him move, took several deep breaths, then concentrated on being absolutely silent.

The howls broke off in midyell. From beneath him came snuffling, snarling, gulping noises. Stench rose around him, like smoke. The miasmic cheesy smell meant it was trolls. Ogres and manticores smelled like rotten meat, chimeras smelled like cats, minotaurs like cows, but manticores, chimeras, and minotaurs didn't hunt at night—strictly speaking, minotaurs didn't "hunt" at all, though they were dangerous enough for all that. Trolls and ogres hunted at night. The tree shuddered as something huge hit it, perhaps only by accident, as the result of the scuffle going on. They could smell him, Lord only knew how, above their own stink. At least, they could smell where he had been, including the tree trunk.

The trunk shuddered again, and again. Something trying to climb? Mature trolls couldn't climb. Their legs bent the wrong way, and they were too heavy.

Abasio put his head on his bundle and concentrated on grayness, noth-

ingness, nothing at all, at all. Grandpa had always said monsters could read
people's thoughts. It was important, so he had always said, not to think.

So he would not think. Despite the vibration of the trunk, despite their
scratching at it, the deep rasp of their claws on wood, the stench, the howls,
he would not think of them. He would think of something else. Horses.
Horses away somewhere else. Delicious horses. Galloping, galloping, why
weren't these trolls out hunting horse? Hmmm?

Silence below. Yammer-snarl-yammer. Moving away among the trees.

Abasio didn't fall for it. Both trolls and ogres had been known to move
away and sit silent for hours, waiting for prey to appear. Trolls were very
patient. One of the Purple legends written in the Book of the Purples was
of Ben the Wolf, who had gone into the wilderness, sought out a monster
in its lair, pursued it underground, and slaughtered it. Abasio had always
considered the story apocryphal. One of Grandpa's words, *apocryphal*. Nothing in the present encounter had made him change his mind. He curled up
on the blanket as best he could. Eventually he fell asleep.

First light found him early awake. The grove beneath him was empty.
Trolls were usually back in their lairs by dawn because sunlight immobilized
them. They were blinded by bright light. Abasio climbed down stiffly, ach-
ingly, yelling a few times and bouncing on the branches, just to bring out
anything that might be hiding. Finally he dropped from thirty feet up in the
tree, falling and rolling, managing not to break anything.

When he looked at the trunk of the tree he'd been in, he couldn't hold
back a shudder. Claws had ripped it deep, shredded the bark so that it hung
in tatters. And everywhere around was the splash and stench of monster,
marking the territory.

He left quickly, making time for a quick bath in the river, breakfast of
cold meat and potato, tracking the horse—which had not gone as far as it
should have for its own good—and continuing his journey. From the hill
where he'd camped he could look east across the river to the highway, a
shiny line where bug-size freight vehicles trundled along spouting smoke.
At one time, so Grandpa had told him, highways would have been full of
vehicles, people going here and there, things being carried back and forth
from the far edges of the world. Goods that could be manufactured next
door, food people could have grown for themselves, both had been carried
across whole countries! People had used fuel prodigiously in the old days,
which left damned little for use now. Of course, most of the people had gone
to the stars, so there wasn't so much need now.

By midmorning, he could see the tops of the Wise Rocks, their flattish
heads seeming to float above a ridge some distance to his right, up the Crystal
River valley that wound westerly into the hills. As he rode higher, the lower
parts of the red pillars came into view: tall, contorted, slightly hunched

figures, their heads together in eternal confabulation. Since he left the Patrol Post, he had not seen anyone except the Farmwife he'd bought food from. Now, hungry for the sound of voices, he found himself listening, as though he might hear the stones talking if he were only quiet enough.

Though boiling with rampant, muddy fury in the spring when fed by the runoff from the western ranges, the Crystal River was clear and burbling this time of year. Along its flow, here on the valley floor, was where the refugee had been, Abasio thought. She'd been seen by hunters who, if they'd been hunting goats, must have been high upon the ridge, among the feathery new growth of forest. There were more goats all the time, and more deer, too, as the forests and meadows came back on the heights, replanted by Sisters to Trees. Abasio's ma's ma had been a Sister to Trees, according to Grandpa, and there were others of them among the Farmwives in the valley.

The hunters would not have been the only ones to see the refugee. Someone on a farm would have seen her as well. Abasio would ask. If that failed, he would ride on to Whitherby, the nearest village down the Long Plain, a few hours ahead. But first—first he'd ask at the farms. Perhaps at Grandpa's farm.

He pulled up the horse as though needing stillness to contemplate that idea. Grandpa's farm. Well, maybe he wouldn't go there. He took a deep breath. Maybe he'd ask about Grandpa, but he wouldn't go there. He was honest enough to admit the reason. He'd had certain dreams of himself when he was a child. He and Ma had sometimes talked about what he could do or be. They had talked of traveling west to join the Guardians. Grandpa had been full of tales of the Guardians. Or he would explore the lands to the south, where new towns were said to be growing out of the low jungles, maybe become an Animal Master or a Sea Shepherd.

When he'd run away, he hadn't planned to be a ganger. That had just happened. The dreams, the plans, the visions he'd had of himself when he was a kid didn't match what he was now. He didn't want to deal with that difference. That *dissonance*.

It was not a word Abasio would have said aloud in Fantis. The gangs were suspicious of polysyllabic talk, of meanings that were too precise. They used few and sharp words to serve aggressive use; few and hard words for threats; few and sodden words for everyday; flabby words with variable meaning, words that took their sense mostly from the tone and the rhythm of speech, that could equally well be endearment or deadly insult, depending on how things came out. The same words could be an invitation to a woman, a challenge to a ganger, an order to a slave, a greeting to a shop owner in the district, the repeated refrain of a song, or a final insult to a dying man.

"Like apes," Grandpa had said, the one time Abasio had gone back, looking for Ma. "Like apes, Abasio. No oral tradition, rejecting literacy as

unmanly. It's a decadent tongue, Abasio, an impoverished tongue. As vocabulary is reduced, so are the number of feelings you can express, the
number of events you can describe, the number of things you can identify!
Not only understanding is limited, but also experience. Man grows by language. Whenever he limits language, he retrogresses!''

Maybe Grandpa had been right. Certainly now Abasio needed some of
Grandpa's words. Like the word he had just thought of in reference to the
unquiet jangling of his spirit and of the world at large: a *dissonance*.

It was noon before he arrived at Wise Rocks Farm. The people there had
been named Suttle. The man had often been away, so the farm had been managed by his wife along with a bunch of children and other people, including
some female relative with a simpleton-son. Likely they were still there.

So recalling, he turned in at the gate. A tributary brook ran beside the
lane, bits of bark and leaves bobbing along beside him as he rode, losing
themselves among the willows and sedges that lined the banks, washing
ashore on grassy ledges. Rising around him was the fresh smell of wet soil
and leaves, the scent of moist growth, and he stopped to breathe deeply,
suddenly alive with a feeling of intense and totally unexpected joy. Beside
him the small stream ran through a chain of shallow pools, where the silver
water had been dammed with leaky lines of stones, constructions a child
might have made.

And there was the child, up to his or her thighs in water, hunting something.
Frogs, perhaps. Or crayfish.

"Hello," said Abasio cheerfully.

The child looked up briefly, then went back to whatever it was doing.

"I wonder if you could help me?" Abasio asked, getting down from his
horse.

"Doubt it," said the child. "Ma says I'm as unhelpful a whelp as any
she's had."

Abasio laughed dutifully. The child was looking at him mildly: unafraid,
certainly, but with a proper wariness, nonetheless.

"No big matter, young'un. I heard that a refugee was spotted here in the
valley two days ago. I'm looking for such a person, that's all. I thought
perhaps you knew where the refugee had gone."

"That wasn't a refugee," the child asserted, turning back to the bank and
continuing its search. "That was my cousin Olly. She went too far up the
river, is all. She's never been here before, my cousin, so she went too far.
Then she had to come back down, so maybe somebody thought she was a
refugee."

"Your cousin." His heart sank. He felt it thudding away in his boots.

"From over near Longville. Olly Longaster."

"Wandering around all alone?"

"Well, she came in a freight wagon as far as our road," the child said. "She just walked right on past us." The child turned limpid eyes on Abasio and smiled at him.

Abasio knew at once that the child was a girl and that she was lying to him. How many times had he seen that glance, all innocence? How many times seen that smile, all sweetness? Girls, girls, girls, and this one was lying through her teeth. Which meant it wasn't her cousin at all. Which meant . . .

"I'll ride on down and see your ma," he said with a smile. "She's Ori Suttle, isn't she?"

"How'd you know that?" the child snapped, glowering at him suspiciously.

"Oh, I was born and brought up over there," he said, pointing west and south, symbolizing the distance between thumb and forefinger, a little way only. "On a farm."

"You're a cityman," the child challenged. "Citymen dress like you. Mud-colored. Hair all covered up. Bet you your hair's a funny color under that cap."

"I'm a cityman now," Abasio agreed. "But I wasn't then. I remember your ma, Farmwife Suttle. And your aunt, what was her name? Upton? And her son. Is he still here?"

"Most everybody who ever was here is still here," the girl said, dismissing him as she turned back to the muddy bank.

Including the refugee, Abasio assured himself as he rode on down the lane. Certainly including the refugee.

Ori Suttle sat just inside the open door of the dairy, skimming cream with the assistance of the Widow Upton. Abasio dismounted and carefully tied his horse, taking his time about it so they could get a good look at him, then went close enough to bow and introduce himself as a former neighbor, now a cityman, out looking for a refugee who had been reported in the neighborhood.

"And what would you want with a refugee, cityman?" asked Farmwife Suttle, drawing her brows down in a scowl at him. "Some poor soul from some troubled place, already with enough worry on his poor head, driven out, no doubt, only to have you city hounds after him as well."

"I've been helpful to refugees in my time," said Abasio mildly. "Sometimes I can offer a job, or some advice as to where one might be found."

"I know your jobs," snorted the Widow. "Jobs for harlots and songhouse barkers and poor fools to be killed in the arena."

"I've never put anyone in the arena, fool or not," said Abasio stiffly.

"And I've never made a harlot of anyone, either. It's true, I've recruited concubines a time or two, and carnival folk—a magician, and a strong man. Why do you assume I'm a villain, Farmwife?"

"Your hands are covered, boy, which means tattoos to me, and that means gangs—though you don't speak like them, or at least not when you're speaking to us, though I've no doubt you can and do, most times. Well, it's no matter what you are. There's no refugee here. Only my niece, Olly Longaster from Longville. She missed the turning and went too far up the valley, where she was seen by Farmer Chyne. And if you were born here and raised here, as you claim, you know about Farmer Chyne."

"He was never fond of strangers," said Abasio.

"True. And what with these monsters breeding in the hills, more of them every year, he's got other things not to be fond of. Was his manner as much as anything that made my niece sure she'd gone too far, so she turned and came back again. And that's the whole story of that." She tapped her skimming spoon on the edge of the jar. "May I offer you some biscuits, cityman—"

"Abasio," he offered.

"Abasio." She nodded. "Then it was old Cermit was your grandpa."

He got the name out with some difficulty. "Cermit. Yes."

"Poor old man." The Widow gave him a sharp look. "All solitary up there in the woods. So you're the boy who ran off to the city and broke his ma's heart."

"Hush, sister," said the Farmwife. "Let old dung lie."

"Do that," said Abasio stiffly. "I did no more than she had done in her own youth. And I've not regretted it."

"You're young still," said the Widow with a sniff. "Your time for regret is yet to come."

"I offered biscuits and fresh butter and cheese. The good cheese, boy. The stuff we keep for ourselves."

Abasio found his mouth watering. The good cheese, the aged stuff that the farmers kept for themselves because there was no point wasting it on cityfolk. He hadn't tasted that crumbling yellow wonder in years.

"Yes, ma'am," he told her fervently. "I'd be most grateful."

He told himself later it was fate, certainly. Fate that the Farmwife mentioned the cheese, and that he accepted it, and that he had his mouth full of it when she walked in. She. Her hair a cloud of darkness and her eyes glowing at him. Her skin shiny as a piece of handled wood, polished and gleaming. Her skirts pulled between her legs and hiked up into her belt as women did when they worked in the garden, the fabric damp around her knees, knees so softly rounded he could feel them in the palm of his hand, shapely calves, sweetly turned ankles, and feet that made him think of dancing on meadows. Barefoot and laughing she was, coming in and catching sight of him and her brows going up like wings, saying, Who's this? Where've I seen this one before?

And he, he caught his breath through that mouthful of bread and cheese, and choked like a fool, and almost strangled himself, gasping, so there was somebody pounding on him and the Farmwife clutching him around his middle, and when he caught his breath at last with a great whoop of air, she'd gone.

"Smaller mouthfuls, boy," counseled the Farmwife. "Did your ma teach you no manners before you left her?"

"It wasn't that," he said, unthinkingly truthful.

"No, I hardly thought it was," she said dryly. "That was Olly Longaster, my niece, as you've no doubt guessed."

Which was a blatant lie, but he would not argue with her. "She's—she's a very lovely girl," he said.

"She's a lovely young woman, yes. She'll make some lucky farmer a fine wife," said the Farmwife.

"What a waste," he blurted, still unthinking.

"A waste!" Farmwife Suttle exclaimed. "Isn't that a cityman talking! How would you not waste her, boy? Let's see, she could be a gang concubine, sold to a Chief, and passed on by him to his boys when he tired of her or when she caught one of the IDDIs or grew old. Or she could go to a brothel, where she'd fetch a good many silver rats for her owner until she sickened there. They don't last long in the brothels."

"I was thinking of the Edge," mumbled Abasio, redfaced. It wasn't true. He'd been thinking of himself.

"Oh? And since when have the Edges been recruiting from outside? You know as well as I do, boy, that the Edges are closed, them with their lawns and their trees and their tennis and their guard dogs. Them with their clean white clothes and their clean soft hands. Them with their patrols! You have to be born to one of their families, go to one of their schools, be confirmed in one of their faiths, and dress and talk as they do, and if you don't, out you go. No outside wives for them. Nossir."

The Farmwife leaned forward to rap him on the knee with a hard knuckle. "Let be, boy. She'll make some farmer a fine wife, bear him several handsome children, and grow old no unhappier than most of us."

Abasio had no desire to let be. He wanted to rage at her. He wanted to run after the girl. He would have done, except he'd seen her go, and the way she had gone bothered him. She'd fled. She'd taken one look at him and gone out like a cat spooked by a dog.

He finished his bread and cheese, unashamedly begged a bit more for his homeward way, and went out the way he'd come, trying to decide how he'd manage to find the girl, or talk with her if she was so unwilling. As he rode back along the brook on his way to the gate, he saw the girl-child once again, this time sitting on the branch of a gnarled tree, watching him closely.

"Olly says she saw you," said the child.

"What's your name?" asked Abasio.

"Seelie."

"Seelie. Well, yes, she saw me and I saw her, but she didn't stick around. She came out here, did she?"

"That's her business. I'll be watching, so don't you try anything."

What did she suppose he would try? Abduction? Here in farm country, where the tocsin would bring the farmers and their families swarming at him like bees? Rape? With the same consequence?

Then all such worries departed him, for he saw her, standing as Seelie had stood, knee-deep in one of the pools, hunting something or other, a plumy creature on her shoulder that at first he thought was a bird, then thought was something else.

He didn't speak until he was near her. "You're Olly," he said foolishly. So far as he knew, it was the only name she had.

She looked up from the fat crayfish in her hand, then dropped it into the sodden sack hanging from her belt. "And you're the man from the city," she said, carefully keeping her eyes away from his. He was just as she remembered him, though the cap and gloves he wore contributed nothing to his appearance. Dark, he was, like walnut wood, darker than she was, and she was dark. Eyes with fire in them. Hands that moved gracefully, as though of themselves.

Handsome or not, she had been warned against citymen. Burned Man had warned her with every word he said. Oracle had warned her with some of the words she hadn't. Though it took all her resolve, she accused him.

"You're a ganger," she said flatly. Her eyes told him she'd seen him before in ganger company, though she didn't say that. She knew he recognized her and knew she was not Ori Suttle's niece. Still, she would not admit it. Not to him. "A ganger," she repeated.

He flushed. Just so had his grandpa used to say the word. A ganger. As though he had said, a cockroach. A poison snake. A rat in the granary.

"Some here in the country don't approve of gangs, it's true," he said, trying to keep his voice flat and unchallenging. "But in the city, most men my age either belong to a gang or pay dues to one. As for me, I'm a member of the Purples."

She gave no sign she had ever heard of Purples. The very fact she did not made him ache with doubt. Had she not felt anything, then? Had she merely looked at him as at any wandering ganger? Was this flaming heat in him all on his side, none on hers?

It was much on hers, as well, but she was using all her strength to deny it. "That's all right." She waved her hand, dismissing the question and him along with it. "We've all a right to our own way of life. So I've been taught, at least."

Oh, go away, she said to him silently. Before I throw myself at you, like some stupid Ingenue. Go, go, get you gone!

He refused to be dismissed. He wanted to winkle her out of her deception. "What brought you here from Longville? I think I went there as a child, to market, probably. Isn't the Longville market famous?"

She looked up at him briefly, her eyes opaque. "I suppose all markets are famous to those who buy and sell there. Here in the country, markets are our entertainment."

"You found the village dull?" he persisted, purposely leaving the village unnamed.

She shrugged. "It was home, but sometimes we . . . sometimes we need new surroundings. Else we stultify."

Stultify. Another of Grandpa's many words. She too had been reared by a lover of words. "You find Wise Rocks less stultifying?"

"It's too early yet to say," she said, stooping to the bank, eyes probing the ripples. It was easier to keep a proper attitude toward him if she did not look at him. The angel flew from her shoulder to his, landed there, much to his surprise, and pecked him sharply behind the ear.

He clapped his hand to the spot, feeling blood. The winged creature went back to its mistress, who scolded it wordlessly. He looked at the blood on his hand, feeling inexplicably angry, more at her than at her pet. She was almost contemptuous, certainly disrespectful to him who'd grown accustomed to respect. Or what passed for it in the cities. He had no idea what it cost her to appear so.

"Perhaps you'd find the city less stultifying," he challenged. "I'd be glad to escort you there, if you'd like to see it."

It was the worst thing he could have said. Her face closed, like an iron-bound door, shutting him out. "Do you think I'm a fool, cityman? I've been told what sleazy life awaits women there." She gave him a contemptuous look, hating him for being what Oracle had said citymen were. Not her Prince Charming, but a serpent, his darting tongue laden with false words.

He looked so shocked, so bereft, she almost regretted her decision to have no more to do with him. More gently she said, "There's only one thing you could do for me, cityman, and that's to let me pick your brain. I was recently told by a—fortune-teller that my fate is entwined with some mystery. In your travels about your exciting and no doubt wonderful city, have you by chance heard of *three thrones that tower*?"

He shook his head, baffled at this change of direction. "If it's a matter of prophecies, half the city is hearing prophecies on any given day. Every carnival has fortune-tellers, the odds-shops have palm readers, there are astrological forecasts on the public amusement screens. Anytime a gang goes to war, it seeks some prophecy or other.''

''Would you have heard, perhaps, of five beings called champions or six who seek salvation?''

He became sly. ''I'll be honest with you, Olly. Yours is the kind of question that needs to be taken to a real soothsayer, an archetypal Oracle, perhaps. Even we citymen take some kinds of questions to Oracles. My Chief went to one not long ago, in a village near here, as a matter of fact.''

Slyness achieved nothing. Her face closed once more. ''It's of no matter, cityman. Forget that I asked.'' She turned away, dismissing him once more, this time finally.

Memory tugged at him, faint and illusory. He couldn't pin it down. He called after her, ''I'll ask when I get back. Perhaps someone there will know.''

She was splashing her way down the stream, ignoring him, wondering why she had even bothered with this spate of talk. Oracle had told her it was better to say nothing to such men, but there for a moment his face had been open and likable, not conniving at all. There for a moment she might almost have trusted him.

He cried after her desperately, ''You might consider the three thrones that remaineth!''

She turned and came back a little way. ''Remaineth?''

Now, where had that memory come from? He groped for more. ''Something to do with the world,'' he said, astonishing himself. ''Something about—after men went to the stars, the thrones that remaineth to . . . protect the world from upheavals.''

''Is there, then, some such protection?'' she asked. ''I've not heard of that.''

''It may not exist. Or perhaps it's fictional. It's simply something I heard of a long time ago.'' It was Ma, or maybe Grandpa who had mentioned the thrones, he remembered now.

''Ah,'' she said. ''Well. How interesting.'' She smiled an almost-real smile, and he felt himself melting. ''Thank you for that.''

She went away again, downstream, where she was joined by Seelie. The two bent their heads over the sack of crayfish and then, evidently deciding they had enough, they went on to lose themselves among the willows.

Abasio was left to stare after them, a foolish look on his face. So he had found her, and now what? He had come all this way, been almost eaten by trolls—and she would have none of him. This wasn't the city, where he could demand to see her pass and if she had none, take her for his own, or if she had one, kill the man who had issued it and take her anyway. This was not the city, where he could call out his gang to help him kidnap her and keep her thereafter.

What was he to do?

What he did, after some little time, was to shut his mouth. After a moment more he cursed, almost silently. When he got onto his horse, he was amazed to find his eyes wet and his body trembling.

"Farmwife Suttle?" Olly asked. "Have you heard of three thrones of remaineth? Or anything about three thrones?"

The Farmwife, who had her cheek against a cow's flank as she stripped the last of the milk from the teats, drew back with a puzzled look. "Seems I've heard something like that. A story maybe? Some kind of fairy tale?"

"That man who was here, he said there were three thrones at remaineth or of remaineth. He said it had to do with the world, with upheavals."

The Farmwife's expression cleared, and she smiled. "Well, of course. That's where I've heard it. That cityman was old Cermit's grandson, and Cermit is always going on about upheavals. He's a great reader, Cermit. Spends half the mice he gets for his crops buying books." She picked up her bucket, slapped the cow on the flank until it moved toward the barn door, then moved herself and her milking stool to the other cow.

Outside the barn the guardian-angel whistled and chortled, then came fluttering in to seat itself on Olly's shoulder, where it pecked at her ear gently.

"He said his name was Abasio," said Olly, ignoring the angel, who had been extremely active of late, coming and going all the time, even at night, taking off on little flights into the forest at the least provocation. She hadn't dared talk with the man, but since he left, she had very much wanted to talk about him.

The Farmwife gave her a look from under her lashes, one that understood a good deal more than Olly knew. "Abasio Cermit. Cermit's daughter Elisa ran off when she was only a girl. Little more than a year later, she was back again—tattooed, hair dyed, pregnant, scared out of her wits those from the city would come after her. Nobody came, though, and in due time the babe was born. Abasio. Thirty-some-odd years ago, that was. I was only a child."

"And he also ran off to the city?" queried Olly.

"When he was about fourteen, fifteen. Poor Elisa had so feared he'd do it, she was always warning him against it. Which, in my opinion, practically guaranteed he'd do it, boys being contrary as they are. When he did leave, she went into a black fit, one nobody could lift her from. In the end, she killed herself, or as good as."

"As good as?"

"Drowned herself. Old Cermit went frantic, set off a distress signal that brought a resurrection team from the Edge, and they brought her back. They'll do that, you know, if you pay them. It took all Cermit's savings, and little good it did the poor man, or her, either. They should have left her dead."

"Drowned Woman!" said Olly, trying to remember where Drowned Woman had been when the Purples came to the village. Not where Abasio could have seen her, obviously.

The Farmwife misunderstood this for mere commentary. "Elisa was a drowned woman, indeed. She could not remember how to milk, how to plant or harvest, how to wash a dish or churn butter. Cermit tried to care for her, but she didn't remember him. All she wanted to do was dabble in the water and sing little songs and cuddle baby animals, as though they were children. Eventually, she went away. Old Cermit never told us where."

Olly locked her lips. So. Abasio's momma was the Drowned Woman in the village. Now that Olly thought about it, she could even picture the resemblance between them.

She found herself considering his appearance, his size, his build, the set of his shoulders. She shook herself, embarrassed at her own thoughts. Oracle had spoken of men being attractive, of the feelings a woman might expect to feel. Certainly Abasio was attractive, but she didn't recognize however it was she felt. Interested, maybe? But he was a cityman. Oracle had been more than clear about what a woman could expect from citymen.

Nonetheless, since Abasio's momma had also been Orphan's momma, in a manner of speaking, he might almost be her brother. That thought she could deal with. It would be good to have a brother. And one didn't need to worry about feelings with a brother. One simply felt . . . familial. As she did toward Oracle. And Drowned Woman. And the Farmwife herself, rather.

"Would the old man, Cermit, tell me about these thrones if I asked him?" Olly asked the Farmwife.

"If I took you over, he might well. In the morning we'll ride over, you and I."

"I've never ridden on a horse."

"It's like sitting in a chair. Nothing to it."

It wasn't at all like sitting in a chair. Olly was so sore by the time they got to the Cermit Farm that she dreaded the thought of riding home again. Perhaps she'd let the Farmwife go on ahead and follow her afoot. Though come to that, she realized when she dismounted, it hurt almost as badly to walk. She gasped, and the angel on her shoulder made a troubled noise, as though in sympathy.

The old man had come out onto his porch to stare dourly at them as they approached, his face breaking into a smile when he saw who it was.

"Ori," he called in a surprisingly firm voice. "Who's this you've got with you?"

"Olly," she rejoined. "A cousin of mine, from Longville."

"Come in, come in," he invited them. "I've some rhubarb wine I've been saving for welcome visitors!"

They went in. They ate muffins and drank wine. They talked. Olly looked around herself. This was a room he had occupied. That bed on the porch— he'd probably slept there in the summer heat. He'd drunk from that well. . . .

"Olly," said the Farmwife, "Cermit is showing you something."

She flushed bright red and looked attentively at the two books Cermit had bought from a peddler who'd come through Whitherby. Old ones. Over a hundred years old, he whispered. They could even be books from before the last upheaval. Olly pricked up her ears at the word, and Originee took the opportunity to ask about the thrones.

He said: "The thrones are a story my wife told me. She was from Artemisia, ran off from there because it didn't suit her, so she said, but she was full of stories that nobody else but Artemisians knew, about Coyote and Bear, about Talking God and Changing Woman, about things that happened long ago. Seems long ago, after most people left for the stars, the world was in upheaval."

"What sort of upheaval?" Olly breathed.

"Well, as to that, she wasn't specific. Could have been most anything: the climate heating up, or an ice age coming; chemicals getting in the oceans that killed the coral, killed the fish; too much ultraviolet getting through the atmosphere, burning everybody. Or it might have been one group fighting another. Who knows? I do know men went to the stars just in time, for if they hadn't gone then, there'd have been nothing left of the earth at all! So she told me.

"Anyhow, in the midst of this upheaval—whatever kind it was—my wife said, 'In a place where power remaineth, three thrones were raised up to keep the world's peace.' I thought later, her talking about peace and all, that's probably when they passed the half-century rule."

"Half-century rule?" asked Olly.

"The rule that says there's to be no history written going back more than fifty years. So's to allow changes to take place without too much grieving over old times, so's people don't dwell on old hatreds the way they used to. Oh, ladies, the wars they used to have! She told me! Old wrongs going back hundreds of years, and people still fighting over them! So they made the rule. Anybody had an old grudge more than fifty years old, it couldn't be written of anymore! Of course, you can make a rule about what's written down, and you can go through the libraries every year and take out any histories that are fifty years old, but you can't keep people from telling tales, now, can you?'' He nodded and sipped, then concluded:

"I'll bet that's when the villages were set up too.''

"Why was that?'' Olly asked.

"Well, according to my wife—Honey was what I called her—certain people come along from time to time who seem to cause upheavals. They just do it, maybe not even meaning to, for it's the type of people they are. So it was thought safest to put these kinds of people where they'd do the least damage, in little villages where they couldn't stir up much. They started out putting away all the Prophets and Preachers and like that, but once the villages were there, people started putting other folks there, special people, to keep the tranquillity and preserve the peace, you know, kind of like in zoos. You can't have tigers and artivorkes roaming around in town, but it'd be a pity to kill them all off too. So anybody troublesome but special enough to need preserving, that's where they go.''

Olly bridled at this as Originee put a cautionary hand on her shoulder, reminding her that Originee's niece Olly would have no reason to resent villages being called zoos.

Still, she seethed. What possible trouble could an Orphan cause? A toddler so tiny she would fit into the pannier on a donkey?

The Farmwife interrupted her agitations. "What were these thrones, then? A kind of government?''

Cermit shook his head slowly. "My wife never said what they were. But she didn't speak of them as though they were a government.''

"We don't have any government, do we?'' asked the Farmwife.

"Not that I know of. There's certain—what would you say—*powers* we don't get in the way of. Like the teams that burn the books and the messengers who tell people they're archetypes and take them from their homes to the villages. But they don't add up to any *government.*''

"Do you think the story about the thrones is true?'' asked the Farmwife. "Do you think they could still be there, be a kind of government, but nobody knows about them? A kind of secret?''

"But why?'' blurted Olly. "Why would it be secret?''

"Oh, girl''—the old man chuckled—"I can tell you one real good reason. Nothing's so galling for us folk as to feel we're being managed. Lord, I've learned that from life. People don't take to being ordered about.'' He shook his head, looking off into the distance. "Us folk don't like laws, and we don't like rules, and we don't like people watching us to be sure we do right. Even when it's rules or laws we set up ourselves, we can't wait to change them or figure out some way to evade them entirely. My ma told me stories about the old times, when they had a whole army of men who did nothing but make laws and change laws and figure out how to get around laws, year after year after year.''

"All men, I suppose," said Farmwife Suttle with a sniff. "That sounds like men, trying to make rules to cover everything. First thing little boys do when they get together is make up rules for their games. Somebody has to win, somebody has to lose. When they grow up, they do more of the same, then go fiddling with their laws and rules everlastingly because they don't work. Any woman knows rules have to give in to needs! There's things that're right and needful that no rule can be made to cover."

Cermit nodded acceptance of this, unoffended. "I suppose it could have been mostly men, Originee, but since mankind went to the stars, there haven't been any rule-wrights that I know of."

"Law-yers is what they were called," said the Farmwife. "And they all went, my ma told me. Every last one of them. They didn't think folks could get along without them, out there among the stars."

All of which was interesting, but no help to Olly. "And you've no idea at all where this 'power remaineth' is?"

The old man shook his head. "None at all. If I had to go looking, I'd go to Artemisia—"

"I've heard of Artemisia before," Olly interrupted. "They have a library there."

"—where they've got the library." He laughed. "We've both heard the same, then. My wife told me there's books in that library go way back. Don't ask me how they manage to keep them. I don't know."

He shook his head in wonder at this, which Olly barely noted, for the mention of Artemisia had set off rockets in her head. She should go. Now. She should . . . travel toward Artemisia! She should find out now, without a moment's delay.

She fretted, controlling herself with difficulty as the talk moved on to other things, such as wine recipes, sourdough starter, and treatment for boggle fly on sheep.

"What's the matter with your windmill, Cermit?" asked Farmwife Suttle. "I noticed when we came in it wasn't working."

He leaned back in his chair, pointing upward. "Oh, it's nothing wrong. Just my own gadget up there. See that heavy little wheel behind the big one? It takes a big wind to turn that heavy wheel, but when a big enough wind comes, that wheel turns and pushes down a latch, and that latch shuts it all down, automatic like, so the pump rod and the gaskets and all don't rip themselves up. Saves me getting up in the middle of the night because I forgot to shut her down. I call it my automatic shutdown system!"

"We haven't had a big wind."

"Did two three days ago. Plenty of water in the cistern. I just haven't gotten around to turning it on again."

Olly stared up at the windmill, thinking how sensible it was to have an automatic shutdown system. Bastard should have had one. Burned Man should have had one, when he got too upset. Fool should have had one, and Fool's mother, before she got IDDI.

Originee stood up and told old Cermit they had to be leaving.

"Well, then," he said, "there's something I want to show you. Come on out back."

They went out back, past the garden and to the corral, where three horses stood head to tail, flicking each other's faces and necks with their tails.

"Why, that's Big Blue!" cried the Farmwife. "I thought he died."

"He did." Old Cermit nodded. "He died. This is his son or his grandson."

"Big Blue was a gelding," the Farmwife objected.

"Well, he wasn't a gelding all his life. Before he was a gelding, he was a stallion, and he fathered a whole string of foals over Whitherby way. Happen not long ago, I was talking about him, and this fellow told me he had a son or grandson of Big Blue that looked just like him."

"He certainly does," said the Farmwife. "Just like him. Same color, same white feet and mane, everything." She patted Cermit on the shoulder. "I know you've missed Big Blue."

Tears gathered in the old man's eyes, and he turned away quickly. "You miss lots of things," he mumbled. "I guess that old horse was one of them."

"What's this one's name?" asked Olly.

"Big Blue Too," said Cermit.

Olly sighed. "He looks like a very nice horse. But I'm so sore, even the most wonderful horse in the world wouldn't appeal to me at the moment."

"Poor child." The old man shook his head. "Let her soak in a hot tub when she gets home, Originee. By tomorrow, she'll be ready to ride over and see me again."

Olly thought it unlikely, and nothing on the trip back served to change her opinion, even though Originee tried to distract her by asking why it was that Olly was so set on knowing about thrones. Shifting painfully, Olly told her of Oracle's foretelling, concluding with:

"Cermit may think it's a zoo, but I was taught it's an archetypal village, and all who live there are real. That certainly includes Oracle."

"I'll accept she's a real Oracle," said Originee. "Cermit didn't mean to hurt your feelings. But he had a point to make, you must admit. Having a real Oracle in an ordinary town, for example—that could cause some upheavals!"

"Oracle herself said that was true," grunted Olly, standing up in the stirrups to ease her aching thighs as she told the Farmwife something of

Oracle's history. "She was sent to the village to keep her from causing upheavals at home. As were Bastard and Burned Man. Supposedly, that's why I ended up there, too, but I'd like to know what kind of upheaval an Orphan could cause!"

Originee looked at her thoughtfully. "Wouldn't it depend on who the Orphan was, really? What was it your Oracle prophesied?"

Olly furrowed her brow and repeated:

> "Ask one only child.
> Ask two who made her.
> Ask three thrones that tower,
> Gnawed by four to make them fall.
> Find five champions,
> And six set upon salvation.
> And answer seven questions in the place of power."

She fell silent, considering what the Farmwife had said. Perhaps some Orphans could cause upheavals, depending on who they were. Certainly the Orphan who had been brought to take her place was *somebody*, though little about her own arrival in the village argued that she herself was . . . much. A little man with a donkey remarked in passing that she had a high destiny.

Destinies could be high and still be quite horrible. Perhaps—perhaps she had been put there for some quite terrible purpose. As bait, perhaps, for those creatures that were hunting her. That thought had come to her more than once. It fit the situation as little else did.

Originee interrupted her thoughts. "It's a mysterious prophecy, indeed. Were you intending to do something about it?"

"Well, I should go to that library the old man mentioned," Olly said.

Originee shook her head. "A sensible idea, child, but I wouldn't go rushing off alone. It's a long way to the border, and women traveling alone have little chance of getting through the cities unmolested."

"I know the roads go through cities, and Oracle herself suggested I go around. But going around means monsters, and I've *seen* monsters."

"A person might go around, but two or more persons traveling together would be better off." Originee nodded thoughtfully to herself, worrying the matter. "Are you feeling some sense of urgency?" Young people had a habit of feeling urgent about all sorts of things, and in Originee's opinion, haste led to disaster, often as not.

"Urgent! Yes. Half the time it's hard to stay still with all the ferment going on inside!"

She didn't realize she'd shouted until she saw the Farmwife's face, shocked at the vehemence.

Olly shook her head apologetically. "Farmwife, my friends Burned Man and Oracle often advised me to be honest with myself, and though it's hard

to do, I do try. I'm a grown woman, as Oracle often pointed out, but as
Oracle also often told me, I've very little experience. I've always been just
Orphan. I've got no sense of—of me-ness. I don't know what I'm like. I've
never been in love—'' She stopped, conscious that this might not be true.
Or was it? ''Or had a baby,'' she went on doggedly. ''I've never been on
a journey, or learned how to work at anything. There was nobody in the
village I could look at and want to be like when I grew, for each of them
was what he was, just as I was what I was. Each an archetype.''

She heard her voice rising and calmed herself. ''None of us needed to do
anything or accomplish anything, we just *were*. I hear Seelie talking about
what she wants to do with her life, who she wants to be. She knows a horse
doctor in Whitherby, and she intends to be a horse doctor herself. Or she
says she'll become a Sister to Trees. I ask her if most young people have
such plans, and she says they do, but I never had any ideas like that. No
matter how I might have imagined being a Princess, a Pirate, a Heroine, I
was still only Orphan. We don't grow out of our roles in the village. No
one in the village had ever planned to be what they were or planned to be
something else later on. They could not escape from what they were, and
they would be that until they died.''

She rubbed at her cheeks, dismayed to find tears there. ''But with me—
with me, seemingly the role only lasts so long. Then, suddenly, I'm supposed
to be someone else. I don't know who. I don't know why! Am I urgent
about finding out? Yes! Yes, I am. My only problem has been, I haven't
been sure where to go. But when old Cermit mentioned Artemisia—it was
like my mind sat up and said, 'That's it!' ''

''You sound angry,'' said the Farmwife.

Olly shook her head, tears flying. ''I—I am angry. It isn't right, not
knowing where one's place is, not being someone!''

''True,'' the Farmwife said, as though from personal experience. ''We
all like to imagine we are something mysterious and wonderful.''

Olly managed a wry chuckle, though it hurt her throat, which was tight
and burning with tears. ''Well, with me, Farmwife Suttle, I won't insist
upon wonderful, though the prophecy does make me out to be mysterious.''

The Farmwife gave her a penetrating glance. ''I should insist upon wonderful, if I were you.''

''Why should I do that?''

''Because, child, if you believe you are capable of wonders, then wonders
you can do. At least, so has been my experience.''


Nelda, manager of the songhouse in Happy Street, had formerly been a
hag working in the Renegade Headquarters. Before that she'd been nursemaid

to the Bloodrun tots, and well before that time (at age sixteen) had been concubine to the man now known as Old Chief Purple. She remembered him well. She had seen him in the interim, here and there, from behind the veils women wore on the street. She recognized him when he came to her song-house to drink and listen to the music, though he showed no signs of rec-ognizing her. It was not surprising. Women came and went in the gang houses. A few were treasured into middle age and beyond, but it was more common to get a tot or two out of them and then sell them while they would fetch a decent price. Why should Old Chief Purple remember her, who had been his bedmate for only a year or so? Particularly inasmuch as she had changed even more than he.

He had changed in several respects. Though he came now and then to hear the music and drink the wine, he did not partake of the women. He had acquired battle wounds that did not contribute to his appearance. He had spent some years in dissipation, which had disfigured him more than the wounds. Sometimes Nelda looked at him from her post near the door and grieved sadly for all the masculine beauty he had once possessed.

Thus it was that very early on a Third-day morning, Nelda was astonished to see the Old Chief drinking at one of the small tables in a shadowed corner of the songhouse atrium. He looked almost as she remembered him from thirty years before. He was alone, which was unlike him, but in other respects he was completely himself.

She had been on her feet for hours and was in such a state of troubled weariness that for a long moment she felt adrift, as though dreaming, be-lieving she had somehow come loose from herself and her proper time to become young again. The illusion lasted until she had worked her way close enough to see that it wasn't actually Old Chief at all. The ears were different, and the set of the shoulders. Even with the differences, this young man was very like the Old Chief. He was not the Old Chief, but she would bet what was left of her life that he was the Old Chief's get!

And what a pity that this one was not Chief of the Purples instead of the poor baby who had taken that office. If this one were Chief, then Sybbis would have nothing to complain of. . . .

The thought resonated: If this one were . . . then Sybbis would have nothing to . . .

Well and well. How strange the workings of fate!

She stopped beside the shadowed table, putting on her motherly face.

"Are you enjoying the entertainment?"

He looked up at her bleary-eyed. He was too drunk to be anything but truthful.

"No," he said. "Not. Not ennertained. Came looking for a girl . . . a girl. A girl like another girl."

To anyone but a songhouse keeper, it would have been gibberish. To a songhouse keeper, it was one of the melodies of life. He was here looking for a girl who looked like another girl, a girl he could have in the place of one he could not. And what kind of girl could he not? A girl who had been sold to someone else, perhaps? A girl caught dallying with the wrong man and disfigured by her rightful owner? A girl who had died? Or even a girl he had loved as a boy and not seen since? Nelda was often amazed at the sentimentality of men. They gutted other men all day, then wept over their mothers. They took payment in silver mice to disfigure some poor wench who'd offended their Chief, then they spent the evening weeping over the fate of a sweetheart they had last seen in the roof garden when they were eleven.

"What did she look like, your girl?" Nelda whispered, drawing out a chair and sitting near him. Not so near as to intrude upon him, just near enough to hear without being overheard.

"Hair all cloudy," he said, nodding. "Like clouds at night, with the moon behind, you know."

"Black hair." Nelda smiled. "What else?"

"Legs all shiny." He sighed. "Pretty knees. Pretty feet. Rosy feet."

Rosy feet. But of course. "What else?"

"Doesn' talk like—like one of us. No. Talks like my granpa use to talk. Lots of words. Inneresing words . . . " His head sagged toward the table.

Sybbis had a spoken vocabulary of a few hundred words, which were all she needed. Well, Sybbis would simply have to keep her mouth shut. The rest of it—the hair, the rosy feet, the shiny skin—was a simple matter of oils and lotions, of keeping the room mostly in darkness, of having her wear a mask.

"I know the girl," whispered Nelda. "She's a friend of mine."

He looked up, wonder and delight chasing one another in his glance, too drunk to doubt her. "You know Olly?"

"Oh, I do know Olly, indeed. She's from—"

"Not from the city," he whispered. "From . . . somewhere else."

"The farms," she suggested. Where else but among the farms and in the Edge did they use many interesting words? Certainly this young man had not penetrated into the Edge to be fascinated by one of the women there. No, it had to be the farms.

"Farms," he agreed.

"Oh, yes, I know Olly from the farms. She said she'd met you. She thinks you're very handsome, you know."

"She . . . she thinks . . . "

"She'd like to know you better."

"She's . . . she's here?"

"Close by. If you'd like to see her, I could arrange it. You'd have to meet her somewhere else. She wouldn't want to come here."

"No," he agreed solemnly, looking past her at the bedraggled women writhing wearily on the dais. "No. Not her. Not here."

Nelda raised a hand, summoning. Two of her stalwarts materialized beside her. "Take this young man to my house. See that he has some of my private stock to drink. He'll like that."

The man was struggling to his feet. "Where? Where's she?"

"Get some sleep." Nelda smiled. "A little sleep. She'll meet you in my rooms, later this morning."

The two stalwarts, silent as was their wont, took the young man away while Nelda summoned another man and sent him for the physician under contract to the house. "Tell him he's to meet me at my private house in an hour," she instructed. "Tell him I mean it. He's to be there."

Three hours later, Nelda and the physician talked quietly in Nelda's private sitting room while Abasio slept a drugged sleep in the bedroom nearby.

"So he's got no diseases. You're sure?"

"I put his blood through the analyzer three times, and it says he has none of the diseases you're worried about, Nelda. What are you up to?"

"Never mind. Better you don't know. You've got his hands bandaged, right?"

"His tattoos are covered. That's what you asked me to do."

"And his head."

"And his head. And parts of his face."

"And what was it you gave him?"

"A dose of something to keep him disoriented, out of touch with reality, as you asked. Since that could interfere with what you have in mind, I've also given him a new drug. It's called Starlight. It will assure . . . competence in the area you're most concerned with."

"So he's dreaming?" she asked. "But physiologically functional?"

"Madam, you have no idea how functional. The drug is expensive, however, and you'll have to pay extra."

She put three silver rats on the table before him. "These are yours for today. There will be an equal number tomorrow, and perhaps the day after. By that time we should know whether your Starlight has worked well, and if it has, you'll be paid for that as well."

"A sparrow," he murmured.

"That expensive? Well, even so. I hope you're wise enough to forget everything afterward, friend doctor. If you find yourself remembering, don't. It could be very dangerous to remember."

He gave her a tight-lipped smile and departed. Remembering too much and telling about it while drunk had gotten him kicked out of the Edge. The

Edge had its own rules, its own customs, just as the city did. Of course he wasn't going to remember too much!

Left alone, Nelda went into the bedroom and examined the sleeping form there. A handsome but anonymous figure. The bandages would keep Sybbis from seeing who it was. He was healthy, which was all that mattered.

Nelda put on the heavy black veils worn by women who went unescorted on the streets, hung her street pass on her belt, bundled a spare set of veils beneath her bulky garments, and went down the street to the baths.

Sybbis had come to the baths that morning in no great mood of expectation. She thought it unlikely Nelda could have acted in the brief time since they'd talked. Her only expectation was to enjoy her bath and the usual massage. The moment she arrived, however, one of the bath-girls whispered in her ear and led her down the corridor to a private room.

"I hope you're in the mood for dalliance," purred Nelda.

"Now?"

"What better time, girl?"

"Who did you find?"

"I found a healthy young man moping for a girl he can't have. If you're clever, he'll think you're the girl."

"He'll know—"

"He doesn't know his own name. He's drugged."

"Then what good will he do me!"

"He'll be capable, never worry. Are you going to stay here and argue with me, or are you going to put on this blackie and come to my house, now, to spend a few hours?"

"Hush," said Sybbis imperiously. "Wait a moment." She left the room and returned, after a time, with Posnia. There Posnia hung her red and green garb across a chair and dressed herself in Sybbis's purple veils while Sybbis put on the black garb of the street. When the corridor was momentarily empty, two black-clad women departed. Behind them Posnia did as she had been directed, moving to and fro restlessly behind the ornamental grill in the door, now in purple, now in green and red, murmuring as she went, now high, now low. The colors of the two dresses could be seen by those passing by, as could the restless movement. Voices could be heard. So far as the bath attendants knew, Sybbis and her sister were having a lengthy conversation. Though it was not unlike the games they had played as children, Posnia sweated, nonetheless. All would be well, Sybbis said. Posnia agreed that all would be well, only so long as they didn't get caught!

In Nelda's living quarters, the brothel mistress stripped Sybbis to the skin and set about making her look like someone else. "Your name is Olly," Nelda instructed as she oiled and dyed, combed and fluffed. "Make up your own reason for wearing this little mask, but tell him your name is Olly and you've been thinking about him since . . . ever since the last time you saw him.''

''When was that?''

''How in hell would I know, girl? Now, go on in there and wake him up. The doctor says he'll be most receptive. And remember, the fewest possible words! Don't talk!''

''I don't see why,'' Sybbis whined. Now that the moment was at hand, she was having certain misgivings.

''Because he knows her voice, stupid girl. A different voice might put him off. You've got a couple of hours before people start wondering where you are. Use the time as I taught you when you were a girl. I taught you how to bed a man, how to delight him.''

''I'd need . . . and I've never . . . ''

Nelda stood back to check her handiwork. In the dimness of the adjacent room, Sybbis would pass. Cloudy hair, shiny skin, rosy feet and all. It was unfortunate the mask was necessary, but behind it, Sybbis was safely anonymous.

''Everything you'll need is there, on the table by the bed,'' Nelda directed her. ''And I know you've never, more's the pity. It may be a bit painful for you, but then, you knew that before you asked. So go! Exert yourself!''

Neither Sybbis nor Nelda remembered the birthmark on Sybbis's inner thigh, a red mark like a tiny crescent moon.


One of the lobbies of the Dome had been chosen long ago by the Founding Families as an appropriate site for a Founders' meeting room. The floor-to-ceiling glass had looked out then, as it did now, upon a dramatic panorama of the canyons. The carpets had been thick and sumptuous then and had been replaced with others almost as lavish. Furnishings, likewise, had been maintained to give an overall impression of age without senescence, stability without stuffiness, luxury without ostentation. At least, so thought the Ander Family, members of whom had invariably been in charge of renovation.

The room still reflected, so the current Ander thought, his family's un-failing good taste, and it was to this room that he invited several elder members of the other Families on a late autumn afternoon, fluttering from guest to guest with relentless charm as they wandered in one by one, The Berkli, as usual, being the last.

''What wonderful news do you have for us?'' Berkli asked, looking around for Ellel, who was not present. He strolled to the table where their preferred refreshments had been set out by Domer staff. ''I assume it is wonderful news. You'd hardly have bothered with all this otherwise.''

''All this'' included the produce of the greenhouses and the apiaries, boughs in blossom and beeswax candles, as well as unusual munificence in the matter of food and drink. Berkli helped himself to both before finding a comfortable chair and arranging himself in it.

Mitty was already at a nearby table, setting up the pieces for one of the interminable games he played alone if no partner presented himself.

"Aren't you eating?" Berkli inquired, biting into a succulent meat-filled pastry and licking the crumbs from his lips.

"Later," snorted Mitty. "After we see what Ander has to say."

"What have you to say?" Berkli challenged his host. "What's it all about, Ander?"

Ander seated himself near the laden table, snapping open his fan, fluttering it with a pretty air of having a secret to share. "You're so sure I've got something to tell."

"Indeed. Certain sure." Berkli sipped at the wine, regarded his glass with amazement, and got up to look at the bottle once more. "Where did you get this?"

"Out of the cellars, Berkli. Where your father put it."

"You've raided my private stock?"

"Ellel wanted the occasion to be perfect." Ander smiled sweetly. "So you'd have absolutely nothing to complain about."

Mitty regarded him from deep-set eyes, his fingers making a repeated ta-rum ta-rum on the arm of his chair. "You're toying with us, Ander. What is it?"

"You're ready to listen, are you, Berkli? And you, Mitty?" He glanced around the room, receiving nods from the few others present, mostly his own family.

"Oh, yes," Mitty said, turning his massive body slowly to and fro in the swiveling chair. "Yes, indeed. What is all this?"

The fan fluttered for a moment longer before Ander clicked it closed and laid it on the arm of his chair. "Ellel wishes me to announce that she is only days away from having in her custody the Gaddir child—no, the Gaddir young woman."

Ander simmered delightedly under their incredulous stares.

"You're fibbing," whispered Berkli. "At the very least, you're exaggerating!"

"No, he's not," said Mitty, gravely. "Look at his face. Ellel is quite sure, or she wouldn't let him make the announcement."

"Quite sure," Ander simpered. "Oh, quite sure, gentlemen. After all your doubts and jeers and sneers, you may be sure that she is sure. I don't know how he did it, or when he did it, but it seems old Werra begot himself a child. At least, the genetic structure matches!"

"He must have done it just before Ellel killed him," muttered Mitty.

Ander snarled at him. "Before she acted in our own best interests, to preserve our security," he hissed. "You yourself heard him utter threats against us!"

"I heard him say it was dangerous for Jark the Third to bring all those walkers out of storage," said Berkli, tipping his glass to examine the lees of the wine. "I wouldn't have called that a threat. And he called finishing the shuttle a foolish waste of resources, but that wasn't a threat, either!"

"You say!" snarled Ander.

Mitty glared. Berkli gritted his teeth, then made himself relax as he put out a calming hand toward Mitty. The Werra matter had caused a level of enmity that it would not be wise to renew at this time.

"That's in the past," he said calmly. "Let it go."

"How does Ellel know this person exists?" Mitty asked, forcing Ander to turn his outraged eyes from Berkli and onto himself. "How does she know?"

Ander took a deep breath before answering. "The girl was in an archetypal village. A man left the village. For some reason, he disliked the girl. He had a notion that she was wanted, so he brought out with him a blanket that the girl had slept in. He gave it to a pair of walkers, and they returned it here. There were sufficient biological traces in it to identify the user as a Gaddir. Of that lineage, at least."

"Where's the girl?" Berkli asked.

"Ellel's walkers are looking for her now."

Berkli could not keep himself from smiling. "So she doesn't actually have the girl."

"No, she doesn't *have* the girl. But she damned well knows there *is* a girl! And she knows more or less where. The girl can't fly away! She has to walk about like any ordinary person. She could only have gotten so far from that village, and Ellel's walkers are all around it!"

"So you think Ellel will find her?"

"I know she will. Probably within the next few days."

"And then what?" asked Mitty.

Ander smiled. "We don't need her until the shuttle is finished, do we? A few days should be plenty of time to convince her of our cause."

"She has to be willing," said Berkli. "Ellel can't drug her, or hypnotize her, or—"

"I'm sure Ellel knows what Ellel can do," said Ander stiffly. "She probably knows better than you do."

An uncomfortable silence fell. Mitty got up heavily and came to sit next to Berkli, while Ander rose, beckoned to several of his Family members, and began to select food from the table.

Mitty half turned his back on the Anders, stretched chubby fingers between two buttons of his tunic, and scratched his hairy belly as he looked across at Berkli, who murmured:

"Speaking of experience, Mitty, since she's just now found the right girl, what has she done with all the wrong ones? All those babies and girls the walkers have been bringing in over the years?"

"Don't ask her," whispered Mitty, his face twisted in revulsion. "Really, Berkli. And don't ask Ander, either. He might tell you, and you don't want to know." He cast a glance at Ander's back, then focused once more on his scratching fingers. "I'll tell you what I know, however. Almost twenty years ago, she had Dever, the engineer, build her a replica of the guidance helmet and the input and output consoles."

Berkli drew in his breath sharply.

Mitty mused, "I'm not sure of anything, mind you. There's no obvious evidence to—confirm anything. Perhaps it's not something one really wants to confirm. And what would I do about it if I found out?"

They shared a long glance, both of them thinking of the thousands of walkers at Ellel's command. Berkli's fears were amorphous, based more on instinct than knowledge. Mitty, however, had a very good idea what similar mechanisms had once done, long ago, before men went to the stars.

"What can the walkers do?" Berkli whispered, as though reading Mitty's mind.

"You mean in addition to destroying all life on the planet?"

"Surely that's exaggerating."

"You yourself told Ander what they can do. So far, Ellel's kept most of them out in the world, searching, moving quickly from place to place. When they move fast enough, the damage they do is limited. But have you thought what will happen when they aren't needed to search any longer? When they gather all in one place?"

Berkli thought about it, feeling himself grow pale.

Ander had turned to watch them, his eyes narrowed.

"We were just saying we hoped you'd keep us informed," Berkli said, forcing himself to look up with a kindly, civilized smile. "Please do, Fashimir. We can't wait to hear."

# CHAPTER 7

armwife Chyne, high up the valley of the Crystal, heard a commotion out by the pigpen one evening and went out to find a young troll breaking down the gate to get at the pigs. Luckily, as Farmer Chyne was later to say, it was a young one. Had it been an old one, or one more alert to her presence, likely his wife would not so easily have dispatched it with the splitting ax. When Farmer Chyne came home, he buried the troll and built a fire on the grave to confuse the scent if its kin came looking, then he repaired the pen.

The following morning, Farmwife Chyne was struggling to get a reluctant sow into the newly repaired sty when the two strangers came. They approached so silently that the first she knew of them was when a huge hand reached over her shoulder to take hold of the gate. She turned in fright as the sow was catapulted past her with a terrified squeal; then the gate was shut and she was alone with her back to it, facing two tall, helmeted figures who regarded her with bleak, expressionless eyes.

"Who—" she gasped, unable to breathe. They weren't menacing her. Some tiny part of her mind noted that, even as it also noted that she was icy with fear. The pig had weighed three or four times what she did, but it had flown through the air like a bird. And yet they weren't menacing her. No. No.

"Have you seen a girl . . . ?"

The voice was soft but hot, like a searing wind coming under a door. Like the hot wind, it caressed insinuatingly, letting her know it could dry her to a shriveled twist of leather if it liked. The two looked almost exactly alike. One was a little bigger than the other. Except for that, they could be twins.

She clutched her bulging stomach and leaned back against the fence, sagging onto a feedbox. One of them reached toward her, perhaps startled by her action. Her flesh shrank from his touch as from the touch of a serpent or a great hairy spider.

She gripped herself, forcing calm, trying not to look at them, wondering who they were looking for. Who? Some slave escaped from the city? Some concubine? The first words the creature said made her believe she was right.

"We're looking for a girl."

She had a split second of vision: fire, burning irons, a scream shivering the air, the stench of burning flesh. She gulped down hard, trying to control herself. "A girl?" She shook her head. "There's no one here but me and my husband, when he's here. Just now he's down the valley a bit, cutting hay."

"A girl who might have been passing through," said the other creature. He—it turned away from her, and she saw the naked blade at its belt. Such blades should be shiny. This one wasn't. It was stained, as though he disdained to clean it, preferring it to declare its purpose.

"Who are you?" she asked without thinking, the words coming of themselves. She choked back, biting her tongue.

Both of them regarded her with blank, impersonal stares. "Why do you ask?" whispered one.

"You're not—not citymen," she said. "You don't look like citymen. I've seen them on the screen. You don't have any tattoos." Oh, heaven, heaven, help me stop talking! she thought. Help me be still!

The taller of them said, "We're not citymen. Who we are is none of your concern. We're looking for a girl who might have been passing through. She's about twenty, slender, with black hair and dark eyes."

She stared into their eyes and knew that death waited there. For her and the child she carried and the man down the valley. Unless they were convinced she was too frightened to dissimulate, unless they were convinced she was stupid and above all, truthful. Truthful!

"I saw such a girl," she said, gaping at them. "But it was a long time ago. Weeks. She asked me the way to the nearest city." Truth, or almost truth, spontaneously uttered out of some spring of deception she had tapped in her panic. She did not want to die, but the girl had been mannerly and kind. She didn't want the girl dead, either.

"What did you tell her?"

"I said she'd find the city by turning north at the bottom of the valley," said the Farmwife. "She thanked me and went on." Almost truth.

"Nothing else?"

She screwed up her face, sorting through her memories. She had to give them something else, something . . . conclusive. "Ah—she asked when my baby was coming. I told her not to tell anyone she'd talked to me." She swallowed, trying to moisten her throat. "My husband doesn't like me talking to strangers."

That brought a grimace, like a scythe edge, a drawing back of the lips before biting. . . .

"But we are not strangers," said one.

They turned and strode away from her, out the gate and on down the road. She leaned back against the wall, heaving, her breath coming and going as from a bellows. Oh, she was sick. She had been touched by something venomous, and she could not say what. Beside her, on either side, the blackened ground smoked as though a fire had burned there, and all around the sty a bitter smell hung like a pall.

After a long, long time she crept into the house and lay down in her bed, the covers pulled over her face, breathing her own warmth as though in that comforting dark she might be safe. So one shuddered when one heard the rattle and knew one had almost stepped on a snake. So one shuddered when one saw the smooth brown body of the spider, just in time. So one shuddered when one stopped, just at the edge of a hidden precipice, knowing death was only inches away, a breath away.

What were they? Oh, what were they?

She clutched her belly again, realizing there had been no movement in there for some time. The baby had been kicking like a little mule, day in and day out, but now it was as quiet as she herself had been.

When Farmer Chyne came back that evening, he said he had been accosted in the hayfield by two strangers who asked if he had seen anyone on the road. He had seen a woman, he told them. Some time ago. He had told her to keep moving.

When he had said this, he stared at her as though in the grip of some great doubt. "Did you see them?"

"They came here," she admitted. "They asked me what they asked you."

"What did you tell them?" he demanded, anger burning at the back of his eyes. Anger and fear.

She shook her head. "What could I tell them? I see no one." Then, to distract him as much as anything, "But it is time I must."

He shook his head in turn, clamping his jaw shut. "We're better alone."

"Husband, needs must. I need you to go down to Wise Rocks Farm and ask some help from Farmwife Suttle."

"We ask help from no one," he said stiffly.

"If you want a live child, you will go to Wise Rocks Farm and tell Farmwife Suttle I have need of her. There's something not right, not with me, not with the child. If you want a dead child and a dead wife, then we will ask help of no one."

He fumed. He cursed. He had been as disturbed by the two strangers as she, but he would not admit it. He would never admit to fear or to doubt. She persisted, calmly, saying the same words over and over.

"The ewes bear without help!" he cried. "What different are you?"

"I am not young," she said. "And old ewes sometimes die lambing, as you well know. But it's up to you."

He fumed; he said he might go; he did not say exactly when that might be.


Abasio returned to his home in Fantis.

"Where the hell you been!" CummyNup cried from behind the protective wire barrier at the top of the stairs leading to Abasio's rooftop shack.

"Don't shout," begged Abasio, tottering on the rickety landing. "My head . . . "

"The resta you, too, from the looksa you. Where you been?"

CummyNup unlocked the barrier and dropped the wires with a clangor of bells and janglers, designed to wake the dead if disturbed in the night.

Abasio shuddered. "What day is it?"

"Sixt'-day. So where the hell you been?"

Abasio stared at him owl eyed. "I went riding in the country."

"For a week?"

He shook his head. No. Not a week. Not possibly. "Greens were going to fight the Survivors," he managed to dredge up from a memory not merely foggy but virtually opaque.

"Last Sevent'-day. Right. It'uz on the Big Show. Wally Skins was the firs' dead, and nobody Green was lef' standin'."

"Oh," he said bleakly, unable to remember why he had cared about that. "Well, it was two days before that."

"Nex' to las Fift'-day."

"Then. Right. Soniff told me to find Litt—Young Chief some kind of amusement, so I went riding. There was a refugee."

He'd found the refugee. Olly. And he'd been in bed with her. No, he couldn't have been in bed with Olly. That must have been a dream. What would Olly have been doing in the city, in that place?

"So where'd you go?" CummyNup demanded.

He explored his memory, finding what he sought after some delay. "Out to farm country. South."

"How long it take you?" CummyNup shook his head. The days didn't add up.

Abasio grimaced. It had to have taken him at least three days to get there and get back. Which meant he'd returned on Seventh-day. Probably. He seemed to remember something about that.

"I musta got buzzed," he said, unhelpfully.

CummyNup shook his head. Abasio didn't drink. Not much.

"Where?" he asked.

Abasio shook his head. He couldn't remember. In fact, he couldn't remember much. The dream. If it had been a dream. He'd ridden out, gone to Wise Rocks, met the girl. Olly. Ridden back. He'd thought of her all the way back. He couldn't get her out of his head. No, she hadn't been in his head. She'd been in his body, in his bones. He'd actually hurt, wanting her. He'd been shaking. So he'd told himself, you want a woman, find a woman. So he went to a songhouse but none of the women . . . none of them. Then— then he'd gotten drunk and found her again. Or maybe not. But he'd been somewhere. . . .

"Where you wake up this mornin'?" CummyNup persisted.

"Truckers' hostel," he admitted. It was the practice for songhouse keepers to have their better class of customers dumped at a truckers' stop when they became unruly or unconscious. Lesser folk were simply dragged into the street.

"Well, Basio, I say this for you," CummyNup said. "You don' usual go off like that, but when you do, you sure do it all! Baby Purp, he been lookin' for you five days. He bored all to hell."

Abasio shuddered, saying, "I need sleep. You get word to the Young Chief I'm home but I'm sick. Tell one of the boys."

"I'll tell Warlord, tha's who. He been lookin' for you too."

Abasio merely gaped, unable to think of a reply. CummyNup gave him a look and stepped over the wires onto the stairs, waiting while Abasio rigged the alarm once more, fumbling the job badly before he turned and went into his shack. He was walking funny, as if he hurt somewhere.

CummyNup stared after him. If Abasio got buzzed, he hadn' got buzzed where anybody could find him, not since late Second-day. Usual, a man went off and got buzzed, somebody fall over him, somebody see him somewhere, but Abasio, he jus' gone.

Sighing, CummyNup clumped to the bottom of the stairs where Soniff himself was waiting.

"He back?"

"Yeh."

"Where was he?"

"Don' think he know," CummyNup said.

"Well?"

"He sick. He be comin' along, soon's he's feelin' better."

Soniff growled, but he let it alone. If Abasio was really sick, he couldn't do anything useful anyhow.

Abasio took a full day and a handful of stimulants to recover himself sufficiently to wait upon the Young Chief, who was disinclined to forgive Abasio's absence.

"I was worn out, so I overslept," Abasio said for the fifth or sixth time.

"That's no reason," snapped his leader. "You could've slep' here at the House jus' as easy."

"I was out looking for something new and different for you, Chief."

"Nobody could fin' you," growled the Young Chief, sounding like an angry puppy attacking a slipper.

Abasio gritted his teeth and groveled. "I'm sorry, Young Chief. It won't happen again."

Young Chief pouted. "I was waitin' and waitin' for what you foun' for me. What was it?"

Abasio thought frantically. What had he found, besides a girl he could not get out of his head? "I've found a new drug," he said. "Whistler's just down from the hills, and he's brought a new drug."

"Where's it at?" Young Chief asked with mild interest. He enjoyed drugs, though Soniff would not let him have them often.

"Whistler should have it ready for me now," said Abasio. "I'd have had it for you earlier, but—"

"I know," sneered his master. "You overslep'."

Abasio didn't move. He was suddenly overcome by a wave of futility and despair. What was he doing here? Why had he come back to the city? Why was he submitting himself to this petulant child-man whom most of his own men, including Abasio, despised? Why hadn't he stayed out there, gone on to visit his grandpa, maybe stayed with him? Why hadn't he stayed where Olly was!

"Well!" demanded his Chief. "How long I suppose' to wait?"

"I'll get it," Abasio said. "Right now."

He backed out of the presence, out of prudence rather than respect. Young

Chief kept a set of throwing knives by his chair, not that he could usually hit anything with them, but he'd been known to try with people who displeased him and who presented a broad enough target.

At the top of the stairs he encountered the other of his two unfailing supporters, TeClar Chingero.

"Whatso, Basio?" TeClar greeted him. "You been missin'. We been lookin' for you all over everwhere."

Abasio shrugged. "Listen," he muttered. "CummyNup's already been at me. You don't know where I was, and I don't know where I was, and let's just leave it, okay? I went out looking for something for the Young Chief, and next thing I know, I'm waking up in some truckers' hostel."

"You got buzzed is what CummyNup say."

"Well, he's probably right, and so what? I suppose I'm the only damned Purple ever got buzzed? Neither of you ever did that, huh?"

TeClar grinned at him. He was a faithful friend, like CummyNup, faithful forever, at least so their mama had told Abasio when he'd accompanied the brothers on a visit to her home near the edge of Green territory. The District was not a safe one. TeClar and CummyNup had been born as the result of a night-rape, but Mama would not leave because the building was among the newest ones in Fantis and surprisingly free of vermin. Though the twins wanted her to move into Purple homeground, they hadn't been able to find a place that was clean enough to suit Mama.

"You need any help, Basio?" TeClar asked.

Lord, he needed something. "You can help me find Whistler."

TeClar nodded solemnly and moved behind him down the stairs, past the glass case that held the Book of the Purples, past the Wall of Respect covered with the likenesses of Purples killed in battle or on tallies, and onto the front stoop, where the two men on guard duty were drinking honey-beer in a state of considerable relaxation.

"I goin' with Abasio," announced TeClar to one of the guards. "You don' need me for escort. The women say nobody needs gettin' clean today."

"That Sybbis, she's about clean enough," mumbled one of the guards. "Ever day and ever day, down to the baths and back again. Down to the baths and back again. Three days, nothin' but goin' to the baths. Glad she finally got cleaned up."

"Don' know what she's doin' makes her dirty," the other guard offered with a suppressed snigger.

Abasio glared at him. "Meaning?"

"What I say?" the guard said indignantly. "Me? I din' say nothin'."

"Better say nothing," snarled Abasio. "If you know what's good for you." And better Purple up, too, he said to himself. Anybody attack the Purple House today, those two'd be dead before they knew who.

"I got to ax you a question, Basio."

Abasio grunted.

"You know out there where the Greens burn all those old folk? You know, whole lotta those buildings out there got nobody in 'em. Howcome they don fix the old places, Basio?"

"Nobody needs them fixed," Abasio replied. "Lots of people went to the stars or moved out to the Edge—the ones that had money enough—and that left lots of empty buildings. We won't need to fix them until all the tots grow up and we need more room."

"Tha's in the Book," agreed TeClar.

Abasio nodded. Yes, it was in the Book of the Purples, along with a lot of stuff about how strong the Purples were getting to be, stronger every generation. Deep as space, said the Book. Something tantalizing about that thought, but Abasio couldn't identify what. He wasn't able to identify much this morning, and that was the truth!

"Whistler, he in the back market yestaday," TeClar offered, leaving the cracked sidewalk to sidle down a narrow, trash-piled alleyway. "Down here."

Abasio followed without comment, kicking the debris aside. The alley debouched onto a flat, open space where a highway had once run, now crowded with individual canvas-shaded booths and carts, its aisles already clotted with shuffling crowds. Though the concrete was cracked everywhere, it was still solid underfoot, all the way to their destination, a cavernous area sheltered among the pillars of a lofty overpass. Though the overpass had fallen in farther on, the space beneath was still accessible from the old on- and off-ramps, and among this "back market" warren of wagons and ancient trucks, both Whistler and Sudden Stop had outlets for their wares.

They had come to the outermost of the ancient concrete piers supporting the road above when Abasio came to a halt.

"Whatso?" grunted TeClar, bumping into him.

"Shh," Abasio hissed. "Come on." And he pulled the boy with him behind the shelter of the thick pillar.

Obediently, TeClar was quiet, peeking curiously from behind the pillar to see what Abasio had noticed. Nothing much was happening. Just people in the market. And what was Abasio doing?

Abasio was staring at his feet, his mouth open, as though listening very intently.

TeClar squirmed uncomfortably. There was something. Some little—what was it? A kind of stillness running down through the market? People getting out of the way of something, very quietly, not talking or moving until whatever it was had passed them, then drifting off, leaving the stillness behind them.

Like a little tide of silence coming, Abasio thought. He had not seen tides, but he'd read about them. The rush of water, the glissade of foam, and the slow withdrawal before the next rush. And there, as at the edge of foamy silence, two striding walkers. Like those he'd most recently seen near Echinot. He must have noticed them, maybe out of the corner of his eye. Seen and responded, though he'd seen them only twice before. Them, or two just like them.

"Whatso, Basio?" whispered TeClar.

"Hush," he hissed so fiercely, the boy gaped at him.

The walkers came along the marketplace, striding evenly over the slime of refuse and the broken slabs, not seeming to notice the cracks or tilted blocks that made others stumble, preternaturally smooth in gait, their sleek faces without expression. They were like the ones Abasio had seen on the highway, the same skintight glisteny suits, the same shiny, close-fitted helms.

*Awful. Dreadful. Terrible.*

The words had come unbidden. Abasio concentrated on the pillar he was standing behind, stared at it, emptying his mind of anything else. The pocked and dingy surface an inch from his nose was scarred from collisions, stained by weather and birds, blotchily overpainted here and there where some kid-G had painted his colors or his slogan in defiance of the neutrality treaty. Colors weren't allowed in the market. Abasio concentrated on gray. No color. No color at all.

The silence moved, coming nearer, stopping behind the very pillar where they stood. The walkers had cornered someone against the pillar and were asking questions, not loudly but clearly, with a peculiar quality of penetration.

"We were told a dark-haired female person, one about twenty years old, asked directions to this city. Have you seen such a girl?" The words were like ice in the ear, or like fire, painful to hear.

Abasio smelled terror, an acrid stench of sweat and urine. The man who was being interrogated had lost control of himself, but he was answering: He'd seen a girl here, a girl there, perhaps the girl they wanted. The stillness moved away while Abasio held his breath. When he peeked around the pillar he saw the man sagging against the pillar, trousers stained, tears leaking unheeded down his gray face.

Why were the walkers still asking the question they had asked him so long ago in Echinot? Why were they seeking . . . a dark-haired girl about twenty? In Echinot it had been thirteen. That had been seven years ago. Had it been that long?

Awareness trembled in him, making him afraid to move. He knew who they wanted. They mustn't question him. They mustn't even see him!

As though reading his mind, TeClar sagged behind the pillar, holding his breath as the helmeted duo stalked through the back market, out of it, elsewhere. They could tell how far the walkers had gone by the silence that flowed after and around them, the sound resuming only as a subdued murmur.

They moved from behind the pillar to find the gray-faced man collapsed against the far side, sucking in rasping, agonized breaths. The surfaces around him were blackened. Abasio grasped the man's shoulders and pulled him away from the darkened pave before he knelt beside him. There was a bitter smell, one he recognized.

"Whatso?" whispered TeClar.

"He's dying," said Abasio, loosening the man's collar. "See if you can find someone who knows him!"

TeClar moved off, returning within moments with a younger man, a young woman, son and son's wife to the fallen man, farmers come to town with a load of sweet corn.

"What happened?" demanded the young farmer.

"Walkers," said Abasio, laconically.

"Aaah," the woman cried, putting her hand to her lips and looking around herself fearfully.

"Papa, Papa," the boy murmured, lifting the unconscious man, carrying him away. "Oh, Papa, Papa."

Abasio moved slowly away, trying to remember why he had come here. Before the walkers had killed the man, or as good as, they'd been asking after Olly. He knew it as a certainty. Olly was who they had always been looking for, a special person, a unique person. Who else but she? He had to go back to the farm and warn her. Soon. As soon as he could.

"Who those men?" whispered TeClar.

Abasio shrugged, trying desperately to make his voice sound casual. He knew what they were called. He knew what they could do. Maybe. He didn't know what they really were. "In Echinot, they call them walkers. If you're smart, you'll keep out of their way."

TeClar swallowed this with some difficulty. Both the Chingero brothers were naturally audacious without being bright enough to assess the risks they took. Still, he was accustomed to taking orders from Abasio. "We goin' to fin' Whistler, now, Basio?"

Of course. That's why they had come. Abasio nodded absently as they moved into the crowd once more, a crowd that seemed unnaturally noisy now that the silence had passed.

"There," whispered TeClar, his finger pointing before Abasio's nose. "There Whistler, Basio."

Abasio thrust through the throng milling about Whistler's wagon. Whistler always brought a wagon, always had a high, stout counter between him and the customers, always had two or three hired Survivors standing by just in case. Sometimes people wanted stuff they couldn't pay for. Sometimes they got so desperate they tried to take it without paying. They never got it from Whistler, not that way.

Abasio had seen lots of druggies die since he'd seen the dying men at Purple House. He'd seen them unconscious in doorways, barely breathing. He'd seen them screaming and shaking and spouting from both ends, like poisoned dogs. He'd seen them throw themselves off roofs trying to fly and root in the gutter filth looking for gold. He'd seen them fade fast, seen them die slow. Ma had said it was bad; Abasio knew it to be true. Since that first sight of death, he'd bought few drugs, and those carefully. Nonetheless, he, like everyone else, knew Whistler, not only from the almost encounter on the road near the farm, long ago.

"Whatso, Whistler?" he greeted the merchant.

"Abasio," the other rumbled, giving him a basilisk stare, cold as the walkers' glance but more personal.

Abasio, remembering the fate of certain people who'd annoyed Whistler, talked only of business.

"Man at the Patrol Post told me you have something new. Starlight, is it?"

"Starlight it is."

Abasio put an elbow on the counter, attempting to appear sanguine, though being at ease around Whistler wasn't either simple or sensible. "What's the risk, Whistler? Tell me true, now. I'm not buying for me, but I'm the one to blame if it isn't good stuff."

Whistler leaned forward and whispered, "You buyin' for the Purple Chief, the Young Chief, the sweet Baby Chief with his smoothy skin?"

Abasio didn't answer. Any answer was dangerous. Someone might hear. Someone might quote him as having said. Someone might even quote him as having listened without objecting, which in itself could be dangerous.

Whistler sniggered, an ominous sound, like the laugh of a crow settling to dinner on something not quite dead. "Let me tell you the truth. If you was buyin' for a child's hobbyhorse with no balls at all, Starlight would make a stallion of him. 'Starlight, starbright, first star I see tonight, wish I may, wish I might,' and the wish is granted, absolute! Starlight puts starch in ancient cocks, pours molten metal down droopy dicks, paralyzes pricks so they don't come down until six days later. Starlight makes maidens tremble in fear. Even tired old whores with cunts so loose they'd go round you twice, the mention of Starlight makes 'em stutter and run for cover. Starlight puts steel in a man's business, mainman. Starlight is what your Young Chief most needs."

Abasio stared into Whistler's eyes, which showed nothing at all. No emotion. No fun. No hate, no love.

"Moreover," Whistler went on, "Starlight stirs up the eggs, mainman, stirs up the nuts, the balls, the jewels, makes them crank out the juice like so many little pumps. Childless men wish upon Starlight and are childless no longer. If they've got a capable woman, they're bein' called Daddy before they know it.''

"How much?" asked Abasio from a dry mouth.

"A golden sparrow the vial. Which is good for several nights' pleasure, mainman. And as many babies in the oven as the ladies involved can manage among 'em. A single golden sparrow guarantees a man his posterity.''

Abasio's jaw dropped at the mention of the amount. "You're joking!"

The eyes turned colder than before. Inhumanly cold.

"Do I ever joke?"

And of course he didn't. Whistler never joked, not even now, when his price was a quarter of what Abasio had managed to squirrel away over the past several years.

"Pass the cost along, Abasio," whispered Whistler, leaning across his counter to get close to Abasio's ear. He pursed his lips and made music, a pure strain of melody that drifted over the marketplace, making a sudden hush.

It was the same melody Abasio had heard long ago, long and long ago. Then it had intrigued him. Now it made him shiver, for he had until the song was over to make up his mind to buy. If he waited longer, the goods would no longer be available at the price mentioned. Such were Whistler's rules. He was not a patient man.

"I'm not carrying that much," said Abasio.

The melody stopped, cut off.

"Your credit's good." Whistler turned up his lips at the corner, an uncharming smile with the effect of a snarl.

The marketplace noises resumed, almost in relief.

Whistler reached beneath the counter and brought out the vial. "One drop on the skin," he murmured, opening the vial and waving it under Abasio's nose. "That's the smell of the real thing, mainman. One drop anywhere on the skin. No more.''

The smell was familiar. Abasio got a sudden flash, a cloud of dark hair, this smell coupled with the smell of sweat, a gleam of slender legs, a little moon shining . . .

He shook his head, suddenly dizzy. "This stuff is new?" he asked, puzzled.

Whistler simply stared.

Abasio shrugged apologetically. "The smell seemed familiar, that's all."

"You're not my only customer," Whistler said softly. "Between the physicians and the songhouse managers, my stock is much reduced. Of course, later on, when supplies are larger, the price will be reduced as well. Eventually, it will be cheap. Eventually, most things are.'' His smile was bleak. He knew Abasio couldn't wait until then, not if he was buying for the Young Chief.

Abasio reflected that there'd been several days he couldn't remember. He could have smelled it in a songhouse during that time. Perhaps he had mixed it up with memories of Olly, memories of people he'd seen while he was drunk. Probably.

Then who was the woman he remembered? That wasn't Olly, was it?

"It's my neck," he repeated softly. "Is there anything I should know about it, Whistler? If somebody gets hurt, I'll get chopped."

"Couldn't hurt a baby."

"I'll bring the money today," Abasio promised.

"I know you will," said Whistler, smiling his cutthroat smile once more while his dead eyes looked past Abasio at nothing.

It came to Abasio that Whistler looked a lot like Sudden Stop. Unlike Whistler's guards, the Survivors, who stared into Abasio's face, storing it up in case they needed to come after him later, both Whistler and Sudden had eyes that looked on past you at something only they could see.

Abasio put the vial in his breast pocket, placed his open hand across it, and turned to go back through the market, hearing himself hailed from a nearby booth as he did.

"Whatso, Basio!" The words were like distant thunder.

"Sudden Stop." Just the man he'd been thinking of.

"Heard your little dealings there. Happy to lend you a sparrow if you'd like to get Whistler paid."

Abasio pulled his lips into a semblance of a smile. Sudden Stop was huge and bald and wondrous strong; he could handle weapons with one hand that other men struggled to carry with two. He was known to be a fair man, but his interest rates were high. Men who didn't pay were likely to find themselves being used as a demonstration in a weapons test.

"I thank you kindly, Sudden Stop, but I've the money to pay him," murmured Abasio, thankful that CummyNup was standing guard over Abasio's home, for there were ears all around the marketplace.

"Another time then," rumbled Sudden Stop.

Abasio put his head down and trudged homeward, TeClar at his side.

"Me'n CummyNup, sometimes we wonder 'bout those two," said TeClar. "Whistler an' Sudden Stop."

"Wonder what?" breathed Abasio, concentrating on putting one foot in front of the other. Lord, he was tired!

"Never see those two at a songhouse. Never see those two drinkin' beer. Never see those two havin' any fun, you know?"

"They spend a lot of time out of Fantis," murmured Abasio. "Maybe they have their fun somewhere else."

"Could be." TeClar nodded. He cast a sidewise glance at Abasio's pocket, where the drug reposed. "You gonna try it, Basio?"

Abasio snarled, "I am not. It's for the Young Chief. All of it. So don't suggest I let you have a try, either."

"Don' need stuff like that," asserted TeClar in a lofty tone. "Do fine all by my lone. You really got the money, Basio?"

"Yeah," grunted Abasio, wondering how much of it he was going to be able to collect back from the Young Chief.

"A whole sparrow. Tha's a lot," said TeClar sadly. "Tha's a real lot. Whistler, he charges plenty. And ol' Sudden Stop, he charges plenty too. I figure every man in Fantis buys from one of them or the other."

Probably every man in Fantis had bought from both, Abasio reflected. And a golden sparrow was indeed a real lot. It was ten silver rats, one hundred silver mice. It was one-tenth of a golden crow. But there was enough in the vial for several . . . sessions. So, if he divided the stuff, put a little in a separate vial, then if the Young Chief liked it, Abasio could tell him he needed money to buy more. And if he didn't like it, Abasio could sell it elsewhere. Which was the only way to recoup he could think of at the moment.

"You," he said, giving TeClar a hard look. "You don't talk about this, right? You don't say what I bought, what I paid, right?" He was suddenly desperately weary, so tired, he wanted to lie down and sleep.

"Right, Basio," agreed TeClar. "But we wasn' the only ones there."

Which was true enough. Nothing that happened in the marketplace could be considered private.

Weighing his commitments, Abasio decided he would deal with the Young Chief first, then with Whistler. Within limits, Whistler was patient. He knew Abasio would show up with the money because Abasio wasn't stupid. The Young Chief, on the other hand, was incapable of making such a judgment.

Abasio dragged himself to his own place, where he picked up a sparrow from his most secure hiding place and divided the drug into two vials, hiding two-thirds of it with the remainder of his cache. He gulped a few more stimulants, something to keep him moving. He could not recall ever being so tired.

Upstairs at Purple House, Abasio paused at the door of the Young Chief's quarters. Young Chief and Soniff were inside, playing cards.

"You got it?" the Young Chief asked, glaring at Abasio.

Abasio nodded, glancing sidewise at the older man.

"What?" Soniff asked. He was over forty-five. Maybe even fifty. His hair was mostly gray. He'd been Warlord most of his life. "What you got, Abasio?"

"New stuff," Abasio said. "Whistler brought it down. Called Starlight."

"Lemme have it," demanded the Young Chief.

"Wait," demanded Soniff. "This stuff's new, you say?" He got up and held out his hand.

Abasio gave him the vial, lowering his voice. "I figured you'd want to ask about it, Soniff. There's only a little bit here."

"What's it do?"

Abasio felt himself flushing. It wasn't the kind of thing you could say out loud in front of the Young Chief. He leaned forward and whispered. Soniff's brows went up.

"Well, well," he said. "Now that's interesting." He turned and gave the Young Chief a speculative glance. "Maybe this is what the prophecy meant. . . . Even so, if it's that new . . . "

Abasio shrugged. "Soniff, I don't know, so I can't tell you. Whistler says it's safe. Whistler says it couldn't hurt a—a child. 'Course, there's always the possibility this stuff is so new, he doesn't really know."

"Cut all the gabble," the Young Chief whined. "Soniff, what you messin' with?"

"Calm down," Soniff soothed. "Old Chief said I was to keep you safe, and that's what I'm doin'. Not about to give you somethin' could kill you." He nudged Abasio toward the door. "You run on, Basio. I'll figure out how to test this."

Abasio sighed with relief. It was no longer on his neck if something went wrong. Soniff had cut him out, and more power to him. He clattered down the stairs, furiously making plans. First, he'd go to the marketplace to settle his debt. Then he'd sleep. Then he'd start figuring how he could get away again, to go south, to warn Olly about the walkers.

After the last of Sybbis's repeated visits to the baths, she had returned to the House in a mood of such fractious half-hysteria that it frightened her. Feeling the way she did, it would be all too easy to do something stupid, and now was a time she couldn't afford any mistakes. She had to be careful!

Part of her discomfort was simple pain. She was so sore, it hurt to move, but she could deal with that. She had pills for pain. Less easy to deal with was the desire to continue doing what she had been doing for the past three days, despite the pain. The desire was infuriating! Why should she have only the Young Chief to look forward to when—when there was this other kind of pleasure?

On the other hand, she also felt profound relief. No doubt she was pregnant. She had to be! If she assumed she was, that meant she had to entice the Young Chief into going through his tiresome, ineffectual act so he would be convinced he had caused her pregnancy. He didn't often visit her, and she had never tried going to him, though she understood Elrick-Ann had done so all the time.

Never mind. At the moment, she was incapable of enticing anyone. She was, finally and lastingly, exhausted. She had not slept except for tiny little naps during all that time. All she wanted to do was sleep forever.

She was still drowsing a day or so later when she heard men's voices and glanced through the grillwork of her room to see the Young Chief and Soniff come in and seat themselves beside the fish tank, where water from the rain-tank was endlessly recirculated by a treadmill slave in a room below. The two hags who had been sewing in the arbor rose and bowed themselves away. The women who had been playing games gathered up the tots and went into their sleeping rooms. Within moments the roof garden was empty except for the two men who sat with their heads together for a few moments before the Warlord went off toward Carmina's room and the Young Chief rose and came purposefully toward Sybbis.

She listlessly straightened the sheets, reminding herself to be seductive, only to find that seduction wasn't necessary. The Young Chief was in a state of some excitement, which became more frenzied over the next few hours. The fact that he was both unable to bring his own desires to a conclusion and quite unaware that Sybbis had any desires of her own made it more frustrating and painful for her than for him. He went on enjoying himself very single-mindedly until exhaustion set in.

Much later, with the Young Chief lying across her body and gasping like a dying fish, she opened her eyes through a haze of fatigue to see Soniff leaning above her. Surely this was a dream. Soniff wouldn't dare come in here. Nobody could come in here but the Young Chief and the hag who cleaned up. Her eyes fell closed and she forgot it.

Downstairs, shortly thereafter, Soniff happened upon Abasio, who was uncharacteristically asleep in a corner. He sat down beside him, out of earshot of the other Purples, and shook him awake.

"How much did you pay for that stuff?" he demanded.

"A sparrow," Abasio yawned. He needed more sleep. He couldn't wake up.

"By the Purples' honor! A whole sparrow!"

Abasio nodded.

"Well worth it." Soniff nodded with a sneaky grin. "You'll be repaid, Abasio. I've never seen anything like it."

Abasio raised one eyebrow and said nothing. He'd come to Purple House looking for an excuse to get away.

Soniff lowered his voice. "I tested it myself. That way if the Old Chief asks, I can say I didn't give the boy anything I didn't take myself. You don't

need to pretend you don't know, Basio. I know what people say. Old Chief
knows what they say. But you know, the Young Chief is the only son he
has left. Three sons who lived to grow up, the Old Chief had, two good
ones and—this one.''

Abasio nodded again. Under these particular circumstances, it was safe
to nod and say something factual. "They were brave, I know."

"Very brave. Too damned brave. They got killed, and he was left with
this one, Kerf. He wasn't promising, Basio. No. Not promising." Soniff
shook his head, remembering. "But there was always the possibility he'd
grow up into something, you know. And even if Kerf wasn't much, maybe
he'd have a son who . . . well, so the Old Chief retired and left a few of us
old-timers to watch out for the boy. I told Old Chief—well, never mind what
I told him, but he said give it time. Well, we've been giving it time. Didn't
seem like there was hope in that, either, until now."

Abasio cleared his throat. "Now?"

"When things got quiet in there, I went in," Soniff confessed in a whisper.
"There she was, all sprawled out. What a woman, Abasio. She's a wonder,
that one. She's got . . . " He waxed eloquent about several of Sybbis's outstanding attributes, as eloquently as a ganger could, mostly expletives, shaking his head in wonderment the while. "And she's got this little kind of
birthmark on her leg, like a skinny little moon."

"On her leg," Abasio said, unaware he had spoken at all.

"Up high, inside her leg. She shoulda been enough, all by herself," Soniff
said. "The shape of her. And that sexy little birthmark—"

"Birthmark," said Abasio from a dry mouth. The word had brought a
scene back to him vividly, in color. Himself and a dark-haired, masked girl
with a crescent mark high inside her thigh. And wherever he had been at
the time, that was where he'd smelled Starlight before he'd smelled it in the
market!

"Right," said Soniff. "And I'll swear, boy, she'd been done. I've watched
other times. This was the first time I could swear—"

"Well, we'll hope she got pregnant, then," said Abasio, feeling the blood
drain from his face. "For the Old Chief's sake."

"If so, Old Chief'll owe it to you, Abasio. You've been a faithful soldier.
I know he'd want me to offer. If there's anything you want, you tell me,
and it's yours."

Abasio tried to look modestly interested without showing his frantic confusion. Old Chief might owe a good bit more to Abasio than Abasio cared
to admit. One memory had triggered others, and all at once he had whole
chunks of the lost time coming back to him: himself coming back into town
and stopping off at the songhouse, himself drinking and talking about Olly.

He must have talked to anyone who would listen. So, so what? Well, someone had heard him babbling and set up an encounter. Him and Sybbis. Him because he was buzzed out of his head and available. Sybbis because—

Well, that part was easy. Because Sybbis didn't plan to go the way of Elrick-Ann!

Who had set it up? It could have been Sybbis herself. Or maybe someone from the Bloodruns, where she came from. Or—well, who knew who'd set it up? Who cared? It was a good idea, no harm done. At least no harm done if neither of them had known the other one. But if he had seen the birthmark and remembered it, what might Sybbis have seen that she remembered? His tattoos? His crest? Maybe she hadn't needed to see! Maybe she'd known exactly who he was. Maybe she'd even arranged for it to be him specifically. She was a Chief's daughter, you had to remember that. Chief's daughters could sometimes arrange things.

Why him? Because—because he was big and fairly good-looking, at least some said so, and because he was healthy. That was really it. No matter how big he was, how good-looking, the important thing was that he was healthy, because he knew she was, and if she had a baby with an IDDI, Little Purp would know it wasn't his. That was one thing about Little Purp— he didn't have an IDDI. No cuckle for him, no dirty drugs. Soniff took good care of him.

But Abasio was healthy. Basio the Cat had kept his feet almost totally dry. So she might have set it up, naming him specifically, in which case— in which case, if she ever got high or buzzed or had one of her famous tantrums, she could throw it in the Young Chief's face, after which neither of their lives would be worth a black-penny. Not Sybbis's. Not Abasio's.

And if she hadn't arranged it, then somebody else had! Somebody knew. What was to keep that somebody from talking?

" . . . anything at all you want," Soniff was saying yet again.

Abasio felt as he had when he was a child and had done something totally forbidden while knowing, beyond any doubt whatsoever, that he was going to be caught and killed. Grandpa would never actually have killed him, but the Purples would, if Old Chief told them to.

"Yes," said Abasio. "There is something I'd like a lot."

"Name it!"

"I'd like to have a—a vacation."

Soniff looked confused. Abasio tried to think of a different way to say it. Leave. Time off. Gangers didn't take vacations, but Grandpa used to talk about them. "Let's get this work done, boy, then we'll ask a neighbor to look after the animals and you and your ma 'n me, we'll take a vacation." Grandpa's vacations had usually involved going to the nearest lake and spending several days standing hip-deep in water in an effort to catch fish that Abasio had come to believe were entirely imaginary.

Abasio swallowed deeply. "I've always thought I'd like to go traveling," he said. "I've this urge to see something of the world."

"Some of the other cities, you mean."

"Right. Some other cities."

"Well, why not?" asked Soniff, expansively. "The Purples have affiliates in a lot of the cities, and it's always good to see the way things get done other places. Why not? I'll see you get your sparrow back, and that should take you a good way. Take a few weeks."

"Thanks, Soniff. The Young Chief won't mind?"

Soniff grinned. "I've got a feeling he's going to be busy for a while. He won't mind."


Though Abasio wanted to leave immediately, as soon as he reached his own place he fell once again into exhausted sleep, full of strange and threatening dreams. When he dragged himself awake, he found Elrick-Ann was waiting on the firestairs, herself heavily veiled. He remembered now that he'd invited her to come, as soon as she was able.

"How you feel?" he murmured when he'd let her in.

She answered in a throaty rasp, unlike the voice he knew. "Shoulda died, Basio. You shoulda seen I did."

"Elrick-Ann—"

"It was you got me out, I know. Who else? And it was you got Wally Skins dead in the arena too. And my pa dead in the battle. And my brothers, two of 'em."

"I didn't know," he said helplessly.

"They'da died soon or later. Gangers die. That's what they do bes'."

He could think of nothing to say to this. "I'm going away for a while, Elrick-Ann. I want you to live here while I'm gone." It had come to him all at once. Even though he felt it unlikely he'd ever come back, it was easier to say it that way: "Just while I'm gone, Elrick-Ann."

"Why you really goin' away, Basio?" she asked from the bed where she had curled against the pillows.

"Young Chief gave me some time off so I could see the world."

"Oh, sure. He so thoughtful. The Young Chief."

She looked at the things Abasio had piled on the table. His canteen, a blanket roll, and weapons.

"You takin' weapons to see the world?"

"Last time I left the city, I got treed by monsters. I need somethin' to keep them off.'' There was a fire shooter in the pile. Fire was best against monsters. He'd need all his money, including the sparrow Soniff had refunded him. He'd sent TeClar to the market for a few odds and ends, and no doubt TeClar had mentioned Abasio's journey northward. Abasio had talked at length about Vanders City at the big lake and how much he wanted to go there, counting on TeClar and CummyNup to spread the word.

Meantime, Abasio would go the opposite direction. He had to warn Olly. Why did the walkers want her? What had she done? Or was she merely a victim? He visualized what would happen when he saw her again, what she would say to him, what she would do. The dreams were hampered by reality. She didn't respect gangers; he was indisputably a ganger. He might be more acceptable if he shaved his purple crest, but it would be safer to do that after he'd left the city. Slaves had shaved heads, and anybody with a bare scalp was suspect. If he was going to let his natural hair grow out, he'd have to be someplace else when he did it or they'd think he was a runaway.

"It must be nice,'' Elrick-Ann said wistfully. "Goin' somewhere.''

He gritted his teeth and didn't answer. The idea had actually crossed his mind of taking Elrick-Ann with him. But what would he do with her? She'd hate farm life.

He could borrow a horse from the same Patrol Post where he'd borrowed the last one. If he did, though, the officer would know he'd gone south. Better not. Better go on foot. Or tired as he was, maybe steal the horse, making it look like the animal had broken away.

That meant no saddle. Well, he didn't need a saddle. He'd never used a saddle when he was a boy.

"What about when I have to go buy food and stuff?'' she asked him. "Who goin' to guard your place then?''

"The Chingeros will be here every day, turn and turn about. You can send them to market for you, or they'll stay here while you go. Whichever you like.''

"I goin' go myself. They didn' cut much on my legs. I can still walk. Got one arm I can't use, but I can still walk.''

She didn't mention what they'd done to her face and breast, but Abasio had seen that for himself.

He sat down at his table and wrote rapidly. "Here's a letter from me, saying you should live here. Just in case somebody asks.''

She took it and looked it over without comprehension. Watching her, he realized suddenly he had written it out, not printed it. Few people in the cities could read script. Mostly it was used by Edgers or farmers, taught at home or in their schools. Everyone else used printed letters. Cursing, he took the paper from her hand and tore it to shreds. It just showed how distracted he was.

"Wrong paper,'' he said, seating himself at his table and taking a clean sheet from his small supply. This time he printed the few short sentences, affixing his official gang sign and name at the bottom.

Elrick-Ann bounced gently on the bed. "This a good bed, Basio. I don' mind sleepin' here." Her voice was more cheerful than it had been. The thought of something new in her life had pleased her.

"Sleep here. Live here. Cook your dinner here. When TeClar or CummyNup comes over, you use them for whatever you need. I told them to work for you just the way they'd work for me."

Her veil dropped aside, and he saw her smile with half her mouth. Abasio turned away, hiding the tightness that had come around his eyes. When he'd first seen her at the Greens', tied to the chair in that room, blood everywhere, herself barely breathing, all he could think about was getting her out. But she was right. What he should have done was put her out of her misery. He'd had no right to bring her back the way she was. If it had been him, he'd have wanted somebody just to kill him quick, get it over. Much of the time she was in despair these days, in despair and misery, wanting to die. He knew it. He could tell it from her voice.

All he wanted to do was give Elrick-Ann something that would make her feel better. He ought to be doing something for her, but there was nothing he could do! It confused him, making him angry at her, at himself. Sometimes there just wasn't any good solution to things. Sometimes nothing you could do was what you would do.

Set that aside. He owned the rooftop shack; she had her pension; living here was better than her living in Purple House. Better than any other place she might find for herself. Unless the building burned down, she could stay here practically forever.

She regarded him with narrowed eyes. "You want me to keep the place safe, that it?"

"Exactly. I want you to keep it safe."

"When you want me to come?" she asked, folding the letter and tucking it into the pouch that held her street pass.

"Tomorrow morning," he told her.

"Okay, Basio," she said in a sad, faraway voice. "I'll see you in the mornin'."

She wouldn't. TeClar was going to sleep in the place overnight. Abasio intended to leave in the dark hours when he'd be least likely to be observed. If he could keep himself awake until then.

TeClar turned up about dusk, with CummyNup. Abasio went over his instructions about Elrick-Ann until he knew they understood. He'd laid in a stock of the beer they favored. By the time Abasio had gulped down another half-dozen stimulants and left the rooftop, the brothers were barely able to hitch up the alarm and mutter garbled good-byes.

Keeping quiet and largely out of sight, Abasio slipped through neutral territory to the slicks and slimes of the marketplace and through that to the no-man's-land of the burned-out area, where unclaimed bodies still lay about, awaiting eventual disposal by the crows and wild dogs that had thronged the area since the fire. Then he darted across the bridge to the Patrol Post, where he skulked silently, seeing who was around. Nobody much by the look of it. Anyone inside was asleep.

He felt his way along the paddock, testing this pole and that until he found a loose one. It came down with the barest creak, still alarmingly loud in the quiet. The one above it was better fastened, but not by much. Repeated tugging got it loose, and he dropped the end on the ground as though it had been pushed there from inside. He'd brought enough belts and straps to buckle together a serviceable bridle, and he held it with one hand as he shoved his way among the horses, muttering to them, patting them, selecting the animal who seemed friendliest.

He used the corral rail as a mounting block and got onto the horse's back, awkwardly unbalanced by his blanket roll. Several horses found the break in the corral before his mount did, and when he moved south at the center of this small herd, the rest of the animals came ghosting from the corral to trail along.

He worried about the trail they were leaving, but the horses began to drop away, one here, one there, as succulent bits of browse presented themselves. Only half a dozen stayed with him until he reached the near side of the Edge, where he rode close to the wall, distancing himself from it only when he passed the lighted windows of the guard posts. In each of them uniformed men were awake, but none of them seemed to hear the grass-cushioned plopping of the hooves.

Small dark shadows fled before him. He heard giggling from the grassy strip between the roads. Goblins, probably. Or gnomes. Some said they were the same thing. No ditches though. At least he didn't have that to contend with.

By the time dawn leaked its way along the eastern horizon, he and his mount were alone and far from the city. He tried to dismount and succeeded by falling off the horse. He struggled erect, slapped his mount weakly into a tail-streaming canter back the way it had come, and dragged his pack into a nearby copse, where he fell at once into an exhausted sleep.


Despite Abasio's worries, and even in the midst of her usual tantrums, Sybbis had sense enough not to talk. Even if she had talked, she didn't know who her partner had been. Raging curiosity had made her try to find out by peeling the bandages off his hands while he slept, but old Nelda had materialized out of the shadows with a stern command to leave off. Nelda herself was too sensible to talk. Her stalwarts were mutes, which took care of their discretion. Posnia was afraid to say anything to anyone.

The doctor, however, was another matter. He had the twin problems of drink and needing to appear more clever than he was. He could not resist sharing the story with a fellow roisterer, who had no reason not to repeat it. As such stories will, the tale gained in color what it lost in specificity. When, some time later, it came to the ears of Old Chief Purple, nothing remained except amusing generalities. The beautiful young conk. The impotent gang leader. The assignation. The doctor's extreme cleverness in drugging the anonymous donor.

It was the doctor's misfortune that to the Old Chief, generalities were enough.

Old Chief sent for Soniff, who met him in a private room of a songhouse in which the Old Chief had a large financial interest.

"I hear the Bloodrun girl's pregnant," the Old Chief said in clear Edger accents. He'd stopped talking ganger when he'd retired and bought himself a place in the Edge. Not that it had done him any good. Edgers took his money, all right, and they let him buy a big beautiful house and live there among the trees and grass, but he couldn't have conks there, or ganger visitors. Still, he was safe in the Edge. That was worth something. He could always come into the city to do business.

Soniff nodded. "That's what the hags say." He held up a hand, tipping it this way and that. "Of course, it's real early yet."

"How did Kerf manage that?" the Old Chief asked in a mild tone.

Soniff explained about Starlight, about Abasio, and about the reward Abasio had been given.

The Old Chief ruminated, sipping his wine and staring into the candlelight. "Tell you a story," he said, and proceeded to relate the doctor's story as he had heard it.

Soniff felt himself growing pale. "You don't think . . . ?"

The Old Chief shrugged. "Way I heard the story, the one the doctor drugged was from the same gang as the conk. A real joke, funny, so? Suppose it's true. Who was away from the house about that time?"

Soniff thought. Before Abasio had showed up with the drug, he'd come in to see the Young Chief. And Young Chief had been angry with him, because he'd been gone. . . .

"Abasio," he blurted.

"Mmm," mused the Old Chief. "Where is this Abasio?"

"North," murmured Soniff. "Said he wanted to see the lakeshore country."

"Who is he?"

"Why, he's a Purple. Been one for eighteen years or so."

"Before that?"

Soniff didn't know.

"Who recruited him?"

Soniff didn't remember for sure. Lippy-Long, maybe, but it had been a long time ago.

"Find out," said the Old Chief. "And send somebody after him. Send some Survivors."

"You want him brought back, Chief?"

"No. No reason to do that. Tell them I want him dead."

# CHAPTER 8

*I*n his workroom in the bowels of Gaddi House, Tom Fuelry put together the notes he had been accumulating for some days and sat regarding them thoughtfully for a time as he whistled tunelessly between his teeth. There was enough new information to warrant an interview with His Wisdom. He tapped the notes into a neat pile, folded them once, put them into his pocket, and stood up with a grimace. He'd been sitting too long. He needed more exercise.

Despite this acknowledgment, he didn't work up a sweat making his way through the labyrinth of the house. He strolled, pausing now and then to speak to certain of his fellow workers, giving himself still more time to think before he reached His Wisdom's living quarters.

Only to learn from Nimwes that the old man was not there.

"Where is he, Nimwes?"

"Where he goes, Tom. You know better than I do." Nimwes bit her lip and looked elsewhere.

"I didn't think he did much, not anymore," Fuelry said in a hushed voice that he struggled to keep from sounding either fearful or resentful.

"Well, he does. Just because his friends are . . . gone, doesn't mean he's forgotten them. Every now and then, he goes there and spends a few hours remembering them."

Tom thought there might be other reasons, but he couldn't have explained them if he'd tried. "How long has he been gone this time?"

"Maybe an hour."

"I don't like his being down there alone."

"I don't either, but I can't go with him. I can't get through the security. I've asked him to arrange it so I *can* go with him, but he says he doesn't want me burdened with—with that."

Tom tapped his front teeth with a fingernail, sighed, muttered, "I can go. Prob'ly I'd better."

He went back down the fairly well-traveled hall, nodding to this one and that one as he passed them, came to the end of the hall, unlocked a door, went through it, and locked it behind him. From where he stood now, he could hear distant voices, people talking quietly in some nearby laboratory or workroom, only these murmurs telling him he was still near inhabited space. The first secured checkpoint was a little way down the hall, and he negotiated two more after that before he was dropped into a dusty, utterly silent tunnel, deep beneath the labyrinth of Gaddi House proper.

Tom had not come this way in a long time. He was one of only three or four persons who could come here at all. He had always felt it was like a tomb, and every year that passed made it seem more so. The air was dank, and the floor dust-laden. The tunnel was round, as though bored by some monstrous worm, though enough dust had fallen over the centuries to make a narrow, level floor. This slender walkway showed the tracks of wheels, some fresh, some half-covered, some virtually vanished under the coating. If he had not already known the automatics were shut down, the dust would have told him, or the air, which was chill and stale and smelled of something alive but old, some ancient awful thing that lurked and sensed and that might, if one attracted its attention, come heaving out into the light. At least, so Tom always thought when he came here, even when he told himself he was being silly. The tunnels really hadn't been bored by a worm. His Wisdom had told him so.

Though he was following wheel tracks that marked only one route, he still recited the code to himself as he twisted through the silent tunnels past great round doors with complicated locks: *Two right, two left . . .* It always surprised him to see wheel tracks leading up to doors that Tom himself had never seen opened. The tracks showed that His Wisdom had been into those rooms, into some of them fairly recently, though he had said nothing about it to Tom.

*...two left, one right, one left.* The room ahead was the heart of the place. So far as Fuelry knew, it was impregnable. Or would have been, if the monstrously thick metal cylinder door had not been standing open, blocking further progress down the tunnel. One either stopped here or went in.

Fuelry made a face, took a deep breath, and stepped through the circular opening. The space inside was as he remembered it, full of stone pillars made to resemble—or perhaps *grown* to resemble—a forest of ancient trees. Though not identical, they were all much the same size, not evenly set but spaced as though by chance. The pillars went up into darkness. One of the worst things about the room from Tom's point of view was the darkness up there, hiding whatever it hid, if anything. Spiders, perhaps. Bats.

He knew this was foolish. Spiders and bats couldn't live down here. What little ashen light there was leaked from the pillars themselves, and as tree trunks hid distances in a forest, so the thick pillars hid distances here. The space they occupied might be as small as a room or as large as a county; it could be any shape at all, there was no way of knowing. Lichens spread patchily upon the pillars, and mosses grew on the floor in convoluted and oddly colored patterns that looked purposeful, like letters spelling something one could almost read.

Tom had never felt that the pillars were quite rigid. He thought they *squirmed* somehow. To avoid looking at them, he focused on the winding tracks of the wheels, a long, twisting way that brought him, as always, almost to the verge of panic before he came to open space. He had dreams, sometimes, of following tracks that never ended, that just wound on and on and on forever. Eventually the tracks came to space, however; the dimness ended at a place of misty veils and lofty, crepuscular rays that moved slowly, like pale searchlights focused from above. The old man's chair sat in the open space in a puddle of light, only a few yards from the low dais.

Tom risked a quick glance upward from the floor. It was one of the misty days, and he could hardly see the dais, which was fine by Tom. He didn't want to see the dais. He never wanted to see the dais, even though he assumed what was on the dais was mostly stone. Chairs, they were. Only three huge chairs, very tall, very old. Carved out of gray stone. Granite, maybe.

He took a deep shuddering breath. The trouble was, things carved out of stone should not appear to be alive, and yet these did. Eyes carved out of stone shouldn't see. Ears carved out of stone shouldn't hear. But he knew damned well they did. Also, they moved. He couldn't catch them at it, but they did it, anyhow.

"Tom?"

The old man's chair stood quite still, he in it unmoving, his slumped form showing no sign of life. Tom took another deep breath and went slowly forward, keeping his eyes fixed on the old man, not on anything else. He was close to the chair before old Seoca raised his head.

"It's you, Tom. I wondered who it could be."

Tom swallowed the hard, bitter lump in his throat and mumbled, "You know who it couldn't be, Your Wisdom."

"True. I suppose Nimwes told you I was here."

"She did, yes."

"I know it upsets her, but I need to come here sometimes. To commune with Werra. And Hunagor. You never knew Hunagor."

Tom flicked a sidewise glance at the dais, catching only a glimpse of the left-hand chair and who sat in it. The glimpse was enough. He pulled his eyes away. Sometimes they'd catch him looking, and then he couldn't look away. Couldn't unfix his eyes, which stayed glued there for—for a long time.

Tom said, "She was—ah . . . "

"Transfigured?" offered the old man.

"Transfigured before my time, sir."

"She chose to be so. She was finished with her duties, Fuelry. She believed her task was done. Werra, now, I brought him down here well before his time. Otherwise, we'd have been too late."

"Brought him to be, ah"—Tom swallowed painfully once more—"transfigured."

"Right." The old man put his hands beneath his armpits and spoke with slight surprise. "It's cold in here."

"Can I take you back, sir?"

"Might as well. It's getting harder all the time for them to . . . communicate. I miss having them to talk with. Sometimes I get confused. Sometimes I'm not sure I'm cleaving to the pattern, adhering to the philosophy, planning for everything. I come here hoping to be inspired, reassured, but today I'm not. Unless you bring me something reassuring?"

"I'm afraid not, Your Wisdom. I have a few bits and pieces, none of them so urgent it won't wait until we get you back where it's warmer." He turned the old man's chair and moved along beside it, wishing desperately that when he had to come here, he could do it more casually, leaving the place behind him when he left it. The damned room or cavern or whatever it was wouldn't allow that! The feel of it followed him every time. The sense of being noticed by, watched by, known by the great chairs—it went with him, destroying his peace, disturbing his rest.

He sometimes felt he would be less troubled if he understood what was going on here, but though His Wisdom had tried to make it easier, Tom only picked up scraps here and there.

"It has to do with deities, Tom. All peoples have gods. Different people visualize them differently, and some people try not to visualize them at all because they know whatever they try to imagine, the truth is otherwise. The being who is seen in one way and called by one name in Artemisia may be seen another way and called by another name by the Faulty Sea."

"You're saying . . . Hunagor . . . Werra . . . "

"I'm saying names are only labels, not identities. I'm saying reality goes beyond what we can see."

Which was damned little help, Tom thought.

His Wisdom sighed. "I wish you were of Gaddir lineage. Gaddirs have a way of just—understanding these things."

But he wasn't Gaddir. He was just Tom Fuelry, whose great-great-grandfather had been a tribesman in the mountains, and whose grandfather had worked for Gaddi House, whose father had worked for Gaddi House. Faithfully, as the Fuelrys did all things. Sometimes His Wisdom patted Tom on the shoulder and said, "To the weak, succor; to the strong, burdens." He should be flattered, he supposed.

"My own fault it's cold," the old man mumbled as they went through the great round door. "The heat and the filtered air come down from above. I turned them off. It didn't seem worth the expenditure of energy. The essential circuits go on running. There's no way to shut them off."

Tom quelled a shiver. Among other disturbing dreams, he sometimes had visions of those mighty engines of the deep, eternally purring, that deep-set, incredible power that had given its name to the Place. Fusion power, the Domers said. Well, it might be, but Tom had a hunch it wasn't what Mitty meant when he said fusion power.

His voice cracked as he said, "When you want to come here again, let one of us come with you, sir. And wear something warm." His voice had become strident on the last few words. He bit his lip. "I'm sorry, sir, I—"

"Quite all right, Fuelry. I deserve to be scolded. Just wait until Nimwes gets hold of me. She'll let me have it!" He chuckled. "Well, what's your news?"

"A moment." Fuelry went through his long-memorized and complicated ritual of setting locks. After a moment's pause, the door swung shut with a deep grinding hum that made the floor vibrate beneath them as Tom sent the chair briskly along the dusty corridor. "Some time ago, you suggested that since I am not well known outside Gaddi House, I cultivate Qualary Finch."

"That wasn't the reason I gave you, but yes."

"Right." Fuelry had been doing a bit more than merely cultivating her, but he did not intend to discuss that. "When you get past her defenses, she's a very nice person." Comely, he thought. Comely and delightful, and— passionate.

"I'm glad you've found the assignment pleasant." His Wisdom bent his mouth into a secretive smile. "What has she told you?"

"She's not a chatterer, unlike most Domers. She doesn't talk about anything private, probably out of fear. However, she feels no constraint in discussing what everyone discusses. Such as the shuttle project."

They had come to the security shafts, which Tom moved them through rapidly, back into warmer and more inhabited space.

"She speaks of it as a salvage project?"

"That, yes, but she also mentions weapons as among the things to be salvaged."

"Weapons?" The old man sat up, his expression suddenly alert. "Well, now. Has she said what weapons?"

"No. She only repeats what Ellel has said. I asked Qualary what the weapons were for, but the weapons, when discussed in front of her or other Domer servants, have been referred to only as a type of salvage, as parts, as material. Qualary doesn't think of them as armament."

The old man laughed. "Because Ellel hasn't spoken of them in terms of armament. The omission's interesting, isn't it? With all the monsters there are about, Ellel certainly should be interested in weapons as armament." He laughed again, seeming quite pleased with himself.

Fuelry said nothing more until they arrived at His Wisdom's quarters. Only after Nimwes had wrapped the old man with a blanket and plied them both with hot tea did Tom continue:

"Another interesting bit: Qualary has remarked that when the shuttle is completed, only Ellel and Ander will go, together with some of their people. And some walkers, of course."

The old man considered this. "I'm sure it was a problem for her. Can she leave behind anyone she does not trust? Would she dare take anyone along she did not trust? Including only Ellels and Anders is her solution to the problem."

Tom scowled. "So off they go, these two sets of ambitious Domers who don't trust anyone, and back they come with weapons, and what happens then?"

"One wonders." His Wisdom shook his head slowly back and forth. "If Ellel spoke openly of using them against monsters, I might believe her. Since she doesn't speak openly of using them at all, her motives are hidden. What motive would she hide? World domination, of course. That's the formula that emerged with the dinosaurs. Megalomania plus weapons equals domination. Of course, the weapons then were fang and claw, and every creature was a me-firster.''

"I don't know why in hell we don't just eliminate all of them," Fuelry snarled. "The whole bunch of them—and their families!"

The old man shook his head in amused wonder. "When I suggested you cultivate Qualary Finch, didn't you question the ethics of that assignment?"

Fuelry flushed. He had, yes. Of course, he hadn't known Qualary at that point.

"Now, here you are, forgetting Gaddir philosophy to become suddenly very bloodthirsty."

"Sorry," the other said, then, feeling explanation was needed, "If you knew how that bitch had treated Qualary—" Though Qualary had been reticent to speak of it, Tom had seen the scars. He condemned all the Domers equally. If they hadn't done it, they hadn't prevented it, either!

"I understand how you feel, but that's not the way Gaddi House operates, Tom. You know that. We do not impose our will on others. All beings must be free to seek their own happiness. Only when one person's search becomes another person's slavery may we intervene, and even then, not with force. We pay a price for everything we do."

Fuelry pursed his mouth, looking over His Wisdom's shoulder in ostentatious silence.

The old man grinned. "You think I'm maybe stretching a point?"

Fuelry flushed uncomfortably.

"Listen, boy. If a man thinks it will make him happy to hit you, and you duck so he ends up breaking his hand against a brick wall, whose fault is that?"

"I suppose the man doing the hitting," said Tom, unwillingly.

"Of course. If people out there are aiming blows at one another, and if we teach some of them to duck, isn't that appropriate?" He sighed and stretched his hands toward the fire. "If we learned anything from history, we learned you can't legislate how creatures ought to behave. We don't try."

"You may not force them, but you do other things. You fool them. You entice them!"

The old man chuckled. "If, as some believe, man is a fallen angel, he doesn't need to be enticed. He has only to remember what goodness is. If man is an ascending ape, however, he first has to figure out what goodness is, and before he can do that, he has to admit he doesn't know."

"So admitting you don't know is equivalent to admitting you were an ape to begin with?" Though he tried not to, Tom couldn't keep his mouth from quirking, just a little.

"Exactly. Depend upon it. Any system that claims to know what goodness is will also claim descent from heaven. Or expulsion from paradise, which

is the same thing.'' The old man laughed until he choked, and Tom had to
bring him a glass of water. ''Do you have any other news for me?'' the old
man asked.

''Yes, though it was stale news when I got it. Qualary mentioned that Ellel's
been very happy lately, so I played along and asked why. It seems a pair of her
walkers brought in an old raggedy blanket that was turned over to their lab.''

The old man became very still. ''What exactly did the lab say? Do you
know?''

''None of my sources there were available. However, we have a few spies
in the Domer catering section, and they tell me Ander threw a party to
announce that Ellel had found a cellular trace.''

The old man licked his lips and took a deep, sighing breath. ''What have
the Domers done about it?''

''Ellel's done all the doing. She's intensified the search, is all. So far.''

''Where?''

''Down there.'' Fuelry pointed to the east. ''South manland, Artemisia.''
He turned back to stare at the old man curiously. ''How did the Domers get
Gaddir genetic material to compare in the first place?''

''Hunagor was as human as you or I. She used to go out among people.
So did Werra. So did I. And what does it take to get a sample? No more
skill than picking your pocket. You get bumped in a crowd, a quick punch,
a drop of blood. Some spy pilfers a glove, a scarf. What else?'' He knotted
his hands together. ''What have you done about it?''

''If your assessment is correct, the Orphan is on her way south. We've
done what we can to prevent harm coming to her. But there are a hell of a
lot more walkers out there than there are allies of ours.''

The old man sighed and rubbed his forehead wearily. Walkers. Damn man
and his lust for power, his fascination with technology! Damn men who
could build such things! ''Nimwes says she can hardly leave Gaddi House
now without encountering them every few steps.''

Fuelry snorted. ''They're like ants. First you see only one, but suddenly
there's a whole line of them. And the damage they're doing! Half the gardens
in the Place are dead. More than half the trees!''

''They used to be mostly elsewhere. Why has Ellel turned so many loose
here in the Place? What is she using them for?''

''I think Ellel just likes looking at them.''

''Surely not! The smell alone—''

''Truly, Your Wisdom. You should see her during her morning ceremony.
She's almost orgasmic! And as Nimwes says, they've started annoying our
people.''

The old man snarled. ''Surely Ellel doesn't wish to stir up Gaddi House
just now? Not with success practically within her reach!''

"I think she mostly disregards Gaddi House. As we, for a long time, disregarded the walkers. Now, however, they're getting unpredictable."

"Oh, Tom, they're perfectly predictable! Jark the Third was not a technician. He was an ambitious and impatient man with some superficial knowledge. Ellel is more ambitious, less impatient, so she's learned a good deal more than her father did, but even she knows far less than she thinks she does. The so-called reprogramming done by father or daughter simply cannot stand up to repeated stress, particularly inasmuch as the creatures aren't being properly maintained. Ellel has been so busy pulling power into her own hands, she hasn't taken time to provide maintenance."

"You think they're going slightly haywire."

"More than slightly. The surface routines are eroding, and they are now beginning to act as they were designed to do!" He shifted uncomfortably in his chair. "Ah, well. It's the last of many worries."

"The last, sir? If this is the last, I'm glad I wasn't around for the rest of them."

"Oh, the rest of them were easy by comparison, my boy. Yes. Have you ever tried to clean out a water tank?"

Astonished, Fuelry shook his head. "I don't believe so, sir. What kind of water tank?"

"Oh, one used to water horses or cattle. If you have a filthy, muddy tank all grown up with algae that you have to clean out, you can get ninety-nine percent of the filth out of it just by turning it over and dumping it. That's what Hunagor, Werra, and I did, over a century and a half ago. We had a problem, and we dumped it. Since then, we've spent all our effort cleaning up the final one percent."

"I didn't realize that, sir," said Tom, his mouth open.

"Oh, yes indeed. I tell myself that whenever I get discouraged. I tell myself ninety-nine percent of cleaning up the world has been accomplished. And it was true until Jark the Third discovered those damned walkers!"

"Which made it a new problem."

"Or restored the old one. For a while, I thought we should have foreseen it, but the chance of its happening was vanishingly small. It would have been easier to handle with all three of us, but when it happened, Hunagor was already gone. Werra went soon after.

"At first I thought, well, Jark being as he was, pretty much of a dilettante, the chance of his doing anything much with them wasn't large. But he disappeared, and Ellel took over. Now who could have foreseen Ellel?" He sighed again. "Still, I tell myself the whole series of events is only a worry, only a last little glitch, one of those inevitable last-minute things one can't plan for until it happens."

"It doesn't seem like a little glitch to me," grumped Tom.

His Wisdom flushed slightly, sitting silent for a moment before he responded, "You're right, Tom. It isn't. It's a return to the main line, to the inexorable process of destruction we thought we had stopped. But we do have a chance. And I will not dwell on how badly we may fail."

"If we fail, all of us here in the Place will be Ellel's minions. Her servants. Those of us she doesn't kill outright."

The old man shook his head. "That time will be brief, Tom. If we fail, life on earth will be brief."

"If I just *knew* more!"

"Believe me, knowing more wouldn't make it any easier. You'll have to trust that I'm doing my best. Be patient."

Tom, shamefaced, merely nodded. He always had trusted, always been patient, though sometimes it was very hard.


Traveling afoot, and only at night, Abasio reached the Wise Rocks road in two days. He should have been quicker, he told himself, trying to be angry about it and succeeding only in becoming shamingly tearful. There was no reason to have taken so long except for the lassitude, the feeling of exhausted impotence that possessed him. It was not until his arrival within sight of the Wise Rocks themselves, however, that he fully realized what was going on. This same weary futility had been with him since he had waked in the truckers' hostel. Only the stimulants he had taken had allowed him to accomplish anything at all.

He was certain somebody had given him Starlight. Why else would he have known the smell? Whistler had said Starlight wouldn't hurt a child, and Whistler was not known as a liar. Well, maybe he hadn't actually lied. Abasio wasn't *hurt*. He was simply unable to plan further ahead than the next few moments' travel. All he wanted to do was lie down and do nothing, think nothing, plan nothing. Only some deep life-loving core of himself made him go on, only his stubborn will pushed him on. Lying down would be equivalent to death. He had no more stimulants, no food, nothing to drink. If he stayed in one place, it would be only a matter of time before a hunger of ogres or a stink of trolls came upon him. If he wanted to go on living, he had to get home.

The words were thought, not spoken, and it was some little time before he realized the form his intention had taken. Home. When had he last thought of the farm as home? Not for years. Why now?

He couldn't find an answer, at least not one that satisfied him. It took too much energy to think about it. He dragged himself past the Wise Rocks Farm lane and on up the rutted road that led up the valley. The Cermit place was only a few miles farther on. The last mile he virtually crawled, taking five steps, then resting, then taking five steps again.

He staggered into the farmyard at dawn. The old man was already up, strewing corn among the chickens. Abasio saw him as he neared the house, then saw Big Blue in the paddock, heard the familiar whicker, the sound coming to him as though from a great distance. The next thing he knew, he was lying across the back steps of the farmhouse, a blanket wrapped around him and his grandpa spooning something hot between his lax lips.

"What happened?" Abasio begged.

"You'd know better than I, boy. What've you been up to, falling over your own feet that way? Your breath stinks! You look like death warmed over."

"I do?"

"You do. You look like an old ewe sheep: your eyes are yellow, your heart's going ticky ticky like you'd been chased by dogs, and your tongue is furred up like a dirty fleece. What ails you?"

"Just—just tired, I think, Grandpa. Somebody gave me something. I guess it's taking time to—to get it out of me."

"Drugs." The old man spat and struggled to his feet, letting Abasio's head roll onto the boards of the porch with a decided thump. "What would the city be without drugs, eh?"

"I didn't take it," Abasio protested. "Somebody gave it to me."

"Always somebody. Well, you're here now, and there's no somebody to give you anything but hot soup and home-baked bread. Can you get yourself into the house? If not, I'll have to put rollers on you. You're too big for me to move."

He could get no farther than into the porch itself, where he collapsed onto the narrow bed against the back wall of the house. This felt like home, his own bed, where he'd slept in the summers, when the house was too hot.

"That's far enough, I suppose," his grandfather mumbled. "That's a place you're used to. Though the bed's too small for you now, it'll have to do."

Abasio let his eyes close, let his lids glue themselves down. No point trying to keep alert, keep awake. Whatever was wrong with him was getting worse, not better. It had been steadily downhill since . . . whenever.

The day brightened, but Abasio did not. He pulled the blanket over his head, sleeping heavily, almost comatose, as though he would never wake again.

His grandfather roused him and fed him that night and again the following morning. Each time he got as far as the edge of the porch to pee. He slept through the noon hour, but awakened long enough to drink a cup of soup at dusk. The next morning, he awakened on his own, heaved himself onto the side of the bed, and sat there staring owlishly at the chickens in the yard. His mouth tasted like the bottom of their coop. In the kitchen his grandfather stood at the sink washing vegetables, a slumped and yet familiar figure, no matter it was unlike the tall, erect silhouette Abasio remembered from his youth.

"Coming to, are you?" Cermit asked through the open door.

"I guess," said Abasio, slurring the words. He wanted something. Very badly.

"How much of that drug did they give you?"

"A lot, I guess," Abasio admitted. What was it he was wanting? What did he need? Not food. Not drink.

"Too much, I'd say. What was this drug for?"

Abasio didn't answer. He'd suddenly identified the sick hunger he felt. Though he'd had no personal experience with addiction, he'd heard others complain of it, and these were the symptoms. All he really wanted was more of what he'd already had too much of. Starlight. He shuddered and gagged, both glad and sorry he'd given what was left of the stuff to Soniff when he got his sparrow back. The three missing days would turn into a short lifetime if he had a supply available.

Maudlin tears dribbled down his face. Poor Little Purp. Poor Soniff. Were they feeling like this? If they were, if Little Purp was habituated . . . still another reason for hunting Abasio down and cutting pieces off him.

"Oh, shit," he groaned. "I'm sick." He struggled to his feet and managed to make it to the porch steps before he succumbed to the dry heaves.

Cermit shook his head and retreated into the kitchen, reappearing in a moment with a steaming mug. He knelt beside Abasio, grunting in the effort, his old joints popping and snapping like dry twigs. "You probably won't keep this down, but drink it anyhow. It'll give your gut something to spew, and that'll be less painful than what you're doing."

Three mugs later, Abasio managed to keep some of the broth down. He lay back on the narrow bed, letting the dizziness subside. Outside, the windmill whirled against the sky, and he shut his eyes so as not to see the twirling blades.

"You're an advertisement for the city, you are," his grandfather observed. "Worse than your poor ma. She heaved it up, too, but that was because she was pregnant with you."

"I think I'll sleep awhile longer," mumbled Abasio.

"Good idea," the old man said in a dry voice. "You do that."

He slept until midafternoon and awoke without the heaves. Beside him his grandfather sat in the old rocking chair, half-dozing.

"I saw Big Blue," murmured Abasio. "I must be having hallucinations."

"No, you saw him. He's Big Blue's grandson, though. Looks just like the old horse. Acts like him too."

"Dreamed about him," said Abasio. "I really did."

The old man stared at the younger. "When was this?"

"I don't know. A week ago, maybe. Dreamed I was here, at the farm, then dreamed I was going someplace on Big Blue."

"Are you?"

"Am I what?"

"Going somewhere?"

"I'd just as soon not. For a while. Unless they come after me." He sat up with some difficulty, plumped up the wadded pillow, and lay back down again with a sigh.

"Misery me, boy, what are they coming after you for? What did you do?"

"I didn't do anything. Not of my own free will. I may have done something under—coercion, sort of. Not that the Purples will pay any attention to that. If you're sensible, you're supposed to be able to avoid all that."

"If you're sensible," said the old man heavily.

"Which I wasn't," Abasio admitted.

The old man frowned. "So now they're after you. Did you take some precautions? Or did you just come straight home, trolling trouble behind you?"

"I made them think I'd gone north," Abasio mumbled, trying to get angry. Grandpa always had made him furious, which was one reason he'd left, but just now he didn't seem to have the strength to argue, much less be angry.

"You had some wits left, then. Well, no point wearying the day with things past, as the philosopher says. Looks to me like you'll be good for nothing for several days yet."

Though Abasio hated to admit it, the old man was right. He toddled when he tried to walk; he fumbled when he tried to handle anything; he decided to shave his head but cut himself several times in the process. He had to warn Olly, but he couldn't manage it, not yet.

It was her voice that awoke him from a nap several afternoons later, her voice coming from outside somewhere. He struggled awake, got himself to his feet and into the kitchen where he made shift to wash the crustiness from around lips and eyes and make a turban for his bald head. There was nothing he could do about the tattoos. No point in trying to hide them.

"Abasio, come greet our visitors," the old man said when Abasio staggered from the house into the shaded yard where they sat. Grandpa. Farmwife Suttle. And her, Olly.

"We met a few days back," said the Farmwife. "It was he who told Olly you knew of the thrones, as a matter of fact."

"You didn't mention he'd been at your place," Cermit said stiffly. "What was he doing at Wise Rocks Farm?"

"I quite forgot," Originee lied gently. "He was passing through, and he had time for only a few words with us, on the fly, so to speak."

"I was not very nice to him," said Olly, her voice sounding weak and wounded, even to her own ears. He looked sick! He looked sick unto death! All his lovely sparkle dimmed, like embers, hidden under ashes. What had happened to him? She reached up a finger to tickle the neck of the angel on her shoulder, discarding one comment and another. "I took him for a city-man," she said at last.

"Which he is," said the old man heavily. "As his hands will tell you. A ganger. A street brawler. Possibly a killer of innocent bystanders. A slaughterer of children."

"No," said Abasio, too weak to be really angry. "I never did. There's no rep—honor in that!"

"There's no honor in any of it," the old man said wearily.

"Hush," Originee rebuked him, leaning forward to pat his shoulder. "Hush, Cermit. The boy was young. He ran away. Now he's back. Shall we drive him away again, blaming him for what he's been?"

Cermit shook his head. "I know. I know, Originee. I'm not angry at him, not really. But if there's a chance somebody hunting him can find out where he is, if there's a chance they'll even come looking, then he'll have to go away again, no matter what I want. Otherwise the whole valley could be wiped clean."

"Farmers are taboo," muttered Abasio. "Gangers don't bother farmers. Or water-men. Or power-men." The providers of life's necessities were not interfered with, so the doctrine ran.

His grandfather turned on him in irritation. "They say they don't bother farmers, that's true. But if they're looking for escapees, then they bother farmers, and farmwives, and the children and the animals as well! Men on the hunt don't care who they kill."

"Killers, dillers!" cried the guardian-angel. "Watch out."

"Hush, my angel," said Olly, scratching its neck as she considered Abasio's dilemma. "Why are they after you?"

"I don't know that they are!" Abasio cried. "I got into a situation that could be trouble, that's all. I left before anyone found out about it. If I'd stayed until someone found out, it would have been too late."

The Farmwife inspected him closely. "Your grandpa's right in one respect, boy. Those hands betray you." She took his hands in her own, tracing with her thumb the symbols on the backs of his hands. "If you go to the village, someone will notice. If you wear gloves, someone will notice that."

"I didn't plan to go into the village."

"You plan to hide out forever?" the Farmwife asked.

"I didn't plan!" he yelped, tired of all of them, of himself. "I haven't had time!"

"He's not well," said Olly, trying to keep her voice impersonal, as though noticing the condition of some farm animal. "Look at his yellow eyes."

They worried her, those eyes. Was it possible he could have something fatal? Abasio. Surely not. It wouldn't be fair.

But when, Oracle had asked, had life ever been fair?

Abasio felt himself growing red.

The Farmwife patted him. "There, boy. We're trying to help, really. Trying to think of ways to protect you. You remember us farm folk, plain-spoken and meddlesome. Some might say, rude. But if you remember that, you'll remember there's little harm in us. I'll send over some of my good cheese. Olly will bring it. Meantime, I'll put my mind to what might be done about those hands."

"I'm not the only one being looked for," he mumbled.

"Who else?" asked the Farmwife, suddenly alert.

"I think they're looking for her," he said, nodding at Olly. "Walkers were asking about her. In Fantis."

Olly nodded soberly and said in a level voice, "Oddmen. That's what I call them. I know no reason they should be looking for me, but I know they are."

She refused to panic. She had been driven from her home in the village, but she would not be driven from this haven. Not yet, at any rate. Not with him here, so sick, so in need of—of what?

Abasio subsided. If she didn't regard the matter as immediately threatening, perhaps it wasn't. In any case, he felt as impotent to help her as he had been to help Elrick-Ann. What could he do? He could barely stagger on his own!

When Originee and Olly were homeward bound, they rode for a time silently, each of them thinking her own thoughts.

"He could be a dyer," said Originee at last. "Indigo to the elbows. You could be a dyer as well. Nobody looks beyond the splotches, and it does wear off in time."

"What are you talking about?" asked Olly.

"Your thrones, of course." The Farmwife gave her a sharp look. "You want to find your thrones, and if my experience teaches me anything, it is that both you and Abasio should get out of the area as soon as possible."

"Surely you don't think of him as protection!" she cried through teary merriment. "He may not recover! He looks like a soggy dishrag!"

The guardian-angel cried, "A soggy-doggy. He does!"

The Farmwife thought about it. "I don't think of him as protection at this moment, no, but he will recover. He's already much improved from when he came home. Cermit says he has appetite, his lassitude is passing. When he's well, and he will be well, he'll be strong once more. He's probably well schooled in survival. Few gang members live to reach his age. One in four, perhaps."

"You're eager to have me gone," accused Olly, somewhat illogically, her mind on Abasio's recovery.

"No. I'm not. I'd as lief have you stay, if you would, but I'm not such a fool as to think you can hide here in the valley without being found eventually. People watch, people notice, people talk. Sooner or later, someone will say something to bring the hunters down on us, if they haven't already."

"You sound very sure."

"I don't know about your oddmen, but gangers have come before, looking for runaway slaves, fugitive conks. Abasio was right to say that normally we're immune from their riots, but if they're looking for someone in particular, they begin going from farm to farm, working their way out into the countryside, beating on people to make them talk. I know one farm now vacant where a couple tried to hide their own son. He'd run off to the city, been a ganger, got captured in a war, been enslaved, then run away. When the hunters came, they raped the woman and her daughter, then killed her husband when he tried to interfere. The daughter died, as did the slave boy. The woman lived."

"Farmwife Chyne?" whispered Olly.

Farmwife Suttle nodded. "And three graves on the hill above the old deserted farm. Cermit may be angry at Abasio, but he doesn't want the boy dead."

"He'd rather miss him than mourn him," said Olly, quoting the Oracle.

"Indeed," said the Farmwife. "As I would you."


Olly found herself apprenticed to the dyer before she had time to think about it. On the third day after their meeting with Abasio and Cermit, Farmwife Suttle had seized her up and taken her into Whitherby without so much as a by-your-leave. That night she found herself and her belongings in a loft behind the dyer's yard with the guardian-angel shifting from foot to foot on an unfamiliar bedpost.

"Learn," Originee had said, after introducing her to the dyer, Wilfer Ponde. "This man is my friend, and we've spoken together about your needs. Learn as quickly as you may. You will have to teach Abasio, so learn well."

What Abasio thought about it, Olly had no idea, and she was too bemused by the Farmwife's decisiveness to object on her own behalf. Why not learn dyeing, after all? According to the Farmwife, dyers were among the craftsmen and skilled workers who could cross borders with little difficulty.

Though Wilfer Ponde showed no signs of ever having crossed a border. He was a taciturn individual, bent from long hours stooped over his kettles; his sheds and yard were a lifelong accumulation of vats, sacks, boxes, and smelly pools of this or that. He worked in indigo and safflower and cochineal, as well as in a host of less penetrating colors distilled from barks and roots and the skins or husks of both familiar and unfamiliar plants. His arms were colored halfway to the shoulder, as was his neck, where he habitually put up a wet hand to scratch away his puzzlement at the oddities of life.

Olly was one such, and he abused his neck mightily as he took her around the place, beginning with the fabric shed. "Cotton," he told her. "That comes from southern Artemisia. Linen from the flax fields northeast of mainland. Wool from the sheep raised around here on the farms. Silk, imported from the western people, those by the Faulty Sea, and little enough of it, for it takes a lot of hand labor to make. That's the basic four fabrics, plus leather: cow, sheep, goat, pig, horse, each of which has its own problems. This is all fabric in here. Thread and yarn are in the shed across the yard."

"You don't travel?"

His fingers went to his neck as he considered this. "I couldn't carry a tenth of this with me, and it takes all of it to turn out proper products. Each fiber responds differently to dye. Different dyes take different mordants—that's the rinse you use to set the color—to give varying hues. The herbs and barks and roots come to me from all around. Not like in the old days, when dyestuff came from around the world—across the oceans, even—but still, some of it comes from a considerable distance. How would my suppliers find me if I traveled?" He shook his head slowly. "No, the only dyers who travel are those who do custom work, perhaps coloring thread for local weavers or printing patterns on fabric. It's the patterning that Originee thinks may be of value to you. I'll teach you some simple things: one or two kinds of fabric, a handful of colors. The rest is called art."

"Art?" Olly laughed. "I have no claim to being an artist."

Scratch, scratch once more. "Well, as to that, we can fake it. Care and copy can pretend at inspiration." He gave her a penetrating look.

"Why're you doing this?" Olly asked. "Why're you spending this time on me?"

Scratch, scratch. "Originee and I, as I've said, are old friends. We were close in childhood." Scratch again. "People working together, it's part of the pattern of all life." He knotted his hands before him and gave her a frank, determined look. "Why not?"

"And this specially patterned fabric? There's a market for it?"

"Wherever folks want their names or symbols put on the stuff they wear or the banners they wave. In Artemisia, men dress according to society and women according to clan. There's a town west of there that orders a lot of printed silk for fancy silk sleeves and pays me bonuses for it! East of there, men dress according to tribe. South of there, things get festive and ornamental.

"I'll teach you to make dyes of local stuff, safflower and indigo, walnut hull and onion skin and juniper berry. All that grows around here or near enough. If you travel south, you'll find rabbit bush and snake bush for yellow, and cactus fruits to make a rosy red. Farther still, and you'll come to the place cochineal bugs grow, feeding on other cactuses. I'll teach you how to make dye of them as well, and how to print on cloth with pattern blocks.'' He scratched and beckoned. ''Come.''

They went back across the yard and into another building, this one more solid, with a tight roof and screens on the windows, most of the floor taken up with a long, low table spread with a length of creamy cloth bordered with blue figures, half the center decorated in flowers and leaves in yellow and red and green, the other half still blank.

''The pattern,'' he said, indicating a series of blocks lying on a side table. ''Sixteen blocks in all. One for the border corner, three for the border sides. One for the center panel corners, three for the center panel sides. Eight more for the panel itself. Three dyes. And a week's work!''

''I'd be afraid to touch it!'' she cried. It was true, she would, and yet her eyes followed the pattern eagerly, seeming to understand it before her mind did. This block went there, and that one there, and this one was turned so to make the pattern match. It was rather like poetry! Interesting!

''The money I'm getting from an Edger family for this tablecloth, I'd be a fool to let you touch it.'' He laughed. ''And don't let that angel of yours poop on it, either. No, you'll start as any apprentice does, on handkerchiefs and neckpieces, and you'll make the blocks yourself.''

The blocks were of wood with a tightly glued-on layer of hard felt that Wilfer said was made of hammered wool. The felt had to be cut cleanly, with a very sharp straight knife, and the parts that were not in the pattern carved out with a sharp, scoopy little chisel. Orphan copied a pattern Wilfer gave her, a blossom and bud with leaves, a pattern in which a leaf or stem intersected each side of the square at its center. No matter which way the print block was turned, the pattern went on into the next block, and the next. The felt absorbed the dye when dipped into it; pressure on the wooden block forced it into the slightly dampened fabric.

''It looks so easy!'' she cried in frustration, regarding her fifteenth attempt to make the pattern line up cleanly, the dye to be evenly dark or light. ''I'm just not artistic.'' And yet her mind saw how it should look. How it could look, if only her hands would do it rightly.

Wilfer took the block from her hand, dipped it, slapped it onto the dampened fabric, pulled it away, repeated the motion eight times more, three rows of three. A solid block of pattern glowed up from the center of the fabric square. ''Practice,'' he said. ''That part has nothing to do with inspiration or art or any of that. Simple practice.''

She practiced with the blocks in the morning. In the afternoons, she ground roots or berries or fruits, she mixed dyes or prepared fabric. Merely getting a piece of fabric evenly damp but not wet required endless care. Came Sixthday evening, Farmwife Suttle came for her and took her and her angel home, the angel talking all the way, Olly silent and weary.

"Are you learning, Olly?"

Olly took a folded square from her pocket and presented it. Unfolded, it was a kerchief of two colors, rosy flowers among green leaves.

"I did the pattern myself, but it needs to be hemmed," Olly said. "I'll do that tomorrow."

"No." The Farmwife shook her head firmly. "It's a lovely gift, but I can hem it myself. Tomorrow you must teach Abasio everything you've learned this week."

Olly kicked the bag at her feet where several uncut dye blocks rested, along with cotton squares and little sacks of dyestuff. "He'll hate it," she said. "Nothing but the same thing, over and over. He'll think it's dull."

"Do you think it's dull?"

"Now, maybe a little. I think—I think after a while it won't be dull anymore because I'll be able to do things. . . . I have all these ideas for patterns! The way things fit together!"

She did not realize how eager her voice sounded.

The Farmwife smiled to herself.

Abasio, now clear of eye and reasonably clear of mind, did think dyeing was dull, but no duller than other things essential to his survival. Also, it was an excuse to be with Olly. He found her no less enchanting now than the first time he had seen her. He could not be with her enough. Though he now knew very well that he had been with Sybbis during his lost days, his intention had been to make love to Olly, and that was how he remembered it. What he had done, he had done with her. They two had been lovers. He remembered them as lovers, even though he knew it wasn't factual. The worst part was being unable to talk with her about it. He wanted to say, "Remember? Remember when I did this, when you did that." All of this consisted of far more emotion than good sense, but he found the irrationality of it comforting, one of few comforting things in his life at the moment.

So he copied the designs she gave him and cut his blocks neatly—for he had always been good with his hands—and figured out his own system for lining them up to make a continuous pattern, all the time watching Olly, listening to her, touching her fingers with his as though accidentally, soaking her up. When she recited the recipes for the dyes and mordants, he dutifully wrote them down and memorized them. He mixed the indigo she brought, obediently dipped his hands and wrists into the stuff, and watched as his skin turned blue, hiding the gang tattoos.

He considered asking Olly to go walking out in the woods with him. The woods called to him in a way they never had when he was a boy. Their misty distances summoned him; the feathery growth of new trees seemed to touch him with intimate joy; the gaiety of flowers enlivened him, making him smile. These were new emotions, ones he could not remember feeling before. He spoke of them to Olly, and she responded in kind.

"The village . . . ," she murmured, her voice laden with the memory of joy. "The waterfall in winter, laden with ice. The crowded golden bloom at the edge of the meadow. Oracle and I used to sit and look at it for hours."

"I don't remember feeling this way before," he complained. "I don't remember even noticing some of the stuff that grows around here."

"You took it for granted," she said. "It was just there. But you've been in the city for years, where there is nothing like it. I had a friend who told me about the city, about the history of cities. He said before men went to the stars, more and more people moved into cities, and they lost connection with the earth. They didn't understand where their food came from, what kept their air and water clean. They didn't understand how plants and animals and funguses and insects and everything are all connected. They disrespected nature; they held it in contempt. Now, because you've been away, you can see what is here and imagine losing it. Love and grief mixed, that makes a passion!" She knew this last was true because Oracle had told her so. And because she felt it, looking at him, looking at the world around them both. Love and grief mixed, to make a passion. Or perhaps, love alone . . .

He wanted to make other kinds of passion. He wanted to take her deep into that natural world she obviously loved. He thought of having her on a mossy bed, looking at her breasts spangled with sunlight, bathing with her in a shallow pool of silver water. He longed to touch her skin, there at her throat where it changed color inside the neck of her shirt. He longed to lie beside her, holding her. He went over and over these desires in his mind, finding the pictures endlessly attractive. His body, however, could not make the effort. He still slept long and heavily at night and sometimes napped in the daytime, overcome by that same lassitude he had felt since leaving Fantis. Sometimes he wondered briefly if this effect was to be permanent, but there wasn't enough energy left over to worry about it.

"You do look better," Olly told him tenderly. "Your eyes and skin aren't yellow anymore. And your hair's growing out."

"I know. It feels funny. I've worn the crest for—fifteen, sixteen years." He rubbed the bristles with his wet and darkened hands, dyeing his hair tips blue in the process.

She smiled at the blue-tipped hair, considering it totally suitable for a dyer. "Has Originee talked to you?"

"About what?"

"About your going away with me? Or me with you, whichever?"

A brief surge of pure joy was quickly supplanted by his more usual ennui. He shook his head, at once suspicious and confused. "She's told me to learn this dyeing business, for it will hide the tattoos and give both of us other identities, but she hasn't mentioned going away. What do you mean, away?"

"Originee says if gangers come looking for you, they could kill a lot of people, especially if people try to hide you. She says the best thing is for people to admit you were here but say you've gone. It has to be true, though. If gangers find they've been lied to . . . well. You know gangers."

He did know gangers. "That's reason for me to go," he said heavily. "Not you."

"If you're right about those walker things, I've got reason enough. I don't know why they want me, but it can't be for anything good or they wouldn't frighten me so. Besides, I cannot fulfill my prophecy here, and I will have no peace until I do!"

He set the dye pot to one side and cocked his head. "You've never told me exactly what the prophecy says."

She thought a moment. "Well, to start with, I'm not Farmwife Suttle's niece."

"I know that." He smiled. "I've known that all along."

She stared at her feet, somewhat disconcerted. Well, what difference did it make? If they were going away together, it was probably best he knew about her.

He disconcerted her further by saying:

"A long time ago you were brought here by an old man and a donkey. He took you over the hill to the archetypal village. The one over the hill, back there." He pointed back up the valley, toward the crest she had come over. "I met him the day I left home, met you then, too, and before that I used to climb up the trail over the mountains and look down at the village. What were you there? A Princess?"

"I was Orphan," she said, trying to remember him from that long-ago time. She'd been too little. She hadn't had enough words to remember him with. "Just Orphan."

He found it hard to believe, even though the walkers had asked for a parentless child, for she looked nothing like an Orphan. "Tell me your prophecy," he begged.

Olly quoted the prophecy expressionlessly, as though it held no meaning for her.

" 'Ask one only child,' " he quoted softly when she had finished. " 'Ask two who made her.' When I went off to the city, that's the question I had. Who made me? Who was my father? Ma would never tell me; she said I was safer so. So my father was a mystery to me, just as your folks are to you."

Abasio took up his dye pot once more. "If we went, we'd need a wagon, wouldn't we? I have a few golden sparrows."

"I have some money. Oracle gave me some before I left. We'd need a table for spreading fabric. Pots for the dyes. A stock of cotton or linen. Wilfer has extra copies of some of his recipe books. He said he'd sell them to me."

"We'd need a horse," said Abasio, stretching his shoulders.

"A horse," she agreed solemnly.

"But not yet?"

"No." She turned up her hands. "We don't know nearly enough yet to be believable as dyers. We'd be caught in a minute." She looked him squarely in the face, seeking something there, she wasn't sure what. "Besides. I haven't—I haven't decided I want to go with you. I haven't decided to go at all."


The three Survivors hired by Soniff to find Abasio were called Masher, Thrasher, and Crusher. Though originally from various gang backgrounds, they'd had many years as Survivors to give them experience at working together. Their habit of work was to have Thrasher do the thinking and planning while the other two provided the muscle.

"So which way did he go?" Masher asked, twirling the long hammer he customarily carried.

"Warlord says he headed north," Thrasher muttered in reply. He was a wiry individual with a long pigtail wound into a knot atop his otherwise bare head. He wore two whips at his belt, which he constantly patted, as though they were pets. "He may have gone north, and he may not. Best for you two to spend a day or two hunting him there while I make a few inquiries closer to home."

"What scars does he have?" asked Crusher, the largest and hairiest of them, who looked like a bear and up close smelled like one.

"The Warlord said one large knife scar on the left shoulder and a bullet pucker in the right calf."

"Tha's good enough," rumbled Crusher. "If he's there, we'll find him."

"Warlord says he'll take the hands as proof," muttered Thrasher. "We'll meet in two nights at Zelby tavern."

Zelby was one day's foot travel north of Fantis. Thrasher himself intended to make certain inquiries in the city. If Abasio had indeed gone on to the north, the delay of a few days in pursuing him would be of little importance. If, on the other hand, he had gone some other way, they would waste the least possible time looking in the wrong direction.

Thrasher soon learned of Abasio's association with Elrick-Ann. He waylaid her outside the baths and invited her to share a meal with a Survivor who had just won a bout and was celebrating. If Elrick-Ann had not been so lonely, she would probably have refused him, but the little lift she'd had from being given Abasio's place had leaked away. She missed him as her best and only friend, she missed the chatter and activities of Purple House. The offer of wine and talk and music was enough to draw her alongside Thrasher into a nearby songhouse.

Besides, she was wearing street veils, with only the good part of her face showing, and it had been a long time since anyone had asked for her company. This man didn't know what she really looked like, and she didn't intend he should find out.

They ate, and drank, and eventually she became garrulous, talking at great length about her friend Abasio.

"Where's he from?" asked Thrasher in a silky voice, sounding only interested, not at all threatening.

Elrick-Ann remembered her promise. "I don't know," she lied. "But he's smart, Basio is. Real smart. He knows all kinna things."

"What kind of things?"

"Oh, he knows—he knows how to do the writin' they do in the Edges." This was harmless enough, she thought. Besides, she had had a great deal of wine.

Thrasher thought deeply. There was a kind of writing done in the Edge that he himself could not read. If Abasio knew it, then perhaps he had come from there. If he had come from the Edge and had gone back there, the three Survivors hadn't a chance in hell of getting at him. It wouldn't even be worth trying.

It would be necessary to find out.

"Who recruited Abasio?" he asked Elrick-Ann.

"Bashy," she replied after a moment. "I remember it was old Bash. And ol' Lippy-Long."

Thrasher paid for the meal and the wine and left, leaving Elrick-Ann once more alone. He went to the Purple House and asked for Soniff, who was some time getting awake enough to talk. Soniff had been remarkably weary lately, and nasty-tempered when he was awake.

Thrasher asked, "You know that kind of writing they do in the Edge?"

"Script writing? Handwriting?" Soniff yawned, puzzled. He could read script. Old Chief could read it.

"They do that writing in farm country too?"

Soniff nodded. "They do handwriting mostly where they don't have screens. Us, we got the amusement screens, and they use printed words, like our tots learn."

"You have two men, Bashy and Lippy-Long?" Thrasher asked.

"Used to have," Soniff said. "Bashy's dead. Lippy-Long lives over near the North Bridge. He's an old man now."

Thrasher smiled his particularly deadly smile and went away again, not bothering to mention where he was going.

Lippy-Long was an old man, willing to tell anything he knew for a few mice. Yes, he remembered picking up Abasio as a stripling youth at a battery and weapons warehouse. Yes, he'd actually seen Abasio get out of the truck.

"Where had Abasio come from?"

Lippy-Long pulled his pendulous lower lip as he thought, tug, tug, tug, the eponymous feature bobbing and popping under these attentions. He didn't know, but it had been Barefoot Golly's truck. Everybody knew Golly! He could be found at a particular truckers' hostel, when he was in Fantis.

Which is where Thrasher found him. "We're trying to find a man named Abasio," he said. "You brought him to town. Where'd you pick the boy up?"

Barefoot had been drinking for some hours. He remembered Abasio vaguely, but then, over the years he'd picked up a lot of boys and it had been a long time ago. "I dunno," he confessed. "Somewhere out there, in the farms. I remember, he helped me get over a goblin trench."

Thrasher drank with him, trying to elicit something more, but Barefoot had told all he could remember.

When Thrasher met the other two Survivors, he heard their reports without surprise: No one north of Fantis had seen a solitary traveler meeting Abasio's description. No such traveler had stopped at any of the hostels. No such traveler had been seen by any of the truckers. Thrasher nodded to all this, smiling the while, then returned with his colleagues through the city and across the bridge, to begin again.

They would start their search in the farm country east of Fantis, where goblin depredations were most numerous, and if that bore no fruit, they would turn then to the south

Wilfer Ponde, the dyer, had an order for several dozen silk neckpieces and several yards of printed silk. Olly was delegated to make the dye and print them. The printed silk she might design as she would. The neckpieces were to have a single soft green border line with a design of green leaves and purple thistles in one corner.

"Who bought these?" she asked as she crushed handfuls of juniper berries with a pestle.

"The Clan of Wide Mountain in Artemisia," he said, nodding approval at her work. "The thistle is their crest. Make plenty of dye so the color will stay consistent. Take your time with the printing. Be patient."

"What is the Clan of Wide Mountain?" she asked.

"I believe it's their ruling house," he replied. "That's why they wear distinctive neckpieces, to identify people in authority."

"Is there a lot of trade across the borders?" she asked as she ground the pulp with warm water and strained the resultant liquid into another vessel.

He scratched his neck and thought about it. "Well, there's more than you might suspect. In the Edges they make amusement tapes and what they call components and different kinds of parts for all kinds of things. They print books there, too, and make some wonderful expensive kinds of machines. In Artemisia they raise sheep for meat, skins, and wool, and they raise food as well. The tribes of the east trade in lumber and charcoal, which is why they're called Timber Tribes, and the Ore Tribes bring in ores and coal and salvaged metals from the old cities. The people along the Faulty Sea are craftsmen and silk weavers, as well as traders in fish and other ocean produce. Around here the farms grow meat and vegetables and grain. Fruit comes from Low Mesiko, all year round. The truckers, they carry it all back and forth. What doesn't come by camel caravan from the west."

"And the cities?"

"These around here are the last few left. How they've kept going, I don't know. All they have to trade is slaves, and drugs, entertainments, and stolen stuff, and it mostly goes back and forth among themselves. The drugs and weapons have to come from somewhere, but I don't know where that is!"

Olly went back to her task. The picture did not add up properly. Something in Wilfer Ponde's account did not satisfy her. Where did the cities earn the money to buy food and fuel and clothing and the other necessities of life? There they sat, like great pools of honey, pulling in young folk like foolish flies from all the farms around, but what kept the cities going?

She had no time to worry over it. She was busy. She memorized formulae. She learned to recognize certain plants by the leaf and blossom, by stem and root, whether dried or fresh, and by the smell and taste of the powdered stuff as well. She filled a little notebook with the names of suppliers of fabrics and dyestuffs, who they were, how they could be found, what the materials cost. In olden times, so said Wilfer Ponde, there had been wonderful dyes made from chemicals that weren't available now. Red that glowed like gems. Greens as bright as meadows after rain. Pure blues, like the sky. There were no more such chemicals. Most colors now were paler, quieter, more earthy.

She learned all this. She taught it all to Abasio.


Cermit the farmer had words to say to his grandson.

"You think I'm a savage," Abasio shouted, when he'd heard them.

"I think you're a cityman," his grandfather retorted. "What I'm saying to you is simple. Olly is about twenty years old, a woman grown, but she has no experience of the world. Sometimes people think they know things because their minds know about them. They think they know sickness, they think they know danger, they think they know death. But they don't know it. In their gut they don't know it. Look back, boy! Did you know, when you ran off? Your head thought it knew, but inside you didn't know!''

Abasio couldn't deny it. It was true. He would have sworn he knew about IDDIs, but until he saw . . .

''It would be wrong for you to use her in the way you do women in the city, and Originee wants me to make sure you know that before she lets Olly go off with you.''

''Olly isn't that sure she wants to go,'' asserted Abasio, moved by some devil of perversity. ''Besides, we take care of our women in the city!''

His grandfather laughed harshly. ''Your ma told me all about the city, Abasio! You think she didn't know what goes on there?''

Abasio didn't answer. Lately it had been uncomfortable to think of his ma as a ganger's woman. It was impossible to think of Olly in that way.

The old man said softly, ''You're to pretend Olly is your sister. You're not to get her with child. And since you cannot be sure you are not infected with something, don't make her a gift of an IDDI, either.''

''I didn't intend to,'' Abasio said sulkily. It wasn't a lie. He hadn't intended, didn't intend to. Hell, he'd done virtually without for most of eighteen years, just so he didn't catch an IDDI himself! But he didn't like being told not to, either. As if he were still some kid, some brat at home, with Grandpa making the rules.

''It would be dishonorable,'' his grandpa said, not even looking at him. ''Not only dishonorable, but uncivilized.''

The old man hobbled out the door, leaving Abasio to steam alone. Gangers counted coup on women. How many cuckles in one hour, in one night, in one week. It had been a thing Abasio had had to avoid, getting into any coup rivalry of that kind. He himself had known it was silly and damned dangerous, but he'd never thought of it as dishonorable.

He complained to Olly about Grandpa's attitude, finding too late that she agreed with the old man.

''Burned Man told me that women are treated dishonorably in the cities,'' she said unequivocally. ''Everyone in my village would consider it so except Bastard, and Bastard could be one of you citymen himself.''

''But in the gangs, getting a woman pregnant is a good thing!'' asserted Abasio. ''To make the gang stronger. To make it grow.''

''Is that a fact?'' she said. ''They must be very strong, then.''

Possibly they were numerous, she thought, though according to Burned

Man they died young. She did not think of them as strong. Burned Man had not spoken of them as strong, merely as willful.

Except with his ma, who had mostly talked at him, Abasio had never conversed with a woman except as gangers did, to tease or to give them orders. Actual conversation was troubling, and he wouldn't have done it with anyone but Olly. Even with her, he tried the more familiar patterns of teasing and flirting and bragging, only to find that phrases meant to sound seductive came across as ugly and unenticing, the meaning muddy and uncertain, even to him.

"You're talking and talking," said Olly, angrily. "Words come out of your mouth like water out of a pump, all gush and splash, but you're not really thinking about me and you."

"How can you say that?" he'd demanded.

How could she say it? She simply knew it. It was part of the pattern of his life, and she could see that pattern as clearly as she was beginning to see the patterns dye blocks would make, one thing leading to another, certain as sunrise. Things she had been told. Things she had seen. And this man saying words he knew too well.

She spoke softly. "Listen, Abasio. I don't know who I am. I don't know anything about me. Do you know anything about me that I don't know?"

He didn't.

"What I'm saying is this: You see two frogs mating, do you think they love each other?"

He stared, not answering.

She went on doggedly. "Or if it was two people, but one of them was drugged unconscious? Seems to me, the only way people can make love with each other is if they both know who they are and who the other one is! Otherwise it's just the bodies coupling, like two frogs! And I can't respond to your words, because I don't know who I am yet, even if you do know who you are, which I doubt!"

"Suppose I do know you better than you do?"

Oracle had told her about that one. "You know more about sex than I do. According to Oracle all women have a hen-crouch part, so you know more about that part than I do. Burned Man told me how ganger men make up these struts and crows, and cock-a-doodle back and forth, just like a rooster showing off his feathers to get the hens to crouch for him. Doesn't matter to the rooster which hen he jumps! Hens are interchangeable, like socks: Wear out one, put on another. If she won't crouch, peck her until she's bloody. Rooster doesn't care what the chicken thinks! Rooster doesn't care *if* the chicken thinks.

"Sure, I've got a hen-crouch part, just like any other female, but that's biology, not brains. Which is why you gangers are breeding down and breeding down. Burned Man says you men have a saying about quick cuckle: When a man's in a hurry, there's nothing like quick cuckle. So you take the women who spread their legs quickest, they're the ones with the least brains, and every generation of you is dumber than the last!'' Burned Man would never have used those words to her, but then, he had never been as angry as she was now! She yearned toward this stupid, stupid man, and all he did was cock-a-doodle!

''I'm not just crowing! I mean what I say to you,'' he said, matching her anger with heat of his own.

She turned her back on him, tears in her eyes. ''Well if you do, the more shame you, for it's nothing but cock-crow, Abasio. Nothing but habit. You're not talking to me any different than you'd talk to any other chicken!''

She left him there and went back to Wise Rocks Farm. He didn't see her again for days.

And she was right. His talk had been only habit. Now. But when he had seen her first, he'd been on fire, wanting her, Olly, separate and distinct from all other women. He wanted . . . he wanted . . . he didn't know what he wanted!

He lay abed, summoning sexual fantasies that plodded flaccidly to no perceivable conclusion. He snorted and bellowed around the house, trying to stir himself.

''What's the matter with you?'' old Cermit asked. ''You're acting like a ram-lamb with a burr up his tail.''

''I'm afraid that drug has . . . altered me,'' Abasio said, using the phrase his grandpa had used when he spoke of gilts and steers. ''I can't—that is, I don't—''

''Wouldn't that be interesting,'' said the old man reflectively, without the least tone of sympathy.

''Damn it, Grandpa!''

''Shh. I doubt you're permanently altered. That would be too much to hope for!''

''You'd like that, wouldn't you!''

''It would be one way of keeping you out of trouble and alive. Possibly.''

The old man looked after him with a troubled frown when Abasio turned and stalked away. Some men, in this age of IDDIs, took a knife to themselves to stay out of trouble and alive. Others said they would rather die, and did. Among the farms, betrothal of infants was coming back, with marriage taking place as soon as boy and girl were sexually mature, or even before. Cermit had no idea how Abasio had avoided infection all those years in the city. Or if he had. Because he didn't know, and because Abasio wouldn't tell him, he gave the boy less credit than he deserved.

• • •

Came a morning there was ice on the horse trough, ice in the chickens' watering can, and over the hoarfrost on the lane came Originee on hurried horseback, looking distraught as she called to Cermit and Abasio.

"I've just come down from the Chyne Farm. Farmwife Chyne was weeks late about it, and the child was born dead."

"Ah, that's sad news," said Cermit, brow furrowed at her expression.

"It was those walkers that did it. They touched her. She says the baby stopped moving the moment they touched her and never moved again." Farmwife Suttle wiped her eyes. "And Farmwife Chyne was not unscathed. She shivers and cries and worries over Olly, for the walkers were seeking the girl. Farmwife Chyne knew who they were after, even at the time."

"Ah," grunted Cermit, distressed but unsurprised.

"They asked for a certain girl. Farmwife Chyne told them she'd seen such a girl and had directed her toward the city. Abasio said they were seeking in the city, and that was sometime ago. Now we know they are not looking at random. They are following a particular trail. When they don't find Olly in the city, they may well backtrack here. They'll return, I fear, and it could be soon."

"Time then," said the old man heavily. He had grown accustomed to having Abasio about the place, and even though they argued constantly, he did not want his grandson to go.

"Time for Olly," she agreed. "Which means time for them both. I should get back to Chyne Farm, but someone must go to Whitherby to fetch the girl."

"I'll go," said Cermit, and he turned purposefully toward the barn.

So Olly was fetched, she and the angel, with barely time to say good-bye to the dyer and pick up the books and supplies she had bought from him. She fretted, sure of her decision to go, but troubled by this haste, barely able to keep herself from howling. Now that the time had come she felt as much fear as anticipation.

"Take these," Wilfer told her, offering a neat bundle. "It's the neckcloths for the women of Wide Mountain in Artemisia, also the printed silk you did. It's for a Fashimir Ander, and he ordered through the Artemisians. He's ordered from us before. In case you need one, the bundle gives you a reason for traveling south."

She took the bundle, put herself together enough to remember to thank him, and perched herself on the wagon seat next to old Cermit, forcing herself to breathe calmly and not show her agitation. They started down the village street toward the outskirts but had scarcely arrived there when three men came striding from behind a fence to catch the horse's harness and stop the wagon. The man who held the horse was huge; the other two were fierce; and Olly's heart rose into her throat in fear that these were the ones looking for her!

But no. They were not dressed as Abasio had described the walkers, or as she had seen the oddmen in the village. She made herself stop trembling.

"A moment," said one, a man with a hammer at his belt. "We're looking for a man!"

"Ayeh?" said Cermit, letting his jaw drop open. "What you want with me?"

"Not you, old socks," laughed the smallest of the three, a man with whips at his belt. "A young man. Black brows, dark skin, purple tattoos on both hands. A knife scar on one shoulder, a bullet pucker in one calf. Seen him or anybody could be him?"

"I hardly ever come to town," old Cermit whined. "I hardly see anybody. Most folks travelin' through, they don't even come into Whitherby. They stay over 'long the highway."

"How 'bout you, girly?" the man asked, laying a heavy hand on Olly's thigh.

They were not looking for her, but she felt no relief. How could she distract them from Abasio? Could they know old Cermit was Abasio's kin? "There were some strange young men in the village yesterday," she said in a frightened voice. "I saw them down by the tavern."

"Up close?"

She shook her head, mumbling from a dry mouth. "I was in the loft at the dyer's when I saw them."

"We'll ask around," said the whip carrier, stepping back.

Olly sat as though paralyzed. Cermit nodded and clucked to the horse.

"It's Abasio they're after!" she cried, when they had gone far enough not to be overheard. "Cermit, they're after Abasio!"

Cermit nodded heavily. The three were gangers, pure and simple, and there was no doubt at all they wanted Abasio. He put his hand on the girl's hand and drove for a time in silence, letting Olly swallow her fright and breathe normally once more.

Then he murmured: "Doesn't really matter whether it's you or him they're after. You've both got to go quickly." He gave her a look intended to be comforting, though he could not keep his distress from showing. "Abasio and I haven't been idle. We've made a house-wagon ready, such as itinerant craftsmen travel in. We've worked on it in the barn, secretlike, where no one would hear or see and wonder. Originee's used your coin to buy all the stuff you need, here and there, a bit at a time, so as to start no talk."

"We'll need dye pots," mumbled Olly, as full of panic at the idea of leaving as she was full of fear at staying.

Cermit went on implacably. "She got you pots, both for dyeing and for cooking. She laid in a stock of woven cloth. I've added some bits and pieces I think you'll need." He patted her clumsily.

Orphan nodded, her teeth clenched. She wanted to go but she wasn't ready to go. Nonetheless, the threat was imminent and she was not a fool, to balk at necessity. She could spare no time questioning who or what the oddmen were, or why she was being hunted. Or why Abasio was being hunted, for that matter. He who had talked about everything else had been strangely reluctant to share this with her.

"Where will we get a horse?" she asked.

"You have a horse. Big Blue. Abasio says he dreamed of riding away on Big Blue. Seems like it was meant to be."

It was late afternoon when they arrived back at the farm. The little time before dusk was spent in packing and collecting things together, and when dark came, Big Blue was hitched to the new wagon and driven out of the barn. They were ready except for filling the water barrel mounted on the back.

At the last moment, Originee came riding down from the Chyne place to say farewell. She muttered her dismay when she learned there were searchers hunting Abasio as well, but she spent no time lamenting. Instead, she made a final tally of what the wagon carried, assuring herself the two young people could live in reasonable comfort. Olly's belongings were few, and during his struggle to get home, Abasio had lost everything he'd brought from Fantis except his weapons and his money. The wagon held everything they had and all that had been provided for them; nothing was to be left behind.

"It was meant to be," Ori whispered to old Cermit as she closed the wagon door and folded the steps against the side for the last time. "Meant for them to go together."

"Could be." The old man sighed. "But I fear for them both."

Olly did not hear this exchange, which was just as well, for she was quite fearful enough already and was holding herself carefully quiet for fear she would start crying. Despite her fear, what troubled her most was her feeling of leaving friends, of being uprooted and lost.

As she turned from the well with a last bucketful of water for the water barrel on the back of the wagon, she saw on Abasio's face the same expression she could feel on her own.

"You don't feel ready to go, either," she whispered to him, tears running freely from her eyes.

He shook his head. "If it weren't for them—for the danger to them, to you—"

She nodded. "At least you know why somebody's after you. I haven't any idea why they're coming after me. Or who."

He tried a fairly successful grin. "If it makes you feel any better, Olly, I can swear it's no comfort to know why."

"What am I to call you?" she cried. "You can't go on being Abasio."

He hadn't thought about it. He turned to the Farmwife, asking, "What's my name, Farmwife Suttle? You named Olly, now you should name me."

"Samson," she said without a moment's pause. "He was in an old story my ma told me. All I remember about him was he got strong when his hair grew out. So you'll need to do."

Cermit stopped in his tracks. He knew the tale. Destruction had followed debasement in that story, and he did not consider it a good omen.

Unwitting of this, Abasio ran his blue fingers across the bristles on his head. Perhaps he would grow strong. Perhaps he would even be strong enough to keep them both safe.

"Samson," he said, with a wry twist to his lips. "Sammy?"

"No, Sonny," said Olly with a fairly successful chuckle. "Sonny Longaster. Burned Man told me the kind of names gangers favor. No gang member would ever be called Sonny Longaster."

They made their farewells, then Olly crawled across the wagon seat to hide herself and the angel inside the lower box bed in the wagon while Abasio drove them away. Cermit's instructions had been clear as to which back roads would keep the wagon well away from Whitherby. The lurching and rocking of the house-wagon lulled Olly to sleep almost before they reached the bottom of the valley, though the angel sat wakeful upon the slowly swinging door of the box bed, talking quietly to itself.


In Fantis the Old Chief, his thirst for vengeance only whetted by sending assassins after Abasio, had put certain other inquiries into motion. All rumors had branches and twigs that had to be followed back to the main trunk, and it took some days before his people found the doctor. Once they had the doctor, however, they had Nelda within the hour.

"You can tell me now," the Old Chief whispered to her. "Or you can tell me when you're half-dead. I don't care either way."

Nelda, on her knees before the Old Chief, held by two strong men and driven by absolute terror, shouted the first thing that came into her head.

"He was your son! Just as much as that other one is! More. More your son!"

Silence. The two men who were holding Nelda looked at each other in confusion. The Old Chief sat back, his mouth fallen slightly open.

"He *is* your son," Nelda asserted again. "You think I don't recognize your get when I see it? Abasio's just like you were at his age. He's got your forehead, your eyes, everything like you. Bigger and handsomer than either of your sons who died, and he's yours!''

"How old?" asked the Old Chief after a long silence.

"Over thirty," she said. "And it was that long ago you sold me, Old Chief, because all my babies miscarried, and you found you a new concubine you liked better. Remember her? The tall, slender one? From somewhere else, she was. You told me she'd never used drugs. You told me she'd never been sick, so she'd have healthy babies. And didn't I hear she ran off first time she was pregnant?"

The Old Chief's mouth shut with an almost audible snap. There had indeed been a conk who'd run off from him. He'd never forgotten her. Elisa. Young—only fifteen or so. Strong and healthy. She'd been hysterical when he'd first taken possession of her, but after he'd disciplined her a few times, she'd turned quiet. She got pregnant and after a time seemed reconciled. He thought she'd settled down. She went to the clothiers one day and was not seen again. Somehow lost herself and was never found, was presumed dead.

"She died," he sneered. "Otherwise I'da found her. She had noplace in this town to go!"

"Not if she got clean away from this town. Not if she was a farm girl, with someplace else to go. And she was, Old Chief. She was. When that Abasio was all drugged up, he talked about the farm country. Talked about his ma. Talked about riding, riding, going somewhere in the country."

Silence again. Greatly daring, Nelda decided to press her momentary advantage. "So when that Sybbis comes to me, I think, what the Old Chief wants is a good grandson. And here's his own son, his own blood, his own lineage, even his own gang to pass it on. To do what maybe—somebody else can't do."

"Take her away," said the Old Chief. "Put her somewhere. Put her with the doctor. Don't hurt her yet."

It was a reprieve, for the moment.

The Old Chief sent for Soniff. Soniff, who reported eagerly that the assassins were on their way.

"Get them back," the Old Chief commanded.

Soniff gulped. "Back?"

"This Abasio. He's my boy."

# CHAPTER 9

*A*basio and Olly drove southward along the eastern edge of the mountains, the undulating flatness of Long Plain to their left and the promise of Artemisia somewhere ahead of them. Grandpa Cermit had told them if they followed the ruts they were on, avoiding all side roads, they would eventually come to a wooded pass through the mountains. Then would come desert, and finally Artemisia and the library. Grandpa hadn't been there himself, but so he had been told, so he had read. All they had to do was follow the trail they were on.

They had not done so for half a day before Abasio gave Olly a nickname: Whazzat.

''What's that?'' she would ask, staring from the wagon seat at some marvel she had never seen before.

''A bird,'' he would answer wearily, for the dozenth time.

''But what kind of bird?'' she cried, wanting to know its name and antecedents and whether it nested here or merely visited on its way somewhere else.

Abasio had to confess he did not know. "It isn't a bird I ever saw when I was a boy," he told her, no matter what bird it was. Truth to tell, unlike Olly, he had not paid that much attention to animals or birds. He had been more interested in stories, in tales of adventure, in epics and sagas and heroics. Though he was now becoming interested in them, at the time animals and birds had not seemed adventuresome.

He said, "There are no birds much in the cities except crows on the garbage, and pigeons, and little brown sparrows. I've never seen that little gray and yellow"—or black and white, or red and brown—"one before."

Nor had she. Crows she knew, and magpies and jays, and several kinds of ducks that had visited the pool in the village. Herons she knew, for they had waded among the reeds, hunting frogs and talking together in guttural voices. Owls she had heard but seldom seen, and hawks she had both seen and heard, crying from the top of the sky. But she had never seen all these other birds before.

The farther from the cities they went, with even the farms becoming more and more lonely and scattered, the more birds there were. Olly gave up asking what they were and went to naming them instead, this and that kind of warbler, this and that kind of long-legs, this and that kind of duck or owl or hawk. She was up to forty kinds before she realized some were the females and some the males of the same kinds but quite different colors and patterns. She tore up her list and started over again, making little drawings of them in the book Farmwife Suttle had given her. Later, she might use them in designs. Her head was full of ideas for designs. She was beginning to think of herself not only as a dyer but as a designer as well.

From across a valley they spied a large furriness shaking the oak brush and rearing up on its hind legs to pull the ripe fruit from an old apple tree on an abandoned farm. At first they thought it was a monster, an ogre or a young troll, but such monsters didn't eat apples. "Bear, I think," said Abasio, remembering stories his grandfather had told.

"I thought bear were mostly gone," whispered Olly, awed by the size and shape of the distant creature, like a fat man wearing a fur coat, walking on its hind legs almost like a person, like the three bears in her childhood story, like Bear in Oracle's stories, vehement and fearsome.

"I thought they were gone too," Abasio agreed. "Still, I think that thing is a bear."

They saw creatures like deer but as big as cows, with wide racks of antler, standing at the edge of meadows in the morning mist, bugling their challenges into the forests. They saw speckled fish that flickered into visibility along the bottoms of clear streams, then vanished as though made of smoke. Abasio grunted when he saw them, remembering certain lessons Grandpa had taught

him. The next day, he manufactured a rod and line and caught several silvery
flappers for their supper.

Hills appeared on the horizon east of them, growing nearer and taller day
by day. The ground began to rise. The leaves of the shivering white-trunked
trees upon the heights gleamed palely gold among the dark pines. The nights
were chill. One morning snow covered the high blue peaks, and that day
the ruts went around a rocky corner and lost themselves among trees. From
that time on they were traveling in the forest instead of alongside it, seeing
only pale slits of bright sky among the branches. The ground went on rising,
more steeply now. To save Big Blue, they got out and walked, plodding up
each slope and down into each little glade, each rise taking them higher than
the last.

More than once they saw small eldritch shapes moving among the roots
and heard gnomish laughter in the night. At Abasio's suggestion, they set
out pan bread and found it gone each morning, though they could not tell
whether it had been taken by gnomes or goblins or raccoons. Olly met
raccoons, with mixed laughter and curses, when a tribe of them invaded the
wagon. Abasio knew raccoons from his childhood, and he chased them out
with the broom.

Returning from this chase he collided with Olly in the doorway of the
wagon and found his arms tight around her. He did not move, and for a
wonder, nor did she. Her body rested against him like a young willow, supple
yet strong, and for a long moment they stood together, thinking nothing,
deciding nothing, merely letting themselves be together. Had the mother
coon not returned, intent upon finding supper for her brood, they might have
remained lost in their wondrous contentment forever, but the mood was
broken. Scarlet-faced, Olly returned to her usual arm's-length behavior.

As they moved higher, a leaping streamlet came down from the heights
to meet them, growing narrower the farther up they went. At last its waning
trickle disappeared westward, toward higher ground yet, and an hour later
they were upon the promised pass, looking out over distant, misty horizons.
Now they went down through the trees.

Two days later, the tall pines became scattered, then sparse, and they
came out onto a short-grassed, arid prairie, its rounded hills and square-
edged mesas dotted with stout little cone-bearing trees and blue-green plumes
of sage. Even though the forests they had come through could have hidden
whole tribes of monsters in their shady depths, Abasio and Olly had felt
more secure there than they did on these brushlands. In the forest there had
been fringed branches and gnarled trunks reflecting the warm glow of their
fire, making a roomlike space with a comforting illusion of walls. Here was
only the empty darkness going all the way to the stars in every direction,
soaking up their little puddle of firelight like a thirsty black sponge.

Also, the forest had been populated with sounds of bird and beast and wind, a comforting mixture of natural and animal noises, but the desert was quiet, so quiet that sometimes Abasio brought the wagon to a halt and cocked his head, listening for whatever it was that had put an end to all other sound. Several times in the night they awoke to a distant clamor, confused and indistinct, only loud enough to ruin their rest without coming close enough to be truly threatening.

The farther they went into the desert country, the more apprehensive they became. Abasio said several times he wished they had a dog to scent danger and warn them of it. And eventually it was dogs of the coyote persuasion who did warn them with a frenzy of yipping and howling back along their trail.

They had stopped the wagon at the top of a rise where they had a good view of the surrounding country. It was shortly before sunset. Abasio, who had just unharnessed Big Blue, stood with the harness over his shoulder, peering back the way they had come. "I don't like the sound of that," he said.

Olly, busy lighting the evening cookfire, didn't like it, either. There was something almost hysterical about the noise, a wild, uncontrolled howling and yipping.

Abasio hung the harness across the seat and climbed atop the wagon. Olly went up beside him like a squirrel up a tree, and the two of them stared northward. Of the two of them, Olly's eyes were sharpest, and she saw movement first.

"There," she breathed, pointing.

Abasio at first saw nothing, then saw entirely too much. Two shambling forms. Larger than men, walking not on all fours but more or less erect. Long arms. Heads that seemed to jut directly from the shoulders, with no necks. Around them, leaping shapes that kept just out of reach of those arms. Coyotes, teasing.

The monsters were following the two ruts the wagon had traveled, following those ruts, or the tracks of the wheels, or the scent of the horse, or the smell of the two humans. The fact that Abasio could see them at all meant they were too close for safety.

"What shall we do?" Olly whispered.

Abasio made a quick turn, looking in all directions. The wagon wouldn't offer much protection. Ogre talons could rip through a two-inch board in a matter of minutes. On the other hand, the wagon might keep the monsters occupied for a while. Concealment would be an appropriate action, but this open ground offered no hiding place.

"Close up the wagon," he directed, leaping down from the wagon roof. "Leave the fire to attract them here. I see hills east of us, and we may be able to hide there. We'll ride Big Blue."

Abasio rode as he had when he was a boy, bareback, clutching the horse's mane; Olly, with the angel on her shoulder, clung to him from behind. The sun set behind them as Big Blue plodded quietly off into the dusk. The first stars gleamed in the eastern sky, and Abasio took note of those on the broken horizon. It would be dark soon. They might need something to steer by.

Behind them, the howling and yipping came nearer, moving along the ruts they had traveled in the wagon. Ogres hunted by sight, scent, and sound, so much everyone knew. Country people knew ogres were attracted to fire, though they could not make fires of their own and had to steal it when they could, sometimes setting forests or grasslands alight as a result. They habitually hunted in the dark. They had huge, night-seeing eyes and did not come from their lairs until near dusk.

Before darkness settled completely, Abasio urged Big Blue into a clumsy canter, clinging for dear life, finally slowing to a walk again when it became too dark to see. Abasio stroked the horse's neck with a peculiar sense of having lived this scene before. Then he realized he had dreamed it. This was the dark, the quiet progress, the same horse. He lay quietly along Big Blue's back, feeling Olly's body tight against his, willing the monsters to content themselves with the wagon, with the fire.

The sounds behind them continued unabated, becoming even more tumultuous, as though a whole pack of coyotes were following or chasing or being chased by the creatures. Abasio felt for his weapons, finding them both hooked securely to his belt. He doubted they'd be very useful. He was short on ammunition for both the missile gun and the flame shooter. He could cause some damage up close and as a last resort, but if an ogre got that close, it would be a last resort. For him and Olly both.

As they came to the slope of the nearest hill, they heard a screaming roar, a huge and furious sound as of a creature hurt past endurance.

"Our fire burned down, and something stepped on it," muttered Abasio. "I'll bet you anything."

The deafening sound came again. Big Blue swerved to the left, to avoid something only he could see. Abasio got down to examine the terrain as best he could in the darkness. There was only deep blackness and deeper blacknesses, with little to tell which was traversable, which might be safe and which not.

"This way," piped the guardian-angel. "This way."

Big Blue stepped forward as though in response to this invitation. Startled, Olly clung to his back and Abasio to his tail.

"Does your angel know what it's saying?" Abasio asked in a baffled mutter.

"Sometimes it seems to," she admitted. "It found a path for me when I left the village."

If their progress was any indication, the angel had found a way again, for they were moving steadily, curving to the south, as Big Blue picked his way among tumbled stones along some invisible but rising path.

"Through here," called the angel. "Here, here!"

They bumped between stony prominences, the path narrowing, then opening once more.

"Here," whispered the guardian-angel. "Stay here."

Big Blue dropped his head and stood absolutely still, only his skin quivering as though bitten by invisible flies. Olly slid from his back, whispering, "Where are we?"

"I don't know," Abasio answered. "Just a sort of stony place. Look. The moon's rising."

The moon, almost full, shouldered its way above a line of cloud, illuminating the place they stood. They had come from the north, up a winding and hidden path, into an east-facing hollow scooped from a rocky hillside. At either side of the hollow, stony pillars cast ebon shadows; at its lip a scatter of boulders hid them from the moonlit place below; and there, ominous figures stood silently black against the silvered soil.

At the sight of them, Abasio and Olly instinctively leaned toward each other before freezing into immobility. Even in the inadequate light the figures were unmistakable: the stance, the curled helmets, the uncanny silence—all spelled walkers. Their motionless figures were turned slightly northward, toward the wild cacophony that flowed past the hill.

The tumult grew louder, finally surging around the foot of the slope Olly and Abasio had climbed, and onto the plain where the walkers stood.

"Shhh," hissed the guardian-angel, almost soundlessly.

Hunchbacked and hairy, the ogres shambled into the open, huge hands curled, knuckles resting on the ground, heads lowered between those hands, long torsos bent forward on short legs as they sniffed the earth. It was Big Blue's trail they had been tracking—or trying to—for the ring of coyotes that circled them had disturbed the scent.

Olly let herself sag against Abasio, gripping his arm in panic. "What?" she whispered, a mere breath. "What are they?"

"Ogres," he murmured in return, pulling her tight against him, his mouth next to her ear. "Big ones!" Oh, yes, they were big ones. The kind that had populated his nightmares as a child. He had seen young ones before, though rarely, but never any this size or this close. If they could stand erect, they would be twice the height of a man. They would be taller yet if their heads did not thrust so necklessly forward from their woolly chests.

They roared in frustration, clutching at the circling coyotes with their taloned hands. Abasio knew that no weapon he carried, nothing he could do would cause either the ogres or the walkers any but the slightest discomfort or delay. Only something as fleet-footed as the present tormentors would even try.

The coyotes did more than merely try. They leaped and scuttered, twenty or more of them, nipping a hairy ankle, jumping away, coming teasingly close, then darting away, tempting the enormous creatures farther from the scent trail.

Where the whole cacophonous coyote-ogre circus froze into silence, suddenly aware it was not alone.

Abasio and Olly heard the icy walker voice as clearly as if it had spoken only an arm's length away.

*"Go away. We are not your prey. Go away."*

The ogres roared, pounded their chests with clenched fists, waved their great paws aloft, and roared again.

*"Go away."*

The ogres did not go away. They plunged forward, huge arms grappling, closing the distance.

Olly buried her head in Abasio's chest. He saw a spurt of flame, heard a burst of horrid sound. One of the coyotes yipped in pain and scrambled away from the conflict along with the other doggy forms, all leaping and tumbling, head over tails, leaving behind them a towering cloud of dust, silver and gray and black, rising and roiling in the moonlight, growing into a wide pillar that hid the monstrous struggle that had been joined.

Abasio pulled Olly with him as he edged farther into shadow. He couldn't see what was happening. The dust was so thick, he could see only the tumbling cloud, silvered by the moon. The hideous sounds went on: roarings, howlings, shrieks that sounded more mechanical than fleshy; great poundings that made the earth shudder beneath them. Abasio and Olly clung together, both of them terrified at the certainty that, when the battle was over, any surviving monster would find them and finish what the ogres had set out to do.

The sound did not stop all at once. It faded very slowly into a stillness punctuated by occasional howls and roars by a single voice. Out of the dust, one of the ogres emerged to bellow at the moon. *Araungh!* Then again: *Araungh!* As the echoes died, it stared up the hill, its piggish snout moving as it sniffed.

Abasio threw his head back, trying not to breathe. It did no good. The wind was from behind them! The monster was coming in their direction, lifting one hand to strike itself on the chest with every other step: thwomp, then a step, then thwomp, like the slow beat of a drum.

Abasio fumbled for his weapons. Olly caught at his arm, stopping him. She was looking up, listening, hearing what he had heard without realizing it was not part of the continuing struggle, a huge hawk cry, a shriek, a descending scream that ended on the edge of the hollow before them in a great flurry of widely spread wings that extended before them like a ribbed screen. Beyond those wings the ogre made a sound of baffled fury.

The wings beat down, lifted, dived toward the shambling figure, which turned with its huge hands over its head and ran away toward the east, uttering a guttural cough that could have been a summons to others of its kind or the cry of a creature wounded. The wings rose and dropped again. The ogre increased its speed.

Abasio and Olly stayed quiet. Words came from the sky above them, each distinct, falling on their ears like separate blows, soft but clear:

"I remember!"

"Who?" whispered Abasio. "Who remembers what?"

"I don't know," said Olly, staring into the sky. "Or—or maybe I do. I met a griffin once. I think. Though up until now, I'd thought maybe I'd dreamed it." She gazed, mouth open. Had her encounter with the griffin been true? Well, why not? Other, equally unlikely things had been true. Were true.

The ogre's cough receded into the east. The dust settled. Whatever had flown to their rescue was now gone. They moved to the edge of their hollow, far enough to see several dark blotches on the battleground below. Bodies, perhaps. Or body parts. They watched long enough to be sure there was no movement. Neither of them wanted to go any closer.

As though in agreement with this sentiment, the coyotes began to yip and howl once more, emerging from folds in the ground and gathering in a dance of leaping, tumbling forms that flowed back toward the west, taking their yip-yowl music with them. The last member of this departing troupe stopped in its tracks, turned toward them, nose in air, and howled a farewell that sounded suspiciously like laughter.

"They knew we were here," said Olly, wonderingly. "The coyotes. But did the others know? Before that last one smelled us?"

"They knew," whispered Abasio, certain of it. "One set was waiting for us, the other set was following us. They just didn't get a chance to do anything about it."

The angel whistled softly and flew to the pillars at their left, where Big Blue remained hidden in shadow. Abasio and Olly scrambled atop the horse and went back the way they had come, down the twisting path to the north, then around the hill and westward once more, lit by the moon. When they arrived at the wagon, they circled it once from a distance, seeing it was as they had left it except for deep parallel grooves down the wagon door. The assault on the wagon had evidently been interrupted when at least one of the monsters had trodden upon the fire, for there were ashy footprints on every side together with a lingering ogre-stink of rot and filth.

Without even discussing it, Abasio harnessed Big Blue to the wagon, and they drove on southward until they had put a good distance between them and their previous campsite. They had no illusions of safety. If another ogre was looking for them, if the surviving one came back, they could be found by their smell, by the impressions left by the wheels, even by the sound of the wagon as it creaked through the darkness. None of that mattered as much as getting away from where those tracks were, where that stench was, where the terrible monsters had been.

The border of Artemisia, when the wagon reached it at last, was marked by signs printed in several languages, a widely spaced line of them stretching into the distance on either side. The signs forbade unauthorized entry. The highway, which they had not seen for a while, now appeared east of them, gleaming under the late-day sun of autumn, and they could make out a considerable gate standing athwart the pavement with a line of vehicles inching past it, smoking mechanical trucks and vans as well as horse-drawn wagons.

No barrier prevented their crossing in the same two ruts they had followed for days, ruts that ran past the signs and thence southward across endless vistas of dried tufty grass interrupted by thorny growths and feathery yellow puffs of rabbit brush. Olly had been in and out of the wagon all day, gathering the blooms for the golden-yellow dye they produced.

"Now what?" she asked over the armful of flowers she was tucking into a knotted string bag. "What do we do now, Sonny?"

He had said the name pinched him like new boots, so she used it every now and then, getting it broken in, she told him, against a time of need, often watching him as she did now to see his reaction.

There was no reaction. He merely braked the wagon and sat silently as he examined the surroundings. South of them was mostly flat, pinkish desert, dotted with dark balloons of piñon and juniper, gray brushes of sage and chamisa. Dropping the reins, Abasio climbed to the roof of the wagon, where he turned to make a full-circle examination of their surroundings. West were carved buttes and long rock-rimmed, tree-splotched diagonals thrusting toward towering clouds scudding along on their flat gray bottoms. Beyond the crenellated tablelands, indigo mountains lay in rumpled heaps, like dropped laundry, in some places rising into snow-capped peaks. Eastward was desert, and highway, and gate. In that direction the view had changed slightly, and he pointed with an outstretched arm.

"Somebody," he said.

"Somebody coming, galope, galope," murmured the guardian-angel from its customary position at the front of the wagon. Cermit had indulged himself with a bit of fancy work on the shutters behind the wagon seat, and the angel found the carved oak leaves an ideal perch.

Olly looked up, startled.

"Where?" she demanded.

Her companion pointed again toward the east, where a wobbly blot could be discerned moving toward them. At this distance, all they could really see was the scurrying motion of multiple legs and a minuscule increase in size. The rider appeared to be a large bird.

"Whoever it is, they're coming from the direction of the guard post," said Abasio. "Probably someone official. We might as well wait." He draped the reins over the wagon seat and climbed down to join Olly on the ground. Big Blue heaved a sigh that made the harness creak and dragged the braked wheels forward until he was within reach of the tuft of green he'd been eyeing.

Olly stuffed the last of her clipped blossoms into the bag and hung it among others on the wagon's side as she climbed into the wagon through the side door.

The rear of the inside space was taken up with the two box beds, set at right angles, one above the foot of the other, with drawers beneath for clothing and blankets. On either side of the box beds, capacious cupboards held their equipment and supplies, and at the front of the wagon was a comfortably padded bench with shutters opening behind the driver's seat, allowing them to drive the wagon from inside when the weather was bad. Reefed tight to the wagon side was an awning with side curtains that could be drawn out to make a shelter for Big Blue or an open sided tent for cooking in wet weather, and hung on the same side was the fire grill, made to order by the smith in Whitherby, its legs folded flat. A rack on the roof held more bulky items including the dye table and the large dye pots, nested one inside another.

At Olly's suggestion, Abasio had hung a stout basket on the wagon side, and any chunks of firewood encountered along the way were tossed into it. Now Olly got out the teakettle, filled it from the water barrel at the back of the wagon, unhooked the grill from the door, and set about building a fire from the contents of her woodbasket, all with much practiced economy of motion. If they were to receive a civilized visitor, they should at least offer tea, and by this time they both knew that her fires were better than Abasio's. He seemed incapable of building one that didn't smoke.

The kettle was steaming by the time the rider came near enough for them to identify him as a much-befeathered person. The horse slowed as it approached, ears forward, looking with interest at Big Blue. The rider pulled it to a halt and leaped from his large, much-ornamented saddle to stride gracefully toward them, a tasseled and bell-dangled lance in one hand, tall headdress and plumed shoulders nodding with every step.

Abasio stood up politely from where he'd been sitting beside the fire and held out his hands, palms up. Olly remained seated while duplicating the gesture. Though the fancy being before them merited more than a casual glance, they were careful not to stare.

He said something in a deep orator's voice, raising the lance and shaking it so the bells rang wildly.

They shook their heads gently, hands out and empty, indicating that they could catch no meaning from what he said.

"Would you share tea?" asked Olly, holding up a cup.

The visitor heaved a dramatic sigh, shook his lance into a frenzied jangle once more, and asked, "Who are you and what are you doing here?"

Olly bowed from where she sat by the fire. "We are Olly and Sonny Longaster, dyers, hoping to travel through Artemisia."

"What business have you there?" he demanded, scowling with unbelievable ferocity, an expression no doubt chosen to accord with the painted frown lines on his face.

"An order of printed silk neckcloths to deliver to the Clan of Wide Mountain," said Olly, trying not to smile. His dreadful expression was so formalized that it conveyed no menace at all. "Also, we would be glad of any work your people might give us while we are here."

At the mention of their business, he seemed to relax. The scowl departed. "Are you taken care of?" he asked in a more pleasant voice.

Olly looked at Abasio and he at her.

"Taken care of?" Abasio asked.

The man frowned again. "Cut. Fixed. Neutered. Altered. Do you have a certificate issued by the Mankind Management Group saying you are permitted to enter our country?"

Mutely, Olly shook her head.

"Are we supposed to be?" Abasio gaped.

"Must be," said the man. He made the hideous face once more, then said calmly, "I will have tea."

He sat down cross-legged beside the fire and held out his hand. Olly put a mug of tea into it, her own minty brew of monarda, catnip, and wild rose hips. He sipped once, twice, then smiled. "Good," he said, setting down the cup. He burrowed into his loincloth, coming up with a small notebook. He drew a pencil from among the feathers behind one ear.

"Now. First things first. Have you seen any monsters? Where, when, and how many?"

Olly shuddered as she replied. "We saw two big ogres. About—what was it, Sonny? Three days back?"

"Three nights," he verified. "The moon was almost full. They fought with some . . . walkers. We're not positive, but we think one ogre and two walkers got killed.''

''They didn't threaten you?'' the feathered warrior asked, putting down the pencil to pick up the tea once more.

''We hid,'' said Abasio. ''I don't think they saw us. . . . '' He was going to go on with the story, but his feathered interrogator gave him no opportunity.

''What animals have you seen?'' he asked.

''We saw bear,'' Abasio offered. ''I think. Fish in the streams. Raccoon. Squirrels, different kinds. Little stripey ones, mostly. Rabbit. All kinds of birds. And a number of big deer, big as a cow.''

''Elk,'' said the feathered person with a pleased expression, making notes before tucking away pencil and notebook and settling himself as though to stay awhile. ''Now, it's clear you haven't been here before.''

They nodded agreement as they sipped their own mugs, glad of the warmth, for the sun had sunk below the buttes and chill shadow flowed over the valley, leaving light only on the silver-pink lines of rimrock high above them.

The visitor said, ''Then I'll enlighten you. It is the ruling of the Mankind Management Group that there be no obscenity in our land.''

''In Artemisia?'' asked Olly.

He laughed. ''You say Artemisia. That name is a kind of joke, for our country is called Land of the Sages, meaning land of the wise, but another name for a kind of sage, which is a plant that grows throughout our land, is artemisia. You see? A joke. In my own old language, the country is called the Sacred Land in words you cannot pronounce. No matter. In Sages' Land we have no nonsense, no children without proper preparation and care. No sexual diseases passed about to kill us or our children.''

''We have to be—neutered in order to enter?'' Olly asked, remembering certain things Oracle had told her.

''Examined, certainly. Then neutered, or implanted, or properly outfitted. Surely you have heard of this! Our customs are well known.''

''I've heard of it,'' Olly admitted. Oracle had told her.

''No one may impregnate or become impregnated in the Sacred Land without a certificate from the Mankind Management Group. No one may spread disease.'' He nodded to himself in approval of this arrangement. ''We have none of your IDDIs in our land, and none of your little misborns, either.''

''That's remarkable,'' murmured Olly.

He bowed slightly, accepting this as praise. ''My name, by the way, is Black Owl.''

''How do you do,'' said Olly.

Abasio merely nodded, trying to keep from showing on his face what he felt. In his own case it was absolutely unnecessary to do anything at all. No cutting, neutering, implanting necessary. He was no threat. He could hardly remember, in fact, if he had ever been a threat.

"How is this matter to be accomplished?" Olly was asking.

Black Owl hunkered down. "Since you have no certificate, you must come to the gate where someone will examine your health and discuss your choices. There are various ways of assuring you do no harm. There is a belt thing to be locked on. Most uncomfortable and unsanitary, in my opinion, though some who are only traveling through prefer them."

"I would not like that," grated Abasio.

Black Owl interrupted, one hand held out as though to silence him. "Or, members of the Clan of Wide Mountain may travel with you to certify no indecency is done. This is a very expensive alternative! The Wide Mountain women do not work cheap."

Abasio made a face and looked as though about to protest. Olly shook her head at him warningly.

"Some people are distressed," said Black Owl impassively, leaning forward to catch Abasio's eyes. "The people from the west who call themselves holy, they always hire escorts, for it is against the faith of the Guardians to be altered. They spend their lives resisting their appetites. A great waste of effort, to my mind. Also, very stressful." He drank more tea. "We in Artemisia control stress and also our numbers, but we do not interfere with our enjoyments."

"Ha," snorted Abasio.

"Truly." Black Owl patted him on the knee, then pointed to his own shoulder. "See, I have an implant. Most men choose to be cut, but me, I am a sissy. I do not like the knife." He laughed silently. "Still, I enjoy making p'nash very much."

"P'nash?" asked Olly.

"Crotch music," he said, smiling at her. "You know!" He made a graphic motion with both hands. "P'nash."

Olly reddened.

"We're—we're man and wife," said Abasio in a gravelly voice. "We shouldn't have to have—"

"In your own land, wherever that is, no, of course. I understand. There you pretend to be as the wolf, as the goose, mated for your whole life. It is a pretty pretense to be faithful as these creatures are faithful, but we men are more like the lion, the dolphin, or the promiscuous apes, our closest kin, are we not? Sex would be less troublesome had we descended from geese or wolves, but it was not so."

He sighed dramatically. "Our Sages know man cannot legislate behavior, so we must accomplish by good sense and custom what nature and law will not do for us! In our country there are no mans and wifes. Only protected women, too young yet for childbearing; readying women, who will have one or two very soon, while they are young and strong; new mamas, altered women, altered men, and the Quab-dus, the men who have been selected to father babies." He shook his head. "Such a burden for them. Though they too are young, with the appetites of youth, they may not overeat. They may not drink cider. They have supervised exercise, much sleep. No staying up late at the dances. No preference among partners." He rolled his eyes in exaggerated horror at this regimen. "Often I give thanks I am no longer a Quab-dus."

"How do they get chosen?" asked Abasio, openmouthed.

Black Owl shrugged. "It is up to the Management Group, the Wide Mountain women. Since women must bear, women must choose!" He nodded at them firmly. "So, do you come to the gate?"

"I need the library that's inside Artemisia," murmured Olly to Abasio.

"I know," he growled in return. "And I need to—go with you." Regardless of his other problems, he still wanted to be with her. He hated the idea of someone fiddling about with his sex, but the more he thought about it, the more it seemed this matter of altering or neutering might actually increase their safety! Surely no ganger sent by the Old Chief would consent to this business! They would stop at the border, presuming they ever tracked him this far.

"I guess we'll go with you to the gate," he said. "Though we'd like to have supper first."

"No, no. Take your time," said Black Owl with an open-handed gesture of permission. "The gate closes at sunset, so you would have to stay outside until morning regardless. We have you on our border viewer. So long as you come toward us at the gate, no one will bother you. You go any other where, we will find you!" He made an explosive gesture with both arms.

"Border viewer?" Olly asked.

"A thing we have, made in an Edge, I am told. We trade food and wool to the Edges, in manland. We trade also with the Place of Power."

Place of Power! Olly cast a quick look in Abasio's direction, but he had paid no attention to the reference. She opened her mouth and shut it again. Perhaps now was not the best time to ask questions.

Black Owl was continuing, "It protects us well. We lock it on you, it follows you, we follow it, so best you stay put!" He laughed immoderately.

"We'll stay here tonight, then," said Olly in a carefully neutral tone. "That'll give us a little time to get used to the idea."

"You will get used to it. I understand. Many people feel so." Black Owl put down his mug with a little bow, leaped upon his horse, made it rear up dramatically, and rode off in a great jangle of bells.

"Well," Abasio remarked uncomfortably. "I suppose we have no alternative."

He sounded so forlorn that she got up and hugged him. "It's only temporary."

"I wish you wouldn't do that," he growled, stepping away from her.

She looked up at him, confused.

He cried, "You don't mean anything by it! You treat me as you would . . . a brother."

"Of course I mean something by it! I mean you are my friend!" She came close to him again, touching his face, his shoulder. "Abasio—Sonny. Isn't all this complicated enough without your being—like that!"

He gritted his teeth. Here she was, looking at him tenderly, one hand on his shoulder, smelling like . . . woman, sweaty from the sun, her hard little hand feeling like another sun, spreading warmth throughout his body. He had been conscious of her breasts when she hugged him, totally aware of that yielding and entrancing softness. Associations had engulfed him, other such softnesses, more or less yielding, and yet nothing had stirred. In his mind he desired her constantly. In his body he could not. And it had been weeks that he'd been this way!

She, meantime, spent half her waking hours lusting after him, in a formless kind of way. She had resolved not to mention this to him, for her prophecy spoke of an only *child;* her current status was a *child*'s status; until that part of her life had been discovered, she must not do anything that would change her status from that of child to something else. Lover, perhaps. Or adult. Or mother. It was one of those patterns that she recognized without understanding.

Still, she reached out to him, unable to stop herself.

He didn't see the gesture but growled as he moved away from her. "It isn't your fault. I haven't felt right since they gave me that—that drug in Fantis. I feel like a eunuch! And whatever they do to me at the gate will probably just make it worse." Though how it could be worse, he could scarcely imagine.

She regarded him for a long moment. How could she help him now? "Whatever they do at the gate, it's something these people do all the time," she offered tentatively. "They probably know a lot about it. If they say it would make the matter worse, I'll go on alone. You can find someplace safe to wait until I get back."

This did not remove his anxiety, but it distracted him momentarily. "You'd do that? Go alone?"

"Possibly. Depending on how far the city with the library is. Depending on whether they say it's safe or not."

"They who? More like Black Owl and his crotch music?" he snarled. "Him and his p'nash."

She shook her head at him chidingly. "Don't be that way, Sonny. Black Owl is no rapist."

"You know so damned much!" he shouted, irritated beyond control. "Too damned much for a virgin!"

She flushed angrily. "It's true, I know a lot. Oracle told me all about sex and rape and men and diseases and everything, over and over again! And there was Bastard, a perfect object lesson. Lately, I've wondered if Oracle prevented my having any joy of discovery about it, telling me as much as she did. But she was trying to keep me alive, Abasio. She didn't want me to die of an IDDI. Or get slaughtered by some sex-mad, drugged-up bunch."

Abasio glowered and stirred the fire. He knew what she was talking about; he had seen tally groups in Fantis who started out drinking and yelling war cries, working themselves up into a howling mob that ended up pursuing some hapless songhouse woman with such mindless violence, she ended up dead, or as good as. Which had nothing to do with him!

Olly tried to ignore him. She had gone to the wagon to rummage among the foodstuffs. "What will you have for supper?" she called. "We have grain left, and dried meat, and six eggs. We have potatoes and a head of cabbage from the last farm we passed. . . . "

Abasio stepped away from the fire, without answering. He had quit listening. He'd wanted to shake her, but if he did, she'd think he was one of the men Oracle had warned her against! He wanted to kiss her, but if he did that, she'd think something else, equally unpleasant. Most of all, he wanted to love her.

He could do nothing about it. Instead he breathed deeply as he brushed the dust from his clothing and from the inch-long ringlets that covered his head and jaw. He had never had a beard before. The new Abasio he saw reflected in the water barrel might confuse those who knew the old Abasio. Perhaps it would confuse those who were hunting him.

His bemusement was broken by a soprano yipping that came from the darkness before him. Even Big Blue stopped his nose-down shuffle, raised his head, and whickered softly.

"Coyote," Abasio said half-aloud as he turned his head, trying to locate the sound. Ever since the episode with ogres, he had paid close attention to coyotes.

"Close," she agreed, assembling foodstuffs from the wagon.

The yipping continued, first here, then there, intermittent, gradually growing in volume until it sounded as though it came from a hollow behind a nearby clump of thorny choya where a pool of darkness dwindled and welled as the fire leaped and fell.

Abasio took a stick from the fire and walked toward the clump. As he approached it, a coyote came out of the darkness, trotting toward them confidently, laughing sidewise at Abasio as he trotted past.

Olly stood very still.

"Mangy, rangy, yipper, yeller!" cried the guardian-angel from its perch on the wagon. "See, here comes a tricksy feller."

"Good evening," said the Coyote. "I see you've decided to stay the night."

Abasio stayed frozen in midstep. Someone was playing a trick, perhaps a dangerous trick. His immediate reaction was to kill the animal, but he couldn't reach his weapon.

Olly seemed to be better able to deal with the situation. She cleared her throat, gesturing aimlessly with the stewpot she held. "What are . . . ?"

The Coyote trotted over to the fire and sat down facing her, wrapping its bushy tail around its feet. "Hardly flattering to be called a *what*. Why not a *who*?"

"Who are you, then?" she asked, coughing to clear her throat of the hard lump that had come from nowhere.

"Coyote," he replied. "One of many."

"Do coyotes still . . . talk, then?"

"Still?"

"Changing Woman taught you to talk. In one of Oracle's stories."

"I've heard that story," he said. "I think that kind of tale is called a fable. It is true that coyotes talk, but not all of us talk human."

Abasio turned and came back to the fire, dropping the firebrand into it as inconspicuously as possible. "But you do, obviously. How did—I mean—"

"You mean, why is it I can talk? Well, as to that, it has been suggested to me that certain of my ancestors may have been part of an experiment humans made before they went to the stars. Perhaps something to do with changing the sequences of DNA that control the shape of the skull, the development of the vocal cords and tongue, as well as certain centers in the brain. No doubt you understand all that better than I."

"I'm afraid we don't understand at all," said Olly. "I've never heard of such things. Have you—Sonny?"

He shook his head. "Never."

Coyote shrugged, an almost human shrug. "It was only suggested; it may not be the case. Perhaps I'm a mutation. Perhaps I'm a throwback to that fabulous time you speak of. In any case, the talent does not breed true. Only about half my pups can do human talk, and not many of my colleagues. Sometimes I get hungry for conversation."

"How do you learn it? Talk, I mean," Abasio asked.

The coyote scratched behind one ear with a hind foot. "I was found on the desert by a hermit, a man of considerable intelligence and vocabulary. I was only a pup at the time, but I was making noises that interested him. It was he who speculated as to the origins of my forecoyotes." He laughed silently, his tongue dripping. "I would have said forebears, but that's obviously the wrong genus. At any rate, my human taught me language. He was old when he found me. Eventually, he died. My kindred and I howled him away while the buzzards ate him."

"Poor thing," said Olly feelingly, not specifying whether it was the Coyote or the hermit she pitied. "We're—we're happy to talk with you. As a matter of fact, you can join us for supper. I was just putting on some stew."

"Thank you, but I had a rabbit along about sundown. Generally, I prefer raw meat. Biologically, it suits me. I am not at all civilized, only talkative. At least, so my mentor assured me." He smiled, again lolloping his dripping tongue at them while showing long, slightly yellow teeth.

"You don't mind if we go on with our cooking?" asked Abasio, seating himself once more.

"Not at all. As a matter of fact, if you'd like a fresh rabbit, I'll catch one for you. They're quite fat. We had a good bit of rain sometime back, and the grass is unusually plentiful for this season."

"Why would you do that for us?" asked Olly, curiously.

"Tit for tat." The Coyote grinned. "I want to go into Artemisia. The people there are experimenting. They say they are trying to structure a society that includes nature rather than destroys it, a society that controls technology instead of being controlled by it. I want to see what they're doing. Perhaps they're succeeding, but it may be only talk!"

He shook himself. "Now, supposing it's only talk, I'd be unwise to go there without some form of protection. Whether they're attempting to live with nature or not, the men of Artemisia hunt with bows and arrows, with lances, with snares and traps. They deck themselves in feathers and fur, including the skins of my brethren. They like our tails for their dance bustles. They say they're preservationists, that they're careful not to kill too many of us, but what a pity if one they killed was me!"

"But surely, if you talk to them—"

"Hah!" Coyote barked. "According to my hermit, though intelligence is a continuum that does not begin and end with man, most men have traditionally believed themselves to be the only intelligent living things. When our supporters have suggested otherwise, they have been accused of anthropomorphizing animals." He sighed, a very human-sounding sigh. "Of course, it's worked both ways. Man has been reluctant to animalize humans, too, even though he'll never get society to work until he does!" He scratched his ear once more, two wrinkles in his furry forehead. "Man expects far too much from his kind and does too little to help himself achieve it. Artemisians know this. Or so they say. I need to see if they speak the truth."

He reached out with his front paws, stretched himself hugely, rear end in the air, then sat back down again. "Also, Artemisia has its mercantile side. If they didn't kill me, they might sell me! There are men in this world who would pay much for a talking animal.

"No, if I am to see Artemisia, I must belong to someone. Someone like you: an unremarkable couple, just traveling through, no threat to anyone. You put a collar on me, attach it to a leash—whatso, I'm a pet dog."

"You don't look quite like a dog," objected Abasio.

"I'll grovel. I'll slink." He turned to Olly, his eyes glittering. "I'll let you beat me. I'll lick your feet."

"I wouldn't want you to do that," Olly said.

He laughed at them again. "Our relationship wouldn't be one-sided. There are things I can do for you. I can warn you of danger, as I think you already know. I can help you avoid danger, as I have already done."

"You were—"

"I led the group who teased the ogres away from you and into harm's way, yes. I can tell you, woman, that some who are looking for you have moved much faster than you have. They are there"—he nodded to the east—"moving among the truckers. They will go through the gate in the morning."

"I had hoped they were the ones who—who got killed," she cried. "What do they want with me?"

"They have not said," Coyote admitted. "I can understand speech, but I cannot read minds. I can smell fear and excitement and lust, but the walkers stink of nothing I've ever smelled before. Nonetheless, they are looking for you here and there, by twos—inquiring for an orphan female of some twenty years."

He turned toward Abasio. "You're being hunted, too, but your hunters are behind you. I lay outside the light of their fire one night while they talked about you, congratulating themselves on how clever they had been to learn where you were born. They had been to your home; they had questioned your ancestor. He had told them yes, you had come there some time ago, but you had gone away. They have not yet picked up your trail. They do not know you are traveling with someone else."

"Did they hurt him?" Abasio asked. "Grandpa? Did they?"

"I think not. From what they said, he whined and groveled and said he had driven you off, so you'd not endanger him or his neighbors."

"If they've sent gangers after me, they won't go into Artemisia," Abasio asserted. "No ganger would accept being neutered."

"Oh, a professional hunter won't be balked of his prey or his pay by a little thing like a chastity belt! You may be right in saying most gangers would not, but these men do not need to make children to boost their self-respect!'' Coyote nodded to himself.

"How do you know all this?'' cried Olly.

"I run. I slink. I listen. I think. Though my talent is still quite rare, I am far from the only coyote who speaks human. I ask others to help me, and we lie beyond the light of campfires, outside open windows, hearing what men and women say to one another. Information has value, and I offer it to you as value, so you will return my gift with one of your own.''

"Just so you can look around?''

"So I can study Artemisia, yes. Will you do it?''

"What exactly is our bargain?'' asked Abasio. "That you travel with us, warn us of danger, keep us out of trouble, and we pretend you are our pet? For how long?''

"Until we tire of the arrangement.''

Man and woman looked at one another in surmise.

"I see no harm in it,'' said Abasio, half to Olly, half to the animal, "unless you are playing some game with us.''

"I have heard that Coyote is a trickster,'' Olly said softly. Oracle had often spoken of him as a clever creature who had outwitted other animals and man over the centuries they had lived in the same world.

The Coyote nodded. "It's true. I am a trickster. We all are, we coyotes. Those animals who have survived mankind tend to be, one way or another.''

"I'm willing to make the bargain,'' said Abasio. "But don't play false with us if you value your hide.''

"My word is my word,'' Coyote said, rising. "Better than most contracts. I'll be here in the morning by the time you're awake.''

And he strolled behind the thorny bush from which he had emerged, leaving them both staring after him.

Abasio stood silent for so long that Olly asked, "What are you thinking?''

He was surprised into an answer. "Just that the color on my hands is wearing off.'' He hadn't been conscious of the thought until he spoke it.

She came to him and took one of his hands in her own. The purple tattoos were faintly visible through the fading dye.

"I'll mix up some indigo,'' she said, then whispered, "and just in case someone is watching, we'll get out the table and do a few neckerchiefs as an excuse. Maybe we can bribe the gate guards with them.''

She went to bustle around the fire, and Abasio, heaving a great sigh, began the evening chores. By the time he was finished, the stew was done, the dye table was down, and a few squares of blank cloth were laid out in the light of the lantern.

She offered him the dye pot. He sat down with it between his feet and dipped his hands and wrists, letting them soak while he considered what had happened, what would happen in the morning. If what Coyote had said was true, the two humans should not be too quick to move in the morning. Give the Orphan-hunters time to get through the gate before Olly and Abasio came there. And proceed through the gate with the least possible fuss and no tantrum of outraged masculinity.

He returned the dye pot to Olly and went on to the barrel for water to rinse his hands and arms. Behind him, he heard the even thwack, thwack, thwack of the dye block slapped down on the cloth squares. When he returned, she was adding another fluid to the bucket, one she'd been steeping so she could amplify her pattern with another hue. She was working with a troubled, distracted air. Abasio watched her, head cocked, worried by her silence.

The firelight jumped, gleaming from bright runnels on her cheeks.

"You're crying!" he exclaimed, suddenly guilty over his recent anger and irritation. The silent tears dripped from her jaw, and she licked them from the corners of her mouth. "Olly, sweet . . . ''

She leaned into his arms, crying, "Abasio, why are they hunting me? I haven't done anything to anybody." She shook her head, the tears flying. "I was just beginning to think I knew something about me. I try to forget there are people—things hunting me, but then something reminds me, and it makes me so—scared.''

It was the voice of a child, lonely and forlorn. It was Elrick-Ann's voice, the voice of his ma when she had looked in the mirror at the tattooed emblems on her breast and wept for her youth. It was the cry of the lost lambs he had been sent after in his boyhood, to find them and return them to the fold. It was his own voice, a few times he remembered, when all had seemed past understanding or acceptance.

Abasio held her more tightly, rocking slowly back and forth by the coals of the fire where the stewpot steamed and bubbled and the little fire made cracking noises in the night. It was Coyote's talk of the hunters that had set her off, but he had laid the groundwork for her misery. He silently cursed himself and things in general. For the moment it didn't matter that he couldn't lust after her. He cared for her in her trouble and pain, and for this firelit time, that was enough.

The walkers were among the first through the gate the following morning. They had passes that, they said, allowed them to cross any border. The type of pass was so unfamiliar, however, that the person in charge at the gate had to summon her captain before opening the barrier and letting them through.

"Enjoy your travels through Artemisia," the captain said, nodding politely but distantly, wondering at the difficulty she was having in keeping her voice at its natural pitch and intensity. She wanted to gasp, to squeak. She wanted to run and hide.

"One moment," said the taller walker, refusing to be dismissed.

The captain summoned all her discipline to quell a shudder and put on an attentive face.

"We're seeking a female person of about twenty years. We are told she has dark hair and eyes. It is likely she is traveling alone. Have you seen such a one?"

The captain shook her head. "What has she done?"

"I did not say she had done anything," the taller walker said, raising his brows. "Why we seek her is our business only. Not your business."

The captain swallowed the bile that seeped bitterly at the back of her tongue and said carefully, "I merely thought more information might help me assist you better."

"You need no more information. Answer the question."

The captain turned to the gatekeeper, who shook her head wordlessly.

"No," whispered the gatekeeper. "Only men, traders, truckers, a few older couples, but no woman travelling alone."

The questioners turned without further word and left, stalking out through the gate and into the countryside along the road that led to the town.

"What kind of a pass did they have?" the gatekeeper asked her captain in a trembling whisper. "Who are they?"

The older woman shook her head. "It was issued by the Place of Power. It's rather like the ones the name-changers and the book-burners carry. These . . . people are called walkers; the people from manland talk about them. I've not seen them before; they don't frequent Artemisia much; but that is no doubt what they are."

She dusted her hands together, furrowing her brow. "I'd better get to town before they get there. I need to talk to Wide Mountain Mother about this."

She galloped away on one of the swift horses reserved for officers on urgent business. She left behind her a gatekeeper bursting with curiosity. Most days at the gate were boring enough that any exceptional happening made a welcome break in the routine. The gatekeeper hadn't been told to be quiet about it, so with hints and whispers and dramatic shudders, she told everyone who came through about the two strangers and their pass.

"So they said it was none of our business why they wanted her," she murmured, as she shunted Abasio and Olly's wagon off toward a small structure under the shade of several large trees. "Can you imagine?"

"And they had a pass?" Olly asked, not needing to pretend interest.

"They did. Not that they'd have needed one, if they'd wanted to come in regardless, for it's clear they go where they will! Their pass was issued by the Place of Power, my watch captain said, and that's a mystery, isn't it? We get some of our machinery from the Place, west of us, though I've never been there myself. The book-burners come from there. But why should the Place of Power send beings like that wandering about? I tell you, it made me shiver just hearing them speak. Like when you wake in the night to hear—I don't know. Some strange sound outside your window where no sound should be.''

"Our dog often barks at such sounds," rumbled Abasio, tossing a wicked glance in Coyote's direction.

"Dogs hear things we don't!" cried the gatekeeper, looking directly at Coyote, who lay on the wagon seat looking perfectly doglike and servile. "So do cats, or even birds. Earthquakes, for instance. Animals hear things and they howl. I'll tell you, these beings made me want to howl, as though I'd heard something horrid without knowing it." She flapped her hand at them, miming her discomfiture, and pointed to the door of the small structure. "Now you go on in there. The Mankind Management officer will be with you in two pumps of a ram's rump."

"Lamb's tail," said Abasio gravely, remembering his youth among the flocks. "It's the lambs that shake their tails."

"Maybe in your country," giggled the gate guard. "But our rams seem to do most of it here."

Then she was gone, and the two of them were left staring at each other in a small, bare room that smelled strongly of chemicals.

The woman who joined them was lean, horsefaced, and pleasantly matter-of-fact. She explained the controls she could offer, the belts, the surgery, the implants, the escorts; she agreed that Abasio's condition was worrisome, took samples of various body fluids, and went off to consider the matter. When she returned some time later, she looked thoughtful.

"In one sense, you're healthy," she said to Abasio. "You have no sign of IDDIs, rare for a ganger—and I assume you were a ganger, from the scars you bear. You have no evidence of plague, which is more or less endemic in manland. You are ailing, however, and we have no antidote to what's ailing you. So far as we know, there is none. None, that is, except the drug you took in the first place, one available in the cities, which is no doubt where you got it."

"I didn't take it," said Abasio stiffly, giving up any pretense of hiding his history. "Someone gave it to me without my knowledge."

"Whichever," she said. "More of it would make you feel quite your old self, for a time, but it would not be a good idea for the long run, as I'm sure you've figured out."

Abasio nodded dismally.

"We have records of this stuff, but this is the first evidence we've had of it in circulation. By itself, it does not kill."

"I felt half-dead," Abasio objected.

"I know. You were debilitated by the dose given you, but you were not in danger."

"I don't understand," complained Olly.

The woman explained: "There are a lot of sexually transmitted viruses floating around in manland. One particular group of these we call possum viruses, because they play dead. They don't manifest for years, or even decades, if then. This allows the virus to permeate virtually an entire population. Then, given certain stimuli—Starlight is one—the viruses are jolted into life, into virulence. The stimulated virus can be transmitted sexually, also, and it is inevitably fatal. Though many victims die quickly, someone who is lightly infected and received a minimum dose of the drug might last some weeks, or even months during which they could be infecting others."

"So Abasio wasn't infected?"

"No, surprising for a ganger, he was not. He neither had the bug nor gave it to anyone. Even more surprising, considering how addictive the drug is."

Abasio said, "There are lots of addictives, and lots of people using them. Eventually, they all die."

The woman grinned without humor. "It's that *eventually* that makes the difference to us, cityman. We're not overly concerned about drugs that kill one off after five years, or ten. If one of our people gets taken with it, we have time to correct the matter, and we do. We always neuter addicts, and their children, if any, to make sure both the genetic inclination and the addiction itself is limited. If there's any reason to think that may not work, we go further!" She nodded grimly. "However, we do worry about drugs like this Starlight. There's no time to save a life when *eventually* can mean *tomorrow!*"

Abasio grimaced, rubbing his forehead. Seemingly, he had had a lucky escape. Sybbis hadn't been infected when Little Purp bought her. Little Purp had no sexually transmitted diseases, so Sybbis had acquired none. He, Abasio, wasn't going to die. Eventually, he'd get over the effects of the drug. Eventually.

The woman went on: "You're young. You're strong. Our people believe the effects will wear off. Since we don't know how rapidly your body is getting rid of the stuff, it's hard to say how long recovery will take."

She twiddled her fingers, considering. "While we're rigorous in protecting the health of Artemisians, we've a certain reluctance to destroy lives in the process, and putting you under stress or dosing you with more drugs certainly won't do you any good. Are you planning on going straight through our land?"

The question was asked of Abasio, but it was Olly who answered. "I need to stop at the library in Artemisia. And we have a delivery for the Wide Mountain Clan."

The woman went on staring at Abasio, waiting until he met her gaze. "I'll let you travel on a special pass specifying that in your present condition, you're no threat to us."

Abasio tried not to be offended by this, without much success. He was offended. And embarrassed.

The woman turned to Olly. "As for you, young woman, since you're healthy and not sexually active, and since you're going to the Wide Mountain Clan, I'll give you a pass that far, and they can decide what to do with you from there."

"What did the person in the house say?" asked Coyote when they were in the wagon once more headed south.

"She said they have a population that's in balance with their environment; they intend to maintain it that way. She said they have no sexual diseases and don't intend to let any in."

"How very sensible of them," said Coyote, turning to dig his teeth into his flank and burrow there furiously.

"You're lucky she didn't know about your fleas," snarled Abasio. "She said we were healthy, more or less, but we didn't think to have her check you as well. You may be harboring plague in those fleas of yours."

The Coyote, growling deep in his throat, did not reply as he continued his pursuit of whatever was biting him.


The city of Artemisia, when they arrived there after several hours' travel, did not meet Abasio's expectation of a city. On the ridges above the river a dozen or so large, complicated buildings faced one another with facades of shimmering tiles laid in swirling patterns as of flame or boiling cloud or the movement of blown leaves. The shallow stream in the valley was a mere wandering trickle, a silver glitter among braided flat banks of pinkish gravel, an endearing infant creek, dappled by sun and dwarfed both by living trees, golden in the autumn sun, and the huge sun-bleached carcasses of dead ones that lay on either side. These white hulks, so Coyote told them, came shuddering down the arroyo when spring floods sent a muddy fury rioting between the banks. Well above this line of debris, the low adobe buildings of the town sprawled like sand castles.

Artemisia shone like gold and polished gemstone, all softly glittering. Nothing in it obtruded upon the sight. All was a whole, organic as a forest.

"Who lives up there?" Olly wondered, pointing at the larger buildings on the ridges.

Abasio did not reply. He was making a careful examination of their surroundings, both for any sign of the walkers and for a building that looked like a library. He had no very clear idea what a library should look like, but he expected something imposing, certainly something larger than anything he could see.

Noticing Abasio's confusion, a woman left a nearby group of chatting women and came toward them. "Can I help you find something?"

"We would thank you for directions to the Clan of Wide Mountain," said Olly.

"Wide Mountain House is at the bottom of the hill, on the left of the plaza," the woman directed. "Look for the sign of the thistle." She returned to her group and the half-dozen women in it and whispered to the others as they stared after the wagon, heads together in intimate exchange.

At the bottom of the hill the roadway opened into a gravelly clearing centered upon an open-sided, peak-roofed platform where a trio of musicians were plucking and strumming on guitars, a practice session that was frequently interrupted by one or the other of the participants. The clearing was bordered all around with courtyard walls and tall gates, some open, some closed. The sign of the thistle hung above a timbered archway that gave onto a stone-paved enclosure bright with potted flowers. Inside, Olly found an official with whom she was allowed to leave her packages.

"Very nice work," said the woman when she had unpacked the neckerchiefs onto the counter between them. She knotted one loosely about her throat, patting the knot and adjusting the folds. "Our old kerchiefs were faded to nothing, and any respect shown their wearers was purely from habit. What's this other packet?"

"Silk yardage, printed," Olly replied. "Ordered through you."

The woman referred to a notebook, nodding. "Ordered by Fashimir Ander, yes. Good enough. There's a trade group heading west this afternoon, and they can deliver it. Shall I pay you the balance, or shall I send it to the dyer?"

Olly passed over the note Wilfer had given her. "Half the remainder to me," she said. "Because it was my work. The other half sent to Wilfer Ponde, for his profit."

The woman unlocked a strongbox and rapidly stacked silver rats, passing the coins across the counter. "I'll send a draft on our bankers in the Edge at Fantis. They will send the coin to Whitherby."

"You have a banker in the Edge?" asked Abasio curiously.

"Indeed," she replied, giving him a sharp look. "Surely you wouldn't expect us to send coin through that gang-ridden and lawless realm?"

Abasio remained impassive. He wouldn't expect it, but then, he'd never considered how payment might take place across borders. Edges were evidently more complicated places than he had thought they were.

"Anything else?" queried the woman, seeing Olly's hesitation.

"I—I was given a pass only this far by the woman at the gate. She said you could decide . . . what to do with me. And I need to visit the library of Artemisia."

"Now, why would you want to do that?" the woman asked, with an interested expression.

Olly knotted her hands in her pockets. "I have—personal reasons."

"I see." The woman arranged several items on the counter, lining them up, disarranging them, and lining them up again. "I'll have to inquire." She went swiftly out, and they heard her footsteps tapping away down a long, hard-surfaced corridor.

"Of course she wants to know why," Olly whispered to Abasio. "But I shouldn't tell her who I really am, should I? Not with those creatures hunting me."

Abasio started to speak, then fell silent as footsteps approached. A large gray-haired woman came into the room and sat down to face them.

"I'm the Wide Mountain Mother," she said, staring at them with lively interest. "What business do you have with our library?"

"Excuse me, ma'am," said Abasio, shuffling his feet like a scolded school-boy. "But my wife here—her folks died just a year or so ago, and her old aunty told her the rest of the family came from somewhere near the thrones. And neither of us ever heard of that place, so we thought there'd be something about it in your library, it being so famous. That's why we brought your neck scarves ourselves, so we could ask about that."

Olly stared at him, wondering where this bumpkin had come from!

"The thrones," said the woman, leaning back to give him a long, level look. "Now, that's interesting. The thrones are a part of our legends, but I had thought them entirely mythical. What do you know about them?"

"Just that they were set up at the Place of Power," said Olly.

"This is the second time today someone has been concerned about the Place of Power," the woman said. "At a meeting of the Group this morning, here came a border captain bursting in full of questions about passes issued by the Place of Power."

"Yes, ma'am, we heard about that at the gate, ma'am," said Abasio bashfully.

Olly kicked him on the ankle. He was overdoing it.

"The holders of the passes were looking for a dark-haired girl about your age," the woman said. "And though you claim to be married to this man, who pretends at being witless, showing more skill at it than he no doubt intends, the medical officer says you are a virgin yet."

Olly held her tongue. What could she say?

The woman went on: "We trade with the Place of Power, as we do with the Edges, in manland. I see no problem in your going there with whoever next makes the trip westward. However, I cannot guarantee you will find any thrones."

Olly rubbed her forehead. "Since you're not sure the thrones are at the Place of Power, I'd like to see if there's any mention of them in the library."

"Well, as to that—I think you should talk with a librarian. She would know what books there are, what books have been preserved or remembered."

"You're talking about the fifty-year rule?"

"The fifty-year rule, yes. Works of opinion are often destroyed while works of fact are left undisturbed. Now, I'm sure at one time many books might have told all about the thrones, but it may be that those books no longer exist."

"But the librarian will know."

"The librarian." The woman smiled. "Of course."

"How do I find—a librarian?"

The gray-haired woman smiled again. "One of them happens to be my daughter Arakny. She'll return from work shortly. If you'd like to drive down the little alleyway beside Wide Mountain House, you'll find a place to camp above the stream. I'll tell her where you are. As for your companion"—she smiled at Abasio—"I'll send someone to show him about."

Olly started to leave, then turned back. "The pass," she said. "The woman at the gate said—"

"Leave it for now," the older woman replied. "Arakny will sort it out."

She rose to show them out, watching as they crossed the courtyard and mounted the wagon seat once more.

The younger clanswoman had returned to lean in the inner doorway, arms folded, brow furrowed, remarking, "Do you think she is the one?"

"Which one, my dear? The one the walkers are looking for? I should think so, yes. The one your contact in the Place of Power mentioned might be coming this way? Possibly. The one our Seers have said will come, the key for the lock, the pivot on which the world balances? I wouldn't presume to guess."

"I sneaked around front and looked in their wagon. There's a coyote with them."

"A coyote? Ah. How very Artemisian! You think it means something?"

"I don't think anything. If I think too much, those walkers might come back here to ask me what I thought."

Wide Mountain Mother sighed. "Is there anything further on the walkers?"

"They went through town this morning, shortly after we got the first report. They stopped several women and asked questions. The women who were questioned were examined within minutes. Their blood pressure was up. Adrenaline was up. Strong gut reactions, almost as though they had eaten something poisonous. The physicians say it's a panic reaction, like the reaction primates have to snakes, purely instinctive, so far as they can tell, though they're not ruling out subsonics or an unknown pheromone. We'd had enough advance warning to detail a dozen observers, men and women with different fields of experience, including Shabe.''

''Why Shabe? She's a painter.''

''She's a painter, yes, but she's also the closest thing to an anatomist we had available. She says they walk too fast.''

''Too fast?''

''Like an engine, she says. With the wrong rhythm.''

''You're saying they're not human, daughter?''

''I'm only telling you what Shabe said. Shabe doesn't think they're people, and I don't, either. The places where they stood for any length of time are burned bare. The soil stinks. And you no doubt remember what the captain said when she told the Group about them this morning.''

''She said they scared her. She said they were perfectly polite and not at all overtly threatening, and yet she was so troubled by them, she was sick.''

Mother rubbed hands along her upper arms, where gooseflesh had risen from a sudden chill. Over the past decade or two, walkers had become ubiquitous in the surrounding lands, so travelers said. The library said they were beings returned from a former time. Monsters were also returned from a former time. They had come back soon after men went to the stars, but only recently had they become common. Neither monsters nor walkers had often been seen in Artemisia. Mother would have preferred that state of affairs to continue.

The younger woman interrupted her train of thought. ''Will you really send Arakny to talk with the girl?''

''Of course. Arakny is a librarian, a procurer and keeper of information. She gets it from everywhere, books and tales and art—and people. Sometimes she has to trade. Sometimes, as in this case, we must give a little to get a little.''

# CHAPTER 10

*T*he doctor who had drugged Abasio at Nelda's behest had been returned to his practice and Nelda herself to her songhouse, both by the mercy of Old Chief Purple. The sudden prospect of a worthy son, or even a worthy grandson, was very attractive to him, and he decided that Nelda had, everything considered, done him no harm.

Nelda, thanking every natural or supernatural force that she could identify or imagine, went back to her songhouse and took up her duties once more. She heard from several sources that Sybbis was pregnant and from the same sources that Young Chief Purple was said to be seriously ill. There was other gossip about the Purples, something about one of the members of the gang having disappeared. Nelda listened to all of this, exclaimed over it, and considered herself well out of the whole mess, even though the possibilities of extortion from Sybbis no longer existed.

Several ordinary weeks went by as she pursued her daily duties, beginning at midmorning most days and continuing into the night. Came a certain morning, however, when she arrived at the songhouse with her stalwarts to be greeted by a duo of weeping girls.

"Liliane, she's sick!" cried one.

"So's Telline," cried the other.

Such news was not unusual. Girls were always getting sick. Thirty was old in the songhouse trade. Few of them lived past thirty, and those, so went the current wit, were the ugly ones. She herded the weepers in front of her as she went back to the long, low dormitory room where the girls had their own cot cubicles.

Liliane was indeed sick. The flesh around her eyes was livid and swollen, the tight skin glistening as though it were about to burst. Her lips were dry and cracked. She had a high fever and a sickening smell. She did not seem to see Nelda but moved restlessly on the bed, rocking from side to side in a ceaseless, mechanical motion accompanied by panting exhalations of quick, shallow breaths.

"Carry her out back," Nelda directed, and four or five of the other girls seized handholds of blanket and carried it with Liliane atop out into a chilly back storeroom, which Nelda's ganger boss called "the infirmary," which Nelda called "out back," and which the girls themselves called "the dead ward." Justifying the infirmary title were half a dozen cots along one wall, and Liliane was put onto one of them, soon to be joined by Telline. By noon, three of the other girls were beside them. By midafternoon, Liliane was dead.

During these early hours, there was virtually no traffic in the house, so the customers were not inconvenienced. Nonetheless, Nelda did as her job required and sent messengers to the doctor and to the owner of the songhouse, a ganger who arrived an hour later to see for himself, for Telline, he explained to Nelda, was a favorite of his. He was sweating when he arrived, sweating and shivering at once. Before he looked at the girls, he said, he would have a drink of something cold. Two swallows later, he collapsed, and by the time the doctor arrived, looking pale and rather frightened, the ganger too was dead, along with three more of the girls, all their eyes shuttered beneath livid masses of swollen flesh.

The sickness was like no sickness he had seen in Fantis before, the doctor said. It was everywhere, all at once, a few here, a few there, in the gang houses, in the marketplace, in the songhouses. Sparing children and the old, alighting here and there among the townfolk, it seemed focused on the gangers and the songhouse inhabitants, whether boys, girls, or eunuchs.

TeClar and CummyNup Chingero first heard of the disease from the house-hag who nursed sick or wounded men. Two of the Purples were dead, she said to them furtively, two who had been well on the previous day. Their bodies were out back, not even disposed of yet. Also, a woman upstairs was sick.

TeClar and CummyNup did what they usually did when they were bothered. They went to talk to Mama.

Mama's place was outside Purple territory. Normally, the brothers would have been challenged a time or two on their way there, but this morning no one seemed to be in the mood for challenging anybody. When the brothers knocked on Mama's door, she opened the little window to see who they were, but unlike her usual self, did not unlock the door with cries of welcome.

Instead she asked gently, "How you boys feelin'?"

"Fine, Mama."

"You feelin' sweaty? Hot? Weak?"

"No, Mama."

"You been goin' to the songhouse lately?"

Actually, they had, but not often. "Mama, you tole us not to go there."

"You do like I tole you?"

Both of them nodded. The Chingero boys actually enjoyed beer and conviviality more than they did sex, and they had resorted to the girls in the songhouses only occasionally. Since they had followed Mama's instructions most of the time, neither of them felt she needed to know about their lapses.

"Then you can come on in." She opened the door to admit them, and they came in to find Mama's two younger children, Billibee and Crunch, seated quietly side by side, very wide-eyed and scared-looking.

"What you hear 'bout this sickness?" she asked them.

TeClar told her about the Purples, while she nodded and frowned.

"I hear the same," she said. "My frien', upstairs, she has a boy with the Blues. Some of 'em dead, the Blues. You know what I think, boys. I think time's come to get outta this place."

TeClar and CummyNup were surprised, then doubtful. They needed to go back to the house to get this or that. They shouldn't just run off. They didn't have any money.

"I got money," she told them. "All these years you been bringin' me money, I kep' mos' of it. No sense you goin' back for anythin'. Likely you go back, you catch this sickness an' you die!"

They stayed at Mama's until the late, dark hours, then left in a vehicle CummyNup had stolen for them. For no particular reason—except that it was the direction Abasio had said he was going—they headed north. At the end of one night's travel, they took refuge in a truckers' hostel. When Mama began asking questions of the truckers, however, she heard rumors of sickness in the cities to the north, along the lakeshore.

"We goin' the wrong way," Mama said, settling her plump self into the cushions she had piled around her. "North is wrong. I don' even think Basio wen' there."

"He said!" complained CummyNup.

"Don' care 'bout that," she said firmly. "I don' think he wen' there. One thin' 'bout Basio, he lucky. He always lucky. You don' go wrong followin' a lucky man."

"Can' follow him. Don' know where he is!" complained TeClar.

"We don' have to fin' him," said Mama. "Jus' go the same way and take care of ourselfs."

"Like to fin' him," said CummyNup stubbornly. "Jus'—you know, see if he need help."

"Well, mebbe we will," said Mama. "'Cause if he say he goin' this way, he prob'ly go that way instead."

Though they discussed it further, Mama's reasoning prevailed. Abasio was lucky. If there was disease northward, then Abasio had probably gone the other way. Crunch and Billibee didn't care what direction they went. They had never been out of the city and found the whole thing wonderfully exciting.

Accordingly, on the following morning, the family turned east, intending to make a wide clockwise circle around Fantis. The day was cloudy. They could not see the mountains to the west, nor could they see the sun. There were no maps. The world east of Fantis was farm country, rolling ground with rutted roads going hither and thither, no signs, few villages, unfamiliar landmarks, very few places to buy fuel for their smoking, sputtering boiler on the back of the vehicle. Inevitably, they got lost.

They camped out—an uncomfortable new experience, for they had brought little bedding with them. Mama showed them how to snare rabbits, a skill she had used to snare rats in the city. Mama showed them how to roast rabbits over a fire, and how to build the fire itself. When they encountered a village on the following day, Mama bought more bedding, canvas, and a grill to hold the cooking pots she had refused to leave behind in Fantis. Night found them lost again, but more comfortably.

Slowly, day by day, they worked their way more or less south, though they often ended up going the wrong direction when they could find no roads going in the right one. Though CummyNup was fond of the smoky vehicle, they finally decided it was more trouble than it was worth. Mama sewed packs for them all and they left the machine in a ditch one morning, thereafter moving more consistently south, across the fields when there were no roads to follow. They found they could buy food at the farms they encountered, and they learned it was best if Mama or the children made the approach, for the farmers were wary of gangers.

Though they did not keep an accurate account of the days, it might have been four or five after they abandoned the vehicle that they first saw refugees.

They had laid up for the night in a grove along a stream bed with a trickle of water in it, not enough to bathe in—which annoyed Mama—but enough to fill their canteens and cook their supper. North of them was a road that led along the side of a hill, and as dark fell they saw clots of people on it, moving eastward.

"Where they goin'?" asked Crunch in too loud a voice.

"Hush," said Mama. "Don' know. An' better they don' hear you yellin' an' come on down here. We don' have food to spare."

She watched the people moving along the road until it was too dark to see them, now and then cautioning quiet. When they awoke in the morning, there were still people moving on the road, small groups of them trudging wearily, some empty-handed and others carrying burdens or pushing loaded carts. Now and then a vehicle would come smoking importantly along, pushing the hikers out of the way.

"I goin' fin' out wha's goin' on," said CummyNup. "You stay hid."

Mama was as curious as the rest, so she didn't try to dissuade him. He snaked his way north until he was near the road, then took up a position under a tree.

"Hey!" he yelled to the next group that came within hearing.

The group halted, two women, one man, a staggering toddler at one of the women's skirts. They weren't gangers. From the looks of them, they were probably shopkeepers. Dues-payers.

"Where you goin'?" cried CummyNup.

"Away from Fantis!" called one of them. "Where's the nearest village?"

"Why?" CummyNup cried. "Why you leavin'?"

"Sickness," the man replied. "Ever'body dyin'."

"What kind of sickness?"

"They just fall down an' die," the man said, mopping at his face. "They say it's that new drug, Starlight."

"Where's the nearest village?" the woman asked. "We need to buy food!"

CummyNup had no idea where the nearest village was, but it stood to reason the road they were on led somewhere. "Jus' keep on the road!" he cried. "You'll get there."

He waited until they were out of sight before snaking his way back down the slope to the grove where Mama and the others waited. By the time he arrived there, more people had appeared on the road. He told them what the people had said, but he didn't mention Starlight. He had reason not to.

"Look like we got out jus' in time," TeClar commented.

"Now we got to stay away from those folks," Mama said grimly. "If Fantis got a sickness, those folks prob'ly carryin' it with 'em."

Then began what they later called the sneaky trip, during which TeClar

or CummyNup reconnoitered their path during twilight hours and the family
traveled mostly after dark. They stayed away from the roads, most of which
were cluttered with fleeing cityfolk. They bought all their food at isolated
farms, and Mama insisted that the boys shave their heads to let their natural
hair grow out so the country people would feel less hostile toward them.

It was Mama who reminded them winter would be coming and there might
be better cover in the mountains, so they turned toward the west. One night
they crossed the highway, which was edged with small groups of refugees,
and began to work their way south along the foothills. Right about midnight,
TeClar, who was leading the way, sat down suddenly and put his hands on
either side of his head.

"Wha's wrong, TeClar?" asked CummyNup in a worried voice.

"Don' know," he replied. "Jus', all of a sudden, got this pain, like."

Crunch and Billibee cut some pine tips to make a mattress, and Mama
helped TeClar spread his blankets while CummyNup built a fire.

TeClar lay down on the blankets and shivered until Mama wrapped him
tightly.

"Wha's wrong?" CummyNup asked Mama. He knew what was wrong.

She didn't answer him, just shook her head and suggested to Crunch and
Billibee that they take firebrands and look around close for water since she
had filled the kettle with most of what they carried.

Billibee found a pool of rainwater in the top of a hollowed rock. They
dipped it out by the spoonful to fill the canteens. Mama, meantime, made
sugared tea and spooned most of a cup down TeClar's throat, after which
he seemed to go to sleep.

Mama sat beside him, staring into the fire, trying to hold time tight inside
herself, binding it so it couldn't pass away. The skin around TeClar's eyes
was puffy. She had seen that right away. Now it was darkening, as though
it had been bruised, making his face look skull-like.

Crunch and Billibee were burrowing in the packs, wanting something to
eat. Well, let them eat. Might as well. If she knew anything, there'd be one
fewer of them to eat a meal tomorrow.

She felt tears in her throat and looked up at the sky, making the tears run
down inside, swallowing them. CummyNup and TeClar. These two boys—
she had seen the skull in their faces when they were born, even before that,
when the man came through the window with his knife. There was doom in
that beginning. Who could question that? Doom in that beginning, with no
daddy to teach them and her only sixteen. Little tots, they'd been, full of
questions. Little tots, then bigger, then suddenly ganger boys, gone from
home, following the purple-crested ones, strutting and crowing like little
cocks. Lookee me, lookee me, Mama.

Lookee me, lookee me. Me with my crest and my tattoos. Me with my colors on my back. Me with my victories to tell. Me with death peekin' 'round the corner at me.

What was there for them except that? What could she give them instead of that? Still, she'd made them promise her: Don't abuse old folks or babies. Don't kill people just tryin' to live. Don't you ever force a woman says no. If you got to fight, fight people as strong as you, otherwise it's just hateful.

So, so, they'd lived this long, and they'd been decent as they could. They'd whored and they'd drugged, and this was the end of that, the skull that had shown in their faces when they were born. Thoughtless and heedless like all the gangers, boastin' and braggin' for today, tomorrow unthought of, but still good boys.

Faithful to her. Faithful to Abasio, too, and where was he?

She rested her head on her knees tiredly. Oh, they'd had a good chance of getting away. If only, if only! What had TeClar done? Gone to that songhouse when he'd sworn to her he hadn't? Probably. Taken just the tiniest bit of that drug, when he'd said he hadn't. Even if he hadn't, even if he'd had his way with some town girl, who was to say she hadn't been infected too. The end was in the beginning—her own mama used to say that. You start a certain way, that's the way you end.

"He look bad," whispered CummyNup in her ear.

He did look bad. The flesh around his eyes was swollen now. His breath came in harsh little pants, whuff, whuff, whuff. She laid her hand on his face and almost jerked it away from the heat of him.

"Mama? He dyin'?"

"Hush," she said. "Don' you scare the chil'ren."

"He is," CummyNup whispered. "He is."

"You go get those two settle' down. Mebbe they can sleep some."

After a time, they did sleep, and she sat alone listening to the whuff, whuff, whuff, not realizing she herself had nodded off until the silence brought her awake. No breathing. The body beside her cold.

And then she cried, silently. Now, now would it be CummyNup? Or might he be spared? Would it be Crunch too? And Billibee?

Morning came. Looking southward, she saw five tall pillars of stone at the bottom of a valley where a stream ran clear and pure. CummyNup got up, looked at his brother, then stared around himself, tears washing down his face.

"I know where's this place," said CummyNup in surprise, licking the salt tears from around his mouth, wiping his face on his arm.

"Where?" Mama asked.

"Those be Wise Rocks. Basio, he talk 'bout this place, talk 'bout this place like he know 'bout it. Right near here, he say they a farm . . ."

They had no tools to dig a grave, so they rolled TeClar's body in his blankets, shoved it into a crevice, and covered it with stones before striking out toward Wise Rocks Farm. On the way there, they passed several bodies, some of them almost fresh, one of them bringing an exclamation to Mama's lips, a cry, almost of fright.

"Wha'?" demanded CummyNup, turning the corpse with his foot. It was just a man, with letters branded on his forehead. He did look familiar, but CummyNup couldn't remember him. "Wha', Mama?"

"Somebody mebbe I saw once," she said. "Long time ago."

"Somebody broke all his bones," said CummyNup. "This one didn' die from no sickness."

"Well, an' he had that comin'," said Mama, in such a voice as CummyNup had never heard from her in his life.

It was Mama who approached Wise Rocks Farm to ask Farmwife Suttle if she knew Basio. And it was Farmwife Suttle who opened her arms to the family, gangers or no. If they were Abasio's friends, they were hers, though she set certain rules for them to minimize the possibility of their transmitting disease. For a time, she said, they would cook their own foods separately, dig and use a separate privy, wash their clothing and linens in a separate place. To all of this they agreed, so glad to be given a roof over their heads, an old but solid shed out past the barn, they would have consented to almost anything.

Privately, the Farmwife felt the risk of disease was low and getting lower every passing day. Very few who had come as far as Wise Rocks Farm had been carrying the fatal disease, though some had had illnesses of other types. Besides, she needed help, as she told Mama Chingero.

"I can use extra people," she said grimly. "I'll feed as many of the refugees as I can, and the farmers up the Crystal will help me do it, but I can't have them overrunning the place, trampling the fields, killing the livestock, and threatening our peace. Do you have weapons that will keep them at a distance?"

CummyNup allowed that he did. Gangers seldom went anywhere without weapons, even when they were pretending not to be gangers. And he had TeClar's weapons as well.

"Well, then, you join the men who are guarding the road. I'm surprised you missed them on your way in."

Mama explained that they had come under cover of the forest, not on the road, and she asked what she and the children could do to help.

There was much that needed doing. People from the farms up the valley brought grain and winter vegetables down to Wise Rocks Farm. Each day Farmwife Suttle and the Widow Upton cooked up a huge pot of this stuff, making a kind of porridge, to which they added eggs and vegetables and scraps of meat. While the food was still warm, they put it in the wagon and sent CummyNup and Mama Chingero down to the foot of the valley, where the road was, to distribute it to any hungry person coming by. By bringing the food to the road, they explained to the Chingeros, they forestalled people coming up the valley looking for it, people who might kill livestock and damage the cropland.

"Whitherby has a tent village outside it," the Farmwife told Mama Chingero after a few days. "I'm told the people there are mostly healthy enough. Those who were sick didn't make it this far."

Yes, Mama said to herself. That was true. Those who were sick hadn't quite made it this far.

"Me, I'm surprise' the gangers don' take over," whispered CummyNup, looking over his shoulder. "I keep waitin' for them to come. Renegades. Blue Shadows. Cranks."

"They gone like your brother gone," said Mama. "They the ones got sick an' died."

Each day teams of men from the farms went up and down the road, digging graves for the bodies left along the road. Shortly after they arrived, CummyNup borrowed a shovel and went back to bury TeClar.

Then, in a matter of days, the flow of refugees stopped as though it had never been. The last few brought descriptions of Fantis empty, Echhot empty, both wiped out in the space of a dozen days, though the Edges were still there. Hearing this, CummyNup told Mama he wanted to see what had happened. Against her advice and the advice of every other person at Wise Rocks Farm, he packed a sack of food, took a firelighter and a full canteen, and hiked along the empty road, back toward the city.

He passed the remains of campfires, places where magpies and crows gathered thick upon carrion, these growing more common the farther he went. The Edge was as it had always been. From behind the great steel gates, men watched him go past without a word, certainly without a challenge. Was it only his imagination, or did it seem there were fewer of them than before?

As he approached the Patrol Post he was confronted by half a dozen armed men gathered around a large open wagon, all of them dressed in leather clothing with green hats and mantles.

"Whatso!" he called, wanting to be friendly.

"Where do you think you're going?" growled the largest of the men.

"Jus' thought I'd see if there's anybody left," he said, gesturing toward the city.

"No more than deserve to be," the man replied, going back to loading the wagon from a nearby pile of coops and cages, kegs and bags. From inside the coops and cages came a scurry of movement, a flutter of feathers. Several others of the brown and green came around the corner of the building mounted on some of the patrol's horses and driving the rest of the herd before them.

"Where you takin' them?" asked CummyNup.

"The geldings we'll let loose on the prairies east of here. The mares go to the horse farms in Low Mesiko," said one rider. "We've already been through the city, letting animals go. Lots of dogs and cats. Lots of chickens. We found some exotic pets too. Critters from far away, and those're in the wagon."

"Nothin' much lef' but cockroaches, I 'spose," said CummyNup.

"Lots of rats, and maybe a few people," said the man. "But we don't concern ourselves with people."

"Why's that?" asked CummyNup.

"First place, there's plenty of 'em. Second place, we're the Animal Masters," said the other. "Fence cutters, cage destroyers, pen wreckers. If you see any animals we missed, turn them loose. You see any really strange ones, stop on your way out and tell us. We'll have people here for several days yet."

The speaker waved a casual farewell and went off after the horses, leaving CummyNup to go across the bridge and get himself promptly lost in the warehouse district.

Half the buildings he knew were gone; half the streets he sought were blocked with the wreckage of burned buildings and fallen walls. Here and there in the open streets he came across green-gowned women bearing canvas sacks at their belts and iron-tipped staffs in their hands. They were working their way systematically from crack to crack, from dirt alley to dirt alley, making holes with their staffs and dropping seeds into the holes. CummyNup didn't need to ask who they were. Farmwife Suttle had told all about them. These were Sisters to Trees. He greeted them politely and went on past.

He went first to Abasio's place, where Elrick-Ann had been. If he ever saw Abasio again, he would want to know about Elrick-Ann. He saw no sign of her, but there was a sheet of paper on the bed, held down by a heavy book. Reading wasn't something CummyNup did well, so he folded the paper into his pocket. Farmwife Suttle would read it for him.

Leaving Abasio's place, he went to Purple House, finding it unburned, seemingly untouched except for the corpses here and there. Young Chief lay in his room upstairs, half eaten by rats. He hadn't died of the plague. Somebody had slit his throat for him. CummyNup went on up to the roof, pushing open the door to the women's quarters with some difficulty. Someone had blocked it from inside.

He saw movement and went toward it. A woman dressed in mud-colored robes screamed at him to stay away, then attacked him with a knife, but CummyNup was too quick for her.

He held her wrists in one big hand as he drew the veils away from her face with the other. "Sybbis!" he gasped, unable to believe it.

"Who're you?" she cried. "Who're you?"

"CummyNup Chingero," he said. "I was a Purple. Me'n my brother TeClar."

"Where you been?" she screamed. "Why ain' you dead? Everbody's dead!"

He let her go, prudently taking the knife. He gave her water from his canteen and food from his stores, which she gulped like a famished dog. It had been days, she said, that she'd been alone, surviving on what edibles she could find in the house. Everyone else had died. Carmina, Soniff's woman, had run off with her baby, and Sybbis didn't know if she was dead or not.

"I'll take you out of here," said CummyNup.

"Take me to Bloodruns!" she cried. "Take me home!"

Even after she had seen the wreckage in the street, she insisted on going home. CummyNup tried to find it for her, without success. It could have been on one of the blocked streets, maybe in an area that was burning briskly.

"If you're wise, you'll take her away from here," said one of the Sisters to Trees who had been watching them trying to get through a blocked street. "There will be nothing left alive here in another few weeks. Even the rats will starve." She jabbed her iron-tipped staff into the ground, dropping seeds into the hole. "Here as in the east," she chanted. "Here as in the west. Where cities die, come Sisters nigh, and seeds will do the rest."

"Why you doin' this?" CummyNup asked.

"Why, look at this mess!" exclaimed the Sister. "Filth and wreckage, offal and death! In time, the trees and shrubs and grasses we're planting will grow up green to cover the scars. The insects will return, and the birds. Then the Animal Masters will bring prairie dogs and ferrets, foxes and hawks and rabbits to nest in the old cellars and make nests on the rooftops."

"Why?" cried Sybbis. "I don' unnerstan' why."

The Sister gave her a long, level look, then shook her head and went back to her planting.

"I wanna know why!" Sybbis screamed.

The Sister turned and came back to her, taking her by the shoulder in a large, calloused hand and speaking softly. "When places grow too large for peace or health, with people who are not countrymen but warring tribes, they inevitably die. All such places carry their own destruction within them."

"You did it!" Sybbis sobbed. "You a monster that kill everbody so's you could plan' trees."

"Someone did so we could plant trees," whispered the Sister. "But if it was a monster, it was one greater than I." She turned away again, and this time Sybbis did not call after her.

Though Sybbis continued to threaten a tantrum, CummyNup eventually convinced her it would do no good to go on hunting the Bloodruns, that it made better sense for her to return to the farm with him. They made their way back to a familiar intersection, and from there CummyNup was able to guide them among the wreckage until they came to the bridge.

At the near end they were stopped by men dressed all in black except for red and white insignia upon their shoulders and above the clear visors covering their faces.

"What weapons will we find in this place?" one of them asked CummyNup. "What chemicals?"

CummyNup scratched his head and told them what he could about the weapons that had been in use, while the visored men conferred with one another. Sybbis knew something about chemicals, for the Bloodrun gang had controlled the trade of salt, and of lime for privies, chlorine for the baths, lead and zinc for paints, and arsenic for killing rats, as well as certain other necessities. The Bloodruns had kept stores of all these things in a warehouse near the bridge, one painted in Bloodrun colors.

They questioned her closely, and when they had finished, she demanded to know who they were.

The foremost among them took off his helmet and scratched his short, graying hair. "We're an advance patrol of the Guardians. We've been sent to see to the destruction of weapons and the long-term storage of chemicals."

"Why?" asked Sybbis yet again.

"So the water and soil don't get poisoned," he replied, giving her a curious look. "Are the Sisters here yet? Have you seen Animal Masters?"

CummyNup told them they would find members of both groups in and around the city, then he half-led, half-dragged Sybbis across the bridge, glad to be out of the place.

They took their time returning to Wise Rocks Farm, where Sybbis, between throwing tantrums over this thing and that, wept over her sister and her father, not knowing if they were dead or alive. Mama Chingero, hearing one such brouhaha, said to the Farmwife, "I take care of that Sybbis. You got to talk serious to a girl like that. No more conks here, so she got to make somethin' of herself, startin' out by heppin' you!"

Though Sybbis complained bitterly, Mama would not let up on her, and eventually she became what the Farmwife called reasonably useful around the place, though the Widow shook her head over unswept corners and greasy pots. The refugee flow dwindled to nothing, leaving only the people in the tent town and a few marauders who lived by killing livestock and robbing people until they were hunted down by posses of farm folk, irritated beyond endurance. By the time the first snows of winter came, Fantis and Echinot lay empty under the snow, with even the corpse-fed dog packs run away or dead themselves. Word came that the cities north and east of Fantis had also been emptied by the plague.

The tent town outside Whitherby began to dwindle as the refugees moved on. Some were hired by farmers or truckers. Others with particularly citified skills announced their intention of going on south, through Artemisia, to the towns of Low Mesiko, or west, to the stilt towns along the Faulty Sea. A few found work in Whitherby itself, and word came of this pattern repeated over and over again among the villages in manland. Three-quarters of the city population had died, including virtually all the gangers. The other quarter had been widely spread among the villages or across the borders.

The Edges, so travelers said, appeared untouched. Some travelers had actually gone to the gates and asked the guards. They had been told there was no sickness there. Still, few people were seen through the gates, and no one from outside had been in to make sure.

When things had been quiet for long enough that everyone had settled down, CummyNup found Originee alone in the barn and asked if she would read the writing he had found in Abasio's place.

"It was written by a Sister to Trees," Farmwife told him. "Dictated by someone called Elrick-Ann. Elrick-Ann did not die of the plague. She has gone with the Sisters to an encampment in the western mountains, to be a cook for them. She wants Abasio to know she's all right."

CummyNup heaved a sigh and asked if Mama, Billibee, and Crunch could stay at Wise Rocks while he went south searching for Abasio.

"He my frien'," said CummyNup. "Maybe he need me. An' I oughta tell him what Elrick-Ann say."

"I'd be glad to have your mama stay," Originee answered. "She's been more than helpful. As for the children, Seelie would be most unhappy to see them go. I think they'd benefit from some schooling, too, don't you?"

CummyNup could only agree. Very few of the things learned in the cities had stood him in good stead in the countryside. Even his appearance had been against him. Now that the farm people knew no reinforcements could arrive from the cities, and now that his hair was partly grown out, CummyNup was more acceptable. He thought he wouldn't have much trouble working his way south, the way Originee said Abasio had gone.

Sybbis wanted to know all about Abasio, and CummyNup had no reason not to tell her. Sybbis narrowed her eyes, thought long thoughts, and asked certain odd questions, such as had Abasio frequented the songhouses and had Abasio used drugs much, and did he by any chance have a knife scar on his shoulder. She found more meaning in the answers than CummyNup did, for she demanded to go along. They argued over this for some days until Sybbis took advantage of a private moment in the haymow to convince CummyNup she would be a good traveling companion. CummyNup had had girls before, but never one like Sybbis!

Originee, who heaved a sigh of relief at the idea of Sybbis's imminent departure, told CummyNup about Abasio's wagon and horse, that he was escorting an Orphan, that he had become a dyer, and that there were gangers after him and walkers after the Orphan.

"Maybe the gangers are dead, so if Abasio thinks it's safe, tell him to come home," said Originee. "Tell him I'm looking out for his grandpa, but he'd be better home."


Behind Wide Mountain House in Artemisia, Abasio drove the wagon down the alleyway and parked it in the shimmering grove above the stream, as he had been directed to do.

"I'm not getting much out of this bargain so far!" Coyote complained with a yawn. "Tell me what happened."

Abasio merely grunted as he went to unhitch Big Blue, leaving it to Olly to mollify Coyote.

Olly repeated as much of their conversation as she remembered, concluding, "And they sent us here, where we're to wait until a librarian named Arakny shows up."

"Is that all?" Coyote sounded disappointed. "Are you sure that's all?"

Abasio had led Big Blue down to the stream and now returned with him to the wagon, the horse's muzzle dripping with moisture.

"I'm thirsty too," Coyote whined. "And you're not telling me everything!"

Olly filled the kettle from the barrel, splashed water into a bucket for him, and knelt beside him as he drank.

"We're not keeping anything from you, Coyote. They just didn't tell us much. I get the impression they're being sneaky here in Artemisia."

"Sneaky?" Coyote pricked his ears.

"I think they're letting books be destroyed, but they seem to have some way of keeping the information alive. They're going to let us talk to a librarian. And they'll let us go with them to the Place of Power."

She stood up, brushed her hands together, and said fretfully, "You know what I wish we had? I wish we had a map."

"A map?" asked Abasio.

"A map!" she said. "A chart. Oracle told me about them. Diagrams that show what lies along the way. Rivers and mountains and so forth." She sought a straight stick, broke it to gain a sharp point, smoothed a patch of dirt, then drew a map of their journey to Artemisia, marking rivers and mountains along the route. Coyote watched, turning his head from side to side, nodding intelligently as she explained.

Abasio wondered why he had never thought of maps before. The gangers customarily drew diagrams before a battle, showing where each group was to assemble, which streets or alleys they would attack, but he had never thought of having a diagram that extended outside the city. "That could be useful," he mused.

She said, "I'd like to know what countries are where! What's south of Artemisia? What lies east and west?"

"As to that," said Coyote, "High Mesiko lies south of Artemisia, and south of that Low Mesiko, both populated by small busy brown people in temple towns. East begins a wilderness of forests, going on forever, where the Black clans and the White clans make their clearings and plant their crops. West of here is the Place of Power, and beyond that is the country of the Sisters and the Guardians, who live among the high mountains, and beyond that the dry desert and then more mountains and the seashore, where the yellow people live in boat-bottomed towns."

"I know of that place beside the Faulty Sea. Oracle came from there, though she's more sort of tan than yellow. And hearing about it is interesting, but it doesn't take the place of a map."

Coyote said, "My hermit said no one is allowed to make maps now. Those who burn the books also destroy maps. If people do not have maps, they are less likely to travel. If they travel seldom, they stay on the roads. The Guardians do not like them going off the roads. Or the Sisters to Trees, either."

"Besides," said Abasio, "people are safer from monsters on the roads."

"That's true," said a familiar voice from among the trees. To a jingle of bells, Black Owl stepped out of their shade. "Monsters generally avoid the roads."

Coyote ducked beneath the wagon and curled up behind a wheel.

Olly cried, "It's like a puzzle! No maps, so nobody leaves the roads! No old books, so nobody wonders what happened or what used to be! Why would that be?"

"You won't solve the puzzle by shouting," said Abasio, looking around with a slightly furtive air.

"True," remarked Black Owl, with a laugh.

"It's very nice to see you again," said Olly, remembering her manners. "We didn't expect you."

"I've come to show the young man the wonders and delights of Artemisia!"

Abasio mumbled, "I should—stay with her."

"Oh, no. Arakny is coming to talk with her, woman talk, probably. We would only be in the way."

Coyote moved restlessly, glaring at Olly. She ignored him.

"Go on, Abasio," Olly said. "I'll wait here for what's-her-name."

"Arakny," said a voice from among the nearby trees. "Arakny, the librarian."

She came from the wind-flickered shade to join them, a slender woman, no longer quite young, her dress and boots of fringed sheepskin, her graying hair in braids, one of Olly's scarves loosely knotted around her neck.

She gave them both a long looking-over before waving Abasio and Black Owl away, like a mother shooing out the children. "Go, now. Olly and I have much to talk about."

They went off, Abasio turning to look over his shoulder at them. Coyote peered through the wheel spokes, his eyes alert. Olly saw Arakny watching Coyote, a strange expression on her face. Amusement, perhaps?

If so, Arakny said nothing about it as she turned and looked over the horse and the wagon, the wood basket and grill on its side.

"Why don't you build a fire and we'll have tea?" she suggested. "Do you have chairs?"

"Folding ones, up top," Olly remarked as she went obediently to the wood basket. "I have woodmint, or raspberry, or chamomile."

"Woodmint. It's soothing to the nerves." Without ado, Arakny climbed atop the wagon and lowered two of the folding chairs old Cermit had made, bent wood and laced rawhide. She hefted them approvingly, judging them to be both comfortable and light.

"You've come to ask about the thrones," she said when Olly had set the kettle to boil and the pot ready beside it. "It isn't but once in a coon's age someone comes to ask about the thrones. Those who do, so it is said, have reason to ask, for they are of a thronish kindred."

Olly turned to her in astonishment. "Others? Besides me?"

"So our library records. Every now and then. From here, from there. A woman or a man will show up, asking about the thrones, for they've had a prophecy or a dream or a vision of one kind or another. What was it with you?"

Olly paused only momentarily before deciding upon the truth. "A prophecy. Told by an Oracle, in an archetypal village. I was the Orphan there."

"And this old aunty whom your friend mentioned to Mother?"

"Was the Oracle. The only aunty I ever had."

"Ah." Arakny leaned back and looked up at the sky through the glittering leaves. "It is said the thrones are at the Place of Power, but I've never seen them there. Or heard of anyone who has."

" 'It is said, it is said,' " muttered Olly in an annoyed voice. "By whom is it said?"

"By our library," said Arakny, shifting the kettle a finger's width on the grill and whistling tunelessly between her teeth.

"Look," said Olly with some irritation, "either you tell me what you know or you don't. I didn't have a lot of sleep last night, and there's no point in my struggling to stay awake when I'm learning absolutely nothing!"

"I'm not holding back. I'm just deciding where to begin. I guess I begin when man went to the stars."

"That seems to be where everything begins," snarled Olly. "I'm really sick of hearing about when men went to the stars. We seem to date everything from that, as though it were the single important event in history, and it isn't even *our* history. It's theirs, the ones who went!"

"That event happens to be central to our current thinking, nonetheless," Arakny said crisply. "Central, because it both relieves us and tantalizes us."

Olly cocked her head. "Relieves us?"

"We who remain behind. The fact that man has already gone to the stars relieves the rest of us of the responsibility for being intrepid and marvelous. Of *becoming* something wonderful. Of seeding the universe with intelligence."

"I didn't know we were responsible for that."

"Many philosophers thought so, for generations. They wrote so. They claimed that that was the purpose of man, why he had license to use up the world as a chick uses up its egg: so we could hatch from it. So we could leave it behind, like a broken shell."

Olly sighed. "I can see people believing that. But once it's been done, the rest of us can just live. Even though we have only the eggshell to live on."

"The rest of us *can* just live. We in Artemisia *do* just live, making the most of our eggshell and being quite sure that other living things are allowed to live also. Our country is based upon that principle. But still we're tantalized by questions our library doesn't answer. Like: Why didn't everyone go?"

"You wonder how they chose who went and who stayed?"

"Yes, we wonder that. What gave them the right to leave some of us here?" She stirred the fire, pushing an unburned branch farther into the flame. "Also, why haven't some of them come back to fetch the rest of us? Or why haven't they sent us word where they ended up?"

"Maybe they're still on their way," murmured Olly, remembering things Burned Man had told her. "I had a friend, an ex-Edger, who said it would take men generations to reach even the nearest stars."

Arakny sighed. "Perhaps that's it. Whatever the reasons, our library speaks of the chaos of that time, nations falling apart, holes opening up in the sky-blanket, all the forests being destroyed. And it goes on to say that in a place of power, there rose up three great thrones.''

''*A* place of power. Are there more than one? Is it a different place of power from the one you know?''

''I don't know. Now, some versions mention only the thrones. Others say that upon them sat three great and ancient rulers who would bring order and hope to the world. As a librarian, I find no dichotomy between the versions, for in olden books *thrones* has more than one meaning. In some cases, *thrones* meant beings, not chairs.''

''Beings?''

''An order of angels.''

''Surely angels are mythical!''

Arakny laughed shortly. ''At one time ogres were thought to be mythical, and trolls, and dragons. At any rate, in some old books, thrones were a very high order of angels, just below the cherubim and seraphim.''

''What did the thrones do?''

Arakny shrugged. ''They came to restore the balance, so the old stories say. The world was out of balance, so the thrones rose up to restore it.''

''How?''

Arakny shrugged again. ''I've sought the answer to that in the library, without success.''

''If they arose to restore balance,'' Olly said in her most reasonable voice, ''then they must have made some changes. So what changed at that time?''

Arakny stretched widely. ''So many things. Archetypal villages were set up. Monsters returned. The eastern cities died, and those on the western sea.'' She rose to take up the steaming kettle and rinse out the pot before adding the tea leaves and pouring the boiling water over them. ''The fifty-year rule happened then, and the name changes.''

''I know about the fifty-year rule, but name changes?''

''Teams of people changed the names of things, or places. Sometimes they took away the names of cities, or streets, or even whole territories.''

''What do you mean? How can you—''

''Well, let's say a clan has always lived in a place they call *Sacred-home-of-our-fathers,* but the clan moves away because there's a drought. Somebody else moves into that same place, and they call it *New-home-of-our-people's-gods*. Then the first clan comes back. Both groups say that place belongs to them. Both claim a holy right to the same territory, and they're killing each other over it. Then one morning, a team shows up and tells them they can't call it either one of those names anymore. They have to call it *This-quite-ordinary-and-not-very-attractive-place-that-is-disputed-because-of-intermittent-habitation-patterns-due-to-conflict-and-climatic-changes*.''

"Which makes oratory somewhat difficult," Olly said with an appreciative grin.

"Well, it certainly doesn't make a good war cry! If they persist in fighting, then the teams come back and take other names and words away. Words like *invaders* and *enemy* and *terrorist* and *retaliation*. Anyone who says those words falls asleep for days and days."

"How do they do that?"

"I haven't any idea, even though it once happened to us. We didn't used to be Artemisians. We used to be Dine, and Zuni, and Hopi, and Apache, and Ute. Some of us were Tewa or Tiwa or Anglo or Hispanic. We all had separate languages and separate histories and rituals. Some of us had books, and some of us had oral traditions; some of us had sandpaintings and some of us had dances; and we were all fighting over who had which bit of land or how much water we could use from the river. So the name-change team took all our fighting words away, and when we couldn't say the words anymore, we couldn't fight over it."

"But you can say the words now!"

"Nobody gets mad about them now. People only fell asleep over words that made them angry. Angry enough to kill people over."

Olly shook her head in bewilderment. "Then why didn't they do it with the gangs in the cities of manland, where everybody's always fighting and killing one another?"

Arakny furrowed her brow and made a rocking motion with one hand, maybe this, maybe that. "Wide Mountain Mother says the name-change teams were only interested in certain places. Places along the western sea, and Artemisia, and in the Mesikos. It's like when we bring certain animals back. We don't put them everywhere. Just certain places, appropriate places. . . ."

Her voice trailed off into quiet, and she stared musingly into the smoke. "We don't put mountain goats on the prairies or bison on the peaks. Each thing to its proper place. It's probable that there are proper places for man and places man should stay out of." She sighed. "Anyhow, the name-change teams came from the Place of Power. I've been to the Place of Power—well, to the marketplace outside—but I've never seen or heard of any thrones there.

"And that's all you know?"

Arakny measured tea into the pot and poured boiling water over it. She shrugged. "I don't *know* that, as an absolute. I'm only quoting what our library says."

"Is that *all* it says?"

"No. That's merely all it says to me. It may say something else to you."

Olly gave her a puzzled look. "Well then, I'd like to—go there, see what more there is," Olly said.

"You don't need to go there. It has already come to you."

"I don't understand," she gaped.

"It has come to you. I bring the library." Arakny reached into her pocket and brought out a small packet, the size and shape of a not-very-thick book. Attached to it was a silvery mass, like a number of linked chains. Arakny flipped them open with one hand, and they locked into the semblance of a lacy cap. "It is here."

"A library!"

"More than one. All the libraries we've collected since men went to the stars. And not only books but songs and stories and paintings and dances, all the tales and histories, however told, however remembered."

"So when the book-burning teams come—"

"They burn books. They do not look in librarians' pockets. They do not burn this."

"Where did you get it?"

"We get them from an Edge. They make marvelous things in the Edges. This library can record words or sights or smells. Anything I can sense, the library can pick up. It can read books. There's an attachment to turn pages. It can read tapes and discs and cubes. It's a marvelous thing!"

"You have more than one of these?"

"Every librarian has one, plus there are a few extras. They can all be linked, too, so that information that one has can be shared among all of them."

"May I?" Olly asked, pointing to the silvery cap.

"Oh, indeed," said Arakny. "You may make your way through the library while I have tea. And when you have finished, we will join your friend at the men's houses on the height."

Arakny helped her put on the cap and showed her the controls on the side of the packet. "It's just an on-off switch. When you turn it on, you think your question. The library gives you what information it has on your question, which leads you to another question, and so on. Some people spend days hooked up to it."

"Days," breathed Olly.

Arakny patted her on the shoulder. "Don't worry. I'm here. I'll take care of you. I won't let you starve."


In the marketplace outside the Place of Power, Tom Fuelry and Qualary Finch wandered among the booths, buying a bit of this and a bit of that. Though they met often by appointment and had become close friends—which is what Qualary insisted they were, no more than that—Tom had formed the habit of showing up in this neutral territory to meet her as though by accident.

This was for her protection, in case she should ever need to say how she had met him or come to know him. At least, so Tom believed, ignoring the pleasure he took in her public person, which was quite distinct from her private one. In private she had become wanton, luxurious, instinctive, ignoring everything around her as she focused completely on appetites she had never known she had. In public she was as alert as a little squirrel, noticing everything that went on around her and commenting humorously on it under her breath, a running monologue that delighted him. As he had commented to Nimwes, it was like being in love with two different women without the complications of infidelity.

Today she was commenting on the weather, the shoppers, and the goods offered for sale, and he was trundling along behind her, listening with enjoyment, when she stopped so suddenly that he almost ran into her.

"What?" he said, following her gaze.

"Something," she muttered. "Oh, Tom."

She was staring fixedly into the sheltered space made by two vehicles parked at right angles where half a dozen children, Domer children and outsiders, had drawn a circle in the dirt and were playing marbles. So much Tom saw at once, though it took him a moment more to see what had attracted Qualary's attention.

Near the vehicles, almost hidden by them, stood a black-helmed walker. There were other walkers scattered throughout the market, but for the most part they were behaving as walkers did, either standing totally immobile or striding about on their incomprehensible business. The one Qualary was watching, however, was acting as no walker had ever acted. It was twitching. It bent its head jerkily forward, then back. Its arms flicked forward, then back. The children, who were only a few feet away, did not seem to notice it. They went on playing, moving around their circle, their voices rising in derision or complaint, while the walker grew more and more agitated.

One of the players made a good shot, jumped to his feet, and waved his arms in self-congratulation as he gave a victory yell.

"You will surrender!" the walker shouted suddenly, darting forward to grasp the waving child by the shoulder. "You will surrender!"

The child screamed as he went up into the air, suspended by the shoulder. He screamed again. There was a noise, a cracking, as of a dry stick broken, then the child went flying even as the walker moved forward again. Another child flew screaming through the air to strike the pillar of stone where the first one lay unmoving. Several onlookers howled with rage as the walker teetered and jittered, shouting at the remaining cowering children, "You will surrender, render, render, render!"

A flung stone caught the walker on the head. It turned and began to stalk the thrower, only to be overwhelmed from behind by three large men who bore the walker onto the stony ground and began bashing it with whatever stones or tools had been closest to hand.

Qualary ran to the place the children lay, joining a mixed group already there, Domers, Gaddirs, and outsiders, women weeping, other children screaming in dismay.

An Artemisian woman still holding the skeins of wool she had come to sell stood up from the crumpled bodies and said in an expressionless voice, "Both. Gone."

Weeping adults went to their knees beside the bodies.

The men battering the walker stood up and backed away from the wreckage that still twitched, jerked, twitched, black fingers scrabbling against the gravel. The men were themselves battered and bruised and splotched with the walker's body fluids. One attacker held his arm protectively in the other hand, the injured wrist dangling at an unnatural angle.

"Tom, Tom," Qualary whispered, clutching at him.

He put his arms around her. "Let's get out of here," he said, wanting desperately to get back to Gaddi House and tell His Wisdom what had happened. His Wisdom wouldn't be surprised, he told himself, anymore than he himself had been. Appalled, but not surprised.

He led her back to the wall. They had just cleared the gate when he saw a column of black-helmeted walkers approaching, Quince Ellel's robed form in their midst. Tom darted to one side and through an open door, pulling Qualary after him and holding her there until the last of the procession had passed by. Ellel had not seen them.

"Why?" she cried, seemingly unaware of Ellel's passage. "Why did it kill them?"

He shook his head. If His Wisdom was right, the walker had killed the children for no reason at all, but he'd rather not tell her that. It wasn't something he wanted her worrying over. Or talking about.

He took her with him into Gaddi House, left her weeping in his quarters while he went to His Wisdom, then returned to lie down beside her and hold her close. She wept for a long time before falling asleep with her head on his shoulder.

Some time passed. Outside the window, darkness filled the garden, which turned on the lights. The fountain played softly, peaceably, quietly glimmering. Tom stretched his arm, relieving a cramp in his shoulder, and the motion brought her half-awake.

"I'm too heavy," she murmured, moving away from him.

"Shh," he said, pulling her back where she had been. "You're not too heavy. We just haven't moved for hours."

She wiped at her tear-smeared face. "I have to go home."

"Why? What do you have to do?"

"Tonight—tonight I have to get ready, get my things together. Tomorrow I do Ellel's quarters."

"Does she know you have a Gaddir friend?"

Qualary pulled herself up and considered this question. "I don't think so. I think she stopped being interested in me a long time ago. Once she has things under control, she pretty well loses interest."

"Have you thought what you'd say if she ever found out?"

Qualary shifted uncomfortably. "She'd kill me."

Tom smiled at her. "I wouldn't like that. I wouldn't like that at all. I'd rather you protected yourself."

"Against Ellel? Oh, my. She's—she's hard to protect against. She comes at you when you don't expect it."

"But we know what she's like. We know what she's afraid of. And if you offered to find out things for her, things about Gaddi House . . ."

"Oh, Tom, I'd never ask you to—"

He smiled again. "I have no intention of telling you anything that would be troublesome, either for you or for me or for anyone else. But there are things we can tell Ellel that aren't troublesome. Ordinary things, but still, things she doesn't know."

"It would give me an excuse for seeing you?" she asked. "Oh, do you think it would?"

"She might even give you time off to do more of it."

Qualary Finch surprised herself by smiling. Then, ashamed of herself for smiling so soon after what she had witnessed that day, she broke into tears again.

The next morning, when she had cleaned Ellel's quarters thoroughly, she dallied over the last few chores, waiting to be noticed.

"What's keeping you?"

The voice was more toneless than usual. Qualary swallowed deeply, fixing her eyes on her feet.

"Ma'am, there's a Gaddir man been attentive to me lately, and I wondered if you'd like me to see what I can find out from him." She had rehearsed that sentence a hundred times this morning. Now she glanced up through her lashes to see mask and robe standing petrified, like stone.

"He tells me things," she went on. "I don't know if they're important or not. Probably not, but still I thought I should ask."

The robe sagged only a little. The mask tilted.

"*Tells* you things? Not *asks* you things?"

"Oh, no, ma'am, he never asks me anything."

"What kinds of things does he tell you?"

"Oh, history, mostly. Like how many people there were before men went to the stars. And—"

"How many?"

"Five hundred million on this continent, he says. He says there were eleven billion in the whole world."

Long pause. Metallic laugh. "There weren't that many. There couldn't have been."

Qualary swallowed. Fuelry had covered the possibility of contradiction. "Oh, ma'am," she said, "he may not know what he's talking about. He's just a worker over there. But he does go in and out all the time."

"Yes. Go on seeing him. Get friendly with him. Really friendly, you understand me!"

Flushing, Qualary nodded.

"Ask him about Seoca! Ask him about the old man. Ask him if there are any children in Gaddi House. Ask him what they do in there."

"He may not know."

"Well, whatever he knows. He likes history? Ask him when Gaddi House was built. And why, why was it built."

Greatly daring, Qualary murmured, "But, ma'am, don't you and the other Domers know why?"

The answer was only murmured, as though from someone distracted. "It was here when our people got here. But we had no records of its being here. So we don't know who built it. Or why." The robe quivered.

Qualary turned, ready to leave, only to be stopped.

"Qualary."

"Ma'am."

"Did you hear what happened in the market yesterday?"

Frantic thoughts chased one another. Say yes. Say no. Say nothing.

"I heard . . . something," she said unwillingly. "Someone was hurt, was it?"

"Some children teased a walker." That dead, metallic tone again. "That's a dangerous thing to do, Qualary."

"Oh, yes, ma'am. That would be dangerous."

Silence. Then, "If anyone asks, you tell them about the children teasing the walker. Won't you?"

"Oh, yes, ma'am."

She fled.

"And now you're safe," said Fuelry, when she told him how the conversation had gone. "You're only doing what she's told you to do."

"She wants to know all sorts of things."

"Like?"

Qualary repeated what she remembered: Seoca, children, the purpose of Gaddi House, when and why built.

"Well, let's see. Seoca is old, but he's alive and well. Yes, there are children in Gaddi House, but they're all the children of the workers. They have a school here, just as the Domers have a school for Domer children. As for Gaddi House, it was built so long ago that no one knows when. Tell her that.''

His Wisdom insisted that was true, at least for the lower parts of the great building, though the upper and outer shell had probably been built more recently.

"She wants to know what is done in here.''

He ticked a fingernail against his front teeth. "You could tell her Gaddi House was set up to preserve the earth and the place of all life upon it.''

"That has a nice sound to it,'' said Qualary. "Is it true?''

"Oh, I'm sure it is,'' he said, sliding his arm around her. "Haven't you noticed how I'm preserving you and your place in it, for example?''

She made a little sound, as though she tried to laugh but found it hurt too much. "Ellel says the children teased the walker. That's why it killed them.''

He looked at her in disbelief. "She expects you to believe that?''

"She doesn't care what I believe. She only cares what we say. We . . . Domers. She wants us to say it was the children's fault.''

"Does she know you saw it?''

She shook her head.

"Don't tell her,'' said Fuelry. "You'll be safer if she doesn't know.''


After Black Owl showed Abasio the town, which extended through a series of plazas with homes and offices of various sorts grouped around them and nothing anywhere that Abasio thought of as the least citified, they went down the slope toward the stream, Black Owl pointing up the opposite slope as he said, "Wide Mountain Mother thought you might enjoy feast night at the men's house.''

"Men's house?'' Abasio asked.

"On the ridge. Those large buildings are men's houses.''

"The men don't live down here?'' Abasio asked, turning to look over his shoulder. He was looking for the clearing where he'd parked the wagon, and he saw it through the trees. Olly and Arakny were there, sitting beside a small fire with their heads together.

"Off and on, now and then,'' Black Owl said. "But living among men suits men best. Women are peripheral to our lives. The women say they are *occasionally adored, but mostly ignored.*'' He laughed. "If that's true—and who am I to contradict the women—it suits both of us best when we are allowed to live in accordance with it.''

Abasio looked where he was going just in time to avoid tripping over a large stump above the stream bed. "How do you mean?''

Black Owl sat upon the stump and assumed an attitude of oratory. ''We are happiest when our men and women relate to one another naturally, unconstrained by contrary custom. I will tell you how the women say it. They say this: In past times, men never gave up having mommies. When they grew up, they merely took a sexual mommy and went on being boys at home. To keep the women from escaping being mommies, the men made certain rules about what women could do and how women could behave.''

This did not seem totally unreasonable to Abasio, though he was glad Olly was not there to hear it.

''When a mommy got old and fat, sometimes a man would throw her out and get a younger mommy. But,'' said Black Owl, striking a pose, ''our women say being a mommy for anyone is damned hard work, and being a mommy for grown men is boring, so came a time—it was shortly before men went to the stars—that women fought a great battle and refused to be men's mommies anymore.''

''I've never heard that,'' said Abasio, openmouthed.

''Oh, yes. It was called the Old Folks' War, and the women were called feminists. They were greatly revered by our foremothers.'' Black Owl rose to his feet and led the way across the stream bed, leaping over the silver threads of water and winding his way through the white hulks of dead trees that lay along the far side.

''What happened?'' asked Abasio, when he had caught up to him. ''In the war?''

''When the feminists first rose up, they were cursed by certain groups of old men who knew God personally, so the women declared war on the old men and on their God. The oldest women among the feminists, some who had been thrown away by their menfolk and many who had little time to live anyhow, took secret weapons and poisons and began killing the old men. Their battle cries were 'Tit for tat,' and 'Sauce for the gander.' ''

''Did they kill all the old men?'' Abasio was aghast, thinking of his grandpa.

''No, just judges and priests and those who made the rules and spoke for the men's God. The old women were imprisoned or put to death, but other old women took their place, and in time many more old men died.''

''So what happened!''

''So many old men were dying that they decided it was time to reexamine the rules and perhaps even get a new god. Finally, after much shouting, everyone agreed that men were at their best among men, women at their best among women, that their problems arose when one sex made rules for the other, and that they enjoyed one another most when they were least constrained to endure one another's company. So here in Artemisia, each sex makes rules only for itself, and we live mostly apart, but with no walls between. When we want one another, we are here, and when we do not want one another, we go apart.''

Abasio shut his mouth abruptly. He had never considered such a way of doing things. ''Who cooks for the men?'' he demanded. ''Who mends their clothes?''

''Why should anyone cook for us but ourselves?'' Black Owl asked, astonished. ''And if men can make costumes for the dances, can they not sew up a shirt? We do both things very well, as you will see tonight. It is the first dance of the season. The Owl Society has made a feast and invited everyone to enjoy the food, the dancing, and the company. We are having roast lamb.''

''Artemisia has a pastoral culture, then?''

''Some of us graze sheep on the desert in winter and early spring and in the mountains in summer. Some of us farm the lands along the river and cut hay from the pastures there. Some of us keep sun-pit greenhouses for winter food. Our main trade crops are wool and leather, vegetables and meat. We keep goats for milk and cheese. We have different sorts of horses for the patrols and the shepherds.

''Since men are stronger and our chemistry inclines us more to battle, we provide most of the patrols and most of the sheepguards who take the flocks to pasture. We also fight off the occasional troll or ogre that comes too far south.''

''It doesn't sound like the kind of society that would have a huge library and need librarians,'' said Abasio. ''I expected it to be more—more citified.''

Black Owl shook his head firmly. ''Cities are not good for this world! Wherever a city is, there also the land dies and the creatures of the land die. Look at the nests of ants, how around them the land is barren. So it is with people when they live like ants.''

They had climbed the far bank onto a sandy road that led to the ridge above the town. The buildings there gleamed orange and salmon and copper in the evening light. Drum sounds filtered downward, along with the rattle of tambours and the thud of many feet stamping in unison.

''Owl House,'' said Black Owl, when they had climbed almost to the top. The building he indicated was tiled with a design of eyes and wings, talons and beaks. On the hard earth before it, a circle of gorgeously costumed men danced to the sound of the drums, stopping every now and then to confer about their performance, while the drummers and chanters stood impassively on the sidelines and a scattering of onlookers watched from the porches on three sides. Smoke rose from pits at one side of the house, and the smell of roasting meat made Abasio salivate hungrily.

''Do the dances have meaning?'' Abasio asked.

Black Owl cast a quick look around him, then said sotto voce, ''Don't ask that of anyone else. Our men would be much offended that the meanings aren't clear to you after the endless hours they spend in ritual, in making costumes and carvings, in learning the stories of our people and our land.''

He led Abasio toward a circle of chairs set in the shade of the porch, two of them occupied by elderly men with gray braids and bright blankets wrapped around their shoulders. "A guest," he called. "A dyer, from manland, who travels through Artemisia." He turned to Abasio and indicated the elders. "Tall Elk. Night Raven. Now, you will sit here, in comfort, watching the early dances. And when the womenfolk join us, we will eat."

He slipped away among the clustered participants, leaving Abasio to seat himself between the two old men. Despite the color and rhythm going on all around him, his thoughts were back in the river bottom, where Olly was. What was she learning? What could Arakny tell her?

His distraction was broken by the man to his left, Night Raven:

"You are a cityman?"

Abasio nodded. "From Fantis."

"Fantis, alas," said Tall Elk.

"Cities, alas," returned Night Raven.

Abasio took this for a ritual exchange and merely nodded.

Tall Elk nodded in return. "You have a name?"

"Sonny Longaster."

"Ah."

Night Raven rocked forward to get a good look at Abasio's face, saying, "Tonight we dance the return of the bison."

"Bison?" asked Abasio.

Night Raven nodded slowly. "Soon after men went to the stars, the Animal Masters cut all the fences, then bred many bison and returned them to the prairies. I have ridden there myself to see the bison on the grasslands, yes, from the foot of the mountains to the far forests."

"My grandpa told me there are Black and White clans in the forests," Abasio remarked.

Tall Elk commented, "Our storytellers say they were different colors long ago. Long have they fought, capturing one another's women and fathering children upon them. They are all the same color now. Still, those who once were blacks call themselves blacks, and those who once were whites call themselves whites, no matter who their mothers were."

Abasio forestalled any further questions about himself by asking, "The woman who said she was the Wide Mountain Mother—whose mother is she?"

Night Raven laughed, tugging at the long gray braid that lay across his shoulder. "She is all our mother. She was chosen to be mothermost of all the Wide Mountain women."

"But she obviously wasn't your real mother."

"A real mother is who?"

"The one who had you, who was pregnant with you."

Tall Elk gave him a curious look. "Do you, then, know who bore you?"

"Well, yes."

"I don't know who was my birth mother. Do you, Raven?"

Night Raven scratched behind one ear, reflectively. "I always thought it might have been White Rose. People used to tell me I resembled her. And I also thought I was the birth son of Stout Bear. Do you remember him?"

"Of course. He died fighting that winged thing that was stealing the sheep. We sing his praises still."

"So you *don't* know who your parents were?" Abasio persisted.

"They were healthy. What more is needful to know?"

"How do you know that?"

Tall Elk pursed his lips and looked severe. "We do not allow pride to get in the way of the health of our children, that's why."

"Pride *or* stupidity," remarked Night Raven.

"With the Wide Mountain Clan checking on us all the time, who's allowed to be stupid?" laughed the other.

"I don't understand what you're saying," Abasio persisted.

Night Raven shook his head at such ignorance. "Some men and women are healthy, some are not. Some women are good breast mothers, some are not. Some persons care for toddlers well. Some are good at educating older children. To insist on bearing children if one is not healthy, to insist on rearing children when one is unskilled at it, or on educating when one is ignorant—why, that is what animals do! That is how sheep behave! Every ram tries every ewe. Every ewe nurses her own lamb. Can the ewe see if the ram mounting her has runny eyes? Does the ram care that the ewe's udder is collapsed? Does the bad mother among sheep give her lamb to another sheep that will mother better? No, for they are animals! A man or woman who acts so is no better than a sheep!"

"That's rather harsh," Abasio offered.

"Man must recognize his animal heritage before he can humanize himself," snorted Tall Elk. "In the bad old days, man sentimentalized his animal nature. He acted like the sheep but called it love. If bearing unhealthy children is love when man does it, then it's love when sheep do it too."

Both the old men laughed, almost silently.

"But who raises you if your parents don't?"

Tall Elk tugged at one of his braids, as though stimulating thought. "First a breast mother. Then men and women who like raising little ones. Then men and women who like educating older ones."

"And you live with them?"

"All our people, including little people, stay wherever they are happiest. We do not pull at people as though we owned them."

Abasio gestured toward the dance floor, where there were many youngsters of both sexes among the men. "What if a woman wants to do men's kinds of things? Hunt, or be a shepherd, or dance?"

Night Raven shrugged. "Some of the women's households do those things. Most men enjoy one kind of thing, and most women enjoy another, but that does not mean all men and all women are alike. We are not archetypes. We are individuals."

"But this Mankind Management Group of yours makes your decisions for you."

The two old men looked at him with serious faces. Tall Elk reached out a bony old hand and shook him gently by one shoulder. "Listen, young dyemaster. Our Management Group makes only the decisions of where and how many! Think! *These are the most important decisions men can make, yet before men went to the stars, no one ever made them!* Each man fucked as he willed! Each woman bore as she would! Life, they said in that time, was holy, but they meant only their own lives, and so in many places all life died!"

"We in Artemisia say no life is holy unless all life is holy!" commented the other old man. "Here, in the Land of the Sages, no town may overstress the land and its life. Each must be small enough that the inhabitants know one another by name. So is disruption and ugliness avoided! So does beauty and order surround us. The librarians tell us that in olden times people were anonymous and many, and evil was done without shame."

"But not here," murmured Abasio.

"No; in Artemisia, each of us is known. We wear our name upon our faces, in our costume, in our clan insignia. Each of us is responsible for what he does. He does not blame his heritage for what he becomes!"


Olly seated herself carefully in the rawhide chair across from Arakny. She put her hands to her head, feeling the silvery cap with gingerly fingers.

"It's all right," said Arakny. "It won't hurt you."

Still, Olly hesitated.

"I want to know," she said plaintively. "But—"

"But the idea of knowing scares you."

"Yes," she agreed, surprised.

"I know. It's easier not to know too much. You can believe nice easy things if you don't know too much. Like, 'good guys always win.' And 'generosity is rewarded.' And 'life is eternal.' Stuff like that." Arakny laughed. "We librarians tend to be cynics. We have to be brave."

Olly smiled tremulously. "I'll try," she said, taking the little box into her lap. She leaned back, her finger on the button, then turned it on.

Arakny watched as Olly stiffened, as a startled look came into her eyes, then as consciousness fled away. She had gone inside herself, where all the information now was. It was scary. Scary to experience. Scary to watch.

Arakny lifted her cup and sipped her tea, eyes fixed thoughtfully on the girl sitting across from her. No two librarians ever found the same information, because no two ever asked precisely the same question. Even when the words were the same, the mental attitude toward the words was different, the experiences underlying the words were different, the need-to-know was different. So now, this girl would ask the same questions Arakny had asked, but she would not receive the same answers.

Sometimes, when two librarians had explored a similar area of knowledge, they shared their perceptions with one another. Perhaps this girl would do the same.


Olly stood upon mist, with mist around her. On every side, above, below, behind, the mist was a presence. It was there, tangible though tenuous, occupying all available time and space.

"What is your question?" the presence seemed to ask. "You have reached the library. What is your question?"

The question Oracle had told her to ask, of course.

"Ask one only child," she cried.

One only children, dark and bright eyed, blond and pale eyed, fat ones, lean ones, laughing ones, crying ones, an endless river of only children flowed through her mind, great hordes of them, parented and orphans, familied and foundlings, abandoned nameless infants and sole heirs to great dynasties. None of them looked familiar to her. She did not find herself among them. She could not find herself in all this mob.

"Thrones," she thought. "One only child, and thrones."

The hordes disappeared as though they had been smoke. Now were thrones with their heirs presumptive seated upon them, princes, princesses, a procession of nobility, of majesty. Here waved the flag of a country, here sat a crown, a scepter, here were guardsmen and councillors and courtiers. Some thrones were ancient, of times and countries long past, and others were new as tomorrow, but none of them was the throne she knew, the gray throne, the great throne . . . one of three.

"Three thrones!" she cried mentally, sending the plea into whatever and wherever the library was. "Three thrones, and one only child, and two who made her."

A moment's vacancy, as though the mist sought within itself, and then

they were there, as she had dreamed them long ago and often since. Thrones.
Tall and gray, covered all over with strange carvings. Three of them standing
side by side, ponderous and immemorial. Surely such things could not move,
and yet they did. They shifted. The two at the sides moved behind the center
one so that she saw only that one. Then they separated into three. Then they
merged once more. One throne. Three thrones. Three that were, in some
special way, alike. Three of the same kindred. Superimposed. Apart. Superimposed. One kindred. Of one kind.

She looked intently at the one, the single great gray chair where it stood
solidly upon its four legs, its four feet. Huge legs. Monstrous feet. See how
the feet changed, shifted, grew toes, extended claws that extended and
reached. See how the legs lengthened and jointed themselves, bending beneath the throne as though to leap upward. But it wasn't a chair any longer.
The back of it had bent backward, bowed, become a neck, the end of it
shaped itself into a head. Now it turned upon its great legs, its huge feet,
so she could see its mighty head, its ears and mane and enormous glowing
eyes. It had not actually been a chair at all. It had always been an ani—no.
Not an animal, not a beast. A being. A huge, monstrously ancient being that
now stood high upon its legs as it stalked out of its place, out of its cavern,
out of its lair. See it walk onto the mountain peaks. It strides, oh, it strides.
It strides across the peaks, across the sky. It leaps from star to star, galaxy
to galaxy, its fiery mane flowing behind, its great taloned feet tearing at the
nebulae, its mighty shoulders thrusting aside the dark veils where nothing is
and all is about to be.

Ancient it is. Immortal it is. A servant of life it is, created in the dawn
of time before life had yet emerged, to control that life and keep it within
proper bounds.

See how it returns across the sky and comes to rest, how it sits upon its
feet, becoming only a chair once more, splitting to become two, or three,
or more if more are needed. And see how living creatures come into the
cavern where the thrones are, now one creature, now another, to bow down
before they sit upon it, upon them. And those who sit upon the thrones, they
rise, they go away, they do the thrones' command and they return. And
again they go to do the thrones' command. And they return, to go again.
Until at last they return and seat themselves but do not rise again, but melt
instead, but flow, but become part of what it is they sit upon. Liquid substance
absorbed into other substance making an alloy. Water flowing into water.
Fungible. Indistinguishable.

"I have seen you before!" Olly cried. "I have seen you before. Did I sit
there, upon you? Have you sent me away to accomplish some great thing?
Am I to come back to you now?"

No answer, only the chairs, three, then one, then three again.

"The Place of Power," she asked. "Where are the thrones? Where is the correct place of power?"

Sunset over the mesa, a dome black against the sky, a high, blocky fortress to the right, a wall, gates, people coming away from the gates with the things they had traded for. Inside the wall, four families contending with one another and with a great, golden fortress. Outside the wall, green robed women, green-and-brown-clad men, feathered warriors and women of Artemisia moving away from the gates and the sun sinking behind them as the stars pricked out, one by one.

And a tide of walkers along the road. Black-helmed figures like ants, flowing into and out of the place of power, the earth charred beneath their feet, the vegetation dying where they walked.

And from the fortress, a call, a summons, like the call of a mighty commander to an errant armsman: "Come! Now! Too long have you delayed! You are past time! Come now to my aid, before it is too late."

Dismayed, she asked something, something, something.

The world around her melted into nothing.

She saw the pattern. It emerged from what she knew, what she had been told, what she had seen and guessed and speculated about. It was like the patterns the dyer used. This block and that, joined in such a way.

A long, long silence. A long time of learning.

She looked up into Arakny's eyes.

"I took the cap off you," she said. "You've been in there a long time, and you were drifting. Sometimes it does that to people. We never let a woman use the cap while she's alone. You can get lost in there!"

"Do you know what's in there?" Olly asked, her voice sounding harsh and unaccustomed, as though she had not used it for several years.

"You mean, do I know the answers to your questions? No. Even if I asked your questions, I would get different answers. I do know, in a general way, what's in there: all the information from everywhere that the librarians of Artemisia have managed to collect in more than a hundred years. Everything anyone ever wrote or said or danced or painted or sculpted. Everything we know about people now. That's what we're for, we librarians. We catch everything in our webs.

"And the machine—the . . . brain in there—it puts it all together to make more than the sum of its parts." She laughed. "In a way, it's smarter than we are. It can extrapolate better than we can. People, you know, there are some solutions they won't accept. The brain in this thing, it accepts everything."

Olly shook her head in wonder, in awe. "And they make this in the Edge?"

"The device itself, yes. Empty, of course. What we put into it is our
business." She began to fold the cap.

"Don't put it away. I have to borrow it for a while."

"You haven't found what you needed to know?"

"Your Place of Power is the right one. I came from there. I must go there
now, urgently." She reached for the library, tugged at it.

Something in Olly's voice made Arakny release her grip on the library.
"What is it, Olly Longaster?"

Olly looked at the library in her hands, looked up past Arakny at the
glowing sky, soft pink in the lowe of sunset. "Only a pattern, Arakny.
Things I know without knowing how I know. But it is as important to you
as it is to me. I do not ask for your library out of any trifling curiosity."

Arakny ran her fingers across her hair, undecided. "I'm not supposed
to—"

"I know. But if you ask Wide Mountain Mother, she will tell you it's all
right."

"How do you know that?"

Olly held up the library. "I know, that's all."

Arakny stared at her for a long moment, then sighed. "Well, I'll ask.
Keep it for now. I think we'd both profit from a meal and a rest. We'll go
up the hill to join your . . . "

"I can't take time to!" Olly rose to her feet. The sense of urgency in her
had risen like a tide.

Arakny shook her head. "No matter where you have to go, you can't go
now. You can't travel in the dark. No one will guide you until tomorrow.
You must take time to eat and sleep, and tomorrow you can go as fast as
you are able." She started toward the stream, beckoning imperatively.

Coyote barked sharply.

"Go on," said Olly. "Let me take care of . . . my dog."

"Yes," called Arakny. "Take care of . . . your dog." She walked toward
the river.

"What?" demanded Olly of the animal behind the wheel.

"I want to see the dances."

"You weren't invited. But that's all right. I'll tell you about them."

Coyote growled. "Untie me at least!"

She did that, suggesting that he lie still until they were gone. "There's
food in our food box. You can have all of it. No hunting in Artemisian
chicken yards! I want to stay in their good graces."

Coyote snarled, "You're leaving them. You're going to the Place of
Power! You said so!"

"That's where I have to go!" she cried in an agonized whisper. "I want
to start now, but I suppose she's right. There's no way—"

"That thing she had, that—library. Do you suppose I could try it?"

Olly gave him a long look. "Coyote. I promise you. You'll have a chance to try it."

Then she turned and trudged away after Arakny. She felt hollow inside. Perhaps it was only hunger. Perhaps it was something else again. The sound of that voice still rang in her mind: *Now. Urgently. Before it is too late!* And here she was, going to a dance!

Still, Arakny was right. Big Blue needed to eat and rest. She and Abasio could not travel in the dark. Probably they needed a guide, would get there more quickly with a guide. So, early in the morning, then. As soon as it was day!

She caught up with Arakny at the stream and followed her up the opposite slope. Above them the sound of drums and rattles welled and ebbed, voices rose, smoke blew down toward them smelling of meat and resin.

As they neared the top, Arakny paused to say, "Usually the first dance of the season is one of thanksgiving for the return of the rains, and it's followed by the mend-the-world hoop dance. I've heard they're going to dance the return of elk and bear and bison tonight, if they have had time to make preparations."

"We saw elk on our way here," said Olly in a preoccupied voice. "We think we saw bear."

Taking no notice of Olly's preoccupation, Arakny said, "They've been wanting to do those dances for the last five years, but the Animal Masters said there weren't enough animals yet. It's not right to dance it until we've actually done it! Lord of all trees, what we went through! We had forests to replant in certain places, to stop erosion, and the Sisters to Trees were in and out of here every week. Then the Guardians showed up to teach us how to clean the water. Then we had to improve meadows by adding certain forbs that had been wiped out. The Guardians provided seeds, but still, it was backbreaking work!

"After all that was done, we got our breeding stock from the Animal Masters. Then when the elk were breeding again, we had to protect the calves until the population was large enough to sustain itself. This meant raising sheep to feed the predators, to keep them alive also, for they are required in the mended earth just as the elk are required. We had to protect the calves from poachers from the cities too."

"How did you do that?"

"Our men mostly ambushed them and killed them. The cities care nothing for a renewed earth, but our rule is, man may not eat what he does not protect!" She sounded so ferocious that Olly blinked.

They made their way toward the porch, where they found Abasio seated between two elderly men, all three of them talking and nodding and laughing.

Arakny and Olly joined the group, and Olly was introduced to Tall Elk and Night Raven.

Before them, dancers turned and twisted in the light of the setting sun, light gleaming from their oiled skins, from the feathers they wore, dancing to the beat of the drums and the sound of the singers.

"What are they singing?" Olly asked.

Night Raven replied: "They sing in one of the old languages of the blue boy rain walking on the wind, of the yellow girl rain that comes with the sun of spring, of the black male rain that makes the arroyos flow, of the white woman rain that soaks the fields. They beg the rains to come again, to make this place their home, to regard us as their children."

The two visitors sat cross-legged, arms resting on their knees, quietly watching the dancers. After a time, Arakny signaled to one of the young people on the porch who brought them food on wooden trenchers: sliced meat and flat circles of bread and vegetables Olly had never tasted before.

"Beans," Abasio whispered to her. "And tomatoes. Grandpa used to grow them sometimes, but our season wasn't really long enough."

"Tomato and onion and green pepper," agreed Arakny. "And bread made from corn, and melon and beans and roast lamb. And peaches and apricots and apples. And honey from the hive. And milk and cheese from the goats. Bounty. In the autumn we celebrate bounty. It was a habit of one of our groups long ago, and the others of us found it appropriate."

The rain dancers left the circle, and others entered, these bearing bundles of wooden hoops that they laid in piles around themselves and took up one by one as they danced, interlacing them with their arms and legs to make wings, becoming birds; to make manes and heavy legs, becoming animals. Olly watched in fascination as they danced, never missing a beat of the drums, the hoops spinning, shifting, interlocking, working up from legs onto arms, from arms onto hands, now all the hoops joined together to form huge lacy spheres around each dancer, and out of these large openwork eggs the dancers hatched, feet first, ending with the spheres carried triumphantly above them.

"They have danced creation, the hatching of life, the final mending of the earth," whispered Arakny. "The hoops are symbolic of the cycles of life, birth and death joined, each thing dependent upon other things, all existence woven together."

Other dancers entered the circle. The drummers and singers went on tirelessly. Olly ate everything on her trencher and would have gone for more if she had not feared to appear greedy. She wanted to tell Abasio about the library, about what she'd learned, but it did not seem appropriate with so many people about.

Instead she whispered to him, "I need to talk to you. As soon as we can politely leave, let's go."

He nodded, peering at her face. "What?"

"I'll tell you down at the wagon."

He nodded again. Someone came with a jug and a basket of gourd cups. They drank the beverage offered, water and honey and fruit juices mixed together.

"No beer?" asked Abasio.

"We cannot waste our time so," Arakny replied, "or our grain. Water is our drink, usually. Or goat's milk. Though sometimes the cider from our apples turns, you know, becoming something more. We drink that, in order not to waste it." She grinned at them impishly.

It had grown dark; only the firelight illuminated the dancers, giving them an otherworldly look, half fire-colored, half dark, reduced to outlines and flat surfaces, demonic, perhaps, though they were undoubtedly good demons.

Abasio squeezed Olly's hand, the gesture saying he was preparing to leave. "Where will I find . . ." he asked, rising.

Arakny looked up at him. "Over there." She nodded across the fire. "The compost house is behind the crowd over there, beyond those two trees."

"We'll leave when I get back, in just a moment," he murmured to Olly, turning to stride off around the circle.

She rose, fidgeting. She should get back to the wagon, put things away, be ready to leave early in the morning. As soon as it was light!

A chorus of joyful cries came from the watchers.

"Look!" cried Arakny, echoing the others. "Here come the bison dancers, the elk dancers! Oh, look!"

New dancers had entered the circle, men wearing antlers, men wearing bulky headdresses with carved horns. They circled and stamped, they spiraled, shaking their feathered lances. The people cried encouragement as the drums quickened and a new song was sung.

"We've worked so hard on this!" said Arakny, tears in her eyes. "It's taken so many years."

Alert for Abasio's return, Olly detected a restless movement among the watchers across the circle, a heaving, as though they had been disturbed. The fire leaped up, and she caught a momentary glimpse of a huge figure there, briefly lit, then lost in darkness once more.

"Who was that?" she asked Arakny.

"Who? Someone over there?" The woman peered, wiping at her eyes with her sleeve. "I don't see anyone except people from town."

"Someone very tall, very big."

"A stilt dancer from the Rabbit Society, probably. They sometimes end the evening with clowning.'' She turned her attention back to the dancers, leaving Olly to stare into the darkness, disturbed by what she had seen, though uncertain as to why.

"Those strange people who entered through the gate this morning. Those two walkers,'' Olly murmured. "Did they go on?''

"South,'' said Arakny. "Oh, yes. Women from town watched them go.''

"How about people coming in? Did anybody else . . . remarkable come in today?''

Arakny turned toward her, giving her a curious look. "I don't know. I was told about the two walkers. I was told about you. No one else was mentioned to me.''

"Gangers? From one of the cities up north?''

"No one said. What's the trouble, Olly Longaster?''

"I think I'll go find Sonny.''

"We'll go together,'' the woman said, rising, her forehead furrowed.

They moved to the rear of the circle of watchers and worked their way around the outside in the direction Abasio had gone, stumbling a little in the shadows. As they approached the far side of the crowd, almost opposite where they'd been sitting, they found much of the audience standing in small agitated groups, muttering to one another rather than watching the dancers.

Arakny seized one mutterer by the arm and demanded, "What's happened?''

A confused babble answered her.

"Stop!'' she commanded. "One of you—what's happened here?''

The short woman she was holding by the arm answered: "Three men, Arakny. Three men from outside, gangers by the looks of them. They spotted this other visitor walking over toward the compost house, and they grabbed him. Some of the men objected, and they got knocked on their heads. Look over there.'' She pointed through the milling bodies to a place where several costumed men lay, surrounded by others.

"What did they look like?'' Olly demanded. "The three gangers?''

"Why, as to that—I don't know. I didn't see it. Ask Lithel, she saw it. She saw the whole thing.''

Olly recognized Lithel, the woman who had talked to them at the gate that morning, the one who had been so sympathetic to Abasio, who was now busy bandaging one of the fallen.

She answered Arakny's question in a rapid mutter. "One of them was bald, with a beard and a hammer. It was the hammer did this damage.'' She was sponging away the blood that seeped down the man's face. "One wore whips at his belt. He told the others what to do. The other of the three was a giant, hairy as a bison, and he stank.''

"Where did they go?" cried Olly, recognizing the description as the same three who had stopped Cermit's wagon in Whitherby.

"They went down the hill," the woman replied. "Our men were objecting, and the little man was assuring us they would not kill him until they were in manland once more."

"What does she mean?" Olly seized Arakny by the arm. "Kill him? What does she mean?"

"Our treaty with manland forbids gangers killing one another in our territory," the woman answered. "It does not forbid their taking your—husband back to manland and killing him there."

# CHAPTER 11

hey will kill him there.''

At first the words were meaningless to Olly; then they made dreadful sense. She stood briefly in paralyzed dismay, then spun around and ran frantically toward the sandy road.

''Wait,'' Arakny called, trotting after her. ''Wait, Olly Longaster! Where are you going?''

''Back to the wagon!'' Olly cried.

''You can't go after them! You'll get yourself killed!''

''I know,'' breathed Olly. ''Oh, heaven, I know.''

Arakny followed, but Olly soon outdistanced her. She had been running on the prairie for days, back and forth from the moving wagon, gathering dyestuffs compulsively, as though life depended upon the artifice. Her legs had become quick and strong; they were tireless now as she sped down the hill and across the wandering skein of water. By the time she reached the wagon, she was quite alone.

She stumbled against one of the wagon wheels and

held her breath. Where was Coyote? She heard a yawn. He was curled against the wheel.

"Wake up!" she demanded, falling to the ground beside him.

She was greeted by a brief flash of starlight on teeth.

"Araughrrr," he said, deep in his throat. "Who could sleep with all this clatter."

"Are you awake?"

"Of course I'm awake! What is it?"

"The men after Abasio, they've taken him. You said they were far behind!"

"They were," he replied, suddenly ear prickingly alert. "They were a considerable distance, a day's run. Three of them. Two ordinary smellers and a stinker."

"They must have hitched a ride with someone," she said bitterly, "for they were here, up the hill, at the dance. They saw Abasio, and they took him, just like that. Almost as though they knew who he was. Almost as though someone had *told* them what he looks like now."

"Don't talk to me in that suspicious tone," snapped Coyote. "I didn't tell them."

"Someone did."

"Someone may have done, but that's not the problem at the moment, is it? What do you want from me? Conversation? Counsel?"

"Rescue!" she demanded angrily.

"You have a high opinion of my abilities, girl."

"Not yours, no," she whispered, raising her head to listen. Down near the river, Arakny was calling her name. "The two who were following me, looking for me. The walkers you said smelled so strange. What would they do if they thought those three gangers had *me*?"

Coyote scratched himself reflectively. "They'd go find out, most likely."

"You could make them think it was so!"

"Make the two walkers think the three gangers had *you*?" He snorted. "Lying to those two might be the last act of my sneaky life. A very bad idea."

She shook him frantically. "You're clever. You kept the ogres away from us. You can do the same thing with the walkers, somehow, without lying, without their knowing even who did it. You can figure out a way. Make them think the gangers have me and are taking me back to the city. Please!"

"What do I get out of it?"

She cried, "What do you want?"

"I don't know," he said, stretching. "I'll think of something." He licked his jaws thoughtfully. "What do you want him back for?"

She glared at him. "Why . . . because. He's my—well, he's . . . "

"You don't know why you want him," commented Coyote. "But you'll no doubt think of some reason, sooner or later."

"Hurry," she commanded. "Arakny's coming."

"Achr," he growled. "I need your clothes. Something womanly. Something you wear next to your skin!"

She gaped at him.

"Come, girl, don't dally. You want your whatever rescued, give me credit for a bit of clever of my own. Give me your underwear!"

She stripped off her tunic, pulled the soft stuff of her chemise over her head, and dropped it, tugged the tunic back on.

"Where will you be?" Coyote whispered.

"West. Toward the Place of Power. I can't—I can't wait here. I have to—I have to go."

Arakny called again, this time from the grove along the river.

Coyote gave Olly a look, distant lights reflecting from his eyes, then snatched up the chemise and scampered under the wagon and thence into the darkness among the trees.

"What are you doing?" demanded Arakny, coming across the clearing. "You're not going to try to go after him alone."

"Who would go with me?" asked Olly in a bitter voice. "You?"

"Yes," said Arakny gravely. "Though I think it's a fool's pursuit, I'll go with you rather than see you go alone."

Olly leaned against the wagon and laughed hysterically. "I learned to fight as a child, Arakny. A Hero taught me. I learned well, but I remember what he told me. Between two fighters of equal skill, the larger will probably win. Between two groups, the more numerous will prevail. We're both outskilled and outnumbered."

"I know," said Arakny. "That's what I've been trying to say." She stared beneath the wagon. "What happened to your dog?"

"He ran off," Olly replied. She turned hopelessly away from the older woman and stared into the darkness. She wanted to go after Abasio. She longed for him, grieved for him, could not think of anything but him, and at the same time she could not let herself take the time.

"We'll go after him," said Arakny. "I'll get some of the warriors."

Olly shook her head. "No. I can't. There's something more important."

"More important!" Arakny looked at her in amazement. "What could be more important?"

"Oh, Arakny. Arakny. So many things."

"I can't imagine what."

"Let me put you a problem, Arakny. The world will end tomorrow, and you have the power to prevent it if you go very quickly to do a certain thing.

On your way, you see a child drowning in a river. If you stop to help the child, the world will end. Where does your duty lie?''

Arakny merely stared, not answering, her mouth working as though she could not find words.

Olly said softly, ''I cannot help Sonny because I have to go to the Place of Power. And you cannot go after my friend, my love, because I need you to take me where I must go. Now. At once. Tonight!''


Abasio had been captured with such efficient violence, he did not fully realize what had happened until he found himself jerking along in the dark, tied in the saddle of a horse, hearing the sounds of other horses ahead and behind. He'd been hit on the head. He compared his current pain with pain remembered and assured himself it was no harder a blow than he'd had in his youth during any one of several notable ganger wars. No. No worse than that, which was quite bad enough.

His attempt at self-assurance didn't help. He remained disoriented and dizzy, and every time he opened his eyes, his head felt as though it would explode. If he kept his eyes shut and rested his head on his bound hands, the flashing agony dwindled to a sullen throb and he could think. He'd been captured, he told himself. By gangers, no doubt. They hadn't killed him. Maybe they'd been instructed not to.

''Where are we going?'' he asked, angered to hear his voice trembling like that of a pleading child.

The man riding ahead of him answered. ''Be quiet, Purple boy. We're takin' you 'cross the border. Old Chief Purple says bring 'im your han's, so tha's what we'll do. You behave yourself, we'll do you quick.''

Abasio considered this, knowing something was wrong with it but unable to identify just what for some time. Gradually, his mind cleared.

''You can't take him my hands,'' he said. ''Not if he wants to see the tattoos.''

The man behind him rode up beside him and leaned close, a miasma rising around Abasio like that of an untended privy.

''Whachu mean?'' he growled.

Abasio turned his face away, breathing through his mouth. ''I mean you can't see my tattoos. My hands are dyed. You'll have to take all of me back.'' He'd been hoping a live body was less smelly to transport than a dead one, but if they willingly traveled with this reeking giant, one rotting body more or less would make little difference to them.

''Whatso, Thrash','' complained the giant. ''D'ju see's han's?''

The man riding in the lead called, ''Never mind. We'll stop in a bit, have a look then. If we can't take his hands, maybe we'll take his head.''

"Head'll rot before we'd get it there," complained the third man. "Han's're all right. Han's dry out okay. Heads rot till y'can't tell whose. We got nothin' to put 'im in to keep 'im from rottin'."

The lead man was unperturbed. "Talk about it when we stop."

Abasio slumped in the saddle. He'd never planned to die this way. Of course, he'd never really planned to die anyway. And Olly! Would she know what had happened to him? Maybe—maybe she'd try to rescue him!

Maybe she'd better not, he thought bleakly. Better limit the damage. She wouldn't have a chance against these three, and somehow he couldn't see the people of Artemisia helping her out. No, any thought of being rescued was what Grandpa would call a foolish hope. Here he was, ending up just as Grandpa and Ma had always feared, on the wrong end of a retaliation.

He slumped further, head resting upon his bound hands. Given enough time, maybe he could gnaw his way out of these bonds.

And then what? He considered how he might escape, playing the scenes over as the horse plodded into darkness. All his scenarios ended in his recapture and immediate dispatch. By the time the man in the lead called the journey to a halt, he had no ideas left.

"We'll stop until morning," the leader announced as he dismounted and came toward Abasio. He pulled Abasio not ungently from the saddle and stood him on his feet. "May as well know who has you, boy. Give you our arena names, jus' so you'll know who's doin' what. I'm Thrasher. This is Masher, and the big one's Crusher. An' so's you'll know why, Old Chief Purple's payin' us a crow for you."

"How'd you know who I was?"

"Recconized you, boy. We was standin' guard for Whistler when you bought some stuff. He called you by name."

Abasio grew cold in the pit of his stomach. "You're Survivors."

"What else, boy? Survivors, sure."

The other two men busied themselves collecting wood and setting a fire, then Crusher lifted Abasio—casually using only one hand to do it, as though he lifted a stick of firewood—into the light of the fire where Abasio's hands could be seen. Thrasher laughed abruptly and muttered a command, at which Crusher carried their prisoner to a stout tree and bound his wrists behind him around the trunk.

When the giant left him alone, Abasio tested the bonds. He was tied with thong, but there wasn't a long enough piece of it between his wrists to abrade it on the rough bark. He would bloody himself to no purpose if he tried. The men were professionals. But then, he'd known that as soon as he'd heard their names. These were Survivors' survivors. Rulers of the arena, become mercenaries. Almost legendary, they were.

"What'd you do to Old Chief Purple?" demanded Thrasher from his place near the fire.

If they were not yet beyond the border of Artemisia, the story might keep him alive for a time. He told it, stringing it out while the three spread their blankets and collected a pile of firewood for the night.

When the story was done, Thrasher said, almost sympathetically, "Too bad. Nothin' you did wrong, ganger. But you know how 'tis."

He did know how it was. You got paid for doing somebody, you did somebody. It didn't matter whether the somebody was guilty of anything. Most times the victims of tallies weren't guilty of anything. In his younger years, Abasio himself had taken part in retaliations without asking whether the victims had actually done anything wrong. Soniff said fight, everybody fought. That was how it was done.

He complained, half-aloud, "Whyn't the Old Chief send Purples? I'd have thought he'd send Purples."

Thrasher laughed, a sneery cough of amusement. "Purples! Who'd he send from the Purples? Purples are a joke!"

Masher added, "On'y way the Purples stay alive is Old Chief pays off the other gangs not to fight 'em."

Abasio stirred indignantly. "Warlord says the Purples are getting deeper and stronger all the time."

The three Survivors laughed, slapping at one another in their amusement. When they had somewhat controlled themselves, Thrasher chortled, "You're young. And you're a farm boy. You're not old enough to remember. We remember. Was a time, gangers filled Fantis clear up to the edges."

Abasio sat straighter, raising his voice above the coyote chorus that had erupted beyond the fire. "I thought—I thought Fantis got emptied out when people went to the stars!"

"Nah. Fantis was full long after that. Even when we were kids, Masher and me, it was full then."

Abasio forgot the discomfort in his arms and wrists, the rock that was making a hole in his rump. Was Fantis actually getting smaller?

"Is drugs," said Crusher in a sleepy voice. "Lotsa people dyin' on drugs. That new stuff Whistler brought. I hear people dyin' on that."

Abasio stared in Thrasher's direction, seeing only a blanket-covered lump. "People dying . . . how?"

"Hmm," the lump yawned. "Just lay down an' die. Drugs and battles. And sicknesses. Doesn' matter. I won' be around to see the endin'." The lump yawned again. "Your endin', that's diff'rent. I'll be around to see that."

Abasio slumped against the tree, full of questions he couldn't ask. So the city was dying. He'd known that, somehow. All those derelict buildings. All those babies born dead, or dying. All that strut and crow from the gangs, like cocks on a dungheap. Was this the way the cities in the east had gone? And the ones in the west? Were the cities of manland only the tail end of citydom, doomed even when Abasio's ma had been young? She'd said so more than once, but back then, Abasio had preferred not to believe.

Did the people in the Edges know the cities were doomed? Was that why they'd gone out, away? And what about the farms? Surely the farms weren't dying. If the farms died, nobody would have anything to eat! The Edges needed to eat too. So if the Edges survived, likely so would the farms. . . .

The coyote voices rose in a chorus of howls, then fell into silence. One of the horses whickered, half a question, half a complaint. A few moments later another horse—or was it the same one?—whickered from farther away.

Abasio's head sagged onto his knees, full of new ideas. Whistler and Sudden Stop selling death as though it were sweet corn. Gangers dying, not even with the sense to run away. Elk and bear being brought back. Forests being replanted. Rivers being cleaned. Women being Sisters to Trees.

And places like Artemisia springing up, not a farm, not a city, not an Edge, but something in between. The woman at the border had said they were in balance, whatever that meant. Presumably it meant enough people, but not too many. How many was too many? Who decided such things?

The horse whickered again, this time from a considerable distance. Abasio raised his head, listening intently. Horses didn't ordinarily wander so far when they were hobbled. Had that been one of the ganger horses? Or someone else's?

Thrasher turned uneasily in his sleep.

Abasio held his breath. Let it be the ganger horses. Let it be the ganger horses wandering away, far away, so the men would have to spend hours hunting them in the morning. Hours during which . . . what?

Foolish hope, he reminded himself. Only foolish hope.


Not far to the southwest of Artemisia the pair of walkers who had come through the town moved along side by side, a bit more slowly than in daylight but still far more quickly than ordinary men could have marched in darkness. They had settled on this direction after using the daylight hours to search south, east, and west of the town. Eastern routes led to grasslands and forest. Northwestern routes led into high, cold mountains. Other southern routes led mostly through wilderness, but this was the straightest line to High Mesiko, the most logical destination for their quarry to be seeking. People went this way seeking work, so they had been told. There was much commerce going on in southwestern climes.

"Food," said one to the other after miles had gone by in silence. Usual communication between them was infrequent and monosyllabic. Food. Rest. Left. Right. Faster. Slower.

The other expressed no agreement or dissent, merely slowing his pace to fall slightly behind the speaker, who led the way up a slight rise to where he had an unobstructed view of the country around them. Though it was a dark night, they were able to see quite clearly by starshine.

Each sat down to eat a bar of compressed fuel from the pack he carried. The fuel was tasteless. Taste was unnecessary. Sleep was also unnecessary. What was necessary was that energy be replenished and certain automatic procedures be carried out. These took place whenever the walkers stopped, whether for nourishment or to await instructions.

An owl sounded from the nearest brush, single hoots uttered deliberately, with long pauses between. Then it swept above them on silent wings, visible against the stars. Neither of them looked up. In the surrounding desert coyotes yipped and howled, but they did not look at the coyotes, either. They had not been sent after coyotes. They had been sent after a young person with dark hair who had been an Orphan in an archetypal village. They had been sent with a retinue, a new Orphan, a Wet Nurse, other persons costumed variously in procession, including one person with the power of command. The purpose of this unusual show had not concerned the oddmen. They had asked no questions about it, though it was in all respects unique. Their instructions had been specific: Make room for the new Orphan by removing the old Orphan and returning her to the Place of Power.

There had been no old Orphan to return. No one had seen her leave. She had been there, so everyone said, only the day before.

As soon as the procession was out of sight of the village, the two had been commanded to leave the rest and search the mountains. An easy search, they had been told, for a young woman alone, without help, who would no doubt be blundering about among the trees, lighting fires and yelling for help. The oddmen had been given words to use: soft words, gentle phrases, and a special tone of voice.

But there had been no girl. No fires in the night. No voice calling. Only the sleepy mutter of birds and small creatures, the scratch of claw and nibble of teeth. The walkers had gone east, and north, and south, and west of the valley. They had moved outward from it. Eventually, they had come to a woman who had seen the girl and directed her to the city. They had gone to the city. They had not found her. They had returned from the city. They sought her still, as did others of their kind. They would find her eventually. They were not at all impatient.

A voice came from the night, a high, howling voice, clear as a bell:

*"Three men from Fantis took a young person with dark hair. They took*

*the person from Artemisia town. Three men from Fantis are traveling back
toward manland with the young person, on horseback.''*

The oddmen rose. To anyone observing, the motion would have been a
blur, so fast it was. Fire bloomed from their helms, and they spun, lighting
the desert with wheel spokes of light, fierce white beams glaring into the
darkness.

Nothing. Two or three coyotes darting toward the safety of shadows. An
owl surprised on the top of a cactus. They did not care about coyotes. They
did not care about owls.

"I heard," said one emotionlessly, "a voice."

"It was not malfunction," verified the other. "It may have been deception.
Perhaps the person referred to is not the person we seek."

"We must go back," replied the first. "Even if it is deception, we must
go back to make sure."

"Back," agreed the second.

They turned and ran the way they had come. A watcher, and there were
watchers, could have seen only blurred motion, a progress too fast to observe.
One watcher followed nonetheless, trotting rapidly northward even after the
movement of his quarry could no longer be seen or heard.


Abasio was too uncomfortable to sleep. Hours wore by as he sat, sometimes
with his head on his drawn-up knees to ease the pain in his head, sometimes
struggling to his feet, inch by aching inch, to ease his back. After one such
maneuver, he found he badly needed to pee. He didn't want to end up sitting
in it, so he worked his way around the trunk of the tree, shifting his bound
wrist a bit at a time, until he was on the side away from the sleeping men
and the smoking remnants of the fire. The trousers he wore were baggy, and
by dint of much tugging against the rough trunk and shaking of his legs, he
managed to get the fabric located so the pee would run down his leg onto
the soil rather than soaking into his trousers.

So he thought, forgetting the boots he wore. The trousers got a minimal
share, but the soil shared half the remainder with the inside of his boot. He
stood with his head down, cursing silently, interrupted in his discomfort by
a voice asking:

"Where is the woman?"

Abasio held his breath, frozen. The voice had not come from any one of
the Survivors. It did not sound like a human voice. A beam of intense white
light from the Survivors' camp went past the tree trunk, throwing distant
foliage into stark relief, black and white. When the light went out, he could
see nothing but flowing afterimages on the insides of his eyes.

Something rough and hairy pressed against his lips. Coyote's voice whispered in his ear, "Be still."

"Where is the woman from the village?" the strange voice asked again.

"Wha'?" someone responded. Thrasher's voice, sounding strangled.

"Where is the woman?" the first voice asked again.

Fur brushed Abasio's jaw. "Sit down," whispered Coyote from his left shoulder, a mere breath in the darkness. "Quickly, quietly, get your hands down in the grass where they can't be seen."

Abasio's knees sagged obediently, and he sank under the pressure of Coyote's forefeet, ending by sitting in the very puddle he had wanted to avoid.

" . . . don't have any woman!" screamed Thrasher for the third or fourth time.

An inch from Abasio's ear, Coyote breathed. "Now stay silent."

Abasio held his breath while the Coyote went around the tree and sat down on Abasio's hands. So it felt, at least, warm, furry, and heavy enough to renew the pain in his wrists as the weight dragged at the thongs.

"The person you took from Artemisia," said the cold voice. "We want her."

The light of the fire flared up, orange light washing around Abasio, flickering on either side of the place he sat in shadow. Something was being dragged. Something made a keening noise, a scalpel of sound, then gasping noises, as from a person half-strangled.

"Wazza man!" screamed Masher. "Not a woman! A man! Tied to that tree, over there, that tree."

Coyote barked. The glaring white light washed over him and past him.

Abasio shut his eyes, blinded once more.

"That is an animal," said the terrible voice. "Do not lie to us, ganger! Tell us where the woman is, the one from the village."

"No woman!" Thrasher cried. "Crusher. Help!"

The giant bellowed like a bull. The keening noise shrieked briefly. The giant howled. Something fell heavily.

"It is not wise to attack us," said the terrible voice. "It is not wise to lie to us."

Silence. Coyote sat heavily. Abasio could feel his breathing.

"They have ceased to reply," said a terrible voice. "Why have they ceased to reply?"

"They have malfunctioned," said the same voice.

"Lately they malfunction more often during questioning."

A brief silence.

"Perhaps the woman is with the horses."

"We will look there."

Departing movement, too fast to be quite human.

"Pull your hands as far apart as you can," whispered Coyote from behind the tree. "I've got to chew you loose."

Abasio pulled, gaining a little slack as he felt the furry snout pressed between his thumbs. The thongs moistened and stretched slightly. Teeth chewed noisily; the tongue lapped wetly. After what seemed forever, Abasio's wrists parted company.

"Come on," demanded Coyote, nosing Abasio's thigh.

"Where are the horses?" Abasio asked, trying to rub feeling into one leg with hands that were completely numb.

"I sent some of my family to drive them as far away as possible," Coyote answered. "I suppose they managed it, for I don't smell horse near here."

"Can those—can they track me?" Abasio wondered.

"Possibly. My packmates will try to forestall any tracking—if you'll get moving." He punctuated this demand with a nip at Abasio's thigh.

Abasio yelped and moved forward, promptly tripping over a root and falling on his face.

"Hold on to my tail and pick up your feet!" Coyote snarled in frustration. "Move, cityman!"

Abasio struggled to his feet, and they moved slowly into the darkness, the fireglow dwindling behind them.

"How'd you find me?" Abasio whispered.

"Finding you was the easy part. My packmates saw you and howled your location. It was Olly's idea to get the two sets of hunters hunting each other. More or less."

"The gangers—are they dead?"

"I imagine so. If not, so close as to make no difference."

"Those walkers were surprised when the gangers died. Did you notice that?"

"I wouldn't have said surprised," Coyote growled. "I don't think those creatures feel surprise. But I think they didn't intend what happened."

"Right," muttered Abasio. "As though they weren't quite in control of the situation."

Behind them, coyotes yipped and howled.

"My packmates," Coyote explained. "Some of them following the walkers. Some of them crossing our trail. Brushing it out. Peeing on it. Shitting on it. Dragging dead skunks and dead fish over it. Making new trails. When I sent my packmates after the horses, I sent Olly's undershirt with them. It's out there on the desert. Those walkers will find it. It's obviously woman clothes. It smells of woman. It'll make them think she's out there, somewhere, and that'll distract them, maybe."

"You think they can smell—like that? Like you can?"

"Who knows what they can do? They may even be able to hear us now."

Abasio took the hint and moved more quietly, without speaking. Only after a long silence did he whisper, "Where are we going?"

"As far away as we can get. Then I'll leave you someplace safe and go find your sweetheart."

"She's not."

"Maybe not. Still, she didn't think twice about sending me after you. And she was quick at figuring out a plan too. Clever, she is. Like me."

"Cleverer than I am," said Abasio bitterly. "Both of you. I would never have thought of leaving something that smelled of her."

"Speaking of smells," said Coyote, skidding to a halt on all four feet and twitching his tail out of Abasio's hand. "I smell a cavern."

"How can you smell a cavern?"

"I smell moisture and bat droppings. Also, there are swallows cheeping, high on the walls. I can hear them."

Abasio listened. There were rustling cheeping noises, high and to his right. "You want me to wait here?"

"Here is as good as we're likely to find. You'll be under cover. There's water. Olly said she was heading west, but I'll need to pick up her trail, and I can do that faster alone. If I don't return in a day, work your way south and west, and I'll find you." The last words came softly as he moved off into the dark.

Abasio sat down obediently, grateful for the stop, which gave him a chance to take off his boot and the squishy sock inside it. Though he could hear the drip of water off to his right, he'd wait until light to find it. Then he'd drink and wash out his sock and bathe his wrists where the thongs had cut. Meantime he sucked at the skin of his wrists, softening the crusty edges of the abrasions.

Slow time went by, darkness fading slowly until he could detect a wash of fluid gray seeping along the edges of the eastern world, a flowing liquid line of desert and mesa. The sky lightened, imperceptible degree by imperceptible degree. Soon he could distinguish the glimmer of water lying in the hollow, the dark arch of the cavern above him. He remembered his thirst and started to get up, only to stop, frozen in place.

It was sound that stopped him, sound coming from the north, a humming, soft as a bee caught in a jug, a frustrated whine that increased in volume, rapidly becoming painful. Abasio put his hands over his ears and crouched to put his muffled ears between upraised knees. The sound screamed overhead, an excruciating lance of noise that went through him on its way south, leaving him panting.

Something plopped onto the sand, a feathery fluttery helplessness, blood on its beak. It struggled briefly and was still. Other swallows fell, littering the soil around Abasio with agitated movement and agonized complaint that lasted only briefly.

When all was quiet, he stood up, feeling his head with his hands, assuring himself he was largely undamaged, though emotionally he felt he'd been maimed. His ears seemed intact. He wasn't bleeding, and he could hear the resumed sound of bird and insect. There was residual pain in his head, but that was left over from the assault by the gangers. Unlike the helpless birds, he'd managed to block the worst of it with his hands.

Thrashing sounds from the canyon below him drew his eyes in that direction in time to see a large furriness emerging from the brush. It was blackish brown, the size of a half-grown cow, and it pawed at its doglike head as though in pain.

"Bear," Abasio's mind told him wonderingly. Except for the distant forms spotted during his journey south, he had never seen the actual animal. He couldn't remember reading about bears being dangerous, though the thing below him obviously could be. It weighed as much as two large men, at least, and no doubt there were formidable teeth in that muzzle.

The wind blew softly past Abasio's cheek toward the animal. A moment later, the Bear rose on its hind legs and turned in his direction, nose wrinkled, teeth exposed—very long teeth—small eyes peering. It made a muffled noise, of exasperation or curiosity or surprise. Or anger. As though, perhaps, it thought he, Abasio, had been responsible for the painful noise.

Abasio looked around him for a place to hide, a place to run. Could a bear climb trees? His eyes came back to the animal below him, still standing, still watching. Perhaps if he merely stood very still . . .

The Bear dropped to all fours, exposed its teeth in a muffled growl, and started purposefully toward him.


The sound that had killed the swallows was heard by many in Artemisia, including Arakny and Olly, who were traveling west along a little-traveled canyon road that Arakny said was the straightest route toward the Place of Power. Big Blue stopped at the sound, four hooves dug into the gravel, head up, ears pricked and swiveling as the noise went past. The women's heads turned similarly, following the sound, which had a peculiar attribute of motion, as though some shrill machine moved invisibly in the air above them, coming from the north and dwindling away west like a monstrous flying voice calling to another of its kind.

"What was that?" breathed Arakny.

"The walkers," said Olly. She had no doubt that what she said was true. This horrid noise shared certain qualities with the voices that had called to her in the forest above the village. Both sounds had the same insinuating directionality, the same quality of threatening focus.

"The walker ones who came into Artemisia? The ones who were looking for you?" asked Arakny.

Olly nodded. She started to speak, stopped, began again. "I think the sound came from where Sonny—Abasio was." She leaned sidewise across the footboard to blow out the lantern that had dimly lighted their way during the dark hours. "I don't think the gangers have him anymore. I think he's either escaped—or he's dead."

"What makes you think that?"

"My pet dog," said Olly in seeming irrationality, as she climbed down to the road. She was blinking rapidly to keep the tears back, aware it was no time for tears. "I sent my pet dog to look for him, and I think he got there."

"You what?"

"Never mind. Just take my word for it." Olly rubbed her eyes, unable to decide what to do next, deciding in favor of doing nothing at all. Coyote knew she was headed west. If he was still alive, he would come after her. If he was not alive, likely Abasio was not, either. She refused to consider the implications of that as she stood leaning against the wagon, motionless, too tired to move, too tired even to grieve.

"You want to stop here?" asked Arakny.

Olly murmured, "Not want—must. Big Blue is so weary, he's stumbling. He's traveled a long way."

"You say you sent your pet dog," remarked Arakny, as she climbed from the wagon seat. "Are you going to tell me about this pet dog? Is it anything like your pet bird?"

Olly raised her head and stared blindly into the face of her companion. "It's not a bird. It's a guardian-angel."

"I see. How do you know it's the walkers that made that noise?"

Olly sagged wearily. "Because I've heard the sounds they make. Not that particular one, but something like."

Arakny stared at her. "Are you hungry?"

"No. Just so tired I can't think."

"Tea, then. Before you sleep."

Arakny led Big Blue within reach of some foliage he'd been trying to get at, then took the grill from the wagon and set about making a fire, moving through these chores with practiced efficiency, as though she had done them often before.

Olly filled the kettle and brought it from the water barrel, the guardian-angel fluttering to her shoulder as she passed the wagon.

"We're low on water," she said with a shiver. The air had grown cold during the night, and though it was somewhat light, it would be hours before the sun warmed them. The angel's feathers against her cheek were chill, like ice.

Arakny gave her a sympathetic glance as she went into the wagon and came back with a blanket.

"Lie down here, where it's warm." She spread the blanket by the fire.

Olly lay down, pulling one side of the blanket over her and rolling an end beneath her neck as a pillow. The angel cuddled beneath her chin, making broody noises, its slender beak pricking the skin of her shoulder.

"Tell me about this pet dog," Arakny demanded.

Olly sighed. "He's actually a coyote. And he talks. He came up to us outside your borders, in the desert. He offered to come with us and be our— our sentinel, our guard, if we'd let him enter the city. He'd already saved us from the ogres, so we owed him a favor, and he said he was hungry for conversation."

Arakny looked silently into the fire, her face unreadable.

"It's true," claimed Olly, almost angrily.

"Oh, I'm sure you think it is," Arakny responded in a kindly voice. "Just as you think all of it is. I can accept parts of it. The walkers. After all, I've seen them and heard about them from others. I can accept you were Orphan in an archetypal village. There are such villages here and there." She thoughtfully stirred the fire once more. "I can accept you were given a prophecy and that you've quoted accurately what you were told, though I don't necessarily believe the prophecy itself. I can even accept that you call your bird a guardian-angel, that it talks, sometimes pertinently, and I can admit it looks like no bird I have ever seen. I accept that your 'pet dog' is a coyote. I knew that the first time I saw him. But I cannot accept that he talks, no matter that our ancient legends speak of talking coyotes and bears and even birds and insects. My guess is ventriloquism."

"Ventriloquism is a shaman's trick," snorted Olly. "I know all about that. Oracle did something of the kind when she used her cavern voice. I assure you—"

"—Coyote is not a ventriloquist's dummy," said a voice from up the hill.

Arakny jumped to her feet. Branches rustled. Gravel skittered down the bank and sizzled across the road like water on a hot pan. Coyote emerged from the uphill foliage and remarked: "I, too, find myself unbelievable."

Arakny sat down abruptly.

"Did you find Sonny?" cried Olly.

"I did," responded Coyote. "Do you have any water left? I've had no water for hours."

Olly rose, took down the bucket hanging from the rear of the wagon, and half-filled it. "Tell me!"

Coyote stuck his nose in the bucket and lapped thirstily. Arakny got up from the fire and went up the hill, losing herself in the trees.

"Where's she—?" Olly murmured.

"Let her go," said Coyote. "She's hunting for whatever human person or human-directed mechanism is pretending to be my vocal cords. Eventually she'll realize there isn't one."

"So?"

"So I sent some of my packmates north, one of them carrying the garment you gave me. They moved the horses away from the gangers, quite far away. They dropped your clothing near the horses, where it might be found. I, meantime, went south."

"You found the walkers?"

"I howled to my colleagues, who howled back their location. I went there and called to them from the darkness." Coyote turned and grinned at her fiercely. "Cleverly, as you suggested. I told them a dark young person had been taken north by gangers. It wasn't a lie. Abasio is young enough and dark enough to fit the description. The walkers went like the wind, too swift for me to follow."

Arakny returned in a scatter of gravel, her brows drawn together as she stared at the speaking animal. "He talks."

Coyote stared at her, then barked twice, panting and crossing his eyes to make himself look like an imbecile dog.

"Stop that!" Olly demanded. "Tell me what happened!"

Coyote uncrossed his eyes and gave Arakny a wicked glance. "I couldn't have kept up with them, they went so fast, but I knew where they were going better than they did. At least, my packmates had howled me which way the gangers were headed, and that they were on horseback. The walkers had to cast back and forth, searching, while I could run directly there. By the time the walkers arrived, I had come up to the gangers and had found the tree where your friend was tied. I let them see me to keep them from seeing him, and that worked well enough. They killed the gangers, not meaning to, then decided you might be with the horses, so they went off to find you. If all went as planned, they found your garment and will believe you were there, somewhere far north of here."

"What about Sonny?" cried Olly.

"I chewed him loose and brought him partway. Since we didn't know exactly where you'd got to in the meantime, it seemed sensible to let him rest while I located you."

"He actually talks!" marveled Arakny. "It's him. He's really doing it. But how can he, with that tongue, that shape of jaw? His mouth isn't made for speaking!"

"Nor yours for singing," snapped Coyote. "Any bird can do it better, but some of you learn to do it nonetheless. So I learned to talk, with difficulty. Have the courtesy not to tell me what I can and cannot do!''

Arakny subsided, but watchfully, as though she still suspected a trick.

"You heard the horrible noise?" Olly asked him.

Coyote snarled. "I did. A cry for reinforcements, perhaps? A notice they had found you, or almost? An attempt to kill or cripple you? That noise would have maimed you if you'd been close enough to it."

Coyote stuck his muzzle into the bucket and lapped once again. When he had drunk his fill, he said: "I promised your friend I'd be back to collect him. He's not far, but have you something I could eat first? If I take time to hunt—"

"Eggs," said Olly. "And bread. And the remnants of last night's stew. No, night before last's stew. The one I made the night we met."

"The stew," he agreed. "It smelled very tasty when you were cooking it, though I wasn't hungry at the time."

Olly brought the pot out of the wagon and set it on the ground, where Coyote wolfed the contents within moments and then chased the pot about on the gravel as he licked up the last drops.

When he had finished, he sat down and licked his jaws for some time, getting the last of the flavor. "Stay here," he directed. "Get some rest. I'll bring Sonny as soon as possible."

He trotted up the bank and was gone amid a shiver of foliage.

"I don't believe this," said Arakny.

"Believe it or not," Olly replied. "I'm too tired to care."

Shaking her head at her own disbelief, Arakny cleaned up the pan and the cups they had used, then drove the wagon into a screening copse, where she unhitched Big Blue and hobbled him. Full daylight had come by the time she took her place on the wagon seat to stay on watch while Olly and her angel slept and Big Blue chomped his way along the edge of the trail.


Abasio had managed to get five or six feet up the rock wall before the Bear arrived, knowing all the time it wasn't high enough to do him any good. When the Bear arrived, that point was made even clearer as the animal reared up to full height and took a good sniff of Abasio's nearest body parts. Even as scared as he was, Abasio had time to think that everyone and everything in the world seemed interested in his sex life.

He had no time to think anything else before the Bear sat down and said in a conversational voice, "Not eating you."

Abasio was startled into letting go of the rock. The resultant slide dumped him almost at the Bear's feet.

"Not," the Bear repeated. "Did you think?"

"Yes," said Abasio, for the moment incapable of duplicity.

"No," said the Bear thoughtfully. "Fish, yes. Eggs, yes. Ant eggs too. Not big animals much." He sighed deeply and drooled a little. "Looking for woman person. Dark hair. You seen her?"

Abasio's mouth clamped shut, and he felt sweat start out on his face.

The Bear sniffed. "You know where," he accused. "You not telling me."

"Two walkers have been looking for a dark-haired woman," Abasio explained. "I don't think they intend to do her any good."

"Them." The Bear nodded. "I saw them. They look this place, that place. Whuff. Talk funny. Smell funny." He pawed at his ears. "Make noise like— don't know. You hear it?"

Abasio nodded. "It killed some of the swallows."

The Bear got up and nosed among the feathered bodies. "Poor birds," he said sympathetically. "Go to waste. Not eating them. Feathers prickly. About this girl . . ."

"What do you want her for?" demanded Abasio.

"I telling," the Bear growled. "You nervous person. Flesh persons nervous. Right?"

"What do you mean, flesh persons?"

"Like you. Not like those two. Part flesh, maybe. Not all. Smell funny."

"I never thought they were quite human."

"Not animal, either. Find girl. I take girl. Where she goes."

Abasio laughed. "We've already got a coyote who says he wants to serve as our guide."

The Bear sat down again. "Can have two?"

"Where did you intend to guide us to?"

"Where she goes."

"Do you know where the thrones are?"

The Bear pointed with one large paw. "That way."

"That's probably where she'd like to go. I'm not sure Coyote knows where that is."

"Coyote knows." Bear wrinkled his nose, as in disgust. "Coyote goes around. Coyote says much." Bear nodded to himself in satisfaction. "Bear goes straight. Bear says little. Bear says true."

"Coyote isn't honest?"

Bear shrugged. "Sometime. A little." He used the claws on a front foot to comb the hair at his throat. "He good sneaker. Bear good fighter." As though to demonstrate this, he reared up to full height, extended both clawed feet and growled hideously.

Abasio shuddered. After swallowing deeply he managed to say, "So if we want to get there unnoticed, he'd be better at it? But if we had to fight, you would?"

Bear sat down, making a whuffing noise that Abasio interpreted as agreement, or laughter, or both.

"How would he feel about your—joining us?"

The Bear shrugged, a massive heaving of huge shoulders. "Coyote! Today, this way. Tomorrow, that way. Who can tell?"

Abasio slumped. "He said he'd be back to get me."

"He will. Sometime."

Abasio picked up his soggy sock and went to the shallow pool that lay within the cavern's entrance and overflowed in a trickle that led down a face of stone into the soil, where it disappeared without a trace. He washed the sock in the overflow, well below the level of the pool, wrung it out, and smoothed it on the rock face in the sun to dry.

"How did you learn to talk?" he asked the Bear, who was licking his feet with great attention to the furry spaces between the toes.

"Mama talks," said the Bear. "Many bears do."

"Have you any theory as to—to why?"

"Don't know. Some cubs talk. Bigger animal, more talk."

Abasio thought this over. "You mean, the smaller animals don't talk?"

"Rabbits, hardly any. Coyotes, some. Bears, lions, a lot."

"Lions?" gasped Abasio.

"Not many yet. But most talk. Buffalo talk. Eagles talk."

Abasio thought this over. "Coyote wanted to go with us just to hear conversation."

"Coyotes say that."

"You think it a lie?"

The Bear shrugged once more. "Maybe. Maybe helps woman. Bad things everywhere. Woman needs help."

"Help getting to the thrones?"

The Bear shrugged.

"She's had this prophecy about the thrones," said Abasio.

"What's prophecy?"

"A telling about the future. Someone told her she is to find five champions who'll take her to three towering thrones being gnawed by four something elses. Oh, there's six set on salvation in there somewhere."

"Five what?"

"Champions. People to fight for her."

"She got some?"

"Me," said Abasio. "Maybe Coyote. Maybe that woman from Artemisia."

"Me," said the Bear, rearing up on his hind legs to rip the bark from a tree in long, tattered shreds. "Need one more. Find one, stop looking."

Abasio's jaw dropped.

"You think bears not smart," challenged the Bear. "Can't count one an' one an' one."

Abasio nodded, feeling himself flush.

"Bears smart. Coyotes smart. Other animals smart. We don't talk, man says not smart." The Bear made the repeated whuffing noise that Abasio identified as laughter. "You know, we count-smell."

"Count-smell?"

"Smell whole thing. Part gone, smells different. Something more. Smells different. Count-smell. Not one, two, three. Is thing, more thing, less thing."

"I suppose that would work," agreed Abasio, who had seen a mother cat with a litter of seven search for one missing kitten. "Smart or not, why would you want to help Olly? You don't even know her."

The Bear scratched his jaws and head with both front paws, ending with a vigorous ear massage. "Good thing," he said at last. "Like eat fish. Like follow bees. Like—winter sleep."

"You instinctively want to help her?"

"Yes." The Bear lay down and put his muzzle on his paws. "Coyote here sometime. Sleep now."

Amazed at himself for doing so, Abasio lay down beside the Bear. If Grandpa could only see him now!

# CHAPTER 12

*I*f Arakny had had some trouble believing in Coyote, she found it impossible to believe in Bear. She was asleep when he came shambling down the hill in advance of Coyote and Abasio. Big Blue scented him first. The horse's frantic whinnying awakened Arakny. She almost fell off the wagon seat when she saw the large furriness sitting quietly on the roadway some distance from them.

"Not eating you," remarked the Bear between Arakny's shrill ululations.

"Big black bear," remarked the guardian-angel from its perch on the door. "Not eating you."

"He's not going to eat you," Abasio reaffirmed, as he came sliding down the bank.

Big Blue shuddered and stopped whinnying, though he went on snorting, eyes white-rimmed and ears laid flat. Arakny subsided, shamefaced. It had been the surprise that set her off, she told herself. If she hadn't been so startled, she wouldn't have yelled like that.

"Another one!" she blurted.

"Another what?" asked the Bear, unmistakably annoyed.

"Another talking animal!" she gasped.

Bear wrinkled his muzzle and showed his teeth, only slightly. "Six animals talk. Five talk human. Two two-legs. Two four-legs. One angel."

"Sorry. I didn't mean to be insulting," Arakny managed to say.

Coyote remarked, "You weren't insulting. Bear just likes to show he can count and then belabor the point. He has no sense of humor."

"Sense humor!" snorted the Bear. "Coyotes laugh at fleas!"

"How did you know it was a guardian-angel?" asked Arakny.

"Obvious," said Bear. "What else?"

"*Two* two-legs!" cried Abasio, belatedly. "Where's Olly?"

"Asleep," muttered Arakny. "By the fire."

"Nobody's asleep by the fire!" he cried. "Where is she?"

Arakny stared stupidly at the fire, gradually coming to herself. "Gone?" she said in disbelief. "Gone?"

"Where?" cried Abasio again.

Arakny pointed westward, grimacing to herself. "We'll catch up to her shortly. She can't have gone too far. She had this—this compulsion."

"She found something out?"

"I think so. She didn't say what. Except that she had to get there, to the Place of Power. Soon."

Abasio ranted. "We can't let her travel out here alone! It's dangerous. I'll harness Big Blue. You put the grill on the wagon." He took the harness from the peg where Arakny had hung it the night before, calling as he did so, "Which way do we go from here?"

Arakny pointed up the canyon. "There's a fork at the top of the canyon up ahead. The left fork turns south, toward Low Mesiko. The right fork continues westward across the prairie. It's been some years since I've traveled to the Place of Power, but I remember the landmarks. Olly will stay on the trail. It's the shortest way."

"We're short on food," remarked Abasio. "We'd intended to buy food in Artemisia."

"You're also low on water," said Arakny. "But if we leave now, we'll reach Crooked Wash yet today. We can get food and water there."

The angel left its perch on the wagon and flew to a branch near where Coyote and Bear were, where it teetered and peered, chuckling to itself over and over, "Big-fur-bear. Tricksy feller." Abasio harnessed Big Blue, and Arakny fretfully examined their stopping place, searching for anything they might have dropped or overlooked, somewhat handicapped in this effort by her desire to watch the animals.

"Mother won't believe this," she muttered to the world at large, in variations. "Nobody will."

Abasio mounted the wagon seat, and Arakny climbed up beside him. Bear shambled beside them, and Coyote trotted in the shade between the axles. Neither animal had anything further to say. Time and distance went by almost silently, with only the creak of the harness, the clatter of the wheels, and an occasional snort from Big Blue disrupting the quiet. Their way led gradually upward along the side of the arroyo, a serpentlike trail that came at last over the rim onto level ground and into the blinding rays of the late-afternoon sun. Abasio reached into the wagon and found his driving hat, pulling its wide brim down to shield his eyes.

Arakny pointed ahead, toward the blue mountains. "Big River is between us and the mountains. You can't see the valley yet. Crooked Wash is about halfway—"

"We should be able to see Olly! How far ahead could she have gone?"

"We'll catch up to her," Arakny said. "She'll have to stop to rest, or eat."

A mile farther on Coyote leaped into the wagon and went to sleep. Bear disappeared over a ridge and did not reappear for some time and then only at a distance. The angel drowsed on one leg, its head sunk into its feather ruff.

"Coyote told you and Olly what happened?" Abasio asked Arakny.

Arakny nodded. "It was probably the relief—knowing you were alive, were all right. She was terribly grieved about not going after you."

Abasio said, "I thought they would kill me." He swallowed and looked resolutely ahead. "I should tell you about the walkers. Something has been bothering me ever since it happened. I'm almost certain the walkers killed the three gangers without meaning to."

"Accident," murmured Coyote from behind them. "They killed the men by accident."

"Accident?" questioned Arakny.

"As though they didn't know that what they were doing could be fatal," said Abasio. "It was like a bull charging someone with his horns, because that's what bulls do! They just did it, as if they were designed to do it. They didn't think about its killing anyone."

"Maybe they didn't care?" asked Arakny.

Abasio shook his head thoughtfully. "I don't think *care* is the right word. They intended to question the men further, but by that time the men were dead."

Inside the wagon, Coyote raised his head and sniffed. "I smell smoke!"

"Up ahead," verified Abasio. "A town, I think."

"Crooked Wash," said Arakny. "Since we don't want to draw a lot of attention and stir up a lot of talk, it would be wise to keep our visit casual."

"No talking coyotes, right?" asked Coyote with a little sneer. "No talking bears?"

"Frankly, I think we'd be less conspicuous without undomesticated animals of any description."

"I'll tell Bear," Coyote said, shaking himself awake. "We'll rejoin you later."

He leaped from the wagon and was gone, leaving the two humans to go on toward the village. As they came closer, the dwellings seemed to emerge as though from the earth, a dozen sprawling mud houses arranged haphazardly around a dusty square.

"Crooked Wash," said Arakny, pointing toward the narrow, twisting canyon that bordered the dwellings on the south. "Ahead, to your left, there's a footpath down to the water. You fill the water barrel while I dicker for some food." She jumped from the wagon and strode off toward one of the dwellings, where she entered its courtyard without knocking.

Abasio noted the sign of thistles above the gate. "Wide Mountain Clan," he said to no one in particular as he drove on to the edge of the arroyo, where he got out to stare at the stone dam that made a small pool below them. Wooden buckets, iron-hooped, stood beside the overflow pipe.

His presence had been noticed by others, a few here, a few there: women drifting from their houses; children bubbling up from the arroyo; a horseman jogging in from the north; dogs sniffing the wagon wheels, their necks bristling as they growled in the back of their throats. By the time Abasio had brought two brimming buckets up, there were a dozen folk eager to carry water in return for the novelty of talking with strangers.

It was not long until Arakny returned, several children trailing behind her with string bags and baskets. She opened the wagon door and stowed the contents as the children passed them up to her: vegetables and fruit, corn meal, and meat.

Arakny's kerchief elicited respectful questions: Did the Wide Mountain woman need help? Did the Wide Mountain woman desire cooked food? How about company for their journey? To all of which Arakny replied courteously no and no and no, they were going west for a bit, but the journey was neither important nor urgent. Just a young dyer being escorted to the western trail, the one that led toward the Faulty Sea.

They were on their way within the hour. Coyote rejoined them when they were out of sight of the village, and a bit farther on, Bear came from behind a clump of cactus to scuffle along behind, sniffing at this and digging at that, falling behind, then galloping to catch up again.

"Bear knows a good place to stop for the night," Coyote informed Abasio with a doggy grin. "To your right, ahead, there's a spring and a grove of trees."

"I can't stop," grated Abasio. "We haven't found Olly."

"I'll go looking, sniffing her out, as soon as you're settled," said Coyote. "I can catch up to her more easily on my own."

"Then why didn't you—"

"Because I was tired too!" Coyote snapped. "I've had some rest now, so now I'll find her!"

The day had almost gone by the time they came to the spot Bear knew of, only enough light left to see to the necessary chores of firewood, food, and harness. Coyote and Bear disappeared into the surrounding dusk to find their own suppers and to go look for Olly's trail, so they said, while Arakny made stewed meat with corn dumplings and peppers. She claimed it was a family recipe, and she used the cooking time to give Abasio a lengthy history of the Wide Mountain Clan while the fire crackled and their dinner steamed fragrantly.

Before their supper was ready, Coyote returned, licking his jaws, to announce that he and Bear had found Olly's trail and were going after her.

Abasio stood staring after them as they moved off into the darkening landscape, Coyote's nose to the ground, Bear shambling after him. He should go with them. He said so to Arakny.

"You'd fall on your face," she said impatiently. "It's dark. You can't smell out a trail, and they can. They'll find her if she's to be found. Settle down. Get some rest. Tomorrow may be harder than today."

"Is that an Artemisian saying?"

"It's a truth of life," she snorted. "Always. In Artemisia as elsewhere." She stirred the pot.

He sighed, trying to think of something besides Olly. "Does Wide Mountain Clan make the laws in Artemisia?"

"We don't really have laws. We have justice, which is another matter. Before men went to the stars, I have read they had laws instead of justice. Among us, each dispute is settled on the basis of equity, not upon the basis of rules someone has made up."

"You settle your disputes on the basis of what people need?"

"No, on what is needful, not only on man's needs but upon the needs of animals and trees and rivers as well. We are all one. Our needs are one."

Abasio gestured toward the dark, where the animals had gone. "So Bear could ask for justice from your people?"

Arakny flushed, as though slightly embarrassed. "We have persons who serve as representatives of animals or trees or rivers, and we have decided disputes in favor of bears. It would be interesting to have a Bear argue his own best interests."

"You sound very well-regulated."

Arakny shrugged. "It is not onerous. We make sure all our people have opportunities for study, and child-bearing and rearing, and adventure—"

"And p'nash," said Abasio, in a sarcastic tone.

"That too," agreed Arakny, grinning at him. "Lots of opportunity for dancing and singing and p'nash."

Abasio said a few choice words about p'nash, indicting Black Owl first, then most Artemisians by association, and finally Olly because she had defended them, the whole explosion surprising him as much as it did Arakny.

"You're upset," she said unnecessarily.

"I'm worried about her!" he cried. "I love her! Damn it. I've loved her since the first minute I laid eyes on her. We've spent days and days together, and I still love her, and now she's just—gone like this."

"Are you two sweethearts? I know you're not man and wife, so don't tell me that."

"What would you know about man and wife!" he grumped at her.

"Those from the Faulty Sea, they marry one another. I've watched how they act toward one another."

"Well, what would you know about sweethearts, then?"

"I've had a few," she said. "Lovers. We don't just go to the dances and end the evening with a general orgy, you know. That's not what p'nash is, though you seem determined to think so."

"I don't really. It's just—I love her, and I haven't been able to—and she—"

"You don't know how she feels?"

"She's . . . she doesn't feel anything for me, so far as I know. Sisterly, maybe."

"She feels a great deal more than you think," said Arakny, sleepily. "You should have seen her face when she thought you were dead."

Guiltily, Abasio thought about that for a long time. He opened his mouth to pursue the subject further, hearing in that instant a soft little snore from the bunk above. He changed his mind.


Some distance west of them, Olly lay rolled in her blanket under a sheltering arroyo bank beside the embers of her campfire, her food packet and water bottle beside her. Late in the night, she awoke all at once, thinking someone had called her name. She listened, but heard nothing. There was no sound of bird, no distant yip of coyote. Even the insects were quiet, probably because of the cold. It was the cold that had awakened her. Beneath the glassy heavens, the air had turned to ice! She should have brought another blanket. Failing that, she needed to put some wood on the few vagrant coals that breathed beside her, seeming almost to sigh beneath their ashes as they glowed and faded and glowed once more.

She rose, the blanket wrapped tightly around her shoulders, and went up out of the arroyo, onto the desert, away from her sleeping place toward a patch of dead cedar she had seen before she'd lain down. It showed darkly against the sand in the light of the stars. She caught no glimpse of those who waited there until they rose up on either side of her.

Abasio and Arakny found the blanket at first light, still lying beside the patch of sage. Coyote, who had brought them there in some haste, pawed at it with an expression of disgust and said it reeked of the smell of walkers.

Mitty and Berkli were having supper together in Berkli's quarters, served by Berkli's servants, drinking Berkli's wine.

"Ellel's going to do it, isn't she," Mitty said, making no question of it.

"Probably," said Berkli. "I saw her going out the gate at sunset with a couple of walkers and some of her people. She had an air of elation about her. I have no doubt she'll return sooner or later with some hapless young woman." He twirled his glass, staring through it. "Sometimes I think Ellel has willed this woman into being. She has created her, by sheer force of determination and desire."

"I keep wondering why," Mitty mumbled. "I mean, when this shuttle project was first conceived of in my grandparents' time, it made some sense. There really were materials in that space station that we needed, or thought we did. Since that time, however, we've found most of what we need right here."

"Or we've learned to do without."

"But the project goes on, like some monster set into motion that we can't shut down. Do you really want to go into space, Berkli? Or to the moon? Why?"

"Why do we do a lot of things? Why did our forefathers come here in the first place?"

"Why—they came because civilization around them was being wiped out by drugs and disease and monsters. They were faced with retreating into savagery or finding somewhere where knowledge and technical skills could be preserved. They'd heard there was power remaining here, cities remaining here. And there were, of course. Are. And we're sitting on the only fusion power source in the world, one that is automatic and eternal, so far as we know. We can't get into it to check, but, as Ander so elegantly puts it, who cares what's going on inside, so long as the output is what we need." Mitty laughed shortly. He did care, immensely. He very much wanted to know, but several generations of Mittys had failed in their attempts to get into the power source to examine it. "We've done reasonably well by the world, Berkli. We've educated teachers who've educated whole generations of Edgers. Without us, it's possible they wouldn't have survived."

Berkli stared into his wineglass, finding his reflection there among vagrant glimmers of lamplight. "Do you ever wonder where the monsters came from?"

"Hadn't we always had them?"

"Not according to Berkli family history. About the time men went to the stars, monsters started to turn up here and there and everywhere. There was one in Urop, a giant water creature out of a lake somewhere. Nessie, it was called. Then trolls began infesting the forests. Big Foots, they were called then. Then came wiverns and griffins and dragons. And ogres, eating men! It's all there, in the Berkli family notebooks, each new appearance described."

Mitty shook his head. "I haven't thought much about monsters, I'm afraid. But then, the Mitty family's always been single-mindedly devoted to the technical end of things. Since there were so few technicians and scientists left, preserving their knowledge became rather a religion with us."

"Then I wish you'd preserved enough to discover whatever guidance system it was men used when they went to the stars! I know damned well it wasn't a human mind, and I don't like this nasty business Ellel's up to!"

Mitty gave Berkli an astonished look and said offhandedly, "But we know perfectly well what they used! It was complicated, but perfectly within our capabilities. It was earth-based, of course. Transmitters and receivers, widely scattered."

"Where exactly?"

"I don't know. Mitty family history lists the names of the places where they were. Cape Canaveral. Houston. But of course, those names don't exist anymore. Our forefathers didn't record locations. Why would they? They knew where the places were. They didn't expect *places* to disappear. The books that might have told us where they were have been destroyed. Our family histories don't include maps, and we've been unable to find many."

Berkli scowled, his fingers making a rum-atum-atum on the table edge. "Well then, if we could have built a system like that, why didn't we do it? Why is Ellel looking for this Gaddir female when there's another way to do it?"

"It's being done this way because we found the plans and specifications for doing it this way, and because she's her father's daughter! Look at how she's taken over his walkers."

"Which weren't even his!" Mitty fumed. "He was merely lucky enough to dig them up! Or unlucky enough! What made the man go digging just there, blowing great holes in the ground! Other people had seen those same records. My family had seen them! None of them had gone digging for androids."

Berkli smiled behind his hand. The Mitty family had never forgiven Jark for invading Mitty expertise in that way.

"I find Jark's digging for them easier to understand than why some preastral bureaucracy manufactured thousands of android soldiers and then left them in cold storage." Berkli went to the window, seeking movement to release the tension he felt. "Where does she control the walkers from?"

"Why—why—I don't know."

"Jark the Third gave some to your family. Where do you control yours from?"

"I've a control box in my quarters, one set to a specific frequency and a particular recognition code. Jark the Third gave it to my father as a gift, along with a few dozen of the things."

"He gave Ander's father a few likewise, and my father being gone, he offered a few to me, which I refused on aesthetic grounds, to Jark's great amusement and Ellel's annoyance. Almost as though he was buying us off, wasn't it? Soothing us. Making us think they were only toys, amusements. Of course, maybe he thought they were, after he'd reprogrammed them."

"No," said Mitty, with sudden vehemence. "No, he didn't, Berkli! I know we speak of his having done so, but it isn't strictly true. He couldn't have actually reprogrammed them. No one could. The basic functions are so well protected that Jark couldn't have changed them. The original design provided for a series of abort signals to override the basic functions."

Berkli turned slowly, furrows of concentration between his eyes. "I don't understand."

Mitty fumbled for an example. "When a walker is about to kill someone, it receives an abort signal, then a command to do something else, such as— oh, go find something. Because they were built to find things, they can do that. They can do something a little *less* destructive, but they can't do anything that *isn't* destructive because their fundamental nature is destructive. They're nuclear powered, of course, so they destroy even when they're standing still. Their bodies are shielded somewhat, but their feet aren't. They burn the soil they stand on. Nothing will grow there for at least ten years, which is as long as I've been experimenting, trying to find out if the effect is permanent."

"But Ellel touches them."

"Ellel wears a mask these days. She keeps her arms and hands and body covered. Haven't you wondered why?"

Berkli shook his head in dismay. "I had assumed they were more or less harmless."

Mitty frowned. "No, Berkli. No. Haven't you seen the pathways where they walk? Haven't you heard about one of them killing two children in the marketplace?"

"Two of our children?" Berkli asked in a hushed voice.

"Domer children. Not Founding Family children, but they could just as well have been mine. Or since you have none, your sister's. Everyone's talking of it."

"She'll have to call the walkers in!" cried Berkli. "Put them away somewhere. Where they can't do any more damage."

"How do you suggest we convince her of that?" Mitty asked dryly. "Even if we could convince her, how many of the walkers would still be capable of obeying?"

Two walkers had risen up on either side of Olly as though they'd grown out of the earth. She'd felt their presence in the same instant they had clamped her arms in steely hands. She'd started to cry out, but something had pinched her on the thigh, and the effort to make a sound had become, all at once, beyond her. She'd known it was a drug, something they had injected her with, something that made her body an unfeeling, limp bundle of flesh.

Then they had wrapped her in something and carried her away between them. She hadn't been able to raise her head voluntarily, but it had bobbed as the two trotted along, up and down, allowing her to catch a glimpse of the horizon against the stars, a glimpse of the coals blinking slowly in the dark. Then everything disappeared, and there was nothing she could identify. The ceaseless bobbing was making her sick. She had shut her eyes and tried to concentrate on breathing.

They could kill her. Any resistance on her part, and they would kill her. Not meaning to, but because they didn't know how not to. The safest course was to endure silently, to answer any questions they asked, if and when they did so.

They showed no signs of doing so. Their motion was continuous and direct. They did not swerve or backtrack. They were taking her to some specific place.

Gradually, as the night wore on, feeling came back into her body and her muscles spasmed involuntarily, fighting against one another and those who held her.

"Drug wearing off," said a cold voice.

"Put her down," said a cold voice, perhaps the same voice. "We wait here."

She was put down, not gently. Her ankles were bound with something metallic, so her fingers told her when she felt of it. It had no links or end. She was effectively hobbled, like a horse, able to sit up, probably even able to stand and walk a few steps, but unable to run away.

She shivered.

"Cold," said the voice. "Cover her."

Something crisp and crackling was wrapped around her. Not a blanket. It was too light and too rustly for a blanket. More like paper. Whatever it was, it worked. She was immediately warmer.

Silence. She wasn't uncomfortable. Her hands were free, she could turn over, she could adjust the covering. The need to pee was an immediacy, too long delayed. She stood up and stumbled away from the two crouched figures, barely visible in the night, dragging the covering with her.

"I need to pee," she said, hoping they understood.

They did not respond, did not even seem to hear her.

She dared not go too far. When she had finished, she found a soft spot and lay down again, as far from them as she dared go, uncertain where they actually were. Somewhere close, her hair told her, prickling at the back of her neck. Nothing she could do about that. At least they hadn't hurt her. They didn't even seem interested in her.

Exhausted, she fell into a doze.

When she opened her eyes, she was still wrapped in her covering, a silvery foil that crackled when she moved. Wrapped in similar bundles, other forms sprawled around her. As she moved, she saw a person sitting cross-legged beside her, eyes peering through the holes of a glittering mask.

Olly started to ask, then decided not to. She would not ask who, or where, or why. Instead she merely sat up slowly, pulling the filmy wrapping with her for warmth, regarding the woman before her with watchful judgment.

"What's your name?" the masked form asked in what Olly took to be a woman's voice.

"Olly Longaster."

"We've been hunting for you for a very long time, Olly Longaster." The woman rose. "The name is a pseudonym, of course, but no matter. We were becoming afraid you didn't exist!"

"We—who?" Olly asked.

"We Domers. My name is Ellel, by the way. Normally, I'm addressed as Madam Domer."

"Not Elly?" Olly asked, moved by some devil of disrespect.

"No. Not Elly," the woman said with displeasure. "Quince Ellel. Ellel is my family name. Your family name is probably Werra."

Olly's mouth dropped open. "My—"

"Your family name. Werra. I'm fairly sure of that, though it's remotely possible you came from one of the other lines. There are only three it could have been. Werra, Seoca, or Hunagor. Qualary tells me Seoca is still alive. Hunagor's been dead a long time, as has Werra, but reproductive cells can be preserved."

"I have no idea what you're talking about," said Olly.

"Oh, come now," the voice sneered.

Olly did not care for the sneer. It trusted not at all.

"My name, Olly Longaster, was given me by a friend," she said in her most dignified voice. "I know it is not my own. However, I do not know what my own is, or if, indeed, I was ever given a name."

"Well, for ancestors' sake, girl, where have you been?" The woman laughed, as at an ugly joke. "They must have called you something!"

"Orphan," said Olly, "was what I was called."

The eyeholes turned to peer at her. "You were in a village? An archetypal village?"

Olly nodded slowly, regretting that she had let this be known. Though she didn't know why, she felt it would have been better to have kept the matter to herself.

"By the Dome," the woman swore. "So you were there after all! When we didn't find you there, I thought it was a false lead." She laughed again, a dreadful snigger. "I actually sent a dozen of my creatures to dispose of the Bastard who gave us your blanket. I don't like liars."

"You—you killed Bastard?"

"They killed him if they found him," she said carelessly. "Which they probably did."

Olly, thoroughly confused, drew the wrapping more closely around herself. "The things that captured me? Do they work for you? What are they?"

"Devices. Partly a kind of flesh. You didn't think they were human, did you?"

"I didn't think they were anything to do with me. It would be kind of you to explain who you are, who you think I am, and what is all this business of searching and finding."

"But of course, my dear," Ellel said in a gloating, self-satisfied voice without an ounce of kindness in it. "I'm sure you've heard of the Place of Power because everyone has. We Domers are from the Place of Power, and for a number of years we've been looking for a Gaddir child with a particular talent."

"What is a Gaddir? Why do you want this person?"

"A Gaddir is—well, we believe it is someone who inherits a specific genetic makeup, a genetically transmitted talent. And we need that talent for a little project of ours."

"Which is?" Olly breathed, angered by this amused, patronizing tone.

The woman laughed, a brittle laugh, like breaking glass. "Why, to remedy old wrongs, to put things right. To resume the governance of earth!"

"Why me?" Olly pleaded. "I know nothing about governance of anything."

"One wouldn't imagine you would! But you're from the proper family, no doubt about that!" Her hand reached toward Olly but withdrew without touching her. "It's really nothing to do with you, girl. Nothing you need to think about or worry about. A simple errand. I'll verify you can do it, and when you've done it, we'll pay you well. We'll only need to borrow you for a few days." The woman turned away, saying carelessly over her shoulder, "A few weeks at most."

The words fell into Olly's mind like keys into a lock. Part of the pattern. Part of the whole thing. Still, it would be wise to verify. "Borrow me for what?" she cried.

"It's far too complicated to discuss. There's no time now. When we're sure you're the right one, we'll tell you all about it."

The woman went to one of the sleeping persons and kicked, not gently. "Up, Qualary. Get the others up. Time we started for the Place."

"Excuse me," Olly called, "but I was forcibly removed from the company of my friends. They will be wondering what happened to me. If you don't mind . . . "

Her voice trailed off in response to Ellel's sudden change of attitude, the half-crouch, the hands extended like claws.

"We don't need your friends!" the woman snarled.

"I need them," snapped Olly, without thought.

"Don't be annoying!"

The woman snarled a command at one of the walkers who turned and pointed his hand at Olly. She went down like a felled tree, rigid, every muscle spasming uncontrollably. The world turned hazy around her.

"I said we didn't need them," said Ellel in her former voice, with a dismissive nod at the walker. "Though I can't imagine why you'd want to, you'll be back with them in due time. Nothing to concern yourself about."

"Be still," said a voice.

Olly thought it was herself speaking to herself, as one did at times of danger, remembering childhood warnings, restating them under stress. Then she thought it wasn't her own voice, for it went on, repeating the phrase in a whisper.

Painfully, she turned her head to see Coyote lying behind a clump of sage, his nose flat against the earth.

"Don't worry," he said. "We'll be nearby."

His image disappeared in a flash of light from inside her head. She turned her head to see where the woman was, and when she turned back, there was only a clump of sage, no Coyote. She told herself solemnly that she had dreamed him. She had seen a coyote-shaped rock. She had made up the voice. He hadn't been there.

But if she'd imagined him, wouldn't she have imagined him saying something else? Something more comforting? Perhaps something about rescue?

She had no time to go on with the thought. The two walkers who had captured her now lifted her and placed her in a hammocky sling on a pole, then carried her away with great rapidity toward the west.

At least, she told herself dizzily, she was going in the right direction. And she'd been given a label for who she was. She tried to follow that thought to some conclusion but lost it in the general dizzy haze. It was impossible to think when she was being swung and jostled like this. Her head ached. Her stomach felt as though it would heave at any moment. She shut her eyes and tried to think of nothing at all.

They stopped for food during the morning. Olly felt too nauseated to eat, though she drank some tea that the woman called Qualary offered her. Olly tried to ask about the walkers when Qualary returned for the cup.

"Those—those walkers who caught me. Did someone create them?"

The woman, who had seemed friendly enough before, now turned away abruptly, hushing Olly with a whispered, "Shhhh."

"What is it, Qualary?" Ellel called from some distance away, where her own meal had been served to her in privacy. She ate with her mask pushed up onto her forehead, her back turned to the rest of them.

"Nothing, ma'am. I tripped over a rock," the woman said in an expressionless voice.

"Pick up your clumsy feet," the woman said. "Is she all right?"

"Quite all right, ma'am. Perhaps a little sick from the motion."

"That's nothing," said the voice carelessly, with a cackle of laughter. "Feeling sick is the least of her worries."

Olly shut her mouth and resolved to ask no more questions, not to talk of her friends, not to ask about the walkers. Anything she said would be wrong; any question she asked might do harm! They were going westward. For the time being, that was enough.

The sun was midway down the sky in the west when they stopped next. Olly said pleadingly that she had to go and was allowed to go off behind a bush with only Qualary, serious-faced and silent, as a guard. The woman did not respond when Olly used her name, though she offered a sympathetic hand when Olly staggered on her way back.

"Not much farther," the woman murmured without moving her lips. "You'll get a chance to rest soon."

"Hurry her up!" called Ellel, when she saw Olly tottering along.

"May I walk the rest of the way?" Olly asked. "I'd feel better."

"My dear, you couldn't keep up," sneered Ellel.

"As soon as I get the kinks out of my legs, I can walk as fast as any of you humans are walking," Olly said stubbornly.

Ellel bowed, a mockery. "Why then, walk! And she won't fall behind, because if she does, she'll be taught how to keep up!"

Olly had hoped that by walking she might be able to spot Coyote, or Bear, or even her guardian-angel, though if it had really been a guardian-angel, it should have been with her when she was captured! She saw no sign of them. Qualary and one of the other women walked just behind her, guarding her.

Very shortly they came to the western edge of the tableland and descended by a well-traveled path to walk through golden trees and great bunches of purple asters in a river valley old enough to have been much flattened and silted in. Soon they came to the river itself, and the narrow plank bridge that crossed it, the whole suspended on ropes that swayed rhythmically as they walked across. When they emerged from the belt of trees on the far side, it was to look upward through eroded canyons toward another tableland high above them.

By early evening they reached an upward-sloping road, one so wide and smooth it had obviously been built for vehicles. Around the second curve, the vehicle appeared, parked in a wide graveled place, a truck much like those that carried goods between villages and cities, though this one was shinier and newer than any Olly had seen in Whitherby. At their approach, the driver, who had been lounging beneath a tree down the slope, scrambled back to his machine and adopted an attentive manner.

Olly's escorts unceremoniously bundled her aboard; the others, except for the walkers, climbed into the truck with muttered oaths and complaints. It was damned near nightfall, they said. They were sore, they said. They had walked too far. They grouched and murmured to the sound of the engines as the vehicles went groaningly upward. Once in a while they could hear Ellel's voice raised in tuneless song from her seat by the driver.

"Got her, got her, got her," she caroled. "Got her to go, to fly, off to the sky. Oh, got her."

Beside Olly, Qualary shifted her weight uneasily. When Olly looked up, she saw the older woman watching her with an expression of heartfelt pity.


Coyote led the way, sniffing out the trail the walkers had left. Bear roved right and left, to rout out any dangers that might be lying in wait. Behind them, Abasio and Arakny drove steadily westward across the mesa, down the same trail Orphan had traveled, across a shallow in the the river beside the narrow footbridge, on through the trees and meadows and up the far road, arriving a little before dawn at the place the truck had been parked the afternoon before. Coyote and Bear sniffed their way around the place, up and back, before returning to block the progress of the wagon and bring Big Blue to an abrupt halt.

"What?" snarled Abasio from the wagon seat. They had been moving since dawn of the previous day, they had not even stopped to eat, and he was hungry, tired, and furious with Olly for running off and getting captured.

"From here, better go afoot," said Coyote.

"Where is she?" demanded Arakny.

"Up there," said Coyote, pointing with his nose. "Inside the wall. They'd done her no harm this far. She was walking with them until they got into a vehicle, right about here. From what's left of the smell, the vehicle went up the hill about sunset."

"It was walkers who took her?" demanded Abasio.

"Who captured her, yes. But it was humans who brought her here. Some men. Some women."

"So now what?" demanded Arakny, climbing down from the wagon seat to stretch her legs. "I don't imagine we can get over that wall."

Bear whuffed, that peculiar noise he made that Abasio equated with laughter. "Go under," he said. "Not over."

"What does he mean?" Arakny asked the air. "Under!"

Coyote licked his nose. "He means what he says. We can't go over the wall, but we can go under it. That means we have to leave the wagon here and go on on foot. Sneakily." Coyote licked his nose again.

Arakny glanced eastward where the sun just edged above the horizon. "It'll soon be full light. There'll be traffic on this road. If we don't want the wagon seen, we'll have to hide it somewhere."

"Easier said than done," snarled Abasio.

"Easy done," said Bear. "This way." He strolled across the road, back the way they had come, then disappeared behind a clump of piñons up a side canyon.

With some difficulty, Abasio got the wagon turned around and drove Big Blue after Bear. A flat wash of gravel extended past the piñons and up the side-canyon, around an outcropping of stone, and into a good-size pocket of unexpected greenery. Evidently the little side-canyon had a spring in it, for the verdant growth extended halfway up the slope, hidden along its entire length between buttresses of bare stone.

Abasio climbed to the top of the wagon. Even from this vantage point, the road up the larger canyon was quite invisible.

"What do we take?" Abasio demanded of Coyote.

"Bring horse," said Bear.

"Food," suggested Coyote to Arakny. "If we have to wait."

"Wait for what?" she asked.

Coyote merely licked his nose. Bear scratched himself.

Muttering angrily, Arakny filled two canteens and made up a packet of bread, dried meat, and fruit while Abasio unhitched Big Blue and put a bridle on him.

Coyote looked at Bear, his head cocked, one ear up, one down.

"Enough," said Bear.

The angel cried woefully as it flew to Arakny's shoulder.

"Good angel," said Bear. "Can come."

"No, no, no!" cried the angel. "No, no, no!" It flew from Arakny's shoulder to a nearby tree, from that up the slope to another, then disappeared into the tumbled rock.

Abasio cried out and started to climb after it.

"Let it go," said the Coyote. "It's gone to find Olly."

They stood for a time looking aimlessly in the direction the angel had gone before Arakny turned with a sigh and asked, "Where are we going?"

"Through the forest," said Coyote, peering up and down the road to be sure no one was coming. "Follow me."

They went across the road, over its outer edge, and down the embankment into the canyon, where juniper and piñon grew thickly, fogging the air with fragrance. Here, if they were careful, they could walk unseen by anyone traveling the road unless that person looked directly down on them from above. The bushy little trees grew too closely to the ground to walk beneath them.

By the time there was much traffic on the road, the sun was halfway toward noon and they had come through the shorter trees to walk among pines and spruces whose branches hid them from above. It was cooler in this more verdant forest, though the ground between the trees was still the sparsely grown pinkish gravel of the plains.

The farther they went, the farther the road was above them, winding along the south wall of the canyon. From time to time they could see the glimmer of sun on an ascending vehicle.

"Must be a market day," remarked Arakny. "Everyone's headed up."

"Could we join the market?" asked Abasio. "Maybe sneak in through the gates?"

Arakny shook her head. "One of my more vivid memories of this place is the identifying crystals that were fastened to people's bodies, like jewelry. I recall welded-on bracelets or collars or ear studs. Without such identification, no one gets in."

Abasio subsided. Since they had found Olly gone, he had tried to think not about her but only of what he was doing at the moment. He could be an effective rescuer only if he didn't panic, and the thought of her being in the hands of the walkers made him panicky. He remembered too well the confrontation between gangers and walkers, the sounds he had heard from behind the tree. Even though Coyote said Olly wasn't hurt, as long as she remained with those creatures she could be.

Bear and Coyote knew where they were going, although for the moment, Coyote was rivaling Bear in being laconic. Neither one of them intended to reveal the destination, probably wisely. If one or more of them were captured before reaching wherever they were going, it would be better if the humans could not tell their captors any specifics about where they were headed. No one would think of asking the animals.

Coyote had said "under the wall," which was suggestive. It implied what? Tunnels? Caverns? Old worked-out mines, full of rotting timbers? Or a bear hole, a muddy burrow full of the roots of trees?

Abasio sighed and walked, trying to keep his mind only on what he was doing.

Arakny, meantime, was putting one weary foot in front of another, wondering why she was here, what she thought she was doing, whether she ought to be here or someplace else. Certainly, invading the Place of Power hadn't been in the orders the Wide Mountain Mother had given her. "Go spend some time with the girl and find out what she's up to" had been the assignment. Perhaps even now there were clanswomen scouring Artemisia, looking for her. Well, no. Word would soon filter back from Crooked Wash that she had been there yesterday. They would know where she had been headed. Trackers from one of the men's societies would soon find where she had come to, but until the whole matter became clearer, they would take no action except that of following her trail.

"You may leave us, Qualary," said Quince Ellel.

They were in Ellel's quarters, Qualary and Olly just inside the door, Ellel moving restlessly about a few feet from them.

"I'd be happy to stay and help, ma'am," said Qualary, moved both by pity and despair for the girl beside her.

"I said you may leave us!" said the golden mask, in tones of deadly threat.

"Ma'am," murmured Qualary, backing out the door, feeling Olly's body sag against it as it closed. She went down the corridor, past the turn. In a moment she heard the door jerked open, then slammed shut again. She went back and put her ear against it, hearing Ellel's voice rising and falling, like a chant, like a litany.

"Got you, got you, got you," Ellel sang, over and over. "Got you, girl. No matter how you run, how you twist, how you hide, found you."

"I didn't twist and I didn't hide," said Olly. "I was on my way here when you took me."

The eyeholes glared. The hands came up. The mask was lifted, and it took every jot of Olly's self-control not to scream at what she saw there. It was Burned Man all over again, only worse. The eyes were all right. The lips were terrible, but complete. But as for the rest, the riven cheeks, the corrupted nose, the forehead blistered and eaten like the surface of the moon. The twisted flaps of ears. The horror of the oozing chin and the neck . . .

"Don't take me for a fool," the horrid lips said, sucking on the words. "Oh, girl, don't take me for a fool. It suits me to let the others think I'm less than I am. They don't believe I can do what I'm doing, and so much the better. They won't try to stop me until it's too late. Now. We need to talk about you. After all this time I'd been hunting you, I caught you coming here. Why?"

"Curiosity," Olly replied, carefully unfocusing her eyes as she had learned to do with Burned Man. Some things simply should not be looked at. "The Oracle in my village gave me a prophecy about the Place of Power. I was to answer some questions here, so I came here to do it."

"What questions?"

"I don't know yet. Even if I knew the answers, which I'm not sure that I do, that doesn't mean I know the questions."

Ellel began a restless movement, to and fro. After a moment, she took the lid from an ornamental jar, removed a glassy oval, thrust it into her mouth, and bit down sharply, making crunching noises. Her pupils dilated. Her breathing slowed.

Olly moved toward a chair.

"Not there!" Ellel snapped. "That's my father's chair. Over here. On this." She pointed out a much-carved and painted bench that looked uncompromisingly uncomfortable and proved to be so. Too weary to care, Olly sat, her head sagging onto her folded hands.

Ellel moved around the cluttered space, muttering to herself, looking into cupboards, under pieces of furniture, behind draperies and tapestries. Once in a while she asked a question. Several times she slapped Olly with her gloved hand when Olly did not answer immediately. The questions were silly, meaningless, as though Ellel were only passing time, as though she thought someone might be listening. Time wore on, but Ellel's search went on, every corner, under every piece of bric-a-brac.

Olly dozed and woke again at a slap across her face. Ellel was before her, holding her shoulders.

"Time," Ellel said, her voice flat and unemphatic. "Everything secure. No one hiding in here. None of Mitty's little devices. Now we'll find out if you're right for the job!" She tugged Olly erect, pulled her across the room to a locked door, unlocked it, pushed it open, pulled Olly through into darkness.

"Minute," she said. "Minute. No lights. Can't do the job with no lights."

In a moment she returned with a lighted candle, which she carried down a dusty corridor, through another door, and put upon a table near the doorway. The little flame barely illuminated the dust, the curtains around the huge bed, the window across the room.

"Brought her, Daddy," said Ellel in that same flat voice. "Got her."

Silence.

No. Not quite silence.

Olly felt her hair rise at the back of her neck, felt her skin creep.

"Good, good, daughter," came the words, a whisper, a mere crepitation from behind those dusty curtains. "Oh, that's good, Princess."

"Got to check, of course," Ellel went on. Her tone was coldly implacable. "It would be foolish not to check."

She gestured Olly to sit in the chair by the bed, and Olly fell into it bonelessly, so tired she would have sat anywhere.

The metal bands that slid around her arms and legs were fastened before she knew they were there. Ellel stooped before her, eye to eye, peering intently at her from a terrible madness and an equally terrible purpose. Ellel was letting her see the purpose, letting her know there would be no random or erratic behavior, no way of escape. Ellel smiled, and among the ruined teeth, Olly saw death waiting.

"This is an input console," Ellel said, pointing to a device beside her. "Information is fed through here into the helmet. The helmet comes down over your head. That is the output console. If you can understand what comes in, you can make a signal come out. The signal goes to the engines. I'm telling you this so you'll understand. I've told them all."

"All?" Olly whispered.

"All the girls my walkers have found. All they've brought to me here. All who have sat in this chair."

"Where—where are they now?"

Ellel went to the window and opened it. Cold night air came in, raising the dust in clouds, sweeping the sill.

"Out there," she said, gesturing into the night. "Out, through the window There's a pit in the rock below this window. The crows roost there. And the buzzards. Coyotes come there—I hear them singing. None of those who went out this window could do what has to be done."

Olly's head sagged.

Ellel whispered. "I'm not using the full array. I'm not sure we could disconnect if I used the full array. I'm only using enough to test. Just to test."

Olly felt the helmet come down. She felt points pressing at her scalp, then pain, a terrible, searing pain that was everywhere, simultaneously. She opened her mouth to scream, saying to herself she had to scream, to let the pressure in her head escape, and in that instant the pain ended, all at once, as though a door had opened inside her to let it flow through and away.

A question asked itself. This was moving and that was moving and the other thing was moving, too, this thing at that speed and the other thing more slowly, so how should this thing move to meet that one?

In that way, she told herself, knowing the answer the way she had often known answers. It was like catching a ball. It was like seeing the pattern the dye blocks would make before they were printed or knowing what Bastard's motivation had been in talking with Fool. It was the same kind of problem: A joined to B joined to C yielded X without question, incontrovertibly. One needed to move in this way to arrive at that point. It was simple.

Other problems presented themselves. It didn't matter. No matter what the problems were, she could solve them. There was no pain. Only certainty.

The helmet moved. She was aware of the pain again, for the briefest possible moment, then it was gone. The bands released her arms, her legs. She put up her hand and found blood on her face.

"I want to wash my face," she said calmly from a depth of despair. Everything was clear. Clear and unbearable.

"Go, go wash your face," Ellel said, pointing the way.

As Olly got up, staggering, for the moment unable to move, she heard Ellel babbling behind her.

"All we have to do is plug her in!" cried Ellel. "It's finished except for her. Almost. Only a few days left. Then we'll go, Daddy. Just like you wanted to. See the moon, see the stars!"

"Good, that's good, daughter."

"You want to see her, Daddy? You want to see her?"

While Olly stood, wavering, Ellel pulled the curtains roughly apart. The movement set off an explosion of dust in the dimly lit place. Olly gasped and coughed. She knew the smell. Part of it, at least. But only partly.

"Here she is. Here she is."

Olly turned and saw what lay on the bed. Ellel went on talking with the creaking voice, but Olly paid no attention after that.


Berkli responded to a request from Ellel that he come to the Dome after her morning ceremony. Her enormous excitement and his recent conversation with Mitty made him more apprehensive than he otherwise might have been. Though unwilling to acknowledge it, he had to admit she had sounded victorious. He waited until the walkers left the Dome, then came slowly through a side door, slowly, hearing Ellel's voice before he saw her stalking slowly toward him across the mosaic floors. For a moment, all he could think of was the big cats he had occasionally seen from the walls, stalking their prey as she stalked now, shoulders high and eyes intent.

When she came up to him, she stopped, drawing herself up to her full height and uttering a peculiar noise somewhere between the crow of a cock and the bray of a trumpet. She gestured toward the people behind her, two of Ellel's female servants supporting a young woman between them. The young woman looked desperately tired. There were small bloody wounds on her forehead and horror in her eyes.

He had expected to feel something if and when this happened, but he was unprepared for the rage that overtook him. Ellel had done it. She had actually done it. Unforgivably, the bitch had done it.

He took a deep breath and held it, willing himself to be calm. He walked beside her, smiling. He listened, smiled, listened again while Ellel spoke softly, cogently, while she told him she had found the girl, had tested the girl. The girl could guide the shuttle. All was as had been planned.

He felt his control slipping. She preened while his anger welled. Face flushed, neck swollen, but still smiling, he excused himself to turn and walk away from her.

Olly, sagging between her two guards, saw him go, saw Ellel poised behind him, the line of her back like that of a serpent, ready to strike. Her eyes glittered through the mask, the damp snaky tendrils of her hair waved around her mask. Medusa, Olly thought irrationally. Oracle had told her tales about Medusa, and here she was.

This was more of the pattern. Just as she had known the meaning of that terrible chair, so she knew the portent of the total pattern. The only child had come to the right place and her destiny was high indeed! Stratospheric! Extraterrestrial!

She swayed between the two women who were holding her, who had held her all during the strange ceremony in this terribly strange place. There had been more walkers than she could count, the smell of them like a nauseating gas, making her so dizzy that most details had been lost upon her. Ellel's voice reverberating in this pillared hall had been only sound with no sense. These rituals and confrontations had no meaning, but then, no more meaning was necessary. All the veils of fatigue, fear, and hunger did not hide the central fact, the core of certainty.

Now, drawn away from the women by Ellel's hand, she followed blindly, like a toddler too weak to resist.

"Come along," said Ellel, moving rapidly across the vast space and into a seemingly endless corridor. "I want to show you to my colleagues. My dear colleagues, who have supported me so faithfully all these years. Qualary! Come with us."

The woman trotted after them as they went down curving hallways and ramps, through doors, past cavernous, noisy spaces, and into a kind of foyer, where two men were seated in massive chairs facing one another as they played a complicated game with white and black pieces on a figured board.

Olly, breathing shallowly, staggering from being dragged so quickly along, saw them without seeing them, her mind scurrying about like a mouse seeking a hole. Behind the men was a window, and through the window she could see something huge that she had no label for. A tower? One tower inside another? It made no more sense than the rituals had done.

"Gentlemen," Ellel said in a gloating voice. "Mitty. Ander. I'd like to introduce you to the last surviving Gaddir!"

The man addressed as Mitty turned slowly toward her, one hand holding a gamepiece that sank slowly toward the table. "The old man is dead, then?"

"I mean besides him," snapped Ellel

"No," Mitty said flatly. "Not possible."

"Tell me your name, girl!" demanded Ander of Olly.

"Olly Longaster," whispered Olly.

Mitty laughed. "Hardly a Gaddir name."

"Werra!" Ellel blazed. "No matter what she calls herself, the tissue sample says she's Werra! Her ability says she's Werra!"

Mitty gave her a quick, almost frightened look. "Her ability—"

"Really, Ellel?" Ander commented, twisting his mouth into an appreciative smile. "Here's our wonderful Ellel telling us she was right all along!"

"Isn't she always?" Mitty asked in an expressionless voice as he swept the white gamepieces from the board. Ander followed his example, the table gathered the board and pieces into itself and folded into Mitty's chair.

"Well," said Ander, nodding toward Olly with a meaningless smile. "How nice that you've joined us. Particularly just now."

"I was given no choice," said Olly in a stubborn, childlike voice she did not recognize as her own. It was a voice on the edge of tantrum, teetering into hysteria. "I was—was—"

Mitty gave her a look, admonishing, warning, what? She couldn't tell, but she swallowed her words and was silent.

Ander chuckled. "No. Our Ellel doesn't give any of us much choice."

"This young woman looks tired to death," said Mitty, calmly, objectively. He gave Ellel a long look. "I suppose you've had her up all night."

This was so near the truth as to make Ellel mutter angrily.

Mitty spoke to Ellel, but his eyes were fixed on Olly's. "She needs rest. She needs food. She'll do you no good if she falls ill, Ellel. Send her off with Qualary. Let her get some sleep and some breakfast. You'll want her at the peak of her—ability, won't you? Didn't Werra's plans specify as much? It seems to me I remember something of the kind. And now that she's here, we can take our time to discuss how matters should go."

Olly dropped her eyes. He was talking to her, telling her something.

Ellel spoke with only slight annoyance. "How thoughtful of you, Mitty. By all means." She turned toward Qualary. "Take her home with you, Qualary!" She dismissed them both with a gesture. "Mitty and Ander and I have things to talk about."

Qualary took Olly by the shoulder to lead her away.

Ellel's strident voice reached them as they neared the door. "Don't misplace her, Qualary."

"No, ma'am," said Qualary doggedly.

"My walkers will make sure you don't," Ellel said in a razor-edged whisper. "They're watching you, Qualary. And you, Olly Longaster. You can't take two steps without their seeing you, nor three without their catching you!"

She paused, then laughed as she saw Qualary's expression. "Why, Qualary! You don't like them, do you?"

"It's—sometimes hard to get my work done with them around," murmured Qualary, bending her shoulders and back, bowing her head, groveling a little, just a little, for groveling pleased Ellel mightily.

"Oh, my dear, they won't interfere. They'll simply be sure our guest doesn't wander off. Or that you don't let her out of your sight."

"Yes, ma'am," said Qualary again. She bowed her head even more submissively and waited until Ellel had turned back to the others before she drew Olly out into the corridor.

"What was that thing through the window?" Olly whispered, pointing over her shoulder.

"That's the shuttle," Qualary answered quietly. "A kind of spaceship."

So that was a shuttle. Somehow, she hadn't expected it to look like that. She had thought it would have wings, like a bird. "What are they going to do with it?" she asked. She knew. She only wanted to hear the words.

"Fly away." Qualary laughed chokingly, a bitter sound, making fluttery motions with her hands. "That's what they say."

"Where?" Olly breathed.

"I only know what they say," Qualary replied, giving her an impenetrable look. "Can you walk?"

"Rather than be carried by those things," Olly said, "I can walk, yes. I like them no better than you do."

"Hush," the woman said, putting her fingers on Olly's lips and glancing sidewise, to see who might have heard.

"But I do want to send a message to my friends," Olly said stubbornly, moving Qualary's fingers away. "They'll be worried about me."

Qualary shook her head, leaned close, and whispered, "I have no way to send a message to anyone outside the wall. Ellel would have to do it."

Olly felt her eyes overflow, tried to blink back the tears with no success. "I'm so tired."

Qualary, distressed, wiped the tears away, whispering, "You've been up all night, just as Mitty said."

Olly opened her mouth to tell of the wildly disordered apartment where she had spent the night; of that terrible face beneath a shoddy too-small crown, which should have been laughable but wasn't. It had seemed a kind of madness. Oracle had said something once about madness: *The only difference between a futile madman and an effective tyrant is power and will.* Ellel's vision of herself might be mad, but she had the power and the will to make it come true. What could she tell Qualary of this? Nothing that would do any good.

Dismayed at Olly's pallor and her silence, Qualary nudged at her. "You haven't slept?"

"No," Olly replied, falling back on simple complaint, simple needs, simply stated. "And I haven't had anything to eat or drink. And I do have to let my friends know where I am."

"Well, then, food and rest can be had at my house." She dropped her voice to a whisper. "And I have a friend who can send a message. Maybe."

They left the precincts of the Dome and went into an ordinary street, not unlike the streets back in Whitherby, except that it was thronged with blackly glittering walkers who watched with redly gleaming eyes, heads swiveling as Qualary and Olly went by. They went into Qualary's house, an ordinary house. Looking dazedly out the window, Olly thought it a banal setting for the creatures, swirling like eddies in the aftermath of a flood, their bodies moving aimlessly while their eyes kept this house under purposive observation.

"Do all of them belong to Ellel?" Olly cried, on the verge of hysteria.

"All the ones you see out there. Ander and Mitty have a few, but they never use them. Berkli has none. He hates them. But then, Berkli is a doubter." She fetched a pillow, helped Olly lie down on the sofa, and covered her with a soft blanket.

Berkli had been the man routed from the Dome. "What does Berkli doubt?"

"Oh, he doubts everything. Doubts the Domers should have ever left their towers by the seas to come here. Doubts they should have bothered with the shuttle at all. Doubts they'll ever get the shuttle finished. Doubts they'll get the guidance system they need to fly it."

Olly had no doubt they had already found their guidance system, but it was obvious Qualary didn't understand the implications. "Why do they want to go?"

"To the space station? They say there are materials in the space station that they want."

Olly had heard that during her previous night's experience. "They say I am a Gaddir."

Qualary rubbed her forehead. "They say so. I don't know exactly what that means."

"Do you think I am a Gaddir?"

Qualary pivoted on one foot, a swinging motion, back and forth, back and forth, as though perhaps the motion helped her think. "There were three Gaddir families. Hunagor died long before I was born. Werra died when I was just a teen. Tom says old Seoca is still alive, though nobody outside Gaddi House has seen him for ages."

"Ellel says I'm a Werra. Could my mother and father both have been from this Werra family?"

Qualary shook her head, confused. "Girl, I don't know. None of them talk *with* me; they just talk around me. All I know is what I overhear."

Olly sighed. "I've seen the shops the Domers run. I can figure out what they do, how they live. But what do the Gaddirs do?"

Qualary shrugged. "I've asked my friend Tom—he's a Gaddir—but all he does is make jokes. The Gaddirs don't say what they do. Or did."

"Someone here sends people to burn books. And change the names of things."

"People speak of that in the marketplace, but it isn't the Domers who do it. I'd have heard about it if they did."

"Somewhere here are thrones."

Qualary shrugged. "I don't know."

Olly sighed. "Thank you for telling me what you do know, Qualary."

Qualary wrung her hands together. "It's because I know how you feel. I really do. Sometimes with Ellel I've been so—so scared! And when the walkers are around, I just freeze. I hate feeling like that, and the only time I feel even halfway safe is when I know exactly what's expected, what I have to do. I thought—I thought the more you knew, the easier it may be for you. I don't want anything to go wrong. When things go wrong, people get hurt."

She made a sound of distress, bowing her head to hide her eyes. Then she said, "You must be starved."

She went into the neighboring room, where Olly heard at first agitated steps, a few muffled gasps that might have been sobs, then noises that were gradually quieter and more purposeful. She had almost fallen asleep when Qualary returned bearing a tray that she placed on a small table by the sofa.

"Scrambled eggs," she said. "Green pepper sauce. Piñon muffins."

"You're very kind," Olly murmured. The smell of the food awakened her slightly, and she sat up to nibble for a while in drowsy silence before asking, "You've never heard anything about five champions, have you?"

Qualary shook her head.

"What about six people or groups set on salvation?"

Qualary, buttering a muffin, answered without hesitation. "The six set on salvation are the Sisters to Trees, the Guardians of Earth, the Artemisians, the Northern Lights, the Sea Shepherds, and the Animal Masters."

Olly was amazed and showed it. "The who?"

''The six groups set on salvation, dedicated to saving the earth. I've heard there are others elsewhere, but those six are the ones we trade with, in the marketplace here.''

''I met a Sister to Trees,'' Olly offered around a mouthful of eggs. ''And I know some Artemisians. I've heard the Artemisians mention the Animal Masters and the Guardians, but I don't know what the Guardians do.''

''They're mostly involved with water and soil, with stopping erosion and cleaning up pollutants. The Northern Lights run ozone plants. The Sea Shepherds govern fisheries. The Animal Masters run breeding farms, set hunting quotas, and hunt down poachers—though of course the Artemisians do that too. It was the Animal Masters who salvaged zoo and farm stock after men went to the stars, and it is they who bring the camel caravans across the desert from the west.''

Olly started to ask about talking coyotes and bears, then bit her tongue. Any such information given to Qualary could get back to Ellel. It would be unfair to ask Qualary to keep secrets. Instead, she yawned. The food had drawn her blood away from her brain, and she was suddenly overwhelmingly drowsy. ''I'm sorry,'' she gasped. ''I'm so sleepy.''

''Lie down. Sleep.'' Qualary rose. ''I'll be here when you wake.'' Looking down at the weary woman, she thought it was the least, perhaps the only thing she could promise.

# CHAPTER 13

*sk,* dreamed Olly to herself, *one only child.*

She walked in a dark place, her hands held by a person on each side of her. These were her parents, she knew. Father. Mother.

"Where are we going?" she asked them.

"We're there," they said, both at once, with one voice. "Here we are."

And they were there, where the three chairs were, tall chairs, gray and ancient, their arms and backs carved with beings whose bodies were twisted into curly words. Mother went to the left-hand seat, and Father to the seat in the middle. Olly was all alone.

"Here we are," the ones in the great chairs said. "Here we are, child. These are the thrones."

"What do you want with me?" she cried. "Why am I here?"

"We need you, child. You were born because we need you to do something for us."

"I don't want to!" she cried. "I want to go away with

Abasio. I want to go to the Faulty Sea and see the stilt houses. I want to travel to Low Mesiko. I want to . . . want to . . . '' She wept in her dream. ''It's not fair.''

''There's a way,'' said the right-hand chair. ''There's always a way. Everything has happened before. If not here, elsewhere. If not now, then. Every question has been answered before.''

The right-hand chair was empty. She wanted to get up next to Mother and Father, but it was too tall to sit in.

''It's too big for me,'' she said. ''It towers.''

''Yes,'' they agreed. ''It's huge. It's old. It's not for you.''

She laid her hands on the seat. It felt old and powerful and wise. Everything was there, in the chair. Everything she needed. And it connected to everything else, everywhere.

''The end is in the beginning,'' said the chair. ''To the weak, succor; to the strong, burdens.''

Then they were gone, all of it was gone, and she was merely asleep.


A knock at Qualary's door.

''Tom!'' Qualary cried, when she had opened it. ''What brings you here?''

He had a strange feathered thing on his shoulder, not quite a bird. ''I understand you have a houseguest,'' he said, smiling at her.

''Where's my Orphan?'' said the feathered thing, turning its bright black eyes this way and that, stretching its ruffled head from side to side, clacking its rapierlike beak. ''Where's my Orphan?''

''Where did you hear about her?'' asked Qualary, her eyes on the feathered being.

''Oh, someone saw you walking along the street.'' He strolled into the room and gazed at the young woman asleep there, her face peaceful.

''There's my Orphan!'' said the feathered thing, fluttering to the back of the sofa and settling there with a chortling sound. ''My Orphan.''

Tom said, ''So it's true. Well. Do you know who she is?''

''I know what Ellel says,'' she murmured.

''She's a pretty thing,'' he said softly.

''You had some interest in her?'' Qualary asked in a worried voice.

''Now, Qualary''—he smiled again—''of course I do. Isn't this supposed to be the missing Gaddir child? The rumored child? The child who is going to solve all of Ellel's problems?''

''I think she'll be safer if you don't take any interest in her,'' whispered Qualary.

''She would have been safest if Ellel had taken no interest in her, but perhaps you're right.'' He looked out the window at the passing hordes.

"What do you suppose would happen if we tried to take her over to Gaddi House right now?"

"We'd be stopped!" she said, distressed. "Ellel has told the walkers the girl is to stay here. Don't do anything to set the walkers off, Tom! Please! You know what they can do!"

"Well, of course," he said softly, "I wouldn't endanger either of you." He touched her cheek, smoothed the furrows between her eyes. "Ellel will know I was here. If she asks why I came, tell her I found the girl's pet bird, and I was curious about her. Don't worry over it, Qualary. Everything will work out."

"I do worry about it!" she cried in an agonized whisper, looking over his shoulder at the shifting masses of walkers. "I keep watching them. See the one on the corner, jerking and twitching, just like the one did that killed the children!"

He patted her face and was out before she could say good bye.

When he reached the street, he was stopped almost immediately, one walker holding him, one questioning him.

"What are you doing here?" the walker asked, with a peculiar buzzing and rattling in the metallic voice, as though some part were not firmly connected.

Tom also noted the slight tremor in the hands that held him. Well, he told himself, assuring himself he was calm, if they'd all been built about the same time, it stood to reason they'd all break down at more or less the same time. Which, if his luck held, wouldn't be for a few days yet.

"I came to see Qualary Finch," he said in a quiet, authoritative voice. "But she has a guest, so I left."

"What are you doing here?" the walker asked again.

He repeated his words, still quietly.

"What are you doing here?"

He thought for a moment, feeling the hands tighten painfully upon him. "Ellel wanted me to come here," he said at last. "Ellel wants me to be friendly with Qualary Finch."

Still the tremor, but the hands loosened.

"What are you doing here?"

"Ellel wants me here."

The hands released him, the figures stepped back. As he walked slowly and carefully away from them, he heard one of them asking the other, "What are you doing here?"


Abasio, Arakny, and their guides arrived at the top of the canyon late in the morning. They had passed the separate mesas with their deeply riven canyons. They had come by scree slopes dotted with juniper below deep-pocked, horizontally striped walls of gray and ochre. They had looked up at crenellated rimrock rising like shield walls and, behind that, vast tablelands thrusting massively against the sky, layer on layer on layer, a gargantuan earth-cake cut through to show its very foundations. Gradually, the scarred cliffs had closed in on either side, pink and pitted pillar stones fronting shadowy side-canyons, the wall before them looming taller the closer they came. Now they were only ants crawling at its base, unnoticeable ants against the immemorial stone, feeling their own insignificance with every step they took.

This was true of Arakny and Abasio, at least. The animals did not seem in the least awed. Their destination was, as Abasio had suspected it might be, the entrance to a mine. Not a mine, Coyote said. No, Bear agreed. Nonetheless, it looked like a mine, a cobwebbed hole framed in tilted timbers, damp-mottled and gray with age.

Inside they found a sandy cave, both warm and dry, with a pen where horses or burros had been kept, complete with a manger and a stack of sweet-smelling hay.

"Horse," muttered Bear, pointing with one paw.

Obediently, Abasio turned Big Blue into the pen, removed his bridle, and filled the manger.

"Water," grunted Bear, from behind a buttress of stone.

Abasio found Bear with his nose in a bucket set beneath a dripping crevice in the moss-grown wall. When Bear had finished, Abasio took the bucket to the pen and hung it by its handle over a post where it would not be kicked over.

"Now what?" asked Arakny.

"Now you wait," said Coyote.

"For what?"

"For somebody to come."

"Who?"

"I imagine Herkimer-Lurkimer." Coyote grinned.

Abasio sat down on a chunk of stone and asked, "Would this Herkimer-Lurkimer by any chance be your hermit?"

"I said my hermit died."

"That's what you said. Was it a fiction?"

"It was the story of my life. My story. Bear has a story, and Rabbit, and King Buffalo. Stories don't have to be absolutely true, just essentially true."

"All of the storied beings can talk?" asked Arakny.

"Of course. How can we explain things to men otherwise? How can we convince them of our intelligence, our brotherhood?"

"No," remarked Bear. "Brothers too close."

Coyote laughed. "Cousinhood then," he agreed. "We are at least distant cousins."

"My people don't need explanation!" Arakny exclaimed as she sat down next to Abasio. "We understand the kinship of life without animals talking human talk!"

Bear shrugged, a very human gesture. "You tell stories. Children listen. In stories, animals talk."

Abasio said, "He's right. We all tell animal stories where the animals talk. Why do we do that?"

"Same as trees," said Bear. "Same as mountains. Cousins."

Arakny nodded slowly. "I suppose it would be harder to kill off a whole species if you were accustomed to having conversations with it. Easier if you depersonalize it first." Seeing Coyote's laughter, she demanded, "You're not a mutation. What are you?"

"A hungry animal, waiting for Herkimer Lurkimer."

"Are you flesh? Or are you like those walkers?" Abasio asked.

"Flesh," said Coyote. "Oh, yes. Flesh."

"Hungry flesh," remarked Bear. He went out into the daylight and wandered off among the trees, where they saw him ripping up a dead stump to get at the grubs within.

"Me too," said Coyote, slipping out into the light. "Be patient. We'll be back."

Arakny opened her packet of food and offered it wordlessly to Abasio. "What are they?" she asked.

He took a piece of bread, bit off a mouthful, and chewed it thoughtfully before he answered, "My guess is they've been created to talk to men. So men will stop killing them."

"But we had stopped!" she spluttered through a mouthful of bread and cheese. "We've reduced our numbers appropriately. We kill only what we need as part of the food chain."

"Still, we could forget again," Abasio commented.

"That's the problem with civilized behavior," said a voice from behind the pile of hay. "It has to be constantly reinforced if you want it to persist!"

Both Abasio and Arakny jumped to their feet as the hay pile slid forward, toppling away from the wall. From behind it appeared a round-faced fellow brushing hay from his hair.

"Tom Fuelry," he said, grasping Abasio's hand firmly between his own. "Sorry I'm late. I knew you were coming, but I wanted to check on the girl before I met you."

"Olly?"

"Is that her name? She's unharmed. She looks a little tired, but otherwise quite all right."

"She's safe!" cried Abasio, clutching at Arakny.

Tom shook his head. "I didn't say she was safe, I said she was unharmed. At the moment, none of us is safe."

Abasio stepped away from his companion, becoming angry as suddenly as he had become elated. "But Coyote said—Herkimer-Lurkimer. What was all that about?"

"Herkimer-Lurkimer? That's one of Seoca's jokes. It's what he calls himself sometimes. He'd like to have met you himself, but he can't manage the ladder anymore. He's waiting up above."

"Coyote?"

"Coyote has his own way in. Come along."

Wordlessly, they followed him behind the pile of hay where a narrow door stood open. Tom stopped to pull the hay against the opening before shutting the door, hiding the way they had come. Then he led them down a dimly lit tunnel with branches extending on either side.

Arakny made a noise as though she'd been struck.

Abasio skidded to a stop beside her. She glared into one of the side-tunnels where shadowy forms stood against the wall. The closest one regarded them from half-opened eyes, its feet dangling limply beneath long skirts.

Fuelry came back to where they were standing. "Sorry. I should have warned you. It's deactivated, don't worry about it."

Abasio went into the side-tunnel for a closer look. The thing they had seen was only one of many. "Who? What?"

Fuelry fidgeted. "This is a bit-part storage tunnel. The one you're looking at is a Spinster Sister. The one next to it is a Faithful Sidekick, then there's a Sycophant and a Termagant/Gossip. Bit-part players."

"From archetypal villages?" Abasio asked. "But I thought the people there were real!"

"Most of them are," soothed Fuelry. "But many of them require ancillary bit-part players, and it's often difficult to fill the role. We don't think it's fair to ask someone with larger capabilities to spend their lives with half a dozen lines of dialogue and no extemporaneous actions." He nodded toward the Spinster Sister. "She needs only housecleaning and cookery skills plus a few hundred basic words and phrases. *'Dinner's ready, John. Wipe your feet, John. Close the door behind you, John. Are you busy, dear?'* She's basically interchangeable with the Author/Artist's Wife/Mistress model except for the sexual-compliance chip."

"We?" asked Abasio. "Who is we?"

"We people in Gaddi House," said Fuelry. "We people who set up and manage the archetypal villages. Among other things."

He led them rapidly along the wider way until they encountered a vertical shaft lit at the top. He gestured Abasio to lead the way up the metal rungs protruding from the stone.

"There are lifts," he said. "But they're huge, and we'd have to turn the power on. I'll come last. To catch you if you get dizzy." He bowed to Arakny.

Arakny did not get dizzy, though she had to pause twice to rest on the way up. At the top they stepped out into another tunnel, furnished with a complicated door that Fuelry opened with a slow scream of rasping metal.

An old man sat outside in a wheelchair, holding out his hands to Arakny and Abasio while the young woman at his side watched him as a mother watches a child.

"Welcome to Gaddi House," he said. "I'm Herkimer-Lurkimer. Thank you for taking such good care of my Orphan."

Qualary was told to bring Olly to the meeting room at the Dome for a briefing.

"Briefing?" asked Olly. "What's a briefing?"

"It means informed," said Qualary. "They'll talk at you. If you'll take my advice, don't say much. Just listen. It's probably better to say you don't understand something than to ask questions about it."

"Better to appear stupid than contentious, is that it?" Oracle had said that about olden times, that the basic strategy of women and slaves had been to appear stupid rather than contentious. Those in power would allow stupidity because it verified their unflattering view of women and other races.

Qualary gave her a startled look. Indeed, that was it, but it had taken Qualary years to get to the point of understanding it. Olly's perspicacity was somewhat disconcerting.

"I wish I weren't so dirty," Olly said, looking at her clothing with disgust. "I stink of smoke and sweat."

"We're about the same size," offered Qualary. "I'll find you something clean to wear while you have a bath."

While Olly rejoiced in the novelty of washing herself in warm water inside a warm house, something she had last experienced at Wise Rocks Farm, Qualary went through her own garments and selected a shirt and trousers in sunset colors. Olly, gazing at herself in the mirror, relished the unfamiliar silkiness of the fabric in a color that made her skin glow and showed off the shining darkness of her newly washed hair.

The transitory pleasure lasted only until they reached the street. While Qualary expressed surprise that the mobs of walkers had been reduced to a few hundred, still those hundreds parted only reluctantly before them, red eyes following every step they took. The air was redolent of them, a mephitic stench that made Olly gag. She swore under her breath.

"Just a little way," Qualary murmured, giving her arm a reassuring squeeze. "They won't follow us inside the Dome building."

And they did not. Once inside, the air became clear; the corridors were empty; the reception room itself appeared airy and orderly. The four Domers she had seen previously—even Berkli, who had run away in such a hurry—waited for her in one corner together with a scatter of other people to whom she was not introduced. Their dress alone separated them into four groups, one of which wore long, patterned sleeves that could have been done by no one but Wilfer Ponde. Or herself.

"Domer Family members," muttered Qualary, without moving her lips.

"Sit there," Ellel directed Olly, pointing to a chair. She was standing commandingly still, one arm extended. Obviously, this was the Ellel her own people knew best. Calm. Efficient. Knowledgeable.

Olly sank deep into a boneless chair while Qualary faded into the draperies along the wall, her head lowered. The Four Family heads sat behind a table, as though they sat in judgment.

At the right, Ander held a full glass in one hand and an almost-empty bottle in the other. Next to him was Ellel, then Mitty, with Berkli at the left. The other Family members stood around and behind these four, many of them staring curiously at Olly, who returned the stares, examining their faces, keeping her own expressionless. When uncertain how to behave, Hero had told her, give the impression of uninvolvement or affability, for threat begets threat and anger begets anger. It was much the same thing Oracle had said: Be affable. Be stupid.

Olly's attention was drawn from them when Berkli asked in a kindly voice:

"Have you had something to eat? Have you had a chance to rest?"

Ellel snorted. Olly simply nodded.

"Now that you're settled in," said Ander in a much-slurred voice, "we thought it would be a good idea to let you know what we es-espect of you." He cocked his head and waited. Olly looked attentive, but said nothing.

"That is," he murmured indistinctly, put off by her silence, "if you're interested."

Ellel laughed harshly. "Interested or not, she will be told what is expected."

Murmurs from those in attendance, some approving, some not. A few of the older persons present shook their heads at Ellel, as though she were guilty of some breach of manners. One or two threw similar glances in Ander's direction, but he merely filled his glass once more and drank thirstily.

Ellel did not seem to notice. She leaned forward in her tall-backed armchair and held out one hand, finger extended, a pointer that said more clearly than words, *attend*.

"When men went to the stars, they left behind them a space station, moon settlements, at least one partially finished shuttle, and, it is said, a starship under construction. In addition, enormous quantities of equipment and supplies were left here on earth, much of it carefully stored. Some of us believe our kindreds' outward migration was intended to be only the first wave of a continuing process.

"We believe that we, too, may go to the stars."

"If we wish to do so," Berkli interrupted with a studiously impersonal expression on his face, as though he dared her to object.

She's talking to her people, not to me, Olly thought. It's them she has to convince. As for him, he's like a cat, teasing a snake to make it strike. Did he know what poison the snake carried?

Ellel turned on him with elaborate forbearance, every word chosen carefully to sway those in the room to her own opinion. "Of course, Berkli. But even if we choose not to migrate outward, we have already chosen to continue man's upward progress here on earth. The first step in either alternative is to take a look at the space station and the moon settlements to see what vital information and materials have been left for us there."

She turned back toward Olly, as though expecting a comment. Olly contented herself with silence.

Ellel waited. When it became apparent that Olly intended no comment, she went on. "The shuttle is virtually complete except for its guidance system." She waited again, this time fingers tapping impatiently.

Olly looked at each of them, seeking a clue. What did they expect her to say? That she'd be delighted to serve as their guidance system? She felt hysterical laughter building up inside herself.

"I'm sure she understands," said Berkli quietly.

Olly nodded at him gratefully.

The Ellel onlookers nodded similarly and smiled. Good. The system understood what was expected of it. Some few others, standing in corners, frowned in dismay.

"Werra tole us 'bout you," said Ander. "You"—he took a deep breath and pulled himself together—"you're the one. The only . . . child."

"The one what?" asked Olly, totally forgetting Qualary's warning.

Ellel's face flushed, her mouth twisted, but before she could speak, Berkli rose and put his hand on her shoulder, restraining her. She shook him off, angrily.

"Ellel," Berkli said softly. "Surely she has the right to know what Ander means." He leaned across the table, saying, "The residents of Gaddi House used to mix freely with the people here in the Place. My father told me of seeing Hunagor. Many of my generation remember meeting Werra and Seoca. It was Werra who said that a Gaddir child would have the ability to guide ships in space.''

Did he think she didn't know? Well, perhaps he didn't know about the chair in Ellel's quarters. Perhaps he hadn't been told about all the other girls who had sat in that chair. She started to speak, only to be quelled by a warning glance from Berkli as he went on:

''Some years ago, Ellel obtained cell samples from one or more of the Gaddirs.''

''From Werra,'' Ellel confirmed, ''and Seoca.''

Mitty spoke up. ''So if Ellel has established that you are of their lineage, I think you can rely on that information. And that's what Ander meant when he said you were the *only* Gaddir child. You may not be the only one in existence, of course, but you're the only one we've found.''

Berkli sat back, every line of his face warning her. The room simmered silently, a pot just on the boil that might, with only a bit more heat, boil over. If it did, Olly thought, it would disclose something terrible below that steamy surface.

Mitty coughed and said in a conciliatory tone: ''I'm sure none of us expects you to guide the ship tomorrow. I would expect you'd need . . . a time of familiarization. You'll need to see the ship itself. You'll need to talk with the engineers. If you have this ability.''

''She has it,'' said Ellel, an edge of anger audible in her voice. ''I've told you that!''

''But she is unpracticed in using it,'' Mitty interjected, with a meaningful look at Olly. ''If you were expected to guide a ship today, would you be able to do it?''

So. That was where they were tending. Mitty and Berkli were conspiring to give her time. Not escape, which they might be unable to arrange, but time. She shook her head firmly and spoke clearly. ''No. Not safely. To do it safely, I will need more information.''

Silence again. Ellel's eyes snapping with anger. Mitty keeping a quiet face. Everyone else watching, waiting.

''What sort of information?'' asked Berkli. ''Since yours is a Gaddir talent, I suppose you'll need information from Gaddi House?''

''I will,'' said Olly, reading him correctly.

''Never!'' snarled Ellel.

''Then I can't do the job,'' said Olly, keeping her voice flat and unemotional.

The others murmured among themselves. Ellel's golden mask glared at Olly as though to pierce her through. Olly managed to return the look with one that was virtually mindless. She had allies in this room, but she would not keep them long if Ellel knew it.

Abruptly, Ellel's face cleared. She had thought of something.

"Well then," she said, in a voice that was little more than a keening whisper. "I shall take this matter under advisement. It may be possible for her to go into Gaddi House. Under the proper conditions. I will think it over."

Olly took a deep breath, ready to assert herself again, only to see from the corner of her eye a tiny motion of Qualary's hand. It was a warning. Best she not break Qualary's rule again. Don't appear contentious. Though she wanted to scream defiance, she stayed quiet. They couldn't kill her if they needed her to guide their ship! They couldn't hurt her seriously.

But it would be dangerous to say that. She threw another sidelong look at Qualary and found the woman's eyes fixed pleadingly upon her. She bit down her anger and said in the childlike tones she remembered using when Oracle had been grumpy, "Oh, I'll help if I can. I think it's all very exciting."

Several bystanders dressed in silks with fluttering sleeves smiled and murmured to one another. Ander nodded drunkenly, apparently satisfied. Berkli and Mitty carefully did not look at each other.

"Take her away, Qualary," Ellel snarled. "I'll let you know later about where she can go."

"Ma'am," bobbed Qualary. She came to put her hand on Olly's shoulder, and they departed as they had come.

"You did very well," murmured Qualary as they went down one of the long curved corridors around the Dome. "You didn't give her much of a chance to get mad at you."

"Is there some way I could talk to Berkli?" Olly asked.

"Berkli! Why?"

"He may have useful information, and he might tell me things Ellel won't. I'd like to talk to him."

"Trying to talk with Berkli would be a good way to get yourself killed! Ellel hates him almost as much as she hates Gaddi House. Berkli has no power. The walkers belong to Ellel. He doesn't dare cross her. Not him, nor Mitty either!"

Despite this warning, when they emerged into the air, they found the walkers going away, flowing toward the gates in the wall. Only a sparse dozen remained to watch them.

Inside, Qualary went to the window, her mind busy with a thousand suspicions brought about by the sudden departure of the others, the threats Ellel had made.

"You never told me about last night. What happened while you were with Ellel?"

Once more Olly tried to put words to the experience. Once more she failed. "I can't . . . it's hard to describe," she said. "It was just—confusing. Her place is like a . . . I don't know. It's sort of like Oracle's cavern, all cluttered up with meaningless stuff."

"I know," said Qualary, sitting beside her. "I know. I'm her housekeeper. I know exactly what it's like."

Olly threw up her hands. "As for her, she's strange. What she says she wants and what she really wants may be different things. I kept feeling she was lying to me, but also lying to herself."

"Did you mention where you came from?" Qualary asked. "Did she ask anything about your childhood? Did you tell her anything about your growing up, who took care of you?"

Olly tried to remember. "She knew I came from an archetypal village. I'd already told her."

"Did you tell her anything about it?" Qualary persisted.

Had she? Olly tried to remember and couldn't. "I must have told her something," she confessed. "I was so tired, and so hungry, and she kept . . . " She couldn't describe it.

Qualary shook her head, trying to make the motion seem casual. "It probably doesn't matter," she soothed. "It probably makes no difference."


In the archetypal village where Olly had grown up, day had succeeded day as though nothing at all had happened. A new Bastard had come to take the place of the old. There was never any shortage of Bastards, as Drowned Woman remarked—or of Fools, said Oracle, for they soon had another one of those as well. The new Orphan was only a baby, kept so shut away by the Wet Nurse that the villagers did not know if it was a boy or a girl.

Oracle missed having an Orphan to cosset with biscuits and to plague with good advice. Drowned Woman spoke of her fosterling longingly from time to time. Burned Man recalled her as well, saying what a quick pupil she had been, how exceptional her understanding. Remembering in what company the Wet Nurse had arrived, none of them spoke of "their" Orphan in her hearing, though it was likely she overheard them anyhow. Wet Nurse, they all soon confirmed to one another, was a sneak.

Winter came with early snow, and the peddlers told of disease among the cities. This telling was reinforced by the farmers who supplied them with food. The cities were dying, they said. Then the cities were dead. No more gangers.

Hero went out to see what was happening in the world and returned with a look both stern and sad on his face. "Woe and pity!" he cried. "For the cities are no more."

Burned Man sat in his front window and wept as though he would never stop. "All those children," he cried. "All those poor children."

"Come now," said Oracle impatiently. "Hero says most of the children who were born healthy are still healthy, and as for the rest, you knew very well they were headed toward such an end! That's what got you in this fix in the first place!"

"But—but—" he cried.

"There is no but!" she exclaimed. "If a man leaps from a high cliff and breaks his legs, do we say, '*But* it isn't fair! *But* it isn't right! *But* someone should have figured how to leap from cliffs without breaking bones! *But* all the cliffs should have been leveled long ago!' We don't blame the council or the mayor. Instead we say the jumper is a damned fool and lucky that he isn't dead. Surely the end is in the act! And if your gangers go to the songhouses and take drugs when they know it causes disease, surely the end is in that act as well."

"They don't mean to die!" he cried. "And what of the innocent man or woman your jumper pulls over with him when he goes!"

"Few ever mean to die," Oracle replied. "And no one ever means to be pulled over by someone else, but those ends are also in the act. Who one chooses to be with is as important as what one chooses to do. Danger is communicable, like disease."

"I blame the Edgers!" he shouted. "They could have—"

"Man believes what he wants to believe," sighed Oracle, "and he usually wants to believe someone else is to blame. So blame who you like. You might remember what you yourself told Orphan. There are not enough Edgers in the world to have fixed the cities. There are no acceptable solutions to some problems!"

Still, Burned Man would not be consoled for days. He spent his time between fury and tears, until at last both emotions wore themselves out and left him much as he had been before.

It was then that the walkers came.

They came in great numbers in the early morning, along the road and from among the trees on either side of the village, and down the trail that ran beside the waterfall. They found Oracle asleep in her cavern and Drowned Woman playing with the Water Babies, they found Burned Man fixing his breakfast, they looked for Hero but missed him, for he was off on a quest. The three they found they took over the hill with them and down into the valley of the Crystal, where they took old Cermit from feeding his chickens and Farmwife Suttle from milking her cow, and then with all these folk who had succored and loved Orphan, they went at great speed into the southwest, returning to the Place of Power whence they had been sent.

At nightfall, Hero returned to the village to learn from Miser and Artist and Ingenue what had happened there and that the black-helmed creatures had sought him, Hero, as well. Long into the night he sat at the flap of his tent, thinking heroic thoughts. At dawn he rose, mounted his horse, and left the village without a declamation, without a stated quest. For the first time in his life, he had encountered a situation he could not meet alone. He knew of other villages, of other Heroes. He intended to go to them, all of them, and ask for help, for there was a maiden to be rescued. A maiden he knew.

During the long night, he had been surprised to discover that knowing Orphan made a definite difference.

By an inside route through Gaddi House, up certain shafts and across catwalks above otherwise untraversable areas, it was possible to reach the roof, a vast graveled area broken here and there by glass-roofed openings that let light into the gardens far below. It was old Seoca, Orphan's Herkimer-Lurkimer, who suggested Tom take their guests to this vantage point. It was from behind the roof's low parapet that Tom showed Arakny and Abasio the Place of Power, pointing out shuttle and Dome and explaining how the Domers had arrived in the long ago.

When he had finished, Abasio said, "Everything looks calm down there, very peaceful. But earlier, you said none of us was safe. What did you mean?"

Tom leaned upon the parapet and pointed downward. "See those walkers moving about? A lot of them recently left, but there are still enough of them to kill us all. One word from Ellel, and it would be like a scythe cutting grain. Men would fall dead, harvested."

"I've heard the sound they make," said Abasio. "From miles away, but the sound still pained me and killed birds."

Tom went on: "Think how many of them there are! Thousands, getting older every hour. Wires corroding, circuits wearing, crystals fracturing. Even pseudoflesh eventually sickens and dies. His Wisdom thinks these creatures may have been stored away in the first place because they were considered dangerous or unreliable. Otherwise they'd have been used for something, wouldn't they? Well, what happens when their systems break down?"

Arakny and Abasio considered this in silence, which Arakny eventually broke to say, "No one has told us yet what this woman Ellel wants with Olly."

"The shuttle is almost complete. It lacks only a guidance system to be able to carry them out, away, into space."

"They think Olly has one?"

"They think she *is* one."

"I don't understand—?"

"You mean—?"

Both of them shouted, heard themselves shouting, guiltily hushed themselves.

Tom said, "According to what I've been told, certain persons of the Gaddir lineage have the mental ability to do this thing. Have you ever heard of idiot savants?"

Arakny had. "They are persons without competent mentation who none-theless have a single outstanding talent, as for example creating represen-tational art, or rendition of music heard, or instant calculation."

Tom nodded. "The Gaddirs I speak of are savants with normal mentation. They can instantly establish the interaction of seemingly unrelated facts. One facet of this talent is to compute the relative motion of two or more bodies in space. It's a talent many people use when they play games. They see a thrown ball, and they jump to catch it, unconscious of the calculation that has taken place in computing the speed and direction of that jump. Gaddir talent is the same, only vastly more powerful."

"So they'd put Olly in this ship—"

"Install," said Tom very quietly.

"What do you mean, install?"

"I mean, put wires in her head," said Tom. "Install—"

Arakny and Abasio shared glances, hoping they had not heard him cor-rectly, knowing they had.

"—but it will only work if she's willing," continued Tom. "According to His Wisdom, she must be willing."

"Does she know this?"

"Parts of it. I doubt she knows she'd be wired into the ship, though she may know even that by now."

"If she knew, why was she in such a hurry to get here?" cried Arakny.

"If she doesn't know, is she to be allowed to find out about it?" Abasio demanded in an angry voice.

"Necessarily, yes. Since she has to be willing, she has to know all about it. Though they are holding Olly prisoner, in a sense she holds them as well."

"She only came here, or started for here, because of her prophecy," grated Abasio.

"What prophecy was that?" asked Tom.

Abasio quoted it, in full.

> "Ask one only child,
> Ask two who made her,
> Ask three thrones that tower,
> Gnawed by four to make them fall.
> Find five champions,
> And six set upon salvation,
> And answer seven questions in the place of power."

"Well, as to the three thrones that tower," said Tom, "they are here. *Gaddi* means 'throne.' This is Throne House."

"And what are the thrones?"

Tom looked over their heads, as though seeking revelation. "I don't know, even though I've gone with His Wisdom when he goes down to the throne room, where they are. What he sees may be different from what I see. He sometimes tells me the thrones were made before men were made."

Arakny said, "Are they things? Or beings?"

Tom sighed and ran his fingers through his hair. "They look like thrones—great, gray chairs, tall and imposing. But they're carved all over with . . . creatures. The chamber where they are is misty or smoky, sometimes more than others, and it's often hard to see the thrones. I know Hunagor is sitting in one of them, and Werra is sitting in another, and the third one—well, it's more or less empty, though it has old Seoca's name carved on it."

"Hunagor? Werra?"

"Two of His Wisdom's kinsmen. They died some time ago."

"The thrones are crypts, then. Coffins?"

Tom shrugged. "One could say that, I suppose." He shook himself. "If you've seen enough up here, His Wisdom is expecting us."

They returned the way they had come, oppressed by the vast shadowy spaces inside the great house, wondering at all this empty space housing so few, for when they asked, Tom replied that there were only a couple hundred Gaddirs, in space enough for thousands. There had been thousands once, he said. Long ago. When they were needed.

"But there are only two hundred now, and that includes the children and our agents," he said, "who do His Wisdom's will, out in the world."

They were taken to join the old man on his terrace.

"I've shown them the Place," said Tom. "I've answered their questions, so far as I could, but they want to know about the thrones."

"Of course they do," said the old man. He reached out his hands to Abasio and Arakny. "The thrones have been here a long time. Think of the phrase 'seats of power.' When one sits in a seat of power, one can accomplish things. If it is necessary that certain things be accomplished, then the appropriate seats of power rise up. This is natural law. It always happens."

"Rise up from where?" Arakny asked.

"Well, as to that, I'm not sure. Out of time, perhaps. Or some other space. Or the inside of the earth, perhaps, where they were forged at the beginning of the planet. I truly don't know. I'm not sure even the thrones know their origin."

"But one sits there?"

"One can. Briefly. If one is of the right lineage. And then one understands certain things that have to be done."

"Tom says your name is on one of them. You sat there?"

"I did. Briefly. You're welcome to go look at them, so you can tell Olly about them."

"We can tell Olly?"

"If you choose to go to her, yes. Tom tells me she's being kept in a house down there in the Place. She's with a woman we know, a very pleasant woman. Tom can take you down there, or try, at least, though you may be stopped. As with most things, there's danger involved."

"Danger from this Ellel person?" demanded Abasio.

The old man gave him a wide-eyed look, like a child's. "Ellel needs Olly, but she doesn't need either of you. She may feel you are an entanglement, a complication, and Ellel habitually disposes of complications. She may kill you. Or take you hostage."

He waited, but neither Abasio nor Arakny replied.

"On the other hand," the old man continued, "she may let Olly come back here with you. Which would be a good idea, if possible."

"And if Olly decides not to do this . . . guidance thing?" asked Abasio.

"Ellel would be very angry."

"It sounds to me like danger if she does and danger if she doesn't," said Arakny. "What difference does it make?"

"Oh, every decision makes a difference," said the old man. "Though sometimes we lack the ability to distinguish between alternatives."

"How do we get to her?" Abasio asked.

Tom snorted, a sound like a troubled laugh. "We walk out the gate of Gaddi House and stroll across the grass, where there's still some left. We go down the street and knock on Qualary's door. That's how I got there yesterday, though I almost didn't get back!"

Arakny threw up her hands, her voice rising stridently. "It hardly sounds like a mission requiring courage and resolution, to take a simple walk down the street!"

The old man bowed his head over his knotted hands. When he looked up, he spoke softly. "Often the most terrible struggles take place quietly, behind a screen of normal activity and civility, behind a curtain of diplomacy. In secrecy, in silence, a whole race may be destroyed without notice. Whole cultures and species have been destroyed while men smiled and spoke of economics, of employment, of progress, of the welfare of mankind. Is a threat less deadly because it does not scream and rage and threaten force of arms?"

"So out there is danger."

He gave his answer gravely. "Yes. But so long as you remain here, you are perfectly safe."

"Being perfectly safe is not what I had in mind!" cried Abasio, in a fever of impatience. "There was danger all around when we started out on this journey. I don't see that anything's changed. It was gangers and walkers and monsters then, it's just another kind of gangers and more walkers and monsters now. I told Farmwife Suttle I'd keep Olly safe, and that's what I'll try to do. I want to go where she is."

"Ah," said the old man. "Well, that's a quick decision." He turned to Arakny. "And what about you?"

"I don't know," she said. "The girl is a nice enough girl, but she's not family or a close friend. On the other hand, she has my library, and I should take some steps to retrieve it. Also, my whole duty is the acquisition of information, and I am learning things here in the Place of Power that I did not know, things my people do not know. I am weighing whether I should risk my life to learn more, or go back to my people with what I already have."

"Or put what you know down onto paper and send it by messenger," said the old man.

"What messenger?"

The old man turned to Tom. "I was thinking of Coyote."

"He would take the message," said Tom.

Arakny thought this over silently for some moments. "You don't care if all Artemisia knows about this?"

The old man shrugged. "Up until now, we've played a quiet game, but now the gamepieces have begun shouting. Now we win or we lose, and it doesn't matter who knows."

"And if we win?"

"Life has a chance. You Artemisians may go on with your noble experiment at civilizing mankind."

"And if we lose?"

"Death gathers. Tyranny is triumphant once more. Evil stalks the earth, and all life dwindles into death. Yours and mine and Coyote's and Bear's. And your elk. And your bison. And the forests planted by the Sisters to Trees. And all the fish in the seas. All."

She shivered, trying twice before the words would come out. "I'd like to see the thrones so I can tell Olly about them, but I will tell Wide Mountain Mother as well."

"Tom will take you," said the old man.

When they were out in the hallway, Abasio said, "You don't look at all eager."

"I'm not," Tom said flatly. "I'm an engineer, or I like to think so. I like things to be definable, measurable. The thrones are not definable, and they make me feel inadequate. Uncomfortable. No matter. His Wisdom said to show you."

They went with him through the security points and the dusty labyrinth, past huge old doors that Tom said had never been opened in his memory, down the last stretch to a door in every way similar, except that the dust lay less thickly around it. When the gigantic portal swung open, it blocked the entire corridor and gave them no way to go forward but into the room itself.

"Follow the tracks," Tom told them, pointing at the dusty floor, serpent-trailed by wheels. "I'll wait for you here." He had no wish to go into the room again. He had not slept well since he had been there last.

They went alone, laying their hands against the pillars, feeling moisture and a barely discernible vibration, as of some huge engine in motion, some mighty heart beating far underground, perhaps at the center of the earth itself. The dust rose beneath their feet and fell again, half-covering the footprints they had just made. The wheel tracks twisted and coiled, and they followed in the same path, coming at last to the place the pillars stopped, the open place before the dais.

The air was clear. No smoke. No mist. Three great chairs, carved all over with creatures. Carved eyes saw them, carved faces perceived them, carved mouths opened imperceptibly wider, carved nostrils took their scent. On the left-hand seat sat a woman. Not entirely human, thought Arakny. Not entirely dead, thought Abasio. The figure was half-absorbed into the stone, but its eyes also saw; its nostrils smelled their presence. High on the back of the chair was carved the word *Hunagor*. In the center chair, the figure was male, with the word carved high above his head: *Werra*.

The right-hand chair was empty of human form, though it, too, had its crowded quota of other beings. It bore the name *Seoca*. The dais was deep in dust, though none lay on the chairs themselves. The air around the chairs seemed to tremble, as air shimmers over a heated roadway.

Abasio wanted to speak but did not. He knew his words would not penetrate this air. He glanced at Arakny and found her eyes on him, wide and slightly frightened. He put his lips near her ear and whispered, "All the things carved there. They're still . . . alive."

She looked again. The creatures had lived once. Each of them had come to sit in a particular chair. Each of them had been absorbed into it. Maybe they were, in a way, still alive. She shuddered. Maybe they were . . . the thing itself. Not merely thing, not merely being, but both. An indescribable amalgam, ancient as stone, partaking of stone, but sentient and aware and awfully, dreadfully alive.

They stood a moment more, scarcely breathing, unspeaking, finally backing away until they were among the sheltering pillars, then quickly and more quickly following their own tracks back the way they had come. When they stood clear of the great door at last, gasping as though they had run a great way, Fuelry shut it behind them.

"Who are they?" Arakny whispered.

"They? The thrones?" he asked, as though surprised.

"Sitting there?"

"You mean Hunagor? Werra? People. I knew Werra. My father knew Hunagor."

"Not human people," said Abasio firmly.

"What makes you say that?"

"They don't look entirely human. They're—they're different."

Fuelry rubbed his face and chin with one hand, as though scrubbing away cobwebs. "They were human."

"You have only to look at them," insisted Abasio in a hushed voice, as though he were afraid of being overheard.

Tom said patiently, "But you see, I knew Werra. He was as human as His Wisdom is."

"Will the old man come down here? Sit there? Like them?" Arakny asked.

"He says he will. When the time comes. Which will not be for many years."

"Tom," Abasio insisted, "if you know that, you must know other things. What's the purpose of all this?"

He led them back the way they had come. "I can only tell you what Seoca has told me, over and over. The purpose of Gaddi House is to protect the earth and the place of all life upon it. That's what the thrones do! I don't know how they do it, not entirely. I know parts of things. People come here. They talk to His Wisdom. He gives them instructions and supplies. The people leave again. They go out into the world, here, or there, as he commands. They do things, this, or that.

"But I don't know them all. I don't hear what's said to them all, see what's given to them all. I don't know how it all fits together. I don't know what's behind these other doors."

"This place is old," whispered Arakny.

"Seoca says this down here is ancient beyond counting, but I never believed that."

Abasio shook his head. "I think he spoke truth."

Arakny asked, "Will Coyote take the message I'm going to write?"

"His Wisdom says if you write your message, I am to send it."

They returned the way they had come. When they came through the last secured door, which Tom locked again behind them, Abasio stopped short, head alertly cocked.

"What's that?" he asked in a surprised voice.

The other two listened, at first hearing nothing. Then they made it out against the susurrus of moving air, a plaintive whistle, a strain of melody. It came nearer, though still far off, seeming to emanate from a cross-corridor a considerable distance down the hallway where they stood.

Two men emerged from one side, the tune emerging with them. Without seeing Abasio or the others, the two men crossed the hallway and disappeared down the cross corridor, the tune following after.

"Whistler!" Abasio choked out. "And Sudden Stop, the weapons man! What are they doing here?"

"They are agents of His Wisdom's," whispered Tom. "Two of His Wisdom's most trusted men. They have just returned from the cities of manland."

"I know," Abasio gasped. "I saw them both there!"

Though Arakny looked at him curiously, Abasio said nothing more, though his mind was full of confusion. When he had first seen Whistler, Sudden Stop, and the old man with the donkey, he had assumed they had encountered one another accidentally. Later on, when he found out who Whistler and Sudden Stop were, he had been sure of it. But perhaps it had not been accidental. Perhaps they had been traveling together. Why? What had the drug merchant and the arms merchant been doing here?

When they returned to their suite, Arakny wrote her letter, spending considerable time at it. It was almost midnight before she finished. She put her letter into a small bag made of heavy cloth that Tom had provided. Something for Coyote to get his teeth into, Tom had said.

When morning came, Tom arrived to take them to Olly, saying that Arakny's missive was on its way. He stood waiting for them calmly enough, but Arakny saw the little beads of sweat along his hairline and the almost imperceptible twitch at the corner of one eye. He didn't much want to leave Gaddi House. Well, neither did she, though Abasio seemed immune to her terrors.

Terrified or not, they went out the massive gate and strolled, as Tom had said they would. Arakny tried to convince herself it was like an early morning walk in any civilized place, though in places the ground was blackened and the trees were dead. Where there was still grass, it was sere at the tops but green at the roots. Recent warmth and rain had started it growing again. The air was almost springlike.

That being so, why was she gasping? She could not seem to breathe as she ordinarily did. The air did not nourish her lungs. It was smothering her. So too Abasio, and Tom. Panting, both of them, like running dogs.

She looked around, but there was no one else abroad in the place. No person, dog, cat, no song of bird. The air was utterly still. She reached for

Abasio's hand, unaware she had done so until she felt his fingers squeezing hers, looked at his face to see the same apprehension there that she felt. He took a painfully deep breath, heaving at the air as at a monstrous weight.

They approached Qualary's house, the horrid pressure increasing with every step. Each breath came unwillingly, for now there was a smell, too, rank and choking. Even Tom coughed, giving them a swift, apologetic look. They came to the door of the ordinary house. Tom knocked. The door opened.

"Good morning, Tom," said Qualary Finch, her voice reverberating as though echoing from some great distance, the sound coming as through delirium or nightmare: *Goooood Moooohrniiing*.

Tom said something, they could not hear what. Olly came from a bedroom yawning, to throw her arms about Abasio, about Arakny, to weep glad tears at seeing them. All of it veiled, distant, unreal, each act in slow motion, each sound resonating, all of them caught in nightmare and unable to waken.

And then the pressure and the smell surged up around them like a tide of foulness, making them struggle and crouch and turn to look, gasping like caught fish, for the street behind them had filled with walkers, rank on serried rank of them, forms that had slipped silently into place like gamepieces, file after file, black helmets aligned in an obdurate grid.

And there, suspended before them like trophies, exhausted and pale, were Burned Man and Oracle, whom Abasio did not know, and old Cermit and Farmwife Suttle and Drowned Woman. Whom he did.

"Grandpa!" cried Abasio in a huge voice, and then in one of shattered surprise: "Ma!"

Came a crow-call of command to make the enormous rank and file of walkers turn as one and go trampling away, feet stamping down, the road shivering and the air crashing, leaving behind only a hundred or so to surround Ellel, her pale hair a snaky tangle around her face, her mouth open in a toothy grin of amusement, her eyes glittering at their expressions of confounded pain.

"What are you doing with them?" cried Olly, though Qualary reached out for her, trying to quiet her. "Why have you brought my friends here?"

"Not only *your* friends, it seems!" cried Ellel in a triumphant voice. "Not only yours, no. And we are keeping them here for reasons you well know, Gaddir child. Keeping them safe, for a time. Their safety depends upon your doing precisely what we—I—want you to do."


The hostages were taken away. Tom got the others inside Qualary's house and shut the door behind them. Though Abasio and Arakny were boiling with impotent rage, Olly was silent and pale.

"Why does she have Abasio's folk? How did they get your Oracle?"

Arakny cried to Olly. "If she is, as you have said, a true Oracle, then wouldn't she have known they were coming?"

"Hush, hush," Tom soothed. "Arakny, this ranting does no good. We must be calm. We must think. Perhaps the Oracle did see them coming and also saw beyond that! Perhaps she let them take her for a reason."

Arakny, muttering, threw herself into a chair.

Olly broke her silence to say, "Oracle might have done that, for a reason."

Her voice was so quiet that it gained all their attention. Abasio asked, "Was my ma in this village of yours?"

"Drowned Woman," Olly replied. "She took care of me when I was a little child."

"Drowned Woman!"

"She tried to kill herself when you ran off to the city," said Olly. "But your grandpa summoned a resurrection team, and they brought her back. Afterward, she had no memory of you, or him, or anything much, so she was sent to a village as an archetypal Suicide. She was my friend. Is my friend. As is Burned Man."

"Burned Man? He's the scarred one?"

"Burned Man. An archetypal Martyr. Also my friend. He taught me . . . many things."

"Hostages," said Abasio bitterly. "I thought when I came home from the city, I had done with hostages."

Tom raised his voice, demanding to be heard. "There is no immediate threat to them. Remember that. Let's not be impetuous, thereby making things worse."

"I'm surprised she didn't seize up Abasio and me as well," growled Arakny.

"No," murmured Olly. "She wants Abasio here fuming and fussing, for she thinks that may influence what I decide to do. You, Arakny, she does not know, but she'll leave you alone while she assesses your worth to her. That's the way Ellel is."

"That's true," said Qualary, wonderingly. "That's exactly how she is."

"I suppose," said Olly, still in that strangely expressionless voice, "I suppose I have only to do what they want in order to get my friends free of her."

Tom Fuelry shifted uneasily.

Abasio cried, "There are things to consider first!"

"I know," said Olly. "And there is no great hurry."

"There's no great hurry," agreed Tom. "Their shuttle isn't ready yet."

"They admitted that you might need additional information," whispered Qualary. "They even said you might want to go to Gaddi House."

"Did they now?" Tom's head came up. "They said she might want to go to Gaddi House?"

Olly got slowly to her feet. "Berkli said that. I think he and Mitty were trying to be helpful. But it was his saying so that made Ellel decide to take hostages."

She drummed her fingers upon the table. "Well, what is done is done. Now the longer we stay here, the more danger there is to all of you. And to Qualary herself. Ellel brought the hostages to assure that I return from Gaddi House. Let us give her no time to add to their number or change her mind. We'll go now. Though I may have to come out again, at least the rest of you will be safe there.

"Qualary, can you go to Ellel?"

Qualary shivered. "Yes. I can."

"Tell her—tell her I am going into Gaddi House. Tell her I am going there to learn to use my—my talent safely and well. Say that I want to see the shuttle this afternoon, that I will do whatever is needful to obtain the release of my friends."

Tom cried, "Are you sure? Is this really what you want to do?"

"I don't know what I want to do," she said simply. "I'm not sure what I must do. But this will give me time to think about it."

She took Qualary's hand and squeezed it. "Go now. We don't want her to blame you for anything."

Qualary went out, observing the walkers on the opposite side of the street, strung out here and there along the way. They did not stop her, but they watched her, jittering and mumbling to themselves. They were not trustworthy. If she made a wrong move, they'd kill her without meaning to, without caring. She made herself walk slowly, fighting down the urge to run. If she ran, she would die.

She heard the others come out behind her and cast a quick look over her shoulder to see them walking quietly across the grass. The walkers watched them go, jittering, twisting, muttering, but not stopping them. Resolutely, she looked where she was going. Merely doing her own task would be quite difficult enough.


Ellel and the others were in an anteroom of the Dome, while beneath the Dome itself were all the thousands of walkers who had been in the street. Ellel stood motionless, looking at them. Beside her, Berkli moved jerkily from one pillar to another, his voice raised in irritation.

"How long do you intend to keep them here, Ellel?" He gestured at the walkers as though to push them away. "How long?"

"Until I need them for something," she replied in a careless voice. "I may need them for something. Perhaps to quell a rebellion."

"Why? Are you casting me in the part of rebel?"

She laughed. "No, Berkli. I see you for what you are, an uncooperative Domer, one who cares little for our accomplishments and even less for human progress."

"I care a great deal for human progress!" he cried. "I'm just not sure what it is."

"You never will be," she snapped, catching sight of her servant. "Well, Qualary! What is it?"

Qualary delivered her message, her head bowed submissively.

Ellel snarled, "You'll bring her to the silo this afternoon. Is that clear?"

"She said she would need to see the silo," said Qualary. "See the shuttle. She needs to see everything, understand everything, so you'll all be safe."

"Don't push her, Ellel," urged Mitty.

"I don't suppose a few days more really matters," commented Ander offhandedly. "The shuttle isn't quite ready, in any case."

Ellel jerked her head toward the doors, signaling Qualary to go.

Berkli turned from his revulsion at the walkers to his more recent annoyance. "Taking hostages was a nasty thing to do, Ellel. It was uncivilized, even for you. Where are you holding them?"

"Why? Do you want to see them?"

He grinned at her, knowing it infuriated her. "As a matter of fact, yes. I understand one of them is an Oracle. I don't often have an opportunity to get a prediction about important things, such as a shuttle trip into space."

"Trust you to fall prey to superstition!" she sneered. "By all means, Berkli. They're being held in the meeting room."

"A bit luxurious for prisoners, isn't it?"

"It's convenient," she snapped. "Accessible. In case I think of some question I want answered in the middle of the night. In case I want a prophecy of my own!"

Berkli, with Mitty trailing along, went to the meeting room and found that no food or drink or beds had been provided, an oversight typical of Ellel. She would overlook the simplest of human needs and then wonder why people were uncooperative. Berkli summoned Domer staff members and had them equip the room both with the necessities for a lengthy stay and with the luxuries to make that stay bearable.

"Thank you," said Oracle, who seemed to have appointed herself spokesperson. "You have our gratitude."

"I apologize for my colleague," Mitty said. "She overlooks details." He excused himself and departed, looking troubled.

"He doesn't like this," said Oracle.

"No. But he's not a fighter," murmured Berkli. "Mitty will go a long way to avoid confrontation. He eschews evil, but he won't take up arms against it."

"Can you tell us what this is about?" Oracle asked.

"You are the Oracle, why don't you tell me?" Berkli challenged her.

"I can do that without foresight," she said. "Orphan—that is, Olly—was brought here to do something Quince Ellel cannot do. It has something to do with a journey into space. It is something Olly might choose not to do, and we have been brought here to guarantee her cooperation."

"That took no oracular talent?"

"No. I merely listened to the talk that was going on around us this morning," she replied. "I can extrapolate from that. Quince Ellel longs for the stars, though she will settle for an empire on earth, with herself as Empress."

"You foresee this."

"I judge that it is true from what I see of her. Not all the archetypes are in the villages, Dome-man. Some of them still walk among ordinary men. And sometimes I do not need to foresee. Sometimes I need merely look and listen to learn interesting things. Such as the fact that the cities are gone."

"What cities?" he asked, suspiciously.

"The last cities," she replied. "Those few that were left in manland. I thought you here in the Place of Power kept track of the status of the world and its peoples."

He furrowed his brow. He hadn't looked at the information console for days. Had anyone looked at it lately? With all this triumphant strutting that had been going on, it was likely no one had looked at it in some time. Perhaps he'd been the last one, and he certainly hadn't paid any attention to the cities.

Oracle nodded at him, as though she read his thoughts. "The cities are gone," she said. "Fantis and Echinot and all the rest. The plague has walked through them, winnowing their populace, separating the grain from the chaff, consuming the chaff while the grain was flung outward, into the villages, into the farms. Now on all this continent, the cities are as though they had never been. Now we have only towns, as in Artemisia, where people are known to one another. There is neighborhood once again, where before were only unknown men doing evil to faceless victims."

He gaped at her, and she smiled in return.

"You needn't take my word for it. Verify it for yourself."

Leaving the luxurious room at a laborious trot, Berkli went down the long, polished corridor to the Dome. The lift chair sat empty against the wall, but before he could sit down in it, Ellel and several of her walkers came upon him.

"And where do you think you're going?" she asked him.

"I need to check the data. Ellel, did you know—"

"You need to check nothing."

"Someone needs to!"

"No. You have meddled with my affairs once too often," she snapped. "I'm confining you to your quarters!"

"You are what?" he gasped, choking down laughter.

She turned and stalked away. He laughed out loud until the walkers took hold of him, carried him to his own quarters, then shut him in. They stood outside and would not let him out again. He bathed first, to get rid of the stink of them and because Mitty had said their touch was dangerous. Then he sat beside the window, staring out in bemused fury. Of all the Domers, he was the only one who knew the cities had died. And he wondered if it made any difference to anyone.

CummyNup Chingero, on his slow and meandering way south, had encountered this one and that one who had escaped from the cities as he had, this one and that one who had been immune to the plague or who had been of abstemious habit and had not caught it. To these men, and women, CummyNup spoke fondly of Abasio the Cat, Abasio the Clever, Abasio the finest and first among men.

Somewhat to his astonishment, Sybbis spoke even more eloquently than he. Abasio was tall, and strong, and handsome. Abasio was a prince, a warrior, a mighty lord. Abasio was the kind of men other men should follow. She, Sybbis, was his consort and was carrying his child.

CummyNup was more than a little peeved at this claim, and he challenged her about it. How could she claim Abasio as the father of her child?

Because, she said. She had put it together from things she'd heard in Fantis before Old Chief Purple slit Kerf's throat for him. And from things CummyNup had told her back at Wise Rocks Farm. And from things she herself had observed when she got pregnant.

CummyNup had to agree, it sounded like Abasio, knife slash, bullet pucker, and all. He couldn't get over it. She had been a virgin when Kerf got her, which meant she'd stayed a virgin until Abasio had her, which meant she was Abasio's woman and his alone.

" 'Cept for that time in the barn back at Wise Rocks," CummyNup was so injudicious as to remark.

That, so said Sybbis, had been his good fortune and she'd done it only because it was necessary, so he'd bring her along. She certainly couldn't stay at Wise Rocks Farm in safety while her lover, consort, king, and lord was down in the southlands someplace, running into all sorts of monsters and stuff, now could she?

Many of those who heard CummyNup's stories about Abasio were men at loose ends with no particular plans for the future. Some of them were ex-gangers who, at Sybbis's insistence, shaved their heads and wore long white leather vests with a cat-head on the back to show they were all followers of the absent but no doubt potent Abasio. In the meantime, CummyNup was their captain, and he accumulated several hundred followers in this manner.

One night, while he was standing watch, more or less alone because he enjoyed it, he was approached by a coyote who came up to him and wished him good evening.

CummyNup was not much surprised. Being a cityman, he knew very little about the natural world. It would not really have surprised him if a spider had crawled out of its hole and greeted him in ganger lingo. So he wished the Coyote a good evening in return, and the two of them fell to talking.

When CummyNup said he and his group were searching for Abasio the Cat, the Coyote asked if that would be the Abasio who was once a Purple. Abasio who traveled south in a dyer's wagon?

Yes, said CummyNup, that was the Abasio.

Why then, said the Coyote, he'd be happy to tell CummyNup where Abasio might be found: there to the southwest where the mountain cut a broken line into the stars. He pointed with a paw, and CummyNup marked the place against the morning.

When morning came, he told the assembled men and women that he had had a revelation during the night. Actually, he started to tell them about the Coyote, but he knew there were skeptics in the group, so the information took the form of a revelation. Either way, the several hundred men who were following CummyNup all agreed to march toward the mountain where Abasio awaited them.

Wide Mountain Mother found a cloth-wrapped package on her doorstep. The cloth had tooth-holes in it, and inside was a letter from Arakny. The missive was somewhat moist and also pierced with tooth-holes, but not unreadable. When Mother had read the first page, she felt she understood the tooth-holes, but when she read further, she felt she understood nothing at all.

Hurriedly, she sent messengers up the hill to the men's houses. After conferring with the warriors and her own council, she sent messengers out in all directions. By midafternoon, the people of Artemisia were gathering outside the town, and by nightfall, a throng of them, headed by feathered warriors, set off westward toward the Place of Power.

"What did Arakny say?" one of Wide Mountain Mother's daughters asked, this one also a librarian.

"She said she had seen the thrones," Mother answered, without expression. "She said she does not know whether they are intelligent machines or monstrous beings. In either case, she fears what they may intend."

# C H A P T E R  14

*I*n a quiet garden of Gaddi House, Olly told
Tom she wanted to see the old man.

"My Herkimer-Lurkimer," she said,
"who owes me an explanation, at the very least." She
laughed, a little bitterly. "Oh, yes. If he's my Herkimer-
Lurkimer."

"He told us he was," murmured Arakny.

"If that's true, then I was a child here, where you say
the thrones are," she murmured. "I've dreamed of
thrones. Was that because I saw them as a child?"

"Perhaps," said Tom. "That could be so."

"No doubt seeing them again will refresh my memory." She rubbed her forehead fretfully. "Can I see them
before I see him? Can you show them to me, Tom?"

Tom assented, though grudgingly.

"Do you want to go with us?" Olly asked the others.

Arakny shook her head. Even Abasio had trouble meeting her eyes.

He said gravely, "I'll go with you if you ask me, Olly,
but only because you ask!"

Arakny threw up her hands. "I may as well go along."

They went by a longer route than Abasio and Arakny remembered from their previous trip, though it may have only seemed so because Olly stopped so many times along the way—stopped to put her hands on closed doors, to feel the walls, to listen for sounds, to sniff, as though she smelled something they could not.

"How does it make you feel?" Abasio asked her.

Olly stopped dead, her mouth working. "How does it make me feel! All this, you mean? It makes me feel like a chip on a river! Washed along, willy-nilly. It makes me feel as Oracle must have felt, sent away as a child because of what she was, of what she could do! It makes me feel trapped and desperate! That's how I feel."

Abasio reached out for her, but she shuddered away from him, her face closed and angry.

He said, "I only meant, does it seem familiar?"

Olly breathed deeply, calming herself. "Yes. I suppose it's familiar. Mostly it smells familiar. But also, I feel I almost know what's behind these doors, that any minute I'll remember." She dropped her eyes. "If I want to remember."

"The place depresses me," Abasio said awkwardly. "It makes me itchy."

"Oppressed," said Arakny. "There is something here that is . . . not . . . ." Her voice trailed away disconsolately.

"Not human," agreed Olly, turning to their guide. "Would you agree, Tom?"

He shook his head, annoyed. He would not agree. "I've been a Gaddir since I was a child. I've never had any sense it was not a human thing to be."

"Coyote said something about our needing to think of intelligence as human," Olly told him, staring through him. "So if we find intelligence, we assume humanity goes with it. That's our protection, isn't it?"

"Protection against what?" he demanded.

"Against having to learn to communicate with others, who think differently than we do." She squeezed his arm and urged him on.

They came at last to the designated door, which Tom opened while Olly stood at his shoulder, nodding, murmuring, as though committing the procedure to memory. The three stood aside to let her enter.

Without a moment's pause she went swiftly along the wheel tracks, losing herself among the clustered pillars, leaving the other three to shift uncomfortably behind her.

Tom thrust his hands deep into his pockets, hunching his shoulders against the chill. Arakny shivered in the same surge of lonely cold. Abasio merely shut his eyes and listened.

Eventually they heard a sharp cracking, then a creaking, as of something opening. These inanimate sounds were followed by what might have been a voice. If it was a voice, it was not Olly's but that of someone larger, someone, thought Abasio, more female. All they actually heard was a questioning murmur with a periodic upturn.

"........?"

"Who?" whispered Tom.

"Hunagor," grated Arakny. "Who else?"

"Hunagor is dead!" said Tom, his voice shaking.

"To you, to me, yes. But we're not Gaddirs. Maybe she's not dead to Olly."

The murmurs stopped, to be succeeded by others, lower, below the level of any human voice.

"........?" "........?"

"I suppose that's Werra," said Abasio, trying without success to sound flippant.

Neither of them answered. They merely stood, waiting for the voices to stop. When the murmurings ended, however, other sounds began and continued: draggings, crashings, distant reverberations, and echoes, as of mighty portals opening to disclose impossible vacancies beyond. And at last came a great, sure humming as of a mighty engine turning.

Then even that faded away into dusty silence.

Footsteps.

Olly came from among the pillars to join them. They searched her face, finding there a deadly quiet, but no other difference.

Tom shut the huge door behind them, and they returned as they had come, pausing at a turn in the corridor as Olly fell behind. They turned to see her standing before one of the massive doors, ankle-deep in the dust drift that lay before it.

"You can go back," she said to them.

"You don't need me to guide you?" Tom croaked.

"No. I can find my way."

"You can get in there?"

"I believe I can, yes. Before I see Herkimer-Lurkimer, I need to see this. Go on, I'll be all right."

She ran her fingers across the word that was graven deeply into the door, reading it as much with her fingers as her eyes. Graven over and over, ornamentally, cursively, in a thousand alphabets: *Werra. Werra. Werra.*

Tom drew them away, but they heard the rending of the door opening behind them as they went.

"They always open," said Tom, tonelessly. "Even when it's been... ten thousand years. They screech and squeal, they make a racket, but they always open. Sometimes I think they were brought here, maybe from the stars, aeons ago. Or grew here, like great trees.'' He flushed, as though ashamed of this outburst, compressed his lips, and said nothing more as they returned to occupied space.

As they entered their suite, Abasio found himself seeing the rooms with strange eyes. Why did these spaces seem unfamiliar and odd? Should corner meet corner like this? Should floors be softened like this? Should there be a place to sit, a place to lie down? A place to prepare food and serve it? An arrangement for cleaning oneself and one's possessions? Rooms. Human rooms. Rooms that would speak of human needs even to something alien and totally strange.

As other rooms might speak of other creatures. As the throne room spoke of other beings. An alien space.

Arakny went into the next room and shut the door behind her. Abasio dropped heavily into the nearest chair, leaned his head back, and closed his eyes. He tried to think of nothing at all, but his mind kept going back to the great chairs, trying to imagine their occupants as alive and speaking.

He opened his eyes to find Olly watching him from the door.

''It didn't take long,'' she said. ''I just wanted to look at the—at what's there.''

He sat up. ''Olly, what's this all about?''

She sat beside him on the low arm of the chair, putting her arm around his shoulders, her head against his. ''When I was at your grandpa's farm, he talked about his windmill. He told us he had built a device, a heavy little wheel that turns only when the wind is very strong. It shuts down the mechanism so it doesn't flail itself to nothing.''

''I know,'' said Abasio. ''Grandpa's automatic shutdown system. I used to climb up there to oil it, when I was a boy.''

''One might think of these—these thrones as something similar to that wheel. They're a device also, a shutdown latch that takes over when life is threatened. They're also living things. They swim in time, not dying as we do, but living on, epoch after epoch. They may have looked quite different when they were new, but over the aeons they've accreted. They may have been ignorant when they were first made, but now they know things we don't know. No. That's not right. No, what they do is, they accept things we won't accept. And that makes them frightening to us. We're used to believing we're the only intelligent beings around and that our reality is the only one.''

Her voice faded into silence. Abasio swallowed painfully. ''But Tom says Hunagor and Werra were human.''

''Well, they were. They were human agents, but there have been other agents who weren't human. And all those other agents have been absorbed into the primordial thing, the throne, the angel, the whatever.''

"Absorbed alive?" he croaked.

She came to kneel before him, taking his hands in her own. "What is 'alive,' Abasio? Is an entity that thinks and cares and needs still 'alive'? If so, then Hunagor still lives. And Werra too. And all those who became part of the thrones before him. As I would be, or you, if we still cared and thought and needed, no matter what we—looked like. No matter where we'd gone."

She pressed her cheek against him, rose, and turned as though to go, then changed her mind. Instead, she sat down again and said, "Will you wait for me, Abasio?"

"Wait for you?"

"Until I get back in a little while."

"Where are you going?" he asked, fighting panic.

She looked at her twined fingers for a long moment, as though the answer were there. "I said it before. Herkimer-Lurkimer owes me an explanation. Even though I understand some things, there are others that seem foggy. I want to see the shuttle. It's—it's scary to think I have to—to spend my life this way! I've hardly lived at all yet!"

"But, but," he cried, "when the shuttle comes back, surely they'll let you go!"

"I don't think it would matter if they did. I think once you're really hooked up to that system, you don't get loose again. That's one of the things I want to ask him, the old man."

"If that's true, you won't go. You can't. I won't let you!"

She shook her head slowly. "Oh, Abasio, I'm not sure I'd let me, either, but if I do . . . would you give your life for me?"

"If I had to!" he cried, without thinking. "To save you!"

"Well, you see, I'd give mine for you. And you are part of life."

She leaned forward, her forehead pressed against his. "I feel the pattern, Abasio, mostly. I know if that ship goes, there's a chance—more than a chance—that whatever comes back, it won't be me. But if I don't go, I see the pattern of what will happen here. Pain and terror. The walkers changing, becoming something else, something worse. I see them, Abasio. They're human in form, but they aren't alive. They don't care about life. I can see the pattern of their design, their manufacture. They can aggregate, did you know that? They can join themselves together to make bigger things, more dangerous things. Two alone are terrible, but when two join, they are many times as dreadful. And when two join to two more, and those to another two, they are horrible beyond belief. I can see them, towering, thundering, the very planet breaking apart beneath them!

"What they would leave behind would be a cinder, dead as ash."

She rubbed tears from her cheeks. "All the lovely birds! All the flowers.

Arakny's elk she was so proud of! The fish you caught for our dinner. All gone, Abasio. Coyote gone. Bear gone.''

"Why? Why would Ellel want that?''

"She doesn't *want* that. She's *risking* that. People like her have always been willing to risk things they didn't want to happen. Usually for power. Oh, she knows what the walkers may do! Men designed them to destroy the world. One tribe of men said to some other tribe, *If we are conquered, then let the earth perish! If we can't live as we like, then let us all perish!*''

She scrubbed at the tears again. "Will you wait for me?''

"Yes,'' he said, scarcely able to get the words out. "Yes. I'll wait.''

Her fingers clung to his for a moment, and then she went out without a backward look.

He wanted her. All of him wanted all of her, all at once, and so completely that he shook with it. Whatever had ailed him ailed him no longer! In this moment he was unassailably aware of that fact.


Seoca sat in his chair upon the terrace. Olly sat cross-legged before him. She had thought she might remember him, but she did not. He was merely an old man, someone who had used her as a fly fisherman uses a fly: to make the big fish rise.

"You want Ellel to go?'' she asked.

"Ellel should go,'' he replied. "But we can't force her. We don't do that. We can create weapons, but we can't use them. Our lineage unsuits us for it. Even if we could do it physically, we're not allowed to philosophically. Only if the means is correct is the end appropriate.''

She said, "You need me to take her?''

He nodded. "Everything we know about her says she will go only if she believes she has captured you in spite of our best efforts at hiding you, if she is forcing you despite your best efforts to resist, if she is compelling you against your will. If you came to her with open hands, offering to guide her, she would be too suspicious to accept your offer.''

She glanced upward in sudden comprehension. "That's why they didn't just go ahead and build the kind of system they used to use?''

He nodded. "She would never have trusted an electronic system. She'd have been sure Mitty had sabotaged it. Oh, she'd have let the shuttle go. She'd have sent Ander, perhaps. Or some other of the Ellels. But for herself, she cannot trust what she has not trampled and conquered and bent to her will! She cannot trust what she does not hold by force.''

"It was you who gave them the specifications for the Organic Guidance System?''

"It was Werra, actually. He put the plans where they'd be found. He told the Domers you existed. But then we hid you and would not tell her where you were. We frustrated her for years, and now only her triumph over us has convinced her it is safe for her to go."

"Why must she go herself?"

"Because if she does not go, she will stay here, in control of her walkers. She knows what they're capable of. She'll end up using them. On the other hand, if she goes, it will set other wheels in motion. It is not her going but what happens after she goes that will be decisive! One way, or the other."

"Wheels within wheels," she murmured.

"Oh, indeed."

"Oracle used to tell me a story," she remarked. "It was an Artemisian tale, about Changing Woman and the monsters."

"I think I know the tale. Was it about Old Age, and Cold Woman, and the animals needing worse monsters than that?"

"That's the one. Coyote and Bear asked Changing Woman for worse monsters to kill man, so they could keep their hides. But instead, she taught them to talk. I thought it was just a story, but someone did teach them to talk."

He smiled. "There's another version, you know. In that one, she teaches them to talk, but she creates some terrible monsters as well."

"To eat up man."

"No. Just to get him to pay attention. So the story goes."

"I'll have to put that into Arakny's library."

"Do you have Arakny's library?"

She took it from her pocket and showed it to him. After that, they talked a great while longer. Before she left him, the old man leaned forward and kissed her on the cheek.

"Thank you, child," he said. "Thank you, child."


Later that afternoon, Olly emerged from Gaddi House and asked to be taken to the shuttle. Mitty, in a move unusual for him, insisted on being present. He stayed with Ellel in the control section while Dever took Olly through the crew space, the passenger cubicles, the moon lander, the engines. Mitty heard Dever's voice going on and on about galley arrangements and toilet arrangements, including a great deal of tediously graphic information about the difficulty of weightless elimination.

When Dever ran out of shuttle explanations, they went down to the floor once more. During the entire tour, Olly had remained expressionless, as though what was said did not much matter, and now she said to Ellel, "I need some additional information."

Ellel had been waiting for opposition, poised for battle. "You need know nothing beyond—"

"If you want us to get where we're going, I need to know some things," said Olly with a sudden icy hauteur that cut through Ellel's belligerence like a knife. "I need to know who is going, and how many. It makes a difference."

"We're all going," grated Ellel.

"That cannot be true," said Olly, stating it as simple fact. "I counted the spaces in the shuttle. That's why I had to see it, to know how large it is. You can take no more than a hundred humans if you take no walkers. If you take walkers, you can put several in each cubicle, but that means you will take fewer humans. Even if you took no walkers and a hundred humans, there are many more of you than that. Inevitably, some will go and some will stay. I need to know which ones."

"I can see no possible reason why—"

"I don't know why, either," said Olly. "I can't give you reasons or argue with you because I simply know it's necessary without knowing why. This guidance thing is done subconsciously, it's a kind of wild talent, not a science. If it's going to work, I have to know who's going. The cargo enters into the calculation."

Mitty spoke forcefully. "Ellel, that's not unreasonable. Surely you've already decided who's going to go along! You can make up a list for her, can't you? What difference does it make?"

It made a difference to Ellel, who wanted her will to be done, however arbitrary it might be, without question or hesitation, but she glared at him from behind her mask and agreed. She would punish him for his interference when she returned.

"How soon?" demanded Ellel, her eyes glittering.

"Whenever you're ready," said Olly with flat indifference. "When you know who's going, send someone with a list. When you're ready to leave, I'll be ready to guide you."

Ellel was confused, almost disappointed by this ready acquiescence. "I won't free your friends until you do!" she cried. "You understand that! And worse will happen to them if you disappoint me!" She stood, fingers extended as though they were talons, head forward as though to strike.

"She understands that," said Mitty. "Let's not make a battle out of it—"

Olly interrupted. "You needn't threaten me or my friends, Madam Domer. Believe me, I understand you completely."

Mitty took her out, leaving Ellel to stew silently behind them, too set upon battle merely to let the matter alone. If she could not get a fight from Olly, she would get one from the hostages!

But she had no more success there.

"You needn't rage at me," Oracle said calmly. "If Olly says you'll be guided, then you will. She won't lie to you."

Ellel laughed at her. "History is made up of broken promises," she said in a sneering voice as she looked around the luxurious meeting room, which now had the appearance of a hasty camp, with beds scattered here and there and people sitting about looking bored and apprehensive, both at once.

"True," Oracle agreed. "Still, some do not lie."

Ellel gave Oracle a penetrating glance. "My associate, Berkli, said he wanted you to prognosticate for us. About the success of our journey. Did he receive a prophecy?"

"When he found we were tired and hungry and thirsty, he arranged amenities for us, saying he would return later for the foretelling," said Oracle. "I thought it both kind and wise of him to do so. I'm a better Oracle when well fed."

"One could have guessed that," sneered Ellel. "It took two walkers to carry you."

Oracle recognized the voice of an habitual provocateur and did not reply.

"Since you have not yet given your prognostication, I will ask for it now," Ellel said, with a sidelong look.

"The rules require that I be paid," said Oracle. "This guarantees the veracity of what I say."

"Oh, you'll be paid." Ellel laughed. "With your life, perhaps. Or I'll let you keep your sight. Or your tongue. Is that sufficient payment?"

"Indeed it is," said Oracle, in a voice Olly scarcely would have recognized, so sweet it was. "Is there a private place here where I can concentrate?"

Ellel opened a door into a neighboring room furnished with a table and a few chairs. "In here."

Oracle went into it, drawing from her capacious robes a small leather bag, and from the bag an incense burner and a bell. "Simple devices to assist my concentration," she murmured. "One becomes habituated to their use."

Ellel folded her arms and leaned against the closed door while Oracle busied herself. Olly would have recognized the scent, the smoke, the sound of the tinkling bell, the sight of Oracle climbing onto the table with great agility and folding her legs beneath her. Ellel sneered at all of it.

"Ask your question," said Oracle, in a voice unlike her own.

"Will our trip to the space station be successful?"

Oracle's eyes rolled back into her head. She breathed heavily. Her voice came as though from a distance.

"*Four court disaster. Three cannot reach the moon. Two families alone achieve the stars.*"

Oracle breathed more shallowly, panting. Slowly, slowly her eyes came back to normal.

"What does it mean?" snarled Ellel. " 'Four court disaster'—what does that mean?"

"I honestly don't know," said Oracle. "Does it refer to four families? Some difficulty on the flight, perhaps. Some interfamily conflict. Could that be?"

Ellel pondered, her fingers making a rapid tattoo on the door behind her. "Families. Your forecast says families. And why the stars, when we do not intend to go beyond the moon?"

Oracle shrugged. "I am a bona-fide Oracle, Madam Domer. I do not plan what is to be said, and I cannot interpret it. Nor can I pile prognostication on prognostication to arrive at greater and greater detail. What I have said, I have said, and that is all I can say until the situation changes."

"And if I don't believe you?"

"You can ask those who know me. They will tell you the same. You can ask other Oracles; we are all more or less alike. You can bring some other Oracle here, or go to some village where one is."

"Families," muttered Ellel. "Not merely I, then, as the head of the family, but other members as well are to go. But only two families."

Oracle shrugged. "Perhaps you have arrived at a clue to the meaning. The more of you Domers who go, the fewer of your creatures may go. Perhaps your mission depends on there being a proper balance of both, family members plus walkers. As for the reference to the stars, surely the success of this first journey sets the pattern for those that follow. In the beginning, so I have heard, is the end."

"Are you saying that's what is meant?"

Oracle put out her hands, palms out, denying this. "No, no. I would not presume to interpret. I merely offer a possibility. There is one thing I can tell you, however. The fact that I prophesy a journey clearly implies that Olly will cooperate in guiding you. Otherwise, no journey would be possible, would it?"

Ellel became very still. Why had she not seen that immediately? Why, because—she told herself—she had always assumed as much. She had seen herself, even as a child, standing beside her father on the moon. The two of them, standing there together! She had never admitted doubt, not once. She smiled to herself and opened the door to go out into the larger room. She thought she had not decided to go to the moon but she had really known all along she would go!

While Oracle was out of the room, Domer servants had set food upon a long table, where Drowned Woman and the Farmwife were now making a quiet meal, side by side. Oracle went toward them with a surreptitious look at Ellel, who was leaving, head down, as though she were thinking long, serious thoughts.

"What did you foresee?" asked Farmwife Suttle, with a curious glance at Ellel's departing back.

Oracle said loudly, "If they plan correctly, they will achieve the stars as men did long ago."

The door to the corridor snapped shut.

"Olly's going to take them there, then?" whispered Drowned Woman.

"Seemingly so," said Oracle, helping herself to roast lamb. She sniffed the meat, detecting thyme and parsley, basil and mint. Such cookery was a rare thing in archetypal villages. Her own had never been graced with an archetypal Chef.

"You eat with better appetite than I," said Drowned Woman bitterly. "You seem to care little for Orphan. Don't you grieve for her?"

Oracle's voice quavered as she answered. "What is to be is to be. Grieving will not change it. If she guides the ship, we will not be harmed."

Oracle rose, leaving her plate untouched, to stare out the window at the sky. "Herself traded for us."

"Your prophecy," said Farmwife heavily. "I don't suppose you—"

"No!" said Oracle sadly. "Though I was prepared to lie if necessary, when the time came, I could not. Ellel's prophecy is true."


Deep in the night, Abasio lay sleepless on his borrowed bed, wishing he were elsewhere.

The door opened, admitting a sliver of lamplight, a slight silhouette dark against it.

"Basio?" Olly's voice

"Yes," he said urgently. "Yes. When did you get back?"

"I've been back," she said. "Wandering around in this place. It's endless, Abasio. The part down below, it's monstrous huge. I could explore down there for my whole life and probably not see it all."

"What were you doing?"

"Looking at things. Things the old man told me about. Things the thrones have stored away down there. Things that grew, and things that they made. And some things people like Tom have made too. They have workshops and laboratories here. . . ." Her voice drifted off. After a moment she sighed. "And partly I've just been waiting for everyone to settle down. I didn't want anyone fussing at me. Tom. Or Nimwes, or Arakny. You know."

"I know," he said. "They're all upset." He threw back the covers to get up and go to Olly, all unclothed as he was.

He realized his nakedness too late, as she came to him with a little rush, pushing under the cover beside him, pulling it over them both. "Don't get up."

She lay with her face below his, her lips thrust into the curve of his neck, her body stretched along his, her arms around him.

"Did you see the shuttle?" he whispered, not wanting to ask that question or any question, but needing to hear her voice over the drumroll of his heart.

"I saw it," she whispered. "It isn't very big, Abasio. A hundred passengers is all it holds."

"You can't go with them," he muttered desperately. "You mustn't!"

"I haven't decided. I don't want to decide right now. That's one reason I'm here. So I don't have to decide. So I don't have to think about it."

His arms tightened about her. His lips found hers, wet with salt tears. He licked them away with the tip of his tongue, put his mouth to her closed eyes, to the lobe of her ear, covered her jaw with kisses, bringing them to her mouth once more.

"Olly," he whispered.

"Shhh. Oh, Abasio, I don't want to talk. I don't want to think of words, reasons, arguments why, why not. I see why women sometimes don't want to think. I see why they want to be mindless, like the hens with their proud rooster. Oh, if they had to think, if they always had to think, they wouldn't— they wouldn't love anyone. They wouldn't take a chance. They never could. It—they . . . too monstrous . . . "

"What is?" he asked, his arms tightening.

"Don't," she whispered. "Don't talk. No words. Make me not think of words, Abasio."

The clothing she wore was loose, only a robe of some filmy stuff. His arms slipped inside it and drew her against his skin, herself soft and sleek, smooth as polished wood, soft as a bird's feathers. He felt her heart beating against his own, bent his head to her breasts, soft little breasts, no nipples, the nipples turned inward like a little girl's.

He nuzzled, and a nipple came thrusting against his lips, erupting against his tongue, at first soft, then hard and impatient. There was a fever in the skin of her breast.

She murmured something, a command that was not a word, pushing her hips against him, throwing one leg over him. He pulled his arm from beneath her and thrust her robe aside, letting the lamplight from the next room fall along her body, breast and belly and thigh, all flushed bright, all in restless movement, quivering, pushing against him.

He whispered her name, not knowing he'd done it.

"No words . . . Abasio."

No words, then. He sank into a waiting moisture, a waiting softness, feeling resistance, drawing back in fear of hurting her, only to feel her pushing against him hard, crying out, only partly in pain.

And then no more thoughts. Words that were not words. Movement and all the complicated geometry, Abasio thought, unaccountably, of body A meeting body B, both in motion, needing no guidance. Instinctive. Inside himself, herself, idiot savants who knew without knowing how they knew. The thought fled and was gone in an explosion of light behind his closed eyes.

And a long silence, broken by Olly who breathed one word into his ear: "P'nash."

He wanted to laugh but had only enough breath to go on living.

After a moment: "So that's p'nash," she said again, sighing.

He did laugh then, the laughter rising around him like a warm bath, losing himself and all words and all worries in it, holding her close, never to let her go.

They slept as love left them, still entwined. During the night Abasio moved away, tangled himself among the covers, reached for her, found her, reached for her, found her.

And shortly before dawn he reached for her once more and found her gone.


While Olly lay in Abasio's arms, certain servants were summoned to Ellel's quarters, Qualary among them. The door to the locked room was open. Two things lay on the terribly dusty bed; one bundle wrapped in a blanket, long and thin, tied about with cords, the other an open case. In the case were Ellel's clothes and her personal things, and on top, a crown, a scepter. Qualary pretended not to see as Ellel shut the case and latched it before going into an open closet and seating herself at the console inside.

"Those two things are to go into the shuttle," said Ellel, over her shoulder. "Dever is waiting. He'll say where to put them."

Qualary sent the servants away with the case, with the bundle, meantime hearing Ellel's voice raised in little urgencies, commands, punctuations as her hands tapped, as her eyes scanned the readouts before her. She finished up with a flourish and a crow of laughter, then rose, shut the closet, and locked it, before stalking into the larger room.

"Clean up in there while I'm away," she said to Qualary, gesturing through the open door at the room behind her.

"Ma'am."

"Get all that dust out. Wash the window. Get the furniture replaced. It's all filthy."

"Ma'am."

"And take this list of those going on the shuttle to Gaddi House immediately. We leave at dawn."

"Today, ma'am?" Qualary couldn't keep a squawk of astonishment out of her voice.

"Dever says we can. No reason to wait, so we'll leave at dawn." Ellel laughed, a low, chortling laugh, the laugh of a child given a wonderful surprise. "We're going away, Qualary, but don't think you mice will play. No such thing. No, no. Everyone in the Place will wait here patiently, no matter how long it takes me. And don't try to fiddle with my closet, clumsy girl! Any fiddling with my closet sets my creatures off, and then you'll all regret it!"

Qualary could not take in what Ellel was saying. She watched wordlessly as Ellel left, standing for a long moment as though paralyzed, then turned as though drawn by invisible wires into the terribly dusty room.

The bedcurtains were still pulled back. The impression of a body still marked the filthy linens. The indentation of a head still hollowed the pillow. The smell of dust and walker and something even worse still permeated both. Shuddering, scarcely aware of what she did, Qualary pulled the bedding away from the bed, feeling it shred beneath her hands, and kicked the pile out into the next room, from there out into the corridor, all the time rubbing her hands down her sides to remove the feel of having touched it, the paper in her hand tattering as she moved.

Then, realizing what she had done, she put the paper flat on the table and pushed the torn edges together to read what was written there. A list. The first name, Ellel's, followed by the names of two dozen members of the Ellel Family. Then Ander's name, plus two dozen of his people. Qualary knew the names. The list included most of those with influence. Most of those with power. None on it were very old or very young. No Mitty names. None of the Berklis. The rest—the rest, almost a hundred walkers, identified by serial number in Ellel's hand. Her own selected companions.

" 'We will flit on, flit on over to the moon,' " Qualary sang in a mad little voice, quoting Ander, glad that he was going. Glad that Ellel was going. Glad they would both be gone. Knowing they could not be gone long enough.

Shortly thereafter she was at the gate of Gaddi House. "The list," she announced, handing the paper to a hastily summoned Tom Fuelry. "This is the list of who's going, Tom!"

"Qualary," he said softly, caressing her, "come in."

"I can't," she whispered. "Ellel gave me things to do. They have to be done before she gets back."

"There's time," he said. "Believe me, dear one. The flight cannot be hurried. It takes so much time going, so much time returning. You've done enough today.''

"Too much!" she cried. "Oh, Tom, I've done too much!''

She had done too much. Arakny had done too much, and Abasio. There had been much too much already done. Tom knew it was true, but it didn't keep him from going up to the guest suite occupied by Arakny and Abasio where he believed he would find Olly.

Instead, he found her outside that suite, sitting on a bench that looked out over an enclosed garden, dressed in the bright clothing Qualary had given her.

"The list?" she asked in a quiet voice.

He nodded. "Qualary says they leave at dawn.''

"Who's on it?"

"Ellels, Anders, walkers.''

"No Mittys? No Berklis?"

He shook his head

"Don't worry about it, Tom.''

"I want to help you! What am I to do?" he cried in fear and pity.

She sighed. "One very special thing, Tom. I need to talk to Coyote. Can you reach him?''

"I can. Yes.''

"Send for him. I need him here, very quickly. Also, I want you to give a message to Abasio.''

"But Abasio is here! Surely you left him not long ago.''

She shook her head. "It wasn't the time to say what I want to say. He was too —we were both too . . . involved with other things.'' Her eyes lit up at that memory, wiping all trace of apprehension from her face for an instant. Then she looked at the list she held and remembered where she was.

She gave Tom her message for Abasio, repeating it twice, seeing his face grow grim. "One other thing," she said. "One request of him and you both. Come watch me leave. From the roof. You and Qualary and Abasio and Arakny. Wave me good-bye and watch us go. I will take comfort from that, and likely there will not be a sight like it soon again.''


Dawn came on a late fall morning under a lowering sky. Blackness filled the west, cloud and snow mixed with rain, muttering thunder and a turmoil of wind, its breath reaching into the Place of Power, snarling of more and worse to come. Up and down the canyons trees lashed in that wind, bending unwillingly, branches creaking. On the eastern horizon was only a pale green-gray glow, as of a sickened sun crawling reluctantly from a fevered bed.

Only a dozen or so were abroad in the Place of Power. Four of them were there at Olly's request, braving the wind from the top of Gaddi House, quaking in the cold. The rest stalked the path from the silo to the Gaddi House gate: Ellel and two files of striding walkers.

"Can the Witch see me from down there?" whispered Qualary.

"I think she has eyes only for Olly," said Arakny, with a curious glance at the other woman. She had not said "Witch" out loud before. Nonetheless, the word had a much-used sound in Qualary's mouth.

"Where is Olly?" grated Abasio, tears running down the corners of his mouth.

"At the Gaddi House gate," Tom answered. "Below us."

She was there, dressed in the sunset-colored garb that Qualary had given her the day before, moving steadily out onto the roadway where Ellel and her walkers waited, her angel on her shoulder, its plumes fluttering raggedly in the wind.

The walkers moved toward her.

Olly stopped and held up her hand, forbidding them.

Ellel jittered from foot to foot, dancing with scarcely withheld fury. Even from the roof they heard Olly's clear voice calling, "I come willingly or not at all, Ellel."

Ellel shouted an irritated command. The walkers halted. Olly moved forward once more, walking swiftly among them and past Ellel to become their leader as they returned to the shuttle silo. It was she who was first at that distant door.

"I should have done something," gasped Abasio. He could still feel her body, feel the warmth of her breath, smell her skin. "I should have done something!" He could not breathe. There was a hardness in his throat, a pain in his chest as though something there had broken.

"You did all you could," said Tom.

Arakny thought all of them had done all they could, but still there must have been something left undone, or the girl would not be going away, not like this. Why was His Wisdom letting her go? Or was he as impotent as they?

At the door of the distant silo, the rosy little figure turned and lifted a hand in gallant farewell.

Abasio leaned on the parapet, his shoulders heaving. Arakny hugged him, tears running down her own face, unregarded.

From that distant door, Ellel was watching them through glasses. At length, she made a triumphant gesture and disappeared within.

"It will be safer below," said Tom, tugging at Qualary.

They did not hear him. He had to repeat himself several times and then insist, almost angrily, pulling at each of them before they would leave the roof.

"Can't we see it go?" asked Qualary, torn between relief and despair. She did not want Olly lost any more than the others did, but oh, to have Ellel gone, if only for a time! The very thought made her buoyant, as though she had laid down a great weight. "Can't we see it go?" she repeated.

"From inside," said Tom flatly. "His Wisdom says you can watch with him."

They found His Wisdom in a large room with Nimwes and a few dozen other Gaddirs watching the silo through screens and sensors.

"When?" asked Abasio.

"Soon," said His Wisdom. "The walkers and Domers have been getting into the thing since about midnight."

It seemed unconscionably long until they saw the domed top of the silo crack and open, like the bud of a flower, its steel petals blooming on the stem of the walls, the last few workmen leaving, carefully shutting and bolting the thick doors behind them.

After that it was only a little while until a great noise battered at them from speakers set high on the walls. Then the screens showed roiling smoke and a belch of orange fire from exhaust vents at the base of the silo and the shuttle itself protruding slowly, reluctantly from the top of the structure. It moved upward, more swiftly, more swiftly yet, lunging toward the sky poised on its cylinder of white light, thrusting, hastening, then soaring at the tip of a long, fiery diagonal.

Even in the midst of Abasio's grief, something inside him leaped up at the sight of that ship going. He felt again that surge of ownership he had felt as a child, when he had looked from the belt of Orion to the great stars Betelgeuse and Rigel, when Grandpa had told him there were men out there. In that telling, Abasio had taken possession of the stars, and even now something of that wonder and glory trembled in him for a moment before thoughts of Olly returned.

He was still looking up, but the ship had gone beyond his sight.


For some long time after the last trace of the shuttle's flight had vanished into a cloudless sky, no one moved. They merely sat and watched the smoke clear away from the silo, watched the people of the Place of Power come from under cover, a few here, a few there, little by little, to stand in chattering groups around the empty silo, staring at the equally empty sky.

Oracle came from the Dome, with Farmwife Suttle and Burned Man and Drowned Woman and old Cermit stumping along behind. Berkli came from somewhere, twitching with anger but immaculately dressed. His Wisdom whispered to Nimwes, and shortly after someone approached this group with bows and gestures, inviting them to Gaddi House itself.

"I told my people to bring your friends and kinsmen here," said His Wisdom to Abasio. "I count Berkli among that number, and possibly we will count Mitty also, if he has brought himself to take sides."

He motioned to Tom, saying: "Bring them up to my quarters, Tom. Nimwes is preparing tea for us there. I know they'll all want to talk together. At a time like this, we should not be alone."

They came, Berkli first, to stare around the room, his brows furrowed. He strode to kneel at old Seoca's feet and give him his hand. "I would have done anything to prevent this, sir. I kept coming up with ideas, but none of them worked. All these years I've been thinking of Ellel as a child, a mere annoyance, too young and silly to be a real threat. But she was. Is. We let her get too strong."

"I know," said His Wisdom. "Though history instructs us vividly, people refuse to recognize tyrants until the blade is at their throats. Olly herself said it to me just this morning: People believe what they want to believe." He sighed. "Tell me, where is your friend Mitty?"

"I asked him to come, but he won't. He feels even worse than I, for he's just now realized he's as culpable as the rest of us. We should have stopped her decades ago! Now—now it's too late. If she gets back with the weapons and we don't do something then, there'll be no stopping her!" He grimaced. "The only thing I can be grateful for is that all the Mittys and Berklis are still here and maybe we can put our heads together and come up with a plan."

Tom looked up, alert. "A plan?"

"We must be ready when she gets back! We have these few days while she's gone. When she returns, we can't let her go on doing what she's been doing!"

His Wisdom was smiling, though wearily. Tom took a deep breath. "Was that what she meant?" he blurted. "Olly?"

"What?" demanded Abasio.

"She gave me a message for you."

"Why didn't she tell me herself?" cried Abasio, wounded.

"Because—she said you were both—preoccupied with other things. So she gave me the message, to give to you as soon as I might. She said the struggle would begin when she left. She wanted us, you, to be—resolute."

"With her gone, what does it matter!" Abasio cried.

"She said you would say that," cried Tom. "And I was to say to you, if she gave her life for you and everyone, then you must give some of yours in her memory. She said it would give her great peace of mind if she knew you did not despair, not you, or Arakny or Qualary or me. She said there is a struggle coming, the last great struggle, in which life itself is the prize. And she told me to tell you His Wisdom's story about cleaning the water tank.''

His Wisdom chuckled and wept at once, while Berkli looked on, askance. Water tank?

"It matters what you do," the old man murmured. "What will you do to honor her memory, Abasio Cermit?''

"Then she's not coming back. . . . ''

The old man said, "Suppose she did return, but wounded or maimed. What would you tell her you had done to honor her sacrifice?''

Abasio put his head in his hands, refusing to answer. Arakny put her arms around him, shaking her head at Tom. Let him alone a bit, her stance seemed to say. He'll be all right, but let him grieve a bit.

"Was it Ander who convinced her not to take any of us?" asked Berkli, returning to his own line of thought. "No Berklis? No Mittys?''

"Partly," said Qualary, offering him a steaming cup. "But I think it was Oracle who decided her at the end.''

"I did?'' asked Oracle from the doorway. "How very interesting.'' She came in, followed by the other hostages, to be introduced to His Wisdom and accept tea from Nimwes. Drowned Woman took a cup into her hand, but she could not drink it for her tears. The fragrance had brought back the memory of her sitting on Orphan's rickety stoop, talking about the world.

"I presume we can go home now," said Farmwife Suttle in a brittle voice. "Now that Olly's gone.''

Oracle put her hand to her forehead. "Ellel said we would be free to go if Olly guided them on their journey.'' She pressed with her fingers, as though to soothe an ache, then said dazedly, "She lied, however. I should have realized that at the time. Ellel lied.''

They stared at her, wonderingly, glancing at one another. Abasio's head came up. Tom stopped what he was doing and stared at Oracle.

"But surely *you* are free to go," said Tom.

"No," she said. "No, none of us is free to go.''

"Why not?'' cried Drowned Woman.

"I don't know," Oracle replied. "But she's done something. She's set some trap.'' Oracle moved out across the adjacent terrace to the parapet, where she leaned over to peer down into the canyon below. Her silence drew others to her side. There below them, along every inch of the wall that separated the Place of Power from the world at large, stood Ellel's walkers, and those Mitty had considered his, and those of Ander, all the walkers except those on the shuttle, guarding the walls of the Place.

Tom exclaimed, "That's where they went!'' He ran out of the room, calling to someone in the corridor. After a time he returned, shaking his head angrily. "They're posted all the way around. They're at the back gate as well as the front. They're all along the wall."

"Why?" asked Drowned Woman. "Why are they there?"

"To prevent our getting out, I should think," said the old man. "This place and these people are Ellel's place of power. She does not want to lose Mitty's skill—or the pleasure of killing Berkli and me. She wants to find us all here when she returns. She plans to deal with us before she moves on the rest of the world."

Tom blurted, "When she returns with the weapons—"

"Her ambitions extend far beyond the return of the shuttle," muttered Berkli. "Why didn't we all realize that years ago?"

"We are all hostages now," said Abasio tonelessly. Perhaps that was why Olly had gone so quietly. Perhaps she had known it did not matter.

He turned to Oracle, as though hoping she would contradict his words or his thoughts, but she did not. She refused to meet his eyes as she murmured, "There are no acceptable solutions to some problems."


"Well," gasped Ander from his place beside his colleague in the shuttle. "That was exciting. Are you sure we shouldn't bring someone more experienced up here? Someone who knows what buttons to push?"

"There is no one 'experienced,' and we don't push any buttons," said Ellel. "According to Dever, the Werra offshoot does all that, quite automatically, without any intervention from us."

She unbuckled her belt and floated free, awkwardly grabbing at handholds to move herself into position to see the booth where Olly sat, her head and face invisible beneath the helmet, her strange bird resting upon her lap, between her cupped hands. Olly had entered the booth by herself without being forced or assisted. She had held the bird in one hand while she had pulled the helmet down with the other. She had even pushed the button that started the insertion sequence, and she had not cried out when the mechanism had whined its way through her skull. Perhaps, Ellel thought, the helmet first provided an anodyne, though the replica she had used on several hundred infants and girls over the years had never done so. Her victims had always howled like skewered animals when the wires went in. Olly hadn't cried out during the test. She hadn't cried out this time, either. Nor had the bird, which was looking at Ellel now with beady, seemingly intelligent eyes.

So all Ellel's practice had been for nothing. Nothing! All those babies. All those little girls and silly maidens, all that hysteria and howling, for nothing. Well, it had been worth a try. Repeated tries. The very fact that only Olly had been successful proved the truth of Werra's statement. A

Gaddir child. Bred for this purpose. Well, the Gaddir child was meeting her destiny, and a high destiny it was.

"What do we do now?" called Ander, interrupting her train of thought.

Ellel caught at a handhold and answered absentmindedly. "We don't do anything until we get to the station. According to Dever, that will be two days from now. Even when we arrive, we don't have to do much. Our documents say the station has air, warmth, gravity, all supplied by solar power, so we don't need to worry about that. Our families will occupy the station while we inventory what's there and make decisions on what we'll bring back, but the walkers will do all the work." She moved herself about, enjoying the feel of it. She'd rehearsed this in her mind so many times, this floating, this flying.

Ander, watching her obvious enjoyment from the corner of his eye, thought it best not to mention the fact that his family had already studied the inventory and decided what to bring back. Every Ander on board was agreed about it.

"The workers will load the shuttle for us, will they? Before we go on to the moon?"

"Exactly. The moon lander is removed when we get to the station. That gives us room in the shuttle for the—material from the station, and while some of the walkers are loading it, the others go down to the moon in the lander."

"How will you control them, Ellel? How will you give them commands?"

She shrugged. "There's a control box back in my cubicle. Mitty told me how to do it from the station. Then, later . . . " Her voice trailed off. Later she would do it from the moon itself. Later—after the earth was conquered! After the cities were brought under sway, and the forest tribes, and the people of Artemisia.

"How long until we get back?"

"A few days," said Ellel. "Only a few."

"I hope those we left behind don't get into any mischief back there," Ander muttered. "I hope they don't make problems while we're gone."

Ellel stared through him. "They won't. They can't. I've set the walkers to box them in. Nobody in, nobody out. Aside from the fact they may be a bit hungry, everything will be just as we left it when we return." She yawned, unable to control herself. "I told her, in there. I told her we had to get back safe, or her friends would be forfeit."

She turned and maneuvered her way back to the seat she had left, pausing en route to stare warily at Olly once more. Still nothing. Motionless. Like a machine.

She strapped herself into her chair. It would have been fun to bring Berkli along, but Oracle had confirmed Ellel's own instincts. This way would guarantee a better result. The Place was shut up behind her, and no one was able to do anything about it. There were only Ellels and Anders on the shuttle, including all those from either family who might have been likely to seize power in her absence. Virtually all. Forsmooth Ander had been too ill to come along, the old snake! The Anders were up to no good, obviously, but the walkers on the ship would control the Anders. The walkers on the ship were completely dependable. She'd been saving them for decades, just for this trip. They'd never been used for anything at all. The walkers back on earth would control the situation until she returned, and once she had the weapons from the space station in the hands of her own family, she'd put the Mittys where they belonged! In the shops, maintaining her walkers and her weapons! They were hers. Her imperial army. Just as she'd planned. In time, her family would learn to manufacture more of them.

She took from her pocket a slender booklet, its lined pages annotated in her own hand. The weapons that had been left behind in the space station when men went to the stars, noted from the inventory sheets in order of priority. Some massive, some small. It might take more than one trip to get them all. She read down the list again, the smudged lines as clear to her as though they were newly written. She knew them. In her mind she had held them, worked with them, used them against her enemies. The great laser cannons. The fusion guns. The sonic disrupters. The biologicals and chemicals, array after array of them. And all the lesser stuff, eyes to see with and ears to hear with and tiny devices that could kill leaving no trace . . .

She put the book away with an expression of slight distaste. All was going precisely as she had planned. Why then this feeling of vague disappointment? Perhaps because there was nothing to see except the dark. Like a night sky. There were stars, of course. And the sun, if you looked toward it, which would be unwise, or so Dever had said. They couldn't see the moon yet. Dever had explained that their journey was a long outward spiral. They wouldn't be able to see the moon until they got much farther out. Right now they were headed away from it, being pulled by the gravity of earth into the proper path. So Dever had said.

"How are our people back there?" asked Ander. "In their cosy little cubicles?"

"Sleeping," she replied. "Except for the two of us, they'll sleep until we get there. It's what our doctors recommended. If they sleep, they'll avoid any unpleasant effects of this weightlessness, and there'll be one-half earth gravity at the station." This too had been planned, though she had felt no effects of weightlessness, and Ander seemed to have adjusted well.

"Shouldn't we see the station?" he asked, leaning forward to peer sidewise through the portal. "Where we're going?"

She shook her head. "Dever said not until we're almost there."

She relaxed, letting the belt hold her, feeling her vague discontent fade away into a hazy euphoria. A kind of sweetness. She could not recall feeling such sweetness for a long, long time.

"I'm going to sleep, too, Ander. I didn't sleep all last night."

"Of course," he said. "Of course. Neither did I."

They had pills for sleep, and pills for the nausea of weightlessness, and pills for any of the Family who might get upset or hysterical, and pills for anything else that might go wrong. Pills and a sip tube for water, and behind her, in the cubicle, in her own space . . .

Drowsily she considered what was behind her, in her own space. All that long time ago Daddy had said it wasn't a daughter's business to go along. He was wrong. She'd told him they should stay together. Always stay together. . . .

Ander kept his eyes on her face as she swallowed the pills, as she shut her eyes and squirmed briefly against the restraints that held her. Something obscene in that movement. Like the cuddling of a ghoul. The coupling of monsters. What was she thinking? What was she planning? What was under that featureless mask? Being this near her made him uncomfortable. Aside from the revulsion he felt at her physical presence, he was always expecting a stab in the back or, at the very least, a jabbed insult. Nothing. Here she was, all relaxed, beginning to breathe softly, steadily.

He waited until she was quite asleep, then unfastened his own belt and drifted, as he'd wanted to do ever since they had started. It was wonderful! Exhilarating! He tugged himself here and there, actually giggling like a child. What fun!

He stopped, his eyes caught by the motionless figure in the booth, stopped and flushed. What was it she had said to him, just before the helmet went down? She had looked at his sleeves, reached out to touch them, and said, "I dyed that fabric. In Wilfer Ponde's shop in Whitherby."

"You?" he'd asked, suddenly aghast. "Not you!" Craftsmen—craftsmen were sacred to the Anders. If she—if this one . . .

"In Wilfer Ponde's shop, in Whitherby," she'd said again as the helmet had come down.

It was the last thing she'd said. There had been no time for him to do anything. The helmet was down, and she was silent. It was too late. Done, and too late.

Resolutely, he put it out of his mind. She could have been lying. She must have been. Though how she knew the name of the dyer's shop where his fabrics came from, he could not imagine. What would a craftsman be doing here, in this place?

He shook his head. He had to attend to business. Several Family members had seen Ellel's servants bring something odd aboard. Something that might be—well, a weapon perhaps? Something the Anders needed to know about. Now that Ellel was asleep, drugged, unlikely to wake, it would be a good time to look into the matter.

Hé pulled himself back past the guidance system, without a glance at Olly, through the door, past the toilets and galley, into the long circular space with the cubicles all around it, each one with its sliding door, its own little window into space. The first door was Ellel's. The only one with a lock. Ander smiled. He had thought there might be some locked compartments on the space station, so he'd had Mitty's people make him a gadget that could unlock them.

Which it did, in time. The lock beeped, the cubicle door opened. The long bundle he had seen brought aboard lay on the bunk, held down by straps. He unfastened the top one in order to untie the cords and fold back the blankets . . .

And then felt himself yelling, felt the vibration of his own vocal cords, the rawness of his own throat rasping with no one at all to hear him, no one to understand what he saw, no one but himself to see this thing lying on the bunk, this walker lying on the bunk with someone's cut-off face sewn to its head, a face he knew, Jark III's face, and someone's cut-off chest laced around its torso, and someone's—someone's organ prominently displayed below, all dried, dried like leather, shriveled like old gloves, old shoes, all tied around a walker who looked up at him from dead eyes with its red, red glare and said in its dry voice, "Yes, yes, daughter, yes, princess, yes, yes, yes. . . ."

On old Seoca's terrace above the canyon, the group remained unchanged. Mitty had not come to join them. None of them had found reason to go elsewhere. Oracle looked from face to face, wondering if the others found their minds wandering as she did, wishing to be in another place, another time. She caught old Seoca's eyes and flushed. He knew what she was thinking.

It was Nimwes who broke the silence.

"What can we do? Will the walkers let us buy food in the marketplace?"

"I think not," said Tom. "In fact, the traders are leaving now. The walkers are blocking the gates."

"Are any of the walkers inside the Place of Power?" His Wisdom asked.

Tom went away and came back again to say there were none in the Place, which didn't mean they couldn't come inside anytime they decided to do so. Nothing prevented their doing so, so far as Tom could see.

"Are there provisions here?" asked Oracle. "Such a large place should have provisions for a siege."

"That's the word I was reaching for," the old man agreed, nodding at her. "A siege. Ellel's bottled us up, hasn't she? We are under siege."

"Like rats in a trap," said Arakny. "Until she gets back, at least."

"What's going to happen?" Cermit demanded of Oracle. "You're the soothsayer. Can we last until she returns?"

Oracle mused, "I can't see her return."

Abasio asked, "What do you mean?"

"I mean what I said. I can't *always* see the future, I can't always prophesy. This is one of the times I can't. I don't know what's going to happen!"

The group was silent, staring at one another.

"They could be delayed, up there in space," mused the old man. "There are provisions up there that would allow them to stay a long time, if they chose to do so. Long enough for us to become very hungry. If you choose to act, it might be wise to do so while you still have the strength."

"Weapons," said Abasio. "Surely there are weapons we can use against the walkers!"

"Some we can adapt," admitted Tom. "We have some on the roof, but they'd have to be moved to the outside walls. Mostly they guard against attack from above. Dragons. Wiverns once, a long time ago."

"I wish Mitty were here!" cried Berkli. He turned to Qualary, asking, "Do you know where Ellel controls the walkers from?"

"From a closet, in a room in her quarters. It's locked, and she told me not to trifle with it, for if I do, something dreadful will happen."

"Perhaps that is why Olly went," Abasio said to Arakny. "Perhaps she knew it made no difference whether she stayed here or went there, that death waited in either place."

"Must it?" demanded Farmwife Suttle. "Can't men kill those things?"

"I saw three men kill one," whispered Qualary. "In the marketplace, with little more than their bare hands."

"Which is about the odds we'd need," said Berkli in a deadly, matter-of-fact voice. "Three to one might manage. As it happens, the numbers go the other way. There are approximately three of them to each able-bodied, adult one of us, if we included Anders and Ellels."

"It seems we could drag matters out for some time," said Burned Man. "But I have some experience of stretched-out dying, and I do not recommend it."

All during the long day that followed, during which they came and went, taking inventory of what were obviously totally inadequate foodstores, his words came back to torment them.

. . .

CummyNup and Sybbis had added an additional dozen or so ex-gangers, townsmen, truckers, and who-knows-whats during their journey to what had come to be called the Mountain of Revelation, all of these persons willing to fall in with the larger group and each of them soon well versed in the many marvels attributed to Abasio the Cat. The stories had come to be called collectively the Adventures of Abasio the Cat or sometimes simply Cat-tales. Some of them had a fragment of truth at the heart of them, some of them had none, and some of them were stories originally told about other heroes, now foisted onto Abasio. It didn't matter to the hearers, and as they were told and retold, it mattered less and less to CummyNup and Sybbis.

As they approached the Mountain of Revelation, anticipation mounted that they would soon find the Cat himself, who had gone on a courageous quest, disguised as an ordinary human and escorting an archetypal Orphan in the fulfillment of a prophecy. CummyNup said the words without thinking what they meant. Sybbis visualized the Orphan as a dirty-faced waif of some five or six years, with gap teeth and scabby knees, and she visualized the prophecy as something like a highly ritualized tally, after which Abasio would return to her triumphant.

Though a few of those who joined the mob had subsequently died of one thing or another, most often of fighting among themselves, the rest seemed reasonably amicable and immune to the disease that had wiped the cities clean. Among them they counted a respectable armamentarium, and during their progress west they acquired a number of vehicles and a considerable store of fuel. All together, they constituted a larger gang with greater mobility and firepower than any seen in the cities for some generations.

They had established certain habits and customs on the journey west, their own chain of command, their own ways of laying out their camp and setting guards for the watches of the night. Orders were issued by Captain CummyNup to his lieutenants and from them to the troops. Despite being Captain, CummyNup often followed his old practice of wandering around in the dark, and it was during one of these midnight peregrinations that he encountered Coyote for the second time.

"Whatso, CummyNup," greeted Coyote.

"Whatso," replied CummyNup.

"You still lookin' for Basio?" asked Coyote, in a good imitation of ganger talk.

"Still lookin'," said CummyNup. "Got more men than before too. Whatever Basio need, we got it."

Coyote scratched as close to his rump as he could get with a contorted hind leg and thought about this. "You see that canyon over there?" he asked, pointing to a pocket of dark in a landscape largely made up of such pockets.

CummyNup said he did.

"Basio needs you to be down that canyon, cross the bottom, ready to go up the far side by mornin'."

CummyNup sucked his teeth and thought about this. "How far from here?" he asked finally.

"Far enough you should leave pretty quick now," replied Coyote. "And don't make any noise!"

CummyNup agreed absentmindedly. When gangers went off on a tally, they never made any noise. Not until the battle started. He could get the men started and have them where Abasio needed them by morning.

Later, the thought crossed CummyNup's mind that if Abasio came back, CummyNup might no longer be Captain. He worried at it only momentarily before setting the thought aside. Basio, he told himself, was his friend.

In the woods along the Big River, Wide Mountain Mother camped in the midst of the warriors of Artemisia. Though the night had turned chill, the campfires had been allowed to burn down except for those few at the perimeter of the camp, where members of the Owl and Weasel societies stood sentry. It was one of these, Black Owl, who heard the voice in the night.

"Not eating you," it said in a softly furry voice.

"Halt!" cried Black Owl. "Who goes there?"

"Not eating you," repeated the voice. "Not throwing spear."

Black Owl thought this over. After a time, he swallowed, lowered his arm, and said, "Very well. Not throwing spear."

He held it, however, at the ready, as a bulky form came out of the darkness and into the farther edge of the firelight. It took considerable self-control to hold it then, for what sat in the firelight was unmistakably a bear.

"Chief woman," said Bear. "Go get."

"Wide Mountain Mother?" asked Black Owl. "You want her to come here?"

"I go, spears," said Bear. "She come. No spears."

Black Owl jiggled from foot to foot, wondering what to do next. "You're going to wait for me?" he asked at last, rather plaintively.

Bear grunted what sounded like an assent, and Black Owl took off at top speed for the tent at the center of the camp, the one occupied by Wide Mountain Mother and half a dozen of her eldest daughters.

Considering that she had been asleep when he arrived, Mother returned with him in an extremely short time. With her came a group of daughters, each of them armed and all of them suspecting a trick. When Bear greeted them with "Not eating you," they immediately took off in several directions to find out who was pulling the strings.

Wide Mountain Mother herself merely sat down and stared at him. "You talk," she said at last.

"So do you," said Bear in a grumpy voice.

"You're the one Arakny wrote about," she said.

"Possible," said Bear. "I know her."

"You bring me word of her?"

"I bring word. Move now. Go that way." He pointed with a large paw. "Up road. Sneaky, like coyotes. Morning, you fight!"

"Fight whom? For what reason?"

"Fight dead things. For the sake of living things."

A long silence.

"Is that all?" she called. "Is my daughter well?"

She received only a retreating grunt in answer. In a few moments, the daughters returned to say no person had been found. The Bear had been talking on his own. Wide Mountain Mother had already figured that out.

North of the Place of Power, a certain being sat upon a crag and considered themes of life and death, legend and history, good and evil. Beneath and around the large being, others of its kind and related kinds assembled to await the morning.

"This affair reminds me of long ago," said the large being upon the crag to a smaller being nearby. "When men carried swords of bronze and lived short but mythy lives."

The smaller being scratched a mosquito bite and did not answer. Its own memory did not extend that far.

West of the Place of Power, Hero leaned upon his lance and peered toward the wall. Around him burned the campfires of his fellow Heroes. There were a good many of them, more than he had thought there would be.

"We've been talking," said another Hero, coming up behind him.

"Of what?"

"Of proper ways to kill these things. We agree we aren't likely to survive the attack, but we feel we should make some effort to do as much damage as possible."

"Surely."

"One of the things we've come up with is earplugs."

"Earplugs."

"The walkers have this sound they make. It's crippling. But with earplugs, one can stand it."

"Earplugs and a pure heart," said Hero.

"Of course," said his colleague. "And a pure heart."

South of the Place of Power, Coyote and Bear met by appointment.

"One thing you can say for humans," commented Coyote, "they lead complicated lives. Very interesting."

"You say," said Bear, breathing heavily. It had been a long run up the canyon, and he was winded. "Did you see her?"

Coyote made an affirmative sound in which a great deal of sadness was mixed. "She left a message with me. For him. If he's still alive when this is over."

"Ah," said Bear.

Coyote started to speak again, then hushed himself, head cocked, listening. There were sounds all around them in the night. Foliage moving. Branches creaking. The sound of movement and assembly.

"Did you talk to the Artemisians?" Coyote asked.

"Umph," came the answer.

Coyote sighed. "We've been scouting, as you suggested. I think the caverns we've come up with will do the job."

Bear scratched his nose, wordlessly. "Big enough?"

"I think so. Big enough for moose."

"Moose?"

"We found several. Big enough for them."

"Big enough, then."

Coyote nodded. "Think I'll catch a little sleep," he said, curling up and burying his nose in his furry tail. He was not really asleep. He was thinking about his feelings. Before he had language, a time he could remember, he had had a sensory lexicon. There was not only count-smell but also feel-feel, in which grief was a winter's night without warmth or hope of spring, love for one's mate and cubs and kindred was the smell of new grass, hot mouse-flesh, and shared warmth in the den. These things were remembered, even now that he had language, which was not an unmixed blessing. He had words for things most of his kindred did not. Apprehension. Fear. Knowledge of mortality. It was possible he would not live through tomorrow. He might die. He wondered, as men had done for thousands of years, what lay beyond that barrier. "Tired," he murmured, surprised that it came out aloud.

"You say," grumped Bear, throwing himself on the ground. He had no furry tail long enough to bury his nose in, but his front paws did well enough. Heaving a deep sigh, which was echoed from all around him in the night, he slept. He had fewer words than Coyote and was thankful for it.

Abasio moved restlessly on his bed, like Coyote, not really awake, not really asleep, and for much the same reason. He had fallen into a light doze when Arakny pulled at his shoulder, telling him to come at once with her and Tom and Qualary, for something was about to happen.

"What time is it?" he demanded.

"Not yet midnight," she replied.

He struggled awake and into the warm clothing Arakny insisted he put on, then followed her out into the hall where Tom waited to guide them through the labyrinth of Gaddi House to the roof. The night was dark, the stars hidden behind cloud. Beyond the crags to the north, sheet lightning flashed now and again to the low mutter of approaching thunder.

Tom pointed westward, where they could see a flicker of scattered yellow lights.

"Campfires," said Tom. "The sensors picked them up. And there are beings gathering to the north and south. I don't even know what—who they are."

"Who? Where?" asked Abasio.

"Creatures. People. Animals. I don't know. There seem to be five bunches, altogether. Two coming from the east, one up the road, one across the canyon. One bunch north, one west, one south. Something Ellel dreamed up, perhaps. I didn't wake the others. No point getting them all upset, but Qualary said I had to wake you."

"Where north?" Abasio asked.

"Up on that precipice, and all down both sides of it. It's the only place that actually overlooks the Place of Power. The ones to the south and west are in the edges of the forest."

"What are the walkers doing?" asked Qualary.

Tom frowned. "Waiting. Jittering. A few of them have fallen over or attacked one another. Four Domer men tried to go out last night. Foolish of them."

"Were they—?"

"Three were killed outright. One of them was badly wounded, but he got back in. I think the men killing that one in the marketplace that time was only a fluke. The walker was already broken. If they aren't broken, I don't know if we can kill them at all."

"What's that?" asked Arakny, head up.

They all heard it, a yammering squeal that ran in both directions along the wall, like a herd of pigs being driven at great speed.

"Walkers," said Tom. "They see in the infrared."

"Infra what?"

"They can see warmth, think of it like that. Maybe they've seen something."

It was not long before they all saw it, the silhouette of a winged form high upon the precipice, huge and fell against repeated flashes of lightning.

"Griffin," whispered Abasio, dumbfounded.

The griffin opened its beak and cried out, a brazen cry that awoke the sky with echoes, sending them back into the canyons, where they crashed from wall to pillar to wall in an avalanche of sound.

Then from the west, an answering cry, the clatter of swords on shields.

And from the south, the howl of animal voices.

And from the east, the vrooming of engines and the shout of ganger battle cries. Abasio exclaimed when he heard that.

And from the road below the gate, the ululations of warriors.

"Five," said Arakny in wonder. "Five groups! Olly's prophecy spoke of five champions! It's five whole armies!"

"You're sure all of them are on our side?" asked Tom.

"Those war cries came from warriors of Artemisia," she said. "I believe those to the west are likely Heroes from archetypal villages. As for the animals, they are more likely to be on our side than on the side of the walkers, are they not?"

"And the monsters?"

She shrugged. She didn't know. "They're here! That's something!"

Tom nodded slowly, wondering what had brought the groups here at this time. It seemed almost contrived, but he had not been part of any contrivance! Perhaps His Wisdom was right. When the means were correct, the end was inevitable.

"What good are champions when Olly is already gone?" muttered Abasio. "Why couldn't they have come here yesterday!"

Tom laid his hand on Abasio's shoulder and shook him. "Even today, they may save the rest of us. Remember what she told me to tell you, Abasio."

Abasio shook off his hand. "The mere presence of five champions is meaningless. I hear gangers down there, and I know from personal experience they have no idea how to fight these things."

"My people are there as well," said Arakny. "And they have no more idea than gangers do."

Abasio nodded grimly. "The same will be true of the others, I should imagine. We need something more than mere fighters. We need a strategy."

He put his head into his hands, thinking furiously. He had been unable to save Olly. Perhaps he could save those who had been important to her. All those years in Fantis, watching battles, trying to stay out of them as much as possible, talking them over at the barber's afterward. If the Greens had done this. If the Blues had done that. Surely he knew something about fighting after all this time!

He stood tall and demanded of Tom, "Is my horse still in that cavern down below?"

Tom shrugged. "I imagine so."

"The entrance is well beyond the walker lines, is it not?"

Tom nodded.

"Take me there," demanded Abasio.

"And I," said Arakny. "I will carry your word to my people."

Though it was Tom's instinctive response to ask His Wisdom before he did anything, Abasio would not allow him the time. They went at once, down through the bowels of Gaddi House, toward the door behind the haystack. When they passed the tunnel where the bit-part players were stored, Abasio made an abrupt noise, as though he had been kicked.

"What?" demanded Tom.

"Nothing," grunted Abasio. "I stumbled over a rock."

They went through the final door into the tunnel where Big Blue stood half-asleep in his pen.

With a pang of guilt, Abasio saw that someone had given him fresh hay and water.

"Now," said Arakny, "what do you want me to tell my people?"

Abasio had been thinking about it all the way down. He told her, tersely, answering both Tom's questions and hers as best he might.

"Wish me well," he said to Tom, as he climbed onto Big Blue's back. "I should be able to get all the way around by dawn, starting with the animals to the south."

"Remember where you left your wagon?" asked Tom.

Abasio nodded.

"If you go up that canyon, it will lead you onto flat land south of the Place. You can drop Arakny off on your way."

Arakny peered out the tunnel entrance, seeing fires in the canyon bottom. "We can ride along the slope, here," she told him. "My people are on the road."

Abasio leaned down to pull Arakny up behind him, then took Tom's hand in his own. "We will do what we can," he said.

# CHAPTER 15

*A*basio and Arakny rode southeasterly across the slope toward the road. They could hear the yammering of the walkers a few hundred yards above them, a repeated squealing that moved in ripples along the wall, going and returning, a peculiarly bestial and mindless sound.

"What the hell are they doing?" whispered Arakny in Abasio's ear, her voice shaking.

"Counting off," Abasio said. "Keeping track of one another; a kind of roll call."

"How do you know?" she grated, wiping her forehead on her sleeve. Her sweat was cold, and it stank of fear.

"I don't," he muttered. "I'm guessing."

"Have you come up with any more good ideas?"

He shook his head. "Just what we've already talked about. We've got to base our strategy on some assumptions, though I dislike assuming anything where they're concerned. First assumption: They've been ordered to guard the wall. That means they won't leave the wall en masse, though some of them can probably be tempted away. They're not unintelligent. Tom was very helpful about the psychology of the damned things, if you can call it that. We're forewarned about the deadly sound they make, so we can protect against that. When it comes right down to it, however, they're stronger than we are, and there are more of them than there are of us, though the arrival of all these allies has evened the odds a little.''

"So my people are to fight a war of attrition.''

"We should kill as many walkers as possible from the greatest possible distance—we've talked about that. If we all try to achieve that, eschewing any heroics, we may have some success.''

She sighed. "We could refuse to fight. We could wait them out, bring in food through the tunnel—''

"We can't 'wait them out.' When Ellel gets back with the space weapons, matters will be worse. Our only chance is to dispose of them while she's gone and be ready for her when she returns! The shuttle can go from the silo, but not return to it. She'll have to land outside the walls. Mitty and Tom think we can do something about that, maybe!

"Besides, two people sneaking around on a horse is one thing. Bringing in supply wagons would be something else again.''

"You sound much more yourself, suddenly.''

He laughed, sounding almost joyous.

"What?'' she demanded.

"I figured it out,'' he said, turning his head to look at her over his shoulder. "The tunnel. The bit-part players. It wasn't Olly who went at all! It was one of them. Dressed in her clothes. Looking like her. She was Werra's kindred. The old man wouldn't just let her go off like that! He'd have sent one of those things instead!''

Arakny stared at him in the starlight. "Why didn't they tell us?''

"Couldn't. For fear we wouldn't react right. Everyone's told us how suspicious Ellel is. If we hadn't grieved, fussed, cried—Ellel would have known. It was important for her to go. They couldn't risk telling us.''

"Do you really think so?'' Arakny whispered. "I could have sworn it was Olly who went out to the shuttle.'' It had been, she was sure. But . . . what if Abasio was right?

Abasio turned to face forward, rejecting all doubt. "It wasn't her,'' he said firmly. "That's what her message meant: be resolute. She was . . . she was telling me she'd see me again.''

Arakny's question stayed on her tongue, for the way steepened as they neared the road, and she had to hold on to keep from falling. Big Blue dug in his hooves to lunge upward, once, twice, again, and they were on the road, going toward the hidden canyon where they'd left the wagon.

Once there, Arakny slipped from Big Blue's back, intending to continue the conversation about Olly. One look at Abasio's face dissuaded her. Now wasn't the time. She reached up to touch his arm in farewell, then trotted off down the road toward the Artemisian lines. Behind her, Big Blue stepped carefully around the buttress of stone and past the wagon itself, headed up the wandering trail to the top of the mesa. Intermittent flashes of lightning came more frequently as the storm moved closer, each flash silvering the narrow way before them. Several brilliant flashes came simultaneously with a crash of thunder as the storm moved past, and then they were upon the mesa top, the walls of the Place looming blackly off to their right.

A voice came from somewhere around Big Blue's feet.

"Whatso, Basio?"

"Coyote?"

"Who else?"

Abasio slid from the horse's back and crouched. In the next lightning flash he saw Coyote's face inches from his own, tongue lolling. "Who've you got out here?" Abasio asked.

"Bears. Big ones. And moose."

"What's moose?"

"Like elk. Only bigger."

"Can they kill walkers?"

Coyote shrugged. "Not likely."

"So? What are you planning?"

Coyote's plan had to do with deep caverns and underground rivers and walkers being enticed to become lost or drowned therein by this stratagem or that artifice.

"We thought of some of that stuff, but not all," Abasio remarked. "You're clever."

"We like to think so," said Coyote modestly. "My hermit always told me to take advantage of the terrain. What are you doing out here?"

"We thought coordinating our strategy might help our cause. At least that way we'll all know what the others are doing."

Coyote scratched his ear. "You don't need to worry about the monsters. The Artemisians are disciplined and accustomed to taking orders. The ones you need to convince are the Heroes and the gangers. They're both a bunch of rugged individualists."

"I don't know what the hell gangers are even doing here," puzzled Abasio. "Where did they come from?"

"CummyNup brought them."

"CummyNup! How'd he—"

Coyote told him how, in the fewest possible words.

"Sybbis is down there?"

Coyote laughed at him without answering.

Sybbis here! Abasio fought down an urge to howl, to scream, to throw himself off some convenient precipice. Ironic, wasn't it! The one he wanted with all his heart hidden from him; the one he didn't want not only present but searching for him. He couldn't deal with it now!

"If you'll help me get around to the west," he managed to say, "I'll try to talk some sense into the Heroes."

"Don't tell them about Olly!"

"What . . . what about Olly? What do you know about Olly?"

Coyote examined him narrowly, cocking his head. "Why nothing, Abasio. Nothing you don't know."

"What am I not supposed to tell the Heroes?" he shouted.

Coyote nodded slowly to himself. "Shhh. I'm reminding you that rescuing maidens is what Heroes do. That's why they're here. Don't . . . confuse them about their mission."

Abasio shook his head, swallowing the lump in his throat. All right. So he wouldn't say anything to the Heroes about Olly being . . . being all right. Besides, she did need rescuing. She had to be somewhere in Gaddi House, and Gaddi House needed rescuing. "If you say so," he told Coyote. "You'd know best."

Coyote trotted off to the west. Abasio patted Big Blue and urged him in the same direction. They went steadily among the low trees of the mesa top, slowing only when they saw the glimmer of scattered campfires.

"Who goes there?" came a voice from the darkness.

"A friend of the maiden," called Coyote, flashing his teeth at Abasio before he went back the way he had come.

A bronzed and muscular form with a crested helm stood into the firelight and beckoned Abasio forward.

"Are you Orphan's Hero?" asked Abasio, when he came close enough to be heard.

"We are all at the service of purity," replied the Hero. "We are all Orphans' Heroes."

"I'm the one from her village," said another Hero, who looked much like the first, "if that's what you meant."

"That's what I meant," Abasio acknowledged. "I've come under the wall, around the walkers' lines, to see if we can coordinate our strategy."

"Strategy!" cried Orphan's Hero, outraged. "Since when have Heroes stooped to strategy?"

Abasio considered this, taking his time. "It's unworthy of you, I know. If you were facing men or monsters, it would be inappropriate for me to suggest it. If we weren't so badly outnumbered, we'd not think of it. But we're not facing men or monsters, we're facing machines, and what might be unworthy of us in one case may be only sensible in the other. If you want to save your Orphan—''

''Of course I do!''

''Then we need to think carefully about the coming battle. Call it planning, if that is more acceptable.''

The first Hero remarked thoughtfully, ''Several of the younger Heroes have come up with some ideas.''

''Younger Heroes,'' said Orphan's Hero, puckering his mouth as though to spit, ''who have scarcely left their mothers' skirts.''

''Do they need to?'' Abasio asked, surprising himself with the question. Hadn't he himself been all too eager to leave his mother's skirts?

Orphan's Hero said flatly, ''Of course they must! No man may be a Hero until he repudiates the female influence and joins the great company of puissant men! We must strip ourselves of female sensibility, of female constraints—''

''Then why are you here, saving some female?'' Abasio asked in exasperation.

''It's what we do,'' asserted Orphan's Hero in a kindly though commanding voice. ''If the females are worthy and pure. My Orphan is worthy and pure. She is a virgin, brave and kind and sensible. I taught her to fight when she was little—not that a woman could ever be very good at it!''

His colleague stared into the distance. ''Lately,'' he said, ''some of us have been discussing our relations with women, our rescuing maidens and all that. Nothing we can follow up on now, of course, for we've no time, but in the future, perhaps—''

Orphan's Hero snorted. ''What have you to suggest, Orphan's friend?''

Abasio told them some of the ideas that he and Tom and Arakny had come up with. A group of other Heroes gathered around during the discussion that followed, several of the younger ones offering ideas of their own. Though Orphan's Hero sniffed at the thought of anything except ritual declamations followed by direct hand-to-hand combat, many of the others seemed able to accommodate the idea of evasion or even outright deception.

''If this is to work, someone must speak to the monsters,'' said one of the younger Heroes.

''True,'' agreed Abasio. ''And if you know them, you'd be better at it than I.''

''I could go under a flag of truce,'' said Orphan's Hero. ''That is an honorable approach.''

''However you like,'' said Abasio. ''But whatever you do must be done soon. There'll be no time for conferring come morning.''

''Will the monsters even consider helping us?'' asked an older Hero in a doubtful voice.

Abasio said, "I saw a fight between monsters and walkers once. I've a feeling the monsters hate the walkers as much or more than any of us do. I know if that fight was a fair example, monsters can dispose of walkers far better than we can. If we can make our request in a way they will think proper—"

"Humnph," said Orphan's Hero.

Abasio could take no more time. "I need to get to the gangers before light, however. They're massed in the canyon below the eastern wall."

"I'll guide you," the young Hero said enthusiastically. "I know this country well, and I can lead you north of the Place of Power, between the walkers and the monsters, without either of them knowing you are there."

"Sneaking!" challenged Orphan's Hero.

"Just getting the job done," replied the young Hero in an offended voice.

He was as good as his word, though after they had spent most of an hour in slow, silent travel, Abasio thought there might be something to be said for ritual declamations and a full gallop.

Some time after Abasio and his escort had departed, Orphan's Hero put on his helm, threw a cloak around his shoulders, readied a white scarf to use as a flag of truce, and mounted his war-horse.

"The others should be a mile or so ahead by now," he announced. "I will speak to the monsters."

The other Heroes raised their swords in salute, then returned to their assigned duties, most of which would require backbreaking and difficult work through what remained of the night hours.

Hero rode in a long, obvious arc that took him north of the Place of Power and kept him a good distance from the walkers and the walls. Once there, he kneed his horse into a canter and went boldly toward the rocky canyons that led upward toward the crags. The ground was not heavily forested. When the lightning flashed, he looked over his shoulder and saw that both wall and walkers were clearly visible. During a period of prolonged darkness, he could actually see the gleam of their red eyes, which meant they were looking in his direction. He told himself they did not frighten him, but he hurried his horse directly toward the canyons, nonetheless.

Came a yammering from behind him.

He turned the horse and kneed it into a sidling gait that let him keep his eyes on the wall while moving toward his destination. Three of the walkers seemed to have decided to come after him. They were moving forward slowly, like prowling cats, stalking him. The others along the wall had fallen dead silent, but they were watching.

Hero swallowed deeply.

"Who?" said a huge voice from the rock beside him.

He turned his head briefly, just long enough to see a giant half-hidden behind a pillar, its huge and craggy face lit from below by a glowing cookfire, over which something skewered spat fat into the coals. Either the cooking meat or the giant himself had a rank and musty smell.

Hero kept his eyes on the approaching walkers as he spoke. "I am an archetypal Hero come to ask a boon from the—the great legendary creatures assembled here at the Place of Power."

The walkers stopped prowling. One of them began a rush.

"Mine," growled Hero, as he put his lance beneath his arm and turned the horse to face his enemy. "Mine."

"You are mine," said the walker in an icy voice as he increased his speed.

"Mine," asserted the giant disagreeably, taking several steps forward and pounding the walker into the ground with his fist, like a nail into a board.

Though the other two walkers had stayed where they were, the monster took two more giant steps and nailed them into the ground as well.

Hero, much annoyed, dismounted and leaned on his lance, staring up at the giant as he tallied certain scars and traits against others remembered from the past. "I fought you once," he said conversationally, barely able to be heard above the yammering of the walkers along the wall, "at the siege of Bitter Mountain."

"You did," grunted the giant. "Not today, though. Griffin says not today."

"Griffin is your commander?"

A grunt in reply.

"Would you convey our request for a boon to your commander?"

Another grunt.

Hero outlined his request, trying to follow Abasio's suggestion of being as complimentary and as nonheroic as possible, though he found it exceedingly difficult.

When he had finished, the giant nodded and began trampling out the fire with his bare feet. "I'll tell'm," he mumbled. "You go on back. I'll tell'm."


Mitty and Berkli were roused from sleep by a messenger from Gaddi House who stuttered and waved his arms while trying to tell them what was happening. They wakened others of their people, some of whom they sent to the Domer laboratories and shops, some of whom they sent to the aid of the Gaddirs who were dismantling and moving weapons. The rest were told to hold themselves in readiness while Berkli and Mitty themselves went to Gaddi House to see what help they could provide.

Tom met them at the gates. "Council of war inside," he muttered. "The old man says we'll have to do what we can on our own. He's all of a sudden claiming to be no tactician.''

"Not his kind of tactics," muttered Berkli. "I have a hunch that old one of yours usually takes a few decades to plan things and work them out, and that's when he's in a hurry.''

"True," said Tom, unable to repress a smile. "Though once I saw him do something rather important in slightly over a year." He led them inside and introduced them to several Gaddirs who were rummaging through files and stacks of plans.

"You've no doubt worked with the walkers! What do you have in your shops that might be useful?" one of these persons demanded of Mitty, the moment he caught sight of him. "At the moment, we're thinking in terms of a field disrupter."

Mitty ran a hand through his hair as he did a rapid mental inventory. "I might have something," he said. "Can you send a few men back with me?"

Tom delegated this one and that one, who went off behind Mitty looking somewhat bemused. Berkli, who was left behind, got tired of twiddling his thumbs and went with Tom to the roof to see how the crew moving weapons was coming along, remaining there when Tom went down again to join Mitty and his group. Berkli was of help to no one, so far as he could tell. Since he could find nothing useful to do and it was impossible to sleep, he decided he might as well stay here where he'd have a good view of whatever happened, come morning.


Abasio had begun to fume with impatience long before the young Hero brought him to the canyon where the campfires of the gangers glowed palely beneath the lightening sky. The eastern horizon made a broken line against the sky by the time the Hero stopped, saluted Abasio with his sword, and pointed downward.

"A guard there," he whispered.

Abasio slitted his eyes, eventually spotting the sentry beside a giant fir tree. He started to express his thanks, but the young Hero was already gone, back the way he had come.

Abasio kneed Big Blue toward the tree.

"Give the password!" challenged the sentry in a voice so loud that it provoked a squeal among the walkers up the hill.

"I need to talk to CummyNup," growled Abasio. "Tell him Abasio is here."

Silence. "Abasio the Cat?" asked the sentry in an awestruck voice.

Abasio grimaced. "I suppose," he muttered. "Just tell him Abasio. *And don't tell anyone else!*"

The sentry departed. Abasio dismounted stiffly and crouched on his heels beside the tree.

"Basio?" came a whisper from behind him.

"CummyNup!"

They embraced, pounding and insulting one another after the manner of men.

"Where's TeClar?" demanded Abasio.

CummyNup looked at his feet. "He dead, Abasio. You know that Starlight stuff you got from Whistler? TeClar, he knew where you put it. While you over at the house, he took a bitsy drop, jus' to try."

"Oh, no, CummyNup!"

"It make him real horny, Basio. So he go to the songhouse, and then he feel bad, so he take some other stuff. On the trip, I see him gettin' worse and worse. One night he jus' die."

Abasio could find no words.

"You gonna fight with us?" asked CummyNup, changing the subject. "Or you gonna get us all away from here 'fore the fightin' starts?"

"I think this time I have to fight," said Abasio with a wry shake of his head. "That's why I came."

"Figured so," sighed CummyNup. "Men think they're here rescuin' you from up in there, behind those walls, so maybe you better not let 'em know who you are. I tole that sentry you'uz just a messenger. You know Sybbis with us here? She say she carryin' your baby." There was something quite wistful in CummyNup's tone.

Abasio dug his toe into the dirt and tried to think of something sensible to say.

"Old Chief, he thought that was a good thing," said CummyNup. "Way I hear."

"Old Chief sent Survivors to kill me!"

"Yeah, but he send more later to bring you back. He figure out you his son."

"Old Chief Purple's son!"

"He think so. He want you back bad." CummyNup sighed. "Nothin' to go back to now, though. Cities're all gone." He thought for a moment, then brightened. "Could go to the Edge. Old Chief Purple, he live in the Edge. Maybe he glad to see you, anyhow."

Abasio sighed. "That's the last thing on my mind right now. Right now we got to figure out how to make this fight count. Those things up there get loose, start wanderin' around the world, we'll all be as gone as the cities."

"How we gonna fight those walkers, Basio? Way I hear, they hard to kill!"

"Fire," he said. "That's what I came to tell you. Don't get up close to them, and use fire as much as you can. They're hard to wound, hard to kill, but they'll burn. They can still work even after their outsides are burnt off, but the lenses in their eyes crack and their guidance systems act up. Still, even then they'll move faster than anything, CummyNup. Faster than you'd think anything alive can move. . . . '' His voice trailed away as he saw CummyNup staring along the hill where something moved darkly in the grayness of dawn.

"Abasio?" someone called. "Abasio? Is that you?"

"Tom?" Abasio returned the call. "What're you doing here?"

Tom's stocky figure emerged from the dimness, loaded down with one pack on his back and one in each hand.

"Mitty and I put this thing together," he said, indicating the packs and panting with the effort of carrying them. "Mitty thinks it will stop the walkers, if I can find the right frequency. I brought it out because everyone else is busy, and Mitty's got some new weapons he's putting up top of Gaddi House so they can fire down into the canyon."

"Do you need help setting it up?"

"Yes. Someplace where we won't be attacked. If it works, we can maybe put it on a horse and move around the walls. Mitty thinks it has to be fairly close or it won't work at all."

Abasio and CummyNup helped him carry the packs into cover under the trees. By now, it was light enough to see the wall above them with the walkers arrayed along it. Tom began unpacking the parts, most of which seemed to have been put together with tape.

"I better go tell folks what to do," said CummyNup. "See you later, Basio."

Abasio raised a hand in farewell, before stooping to the mechanism to offer whatever assistance he could.


Berkli remained on the Gaddi House roof, watching Mitty come and go, occasionally lending a hand with this or that piece of weaponry. Tom, Arakny, and Abasio were gone. Presumably they were busy. Berkli wished he had enough knowledge to be busy. He had never felt so helpless and futile.

Dawn brooded gray between the black horizon and a line of dark cloud when a group of workers on the roof stopped short, all of them peering toward the north. As they moved slowly toward the northern parapet, Berkli joined them, and together they stared up at the crag where the Griffin was perched, now almost fully visible. The great beast was moving restlessly, its great face turned toward the east, as though waiting.

A rim of white fire rose above the horizon. The line of cloud turned to flame. The sky seemed to run with blood. The Griffin waited no longer. It cried out, a huge, brazen cry, and stooped from the crag where it had been perched, wings trailing, beak screaming like a bugle in the dawn. From the shadows at either side of the precipice came answering cries, followed by the emergence of giants, huge feet thudding earthshakingly, fists like mighty boulders swinging, jaws like the prows of buttes, mighty-thewed, as twin trees that had grown for a thousand years. So Berkli thought.

Behind the first giants came others, and others yet. And after the giants came ogres and trolls, from large to larger to largest, shaggy head behind shaggy head, shambling figure behind shambling figure. And behind them dragons and more griffins, chimeras and wiverns, minotaurs and manticores, rank on rank, file on file, twisting tails and shining scales, hooked wing behind hooked wing, fanged jaws and clever claws, monster after monster, pouring from the crevasses to do battle with the walkers of Ellel: creatures of legend to do battle with the soldiers of a forgotten time.

So Berkli thought, undecided whether to be elated or frightened. If the monsters conquered the walkers, would they then turn their attention to the Place of Power? Other men seemed untroubled by this idea. They were manning the machines at the eastern edge of the parapet, firing downward into the line of walkers against the wall.

Berkli stood alone, peering into the west, where he could see men on horseback coming from the forest, shields held high before them as they slowly cantered toward the wall of the Place of Power. He heard howling and yipping and bellowing from the south. From the east came battle cries, some voiced by Artemisians, the others, presumably, by the ganger army he had been told was there, warbling war cries, inexplicably howling something about a cat.


The walkers along the western wall saw the Heroes as they came from the forest, shining in the ensanguined dawn like creatures carved from ruby, their swords and shields polished to a uniform glitter, their helms gleaming, the brightly caparisoned horses no less effulgent than themselves, the whole enhanced by the lowering cloud to the north that lent a dramatic and threatening quality to the scene.

Walkers knew beauty when they saw it. When they had been built, the destruction of beauty had been built into them. Many men were comforted by beauty; preserving it was natural to them. Such men were enemies of those who built the walkers. Such men were to be debased, humiliated, and stripped of anything they loved. In order to destroy beauty, the walkers had a subprogram that recognized it.

The sight of these perfect Heroes, therefore, brought the subprogram erupting through the fragile glosses, as the smell of a tethered goat brings saliva into a tiger's mouth. All the work done by Jark III and Ellel fell away as the subprogram took over the direction of a number of walkers who moved from the wall, following the glorious images as they deliberately withdrew.

Too slowly, as it happened. Two of the Heroes could not quite mitigate their practiced heroism to meet the current threat. The walkers moved like lightning. Like lightning their feet strode, their hands thrust, and the Heroes fell, one of them surprised by that final inexorable thrust into a high, incredulous shriek of ultimate loss. A murmur ran through the ranks of the other Heroes, a tightening, and faces already grim grew strained in their concentration. Horses walked backward slightly more quickly, keeping just out of reach, step by step into the shadow of the trees and thence more deeply into the forests. The walkers continued in pursuit.

Not all the walkers followed after. In some, the glosses were more complete. In some the deep programming was better overlaid with more recent strictures. They had been ordered to protect the wall, to prevent anyone coming in or going out, so while roughly half their number followed the Heroes into the trees, the others stayed where they were, immobile, their red eyes gleaming.

After a considerable time, a new group of Heroes moved from cover to form a single rank along the forest edge and pose themselves there as their fellows had done before. These men were, if anything, more glorious than the first group, more magnificently muscled, more marvelously armed, and they increased the power of their attraction by dismounting and striking poses, arms extended, arms akimbo, kneeling with back muscles bunched and throbbing, posed as though to support the weight of the world.

Not only beauty, but power. The walkers had been built to destroy both. Some among those remaining could not resist. An additional number of them left the wall and followed the glorious bodies into the woods, leaving behind only a quarter of the original walkers. This was still a sufficient number to stop anyone who might attempt to enter or leave the Place of Power.

And yet again Heroes came forth, another group, this time arrayed in small ensembles standing against the trees as they sang their battle hymns, declaiming the baseness and villainy of the walkers between verses. Not only beauty and power but also flagrant opposition! Again some of the walkers pursued them, and again they withdrew. This was the last time. No further Heroes emerged from the shadows of the trees.

The walkers who were left were not concerned. Sooner or later their fellows would catch up to those who had tempted them into the woods. Walkers did not need sleep, did not need rest. Sooner or later they would come up to the horses and riders, and when they did, neither horses nor riders would go on living.

To the south, a similar effort at attrition was taking place, though here, since the original creators of the walkers had seen nothing beautiful in animals, or indeed in any facet of nature, the animals had to use strength as walker bait. Though walkers had no emotions, they had something that resembled pride, as the animals had come to know. A direct challenge on the basis of strength could not be ignored.

Thus, when a huge bear came from the woods and challenged them in speech, saying that it was stronger than they, the nearest walkers smiled bleak, scythe-edged smiles and went implacably after it into the canyons. When a bull moose or elk made a similar suggestion, it was similarly pursued. Walkers had no humor or sense of the ridiculous. It did not seem odd to them that large animals kept appearing with similar announcements, or that walkers who had departed in pursuit did not reappear.

Coyote, watching from behind a stump, knew very well that these were only early maneuvers in a battle that could be slightly delayed but never won with such methods. The furry bodies that lay on the open ground between the canyons and the walls spoke eloquently of that. Some of them were his own kin. Some of them were Bear's kin. Some had been speaking beasts. There were not enough speaking beasts in the world to trade for these walkers.

Coyote found his sight wavering, ducked his head to paw at his eyes. Was this what men knew as weeping? Such foolishness. Now, when he needed clear sight above everything.

Arakny had found Wide Mountain Mother awake and alert, and had conveyed to her the essence of what was known about walkers. Helmets must be padded around the ears, she said, for walkers were capable of a sound that killed. Also, it was important to stay away from them, out of their grip. They would not be enticed from the wall by rage, which was a good thing. Many of them could be killed where they stood, if the Artemisian warriors stayed far enough back.

"And how do we do that?" Wide Mountain Mother asked.

Arakny went down the list Abasio had given her. "Their eyes are vulnerable to a direct hit by an arrow or spear, provided there's considerable force in the blow. They'll burn, if they can be hit with something clinging and inflammable. They can be somewhat crippled by removal of their limbs with an ax, though their hands and arms are independently motivated and they can walk on them as well as upon their legs. To cripple them completely, all four limbs need to be removed."

"In short," said Wide Mountain Mother, "they are extremely difficult to kill. What would happen if we merely left them to their carnage and departed this place?"

Arakny spoke of weapons and Ellel and an earth enslaved under a tyrant once more, just now when all tyrants were gone.

"I hope there'll be enough humans left alive to celebrate our funerals," said Mother. "I had hoped to live yet awhile."

By dawn, most of the warriors were equipped with helmets with padding over the ears, and the best marksmen were arrayed nearest the walker lines. The ax was not a traditional Artemisian weapon, but every man and woman in the country knew how to fell trees and split wood, so there were axes aplenty in the Artemisian host. The battle began with a slow practice of marksmanship, during which the warriors of Artemisia discovered how difficult it was to hit the eyes of something that could move as fast as the walkers did. It was not long before the doctors of the Artemisians had many wounded to treat, and many who were past treating.

The gangers, meantime, had come up the canyon wall to the slope beneath the Place of Power. All the fire weapons the gangers had were distributed among the front rank, and as soon as it was light enough, the assault began.

Deep in the forest to the west a dozen walkers moved in swift pursuit of three Heroes. At the mouth of a vertically walled arroyo, the Heroes turned tail and fled, using the full speed of their horses to take them out of reach of the walkers. By this time, the only motivation the walkers retained was to destroy the prey before them. Guarding the wall was a distant duty to which they would return when this task was over. Looking neither right nor left, the walkers ran down the arroyo, keeping the Heroes in sight.

At a narrow turn in the canyon, the Heroes vanished. At that same turn, a sound from above brought the walkers' eyes up too late. Behind a fragile barricade of logs, stones had been piled, and now the ropes holding the barricade had been chopped through. The stones came down, knocking others loose on the slope below them to create an avalanche that buried the walkers beneath it. One of them struggled at the edge, like an ant, buried to its chest but with its arms still free. With incredible strength, it began to pull itself from beneath the stones.

A Hero rode back to the stone pile, cut off the arms, then cut off the head. The walker still lived. Its red eyes still gleamed, the arms still moved of themselves, scrabbling.

"They're still alive under there," the Hero called up the hill. "Eventually, they're going to get out!"

"I know," said the giant at the top of the hill. "But the rocks will hold them for a while."

Methodically, he began piling stones behind another cradle, to await the arrival of the next victims.

.    .    .

To the south, walkers followed bears into deep, dark, much-ramified caves from which the Bears emerged by other exits, leaving the walkers lost in darkness below, their infrared vision useless where all was chill stone. Others followed moose, who decoyed them far up into high meadows beside marshy lakes where they sank deep into the ooze, unable to extricate themselves. Walkers, the animals told one another eagerly, delighted at the knowledge, could not swim.

Still, there were bears who did not return, moose who did not return. Their numbers fell faster than the number of walkers. Animals had only their natural fleetness as protection. They were as overmatched by the walkers as they always had been by weapon-bearing men. It was not a fair fight. Those who had designed the walkers had not thought in terms of fair fights.

Below the southern wall, a frantic Coyote leaped and darted on three legs, one dangling uselessly, barely keeping out of a persistent walker's hands. He tripped and rolled, coming to rest with an uncontrollable yelp of pain when the shattered bone encountered an outcropping.

"About time," he mumbled to himself dazedly, catching sight of a troll form looming over the walker's shoulder. "Someone mentioned our getting help—"

"Talk!" grunted Bear, as he punished the walkers with great blows of his claws before turning to flee. "Fight more. Talk less."

Coyote did not reply. His fighting days were past. His talking days as well, it seemed. The walker was getting up again. They seemed always to get up again. The troll was too far away to be of immediate help. He put his head between his paws and waited for the walker to deliver the final blow.

On his way past, Bear scooped him up with one huge and bleeding paw and thundered down the slope into a canyon, where he led the pursuing walker into the jaws of a waiting wivern.

"Thanks," muttered Coyote to Bear, his vision blurring in and out, like fog.

"Anytime," said the wivern, munching.


North of the walls, the monsters fought with claw and jaw, with whipping tail and biting talon. Fire belched from dragon maws; huge clubs thudded to the earth with monstrous regularity, each blow signifying another walker crushed. Though they seemed for a time impervious to the walkers' bone-breaking blows and untroubled by wounds that would kill ordinary creatures, slowly they, too, began to weaken.

Not soon enough for the walkers, who began to keen, a sound their creators would have recognized as one of frustration. Walkers had been built to deal with creatures more powerful than these! They had programs and weapons they had not yet used, programs that had been glossed and covered with others, inhibitions and taboos that both Jark III and Ellel had inflicted upon them. Now, faced with the possibility, however remote, of losing a battle, those inhibitions began to flake away, a bit at a time, gradually revealing what lay beneath.

While in Fantis, Abasio had managed to avoid real fighting for some years, and he found himself woefully out of practice, praying to someone or something that the walkers confronting him wouldn't make what he thought of as The Noise until he, Abasio, could get Tom out of reach. So long as the walkers confined themselves to using their hands, feet, and bodies only, he might manage to stay alive. This thought had no sooner occurred to him than one of the walkers kicked Abasio's legs from under him and then raised its armored foot to crush Abasio's skull. One of the gangers flung himself at the walker, knocking him aside. Before the thing could retaliate, a beam from the top of Gaddi House decapitated it, as well as several other walkers who were fortuitously grouped just behind it. The bodies went on moving, however, striking out blindly in every direction, and several desperate moments went by before Abasio got Tom free of them, somewhat battered and bloodied in the fray.

Tom set up his device on an outcropping of rock, and while he twiddled with it, Abasio and a dozen gangers surrounded him. One of the men handed Abasio a power lance he'd picked up from some fallen ganger, and he faced outward, wishing Tom would accomplish something better than he had managed thus far. Every now and then Tom would hit a frequency that made one or more walkers explode with a loud noise, a stink, and a gout of fire. The explosions seemed to occur at random, some nearby, some farther away. Some walkers exploded while they were attacking, but some that were uninvolved exploded as well. It wasn't good enough. The humans were tiring even as the walkers seemed to be getting better and better at killing them!

From the Gaddi House roof, Mitty supervised the use of the weapons he had brought there, jumping about from one to another, advising, experimenting, cursing, and pulling circuits apart, only to reconnect them and try again.

Berkli watched him.

"Mitty," he said tentatively.

Mitty waved a hand and went back to his weapons.

"Mitty," said Berkli again.

Mitty put down the tool he had been using and came over. "What?"

"I've been watching over the north wall. Some of the walkers are acting differently. I think that thing has happened you were afraid of."

"Oh, for the love of—"

"Well, you can look for yourself."

Mitty did so, hanging over the parapet at the northeastern corner of Gaddi House. The walkers were no longer stretched in a thin line along the wall. Here and there, they were forming up in military fashion. Here and there, two or more of the creatures opened parts of their bodies and joined them to the bodies of others, becoming something larger and obviously more deadly. Mitty didn't need to have the matter explained. He knew that not even the monsters would be able to stand against them once they had reverted.

"Qualary told me Ellel controls the things from a closet in her quarters," said Berkli from close behind him. "I've been thinking, that's really where we ought to be."

"We can't reprogram—"

"Surely there's some way to turn them off!"

Mitty gave him a look of combined surprise and respect. He himself had not thought of that!


Before leaving, Ellel had called together several young Family members who were known zealots and faithful followers. She had given them weapons and a key to her quarters, with instructions to go there at the first sign of any revolt and hold the rooms against invasion.

Shortly after hostilities had begun at dawn, some Ellels and Anders had taken up whatever weapons were at hand and had gone to fight the Artemisians and gangers, plunging through the gates with a fine disregard for the reality of the situation. They were surprised and dismayed when they came under fire from the walkers and were pinned down outside the gates. While these Domers were putting themselves at risk, Ellel's zealots had barricaded themselves in Ellel's apartment to await whatever happened. Strangely enough, nothing happened for some little time, and they were growing weary of their duty and hungry for news by the time the guard they had left at the end of the corridor dived through the door to announce the approach of Berkli, Mitty, and a half-dozen other men.

Two Ellel adolescents had been stationed at either side of the door. "Are they going to attack us?" one of them asked the other. "Should we attack them?"

The youngster he queried answered the question by firing an indiscriminate burst down the corridor.

"We could have asked them first," said the other, plaintively. "We don't even know what's happening."

The Berkli-Mitty group fetched makeshift barriers and, pushing these ahead of them, came far enough down the corridor to be heard.

"When the walkers come in, they're going to kill us all," shouted Mitty. "I don't care what Ellel told you. The walker programming is breaking down! Remember how the children were killed in the marketplace? They're all behaving that way now, and they'll kill you just as dead as they'll kill us!"

There was a momentary lull in the firing from inside before the youth who had shot first shouted an obscene reply and let loose a fusillade.

Those in the corridor waited for the firing to die down.

"Idiots," muttered Mitty.

"He's telling you the truth!" Berkli cried. "If one of you would like to go look over the eastern wall, we'll give you safe passage."

This time a considerable pause, during which those in the corridor could hear voices raised, some angry, some plaintive. A pale young face thrust itself around the doorframe. "I'll go look," said the young man in a voice that squeaked.

"Fine," said Mitty. "But hurry up about it."

He scuttled past, so intent upon glaring at them that he came almost to a stop.

Berkli said, "You're Varis Ellel, aren't you? Well, hurry. Ellel won't want to come back and find her whole Family dead!"

The youngster's eyes widened, and he scampered off.

"Varis?" asked Mitty.

"I get him mixed up with his brother," sighed Berkli. "Twins, about fourteen. Ellel's best followers are about that age. They have good minds and no experience. I was that age once. I, too, thought I could remedy the world with a little direct action."

"What's keeping him!" demanded Mitty.

A few long moments passed. "Here he comes," said Berkli.

The youngster came at top speed. "They are!" he cried. "They're killing Ellels and Anders outside the gate!"

He went on, and again they heard voices raised from inside. Shortly an arm emerged, waving a towel, and the youngsters trailed out, half a dozen of them.

"We didn't know," they said apologetically. "Honestly. Ellel just told us to keep you out of here. We didn't know."

Mitty had no time for recriminations. He found the locked door to the closet Qualary had spoken of, then he and three of his technicians began arguing how to get into it without setting off anything irreparable.

. . .

Deep in the woods to the west, the stones piled high upon the walkers began to shake and tumble. The earth vibrated, as though a volcano were erupting, and a tower of dust rose from the rock pile. A walker arm emerged, then a walker head, then a walker entire, who began dismantling the rock pile and letting the buried soldiers loose once more.

Above them on the wall of the canyon, weary Heroes glanced at one another in what would have been called despair among men less brave. They turned their horses and rode back toward the city. Perhaps someone there had thought of something else to try.

So close to the wall that he was unseen from above, Abasio brandished his power lance and muttered every filthy word known to gangers as he parried and thrust and dodged and leaped. Tom's device would have been very useful if the man could just aim the damned thing. Eventually, the number of walkers destroyed might add up to something. No doubt they had already disposed of several dozen, but meantime, all he, Abasio, could do was try to keep them at a distance while Tom kept yelling, "Give me a minute, just a minute, I ought to get a bunch with this, a bunch, just give me a minute . . . "

A new sound obtruded on the cacophony of battle, a high voice that cut through the clangor, the grunting, and the shouting with crystalline clarity:

"Abasio, Abasio, Abasio the Cat!" the voice shrilled, a cry taken up by a hundred other voices.

Abasio glanced up. Across the heads of the walkers he saw a waving banner and a high chair carried on the shoulders of heaving men. CummyNup was carrying the banner, and Sybbis was standing in the chair, pointing toward him. She shouted again, and her bearers turned in his direction bellowing, "Abasio, Abasio the Cat!"

The momentary distraction had been all the walkers needed. Abasio was struck from one side and felt himself falling endlessly down into a scarlet-black maelstrom.

In the forest, Bear turned on his hind legs, growling a futile challenge, as three of the walkers worked their way closer and closer.

Coyote lay stunned behind a rock while other animals and monsters ranged across him and around him.

Black Owl, recumbent, stabbed with his lance at the walker above him. He was lying in a pool of his own blood and did not think he would rise from this place again.

Wide Mountain Mother watched and cursed while her daughters worked among the bodies of the wounded and slain.

At the gate, a clot of Ellels and Anders tried to flee back through the gate and were pursued by walkers who then began attacking every person they saw inside the Place.

And in Ellel's closet, Mitty sweated, cursed, and said over his shoulder to Berkli, "I wish you'd thought of this earlier, Berkli. I wish it hadn't taken so long to get into the closet. I wish I'd been quicker figuring out what this thing is set for. Really, you should have thought of this first."

"I know," growled Berkli. "Will you hurry!"

"I have hurried. Well, as they say, do or die. This is it, or we're all dead!"

He punched in a signal, then another, and another yet.

Inside and outside the wall the walkers staggered. They moaned. They stopped. They gazed sightless, at nothing. They cried out, a vast inhuman cry of loss or despair or some totally indecipherable feeling, perhaps only an enormous severance, and fell. Row on row. Rank on rank. Black helmets and red and gold, like beads from a necklace, dropping like wheat from the scythe, eyes going blank, voices going mute, falling down in their hordes.

From the top of the sky the Griffin stooped, screaming, dropping in a great flurry of scaled wings at the foot of the wall near where Tom Fuelry still crouched over his device. Any view of those fallen there was lost under the flailing of great wings and a tangle of Gaddirs and gangers, struggling to rise.

The Griffin rose again, half seen through a cloud of dust. It arrowed away to the north.

Silence.

Silence utter. As though the world held its breath.


Sybbis leaped to the ground and ran to the place Abasio had been, pulling and tugging as she searched among the bodies, crying Abasio's name. Where was he? Who could tell if he was there or not? There were bodies in the pile who might be Abasio. Faces were disfigured, torsos and limbs were mangled.

"Abasio!" she screamed. The gangers took up the cry, making the canyon ring with the sound.

"He not here," said CummyNup, as he sadly rummaged among the fallen. "He dead, Sybbis."

She had tears on her face. Over the past days, she had built him into something more than merely mortal, something that could not be allowed to die. "Not!" she cried, whirling to face her followers. "Gone, not dead. Basio the Cat, he got nine lives. Basio, he can't die."

"Gone," they cried obediently, exalted by the moment. "Gone, not dead."

Above them on the road the feathered warriors caught their breaths and raised their own war cry. From beyond them, away south, came a howling and yelping of animal packs, and from farther yet came the bell-like noise of sword hilts striking shields.

As they turned about and worked their slow way northward into the rocky wilderness and forest lairs, even the monsters sang an awful paean of victory.

Berkli clapped Mitty on the back, wordlessly, then hugged the man and wept unashamedly.

Deep in Gaddi House, the old man bowed his head and shook it slowly to and fro.

"Pity," he said. "Always, such a pity."

# CHAPTER 16

*L*ate afternoon, wearing on to the close of a sunless day. Sparse snow, whirling, refusing to settle. Blood turning to dark ice; the wounded cursing or crying out as they are lifted and carried away to warmer places beside hastily built fires, where skilled Gaddirs or Artemisians are gathered to offer succor. Bodies chilling into death as other Artemisians and gangers move sadly among the slain. Everywhere the stink of walkers, their rigid forms, their staring eyes. They are not dead or dying. They are merely inactivated. Merely quiescent. Firelight reflects from their red orbs, giving an appearance of life, and rescuers shudder, looking hastily elsewhere.

In the Place of Power, Ellels mutter in their homes, speaking of their leader's rage when she returns to find what has happened. They are impotent. Every Ellel with any capacity for leadership is on the shuttle. Anders huddle in their pavilion, speaking worriedly of the strange alliance the day has brought forth. Forsmooth Ander is among them. Though he should have gone, a last-moment indisposition (so he said) prevented it. Now he moves restlessly among his kindred, trying to draw the severed lines of power into his own hands.

Only certain Mittys and Berklis are out, working methodically from fallen walker to fallen walker, each of them armed with a small, hastily built device that will, so says The Mitty, do more than merely deactivate. The walkers, wherever they are, must be located one by one and once and forever killed, their bodies dragged to a rocky pit, and in that place, burned.

In the control section of the shuttle, Ellel awakes from a days-long sleep. Ander is no longer beside her. He has gone to his own space to rest; at least, the telltale before her says that space number two is occupied, so she assumes he is resting.

She yawns, leaning forward to look out the windows onto the universe. There before her something sparkles, something glitters, something not natural, a created thing, a gem against the darkness of heaven. Beyond it is the luminous slice of the moon, a slender arc, rimming the earth's shadow.

Tiny explosions of joy erupt inside her, like the explosions of firecrackers, one after another, little poplets of happiness. Herself, here, as she planned to be. The station there, growing visibly larger as she watches. The moon, lovely in its pearly splendor. Soon she will be there, she and her walkers, and her people. The weapons will be dismantled and stowed aboard. Perhaps some walkers and people will stay on the station. There have been discussions of that possibility. And there will be walkers on the moon!

The station is closer. It looks much as she has envisioned it, much as the plans describe it. A huge wheel spinning in space, attached by four spokes to an unmoving hub where the shuttle will dock. And there, protruding from the unmoving hub, are the particular things she is most interested in. The mighty sun cannons that will make her invincible upon earth, their lenses glittering, almost as though in greeting.

"Oh, Daddy!" she murmurs in her delight. "Look at them! Will you look at them!"

To her eyes they have an elegance, a simplicity that she finds lovely. According to the accounts she has seen, they were tested on earth before they were installed here, so she knows they will work on earth as they do here. With considerably less efficiency, true, but they will work. Of all possible earthly opponents, only the Edgers have worried her until now. The Edgers are enigmatic. They are self-contained and self-satisfied. But when the Edgers know she has these, they will not dare stand against her. Not for long, at any rate.

And there, nearby—the unfinished starship! Just as she has been told. Actually, it is less finished than she hoped, but still—nothing that can't be managed. Later. What a pity Ander didn't stay here in the control section. He won't be able to see from where he is! She thinks of waking him and discards the notion. This time is too precious. She thinks of arousing Daddy and letting him watch the approach, discarding this notion as well. Re-creating him was an indulgence. It was a kind of madness. She has known that all along, but when she could not let the world see the reality of Empress Evel, she needed that secret source of support and confirmation. What happened to her face, her body, had not dissuaded her. But now she laughs abruptly at revelation. Here, now, she doesn't need him anymore!

Slowly, slowly, the station comes closer, the great wheel growing until it occupies the entire window, until she can see only part of it: the hub, to her left, its bay gaping.

She shifts uncomfortably. The shuttle should be coming directly into that bay, but instead it seems aimed at the empty space between hub and wheel. A spoke of that wheel slides across her vision. Space. Space. Another spoke slides by, closer. Space. Space. And a spoke yet again, almost touching the shuttle! Barely clearing before the shuttle moves past it!

The shuttle has gone past! Past the station! It has slid between two spokes of the wheel with contemptuous ease. Leaving the station behind.

Frantically, Ellel brings the rear viewers onto the screen, verifying what she already knows. The station is behind them. They have not stopped at the station.

Has the fool girl misunderstood? Does she believe they intended to go to the moon first? Surely not!

Ellel releases her belt, flinging herself up with such force, she bumps her head on the panel above herself. She pulls her way toward the guidance booth. The girl still sits, as unmoving as before. Did Ander give her some other instruction? Is this his fault? Breathing hard, Ellel goes on by, back past the toilets and the galley into the living space, stopping aghast at the sight of her own door open. Unlocked and open. And inside, exposed to the view of anyone, everyone, what has been her own secret.

Ander! Who else but Ander?

Raging, she goes past, to the second cubicle, stops at the open door, storms in, then catches herself with a scream of half-fury, half-surprise as floating red globules stir in the air she has disturbed by her entry, wobble and bump against her, to break stickily against her clothing, against her skin, staining her with blood.

Blood. Ander's blood. And he, bobbing around the space like an unwieldy balloon. And the door beyond his open, and the next. All of them, open.

Raging, screaming, she goes down the long tubelike corridor, seeing in every cubicle the same, bodies still strapped into bunks with great globules of blood floating everywhere. Dead. All of them dead. Anders and Ellels both!

Howling, she catapults back to the guidance booth. Her hand on the girl's wrist. No pulse. Her hand on the girl's neck. No pulse. Her hand on the breast. No breath. The girl is no longer living. Despite the hostages, the girl has brought them this far and then died. Died!

And there, behind her ear, a small wound. A tiny, precise wound. Unlike the other carnage, this wound has bled hardly at all.

Was it Ander who did this? Ander who did all this?

A chuckling sound. She looks up to see the bird, the strange bird, the bird with the rapier beak sitting upon a pipe that runs along the central corridor. There is blood upon its beak, and it is watching her.

Ander did not do this.

Stunned into utter quiet, Ellel looks out the glassy panes once more in the direction of their flight, seeing all too clearly where they are going. Their impetus will take them past the moon, beyond the moon, and on toward the silent mockery of the oh-so-distant stars.

Behind her, the guardian-angel chuckles sadly once more.


The former hostages had assembled on the terrace above the canyons, to lean upon the parapet while Nimwes and Qualary set out tea and hot soup, and Tom, with bandaged head and arm, fumbled with the controls of the air screen that warmed the place. His Wisdom was there, and a scatter of Gaddirs.

"Did your Hero survive?" His Wisdom asked Oracle and Drowned Woman, who were huddled together over their teacups.

"We don't know," said Oracle. "Someone said they're tending their own wounded, but no one has come to say who lived and who died."

. "Ah," said His Wisdom. "And what of Bear and Coyote and our other talkative friends, Tom?"

Tom shrugged and replied wearily, "I don't know, sir. Give me a minute, and I'll go find out."

In a bleak voice Arakny said, "When the battle ended, I went down to speak with Wide Mountain Mother, and she told me Black Owl is dead. Olly and Abasio knew him." She did not speak of the other wounded or dead, many of whom she herself knew well.

At her mention of Olly and Abasio, a tiny ripple of movement ran through the group: pained shifts and glances, compressed lips, a wiping of sudden tears. Olly was gone, and Abasio had been killed at the foot of the wall.

"I was amazed to see giants fighting on our side," murmured Oracle to no one in particular. "I had not foreseen such a thing."

"I don't think they were fighting on our side out of any sense of conviction or alliance," said Tom, half-angrily. "I think they were just doing what Griffin told them to do."

"Orphan told me a little story about a griffin, a long time ago," mused Burned Man. "Remember, Oracle?"

She shook her head, unable or unwilling to remember, stubbornly going on with her train of thought. "I had not thought there were so many monsters abroad upon the earth."

"There were caverns full of them in the deep," said Tom. "Werra's creatures from the time of legend. His Wisdom tells me such things are not allowed to die or become extinct. The pattern for them remains. Werra had freed some of them before he died, to build their numbers upon earth, but before Olly left, she must have decided to turn them all loose."

"You say they were Werra's creatures?"

"Werra's," confirmed old Seoca. "All the legendary creatures, part beast, part demon, part divine. Designed to illustrate the unity of life and destiny. And man started with them well enough. He had man stories and women stories and animal stories, man gods and woman gods and beast gods. But, over time, only the rutting rooster gods survived."

"Cock-a-doodle," whispered Oracle sadly. "Crouch, you hens."

"Speaking of creatures," said Drowned Woman in a surprised voice, "I think one of them is coming here." She pointed out across the parapet, over the canyons, where a great winged thing, so distant it looked no larger than an eagle, was approaching them from the east.

"Griffin," said Tom needlessly, for there was no mistaking that lion-legged, heavily maned form.

They watched silently as it flew toward them, as it rose above them and folded its wings to drop down upon the parapet, holding its wings high, the long ribs vertically together behind its head so all they could see of it was its head, mane, and frontquarters, like some great heraldic escutcheon. It regarded them severally, then individually, peering at them one by one as though taking roll. Only His Wisdom seemed totally at ease before this scrutiny.

"Not eating you," said the Griffin at last, as it had said to Olly in the long ago, when she was only a child.

"I know," said the old man. "You have fought a good fight today, great one."

"A forced alliance, but necessary," said the Griffin, leaning sidewise to whet its beak against the parapet, one edge, then the other, with a sound like steel on a grindstone. "There will be other battles in future times, for me and my kin, both close and distant. Now is our time come again."

"Yes," intoned the old man, as though it were ritual. *"Now are sent monsters and heroes abroad upon the earth; now are sent the inhabitants of faery and the beings of fable; now a new age of legends is ushered in."*

"Now have the thrones brought balance once more," said Griffin, as in response. "Now they may rest."

The old man gave the Griffin a thoughtful look. "I wonder if perhaps you have brought us a gift?"

"A gift, yes," said the Griffin. "In part payment for one little gift returned to me long ago." Slowly, it lowered its wings to disclose the man who sat dazedly within the glistening mane. Drowned Woman cried out, and Farmwife Suttle. Burned Man and old Cermit added to the babble, along with Qualary and Tom. Only the old man and Oracle were quiet as Abasio slid from the Griffin's shoulders onto the parapet.

"I saw you slain!" cried Tom to Abasio. "Struck down!"

"They said you were dead, boy!" cried Cermit.

"I got pulled out," muttered Abasio, looking around him with searching eyes. "At the last possible moment." He stared into old Seoca's face, fixing him with his gaze. "Where's Olly?"

The old man shook his head, said softly, "You know where she is, Abasio Cermit."

"No!" He denied it. "No, that was just a bit-part player. Dressed in Olly's clothes. Saying Olly's words in her voice. Olly didn't—didn't—you wouldn't have let her go!"

Silence. All of them still, waiting for the reply.

The old man sighed. "Abasio. If the price of a gem is a golden crow, can you buy it for a black-penny? Is all life upon this world so shoddy a thing that it may be bought for a worthless automaton?"

"She didn't!" Abasio cried. "She wouldn't have left me! She couldn't have!" And then, seeing the old man's face, "But she's coming back!"

No answer. Abasio backed up until he was pressed tight against the parapet, feeling his knees buckle. He huddled against the parapet wall, his head moving from side to side in constant negation, saying over and over again, "No. No. No."


Arakny went to Abasio, put her arms around him, and held him. Drowned Woman looked at him sorrowfully, thinking how familiar he looked. Was he indeed her son, as some said?

"Where did they go?" demanded Originee Suttle, tears of anger and pity in the corners of her eyes. "Really?"

Oracle answered, "I prophesied for them. I always tell the truth. Those who hear must interpret, of course." She looked down, her mouth twisting. "People always believe what they want to believe."

Arakny held out her hand, invoking silence. "But what of that prophecy? Olly's seven questions. Did she answer them?"

It was Tom who spoke. "She said you would want to know, Arakny. She told me to tell you. Yes, she answered the questions Hunagor and Werra asked her. Who she was, and who they two were. What the three thrones are, and who the four families are who chewed at them. She foresaw the five armies of champions; she knew of the six set upon salvation, and from both champions and earth-menders she took her hope and her resolution."

"And the seventh question?" Oracle demanded.

Abasio raised his head, his face haggard and drained of all emotion.

Tom paused, his voice doubtful, "She said—the thrones wanted to know . . . if she considered her life well spent. She told them yes, she did."

From Abasio, a wordless howl of rejection.

"We spoke of that once," the Farmwife mused, tears in her eyes. "We spoke of people finding out who they are. And was she only for this, then? What was the purpose of it all?"

The old man said softly, "The purpose of it all was to reverse the chain of events that began when Jark the Third uncovered a cavern full of bionic warriors, made by man during the Age of Great Wars. With that discovery, a chain of probability was rejoined, a chain we Gaddirs were seeking to disrupt, a chain begun by man that would have ended all life on earth."

"We are only just saving it from the time before," Arakny said. "We're just getting it growing again!"

"Ellel was that dangerous?" asked the Farmwife. "One woman?"

His Wisdom nodded slowly. "Had she returned from her voyage with weapons from the space station, yes. Had she sent someone else to get them, yes. Had she remained here even without them, yes. To interrupt the chain of events, she had to leave her army and take with her all the Ellels who might rise up in her place. Yes, she was very dangerous."

"Why didn't you just kill her!" cried Abasio.

The old man sighed. "Natural law, my boy. When a tyrant is simply killed, another rises up. The very act of violence causes them to copse, like trees. Quietly, quietly, one has to dig out the root."

"Did you know all this?" Qualary asked Tom. "Did you?"

"Only bits and pieces of it," he said, with a flush and a shrug. "His Wisdom knew all of it."

"Is that why we were friends? Just so—"

"Just so nothing," said His Wisdom, firmly. "Tom was assigned to get to know you, yes. He was not assigned to lie to you or mislead you. His feelings for you, whatever they may be, are his own, and I know him to be a sincere and honest man."

Qualary flushed in turn.

"And now?" asked the Griffin.

"And now what?" Abasio cried in an anguished voice. "What's left!"

"And now, I have an errand down below," said His Wisdom. "Because you are a collector of information, Arakny, you should come."

Slowly, unwillingly, she nodded.

"I, too," said the Griffin.

"Yes," said His Wisdom. "And you, Abasio."

Abasio shook his head. He wanted nothing more to do with these people who had let Olly go, or this place that had swallowed her up.

"Olly asked me to take you," said the old man, his eyes fixed on Abasio's huddled form. "Come, now."

Abasio rose, unable to resist the adamantine will in the old man's voice, unwilling to resist any request Olly had made.

Tom rose to accompany them, but His Wisdom smiled. "No, Tom. You don't need to come along. You and Qualary see to our other guests. We won't be long."

The old man's chair whirred out into the corridor, and then went swiftly, by ways wide enough and ramps easy enough for the Griffin's wings and claws, to an enormous lift that Abasio knew he had never seen before, thence downward, arriving in mere moments near to the vaultlike door Abasio so well remembered.

The old man opened it, taking far less time than Tom had done. The pillars stood as they had stood before. The tracks leading among them showed faintly in the dust, winding as before. When they came at last to the open space before the dais, Abasio and Arakny saw that the light was dimmer than it had been. The thrones should have been harder to see, except that they glowed with a pale light of their own. The woman who sat on the left-hand throne smiled a slow welcome as they arrived, as did the man on the center throne.

"Hunagor," said the old man, nodding to the left-hand figure. "Werra," as he nodded to the center figure. "Some friends have come to see me off."

"Librarian," the thrones said, a word that took forever, nodding in their turn, a nod that took even longer. "Great One," and a nod to the Griffin. And then, while both of them looked at Abasio, Hunagor spoke alone: "Great-grandson."

Abasio shuddered, started to speak, stopped, unable to form words. He stood paralyzed as all the creatures on the stone, in the stone, making up the stone, seemed to greet him, to nod and smile or speak, though Abasio could not tell whether they had actually done so or merely intimated it in some fashion.

"Well," sighed the old man. "It's done."

"Old friend," they said. "Welcome."

All the creatures on the thrones echoed welcome.

Seoca leaned forward, struggling to get his legs under him and rise from the chair that had carried him so long. Arakny came to help him, and at a commanding glance from her, Abasio supported his other side. There was sweat on her forehead, and her hands were clammy when he touched them. They half-lifted the old man onto the low dais and helped him walk to the right-hand throne, where he sat down with a sigh that seemed to breathe throughout the hall for long moments after it was done, a little wind, a dying wind.

"Look at us," the old man whispered. "Don't turn your head away. Hunagor is your great-grandmother. Werra is Olly's father. She wanted you to know about us. Look at us!"

Reluctantly, backing away slow step by slow step, Abasio forced himself to look at them. From the backs and arms and bases of the thrones, the carved creatures returned his gaze. Tentacled creatures and winged ones. Creatures with many legs. Bloblike things with no discernible features. Lizardlike beings. All of them watching him as he watched them, each of them seeming to say, "Look at me. See me. Understand me. You are of our kindred. She you loved understood me. Now you too."

"So you begin again," chanted His Wisdom softly.

The Griffin quoted: " *'Now are sent monsters and heroes abroad upon the earth; now are sent the inhabitants of faery and the beings of fable; now a new age of legends is ushered in. Now may the thrones depart.'* "

Abasio barely heard, for the creatures on the thrones still held his eyes, willing him to understand. Understand what?

He met Hunagor's eyes. She looked up, lifting his gaze to the back of the throne, above her head, where her name was carved. Hunagor. And above the man's, Werra. And above the old man's, *Seoca.*

*Hunagor. Werra. Seoca.* The words writhed and twisted like snakes, re-forming before his eyes.

*Hunagor. Werra. Seoca.*

Visions came to him, rising out of those words: Forests become deserts, the bloated bellies of starvation, the scorched earth of bombed cities, the hideous faces of IDDIs. Famine. Death. Plague. Earth itself endangered by man. Man himself a plague, to be attacked like a plague, to be killed by whatever means the thrones could find. Hunagor. Werra. Seoca.

Hunger!

War!

Sickness!

His breath caught in his throat. He felt himself grow cold.

"Go, now," said the old man, looking from Abasio to Arakny and the Griffin and back again to Abasio. "Go, my boy."

Abasio's breath left him explosively.

Arakny took him by the shoulder and drew him back toward the pillars. Before them, the Griffin was bent into a profound obeisance. The thrones hummed. The Griffin turned and came after them, a wild amber light burning in its eyes. A wavering effulgence gathered around the thrones, and those sitting there began to melt into the stone, joining that throng of others who had melted into those thrones throughout aeons of time.

Abasio was chill and rigid with protest. He did not believe. He would not believe. He was not thinking. He had willfully turned his mind off. He did not wish to think of anything, particularly not of this.

They fled, following the Griffin out among the pillars, out into the corridor. Behind them the low humming intensified, a sound growing slowly and steadily in volume. The Griffin thrust the great door closed with one push of a mighty wing.

"We are friends, Abasio Cermit," said the Griffin. "For her sake."

Abasio choked on the words. "For her sake."

"Go that way, swiftly! I have my own way out." The Griffin pointed with one wingtip, then went away itself, down the long corridor to the right, striding like a lion, wings folded behind it.

The great engine noise had abated, though not the vibration they could feel through the soles of their feet. They ran in the direction the Griffin had indicated, coming to the open lift they had used to descend. They leaped inside it, felt it lunge upward, fidgeted impatiently as it rose up and up and up into the more familiar purlieus of Gaddi House.

"What's happening?" mumbled Abasio.

"I'm not certain," Arakny muttered as the engine noise from below increased, grew to a steady mutter, then to a subdued roar that made the walls shake. "But the librarian in me says we've probably reached the end of one book and the beginning of another."

The doors opened, and they staggered together along the familiar corridor to His Wisdom's quarters, where they found the others crouched along walls or clinging to doorframes, trying to stand or sit while the entire structure shuddered around them. The tremors went on and on, a constant vibration that made their teeth chatter and their muscles rebel, ripping them away from their holdfasts and tumbling them about on the floor like rocks in an avalanche among a clutter of furniture and broken crockery.

Until all at once, without diminution or aftershock, the noise and shaking simply stopped, absolutely and utterly. They lay in an enormous silence, for a moment without even the sound of breathing, then gasped as they realized they'd been holding their breaths.

Tom Fuelry heaved air into his lungs and demanded, "Where is His Wisdom?"

"Where?" cried Nimwes, sounding both angry and afraid, her question echoed by others of the Gaddirs.

"Below," said Abasio. "With his friends."

"I'll go," said Tom, rushing out. "You shouldn't have left him."

Nimwes ran after him. Arakny started to follow, but Oracle caught at her shoulder, shaking her head. "Let them see. They'll need to see for themselves."

Arakny turned, patting her pockets, muttering.

"What is it?" Oracle asked.

"I just remembered! Olly took my library. I forgot to get it back from her. I wanted to record, to make note, to—"

Outside the room, Tom ran toward one of the secret lifts, one he had used a thousand times. He bumped himself against an unfamiliar panel and stood back, rubbing his head. Where the self-opening door should have been was only blank wall. He shook his head, baffled, angry, frightened, while Nimwes cried from behind him. Well, there was another one not far away, where this corridor crossed another beside a ramp.

He ran. She ran. The crossing was there. The ramp was there. The door wasn't. The lift wasn't.

There was a door, one of the big doors, down two levels! He flung himself at the ramp, Nimwes still pursuing, stumbling two levels down, almost falling in his haste. The door was gone. The whole door, the entire, huge, complicated door. Where it had stood was only blank wall! Wall! Everywhere walls!

All the ways were closed. All the routes he had used all the years of his life were gone. The ways his father had shown him. Portals he had opened time after time were gone, nothing remaining to show where they had been. Lifts he had ridden in were gone. Corridors he had traversed to get from this point to that ended now in different places, against different barriers. Gaddi House was no longer as it had been.

When they returned, there was blood upon their fingertips where they had pressed again and again at unyielding stone. From the adjacent room, the others heard their voices raised in a long, confused lament, while Nimwes cried heartbrokenly. "He didn't tell me good-bye!"

Qualary, not understanding anything that had happened, cried, "When Ellel gets back—when she gets back, she'll find all her walkers gone. She'll find things changed. She hates that. She'll be so angry."

Oracle put her arm around the woman. "Don't worry about that, Qualary. Really, you don't have to worry about that."

Qualary sniffed, dried her eyes. "She told me you said the stars were Ellel's. Two Families, you said."

Oracle only patted her shoulder and did not reply. Her eyes were fixed upon Berkli's, and his upon hers with dawning awareness.

Tom's sorrow had reminded Abasio of his own. "I think of her out there!" he cried to Oracle. "Going on and on, forever. Hungry. Tired. Maybe in pain."

"No," said Oracle. "Believe me, Abasio, my Orphan's not in pain. She'll never be hungry, or tired, or in pain." She looked away from him, her face set and grim.

He would not let the subject alone. "Do you think Olly's life well spent?" he demanded angrily. "You sent her here. Was it right?"

"You're referring to her so called seventh question?" Oracle asked fiercely, returning his glare.

"What do you mean, so-called?"

Oracle snorted. "You didn't believe what Tom said, did you? I mean, he repeated what Olly told him, but she didn't tell him the truth. Those weren't the seven questions she was asked. And those sure as hell weren't the answers she gave."

Abasio merely stared at her, openmouthed.

"Believe me," she snapped. "I know her. Knew her. But with all my oracular powers, I do not yet know the truth about her. Or about you."


The group held too much emotion for it to stay together. Every person in it felt the need of surcease, quiet, privacy, whether for thought or grief or merely sleep. All of them soon went off in different directions, to homes or rooms or newly offered spaces in the great silence that had come over the Place.

Abasio went out into this silence, thinking vaguely that he would find a tavern somewhere. In Fantis he had usually sought out a similar sort of place when deeply distressed, but here none seemed to be open. He was near the gate in the great wall when he saw Captain CummyNup Chingero, jeweled and bedecked, accosting this one and that one to ask if anyone there had seen Abasio the Cat or found his body. Abasio darted out, drew CummyNup into the gatehouse, and told him to keep his voice down.

"You alive!" crowed CummyNup, delighted past measure. "Wait till I tell that Sybbis!"

Abasio shuddered. "No, CummyNup! No."

"You don' wan' I should tell her?"

"You—look. I'm . . . going to have to go off on a long, long journey. I'll be gone . . . years, maybe. You tell Sybbis that, it would hurt her feelings. Right?"

CummyNup nodded dismally. It would hurt her feelings, and Sybbis wasn't that easy to get along with even when she was feeling good about things!

Abasio went on, "But she probably thinks I'm dead, fallen in battle, and that's honorable, right? So she's proud of me. And you can . . . go on, just the way you are. You'd like that, wouldn't you?" He nodded forcefully, making CummyNup nod along with him.

Nonetheless, CummyNup was doubtful. "She carryin' your baby, Basio."

"Well . . ." Abasio made an equivocal gesture. "Maybe. Then again, maybe not. I'd be proud to have you be daddy, either way."

"I s'pose to say you—?"

"Dead," said Abasio. "Killed in battle. A hero."

"No!" CummyNup said stubbornly. "Gone, not dead. Like—well, jus' gone."

"Just gone," agreed Abasio, thinking of Olly. Why not? If one, why not both? He would be just gone!

Torn between grief and elation, CummyNup went back to Sybbis and the army. Soon they broke camp and moved away toward the northeast, where they would find an ideal place to settle—so said their resident seer, whom they had requested from an archetypal village, along with an archetypal Lady's Maid for Sybbis and an archetypal Nanny for the child soon to be born. The villages were being sprinkled outward into the world, and archetypes were needed once more.

Sybbis declared the new settlement would be called Abasiostown, to be ruled by herself and CummyNup until her child, Abasio's child, came of age. It was at her direction that much of the gangers' armamentarium was left behind.

"We not goin' to fight," she told CummyNup. "Got nobody to fight but us, and we not goin' to. I been talkin' to these Artemisian women. They got things to say that make sense, CummyNup!"

During recent days, Sybbis had acquired an almost regal dignity, which surprised her only a little less than it did anyone else. She had intended to be Queen of Abasiostown. Now she thought she might call herself Mothermost. Maternally, she extended to CummyNup her invitation that he continue as her consort and her permission for him to fetch Mama Chingero as well as Billibee and Crunch, if they wanted to come live in Abasiostown.


Berkli and Mitty went up in the Dome to check walker locations on the console. They wanted to be quite sure all had been destroyed. As they were leaving, they were confronted by Forsmooth Ander.

"Berkli," he said in his oleaginous voice. "Mitty."

"Forsmooth," they acknowledged.

"The Anders have been talking this over. This—what might one say? Happening?"

"Have you now," grunted Mitty.

"Since none of the other mature Ellels seem to be available, we consider it appropriate for me, as temporary Family head, to take over the control of things in general until Ellel and Ander get back."

"What things would those be?" asked Berkli, with dangerous calm.

"Why, the shops. The—the ceremonies. You know."

"Since there are no more walkers and old Seoca has departed, what possible reason can there be for continuing the ceremonies?" said Mitty. "Also, we have turned the orbital telescope onto the space station, and we see that the shuttle seems to have misfired."

"Misfired?"

"Misfired. Or been misdirected. Or something. At any rate, it never reached the station. It seems to be on its way to Betelgeuse, which it will reach in a few hundred or thousand years, give or take. Now, as for the shops, they can be managed only by people who know something about them, and that doesn't, so far as I know, include any Anders at all. Any of the Family members who want to enroll in the technical school will be welcome there, of course."

Berkli hid a grin behind his hand.

"I don't like your tone!" said Forsmooth. "I'm sure Ellel and Ander will be able to turn the shuttle around. After all, they have the guidance system! When they return, we will take the matter up with them."

At the mention of the guidance system, Berkli's face had hardened. "You do that," he said. "While you're waiting, however—and it will be a lengthy wait—you might get your Family together to decide how they're going to make a living in the future, for I'm afraid the Domer monopoly on the output of the shops is hereby broken."

Forsmooth stalked away with many flutters of his silken sleeves.

"He didn't understand what you were saying," said Mitty.

"It'll come to him."

"That was quite a pronouncement. About the shops."

"So was yours," said Berkli. "But it's high time, even though it means the Berklis will also have to go to work. We've lived off the Power of the Place far too long."


The second morning after the battle, Oracle announced a premonition: All the residents of the Place of Power must leave immediately and go west, up toward the forests. Gaddirs went from door to door, advising the populace, most of whom took heed, though some Ellels thought it a trick, and some Anders refused to leave their pavilion. Within the hour, people straggled out of the western gates, some of them laden with food and drink and blankets, though Oracle had said they would not need to stay away long.

The last of them had barely come away from the wall before the earth shook and the Place of Power was obscured behind a wallowing yellow cloud that rose straight up, a citywide pillar, like the trunk of a monstrous tree. The people turned and gaped at the dust cloud as a shifting wind from the west frayed the column into long, drooping branches extending eastward, branches that sagged like spruce boughs as the heavier dust fell out of the wind. Below the earth the tremors continued, to the sound of cataclysmic grindings and quakings.

Some farsighted few who had climbed trees to get a view cried out that a chasm had opened down the center of the eastern canyon, where it swallowed boulders and trees down its cavernous maw before it closed again like a pair of huge jaws.

When at last the tremors diminished and stopped, people ran back through the gates, wanting to see what had happened to their homes. Within the walls, the Place remained much as before, except that Gaddi House was gone. Where it had been was only a great heap of yellow-gold rubble that, even as they watched it, flattened and sifted itself into a mere stretch of ochreous dust. Not long afterward, when people went to their homes seeking light and heat, they found that the Power for which the Place had been named was gone also. There were no lights, no machinery moving, no warm rooms. That night the people slept in darkness, except for candles and lanterns and the baleful glow of makeshift braziers.

Nimwes went off to console her family, and be consoled, as did other of the Gaddir folk.

"All the shops," grieved Tom to Mitty. "All the machines. I had equipment in there you wouldn't believe! The things I could make! The things I could do!"

"All the power," grieved Mitty to Tom. "All the things I could make! The things I could do!"

In nowise comforted, they wandered off together, Tom pausing to collect Qualary, all of them looking for somewhere to sit down while they considered options for their futures, beginning with designing some kind of power plant. Hydroelectric, suggested Mitty. Thermoelectric, urged Tom, who knew where there were hot springs. Or perhaps solar.

Or perhaps, Mitty said, they should consult the Edges. The Edges, as everyone knew, still had power.

Perhaps, Qualary said, the Edges would even welcome new residents of a proper kind.

Tom and Mitty grew thoughtful at this suggestion.

Abasio, who had been wandering around trying not to think of anything at all, encountered Arakny near the gate of the Place.

"I'm going down to join Wide Mountain Mother," she said. "She's going to be pissed about my losing my library. Though, given everything, it was probably more than a fair trade." She put her arms around Abasio and hugged him. "Besides, I'm dying to tell her all about the thrones and the Griffin and Olly's prophecy. Not that I believe what Olly said to Tom about it."

"What do you mean, you don't believe?" he asked, suddenly alert. Oracle had said the same thing!

"I don't believe that's what the questions were," she said quietly. "I believe what she told Tom was just a story, something to pacify us."

"Why?" he blurted.

"Why? Because she didn't want the truth widely told, obviously. Like those book-burning teams, altering the past, changing reality. She's not telling us what really happened. She knew I'd put it in the library, and she didn't want it there. I assume you don't want it there, either?"

"I don't know what you mean."

"Oh, I think you do. Why not share your impressions of the thrones with me? I have the very definite notion that you saw something down there that I didn't. Heard something I didn't hear. Hunagor said something to you, didn't she?"

Abasio shook his head. "You're wrong. We were both there. You saw them, heard them, just as I did."

She stared at him, tapping her teeth with a thumbnail. "You know, I told Olly once that *thrones* is a name for an order of angels. When one thinks of angels, one gets sidetracked with old pictures, feathery wings, trumpets and harps, all that. But if you consider what an angel really might be, you get a different idea. A creature dreadfully powerful and awesomely old, for example. A creature not necessarily at all manlike. A terrible creature, perhaps."

Abasio pulled himself together with a shudder. "Look, Arakny, I don't know. I wish you'd just drop it. I find the whole thing extremely ... repugnant."

"That's an odd choice of word."

"Well, it's my choice. Talk about something else. What are you going to do when you get home, for instance?"

She refused to be diverted. "As a librarian, there's only one thing I can do. Make a record of what's happened, of course. Write an Olly Longaster song, and have the men's societies create a three-thrones dance. And have a sandpainting designed, with a story to go with it. And refer the question of who and what they were to our philosophical society. All ways of remembering. Why else was a librarian present?"

Abasio stood watching while she went down the winding road to join her people.

Later that day the Artemisians broke camp and began their trek eastward, the last of the armies to depart. Orphan's Hero, who had survived along with about half of his colleagues, had learned of a maiden who was to be sacrificed to a giant sea creature in a seaside town far to the west, and he had ridden off posthaste to take care of the matter. He had taken Oracle with him, for the people needed an Oracle where he was going. Before she left, Oracle explained that the villages were breaking up everywhere, and all the archetypes were going off to find their proper places. Princesses to kingdoms or towers. Misers to greasy old houses along slimy waterfronts. Ingenues into troupes of traveling players. This one here and that one there, as needed.

"What are you going to do?" Qualary asked Abasio when she found him still wandering disconsolately about the Place. "Go back to the farm with your grandpa?"

"I don't think so," he said reluctantly. He didn't know what he did want to do, though he was certain of what he didn't. He didn't want to live in Artemisia, though Arakny had invited him. He didn't want to return to the farm. He wasn't going to Abasiostown to steal CummyNup's thunder. If there had been another shuttle, he'd have gone off in it in a moment, on Olly's trail, hopeless though that no doubt was.

He tried to explain himself to Qualary. "I don't know who she was," he said. "I loved her, but I never knew who she was. The whole world turned on her, but to me she was just the person I loved."

"None of us knows who other people really are," said Qualary, plaintively. "I think there must be some part of all of us that others never get to. Sometimes we don't get to that part ourselves. Sometimes the feelings I get make me know I have such a part in me: a dreadful strangeness, one that goes back, way back."

Abasio did not find this comforting.

It was during this time of confusion that Coyote limped three-legged in through the open gate in the late afternoon, sniffed his way about the Place, until he came upon Abasio's trail and eventually Abasio himself.

"Big Blue's wondering what happened to you. If it wasn't for Bear and me, he'd have starved to death."

Abasio wiped his face with his sleeve and tried to think of a reply. "Who bandaged your leg?'' he asked. ''I thought you were dead! I thought Bear was dead!''

''Well, we're not. No thanks to you. My leg's broken. The Artemisians set it. Besides, I was talking about your horse!''

''I heard,'' mumbled Abasio. ''Is he all right?''

''He's all right,'' drawled Coyote. ''Bear and I took him up where the wagon is before that last batch of earthquakes happened. Nice grass there.''

Abasio considered the wagon. It was his and Olly's wagon. Their dyers' wagon. With Olly's things in it. He didn't know if he could bear to see them again.

Farmwife Suttle, who had been listening to Coyote with amazed interest, interrupted Abasio's cogitations. ''The mention of Big Blue reminds me that Cermit and I should be getting back to our farms. Winter has set in, no doubt, and the folk there will have need of us. Burned Man and Drowned Woman will go with us.''

''You're not paying attention,'' Coyote yapped, nosing Abasio sharply. ''Do you have anything here you need to retrieve?''

Abasio had nothing he needed to retrieve. When he came to this place, he had carried only a few things. The important ones were all in the pack on his back or in his pockets. Enough to go . . . where? The only thing he could decide was not to decide.

He bade his grandpa farewell. ''Was your wife's name Hunagor?'' he asked.

''Odd you should mention that,'' Grandpa replied. ''I always called her Honey. But since being here, hearing that other name, it's sounded familiar to me and I've wondered if she was related to this Hunagor I keep hearing about. Why do you ask?''

''Just interested,'' said Abasio. ''I wondered the same thing.''

And finally, having worn out all his delays, he stumbled through the gates and down the road behind Coyote's limping form. Behind him he heard the industrious babble of people unsettling themselves, the shouts and orders and grumbling of a people cleaning up one mess and moving out to start another. Perhaps not. Maybe not this time.

On the roadway, Abasio's shadow stretched eastward before him, so slender and attenuated that its head fell off the road and bounced along the trees below, a black dot against the yellowish dust that blanketed the forest. As he shuffled along, slowly, so Coyote could keep up, a little wind gusted up to fling the dust along, like clouds of blowing gold, letting it settle again, farther down.

''It'll take rain to settle that,'' he said to Coyote.

''One winter's snow,'' muttered Coyote. ''Most things settle with one winter's snow.''

"I guess," said Abasio.

"So Olly fulfilled her prophecy," commented Coyote. "Five whole armies of champions."

Abasio stopped still in the middle of the road. "I just thought of something! What happened to her guardian-angel?"

"It went with the ship. To help her when the job was done," said the Coyote.

"I don't know where she is," gasped Abasio, feeling the words as pain. "I don't know where she went."

"You do," said Bear, joining them from among the trees along the canyon side. "She went to the sky. She became a star. She will be there always. We will sing songs about her!"

Bear had wounds upon his shoulders and painful-looking lacerations on his back. Withal, there was an air of contentment about him.

As the sun fell below the hills behind them, they reached the gravel run that led from the road back behind the bulwark of stone, the place they had left the wagon hidden. It stood now in full view with Big Blue between the shafts, his harness gleaming, even his hooves oiled and shining as he pawed the ground in welcome. The animals couldn't have done it. Someone with hands had been busy here.

"Your mother," said Coyote, reading his mind. "She doesn't remember you, but she remembers Olly, and she knows Olly loved you very much."

Abasio swallowed deeply. "You all seem determined to go somewhere."

"No point in staying here," said Coyote. "Everything's done and over with. As prophesied."

"Not as prophesied!" Abasio blurted. "Oracle says not. Arakny says not. Both of them say the story Tom told about Olly's seven questions was a— a—"

"A fable?" suggested Bear.

"A lie!" snarled Abasio. "A lie, a damned lie, and why would she lie to me?"

"Well, as to that," said Coyote, "she never intended to. That last night, before she left, she sent for me. She gave me something to give you, when you asked for it."

Abasio merely gaped at him.

"Why you?" he whispered at last.

Coyote shrugged. "Because she couldn't tell you then. She didn't want to spoil what had happened between you. She wanted to take that with her, she said. She needed it unsullied and perfect."

"Perfect," he cried. "So little time—"

"One perfect thing that would last forever, so she said. But she always meant for you to know what no one else knows. No one but me, that is."

Abasio slumped against the wagon.

Coyote sat down gingerly, easing his splinted leg. "She said she had to live in your memory, Abasio. She said her whole life had to be lived through you. All the years you might have had together. She said you had to know everything about her."

"Tell me, then!" he cried.

"No. It isn't for me to tell, it's for her to tell." Coyote stood up and tried unsuccessfully to get into the wagon. Bear came to give him a boost. Abasio heard him nosing around, and in a moment he came to the front and dropped something at Abasio's feet.

"What's that?"

"It was Arakny's library," said Coyote. "But Olly and the old man changed it. Now it's Olly's library."

"Put it on," grunted the Bear. "Turn it on."

Abasio sat beside the wheel, emptied the silvery chains into his lap, and saw them assume the cap shape.

"On your head!" said Bear.

He put it on his head. Bear pointed to the button on the packet, and Abasio pushed it.

*She came around the corner of the wagon, smiling into his eyes.*

*"Abasio!" she cried. She came close. He smelled her scent, felt the warmth of her body.*

*"Olly," he said, reaching out for her. "You went away!"*

*"I did, yes. I had to go, Abasio. But I've left my love behind. For you."*

*"Why?" he cried. "Why did you do it?"*

*"For loving you, Abasio. For loving the life we had. For loving it enough to want others to have it too."*

*"If you went away, how can you be here?"*

*"Old Seoca helped me put myself here for you. My dreams, Abasio. My memories. Everything I am, or was."*

*"Not real! Not the real Olly!"*

*Olly laughed, somewhat ruefully. "Which Olly did you make p'nash with?"*

*He only gaped at her, so she answered the question for him.*

*"Whatever Olly she was, I am that one!"*

*She laughed herself into his arms, and he held her while chasing stubborn, half-angry notions around in his head, none of them sufficiently strong to move him to let go of her. She felt real. Oh, by heaven, she felt real. As real as he himself. As all the monsters stalking the earth probably were, and Coyote and Bear.*

*"Oracle said you lied to Tom."*

*"Not really. I just didn't tell the whole truth."*

*"Will you tell me?"*

*"I always meant you to know."*

*"What happened when you went before the thrones, that time that Arakny and I waited outside?"*

Olly stood away from him, still holding him, looking deep into his eyes.

*"Hunagor spoke to me. She said she had some questions she wanted answered by an ordinary person. I told her I was ordinary enough, and she laughed at that. She said that in all the history of the thrones, they have seldom had to go so far as they went with man, and they were interested in understanding why I thought this was so.*

*"Hunagor asked me why man did not learn from the recurrent famines she had sent upon the earth."*

*"What did you say?"*

*"I told Hunagor what others had told me: that children are proofs of virility, and solutions that leave virility in doubt were not acceptable; that children are a way of controlling women, and losing control over women was not acceptable; that children grew up to make money or armies, and that not having money or armies was not acceptable. I said that men will not solve a problem unless they can find an 'acceptable' solution, and there are no acceptable solutions for some problems.*

*"Hunagor said yes, but even when men saw their own children dying, still they did not limit their numbers. And I told them what Oracle had taught me: that man believes what man wants to believe, and he always wants to believe the next time will be different.*

*"Then Hunagor asked why man, who claimed to be proud of his intelligence, preferred such easy belief to the hard choices intelligence requires. And I quoted Oracle again: The end is in the beginning. If children are taught to ignore their minds and merely believe, grown men will never do otherwise."*

She fell silent, snuggling into his arms.

*"That's only three questions,"* he said wonderingly.

*"Those are the three Hunagor asked. Then Werra asked why man had not been warned by the wars he had created; why men did not change when Seoca first sent IDDIs among them; why it was necessary, finally, for the plague of man to be controlled by the plague of angels, in order to save the earth."*

*"And you gave the same three answers,"* said Abasio, sure of it.

*"I gave the same three answers. Man believes what he wants to believe, and he chose to believe war was merely local or temporary or justifiable. Man could have made the hard choices that would have stopped the immune deficiency diseases in the same way Artemisia controls them now, but those afflicted demanded other choices, their friends demanded other choices, their*

*kinfolk demanded other choices, no government would take a stand that might lose it support, every faction found some part of the solution unacceptable. And finally, man would not stop destroying the earth until he was forced to do so, for he was reared in the belief he was more important than the earth itself, and the end is in the beginning.''*

*"What was the seventh question?"*

*"It will be hard for you, Abasio!"*

*"Tell me!" He shook her. Only gently.*

*Olly sighed, an echo of the sigh the old man Seoca had made when he sat down upon his mighty chair. "The last thing they asked me was this: Since man was so intransigent, why was he allowed to go to the stars?"*

*"What was your answer to that?" he demanded.*

*"I should have figured it out long ago, Abasio. So should you."*

*"To save the earth? To conserve the earth? Why?"*

*"Man never went to the stars."*

*He merely stared, disbelieving.*

*She pursed her mouth, as though she tasted something bitter. "Men never went anywhere but here." She stamped her foot, looking down at the ground beneath them. "His star journey was only a myth. Another in an endless series of man's heroic myths of his own past. Glorious stories to make man the hero, for man always has to be the hero. 'Cock-a-doodle. Crouch, you hens. Here comes the rooster.' "*

*He could not answer. He thrust her away in his mind, her and the knowledge she had brought him.*

*"You are of Gaddir kindred, too, Abasio," she whispered. "Your children will be, and your many-times-great-grandchildren. You will live long. You will see many things—do many things." She leaned forward and kissed him. "There is an archetype we never had in any of our villages, Abasio. The Mysterious Stranger. The one who comes and goes, who sees everything, learns everything. He is needed in this new world."*

*He could think of nothing to say.*

*"Farewell, Abasio," she whispered. "I'll be here if you need me."*

Abasio found the cap between his hands. He had taken it off himself.

Bear said, "Poor man. So proud."

Abasio made a warding gesture. Bear merely grunted.

"You've both—experienced this?" Abasio snarled.

"Just me," Coyote whispered. "Olly promised me. She was my friend too. I know man never went to the stars."

"It's not true!" Abasio denied it. Men had gone. Men like himself had gone, taking possession of the universe for mankind!

Bear growled. "Little shuttle. Many men! But man believes what he wants to believe."

Coyote yawned. "She said you would see the size of the shuttle, when it went. And she said Tom talked all the time about how many men there had been once. She said reason alone should have told you."

"But there was a space station! There were moon settlements."

"But they were never finished. Olly said men could have gone to the stars if they hadn't been so prick-proud. But they were. So they didn't. They just stayed here and bred!"

"Then why didn't the thrones kill us all?"

"Because you belong here," said Bear.

"That's true," Coyote agreed. "Though some of our people think we'd be better off without you, you do belong here." His voice trailed off, and he put his head upon his paws. His leg hurt mightily. He was weary. Though he had never thought it would happen, he was tired of talk.

Abasio cried, "They ate us up! All our glory! They ate up our stars!" He heard echoes of his voice return from the rocks around them, the sound of a child in tantrum, hating all the world. "They ate us all up."

"That's the point. Someone had to," snarled Coyote.

Bear whuffed with laughter.

"Now hush," said Coyote wearily. "It's over. They don't meddle until they must, and once they're done, they're done. They've gone."

"Tiring, this talk!" grumbled Bear, rearing up and sticking his hairy face in Abasio's to give him a close looking-over.

Big Blue stamped his foot, shaking the reins, whinnying a question that Abasio heard clearly as, "Are we going to sit here all day?"

"Where?" asked Bear, staring into Abasio's eyes.

Abasio closed his eyes, not caring where they went. Big Blue heaved a sigh and pulled the wagon out onto the downward road, settled himself between the shafts, looked questioningly out over the canyon, farted loudly, and shook his head to make the harness jingle. Then he plodded down the road at an unhurried pace while Bear shambled purposefully along behind.

Abasio stared up at the star-pricked darkness, the shining vault of heaven that he had thought was his, if only by proxy, finding his own star. Abasio's star. His own private glory. His own Book of the Purples. His own legend of past marvels, making him more than he was.

*"That's why they started the story,"* said her voice in his mind. *"What man has already done, he need not plunder his world to do again."*

Which was true. He could be less . . . heroic. He could be more deliberate. Careful. Careful not only of himself . . .

Something within him shuddered and sat up straight, substituting one vision for another. Instead of glory and power, instead of a gleaming shuttle pushed by its tail of fire, this slow creaking wagon behind this flatulent horse. How long to reach the moon once more, behind a farting horse? How far to Rigel, or to Betelgeuse? Or did one aspire to a different destination?

He stared out over the trees, beyond the canyon. Artemisia. Low Mesiko. The forests of the east. And room, perhaps for . . . a Mysterious Stranger. A storyteller, perhaps. Someone to immortalize the name of Olly Longaster, daughter of the stars. Someone who was destined to live a long, long time . . .

"What now?" he asked.

*"You're asking me?"* she said in his mind.

"Who else would I ask?"

*"The ones in charge,"* she replied. *"It's not just men this time around, Abasio."*

He looked into the wagon to catch Coyote's calculating eye.

"Are you the trail boss on this journey?" he asked

"Us," said Big Blue, keeping his eyes on the road.

"Us," said Bear, whuffing with laughter. "Us all."